AGAINST THE RICH TAPESTRY OF CALIFORNIA HISTORY SHE LIVED FOR VENGEANCE . . . SHE LIVED FOR LOVE.

ALEXANDER TODD—her husband. Together they fled the East with a golden dream . . . a dream the West had tainted with blood and shame. She would do anything for Alex—anything but let him know that she was still alive.

MIWOKAN—her sunbrother, her friend. Their destinies were linked by chains of gold and of desire. The handsome chieftain swore he would lay down his life for her. But she would live to see *him* avenged.

JOAQUIN MURIETTA—They were two strangers, each suffering bitter wounds. How could she know how much he had given her until he was gone?

LUTHER MOSBY—He saved her from a nightmare, then condemned her to hell. His savagery reached out to destroy everything she loved. She swore she would live to see him ruined—or dead!

2 3 8. 7 9 3 1

2 3 5 . 1 4 5 3

DANIEL KNAPP

California
Woman

A DELL BOOK

For Judy England

Acknowledgements

This book would not have been possible without the assistance and resources of Richard Kahlenberg, veteran Southern Pacific Railroad executive John Pitkin, the Los Angeles Public Library, the Bancroft and Huntington libraries, and the California Historical Society.

My special thanks also to: Drs. Adel Jabour and John and James Williams; Antonia Knapp, James Himonas, S. Koscuik, J. Mulcare, Richard Erickson, Colby Chester, Charles Bloch, Paul Kohner, William Kelsey, Linda Lichter, Ilse Lahn, William Warnick; my editors at Dell—Tova Laiter, Bill Grose, and Linda Grey; and the many other friends and associates who provided me with invaluable support, help, and expertise during the writing and editing of this novel.

THE AUTHOR

Know ye that on the right hand of the Indies there is an island called California, very near the terrestrial paradise and inhabited by . . . women . . . living in the manner of Amazons. They are robust of body, strong and passionate in heart, and of great valor. Their island is one of the most rugged in the world, with bold rocks and crags. Their arms are all of gold, as is the harness of the wild beasts, which, after taming, they ride.

. . . Over this island of California rules a queen, Calafía, statuesque in proportions, more beautiful than all the rest, in the flower of her womanhood, eager to perform great deeds, valiant and spirited, and ambitious to excel all those who have ruled before her.

—García Ordóñez de Montalvo
Las Sergas de Esplandían
1510

One

SNOW

One

Sacramento
May 6, 1869
11 P.M.

The woman in Charles P. Crocker's elaborately furnished private railroad car watched and waited in the
darkness. In black widow's dress, a broad-brimmed
black hat, and black veil, Esther Cable Carter virtually
blended into the interior of the unlit car.

Illumination from the gas lamps at the Sierra Hotel
and in the adjacent buildings on Sacramento's Front
Street scarcely reached the empty railroad station.
There, a solitary kerosene lantern flickered ineffectually. Only when a brief opening in the slow-moving
clouds released a spray of soft light from the moon
was she fully conscious of the deep red velvet and
ornate patterns of the soft chairs and settees in the
forward portion where she sat. Only during those moments was she more than vaguely aware of Charles
Crocker's teak and brass military field desk, the
cushioned swivel chair before it, the cupboard and
shelves containing railroad maps and reports at the
front end of the car.

She preferred the longer intervals of cool darkness.
They matched more accurately the circumscribed,
lethally tinted place her thoughts traversed at the
moment. Suspended there, she remained heedless of
the rest of the ceremonial Pacific Union Express train

14 DANIEL KNAPP

she was aboard, of anything, in fact, beyond the small, sharply focused world of her thoughts.

Forward of the private car, the giant locomotive *Jupiter* rested silently for the next day's journey; its gargantuan wheels, pistons, concave-ribbed cowcatcher, glass-encased square head lamp, and oversized conical stovepipe chimney ready. Waiting. Behind the engine, a matching black coal-car; a wooden flatcar with low plank sidings made up the third unit of the train. In the morning a polished laurelwood railroad tie and a small crate containing a solid-gold spike would be placed aboard it, along with two armed infantrymen.

In less than nine hours, in the morning, several hundred prominent Californians would board the three wooden, cap-roofed passenger cars. Politicians, judges, prosperous businessmen, lawyers, bankers, railroad officials, and a few less successful but historically significant men would accompany the laurel tie and solid-gold spike on a journey of nearly one thousand miles. Their destination: Promontory Point, Utah, and the ceremony commemorating the joining of the Central Pacific and Union Pacific railroads.

But for Esther, sitting in the darkened car, there were no thoughts of that historic moment. Another, more eagerly awaited private ceremony and the small rolling stage upon which it would unfold preoccupied her. Out of deference to the widow of William "Bull" Carter, the late superintendent and silent partner of the Central Pacific, Charles Crocker had offered his private car if she cared to take her husband's place of honor at Promontory. Esther Cable Carter smiled in the darkness. Crocker and the other three members of the railroad's powerful Big Four—Mark Hopkins, Leland Stanford, and Collis P. Huntington—had provided her with the perfect setting.

Behind her, the red velvet curtain that separated the two halves of the private car hung on brass rings encircling a brass rod. Beyond it lay Charles Crocker's brass feather bed, private dining table and chairs, small utility kitchen, pantry, and toilet. The windowed rear door of the car, the studded metal observation platform and its runged, three-and-a-half-foot iron-rail fence took shape in Esther's mind. Even in the darkness she could picture every square inch of the area beyond the curtain, every object in it, the door, the platform beyond, as clearly as though it were lighted by the sun at noon.

Once more, slowly, she went over every step, every act, every detail of what would transpire beyond the curtain during the private ceremony she had planned. A ritual that would begin in deceptive gentleness tonight and end with the brutal honesty of winter lightning tomorrow.

Satisfied, she let her thoughts drift back to the present. She gazed through the window at the front door of the Sierra Hotel. Someone sat rocking and smoking on the railed porch on the third floor, but no one was on the one below it or near the entrance. Faint strains of music and then the sound of applause, muffled by distance, wafted past her from the Eldorado Theater. She could see a few figures moving about in Kennedy's Saloon, but it was Tuesday night, and despite the festive spirit that had gripped Sacramento all week, all but a few people were already at home or asleep. For a moment, the irony of it struck her. There, in that hotel and in a number of homes here in the thriving state capital, were more than half of the people whose lives had significantly touched hers during the past twenty-five years.

Among them was John Augustus Sutter, who had ridden in from his farm upriver to make the trip to Promontory. She shook her head. For at least the hundredth time, the powers that be were exploiting Sutter. He was the founding father of American California, or at least one of them. But the only use they had for him now, even while he spent months, years in Washington seeking to regain title to the vast lands he had once owned, was to play upon his egocentricity and good nature, call him back to California, and trot him out on display as if he were some prehistoric fossil. Whatever his faults, Sutter deserved better, and he could not have been more important to Esther had she been his daughter—or even his wife.

He had been there, at her side, when they brought her, delirious and near death, her lips still crusted with human blood, to Sutter's Fort early in 1847, after she had staggered down out of the snow-choked Sierras. He had held Esther's right hand—tightly—while "Doctor" John Marsh amputated two gangrenous, frostbitten fingers from her left.

Esther touched absently now at the cotton-packed pinky and third finger of the black glove on her left hand. She sighed. Sutter was indeed more than a friend. He had imperiously refused Marsh permission to cut off the tip of her frostbitten nose that day. The pale, scarcely visible scar tissue remained, but as much as she hated the mark and often felt the need to conceal it with a veil in public, it was far better than a tiny stump between her nostrils. Beyond that, Sutter was the only one who had known most of the truth from the beginning. The only one aware that Elizabeth Purdy Todd, now known as Esther Cable Carter, had survived those indescribable weeks in the mountains almost two dozen years earlier. He had never known the worst of it. But he had helped her conceal what he did know, and he had kept her secret all these years.

Billy Ralston had also helped her, in a different way. The millionaire banker was smoking and rocking on the third floor porch of the Sierra Hotel at this very moment; no doubt dreaming, Esther guessed, of new ways to milk silver from the Comstock, further enrich himself, and additionally enhance his beloved San Francisco. Billy had made her a second fortune, greater by millions than her first. But tonight that mattered only because it had helped place her in a position to dictate the events about to unfold in this private car; and prevent, if all went according to plan, the worst of those scheduled for Promontory.

Less than a mile away, Alexander Todd lay asleep in the home Esther had sold him. She wondered what the future held for them. He was still her husband, had been for twenty-four years, even though she had married another man whose surname Todd's son bore. It had been a struggle to get seven-year-old Todd Carter to bed tonight. The prospect of riding with the engineer in *Jupiter* at least as far as Reno had kept him rambunctious until the last minute, when he finally slumped in a chair by one of the windows in her hotel suite. Esther felt no concern for him now. The Indian woman, Solana, would watch over him until Esther returned, no matter how late it was.

Out there somewhere in the city, Lewis Keseberg, half-deranged now in his declining years, would be pacing the floor of his shabby little house, shouting at the top of his lungs, as Esther had heard he did almost every night about midnight, insisting in one of four languages that he had not murdered anyone that incredible winter a little more than two decades ago. Esther did not believe or disbelieve him. But it really didn't matter now. Most of those who had survived the endless weeks in the snow, herself included, had done what they had to do. They had eaten the flesh of men and women, even some of the children who had succumbed to the starvation and the cold. Keseberg may have been grossly indiscreet, indeed grotesque, in his recounting and exploitation of the experience through the years, but it was a wonder any of them who had come down out of those forbidding mountains had retained sanity enough to speak at all, let alone discreetly. None of it mattered any longer. What did matter was that after all the years of her hearing stories about Keseberg, he had chanced to learn that Luther Mosby, the man she now waited for, planned to kill Alexander Todd at Promontory. Keseberg had gone straight to his old friend Sutter with the information, and Sutter had come to her. What mattered even more was that Mosby would be on this particular train when it left Sacramento tomorrow. He was in the Sierra Hotel right now. He would be standing before her in minutes, unknowingly joining her in the first, purposely misleading phase of the ritual she had waited so long to perform.

For a moment she wished that Alex Todd had listened to her. She wished that he was not making the trip in the morning with the rest of them. But he was probably right. If Mosby did not try to kill him at Promontory, it would be at someplace else.

So it was in her hands again, as it had been off and on for twenty-two years. Since the day in the Sierras she had later written about on a predated page of her leatherbound journal. The page, inscribed more than two decades ago in her own exquisitely delicate hand, that ended: *"If it is the last thing I do on this earth, I will see Luther Mosby either ruined or dead."*

Two

Luther Mosby appeared in the doorway of the Sierra Hotel. He was just a silhouette, but there was no mistaking him. Still lean in his mid-fifties, he carried himself, stood, and walked as he had two decades ago. Slightly flexed at the knees, his left arm dangling oddly, loose and ready to spring. Moving down the wooden sidewalk now, away from the train—as Esther had directed him to do earlier in the evening—Mosby reminded her of some lean creature of the wilds.

Breaking his rangy stride, he took out a pocket watch, noted the time, and began doubling back on this side of Front Street toward the railroad station.

Mosby stopped suddenly in its shadow. Esther heard the soft whistling of the railroad watchman, who passed directly beneath the window beside her, then angled off toward Kennedy's Saloon. When the watchman was gone, Mosby began walking again, coming straight toward the train. He stopped opposite the engine, glancing about.

Esther laughed inwardly. He had reason to be cautious. More than a few persons in Alta California, as she was still occasionally in the habit of calling it, were not beyond shooting or bludgeoning Mosby in the dark. It was probably the only place any average man would have even a reasonable chance to compensate for Mosby's ferocious skill with the bowie knife and derringer he carried. It was a wonder that he had accepted her invitation. Even at that, she had been forced to reveal factually—and physically—more than she thought prudent to get him here at this hour.

The Indian woman had taken the message to Mosby before dinner, a brief note asking him to come to the door of Esther's suite at eight o'clock. In the dining room of the hotel, Esther calculatedly sat in profile to Mosby at the next table with her son. Mosby had not missed a detail of the lustrous dark hair that fell over her shoulders, the full, tightly clad bosom, slender waist, and curve of calf that was exposed when she "accidentally" snared her long skirt on a nail in the table leg. She knew the black clothes, hat, and loose-fitting short veil and black gloves had not lessened his curiosity. Nor had his awareness that she was "Bull" Carter's widow. Neither had her frequent glances in his direction, each punctuated with the slight hint of an admiring smile. Still, it had taken some doing to persuade him to come.

"I don't know, ma'am," he said, after she had opened

her chain-latched door a crack and suggested the late-night meeting. "It comes of a sudden, and . . . and . . . as you may know, I'm a recently married man."

"To Miss McDonnell."

"You seem to know a bit about me."

"I have been an . . . admirer . . . of yours for some time."

"That so?"

"Indeed it is, Mr. Mosby. We could . . ." She lapsed into silence and summoned up a suggestive smile.

"Yes?" he said, still guarded. "What is it we could do? I take it you have something you want to discuss."

"Not precisely."

"Well, what is it you want of me?" He glanced up and down the hallway.

"It . . . it's difficult for me to speak of it."

"Well, try anyway."

A gust of wind blew the curtains against the sash with a sudden whisper of sound down near the stairway. Mosby turned to it smoothly, his right hand going inside his unbuttoned frock coat faster than she could see it move. He turned back.

"Go on, Mizz Carter."

"It's so difficult." She tilted her head toward the floor. "I . . . I . . . have lusted for you."

He smiled, relaxing a bit. "That so?"

"From a distance, of course."

"Of course."

"For quite a number of years."

"That's plumb hard to believe, ma'am. But I'll take your word for it."

"Thank you."

"Most women wouldn't have the sand."

"I had to speak of it."

"Why is that?"

"The dreams. I can't sleep for thinking of you. Of the two of us . . ."

Mosby's eyebrows rose. "Together?"

"Yes."

Caught by surprise, he coughed uncomfortably. "Maybe it's a result of your . . . forgive me, ma'am, your late husband's untimely death."

"The dreams go back before that. Before I ever knew William Carter."

"That so?"

"Will you meet me in the private car?"

"I don't expect I will."

"Please," she whispered.

"What's the matter with right here? You just open up that door and we'll spend some time together right there in your rooms. You precedin' me until I've seen no one else is lurkin' about, of course."

"I can't do that."

"Why not?"

"My son is with me."

"Didn't I see him leave with that Indian woman?"

"They took a walk. I arranged that so we could speak. They'll be back shortly."

"I see."

"Will you come? Oh, I feel so shameful speaking this way."

"Speaking is all you'll have to feel ashamed about tonight."

"You will not come?"

"No, ma'am. Much as I'm stirred to by . . . by . . ." He could not take his eyes off the swell of her breasts beneath the dress. "It just don't all come together right enough, bein' out there in the dark in that railroad car. Anythin' could happen."

"What have you to fear from a woman? A widow?"

"Nothin'—and everything. Mostly from someone you might be in league with."

"Who, for heaven's sake?"

"Don't know, ma'am. That's why I'm goin' to pass on this hand." He started to move away toward the stairs.

"Wait!"

His black moustache bristled. "Ma'am?"

"We've been . . . together . . . before."

He looked at her quizzically.

"At least once," she said. "A long time ago."

"How can that be? I don't know you. Never knew no Esther personally, 'cept a little girl back in Charleston. And you're plainly no Southern girl. Anywise, she was only seven years old."

"This was . . . twelve or thirteen years ago," she said. "Fourteen, to be exact. In early 1855."

"Long time. And I'm afraid I don't remember . . ."

"It's difficult for me to tell you where."

"Then that's that." He started to turn again.

"It was in San Francisco . . . at . . . Arabella Ryan's."

He came close to the door now, rifling through memories.

"The night of the fire," she continued. "I've never forgotten the fire—or what took place between us before the fire started."

"Well, I'll be damned. I certainly do remember that night. Where'd you disappear to?"

"It doesn't matter."

"Wait a minute. How do I know you're tellin' the truth? You could have learned about that night from someone. Arabella had a big mouth."

"How would I know about . . . ?"

"The fire? Anyone could have told you that."

"Then you won't believe me?"

"It's all too pat, ma'am, beggin' your pardon. But I've got to cover all the windows." He took a step back and put on his flat-crowned, Savannah-style hat. "Good night, ma'am. I'm sorry I can't oblige."

"I can prove it! Come close to the door."

He paused, looked around. "You move back a step or two . . . and keep your hands in plain view."

"My lord, you are suspicious!" She backed away a yard, and he moved toward the opening, keeping his body protected by the wide oak doorjamb and peering into the room.

"Be still a moment." He listened intently for a few

seconds. "All right. You said you could prove you were the woman I was with that night."

"What do you remember most about our . . . being together?"

"What I remember best would be indecent to speak of in a public hallway."

"It was that memorable?"

"It was. Never have . . . experienced the likes of it before or after."

She smiled. "Why is that, Mr. Mosby? You can speak plainly. Just keep your voice down."

"Best way to explain it is that it wasn't just the woman was the most skillful I've ever met, or the, ah, most enthusiastic. That's a good deal of it. But there was somethin' else. I went into Arabella's lookin' for a professional sportin' woman, and this lady, expert as she was—by which I mean she was a natural, better at . . . it . . . than any professional I've been . . . entertained by . . . before or since—there was somethin' different about her. Down deep I knew she wasn't a professional at all."

"And what do you remember about her physically— I mean, what did she look like?"

"She was a strange one. Wore a hat and a veil and long velvet gloves." He paused again. "Like . . . you do. Like . . . you're wearing now . . . the whole time. 'Cept, of course, they wasn't black."

"They were deep lavender."

Mosby's mouth dropped open.

Esther didn't wait for him to comment. "Did she have any identifying marks on her body? I take it she was unclothed except for the hat, veil, and gloves."

"She was. Marks. Let me see. Yes, I recollect she had a pale strawberry, a birthmark, down deep . . . excuse me, ma'am."

"Go on." Esther began to unbutton her dress.

"She had a strawberry down deep in the cleft of her bosom. So pale you could hardly see it."

Esther peeled the top of the dress down over her

waist. "On which side?" She began unfastening her undergarments.

"The . . . left, I believe." His pulse quickened.

"Did it look like this one?" Esther said, smiling as he stood there, mouth agape, licking at his lips, one pale blue eye peering with awe through the cracked door at her still firm, slightly oversized chest.

Now Esther heard the faint sound of Mosby's boot grind against the forward stairway to the private car as he put one foot up, then waited, holding on to the railing and looking up and down the length of the train. He stood there for a moment, listening in a stillness so deep the slightest sound within shooting range would have betrayed anyone's presence. He holstered the derringer under his arm, checked the knife in the sheath stitched inside his right boot, and climbed up to the door of the car.

"Your eyes will adjust to the darkness in a few minutes," Esther said, once he had stepped inside. He moved swiftly to a spot behind one of the stuffed chairs and crouched.

"I can see just fine. What's behind that curtain?"

"See for yourself." Esther stood up and pulled the fabric aside. "You have nothing to fear. Did you honestly think I would want anyone else to know we are alone here together, with my husband scarcely a month in his grave?"

He moved closer and looked over her shoulder into the rear end of the car. "I reckon not," he said, easing her aside and quickly inspecting the sleeping area, the kitchen, and the lavatory. "It's my nature to be mistrustful." He stepped back to where she'd taken a position at the foot of the brass bed, and looked under it. "I did some figurin' after we spoke. I don't mean to sound big-headed . . ."

"But this has happened before, with other women?"

"Yes. Never have been able to figure out why."

"Why, it's simple. You're a fine figure of a man, and

more than that, women are attracted to men who look like they're capable of violence."

Mosby shifted uneasily.

"Raw animal power. . . . So few men have it."

"Well, I don't know about that," Mosby said, uncomfortable though he savored every word. "But I do know you must've enjoyed that night at Arabella's near as much as I did. And want it again, for whatever reasons. So I reckon I believe you. Only thing is, I can't figure out why you waited so long."

"There are many reasons, Mr. Mosby . . ."

"Might as well call me Luther . . ."

"But they can wait. There will be opportunity enough for all that. We needn't waste any time now. Why don't you . . . get undressed?"

Esther slipped out of everything but the veiled hat and long gloves. She forced herself not to stare at Mosby's left arm. Slightly but noticeably smaller than the right, it was encased at the elbow by a notched, leather brace. Above and below the belted, sweat-darkened supporter, an ugly ladder-like scar ran from the bottom of his biceps to the middle of his forearm, snaking ropy white across the point of his elbow. She knew how he had suffered when he had sustained the deep gash, and the thought pleased her. Her gaze drifted upward across his back, where a burn scar, pebbled and two inches wide, extended from one shoulder to the other. As he turned, the memory of the night he had been burned steeled her for what was about to happen.

Stripped, he hung the holstered derringer within reach on one of the brass bedposts. His eyes widened. The sight of her pale, tapered, but almost boyishly slender body, the contrastingly full breasts and the sheathed tongue of flesh protruding faintly beneath the triangle of soft, dark hair made him breathe deeply. Standing there in just his boots and socks, with his penis practically touching his belly button, he felt slightly foolish.

"Do you always wear that veil and those damn gloves?" he asked, trying to recover his composure. "Why don't you take the hat off, at least, so I can see your face?"

"You can see my face tomorrow." She pulled her legs up and exposed herself a fraction more. "Tomorrow, all the mysteries will be revealed. On the way to Promontory."

"Suit yourself." He pulled off his boots and socks, not admitting that the gloves and the veil, in fact, all the bizarre elements, added to his excitement, intensified his lust.

"Now . . ." she said. She began to falter, almost betrayed by the waves of revulsion that buffeted her as she watched the pulsing of his massive organ. She almost gagged on her words. "Now . . . I . . . want . . . to make you feel . . . the way I did at Arabella's that night. With my hands . . . and . . . my . . . mouth . . . and . . . *this*," she added, rolling back on her shoulders and spreading her legs wide on the deep red satin, eiderdown quilt.

Solana said nothing, asked no questions when Esther returned to the hotel and sent her to the adjoining room. The Wappo Indian woman's nostrils flared briefly after she opened the door and saw Esther's hair loose on her shoulders. Esther was certain her keen nose had picked up the scent of sex. But they had known one another almost as long as Esther had known Mosby. By now Solana's unfaltering loyalty would override doubt or concern about the wisdom or propriety of almost anything Esther did.

Esther undressed, cleansed herself with cool water from a tall china pitcher and scented tallow soap, then took her leatherbound journal out of a suitcase and slipped into bed. She glanced at little Todd, who was snoring faintly on the cot set up against the wall across the room, then lay back with her hands pressing the journal against her breast. Staring at the wood-beamed ceiling, she was repulsed by what she intended to do tomorrow. She was disgusted with herself for enjoying it so much toward the end with Mosby, the way she had only with Alex Todd. Even after all these years she still harbored the faint suspicion that there had to be something intrinsically evil about a woman who took such volcanic extremes of pleasure from fornication—with anyone.

For a moment, remembering the contractions, the uncontrollable writhing, and the final, almost mindless soaring as the deliciously warm wave spread from her loins to the tips of her fingers and toes, Esther wavered. No one so weak could possibly bring off what she planned to do tomorrow without stumbling over her own emotions. But then Alex Todd's face supplanted Mosby's in her thoughts, and she was jerked back to cool objectivity. She guessed rightly that hatred as well as love could possibly stretch a woman's mental control over her body to the point of such animalistic response. She accepted the necessity of what she was doing, would still do, and was reasonably certain that God would understand. And if He didn't? Well, that was a price she would willingly pay for Alexander Todd's life.

She was unsettled, but she knew the healing, steadying value of concentration, absorption. She knew the wavering, the weakening of her determination would cease when she began reading the journal. Propping herself up on the pillow nearest the oil lamp, she stared at the pebbled brown-leather cover. Tilting the book, she touched the knotted black ribbon that tied off and separated a small segment near the opening pages. She felt her pulse suddenly thudding uncomfortably in her throat. Forcing herself, she pulled the cover open. On the first page she had written: *"Events in the Life of Elizabeth Purdy Todd, 1845—."* Luther Mosby's smudged thumbprint marred the lower right-hand corner. The faded sworls held her attention long enough to restore all her determination. There was only one day in her entire life that Mosby could have touched this page. The memory of it, as she turned the leaf and began reading the first entry, erased all doubt, all compunction about what she was going to do.

Three

Bent's Fort
August 2, 1845

Six weeks to the day have passed since Alexander, my dear husband, departed for Fort Laramie. I did not know one could love and miss another human being so. Feeling better. Well enough to go for a stroll outside the walls of the Fort this evening. Pray God the illness that began plaguing me outside St. Louis has passed for good and that all will go well with me until John Alexander is born. I know it is a boy. There! Another masculine kick! even as I am writing this. Pray by now Alexander has secured passage to California with one of the trains of settlers passing through Fort Laramie. I know in his heart he did not want to leave me, and the prospect of being separated for a year grows more intolerable each day. It is selfish of me to think so, and I must do some disciplining to correct my weakness. It is purely a matter of plain thinking, to be sure. Had Alexander waited with me, the opportunity to serve in Mr. Larkin's mercantile establishment in Monterey would surely have passed to another. Time and good fortune await no man.

Stifling hot for six days now. No sign of a letup. I do

not know how the Cavalrymen stand it in their wool and twill uniforms. I thought more than one of them would melt in the parade formation today welcoming Captain John Frémont and his party of mappers and explorers. A fiercer looking group of men I have never laid eyes on, some sixty in all. With the exception of Captain Frémont, who looks a boy so frail and sensitive is his appearance among his trappers and mountain men. They seem exceedingly armed, up to possessing a brass Howitzer cannon, for a body setting out to do more than map the desert region beyond the Rockies before passing to California and Oregon. Came upon Mr. Kit Carson practicing with one of the new repeating rifles called Karbeens during my stroll. He too stands apart from the rest. Moon-faced, soft in manner, he does not bespeak his reputation for bravery or fierceness. I would not have known that side of him unless I had seen the look in his eyes and the challenging smile he wore after the tall, hawk-nosed man they (somewhat derisively, I think) call "Alamo" Mosby, cut him short when he began speaking of the possibility that California would someday—soon, he said—belong to the United States and not Mexico. At first, I did not like at all the way Mr. Mosby, whose first name is Luther, looked at me. The lust was so plain. I must be understanding, however; these men know it will be many months before they see their women again, or have the opportunity to. . . . And I must confess it was pleasing to know that such a striking looking man finds me, swollen as I am with child, still attractive. How easy it is to lose grip of righteousness in the face of temptress Vanity and the courtly manner of a Southern-born man—be he dressed in rough-looking buckskin garments or not!

The breeze that came up while I was taking my walk has died away again. It is as warm as noonday in Vermont, though by now the moon adds light to the lamp glow. Strange that I do not think often of cool New England, or Mother, or little Esther, or the school where I taught after Miss Cable died so suddenly. That seems long

ago and yet 'tis but a year or so back. When the heat
oppresses, I think of Ohio, and sitting along the riverbank
under the bare willows with Alex. His boat. The water and
the evening breeze making soft sounds as we sit pressed
close together, his arm around my shoulder. Dear Lord,
how I go on . . .

Dreamt last night (August second, I am adding this at
breakfast) of wading through deep snow in a blizzard,
lost. Surely that is Vermont! and born of this stifling heat
and dust. . . .

Four

Elizabeth Purdy celebrated her sixteenth birthday
gloomily on the eve of her journey from Manchester,
Vermont, to Plymouth, Ohio. It was late October, and
she dreaded the thought of leaving the rolling, flame-
colored hills of New England. She had heard that nowhere else in the United States was fall so resplen-
dent. There would be other things she would miss.
Mountains, maple syrup, toboggan rides, the fireplace
in her mother's red clapboard farmhouse, her charges
at the Crossroads Grammar School. Most of all, her
sister, Esther, who would be eleven in two more
months.

It was inescapable, though. She knew that. It
seemed like only yesterday that the community had
unanimously decided that she, the oldest and most
outstanding student at the school, would take over
Miss Cable's duties, even though Elizabeth still had
been a half year short of completing her course of
study, when the old woman had succumbed to influ-

enza. Then, scarcely before she had brought the class under disciplinary control, her father, a loving if somewhat puritanical Methodist-Episcopal minister, died of the same illness. Before the school year ended, her mother made an extended visit to Boston, bringing home a new husband five years younger than she. Elizabeth took an immediate dislike to Amos Sandler. Burly, a former seaman who limped from a harpoon wound that had forced him ashore for good, Sandler had shown an immediate infatuation with her. As the summer dragged slowly by, it became apparent that something drastic would have to be done before Amos brought a scandal down on all of them. An arrangement was made with Elizabeth's Aunt Clara in Ohio. She could live with her father's sister in exchange for household duties.

Elizabeth's Aunt Clara, a cold, austere woman whose husband had fled the iciness of their bed, owned a small general store as well as the modest dairy farm her man had abandoned in his flight westward. She expected nothing so much from Elizabeth as the labor and obsequiousness of a servant girl, adding long hours behind the counter of the dry-goods establishment to Elizabeth's voluminous chores around the house and in the milking barn.

Men who worked the boats on the Ohio River often patronized the store, but Elizabeth took little notice of them, until the afternoon Billy Ralston and Alex Todd ambled in to buy some work shirts and overalls. They lingered briefly, making small talk with Elizabeth after purchasing the clothing, then left when Clara made it plain they had worn out their welcome. A half hour later, after Elizabeth's aunt had gone on an errand, they were back.

"We've decided," said Ralston, as Alex Todd tried to conceal his discomfort, "that we have both fallen in love with you on first sight." Todd involuntarily rolled his eyes in despair. Unable to look at Elizabeth, he turned away and began absently fingering a pair of overalls. "And it's simply a matter," Ralston went on, "of you deciding which one of us you like best."

"I think you are mistaken," she said, smiling.

"How is that, Miss, Miss . . . ?"

"Purdy."

"Miss Purdy."

"I believe your friend has fallen in love with a second pair of overalls."

They both looked at Alex Todd, and then all three were convulsed by uncontrolled, totally disarming laughter.

For a month or so, while the river was iced over and the two young men waited to go back to work, Elizabeth innocently spent as much time with them as she could manage under her aunt's watchful eye and incessant demands. They were an odd pair, Billy and Alex, both eighteen and inseparable friends. Ralston was the pragmatist, Todd the dreamer. Billy planned to the last detail his next move "up the ladder." Alex didn't know what he was going to do beyond a vague urge to follow in the footsteps of his cousin Talbott to "find his fortune" in California.

Todd was the more attractive of the two. Elizabeth soon found his sandy-haired, ruddy good looks, his quiet, gentle manner, and his appealing if undefined dream of moving west someday a persuasive combination. When the opportunity came to head south for work, where the river was free of ice, Ralston left immediately and Todd stayed behind. It was obvious that he could not bear to part from her, and the sacrifice, combined with the importance she placed in someone caring so much for her, unlocked a depth of feeling she had never known existed.

In less than a month she could scarcely remember Billy Ralston's face or voice. In the evenings, after her aunt had gone to bed and she had made her way to the barn where Alex Todd waited, she found it difficult to stop at kisses and long intervals of standing pressed together in each other's arms.

He took a temporary job as a drayman hauling lumber to Cincinnati. He was gone for a week. The night he returned, she let him in through her window, and immediately took his hands and placed them on her breasts as she kissed him. He asked her to marry him. Her answer was to strip off his shirt slowly and sit him down on her bed while she took off her own clothes.

During the hours when they were not together, her aggressive sexuality puzzled and disquieted her. Her aunt's silent condemnation of her "shameless" behavior—spending time alone with a man—was simply a more severe manifestation of the way Elizabeth herself felt about such things. But only for a time. She never considered evil anything she and Alex did when they were together, never really gave any thought to it at all.

In late March, after concealing her early morning nausea from everyone, including Alex, she realized she was pregnant. When she told him, he insisted they get married immediately. That touched Elizabeth, made her deliriously happy, and she accepted. But it did not assuage her concern about the ostracism she would suffer when the baby was born and it became obvious the child had been conceived out of wedlock.

"There is a simple answer," Alex whispered to her, as they lay on a blanket near the riverbank. "You can't stay here, and I want to go to California, so we'll pack up and go."

He pulled a folded envelope out of his pocket. In it was a letter form his cousin Talbott in Monterey. It had taken more than six months to reach him, coming around the Horn by ship and then inland to Ohio. Talbott's employer, a man named Thomas Larkin, had agreed to hire Alex if he could be in Monterey before January 1846. Larkin had been appointed U.S. Consul in California, and in anticipation of "expanding political duties," as Talbott put it, Larkin planned to turn management of his business enterprises over to Alex's cousin at the turn of the New Year.

"I am certain," added Talbott, "you can learn what I have in half the time and become my assistant manager within three to six months of your arrival."

Elizabeth did not respond as Alex expected.

"Don't you see? It's the solution to our problem."

"But I have to stay here at least through the fall! That was a condition of the agreement I made with Aunt Clara."

"Your slave-driving aunt has already sweated a year's work out of you in return for six months' room and board!"

He bought a horse and buckboard with a small portion of his substantial savings, and they eloped the following Saturday night while her aunt was attending a church quilting bee. They were married in St. Louis by an itinerant Baptist preacher, who raised his fee to three dollars after taking note of Elizabeth's slightly swollen belly and the thickness of Alex's money belt.

On the way to Independence, Elizabeth's incapacitating headaches and nausea began, then intermittent light fever started to plague her. Two weeks after they had sold the buckboard, purchased a Conestoga wagon, and passed beyond the beginning of the Kansas Territory, it became obvious that Elizabeth should see a doctor. Reluctantly, Alex reined his team off the trail to Fort Laramie and headed southwest. Bent's Fort was out of the way, but it was closer.

The regimental surgeon at Bent's Fort, Captain Elisha Canby, had white hair, a handlebar moustache, and unlimited wisdom and understanding. He was sixty and a doctor, and he had seen it all.

"Young man," Canby said after examining Elizabeth, "your wife is having a difficult pregnancy. All I can do is give you some advice. If I were you, I would not allow her to travel until the baby is born."

Alex calculated time and distance for a moment. "She should have the baby sometime in mid-autumn."

"That's what present indications point to."

"By then it would be too late to cross the Sierras."

"Without a doubt. It would take you more than sixty days to reach them, even if a wagon train were traveling so late in the year, which I seriously doubt. By then I should think the snow in the Sierras would make passage impossible."

"That means staying here until spring."

"Or moving on to Laramie or Fort Hall. You could do that a month or so after the child arrives. But I don't see the sense in it. I should think it wiser to remain here, where there is ample room for you and accommodations are better."

"But I have a job, a very good job, waiting for me in California! If I don't reach Monterey this year . . ."

"Is it all that important to you? There will be other jobs."

"This one holds great promise for the future."

"Then you have a difficult decision to make."

"What do you mean?"

"It seems to me you have a choice. Remain here with your wife, or go on alone and have your wife and child join you next year. It's simply a matter of whether or not the job is worth it—to both of you."

"No. I should be with her. She may get worse. She may need me."

Elisha Canby smiled and put a fatherly hand on Alex's shoulder. "Son, aside from moral support, there is little you can do. I fully understand your concern, and I tell you this only so you may have an objective, unsentimental basis upon which to make your choice. Troublesome, vexing as it is, your wife's condition is not extremely serious. If it follows the course I have seen many times before, it will get no worse if she does not exert herself unduly. And the final weeks of the pregnancy will be normal."

"But where would she live? I'm not taken with the idea of her being alone here with a regiment of troopers."

"The men have their outlets, believe me. There are a number of officers' wives here, including mine. And your wife would be welcome to stay with us. In fact, Mrs. Canby, who teaches the children here at the fort, would relish the company."

"I'm much obliged to you, sir, And I thank you for your offer. But I am not disposed to leave my wife. Even if I were, I can't see how it would sit well with Elizabeth."

When Alex casually mentioned the conversation to Elizabeth, she would not hear of him passing up the opportunity in Monterey. "If it were any ordinary job, I could not bear the thought of it. But *Alex!* Sixty dollars a month! And the chance to advance so rapidly. I've had a feeling about it all along. About California. I believe there will be great good fortune for us there, as there would have been had we been among the first to settle, say, in Massachusetts. Think of what happened for the industrious, the foresighted there. The descendants of those who seized opportunity in the beginning are now the merchant kings of Boston!"

So it had been decided. Not without reluctance on both their parts, not without misgivings and equivocation that lasted a full two weeks. Elizabeth had shed so many tears during that final fortnight she felt almost a sense of relief when Alex drove their Conestoga over the crest of low hills to the north of the fort.

Five

She named the baby after her father and her husband. John Alexander Todd was born on his mother's seventeenth birthday, October 26, 1845. The Frémont expedition had long since come and gone on through the Rockies farther west. Her condition, unstable through the summer, grew better with the onset of cooler weather. There were no complications at birth, though little John Alexander weighed only six and a half pounds when Captain Canby held him by his ankles and gave him his first stinging smack on the buttocks. He seemed healthy enough, Canby told Elizabeth. In time, nurtured by her ample supply of mother's milk, the baby should easily gain his way to normal weight.

Lying in bed with her infant suckling at her breast, Elizabeth reread once again the letter from Alex that had reached her in late August. He had joined a train of one hundred wagons heading mainly for Oregon. Fifteen of them, including his, would separate from the main column beyond Fort Hall, veer southwest, and continue on across an even more forbidding stretch of the Sierras to California. By then the greatest danger from the Indians would be behind them, he wrote. He anticipated little difficulty with the savages anyway. There were too many men and arms in the train to fear more than occasional harassment. He expected to be in California by the end of October.

Camelia Canby sat opposite Elizabeth's bed, rocking as she knitted booties for the baby. "Wouldn't that be something!" she said. "If he got all the way to Californee by the time his son is born."

Elizabeth smiled. Silver-haired Camelia Canby was given to talking too much, and too often about things not worth talking about. But she had been a blessing while Elizabeth was still sick, caring for her as if she were her own daughter. Alex had left Elizabeth three hundred dollars, more than half his savings. She offered to pay the Canbys for board and lodging, but Camelia stubbornly refused to accept a penny.

After the Christmas holidays, Elizabeth began helping Camelia at the schoolhouse. John Alexander still lagged in gaining normal weight, but aside from carrying his crude rocker cradle to the school where she could keep an eye on him, Elizabeth trusted in Elisha Canby's optimistic expectations.

In February, Camelia traveled east for a last visit to her failing, eighty-four-year-old mother in St. Louis. Elizabeth took over her teaching duties temporarily. By then she had read through most of Elisha Canby's shelf of classics and medical texts, some books of more recent vintage owned by Charles Bent, one of three brothers who had established the fort as a trading post in the thirties, and had begun borrowing volumes from the regimental commander. The increased demands of the schoolroom were a welcome distraction from boredom and the tediousness of marking time until she could rejoin her husband.

Absorbed by her teaching duties, Elizabeth almost resented Camelia's return, but within a few days she had her hands too full to feel anything but apprehension. Seizing upon the baby's frail little body, the croup quickly developed into pneumonia. John Alexander hovered near death for a month. Then, as quickly as it had started, the fever and the illness left him. With Elizabeth still breast-feeding him, he began a steady climb back to robust health and normal weight, but it took time. It was not until early June that Elizabeth tearfully said good-bye to the Canbys and headed north for Fort Laramie with one of the Bent brothers in a supply wagon accompanied by two squads of dragoons.

They arrived during the third week of the month. John Alexander had thrived during the rapid journey on his mother's milk and Camelia's Canby's finely ground corn mush. Still, Elizabeth let one wagon train, then another pass on from Fort Laramie until she was absolutely certain her infant was as healthy as he looked. Early in the fourth week she arranged to travel west with the James Frazier Reed family. Reed, a well-to-do furniture manufacturer from Springfield, Illinois, and his friend "Uncle" George Donner were the de facto leaders of a group of twenty wagons carrying

some eighty people. They planned to split off farther
west from the larger, Oregon-bound train in which
they traveled, and to head for California.

There was room enough for Elizabeth and her son.
Indeed, happening on the Reeds seemed to her an
extraordinary blessing. James Reed had spared nothing in providing on the long journey for his frail wife
and for Virginia, her fourteen-year-old daughter by a
former marriage, and their three small children. He
had three wagons, the largest of which carried his
family. Appropriately named the *Palace Car*, it
dwarfed the other wagons in the train. On either side,
steps made entrance easy. Inside, what amounted to a
small room was furnished with stagecoach spring
seats. An iron stove, its insulated chimney punching
up through the wagon's sun-bleached sailcloth cover,
warmed them on chilly mornings. On a second tier
laid across the vehicle there were beds for the entire
family. Margaret Reed's aged mother had begun the
trip with them but had died before they were halfway
across the Plains. At James Reed's insistence, Elizabeth and John Alexander took her bed.

Elizabeth thought Reed's occasional haughtiness and
the spoiled, somewhat jealous temperament of his stepdaughter easy enough to overlook, considering his
generosity. Beneath the bed platforms there were
spacious lockers packed with sacks of clothing, provisions and delicacies unheard of on the wagon trail.
From the moment she joined them, the Reeds shared
freely with Elizabeth. When she offered to help, James
Reed proudly told her there was no need. His hired
girl, Eliza Williams, did the cooking and washing and
helped with the children. He had three drivers and a
hired hand to take care of the livestock and anything
else that needed tending.

They celebrated July 4 amid the splendor of the
Rockies. Although Elizabeth had read of these mountains as well as the Alps, she was filled with awe and

wonder that anything could so completely dwarf the
mountains of her Vermont childhood. By July 17 they
had begun their descent down the far side of the Con-
tinental Divide at South Pass.

Late that day a rider coming up from the direction
of the sunset met them with a handbill-letter printed
by Lansford Hastings. The author of a book about
California, which some of the pioneers carried with
them, Hastings was touting a new, shorter trail he
had just explored. Rather than the well-worn route
that passed through Fort Hall and then branched
southwest toward California where it left the Oregon
Trail, Hastings urged them to veer off sooner to Fort
Bridger. He was waiting there to guide them on the
new trail, which angled south of the Great Salt Lake.

Elizabeth paid little attention to the conference between James Reed, George and Jacob Donner, and
several other heads of families who gathered about the
sweatstained frontiersman. After all, she thought, these
men know what they are doing. In addition to their
families, they had cattle, and in the case of Reed and
the Donners, a small fortune in personal possessions
and commercial goods to protect. Surely they would
make the wisest decision about which route to take.
But that night Elizabeth awoke in the darkness of the
huge wagon dripping with sweat. Once again she had
dreamed of a blizzard. This time with more detail
and two additional characters. . . .

*She was wading through thigh-deep snow, John
Alexander slung across her back in a makeshift carrying pouch cut from skins. A man dragged at her arm,
jerking her upright and then forward through almost
impassable drifts. He wore buckskins and had a sharply curved, full moustache, much like the one the frontiersman carrying the message from Lansford Hastings
wore. Then the snow was swirling out of the night
sky, pelting Elizabeth full in the face and blinding
her. She stumbled, and as she fell the baby slipped*

from the carrying pouch. The man cursed at her, then said something that was lost in the roaring of a wind so cold it made her feel as though she were lying naked on an icy lake. Coughing, spitting snow out of her mouth, she pushed to raise herself and sank deeper. She rolled on her back and pulled at her knees until she gained a sitting position. It seemed hours before she was standing again. She tried to breathe and choked on flakes of snow as broad as silver dollars. She covered her mouth with her shawl and took a deep breath. The baby . . . the baby . . . the baby. Frantically spinning, almost losing her balance again, she searched the snow around her feet. The baby was gone. . . . He has the baby. . . . He must have the baby. . . . She tried to find his outline in the driving, wet, stinging sheets of white that nearly toppled her backward. He was gone. The baby was gone. She closed her eyes and screamed. The sound was even more deafening than the wind.

In the morning she waited for the appropriate moment and drew James Reed aside as the hired hand doused the breakfast campfire.

"Is there any possibility that we will be traveling after the first snowfall in the Sierras?" she asked quietly.

Reed smiled. "None whatsoever, dear child. What prompts you to ask?"

"Nothing. Just curiosity. It is a bit late in the season, though, is it not?"

"Not really," Reed said with total assurance. "I thought perhaps you had chanced to overhear one of the worrywarts in this company. Not the Donners, mind you. But we do have a few traveling with us who are—how shall I put it? Limited, somewhat, in their mentality. And others hobbled by their fearful imaginations."

"I have not heard such directly or indirectly."

"Well, never fear. We are among the last trains to

be traveling this year, but there is plenty of time. It is still summer. If it will put your mind more at ease, I am quite certain we will be traveling with an expert guide by a nigher route to California, one that eliminates some four hundred miles from the journey. We should cross the Sierras many weeks before the first snowflake falls."

"May I trouble you with one more question?"

"As many as you like," Reed said, waving his hand magnanimously.

"The man who rode up with the message yesterday —will he be traveling back with us?"

"The mountain man? No. He left early this morning for Fort Laramie. Lansford Hastings will be our guide."

Elizabeth thanked him and returned to the wagon. She felt like a fool.

On July 19, with the going easier each passing hour, they camped at the waters of the Little Sandy. Under the willows that lined the creek, a vote was taken. A few California-bound wagons elected to follow the Oregon Trail to Fort Hall and then cut southwest on the proven route. All twenty wagons under the influence of James Reed and George Donner voted to follow the freshly cut tracks of the Bryant-Russell party and the Young-Harlan contingent ahead of them. They had cut off here toward Fort Bridger, Lansford Hastings, and the new, shorter route.

Elizabeth was surprised when George Donner was elected leader of the party rather than James Reed. But she knew the wealthy sixty-two-year-old farmer and Reed were the closest of friends, and that Reed's judgment, however much the less affluent voters of the party might resent him, would be no small factor in any decisions Donner made. For all James Reed's somewhat lofty, slightly patronizing manner, she felt secure with him, safe. He was forty-six, in splendid physical health, and he had already displayed his fatherly protectiveness of her.

Handsome, blond, strapping Lewis Keseberg had found excuses to visit the *Palace Car*, obviously smitten with Elizabeth. James Reed had finally put a halt to it, extricating Elizabeth from what had become an awkward situation and sending Keseberg permanently back to the wife he beat regularly in the privacy of their wagon.

George Donner's tiny forty-five-year-old wife, Tamsen, was the only one in the party who seemed disappointed with the choice of the new, shorter route. Normally gregarious and high-spirited, she walked along beside her wagon now, gloomy and dejected as the wheels, oxen, and small clusters of beef and dairy cattle raised a thin cloud of dust around the train. It was relatively easy going over this arid tableland, and everyone else was happy. Elizabeth was content. She had long since dismissed her fears after the nightmare as the foolish reaction of a young girl alone with her baby far from home. Holding John Alexander in her arms and rocking him as she stood in the well of the wagon behind Reed's driver, she gazed westward over scattered sagebrush to the point where the earth fell away under a sky dotted with buttermilk clouds. Four hundred miles shorter was four hundred miles sooner. Four hundred miles less before she saw her beloved Alex again.

The next ten days were a series of almost leisurely rides between campsites and campfires. Night meals had a festive air. During the day several men, Reed among them, rode out and returned with kills. Antelope, rabbit, and bighorn sheep dressed and cured in the Rockies, sizzled over blazing logs in the cool, early evening. Later the fiddles and banjos were broken out, and there was dancing under the brightest moon Elizabeth had ever seen. Accustomed to the howling of wolves and the gargled yipping of coyotes in the distance, she and John Alexander slept without stirring each night.

They crossed the Big Sandy, then followed its north bank to the Green River. On their left a small cluster of low bluffs broke the monotony of the flat, barren country, and there seemed to be mountains a long way ahead. But for now all they had to do was follow the fresh tracks of the two parties traveling ahead of them and let the beasts of burden do the rest. Occasionally deep sand and boulders slowed their progress and stirred the men to brief bursts of intense effort. But for the most part their greatest difficulty was staying awake. They crossed the Green and then wove back and forth across Black's Fork Creek, washing their feet in less than six inches of deliciously cool water. A drowsy, lulling contentment settled over everyone.

On July 28, two log cabins surrounded by a log fence took shape in the distant afternoon haze. The sight was disappointing. They had expected more—a fort rather than a twin-structure trading post and corral. As they drew closer, their disappointment grew to apprehension. The wagons of the Bryant-Russell and Young-Harlan parties were nowhere to be seen. Except for the two grizzled mountain men waving their hats at the gate, Fort Bridger looked deserted.

Six

Praise God we have finally rejoined the California Trail somewhere West of the Great Salt Lake. We are at a point, exactly how far from California we do not know, that we likely would have reached weeks ago had we not taken the short cut. Shortcut indeed! There is not a body among us who does not wish we never listened to that man Hastings. And it is a miracle that only one person has died after all we have been through in the past two months.

It is hard to understand why Hastings would lead us into such an ordeal, why he was not there at Fort Bridger in the first place as he promised. How could he just leave word to follow the tracks of the two parties he went off with? Why, Lord, would Bridger and his partner, Vazquez, praise the route we have just taken, knowing what was involved?

Weber Canyon was well nigh impassable, even after the two groups with Hastings laid down a road, if you can call it that. When I think of Hastings leaving a note on a berry bush for one of our party to ride ahead and parlay with him, it makes me want to wring the man's neck! Bad enough, all of it, but he had never seen the canyon route himself! He had relied on the information of one of his illiterate scouts. . . . My God, what gall. And then to suggest that we cut through the mountains instead of the canyon, a suggestion followed, I hate to say, more

out of James Reed's concern for keeping the Palace Car
in one piece than anything else. How could these men be
so blind? We had already yielded four days resting and
repairing at Fort Bridger. By the time Reed got back from
his ride to overtake Hastings and gain his hollow advice,
five more days were lost. Anyone here would pay dearly
for those days now. But they were too blind to see we
should have doubled back then toward Fort Hall and the
proven way! Spilt milk, as Father used to say.

Hastings would not even come back to guide us through
the mountains. I believe they are called the Wasatch, and
none of us will ever forget them. When dark the moon
itself must look no more forbidding to the angels. Underbrush and alder so thick along the streams the men could
scarcely hack their way through with broadaxes. Terrain
so rocky and steep it is a wonder we did not all slide to
our doom. Twenty-one days to travel thirty-six miles! Then,
beyond the Salt Lake Valley and the desert, a veritable
parade of low-mountain chains running north and south.
Praise God for the streams on the Western side of each
of those intervening valleys!

It becomes obvious that George Donner is no leader
of men. He is too old, too soft, and does not have the
manner. Thank God, unpopular as James Reed has become
because of his decision to cross the Wasatch, that he is
with us. No one else in the party, save William Eddy, is
cut out for such extremities as we have experienced. Most
are but a degree better than greenhorns and tenderfeet,
and some lack the spines of men.

Upon reading the last line I almost move to strike it
out, for the labors through the mountains—and Lord
knows, across that Salt Desert—would sorely tax even the
strongest man. But the shirking—not by all, but by many
—the loafing and malingering and unwillingness to learn
lessons that need be learned quickly, have been inexcusable.

By the time we reached the desert, we had lost many
precious days. Heaped on all that, Hastings's claim that
the dry drive was but only thirty-five or forty miles, and

would take but two days and two nights, was criminally preposterous. It was more like eighty miles! Almost a week without water to replenish with, broiled by day and frozen stiff at night. It is a miracle we have it behind us.

Looking around me, I want to weep. We have lost many precious weeks. Eight wagons are strewn across the desert, dry-rotted or axle-deep in sand and alkaline sink slush. Countless oxen, cattle, and horses dead and bloated under the broiling sun. Untold possessions—bureaus, trunks full of clothes, dishes, silks, silver—the objects of a lifetime scattered or buried in mounds the scurrilous Indians will surely strip away. All because of Hastings.

No, I give him too much credit. There were those in this train who were warned, I now know. Warned as early as Fort Laramie by the mountain man named Clyman. And by pilgrims traveling with them until the Little Sandy. And again, unbeknownst to me, by another mountain man just outside Fort Bridger. Joseph Walker is his name, and, I am told, he is among the most knowledgeable men in these God-forsaken parts. And of those forewarned who insisted on this "nigher" way was James Reed himself! I cannot believe it.

But I also cannot but feel pity for him now. All his possessions save one wagon and two horses and the money belt he carries are gone. He is lucky his family has survived, reduced as they are. As for me, I walk a lot. The Eddys and the Breen family kindly let John Alexander ride with them often. Poor young Mr. Halloran is dead of consumption, and would have been anyway even had we been traveling smoothly up there on the zephyrs and the clouds. It would take an entire book to fully describe the agony this party has already gone through. Mr. Stanton and Mr. McCutchen have been sent on ahead by horse and mule to California to bring back help and supplies. But how far California is I cannot even hazard a guess. If they do not soon return God knows what further horrors we will endure, for the company is torn asunder in dissension and the food we have may not be sufficient.

It is a comfort, as we rest up here by the Mary's, to

recall the news learned at Fort Bridger that the Grigsby-Ide Party—and therefore my dear Husband Alexander—reached a place in California called Sutter's Fort a year ago this coming month. But as I gaze at his son, John Alexander, who seems so healthy, so miraculously unaffected by this ordeal, I find myself wondering if we will ever see his father again. I weaken and must not think thus. But dear God, the sun does loop over us further and further to the South each day, and the days grow shorter.

Seven

The Great Salt Desert and the mountains that had nearly broken their backs were behind them now, as they worked their way northwest, then west, then southwest along the Mary's River to its sinkhole. Behind them as well, scattered across the mountains and salt desert, were major portions of their will, spirit, and rationality. Their bodies cried out for respite, but there was no time to rest. Pushing forward in their twelve surviving wagons, their oxen and cattle, their few horses and dogs emaciated, the emigrants strained to put twenty miles behind them each day. Normally, in this high, rolling basin-land dotted with greasewood and sagebrush, it would have been hard work and no more. But they were spiritually and physically exhausted now, terrified by the time they had lost, and each day took a little more of the life, strength, and humanity out of them.

By chance, the Donners' oxen were the least weakened by the torturous days in the Wasatch and the desert. They soon pulled ahead of the rest of the train by a full day's ride. No one thought to keep the wagons more tightly knit. Indians crept in one night and killed two oxen, knowing they would be left behind. Two mornings later a horse was missing. The losses, and the knowledge that Indians were watching their every move, pushed all of them further toward the breaking point.

Everyone walked now. It was easier on the weakened animals. There were still enough possessions in the wagons to make a modest start in California. Food was another matter. Provisions were dwindling at an alarming rate. Stanton and McCutchen and the supplies they were to bring back from Sutter's Fort would soon be a matter of life and death. With all that hanging over them, as they strained to push westward as fast as they could, tension mounted and tempers began to burst. It began with harsh words and curt answers. But then it turned ugly.

On October 5, the second segment of the train reached another long, steep, rock-crested sand hill. It seemed they would have to use double teams for each of the wagons on this one. Two made it over without as much difficulty as the men anticipated. John Snyder, a rawboned man who had joined the party late, near Fort Bridger, was driving the third wagon in line for the ascent. He was certain he could make it up and over with just his own team. He decided to rest his oxen for a few minutes before the long pull.

Behind him, Milt Elliott, one of Reed's teamsters, sat waiting. A second team of oxen was already hitched to the wagon he was driving. Elizabeth and Mrs. Reed walked past it, through the narrow wash that led to the slope, and moved out of the way. James Reed was partway up the hill, ready to prod the teams if Milt Elliott needed assistance.

Elliott grew impatient. He assumed Snyder was waiting until the men ahead brought a second team back down the incline. There seemed to be just enough room to pass, so Elliott snapped the reins and began guiding his wagon around Snyder.

"What the hell do you think you're doing?" Snyder barked.

"No sense in waiting 'til you get your second team hitched up, is there?" Elliott answered, surprised at the sharp edge in Snyder's voice. He shrugged. It was a matter of small concern. But as he moved forward, his two lead oxen balked, moved sideways, butted, and became entangled with Snyder's team.

"You stupid ass!" Snyder bellowed. "Look what the hell you've done!"

Elliott glanced at the women standing nearby. "Mind your tongue, Snyder. . . ."

Elizabeth, watching from a few yards away, felt a sense of dread as Snyder leaped from his seat, bull-whip in hand.

"I'll show you what I'll mind, you flabby little bastard." Snyder's face was flushed. Now all the anger, fatigue, and frustration of the past weeks welled and pushed him beyond the point of reason. He lifted the bullwhip and lashed out at Elliott's lead oxen, slashing at them again and again. Elizabeth screamed and Mrs. Reed fainted as the beasts moaned in agony. Again Snyder's whip sliced into hide.

"For God's sake, man!" James Reed cried. He ran down the slope and caught Snyder's arm. Milt Elliott, too stunned to move, watched speechless as Snyder shoved Reed and sent him sprawling. He lashed out again at the oxen.

Reed had fallen hard. For a few seconds he waited until the pinpoints before his eyes disappeared. He got up slowly, unsheathing the hunting knife strapped to his belt. "*Snyder!* Stop what you're doing or you'll answer for it!"

The sight of the knife further enraged Snyder. "You big-headed son of a bitch!" He drove at Reed, reversing the bullwhip in his hand and swinging the butt down hard across the older man's forehead. Elizabeth screamed again as Snyder grabbed the front of Reed's shirt and raised the butt of the whip.

Reed could hardly see. Blood was streaming down his forehead into his eyes. All he could make out was the dark shape of Snyder's arm, rising again. He jerked his shoulders and head to the left. Almost reflexively, his right arm swung in a roundhouse. Sunlight glistened on the long blade in Reed's right hand as it arced and drove deep under Snyder's collarbone.

Elizabeth rushed between them at almost the same instant. *"Stop it! Dear God, stop it!"*

Snyder was not through. Crazed, he brought the whip butt up again and sent Elizabeth reeling with a glancing blow on the side of her head. Reed held onto the knife. His shoulder was numb. He stared at the handle protruding from Snyder's flannel shirt. Steady, rhythmic surges of blood pumped out and around the hilt. Reed never saw the third blow. It smashed down full on his skull and drove him to his knees. Through the streaming blood, the spreading numbness in his shoulder, and the pain that filled his head, Reed saw Snyder suddenly stop moving and turn ashen. Dumbly, Reed looked at the knife in his hands. It had pulled free when he went down.

The left side of Snyder's shirt was soaked in a darkening red. He felt the strange sensation of liquid filling slowly in the hollow of his left lung. He turned, walked a few steps up the hill, and fell, bubbled blood spilling from his mouth.

Reed was on one knee now. His stepdaughter and his wife, recovered from her fainting but trembling visibly, held handkerchiefs to the deep wounds on his scalp. He broke free of them, tears rolling down his cheeks, and staggered to where one of the men cradled Snyder's head in his arms. "Oh, God," Reed sobbed. "I never meant for anything like this to happen."

Snyder tried to raise one arm unsuccessfully. He

coughed, burbling up more blood. "I'm to blame for all of it," he wheezed. "I don't know what came over. . . ."

They buried Snyder in a shroud between two planks to frustrate burrowing animals who might pick up the scent of death. Most of the afternoon, while Reed sat apart with his family, two factions argued over shooting him here or waiting and bringing him to trial in California. Lewis Keseberg, still bitter about the tongue-lashing Reed had given him over Elizabeth, exhorted them to hang him immediately from a propped up ox-yoke. In the end, they banished Reed from the train. They allowed him his badly deteriorated mare, but no gun and no food. After he left, Elizabeth borrowed a horse, and under the pretext of taking a last message to Reed from his ailing wife, saw to it that he at least had an even chance against whatever waited for him ahead. Tucked inside her undergarments was an 1836-model Patterson Colt revolver Milt Elliott had stashed in a saddlebag on a happier evening back on the trail to Fort Bridger.

They caught up with the Donners a few days later and learned that Reed had stopped for a night with them, then journeyed on with one of the drivers. Reed had left word he planned to send back provisions if he reached California.

Elizabeth was mildly heartened to join the first section of the train again. But her modest rise in spirits was short-lived. Within minutes of arriving at the Donners' camp, she saw a forbidding sight. Dizzying waves of heat rose from the dry sandy country that stretched on either side of the dwindling river, but the sensation she felt was that of walking into an icehouse. Off to the side of the wagons, flies swarmed around the almost bare bones of a member of the Hastings group. Just a few weeks earlier, he had been killed by an arrow. Buried, he had been unearthed by

Digger Indians, stripped of his clothing, and left there to rot. Wolves and coyotes had done the rest.

It seemed to Elizabeth that Snyder's ghost haunted the members of the party now. Another wagon broke down and had to be abandoned. The Diggers swept in early one morning and drove off more horses. Grass for the surviving cattle grew scant as they plodded southwest. Almost to the sink of the Mary's, they camped one night in a spot where there was no grass at all. The cattle scattered to find food. Again the Indians drove them off, eighteen of them, including a precious dairy cow. By the time the party reached the sink itself, the heat and the savages had robbed them of almost a hundred head.

On October 13 they set out across the last stretch of pure desert between the Mary's and the Truckee River. The combined oxen and cow teams pulling the remaining wagons were half-starved. They pushed on through the day and most of the night, resting only long enough to gain a little strength. Water from hot springs kept them from dying of thirst. It was bitter, almost undrinkable, but "cooled" to lukewarm in kettles, a little of it was just enough to keep them going. By midmorning John Alexander showed signs of dehydration. He no longer even cried. Carrying him, Elizabeth dabbed a handkerchief wrapped around a chunk of sugar on his tongue. She was becoming desperate. Her own milk had augmented the amount of liquid he had been taking in. But now, with scarcely any water to drink herself, Elizabeth's breasts were drying up.

Sometime near noon William Eddy discovered that the Breens, normally people who would share, were hoarding half a cask of water. When Eddy asked for a ladleful for his children and John Alexander, Patrick Breen refused.

"You son of a bitch!" Eddy shouted. "I'll kill you if you don't share the water."

Patrick Breen didn't even bother to stop walking. "You don't have the strength. You're unarmed, and you'd kill yourself in the effort."

Exhausted and dizzy from the heat, William Eddy could not think clearly. What Breen said seemed to make sense. He could not remember what he had done with the Colt revolver. Elizabeth's mind was clearer. She was certain Eddy's children and John Alexander were about to die of thirst. She walked slowly to Eddy's wagon and reached in under a buffalo skin. The Kentucky long rifle was in the same place she had seen it when Eddy had slipped her the pistol for Reed. She climbed into the wagon and muzzle-loaded it the way she had seen Eddy do it many times. Then she carried the rifle forward, cocked and pointed it at Patrick Breen. He stopped walking.

"I am not asking for myself or any other adult," she said quietly. "But if you do not give the children some of your water, I will shoot you here on the spot."

"Mrs. Todd, that water is . . ."

"*I mean it!*" she shrieked. "And may God forgive me."

Breen broke out the cask. Momentarily shocked back to his senses, he rationed out as much as he could for Elizabeth and the Eddys as well as the children. William Eddy took the rifle back and smiled as he replaced it under the buffalo skin. The way Elizabeth had loaded the rifle, it would have blown up in her face.

The train moved on in the still, parchingly dry heat. Within a few hours the incident was forgotten. There were more pressing matters to think of. They kept on through the afternoon, stopped briefly at sunset, then, grumbling, pushed on again as night overtook them. More oxen fell. They had to be cut free of their yokes and abandoned. Somehow, held in what was now a near-delirious trance, the emigrants managed to pick one foot up, move it forward, and then pick up the other. They knew if they stopped they would never move again.

Toward daybreak of October 15, they saw the trees of a river bottom ahead. They were certain it was a mirage. But as they dragged themselves the last three miles, they finally realized the trees were real. Gaping in awe, they walked the last few steps to the bank of the Truckee River and lay down beside it. At first they did not even drink. The sight of it was almost painful. The river was clear and pure and flowing fifty feet from bank to bank under cottonwoods. Hesitantly, as though the entire scene before them would suddenly vanish, the ten families, their passengers and hired help cupped their hands and took small sips of water. Around them lay a verdant pasture of lush grass and wild peas. Birds sang in the trees.

Elizabeth, slowly sprinkling small amounts of water over John Alexander's forehead and onto his lips and tongue, wept. She had been certain on that last stretch of desert that they would both die. Now, sitting here in this veritable Eden, as exhausted as she was, she vowed never to give up hope again. She gazed westward over the cottonwoods and the vow caught almost palpably in her throat. Off on the horizon, she could make out the hazy, blue-gray outlines of the Sierras against the lightening sky. Even at this distance, their enormous size made her shudder. John Alexander made a happy cooing noise, and she was distracted for an instant. When she looked back at the mountains, she gasped. Cloaking their heights now, as the first rays of the sun reached them from the east, lay a mantle of brilliantly white snow.

Eight

Truckee Lake
The Sierras
December 15, 1846

Camped at this bitter, freezing place since early November. Tomorrow some of us will make a fourth attempt to cross the pass and go on to Captain Sutter's fort beyond what they call Bear Valley. It will not be without the help of The Almighty if we make it, weakened as we are. But I know that if we do not go with Mr. Stanton and the two Indians from the fort we will surely not survive the winter. The snow is up to the rooves of the three cabins here and the same, I am told, some five miles east where the Donners have camped in bough-covered tents. There are sixty-odd men, women, and children here by the lake. Twenty or so with the Donners. There is scarcely any food of substance left. The dried beef and flour Stanton brought are almost all used up. Most of Sutter's mules and many of the surviving horses, oxen, and beeves wandered off and died in the high, covering drifts. Those bony few that did not stray are now eaten up. The bear William Eddy risked his life to shoot is gone also and no other game has come near enough to be seen. Even the fish below the ice on the lake ignore the bait on the hooks.

We are reduced to killing the last of the dogs and boiling bones and hides. Last night Mrs. Murphy's grandchildren idly tore off pieces of the Buffalo throw they lay on before the fire, speared them with small sticks and ate them after they were crisped. I do not know what will happen here if the men, all but the strongest—nay, even they—sink any further from lack of proper food and the unbelievable cold. It is difficult for them to carry firewood now. If the snow and the storms that sometimes last longer than a week continue, they will not even be able to move about enough to chop and carry what little there is.

John Alexander and I have been staying with the Eddys and Mrs. Murphy's family—all twelve of them! Nothing can describe the odors and the filth here and in the other two cabins, one of which we found built by an earlier traveler. Vermin crawl upon us in the night. It will only grow worse as more weeks pass. I mean to criticize no one here. Eighteen unbathed men, women, and children, some of them sick from time to time, trying to survive amid the smoke from the fires and the things boiling in the kettles, cannot much turn their thoughts to impossible housecleaning chores.

The baby is still feeding at my breast, as is one-year-old Margaret at Eleanor Eddy's. They are both still tolerably healthy if all too thin. I do not like the fact that they cry less and less. It is a sign of growing weakness, I am sure. John Alexander has a cold again, and I fear leaving with him tomorrow almost as much as staying.

It is difficult not to be bitter. Looking back, it seems as if even one day would have put us across the mountains to the fort and safety. Any one of those days wasted at Fort Bridger, waiting for James Reed to reach and return with Hastings when we were in Weber Canyon, or the weeks lost in the mountains and following Hastings's insane roundabout trail. Even one of the five days spent resting at Stanton's urging after he courageously rejoined us at the Truckee Meadow below here. God knows even less than a half day would have put us across before that first attempt on November second. We were but three miles or so from the crest of the pass, according to Stanton. But the rest would not go on, staying instead around the campfire. We found ourselves covered with snow and the pass blocked by ten-foot drifts when we awoke in the morning.

I do not understand some of these people. I know how tired and frozen they were from wading and pushing waist high in snow. But Stanton and Eddy were just as tired, just as reduced in strength by that time as anyone, and they were ready to continue. As were a few others, myself included. It struck me then almost as if the rest were stubbornly, blasphemously daring God to bring his wrath down upon them.

That is foolish, but it is clear to me now that human nature either gets far worse or far better than average under exceeding trying conditions. There have been sacrifice, sharing, cooperation, even heroic efforts by some. But there have also been base greed in the form of forced payments for food, miserly hoarding, and probably worse. I find it difficult to believe that the Germans, Spitzer and Rhinehardt, did not kill Mr. Wolfinger for his money when they remained with him to bury his possessions after the loss of oxen at the sink of the Marys. Dear Lord, I could not even six months ago have uttered such about another human being. And God only knows what sort of person I will be even if John Alexander and I survive this next test.

Test it will surely be, but fearful of it as I am, I feel we leave none too soon. Despair has given way to sluggish resignation here. Eliza Williams's brother, Bayliss, died today. The accidental death back on the Truckee of Mrs. Murphy's son-in-law hangs heavy on the poor woman . . . not to mention her daughter. Harriet Spitzer is failing fast, I hear. No, I do not want to be here when the last of the victuals runs out and hunger begins to madden them all. I have seen them close to that state from thirst on the desert. And I fear if it comes upon them full, nothing, not even killing one another for a scrap of hide or bone, seems beyond possibility.

Eighteen of us will leave in the morning. Stanton, who says it is but thirty or so miles and that we should cover it in six days, will lead us. His two Indians. William Eddy and old Mr. Graves, the Vermonter who cunningly thought to fashion snowshoes for us out of the hickory oxbows and woven strips of rawhide. Of Mrs. Murphy's clan, Mr. and Mrs. Foster and their two sons will be going. So will Mr. Graves's two daughters and son-in-law, Jay Fosdick. The German man, Mr. Burger. Antonio the herder. (Oh, how he must pine for the warmth of his native Mexico!) Mrs. Pike and Mrs. McCutchen, whose husband took sick in California and could not return with Stanton. And young Patrick Dolan the bachelor.

At first they would not hear of my taking John Alexander. Dear William Eddy, who has been as loyal to me as he has to the Reeds, persuaded them in my favor!

The fire grows low now. Only large embers glow as the children quietly whimper in their fitful sleep. Dear God protect us and let it not snow again until we are down out of the mountains. I must now pack the small carryall I will take with me. Dearest husband, I will take this diary with me also so that, whatever happens, you will know that I tried to bring you your son and the money you trusted me with. I pray that I succeed, and know that my love and longing for you give me the strength and courage to go on.

Nine

A shaft of sunlight awoke Esther Cable Carter with
a start. She had slept only three hours, but she was
instantly wide awake. It seemed only seconds since
she had read the last diary entry and halted, staring at
the blank page that preceded the section enclosed by
black ribbon. She sat up and saw that the journal had
fallen off the bed. Putting on the velvet robe that
hung over a bedside chair, she picked the book up,
closed it, and fingered the ribbon for a moment before
tucking the journal away in the smaller of two bags
she had taken with her for the journey to Promontory.
When she snapped the clasp on the bag shut, her son
Todd stirred under his blankets on the blankets on the
cot, turned, but did not awaken.

Esther picked up a thick white towel embroidered
in blue with the words "Sierra Hotel" from the mar-
ble-topped oak lowboy near the door. She went back
to her bag for the small, red-and-gold leather case
containing an exquisite mother-of-pearl-backed brush
and comb and put it in one pocket of the robe. Alex
Todd had given it to her in St. Louis as a wedding
present two dozen years earlier. The towel over her
arm, she stooped and picked up the chamber pot from
under the bed. Crossing the room, she opened the

door a crack and checked the hallway. No one stirred
this early on the upper floors. She folded the towel
over her left arm and put her bare left hand out of
sight in the pocket of her robe. Barefoot, she padded
quietly to the door of Solana's room. As she raised her
hand to knock, the Indian woman, already dressed
and waiting, opened it. Seeing the towel and the
porcelain chamber pot, Solana nodded and turned
without a word to go to watch over young Todd.

After spilling and rinsing down the contents of the
chamber pot in one of the two bathing rooms down
the hall, Esther drew a quarter tub of warm water,
lathered, and rinsed off quickly. Stepping out of the
draining tub, she began toweling off in front of a mirror. It surprised her that she could not see the faint
scar on her nose from four feet away, even though the
sun now streamed through the gauze-curtained window. She brushed out her hair, then coiled, folded,
and tucked it on the back of her head with a finger-
sized tortoiseshell comb.

She looked at her face again and could not understand why two decades had scarcely touched it. It
pleased her that there were few lines, not even the
beginning of a wrinkle in the milky white skin around
her eyes and full mouth. Glancing lower, she noted
that the pale stretch-marks slanting along the sides of
her abdomen were more noticeable, faint as they
were, than the faded splotch that encircled the tip of
her nose.

She smiled. Then she became aware of the rest of
her figure. She looked away from the mirror and put
on her robe. At five feet seven and a half inches, she
towered over most women, and their petiteness made
her feel awkward and clumsy. She did not care for
the conformation of her body. The outlines were
right, generally speaking, but there was not enough
flesh on her hips and limbs to suit her. Conversely, she
thought her breasts were disproportionately big, and
she was puzzled again that the rose-brown nipples still

pointed forward rather than down after nursing three
children.

Back in her room, she found her son awake, dressed,
and staring out the window at the wisps of steam rising slowly from between the giant wheels of the engine at the station.

"Good morning, mother." The boy blew her a per-
functory kiss and looked back at the train. "You
haven't changed your mind, have you? I can still ride
with Mister Sam in *Jupiter?*"

"No, dear, I haven't changed my mind." She walked
up behind him, leaned over and kissed him on the
cheek. In a way, she thought, William Carter's death
had mercifully spared him the confirmation of his
worst suspicions. Todd looked more like Alex every
year.

"All the way to Reno?" the boy said, rapt.

"If you sit exactly where Mister Sam puts you and
do not remove the leather belt from around your waist."

"I promise! I promise not to!"

"If you do, he'll stop the train and send you back."

He was as headstrong as most seven-year-old boys,
but he was in awe of the engineer. Esther knew that,
and the threat of being banished from the engine
would keep him where she wanted him until they had
crossed the Sierras.

She turned to Solana and took the older woman's
leathery, pale-bronze hands in hers. "Will you take
him to breakfast for me? I don't want to talk to anyone this morning."

"Whatever you wish. Will you not eat?"

"Please have someone bring me a tray of tea, bread,
and jam. I don't want you to carry it."

"The bags?"

"I'll take them with me when I'm dressed."

Solana nodded. "I will see that he is safely in the
iron horse when it is time. Then I will wait at the
riverfront for the giant raft . . . launch."

Esther smiled and put her arms around the Indian

woman. "God keep you. I'll see you when I return."

Solana embraced Esther and took the boy's hand. "Come. You must eat as much as Mister Sam does this morning."

After Esther ate, she took off the robe and applied more than the usual amount of lilac water and scented powder on her body. She put on a chemise, but no other undergarments below her waist before slipping into a fresh black dress, hat, and gloves. At precisely 7:00 A.M. she went down the outside stairs on the flank of the building to the wooden walkway. Through a window beneath the stairs she heard the clatter of dishes and the shouts of the German cook over the muted pidgin-English replies of a Chinese pantryman. Breakfast was being served to a full dining room. It was as she had planned it. She wished to see none of the men or women who would be on the train.

At the bottom of the stairs she stopped as she heard a team of horses round the corner of the building. A landau drawn by two extraordinary chestnut mares passed and continued on down the street. After the dust raised by the carriage had settled, she walked quickly, bags in hand, across the street and along the diagonal path to the station. Halfway there, she veered off toward the rear of the train. The trainman waiting at the steps of the private car saw her and began running in her direction. He was a portly man who saw to all Charles Crocker's needs whenever the railroad boss traveled in the special car. The morning was already warm, and he was sweating when he reached Esther.

"Let me carry those, Mizz Carter." He tipped his short-billed cap and swooped up the luggage in almost one movement. He was breathing hard. "I should have . . . waited for you . . . outside the . . . hotel."

"Thank you kindly, but there was no need."

"You're quite early, ma'am. The train won't be leaving for two more hours."

"Yes, I know. I wanted to avoid the crowd."

He nodded his head. Poor woman, she was still grieving for that son of a bitch Carter. "I understand, ma'am. I'll look in on you from time to time to see if there's anything you need."

They were inside the private car now, and the trainman placed the bags behind the curtain at the middle of the car.

"There is a bellpull to call you?"

"Yes, ma'am." He pointed to the braided cord that hung through loops above the windows on one side of the car. "I'll hook it up to the next section right away. If I'm not there, one of the other men will let me know."

Esther handed him a silver dollar.

"Oh, no, ma'am. I couldn't."

She pressed it back into his hand. "I want you to have it."

He looked down at his shoes.

"Would you be kind enough to tell the conductors that I do not wish to be disturbed for any reason. I'm certain I won't be needing anything, at least not until Reno. I didn't sleep well last night, and I want to rest."

"Certainly, ma'am. I understand. Shall I pull the shades down?"

"Yes, please do."

"I'll be sure no one comes through the door of the next car. I'll lock it. Some of the passengers will be, ah, celebrating a bit, and . . ."

"That's very thoughtful of you. We'll be stopping at Dutch Flat?"

"Yes, ma'am. For just a few minutes."

"Then would you do one other thing for me? My son Todd will be riding in *Jupiter*, with Mister Sam. Would you just look in on him to see that he's behaving himself?"

"Why, certainly, ma'am. He's a fine boy, young Master Carter."

"I'm sure there'll be no need. But if for any reason

he should have to be brought back, please take him to his . . . godfather, Judge Todd. Tell Judge Todd I'll fetch him at Reno."

When the trainman was gone, Esther took the leatherbound journal out of her valise and sat in a chair opposite the one she had occupied the night before. She raised the shade just enough to provide reading light. She opened the book again to the black-ribboned entries and stared at the double-knotted bow midway down the first, blank page. *Now?* she wondered. *Yes, now. I will read them now—and again after I have read it all. Twice. If I falter, if I lose my nerve between here and Donner Lake, the words on* these *pages will serve to see me through the last minutes of all this, whatever the result.*

Slowly, trembling, she untied the knots and the bow, turned the page, took a deep breath, and began reading again.

Ten

South Fork Cabin
July, 1847

December 22, 1846 . . .
Predating these pages. Recording after the fact, as best as I can recall. . . .

Separated from the rest of the snowshoe party this day. Down on the west side of the mountain crest, far from the pass. My own fault. Decent motives, but foolish—and in the end unforgivable, considering what happened. Willful *ignoring, forgetting that my first responsibility was to John Alexander, then myself, not the two women. . . .*

The two women had been gone for an hour after dawn that morning. The previous night, a snowsquall had smothered the campfire. They were six days gone from the lake, less sure now that Bear Valley and the settlements west of it were within no more than five or six days' march. By now, they were exhausted, Stanton worst of all, from the effort of scaling, then descending, the pass and slogging west through waist-high drifts. Near starvation, almost out of their meager provisions, all of them were nonetheless still optimistic. Five of them had gone searching for firewood, among them the two women. The three men were back, breakfast of dried meat and coffee had been eaten, but the two women, Mary Graves and Mrs. McCutchen, still had not returned.

"Got to go on," William Foster said grimly. "We'll all die here if we don't."

The brilliant sunlight bouncing off the snow almost blinded Elizabeth as she turned to him. As weak as they were, she scarcely knew whom she was responding to. "We cannot just leave them behind!"

"Have to," William Eddy said.

She turned to "Uncle" Billy Graves. The old man who had contrived the snowshoes looked away. "Mister Graves. You are not going to just stand there and do nothing, say nothing about this, are you? Your daughter may die!"

"No choice," he mumbled, glancing guiltily at his other daughter and her husband, Jay Fosdick.

"Then *I* will look for them, damn you! I will search for one half hour, no more. And then I will come back. Surely you can wait a half an hour."

One after another, they reluctantly nodded.

"Has someone a pocket watch?"

Graves handed one to her. She stared at the gold-encased face. It was seven forty-eight. "I'll be back no later than eight thirty." She glanced at Stanton, who sat propped against a tree, hoping that neither he nor anyone else would check the time. He winked conspiratorially at her. For a moment she thought of leaving John Alexander with them. But then a sweeping glance at their grimly set, almost emaciated faces decided her against it. Adjusting the sling in which she carried the baby, she set out in the direction the women had taken.

She never found Mrs. McCutchen or Mary Graves, nor was she able to retrace her steps through the windblown snow to the campsite that day. Blessedly, it did not snow during the night she spent under the bow of an evergreen, shivering, numb with cold, nursing the baby, starting with every frozen cracking of the surrounding branches, and certain that at any moment they would be set upon by a mountain lion.

She stumbled on the campsite the following day and was seized by terror. All but one of them were gone. Stanton was still sitting where he had been the previous morning, frozen solid. Staring at her lifelessly through a thin shell of ice, his hand was clutched around a folded piece of paper. Beginning to cry, she pried the note loose and unfolded it.

Dear Mrs. Todd:
   Mrs. McCutchen and I got back safely. I tried to make them wait. They would not. Left here 10 A.M. Mister Stanton offered to remain and travel with you. He is so weak it will no doubt be you who helps him. The men say we will be going due West at all times, unless the way is blocked, then South if possible, otherwise in any direction that is open until we find a path west or south again. Forgive me, and bless you for searching. God speed both of you back to us.
                                        MARY GRAVES

Dropping the note, she collected herself, said a prayer for Stanton, asked his and God's forgiveness, removed his boots, and put them on over hers. After she strapped her makeshift snowshoes back on, she thought to search his pockets. One of them contained a narrow, eight-inch piece of hide. Turning away, she glanced at the campfire ashes, then resolutely set out across the clearing.

There were no tracks in the windblown snow as she pushed west. John Alexander gurgled, unaware, in the makeshift shawl-sling. She looked back once, first at Stanton, then at the enormous, white-capped dome of Cisco Butte. Ignoring the fire in her thighs and calves, she crossed a rise, then threaded along windswept rocks on the edge of a gorge. Finally, the terrain sloped downhill, and she plunged on, her snowshoes coming untied every tenth of a mile, into the bottoms just west of the Yuba River headlands. Zigzagging, guessing which way the rest had gone, she crossed a series of ridges and valleys that flanked narrow, snow-covered streams. She noticed vaguely that they seemed to amble almost imperceptibly southward. She kept on, stopping every fifteen minutes to rest her numb legs, let her bursting lungs and heart quiet—and pray.

When the hollow ache in her stomach became unbearable, she got up and began walking and wading again. As precarious as they were, the wind-scoured rocks and ledges along the upper portions of each ridge seemed more easily negotiable. Climbing, falling in the snow, getting up and going on again, she reached a rim and continued southward. At the top of a gradually upward-sloping rise, she stopped to rest. Looking around, she saw the formidable Yuba buttes behind her, to the north an impassable wall of mountains. As she stood there, the air around her suddenly chilled and grew slightly darker. She gazed to the west. The sun had dropped behind the mountains.

Her hands were numb. Above the upper edge of the shawl wrapped around her face, the tops of her cheeks felt as though they were being repeatedly punctured by hundreds of razor-sharp needles. The rising wind mocked her. The bridge of her nose and her forehead ached so much she wanted to scream at the pain. She knew with nightfall it would be even colder.

She looked around again. Deep snow blanketed the undulated floor of the pine forest covering the surrounding mountains. Thirty feet to her left she spotted a rock outcropping. Remembering how the men in the snowshoe party had set green wood on the surface of the snow to lie on, even built small fires on the primitive platforms to warm them through the nights, she began breaking small branches off the evergreens and the few birches in sight. It took her an hour of exhausting labor to set out a rude wood and pine-needle platform on the snow beneath the overhanging ledge.

Finished, she placed one of the larger pine branches behind her and huddled against it in the corner formed by the rock and the mountainside. She did not bother to take the sling off. Uncovering John Alexander's mouth and one of her nipples, she nursed him slowly, wiping the milk off his chin when he dribbled and licking it ravenously off her gloves. She was aware that her breasts were smaller, that the milk was diminishing. For a moment her fear increased almost to hysteria. She looked up, and the trunk of a nearby fir tree rippled before her eyes, took the form of a bear, and lunged at her.

She screamed, startling the baby and making him cry. She hushed him, looked back, and saw just the trunk of a tree again. Fishing in her carrying bag, she pulled out the narrow piece of hide she'd found in Stanton's pocket. For a moment she was almost overcome with the urge to cram all of it into her mouth. Transforming itself before her eyes, it became a salamander. Startled, she dropped it. When it was a piece of hide again, she picked it up, broke off a quarter of the strip, ate it, and put the remainder back in her bag.

Easing down on her side, she turned toward the rock, cradled John Alexander against her belly, then pulled her knees up and lay one arm over him. Staring at the ridges on the base of the darkening ledge, she saw them start to wave before her and wondered if she would live through the night. She closed her eyes. Somehow she remembered to pull one piece of the shawl up over her face and tuck it under her bonnet before she slept.

She was awakened by John Alexander's weak crying. Still tired, she was stiff but, astonishingly, not as cold as she expected. Stretching her legs out, she felt the small drift of snow the wind had blown up along her back, bottom, and the soles of her boots. Without moving further she partly uncovered one breast and fed her child. She took a glove off for ten seconds and felt under his clothing. He was warm. She looked at the gold pocket watch she had borrowed from Graves. It was already past eight. She had to get started no matter how much she preferred staying right where she was.

At noon, after she had repeated the bone-wearying movements of the previous morning over similar terrain, snow began to fall. Nearly delirious, she had no idea it was Christmas Eve. She pushed through the drifts and along the rocks, wobbling as her own shoes slipped back and forth within Stanton's boots. For another two hours she dragged herself westward as the wind rose steadily.

A rim overlooking another frozen stream turned south. Slowing with each step, she fought her way forward for another fifteen minutes, thankful she was no longer heading straight into the stinging flakes of snow. She stopped for a moment to regain her breath. The dollar-sized snowflakes almost choked her. When she tried to pick one boot up through the half foot of new snow covering a thick layer of crust, she found she couldn't. Standing there, snow swirling around her, swaying drunkenly, she reached into the bag and hungrily ate a third of the remaining piece of hide, putting the rest back. John Alexander was sleeping. She leaned over, saw the pasty, solidifying mucus almost filling his nostrils, and heard the faint wheeze of his breath. For a second she gave up hope. But then, slowly, the trailing edge of the snowsquall moved past her and continued east into the higher mountains.

That restored her determination for another hour. By then she could move no farther. She knew if she sat down she would never get up. She cared, yet didn't care. She hated the thought of dying here but felt drawn to the peace of it even more. She looked at John Alexander. His eyes were half open, staring blankly at her. She fed him, squeezed more milk out of her breast onto the palm of one glove, and lapped it up. When she lifted her head again, she saw the narrow column of smoke rising above the next ridge.

There was not an ounce of energy left in her when she reached the top of the rise. She was sure the smoke was a mirage; certain that the tall mustachioed man in furs, the Indian squatting near him skinning a small animal, the lean-to atop the flattened boulder blown bare under the branches of an enormous conifer, the rack of pelts, were all a cruel hallucination. *I am seeing things,* she thought numbly, as sunlight briefly streamed through an unbelievably beautiful blue fracture in the clouds.

She did not feel herself, fall, slide, roll over, and slide again, still clutching John Alexander; she never saw the startled men running toward her from the direction of their fire.

Eleven

Ðecember 24, 1846 (predated)
Came upon Luther Mosby's lean-to in the mountains
north of Lucifer Peak this day. Thought at first it was a
Christmas miracle, the food and fire gifts from God. . . .

She felt warmth first, then fear as she opened her
eyes and was startled by both the man and the coldness of his gaze. She recognized him immediately
from Bent's Fort but said nothing when he failed to
remember her.

"Here, drink this," he said evenly.

She sipped at the broth and took in his hawk nose,
curving moustache, and sharp jawline.

"You been out for quite a walk, you and the little
fella."

"The baby!" She tried to push up but he stopped
her. "John Alexander! Is he—?"

"He's alive. Weak as hell, but alive. Gonna have to
get him to a doctor. You too. Don't know if he'll make
it 'til thaw."

She lay back and rested for a moment. "Can't we go
now?"

"We got horses." He glanced at the Indian standing

outside the entrance of the lean-to. "But just two of 'em."

She propped herself up and saw the baby wrapped in furs at the foot of the sleeping platform.

"I told you he's alive. Lay back down again, you hear?"

She felt under her breasts for the money belt. It was still there.

He saw the movement. "We didn't take your clothes off, if that's what you're worried about. You ain't exactly invitin' right at the moment."

She smiled gratefully. "Are we very far from a doctor?"

"Quite a ways."

"Please. Take me to one. Take me and the baby."

He shrugged. "Ain't easy leavin' here 'til spring. Helluva risk, not to mention the money in pelts lost."

"I'll pay you!"

His eyebrows rose. "You ain't got any money. I checked."

"My husband. He's in Monterey. *He'll* pay you."

"Take quite a bit to make it worth riskin' our necks."

"It doesn't matter. . . . He's . . . he's rich. He'll pay you anything you ask."

"Two hunnert dollars?" Mosby asked hesitantly.

"Three. I'll see to it. I promise you."

"How come you's alone? Who was you with?"

"The Donners."

"Jeeesus Christ! The Donner Party? Wasn't nothin' *but* stories about you folks just before Seeswash and me come up here trappin." He rubbed his jaw. "Who was it brought the news down to Sutter's?"

"Charles Stanton?" She shivered, remembering the shell of ice that had covered his face and body.

"That's it! Stanton. Went back to bring you people through, didn't he?" Mosby thought for a moment. "Lotta rich folks in that train. You say Stanton brought them in?"

"No. He died back there." She pointed, not really knowing in which direction.

"Beyond the pass?"

"This side."

"And the rest of them?"

Not fully in control of her senses, she thought he meant just the snowshoe party. "They must be beyond this point by now. I was separated from them two or three days ago. I . . . I don't remember."

"Here, drink some more of this soup. Real slow, now."

She sipped at it, resting as the warm liquid both stung, then soothed her insides.

"Three days ago, huh? They was on snowshoes, like you?"

"Yes. I don't know exactly how long it has been. I . . . I lost track."

"Mountain man with 'em?"

"Just Stanton, until he . . . died. Two Indians. But I don't think they are from this region."

"Like as not they're still wanderin' out there. Might have missed this place by less'n a mile yesterday or day before and never know'd it." He thought again for a moment, then stepped outside and spoke to the Indian. She could not hear him, but she saw the Indian smile in an ugly way. He came back in.

"See by your diary your name's Elizabeth. Mine's Mosby. Luther Mosby." He stopped smiling. "Three hundred dollars?"

"Yes."

"We figure them other folks got to be somewhere nearby. We'll start out tomorrow mornin', double back a little, then come down the gorge they musta taken if they was travelin' south. Can't figure out for the life of me why they would be. Or how you managed to angle this way. Nigh impossible."

She got up on her elbow. "Tomorrow?" she whispered weakly. "Why can't we leave today?"

He laughed. "Listen to her! You ain't strong enough

even to lift your tail outa bed, let alone onto a horse. Anyways, it's nearly sunset."

"Sunset?"

"You been asleep for over twenty-four hours."

"My Lord! The baby! I've got to nurse the baby!"

"Don't worry about him. We been feedin' him soup."

"My God!" She reached down, so weak she could hardly lift John Alexander, and somehow managed to take him to her breast.

Mosby sat where he was, watching. Aroused, he licked his lips involuntarily. "You was any stronger, I'd take some of that myself." She glared at him, and he laughed. "Got a temper, do you?"

She ignored him and finished nursing, then held her hand to the infant's forehead. "He's feverish. Sick. We've got to leave tomorrow morning!"

"I told you we would, didn't I?"

"Do we have to double back?"

He smiled, then looked away. "Can't just leave them poor rich folks out there to die without lookin' a bit for 'em, now can we?"

She started to argue with him but held back the words. He was the only hope for John Alexander's survival.

"You sleep now. You're gonna have to be as strong as you can be in the mornin'."

She hated him for loading the Indian's horse with pelts as well as herself and the baby. It would slow them down. She knew that much, dazed and disoriented as she still was. But she said nothing. She knew also there was very little chance they would find even tracks, let along any of the snowshoers. She was right. By noon they had gone miles north and west, the horses slowly pumping their legs up and down in the snow above the buried crust. There was no sign of anything human. The only thing that kept her from utter despair was the thought of the three days' provisions Mosby had packed in his saddlebag. She began to pray.

"They're goners," Mosby said, reining his horse southward. "They set out for Sutter's with Stanton?"

"Yes. By way of Bear Valley."

Mosby shook his head. "Jesus Christ! We're halfway south from there to French Meadows. They're so far off the mark they don't stand a chance. Well, maybe we'll still run into 'em."

All that day the horses plodded southward. They camped for the night in a shelter Mosby and the silent Indian made from cut pine-boughs and a covering layer of hand-packed snow. John Alexander opened his eyes only twice when she nursed him that evening. She knew he was getting weaker by the hour.

"You skinny or fat under that dress?" Mosby asked after they had settled in under the fur pelts.

She looked away. "I think you would call me slender."

"Skinny, huh? Well, you sure got beautiful teats."

Apprehensive as she was that he might come near her during the night, she slept as she never had in her life. In the morning, she felt as though the cold, dry air had almost restored her. But there was a frightening dullness in John Alexander's eyes as she took him to her breast again.

A bulge in the long tail of the snowstorm that had been raging just to the west and north since Christmas Day hit them about noon. Leaning into the howling wind, their faces covered except for their eyes, they bent forward as the lathered horses shivered, snorted vapor, and worked through the increasingly higher drifts. At four in the afternoon, Mosby's mount slipped, stumbled, then lost its footing entirely on a rock ledge over a steep ravine. Thrown uphill, Mosby landed face down in the snow to their left. Elizabeth watched, horrified, as his horse went over the edge, whinnying in terror, bounced off a boulder, kept falling, hit again, and slid down to the bottom. Within minutes the animal's legs stopped kicking spasmodically, and the falling snow began covering it up.

"Son . . . of . . . a . . . bitch!" Mosby shouted. He glowered at the Indian. "Don't just stand there gapin', Seeswash! We got work to do plenty."

Huddled in the lee of a giant fir, she watched them build a three-sided wall of packed snow to screen out the wind. Then they lined the wall with pine branches torn from surrounding trees. Mosby's strength frightened her. When he and the Indian had roofed the walls and covered the snow floor with additional boughs, they crawled inside and huddled together for warmth. The Indian built a fire just inside the entrance with flint and stone he carried in a belt pouch. Only when he came back and sat down did she realize all the provisions had gone down the ravine with Mosby's horse.

She fell asleep just after feeding the baby. Her milk was holding out, but without food, she knew it would dry up quickly.

She woke with a start two hours later. Mosby was lying with his arms around her. John Alexander was between their bellies. Mosby was smiling. She could smell liquor on his breath.

"What the hell you lookin' at me that way for? I ain't done nothin' to you. Just keepin' warm now the fire's gone out."

Despite herself and the shrieking wind, she fell asleep again. In the morning Mosby peered in through the hole he had scooped out of the blown snow filling the entrance to the shelter.

"You ready to go?"

She got up, arranged the baby in his sling, and crawled out through the opening. The snow had stopped, but the sky was overcast. She looked around. The Indian was gone.

"Damndest thing," Mosby said, pulling her up behind him on the Indian's horse. "See them tracks?"

He pointed to a single set heading toward the ledge. Beside them were two furrows. "Must have gone to take a look-see at my horse. Probably thought he could go down and get the food. I guess he slipped and fell over."

He eased the horse to the middle of the ledge and leaned over carefully. "See him?" Mosby said, shaking his head. "Must be three hundred foot almost straight down. Damn shame. No way in the world you could get down there without breakin' your neck."

She stared at the snow on the ledge. All but one small patch of blood had been kicked loose and covered up.

"Better git goin' 'fore it hits again. Maybe we'll make it to the Squaw by tonight. Ought to be easier goin' by then. Should be able to make it downriver on the ice pretty quick tomorrow."

Shutting thoughts of the Indian from her mind, she tried to buoy herself with what Mosby had said. An hour and a half later, its heart and lungs bursting from the weight it had carried so long and the strain of pushing through heavy snow, the horse gave out under them. Mosby lashed furiously at the animal with the reins, but it simply lay there, quivering, one eye staring blankly skyward, froth and blood bubbling over its ice-encrusted bit.

Enraged, Mosby stalked off. She followed him. A half mile further south, Mosby slapped at his thigh violently, cursing himself as he suddenly realized how much food the horse could provide them. Almost gently, he sat her and the baby down in the lee of a giant evergreen, then started back to the animal.

His first slice into the soft flesh along the horse's withers was unsuccessful. He tried again with no luck.

"Open up, you son of a bitch!" he shouted, lifting his bowie knife high and stabbing down hard at the horse's flank. As though the fat and muscle had turned to rock, the tip of the knife broke off and he sprained his wrist. Jerking his head to one side in fury and pain, Mosby glanced skyward and screamed, *"Why's it always have to be like this, you son of a bitch? Ever' time it's important! Ever' fuckin' time since I's a kid."*

He lowered his head and looked at the horse. "It's always the same. . . ."

Collecting himself, he probed in several places with no more success. Even the animal's tongue was frozen almost solid. He thought for a moment about building a fire, thawing the animal out, but he realized the woman and the child would be frozen stiff by the time he finished. Thinking of the three hundred dollars, he got up and started slogging back to them. *We'll run across somethin' . . . a deer, a rabbit . . . somethin'*, he thought. *Got to keep movin'*.

With Mosby pulling and dragging her some of the time, they walked the rest of the day and all of the next, stopping occasionally to rest and then pushing on. Near nightfall of the second day, the snow started again. Exhausted, so weak she could stand no longer, Elizabeth lowered herself and sat on her knees.

"Get up, goddamn it!"

She shook her head slowly. "I . . . can't."

He walked over, pulled the shawl and the baby away, and took a step back. "You'll get up or I'll leave you here and go on with the kid myself."

She started to cry.

Mosby looked up. The snow was beginning to thicken.

"Here, goddamn it!" He handed her the infant and began breaking and gathering branches again. Over the uneven terrain the snow pack around them had formed a small, concave depression. Mosby covered most of the snow well with pine needles and boughs, then spread more over the floor of the eight-foot oval. So tired she could hardly lift her arms, she lay down on the branches with John Alexander, staring

at the green needles above her as Mosby cleared a
small circle in the center of the floor. He left her in
terror for fifteen minutes, but then came back with
an armload of wood he had stabbed loose from a
fallen trunk. Removing the wrapping from a cigar,
he started the fire, lighted up, and sat there smoking
and staring at her.

It was much later when she awoke suddenly, her
face pressed through the pine branches into the snow,
the tip of her nose practically frozen, remembering
the baby. Rolling on her side, she tried to nurse it.
She was vaguely aware that there was no feeling
between her nostrils; none in two fingers of her left
hand. Dimly, instinctively, she knew the liquid was
the last she had in her breasts. Involuntarily, she
licked her lips. They were split and caked with dried
blood in a half dozen places. But she was too weak
to do anything but lie there.

Mosby stared at her breast, at the suckling infant.
He knew he would never get out of this alive with
the two of them on his back. He was ravenously hungry. And now, his gaze locked on her pale, pink
nipple, the sucking sounds filling his ears, another
craving rose in him. He got up and moved toward
her.

She tried to protest when she felt Mosby pull the
baby from her arms, tried to scream when she saw
Mosby toss the baby aside, but she was too weak
even to summon sound. For a moment she thought
she was imagining it all, dreaming. But then she saw
the stream of sparks suddenly rise up over the edge
of the fire where the infant had fallen.

She tried to understand what was happening, but
the facts would not stay coupled in her mind. She
closed her eyes and tried again, but then she was
distracted as Mosby tore her dress open and began
draining the last of her milk.

You must not do that, she thought woodenly. *It is
all I have, and John Alexander needs it.* She lifted

one arm partway off the ground to push him away,
but it fell back and she could not raise it again.

*You must not. . . . He can't be. This is a
dream. . . .*

She felt him turn her over when he was through
with her breasts. She opened her eyes, tried to scream
again as he untied the strips of leather securing her
slitted skirts to her legs. Her eyes would not stay
open. No sound came out of her throat.

He didn't bother to position her, remove her undergarments. Instead, he simply ripped through the
bloomers, tore open the lower buttons on the long
johns she was wearing, then yanked them down far
enough to thrust into her just before she blacked out.

He was gone when she feebly lifted herself up the
following morning. The contents of her carryall bag
were scattered all over the floor of the shelter. She
was not aware that Graves's gold pocket watch was
gone. Not comprehending, almost in the preliminary
stages of shock, she picked up the journal and stared
at the sooty thumbprint on one corner of the first
page. Sitting up and cocking her head in confusion,
she turned the journal over. The other half of the
hide strip she had found in Stanton's pocket, wedged
until now between two pages, dropped into her lap.
She stared at it for a minute, not knowing what it
could be, then picked it up. She hesitated for a moment, distracted by the severe whiteness of two fingers on her left hand. She wondered where her gloves
were. *In a moment,* she thought hazily. *In a moment
I will look for them.* She stared at the strip again.
Without knowing why, she put it in her mouth and
began chewing.

While she was searching for her gloves, placing
everything back into her bag again, she found John
Alexander. Her senses blunted completely, she didn't
notice the pale blue color of his skin or the dark,
charred flesh where the edge of the fire had burned

through the shawl and the left arm of his little coat. Dropping the bag, cooing at her son soothingly, she picked him up, rearranged the shawl, and rocked him back and forth until she was sure he was asleep.

Under a bright blue sky she walked again as she had before finding Mosby and the Indian. An unseasonably warm sun crossed over her from left to right. Vaguely, she was aware she was going south. Sometime in the afternoon, she veered west. Near sunset she came upon the snow-well floored with stripped green branches where the snowshoers had waited out the Christmas storm for five days.

There were five bodies lying in the concave hollow. She recognized the faces of four of them: Antonio, the Mexican herder; "Uncle" Billy Graves; Patrick Dolan; Mrs. Murphy's thirteen-year-old boy, Lemuel. She thought she smelled smoke, turned and saw the dead pine tree, fallen now, that the rest of them had set afire after the storm broke. She looked at the bodies again, rocking John Alexander back and forth, and tried to understand.

They were all naked, their clothes strew about haphazardly. The bones of Patrick Dolan's arm and legs were visible where the others had finally stripped the flesh from them. There was an enormous opening in Graves's chest where the skin and muscle had been sliced open, the ribs smashed and pulled apart. Vaguely aware of what she was looking at, she climbed down into the well and sat down next to Antonio's partially stripped body. One of his wrists lay in the edge of the dead fire. Where his hand had been, there was only a ribbonwork of crisp, black ash.

She sat there for half an hour, trying to think it all out. She was unable to. Finally her will to live and the unquenchable desire to get her baby to safety made her get up. Still clutching the child she methodically removed the knife from the sheath attached to Antonio's belt. Then she walked over to little Lemuel Murphy and cut away as much flesh as she thought she would need.

Numbly, she fanned up a fire in the charred, still smoldering trunk of the fallen pine, thawed out some of what she had, ate, pressed some to the baby's mouth and let the liquid drip between his lips. Certain he was nourished, singing to him, she wrapped the rest in the shawl and lay down close enough to the dead pine trunk to stay warm without being burned.

The following day, after removing the soggy boots and shoes on her feet and replacing them with two pairs lying in the snow-well, she reached the west base of Indian Peak. By the time she crossed the sloping, broad bowl beneath the escarpment, she was totally exhausted again. She found a cave at the base of a bluff, slept in it, ate again in the morning, then pushed on. Continuing on an increasingly downhill path, she followed a series of streambeds and stumbled onto the narrow, snow- and ice-covered South Fork of the American River at noon. Somehow—delirious, her nose and extremities half-frozen, her mind almost blank—she sensed the river would eventually flow west and down toward a valley and settlements.

She began laughing and singing when she briefly pictured a ranch house, a dog barking and smoke rising from a chimney. Stopping to rest, she ate the last of what was in the shawl, then continued downstream. An hour later, no longer singing, she approached a point where the river widened abruptly and the layer of snow on the ice was more shallow. For a few seconds her mind was clear. It came upon her that her energy was almost gone, that she would not make it much farther, that she and the baby would perish. She remembered Mosby and shouted at the top of her lungs: *"I will not die! Oh, God, I will not die!"*

Her mind blank again, she kept on shouting it every

few minutes until she turned a sharp bend and heard, amid the sounds of a waterfall, two shrill high notes that could have been made only by a living creature. She was certain it was her imagination.

Twelve

The two Miwok Indian boys squealed with delight as they stared, fascinated, at the trout darting under the clear stretch of ice halfway down the South Fork. The sound of something moving toward them from upstream brought them to their feet. They were only fifty yards from their village, and though they could not see their people through the dense growth of evergreens, they were not afraid, simply alert, the pointed sticks they carried aimed in the direction of the sound coming from around the bend in the river. When the figure came into view, swaying unsteadily as it moved toward them on the ice, they were sure it was a spirit. Sun dancing off its ice-encrusted, wind-blown garments seemed to them a supernatural halo. And they were certain the small blue form the figure carried partially concealed under its shawl was a strange and fearsome weapon they had never seen before. Overwhelmed by terror, they dropped the sticks, scrambled through the crust of snow on the shallow riverbank, and raced toward their village.

Elizabeth had been walking down the river on the ice since noon the day before. When she first saw the blurred figures dressed in skins, she thought they were deer. Delirious from hunger and exhaustion, her senses warped by what had happened in the mountains on this side of the pass, she saw the blurred movement of the two creatures up the riverbank as the reaction of two frightened fawns. She no longer possessed the capacity to reason that it was too early in the year for such young deer to be at large. For a moment the fragmented thought crossed her mind that had she been stronger, if her vision was not so strangely blurred, if she were more cunning, she might have somehow surprised and killed one of them. Numbly she chided herself for losing the opportunity to obtain food for John Alexander and herself. Perhaps the baby could not eat the meat, but the warm blood would have nourished him. Enough perhaps to sustain him until she found a settlement. Even in her present state of mind she had been certain, once she found the river and became hazily aware that it followed roughly the westward path of the sun overhead, that sooner or later she was bound to find the lowlands and people.

If she managed to stay alive.

"I will not die!" she shouted for the hundredth time. "I WILL NOT DIE!"

When the ringing of the words faded, she heard the crunching of snow crust again and turned toward the sound. The creatures had returned. They were greater in number now, and some of the animals were larger than the first two. Larger than any deer Elizabeth had ever seen. They could not be deer. They were all walking on their hind legs. One of them dropped to a crouching position, but to Elizabeth the animal seemed to have gone down on all fours. Now they did not move. Only the wind and the muted rush of water beneath the thick ice at her feet broke the stillness. Then the two smaller ones pointed their claws at her. *Bears,* she thought. *Bears.* The largest of them was enormous, and now he took a step toward her. Somehow, the absurdity of it amused her. After all that had gone before, a family of bears. For a

moment, before she fainted, she shrieked hysterical
laughter as a slowly melting, nonsensical picture of
them sitting around a campfire and tearing the baby
and her to pieces floated erratically across her mind.

Even to Miwokan, the head of this Indian village,
Elizabeth was at first a forbidding sight. Her long
hair blew wildly off to one side in back and lay tangled and matted down over her ghostly white face.
From a distance of ten yards there was no demarca-
tion between her deep brown eyes and the dark circles around them. Her eyelashes and eyebrows were
caked with soot. Even the whites of her eyes, almost
enveloped by dull-red blood vessels, blended into
what looked to Miwokan and his wife, Solana, like
enormous, eyeless sockets in a bone-white skull.

When she began shrieking, even Miwokan flinched
involuntarily and took a step backward. But after she
crumpled onto the ice and the pale blue object slid
out of her grasp, he collected himself and sifted what
he saw. He took several steps toward her. She wore
a puffed-sleeve blue dress and cape that had seemed
something else when the slitted skirts and untied
leather thongs attached to them had flapped in the
wind. He motioned to the rest of them to stay where
they were and moved out onto the ice cautiously,
spear in hand. He looked down at her. Two fingers
tightly gripping the strap of a pouch slung over her
shoulder were a greenish black. Blood was crusted
around her mouth and smeared faintly across one
cheek. A curious shell-color encircled the tip of her
nose. She wore a white man's work boots. He saw
now that the strange, scalloped shape that had danced
along the side of her head was only a blue bonnet
similar to ones he had seen worn by white women
at the Mission Santa Clara.

Reason and wit quickly overcame his apprehension.
He crouched and held his ear to her breast. The
heartbeat was barely discernible and fluttering wildly

like a bird's. She was breathing, but so rapidly, so shallowly that he knew she was near death. He was about to call two men to carry her to the village when he remembered the pale blue object. Walking to where it lay several yards off, he stared down at it for a full minute before motioning the warriors to do his bidding. He called his wife to his side. Standing there, Solana struggled to hold back a moan. Staring up at her were the open, lifeless eyes of a fifteen-month-old male child. Wisps of sandy blond hair curled over his tiny ears. His arms and legs were frozen in a fetal tuck. His skin was almost the color of an early evening sky.

Miwokan bent down and picked up the rigid little body. Only then did he and Solana see the diminutive arm that had been pressed against the ice. It was charred down to the bone from shoulder to wrist.

She was first conscious of a sudden, strange, tingling pain in the last two fingers of her left hand. The dream about talking and screaming at the bears, strange bears that knew how to build fires and tried to feed her clear liquid that tasted like fish, was over. But she could remember the moment, lying prone in their strangely symmetrical den, when the notion that they were bears was confirmed to her. Blurred as they were, standing and crouching over her, the nearest one, lying perpendicular to her on the floor of the den, was clearly visible. She remembered screaming at the sight of his bared fangs and then laughing when he did not open his eyes and she became aware that he was magically capable of flattening his entire body to a breadth of an inch when he slept. She laughed again, and wondered why the bear who climbed under the fur with her and wrapped her in his arms had felt as smooth as silk.

The tingling sensation in her fingers returned as she felt her left arm lifted. She heard two quick sizzling sounds and the aroma of something akin to beef frying in a skillet filled her nostrils for a moment. The nature of the pain in her fingers changed from stinging to burning. Oddly, the sensation was up inside toward the knuckles and not on the surface.

She opened her eyes and was certain she was staring at God's face. She forgot the dull pain, absorbed with Him. Strange. He was not the way she had always pictured Him. He looked more like Father Christmas. Without a beard. Perhaps God shaves His beard off in the summertime, leaving only those marvelous muttonchop sideburns and glorious moustache. It did not matter. It was warm, almost too warm here in heaven, but she was not about to complain. God was smiling and holding her hand tightly, the one that did not tingle. It was marvelous, the way He made you feel as though you were floating when He held your hand. And it was positively magical the way He made Himself appear, disappear and reappear so quickly and yet so gently, so slowly. For a moment she was conscious of the sun behind Him. It was small, so they must be far from earth, she calculated. God and the sun began to spin wildly before her. She closed her eyes again and realized that she was now a graceful white bird, floating, circling, warmed from above by that same sun and from below by warm columns of air rising from a luminously blue ocean.

Captain John Augustus Sutter turned to Doctor John Marsh and nodded. "Neatly done," he said. He motioned to the two Kanakas who had been holding Elizabeth down. They removed the butcher's cleaver, the chopping block, and the two blackened fingers and left the room on the main floor of the fort. When they were gone, he turned back to Marsh, who had moved the lantern away and set the white-hot hunting knife in a pail of cool water. He wanted Marsh's silence about this woman. He did not know why, but he did, and he had long since begun listening to what instinct told him. He knew exactly how to keep

Marsh from revealing to anyone the circumstances, even the fact that the woman was here.

"John—"

"Do you suppose she's one of the Donner Party?" Marsh interrupted.

"I seriously doubt it. A lone woman crossing the Sierras in midwinter?"

"It does seem unlikely—"

"Be that as it may. I want you to listen to me and listen carefully. I have sent many patients your way, have I not? I have always called you in medical emergencies here at the fort."

"Yes, but—"

"Hear me out. I have for some time known that you are not really a doctor. That you have never had a day of actual schooling . . ."

"You don't know what you're talking about!" Marsh snapped.

"I do, but I do not mean to prove it—ever—to anyone. You perform with greater skill than most physicians, surgeons it has been my misfortune to come across."

"Then what . . . ?"

"I simply ask a favor of you. One I do not fully understand myself as yet."

"What favor?"

"I want you to speak to no one of what you have seen here today. This woman, her condition, anything."

Marsh looked at Elizabeth. "What do you know about her? What are you concealing?"

"Nothing," Sutter lied. "No more than you do."

"Then why . . . ?"

"I want to wait at least until she is conscious and capable of telling me who she is and where she came from."

"You think she may be running from someone, some *thing*?"

"I told you, I don't know. But the circumstances

are so extraordinary that I wish to allow this woman, who has gone through so much, to have a voice in what happens to her when she is well. . . ."

"*If* she gets well, you mean. I don't like the looks of that nose. And she's very weak from the continuing fever."

"You have told me what to watch for. If there are signs of it worsening, I will call you immediately."

"It *will* get worse. It should be done now."

"Try to imagine, Doctor Marsh, what it would be like to walk the rest of your days if *your* nose was taken from you."

"Amputated."

"Amputated, then. Do you understand?"

"I suppose I'd rather be dead."

"Exactly."

"All right, we'll wait and see."

"And I have your word no one, I mean *no one*, will hear of this?"

"Not from me." Reluctantly, but with no choice, Marsh shook hands on it with Sutter. "What about the others here at the fort? The Indians?"

"Only a few of the white men are here. I sent Bigham, the blacksmith, to Sonoma. Vallejo needed some horses shod. None of the others know of her arrival. As for the rest, I expect they will soon tire of celebrating their one-sided victory over the Mexicans at Santa Clara and return by the end of the week. I doubt they will think anything of it.

"The Indians?" Sutter went on, thinking for a moment. "Only a handful of Miwokan's people know anything, and they understand none of it. I will speak to Miwokan, and word of it among them will cease."

Marsh nodded. He glanced at Elizabeth again. Under the laudanum he had given her she would sleep at least twenty-four hours. "Cleaned, without those fingers missing and that nose, she'd be a beauty."

"Yes," Sutter said, ushering Marsh to the front door and saying good-bye as he pressed several gold coins into his hand. *Someone's beauty,* he thought. He closed the door, walked to his study, opened a chest, and took Elizabeth's satchel bag out, spreading the contents on his writing table. Once again he thought of the dead child as he fingered the thin gold wedding band he had removed from her finger when Marsh was ready. Then he sat down, opened the leatherbound journal beside the money belt containing nearly three hundred dollars, and read the handwritten pages a second time.

When the whites returned to the fort, they paid little attention to the fact that Manaiki, one of Sutter's two Hawaiian common-law wives, was tending to a sick woman in his quarters. They assumed she was a settler. It was not unlike Sutter. During the seven years he had been here, he had established himself as the veritable baron of thousands of acres of rich valley land granted to him by the Mexican authorities in Alta California. He had not only wooed settlers from Oregon and east of the Sierras, he had gone out of his way to help them. No one was turned away from the fort. When he learned of emigrants in trouble or short of provisions on the trails, he invariably sent several of his men and mules laden with enough food and supplies to get them through. When they arrived, he showered them with hospitality. If they did not wish to settle and farm on his lands—for a percentage of their crops—he helped them find homesteads and work elsewhere.

The fort bustled with activity. High-walled observation towers rose at two corners. Cannon bought from the departed Russian colonists at Fort Ross flanked the main gate. Practically impregnable, the fort was also self-sufficient. Aside from a central, two-story house, the wood, brick, and mortar fort contained living rooms along its walls, a huge kitchen, a tannery, a cooperage, a dining hall, a blacksmith's shed, corrals, a storehouse, a kiln, a still, and a small granary. Three dozen Americans, Europeans, and Mexicans lived in either single rooms or additional houses inside the huge enclosure. Scores of Wappo, Maidu, and Miwok Indians tilled the rich land around the fort.

In the six years before he set foot in California, Sutter's drive to find a place where he could accomplish enough to erase memories of failure and disgrace in Switzerland had taken him to New York, Cincinnati, St. Louis, Santa Fe, the Russian colony of Sitka, and Honolulu. Here, finally, with the profits of a shipload of goods and credit he had charmed out of merchants in Yerba Buena and Monterey, Sutter had ripped a small empire out of a verdant, game-rich wilderness. Through guile, diplomacy, sheer will and a silken, often cagily generous manner, he had tamed even the wisest and fiercest of the subtribal chiefs and shamans. Here he was master, and in a way, although he did not own anyone as a slave, not even the eight unswervingly loyal Kanakas who formed his own Praetorian Guard, he had almost absolute control over the lives of everyone associated with him.

Sutter had felt genuine compassion for Elizabeth when the Indians had brought her in, strapped to a crude travois, the night before. And he had momentarily placed himself in her boots, wondering whether he would want anything known about his whereabouts and condition in a parallel circumstance. But that was not all that moved him to play his trump card with Marsh.

Sooner or later he would have played it anyway, simply to gain a peg on someone who had arrived before him in this rich valley and therefore possessed some vague claim to precedence or superiority. But more than that, more than the sympathy that filled him when he heard Miwokan's recounting of her appearance on the river, it was the simple fact that for the moment, he controlled the destiny of yet another human being. He liked that, in fact, loved it, and not for a moment did he wonder why he needed that control so much. Instead, he searched his mind for something else—that as yet undefined additional reason that made him actually care deeply about the fate of this young woman. Something about her . . .

Sutter was standing now, watching the Indians scooping up a mix of grain, vegetables, and meat scraps with their hands, at the troughs set on one side of the fort's open quadrangle, when Wetler, the German cabinetmaker who was stouter even than he, walked up and brought him out of his thoughts about Elizabeth.

"Die armoire you hef asked vor, she iz vinish."

"Good," Sutter said absently. "Have—no, never mind. I'll send someone for it tomorrow."

"Yez zir, Keptin." Wetler did not move away.

"What is it?" Sutter asked sharply. He suddenly realized how impatient he was for Elizabeth to recover enough to answer questions.

"Die Amerikin lady, she iz feeling bedder?"

Sutter did not like to lie outright. His conscience had bothered him when he had misled Marsh. He knew Elizabeth's fever had broken, and that with a few more days' rest she would be well enough to sit up, eat solid food—and talk. "No," he said finally. "I do not think she will recover. And she is not an American. She is a Californio."

Thirteen

Wearing a simple, Indian-made sack-dress of light yarn, Elizabeth looked down from a second-floor room in Sutter's main building. Wisps of sour-smelling steam from a still chimney rising above the rear wall of the fort came in through a cracked window. Below her, in buckskins, store-bought clothing, even a sailor's outfit, white men and Indians moved ceaselessly, loading furs and hides onto a wagon, tending to horses and cattle, repairing a corral fence, rolling newly made kegs, and carrying crates from one enclosure or another to a storehouse. She picked up the sound of at least a half dozen accents. Captain Sutter stood talking to an Indian who towered over him and the other men, both dark and light. The Indian was dressed more elaborately than his tribesmen. His buckskins were intricately beaded. A necklace of bear claws hung around his neck, and additional claws studded the fur cap on his head. A deerskin cape hung from his shoulders. There was something vaguely familiar about the Indian's powerful build and angularly handsome features, she thought, watching as Sutter glanced up, quickly concluded his conversation, and strode toward the house.

She walked unsteadily to the bed and stopped to slip off the moccasins she had found beside it. The motion and the sight of the pale fabric wrapped around her left wrist and hand made her dizzy. She fell back to a sitting position on the bed until the spots in front of her eyes disappeared, then pushed the moccasins off with her toes. She had just pulled the covers up to her neck when Sutter knocked on the door. She closed her eyes and didn't answer. Sutter knocked lightly again and then opened the door and peeked in. When he saw she was in bed, he walked to a chair, pulled it over almost noiselessly, and sat down.

Manaiki had brushed out Elizabeth's hair. Her face was washed, and she showed signs of natural color now, the pale tint of life in her porcelain-fair skin. It was then, when she gave up hoping he would leave and opened her eyes, that Sutter realized what it was about her that drew out of him an almost paternal protectiveness. Her eyes clear now, her hair lustrous in the sunlit room, Elizabeth looked, Sutter was certain, as he had pictured his youngest daughter in Switzerland would look when she reached this girl's age. His impression was false. The daughter he had not seen for more than a dozen years would never be so fortunate. But there was enough similarity in bone structure, deepness of the eyes, complexion, and fullness of lips to convince Sutter completely. Elizabeth's words startled him.

"I know the baby is dead. I feel it."

Sutter shifted uncomfortably. *He is overweight, jowly,* Elizabeth thought, detached at once from her statement about John Alexander. But she could see vestiges of a handsome face.

"There isn't any need to think about that until you are well."

"It is quite all right to speak of it now. I have accepted it." She could hear herself speaking, feel herself lying there, watching Sutter's face, but it seemed as though she were also somehow outside herself, watching and listening to both Elizabeth Purdy Todd and Sutter at the same time, through some sort of transparent enclosure that cut off contact with normal emotions.

"Yes," Sutter whispered. "The child—"

"Where is it? The body? Has he been buried?"

"It is in safe hands."

"*I want to know!*"

"There are other things for us to discuss if you feel well enough."

She glared at him, tears brimming, biting her lip.

"All right," he said.

Elizabeth relaxed for a moment, suddenly conscious of her rudeness. "I'm sorry. You have been so kind. . . ."

"No one could have done less for one who has endured so much."

"I do so wish to know about the baby."

"The Indians who found you have . . . preserved him and kept him for you."

"Kept him for me?"

"Until you are able and well enough to be present at his funeral. Their beliefs are strong. They were afraid their gods would be enraged if they went ahead without you. It seemed to me that no matter which decision was made, you would not be pleased. So Miwokan's notion that you should be present seemed the better of two difficult choices."

"Miwokan?"

"The tribal chief who brought you here."

Elizabeth still felt nothing. "How many days has it been?"

"Four."

"Good Lord!"

"You were extremely fevered. And it was necessary to administer much laudanum. You slept for two days."

"How . . . how are they, they . . . preserving the body?"

"The women of the village have tended to him." He did not want to say more.

"In what way? It has been four days."

Sutter sighed. "With ice from the river," he said finally. "They have wrapped him in a quilt of rabbit skins filled with ice. One of them, the chief's wife, is always with him."

Elizabeth fainted.

When she awoke again, it was dark, and Manaiki, the Hawaiian woman, sat watching over her in the chair. She got up, and Manaiki fed her some broth, gently brushed the hair off her forehead, and wiped her face with a cool, wet cloth. When Elizabeth laid the small, handmade, short-handled wooden bowl on a roughhewn night table beside the bed, Manaiki left her. In a few moments Sutter entered the room. Elizabeth could not help but smile at the sight of him. The fort was quiet, but he was still in his quasi-military outfit of boots, gold-striped maroon trousers tucked in below the knee, and a dark blue jacket bearing frilled epaulets. The room was warmed by heat held in the stones of a chimney that rose to the roof. Sutter took off his jacket, and Elizabeth absently noted the fine quality of the silk shirt with ruffled sleeves.

"You are feeling better?" he asked gently, enfolding her right hand in his. He had no idea her smile reflected the absurdity of his outlandish costume. Manaiki had rubbed her hands and feet with soothing coconut oil. For a moment the thought of having her here with him permanently accompanied the sensation he felt when he touched her soft skin. *But that is absurd,* he thought. *At least absurd until the facts are sorted out. And even then . . .*

Elizabeth interpreted his tenderness as fatherly, kind, which for the most part it was. She thought of her own father and his words from the pulpit—*"death is not an end, but a beginning"*—at the funeral service for old Miss Cable. Images of her mother and her younger sister, Esther, left so far behind, flashed across her mind.

"It is important, if you feel well enough, to discuss

some matters," Sutter pressed, still holding her hand.

"Yes, of course," she said, already thinking ahead, already knowing in a vague, undefined way what he would ask and what she would have to say.

"First, I would like to know your name."

She had not thought of that, only of what she could not reveal. Yet obviously her name was pivotal. She stared at him silently for a moment, annoyed with herself for overlooking such a simple trap. She looked away. After the silence between them grew uncomfortable, she said quietly, "Esther."

"I see," he said, betraying nothing. "Esther." He looked away from her. "And your married name?"

"Cable," she said. "Esther Cable."

"Where is your husband?"

"Dead. He was lost at . . . lost at sea . . . when his whaling ship went down."

"And where was that?"

"Vermont. No, New England." She began to realize the extent to which her mind was not working at a normal pace. Falling back on that fact, she said, "I don't remember exactly where. I'm a bit confused."

"Yes, I can see that." He excused himself for a moment, then returned with her bag. "It is all here. Your ring, your money—we, Manaiki, removed the money belt from beneath your bosom when she undressed you the first night. Manaiki has washed and ironed your clothing."

"Thank you." She was unable to conceptualize the steps she might now take to conceal her identity. "As long as I had to live . . . thank . . . goodness I was delivered into the hands of such a kind and honest man."

"And, of course, your journal . . . Mrs. Todd."

She sighed and gave up then, certain Sutter had read all the entries in the diary, and that there was no way she could prevent the news of her survival from reaching Alexander Todd at Larkin's Store in Monterey. "Did any of the others get through?"

"No. It is almost certain they all perished in the last storm."

"Those poor people at the lake. Dear God, they will all die."

"It is impossible to reach them now, but relief parties are being organized to make an attempt as soon as it is feasible. Perhaps we will be lucky. In any case, now that we are being honest with one another—"

"I'm sorry," she interrupted. "There was a reason for—"

"I can fully understand." Surprising her even more, he added: "No one knows who you really are but I. And if it is your wish, after careful consideration, no one else has to. Not even your husband."

Elizabeth could not believe her ears. She gazed out through the window toward the river just north of the fort. Manaiki had told her it ran into another, larger river, which in turn snaked south and then west to the great waters of an enormous bay and the village of Yerba Buena. Down the coast from it lay Monterey. For an instant Elizabeth felt herself pulled by the thought of continuing down the river she had walked on, in one of Sutter's several boats, sailing farther to the village on the bay, and then continuing on to Monterey and Alexander Todd. But then a thought of Mosby and the texture of the rough bandage on her left hand snapped her back to the reality she had formed for herself during the near-lucid, waking moments of the last two days.

"Is that possible?" she asked.

"I think it can be arranged. Although word of the Donner misfortune has traveled widely since James Reed, then McCutchen and Stanton stopped here, no one connects you with it. It is rumored already that you are a Californio woman." He beamed. "*I* have seen to that."

Elizabeth visualized Stanton again, propped against the tree, frozen solid, pale blue and enveloped in a thin womb of ice. She shuddered, realized now that his boots over hers had probably saved all her toes.

"Stanton is dead," she said, sounding to Sutter like someone speaking in her sleep.

"You can tell me about that later, when you are stronger." It did not matter to Sutter now. He was quite sure all of them, including his two Indians, everyone he had read about in her diary, were dead.

Elizabeth shut the memory of Stanton from her mind. She was alive, and this man was offering her the one opportunity she'd hoped for. She didn't know, had not had the time to think through, what she would do about Mosby. But she knew she would do something. And whatever she decided, she was certain that establishing the impression that she was dead would be to her advantage. "It would be a godsend if no one found out that I am alive. It . . . it is . . . very important to me now."

"You feel shame and guilt about your child, even though you make a superhuman effort. No one could hold you responsible."

She let him think the dead child was the main reason behind her desire to change her identity. "But I *am* responsible. . . . For many things."

"In time you will come to understand that is not true."

"You do not know all of it."

"No need to. And until you are better, I do not wish to."

"There is another reason I want to remain . . . dead."

"You cannot bear for your husband to see you . . . now."

It was true, but again, it was only part of the truth. "I have seen myself in the mirror. I can see what is left of my hand."

"As bad as your nose looks now, the scarring effect will fade in time. And it should not matter to someone who truly loves you."

"He *does* love me! It would *not* matter to him, I'm sure. But I love him, and it matters to *me!* I want to spare him the sight of me. I want him to remember me as I was. There *is* no Elizabeth Todd anymore."

Sutter drifted back for a moment into his own past. Caught in it, he rocked side to side in sympathy and she thought he was shaking his head.

"You don't understand," she cried, miserable.

"But I do," he whispered, taking hold of her chin gently and turning her face back toward his. "I can understand it more than most would. I have been in a similar circumstance. Not nearly so tragic, but just as final for me. Long ago. It will never be long enough. I can never go back to that first life I had."

Elizabeth could scarcely feel her relief and gratitude as another wave of numbness caught her up and drained away her emotions again. Watching herself from a point somewhere outside her own body, she saw the tears flowing involuntarily down her cheeks. "I will . . . somehow, some day I will repay you."

"Don't trouble your mind about that. If you become that most valuable of all things, a friend, that will be repayment enough." He dabbed a lace handkerchief at her eyes. "All you need consider now— Esther—is what you want to do. Rest. Tomorrow we will put our heads together and I will then make whatever arrangements are necessary."

Fourteen

When Sutter first learned on January 17 that two male and five female Donner snowshoers had staggered down out of the mountains near Johnson's ranch, north of the fort, he quickly arranged for the woman who now called herself Esther Cable to be temporarily housed at Miwokan's village.

"Until the cabin is built," he said, fingering her wedding ring as he sat next to her bed.

"I want you to keep that, as payment for having the Indians build the cabin."

He smiled. "I will hold the ring for you, if you like, but I would rather make other arrangements about the cabin—and the land."

"I have money."

"That won't be necessary now. The land is two miles from Miwokan's village. If you need anything, the Indians will be ready to help you. This quarter-mile-square piece of land straddles the South Fork of the American River. It is wild country. You will essentially be alone. Are you sure that is what you want?"

"Yes."

He sighed. "Then I suggest the following financial arrangement: A total price of one hundred dollars for the land and the cabin. That is fair. Four annual payments of twenty-five dollars, commencing twelve months hence. If you decide to stay. If you do not, you simply sign title to the property back to me. Agreed?"

"It is more than a bargain."

"I will have Custot, my secretary, write it all down with his quill pen in triplicate. One copy for you, one for me, and one to be filed with Consul Larkin in Monterey, so it is official."

"My God, my husband *works* for Larkin!"

"How would he, or anyone else, know who 'E. Cable' is?"

"That will be the only name on the deed?"

"That—and mine, of course."

"But suppose someone asks who—?"

"I will simply tell them 'E. Cable' is a settler. Come

north from the Pueblo de Los Angeles after arriving there a year ago by way of the Santa Fe Trail."

"I will need furniture."

"The Indians are already making it."

"I want to pay for it."

"Ten dollars—for the furniture and enough seeds, coffee, flour, sugar, salt, bacon, and dried beans to last a year. Is that agreeable?"

"It is too little. I should pay you more than that."

"All right. For another ten dollars you may have the use of a milk cow, a horse, and a saddle."

"You are being more than fair. Unreasonably so. I will find a way to repay you."

Sutter clucked, waving it off, then took her downstairs to show her the handsome armoire his cabinetmaker, Wetler, had recently built.

"It is a housewarming gift—for you, Esther."

Although she had chosen the name herself, the sound of it was somehow uncomfortable. It would take time to get used to, as would everything else in this new life she was beginning. Tears filled her eyes. "You have been like a—father to me. I . . . I will never forget this. Ever."

She was apprehensive about being alone even briefly in an Indian village, but Sutter explained that the cabin was a few days from completion, reminded her of the need for secrecy, and told her a number of things about Miwokan and his relatively small, familial subtribe that reassured her. Still, Sutter accompanied her when Miwokan, his wife, Solana, and several other Miwoks left with "Esther" for the village before dawn on January 19. Since he would be traveling back from the village that night, Sutter took two armed Kanakas with him.

"She needs rest and quiet," Sutter told Miwokan, after Elizabeth was settled in comfortably. Lying covered with furs on the same bearskin that had terrified her the last time she was in Miwokan's sunken, beamed, earth- and barkslab-covered hut, she listened groggily as Sutter went on. "There is simply too much activity too much bustle and racket at the fort. The cabin will be ready soon, so she will not be here long."

"She may stay as long as it is needed," Miwokan answered, glancing at her. "My people are happy for her to be here. She . . . is not only a white woman to them. But more."

Sutter did not pursue the meaning of what Miwokan had said. "You have an empty hut?"

"She will stay in mine—Solana and I will move to another until she is well."

Sutter's eyebrows rose. "In the chief's hut?"

"It is only right. She came over the mountains when there was deep snow. By herself. It tells us that she is a great woman, a daughter of the sun."

Sutter let Miwokan think whatever he wanted to. As far as he was concerned, if their beliefs protected Esther Cable, it didn't matter to him whether those beliefs were childish or not. Riding back to the fort with his two Kanakas, he felt an enormous sense of relief. Fitfully asleep now, with Solana watching over her, Esther was out of the fort not a day too soon, he was sure. For already the place was alive with a mixture of half-fact, half-rumor about the seven Donner survivors and those they had left behind in the snow.

William Eddy was starving, emaciated, too exhausted to speak, when Miwoks from another tribelet brought him to the emigrants who lived in and around Johnson's ranch. William C. Foster—in the same condition after the thirty-three-day trek through the snowbound wilderness between Donner Lake and the Johnson place—was so crazed he could not speak coherently.

Amazingly, all the women who had begun the trip —except Elizabeth Todd—had survived. Mrs. McCutchen, Mrs. Foster, Mrs. Pike, Mrs. Fosdick, and

Mary Graves, all in their early twenties, were severely debilitated, but they were not nearly so badly off as the men. They, at least, could sit up, eat, and talk. This much Sutter knew for certain from the rider who brought the news to the fort. The rest: indications that all seven had had to cannibalize the dead to survive; that someone had threatened the lives of Sutter's two Indians, Luis and Salvador; that the Indians had subsequently fled without snowshoes; that Foster had come upon the two pale brown men lying exhausted and near death in the snow and had then killed them and eaten parts of the bodies; these things Sutter could not be certain of until he spoke to Eddy and the women himself.

However exaggerated, he thought some of it was probably true. And even some of it was enough to chill a man's blood. Sutter shivered now, thinking about it as the hooting of an owl added a primeval note to the moonlit shapes and stillness of the foothill pine forest. He was glad the two Kanakas had accompanied him—for reasons beyond the protection they afforded from living things. Just their company was soothing. Not enough, but a balm nonetheless. Sutter was not a man to entertain even the vaguest thought of supernatural interference in the lives of men under normal circumstances. But this night, filled with speculation about primitive, perhaps even subhuman acts in the mountains, his sensibilities chilled and shaken, surrounded by a cold, pale light that seemed suffused with the eeriness of the unknown, even Sutter found himself as disquieted as a young child awakened by a strange sound in the dark.

He was glad Esther had heard none of the news, the rumors. She was in no condition to deal with or discuss them. The sexual stirrings, aroused in him by his first sight of her extraordinarily formed naked body were gone now. He felt again a strong surge of paternal protectiveness. He did not know how much of the horror she had seen, had engaged in herself, and he hoped it was as little as possible. But her words echoed in his mind:

"I am responsible, for many things. . . . You do not know all of it."

As Sutter and the two Kanakas finally rode across the open fields toward the hushed fort just before dawn, he resisted conjecturing about what Esther had been forced to do up there in the snow. *Sooner or later,* he thought wearily, *it is almost certain that I will find out.*

Miwokan was standing in the doorway of the conical hut, watching Esther, when she woke up. Alert now, she immediately experienced the first of many surprises that would fill the next several days.

"Good morning," he said with perfect pronunciation. "Was your sleep a good one?"

"Yes," she said, aware that she felt more rested than at any time since Fort Bridger.

"The forest is a good place for healing." Miwokan moved aside, and Solana entered with a bowl of steaming black acorn and oat mush laced with wild honey and seeds. She was not wearing the fur cape she had on the day before, and Esther saw that she was at least five months pregnant. "When you have finished eating," Miwokan went on, "you should walk. Each day walk a little more and strength will return. Until you are strong enough, use one of my spears to lean on when it is necessary, but do not lean on it until you believe you will fall."

He left then. As she ate the crude cereal, she could see him through the entranceway with a gathering of young Indian boys carrying intricately handwrought snares and traps. She realized now that he had seemed familiar in the fort enclosure because he had hovered closest to her when she lay thrashing and screaming deliriously in this same hut after they had found her on the river. She had a vague recollection that he had also lain next to her in the furs to keep her warm.

"He goes to teach the younger ones how to trap the rabbit, deer, and fox," Solana said, startling her.

"You do not use bows and arrows?"

"Yes. But it is at the same time less work and more, more . . ." She could not find the words and tapped her head. "More challenging," Solana said slowly, examining the word. "More hard putting of pictures together in the head this way," she added, pointing at the small group leaving the village.

"Where did you learn to speak English? Who taught you?"

Solana smiled proudly. "The mission fathers and Miwokan. A small Spanish, also."

Their unexpected facility with language absorbed Esther. During the next several days as she moved about the village, trailed at a distance by curious young children and peered at from huts by adults, her attention was further diverted from her own condition as huge chunks of misconception concerning all Indians fell away like portions of a cliff collapsing into the sea.

Everywhere there were indications of cleverness and industry that belied white men's evaluation of Indians in general, and these western "diggers" in particular. They were called diggers, a derisive term, because the women customarily dug for tubers, roots, seeds, maggots, larvae, and snails to provide parts of the diet. Myopically, the white men thought that was the only work they did and the only food they ate regularly. Esther saw at once how stupid this supposition was. These people were different from what she knew of the Indians east of the Sierras. They hunted no particular source of food, and their weapons were less developed. But that was only a practical reflection of a wide variety of food sources and a basically unwarlike nature. They were inactive, indolent for long periods, but not all year long as white men believed. They simply worked at various activi-

ties when the state of nature and their environment
indicated the most propitious time. Rather than enormous tribes, there were dozens of subtribes and extended family units that lived in harmony with the
conditions of the small area where they had resided,
as Solana put it, "forever." They took from nature
only as much as they needed, and what they took
they had long since developed simple but efficient
ways to process, store, and use.

Esther saw rows of woven broadgrass baskets filled
with nuts, berries, seeds, acorns, acorn meal, and
flour. Solana showed her the watertight baskets in
which the yellow acorn meal, ground down with stone
mortars, was leached of its toxic acids in water
brought to a boil with heated stones. There were
different types of baskets for hulling, pounding, leach-
ing, and storage.

After eating a piece of dried deer meat and a piece
of bread made from finely ground acorn flour, Esther
was shown a hut full of hides and furs, soon to be
transported to Sutter's Fort and bartered. Solana
pointed out another hut packed with enough cured
meat to last through two winters. A third was lined
with a variety of subtly woven weirs and nets for
trapping fish. Walking toward yet another hut from
which steam issued in an aromatic cloud, she noted
that everyone was amply clothed. Save for a slight
cautiousness with this new, unexplained, and disfigured woman who had strangely come down out of
the deep snow, they were all friendly, happy, apparently at peace with themselves and the world. Now
that she was used to seeing the mugwort leaves some
of them wore in pierced ears and noses, she liked
these people and what they represented.

Beyond a large assembly house made of bark, duck
feathers festooned the hut where the steam rose.

"How beautiful," Esther said. "What is that smell?"

Solana took her hand, smiling. "We are not allowed
there. It is the sweathouse—for the warriors. They

go there, they say, each day to cleanse themselves in
. . . what is the word? steam . . . made from water
and floating herbs. They also——." She stopped. "I will
tell you that another time. For now, know that they
also go there to be away from us. Especially the
women who talk too much."

Esther laughed. "It's the same the world over."

"They pay a price," Solana laughed. "In winter they
must rinse in the river or roll in the cold snow. Which
is only fair."

Esther laughed again. "And you. Where do you
clean yourselves?"

Solana frowned. "It is strange. The white believe
we are filthy. We do not use the sweathouse, but we
heat water, which carries the same herbs as that in
the sweathouse. We have . . . what is your word?
rags . . . which the men do not. In the summer we,
too, wash in the river—when it is not so cold that
our breasts would become stone."

An atmosphere of balance, peace, and rightness enveloped the village. Briefly, it soothed Esther between
her frequent periods of dizziness, sleep, and rest. She
had not spoken of John Alexander, and Solana carefully avoided any explanation of the small, recently
built, covered enclosure set off from the rest of the
camp. The evening before Sutter returned, the men
of the village began carrying logs and branches from
neatly stacked rows of firewood behind the huts. In
the center of a clearing adjacent to the new enclosure,
they built a pyramidal structure seven feet high. Up
one side, they set logs in the form of a stairway to
the top, the apex of which was flat and surmounted
by a small platform of thin, interwoven branches.

That night Solana told Esther much about Miwokan. He was a chief, as his father, grandfather, great-
and great-great grandfathers had been before him.
He was related directly and by barter marriage to
other chiefs. Their "nation" extended from the South
Fork, north of which was Maidu territory, far to the

south and deep into the Sierras in a wondrous, narrow valley of enormous waterfalls they called *uzumati*. As an adolescent, Miwokan had felt a need to outdo his rivals in the rituals of manhood, considered himself obliged to earn his preeminent position as well as inherit it. Alone in the woods, as was the custom, he chose not to kill a deer or an elk but singled out the ferocious animal even the Indians avoided at all costs. Digging a deep pit, covering it with thin, leafy branches, and then pretending to trifle with her young, he had enraged a female grizzly bear and provoked her to chase him. On one flank, Solana said, he bore the four broad scars of a swipe the bear had taken at him.

"He fell, just before leaping over the pit, and she caught him. But then *she* fell and was trapped. He killed her with his spear."

"How terrible!"

"It is not terrible. It is our way."

"But the cubs. The poor little cubs." She thought of John Alexander. "Did they die too, without their mother?"

Solana smiled. "No, they did not die. The bears are much as we are. We do not often kill them because their footprint is so much like that of the people. They travel in tribes, small tribes, then go apart, then come together again. When a mother dies, always another, what is the word?"

"Female."

"Fe-male . . . another mother takes the place of that one who is dead."

Esther felt a wave of grief. "And when a cub dies?"

Solana quickly, wisely guided her away from the subject. "There is always a time for another cub." She pointed to the silver-tipped fur throw Esther was lying on. "Miwokan killed that male, is that what you call it?—that male you are on. Six summers later, when he was to be made chief."

Esther looked at the fur of the grizzly and thought

of Mosby. *One day I will kill* you, she thought. *Somehow. Some way.*

Solana went on with Miwokan's history, and Esther was fascinated. His ancestors had worked for and been taught Spanish, agricultural arts, and music by the early missionaries. One of them had been an aide to Father Junipero Serra, who founded the mission chain that flourished from San Diego in the south to San Francisco Solano, just north of Yerba Buena. Miwokan's forebears had either passed down the teachings or seen to it that their descendants received schooling from the Franciscans until the missions were secularized and began decaying.

Esther was becoming drowsy. Solana, purposely trying to distract her from the sounds of preparation coming from the clearing near the new, covered enclosure, smiled. Her drone, her stories of Miwokan and his antecedents, were working. Esther forced herself to stay awake one last time. Solana told her how she had been raised a Catholic near the Mission San Francisco Solano and had been named after the patron saint's home village in a place called Spain. She explained how she, of the Wappos, had come to be married to a Miwok. Miwokan had passed her village, and then the mission, on his way to trade furs for shells and other valuable objects with distantly related families of Miwoks who lived north of Yerba Buena, along the edge of the great waters to the west.

Miwokan loved the statues in the missions, although he had discarded the religion of the white priests after becoming both chief and bear shaman. When he entered the Mission San Francisco Solano, he saw Solana placing flowers on the altar. He immediately sought out the Wappo chief who was Solana's father. Solana fished in a pouch to show Esther the necklace of enormous, multicolored shells he had given her as a wedding present upon his return from the coast. Only after the Indian woman nostalgically watched the colors dance in the soft light from the small circle of glowing embers in the center of the hut did she realize that Esther had finally fallen asleep.

Fifteen

In the morning, on their first walk, Solana led Esther away from the village toward the river. Trailing, Esther stopped for a moment and wondered about the new, pyramidal structure. She noted that it was decorated with feathers, animals carved from wood, symbols painted on hides, and obviously human figures formed with pliant branches, stones, and tufts of fur. Other objects sat on the small platform as well, but she could not make them out. When Solana noticed her staring at it, she quickly eased her in the opposite direction and offered no explanation. Esther decided not to ask about it. She had the vague suspicion that it had something to do with her, but then she became absorbed in the beauty around her.

Lying in the border area between the foothill and transition zones of the Sierra Nevada range, the forest around the village was a floral wonderland of birch, buckeye, laurel, maple, silver fir, cedar, an occasional sequoia, blue, black, and golden oaks, manzanita, and buckthorn, chaparral, spruce, and yellow pine. Hundreds of birds, the loudest of which were jays and woodpeckers, broke the silence of the snow-covered woodland. Squirrels peered around tree trunks at Esther and Solana as they drew nearer the muted sound of rushing water. Tracks of larger birds, rabbits, foxes, and raccoons crisscrossed the path to the river, and Esther, realizing her cabin was located just downstream, drank in what she knew by pure luck would be her own surroundings.

She let out a gasp as they came to the riverbank and saw the waterfall. At a point where sheer stone cliffs rose as high as the evergreens and the riverbed dropped sharply for twenty feet, the ice was broken in a long, serrated edge. The purest water Esther had ever seen rushed out from under it, spilling in a perfect crystalline arc to an oval opening in the ice at the base of the fall, then disappeared again on its long journey to the ocean.

Sutter was waiting for her when they returned to the village. Quantities of food simmered in kettles over an open, rectangular fire pit. A pair of freshly killed deer were being turned slowly over glowing logs by two of Miwokan's men. There was activity in each of the huts, but the village was much quieter than it had been during the last three days. It was obvious that they were preparing for something important to them. Esther guessed what it was but did not speak of it or show any sign that she knew. She ate a small quantity of food with Sutter, rested for two hours, then took another slow walk with him.

"You have been here long enough to know if you will like living in these parts. Are you still certain this is what you want, Esther?"

Again, the unaccustomed sound of the name set off a fleeting train of doubt about everything she was doing. She fought off the uncertainty and took a deep breath. "More than ever, I will be at peace here."

"The cabin is ready for you. I have seen it, and it will do. I left some cooking utensils, a kettle or two, some silverware, and a few pieces of china."

"I want to pay you for them."

"There is no need to. They are not used at the fort. I seem to have acquired far more things than we need."

She took his hand and held it for a moment, thanking him with her eyes.

"I have also left a long rifle, a revolver, and ammunition. These you may borrow as long as you are here."

"Why are you so kind to me?" she asked artlessly.

Sutter found himself unexpectedly flustered. He cleared his throat and finally, not looking at her, said: "I have . . . adopted you—unofficially—as a niece." Somehow, that relationship, even in "adoptive" terms, seemed to him less potentially incestuous than "daughter." The notion that Esther might possibly take a liking to him when she recovered, when she was herself again, was only a vague, fading hope now. He didn't even think about it for more than a second or two at a time. Still, Sutter was not a man to cut off any possibility if he could avoid it.

They walked a little farther before turning back. "Do you think you are ready? Or do you need a little more time here?"

"No," she said. "I am ready." She turned and looked him straight in the eye. "Ready for the cabin—and ready for what will take place here before I leave."

"You have understood what they have been building?"

"Not all of it. But I know it has to do with John Alexander."

Sutter sighed. "Yes. It is time."

"I know it is. I feel it, even though I also dread it. In whatever way is their custom. You see, they are the only people I feel even remotely close to now —besides you."

After she slept again, Sutter waited until Solana dressed and then guided her to the clearing where Miwokan and the rest were waiting. There were two circles, the men in the forefront and the women behind them. Clustered in groups at the edge of the woods, the children watched wide-eyed and silent.

The men were painted. Stripes, sworls, and dots of vegetable dye covered their faces and bodies. Both men and women wore pungent mugwort leaves in their ears. Despite the cold they were all barefoot. The men had on only breechcloths. All but Miwokan, whose shoulders were draped with the skin of a bear.

Sutter steadied her as they walked to the foot of the small pyramid, where Miwokan stood waiting. It was close to sunset, and the dark shadows of the trees blanketed the clearing. No one spoke or made a sound as Sutter and Esther took their places behind Miwokan.

From the far end of the village Esther heard the fire shaman cry out a wailing, mournful succession of notes. The two circles immediately followed the sound with a continuous, low, sadly melodic contrapuntal chant. Solana joined the fire shaman when he reached the edge of the circle and came through it, cradling a small rabbit-skin pouch in his arms. He gave it to Solana, and she moved slowly forward. The rain and snake shamans came forward, and the pouch was passed to them, hand to hand, then back to Solana, and finally to Miwokan. He turned and offered it to Esther. The contrasting feel of the soft fur and the rigid little body inside made Esther dizzy for a moment, but she bit hard on the end of her tongue and recovered. Sutter gestured for her to carry it up to the platform. She turned, and both Sutter and Miwokan supported her elbows as she climbed the crude steps.

On the high platform she saw a wooden eating bowl filled with acorn meal, thatched green perennial leaves cupping portions of dried meat, and a deep shell filled with water. A mat of dry grass-fibers lay centered on it. Esther turned to Miwokan, and he nodded. She lay the rabbit-skin pouch down on the mat and stared at it. Miwokan touched her arm, and she turned to him again. He was holding a small, painstakingly carved spear no longer than the rabbit

skin itself. He gave it to her, nodded, and she placed
it beside her son.

At the base of the pyre, Solana waited for them
with a long knife. She embraced Esther and gently,
unthreateningly, began to tilt her head down. Sutter
held out an arm and shook his head, but Esther silently put her fingers to his lips for a few seconds
and then, submitting to Solana, bent down and let
her hair fall forward until it touched the ground.
Strand by strand, Solana gathered and cut it off to
a length of two inches at a point near the base of
Esther's skull. When she was finished, she lifted Esther's face and kissed both her cheeks.

The fire shaman brought two torches. Miwokan
looked to the west and waited until the sun was just
a sliver of pale orange behind the line of hills. He
passed a torch to Esther and pointed to each corner
of the structure. Slowly, she circled the pyre with
Sutter at her side, dipping the torch and lighting small
clusters of twigs. When she was finished, Miwokan
held both torches toward the sunset and then threw
them through a small opening into the center of the
pyre. Taking Esther's hand, he turned and led her
toward the concentric circles. They expanded, the
men and women retreating gradually as the fire
snapped and took hold. She rocked backward once,
as they stood watching the flames leap and then rush
upward, but Sutter caught her and kept his arm
around her waist. She started to swoon again. But
then she purposely thought of Mosby's part in this,
and her hatred for him steeled her and stopped the
scene from spinning before her eyes. Within minutes
the pyre was an enormous torch pointing toward the
sky, consuming the platform and its contents. John
Alexander Todd had been laid to rest. And with him
the last reminder of a life turned to ashes. From this
moment, too, Elizabeth Purdy Todd ceased to exist,
she thought. A tower of white smoke rose straight
toward the first visible stars, then drifted westward

on the downwind toward the sun beyond the hills. *Yes, let that life, and Elizabeth Purdy Todd, drift away with the smoke,* she said to herself, tears brimming as she thought of Alex. She forced herself not to cry, to put it behind her. From this instant there is only Esther Cable . . . Esther . . . Cable. . . .

She remembered little of the abandoned dancing, the singing, the music played on crude flutes, whistles, rattles, and foot drums. Sutter had given her a large dollop of the first spirits she had ever tasted. It burned her throat going down, but it lent a warmth to the numbness that mercifully took hold of her as she watched the pyre collapse in a shower of sparks and smoke. She asked for more, then drank a third time. She stayed with them around the village fires for some time, chewed feebly on bits of venison and squirrel meat passed to her, but she was already nearly asleep. When she finally passed out, Sutter carried her to Miwokan's hut, covered her, and waited a few minutes to be sure the noise would not arouse her. As he walked back to the ritual feast and rejoicing for the child's journey to the sky, he marveled at Esther's courage and endurance. It was no wonder she had managed to walk down out of the mountains alone.

In the morning, before they left, he stood next to her on the lip of the ice as she scattered John Alexander's ashes at the waterfall.

Sixteen

Near the Rio de
Los Americanos
April 7, 1847

Do not know why I bother writing. So difficult to keep track of my thoughts. Encouraging—my lucid moments either last a bit longer or are more frequent each day. Sick to my stomach again this morning. Dizzy now . . .

There, that is better. . . . Remember now that I wish to reconstruct what happened after we left the lake with Stanton and Eddy. Terrible. Unbelievable, really. See it all in my mind, fleetingly though. As if I do not want or have the strength to deal with all of that now. Wait until you are coherent. . . . Wait until the thought of Mosby—

Later in the day. I have torn this page out of Journal and copied it further on, leaving sufficient space before it when I am able to think clearly on what happened . . . and put it all down. For now, record what has happened since. Perhaps the mind is like a muscle. . . . Exercise may do it good after injury? Can think of no better word. Must rest again now.

Sunset. Strange, spectacular. My eyes tell me it should fill me with awe. The colors. But I feel nothing. I simply see it. Refreshed after sleeping on the remarkably comfortable bed of stretched hides the Miwoks who work for Captain Sutter made for me. He came this morning, Sutter. Remarkable man. Flawed. Vain to a detriment. But helpful . . . generous . . . And kind.

It is so difficult. The simplest words escape me still. And facts. And dates. Perhaps it is a blessing. It seems to take forever to complete the writing of a sentence. Can only read a page or two of the novel, *Pride and Prejudice*, Captain Sutter gave me. Then nothing makes sense and must go back and read pages again to understand. Dr. Marsh told Sutter that will pass, he hopes, with . . . with what? Time. Pass, he hopes . . .

Asked Sutter why he was willing to keep my secret, after thanking him again for doing same. Remarkable. Said he understood. Guaranteed he would continue to by telling me one of his own. That he was in debtor's prison in Switzerland when he was younger! Somehow caused by his mother-in-law! Made me laugh by telling me the best thing he likes about Alta California is that his wife is in . . . foreign country? Yes. Switzerland. Pass, he hopes . . . and that it is probably a result of the fever, the long fever and the shocking events. . . .

Told me also . . . ? I seem to have been lucid for a long period, except for one spell, during Captain Sutter's visit. That augers well . . . yes, told me that there have been recent battles to the south and west of here and that . . .

Had to rest again. It is dark now. Should eat something. California is now an American territory is what I was trying to remember earlier.

This cabin built by Miwoks. . . . Crude, but all I need. I know Sutter has them watch over me without intruding . . . my wish to be rid of human company. Strange that so-called savages bring gifts of food—ground acorn mush sweetened with seeds that is not altogether unpleasant to the taste—and small wrought utensils, artifacts. I hear them at night. They found me . . . I found them, rather. Tired. Oh, wish so, Alex, that you could be here at my side to care for me.

But that part of my life is over. OVER! I could not let you see me the way I look now. And I could not bear to look at you and tell you of . . .

You must learn to deal with this . . . the death, the

death the death, of his son. Your son. There. I have said it, thought it, written it for the first time. He is gone. John Alexander is gone. It grows easier. The ink stains from the tears . . . I will not cry. I will NOT cry. John Alexander Todd and Elizabeth Purdy Todd are dead. Oh, God . . . THEY ARE DEAD! And only Esther Cable survives . . .

Esther Cable must eat something. Esther Cable will survive. Esther Cable will grow stronger and think clearly again.

I am Esther Cable.

I am Esther Cable.

Esther . . . . CABLE. And I remember now why I continue to write and why I am alive.

If it is the last thing I do on this earth, I will see Luther Mosby either ruined or dead.

Seventeen

Two Indians, a male and a female, watched Esther from a discreet distance at all times. Sutter had seen to this. By now, mid-April, they were familiar with her patterns. She still slept many hours, both night and day. She rose well after sunrise, ate a little, used the privy immediately afterward, then unfailingly took a short walk along the river. Sometimes she became dizzy and had to brace herself against the trunk of a tree, holding her hand over her eyes. Increasingly during the last few weeks she became sick in the mornings and sometimes vomited.

They reported this to Miwokan. The remainder of her day was unchanged: walking and resting, reading briefly, preparing small quantities of food, talking to herself out loud quite often, occasionally working the earth beside the cabin where she had set off a small plot for a vegetable garden. She wore a man's hat, baggy shirt and overalls, and work boots the Indians had seen Sutter bring to her earlier in the month. Sometimes she fell asleep sitting in the doorway after vacantly watching the scores of small animals and birds that now filled the budding woods within view.

Miwokan weighed what the watchers said and decided to wait until Solana visited the cabin on the day she planned to help Esther plant seeds. Solana could then inquire about the sickness. He sent his man back to watch, instructing him to continue reporting anything that was new or different in her activities.

The two Indians peered through pine boughs now as Esther picked up a small, bright stone that glinted in the sunlight in a shallow recess along the riverbank. She turned it in her hand, studying it. Several ducks, fighting the downstream current to reach shelter behind an outcropping of earth on the opposite shore, distracted her for a moment. She turned her attention back to the stone. Suddenly she dropped it and doubled over, folding her arms against her stomach and vomiting. When it was over, she washed out her mouth with a handful of water and returned to the cabin and stood staring at the mountains to the east for a long time. Suddenly her face contorted in anger.

"Oh, God, how I *hate* you, Mosby!" she cried, tears spilling down her cheeks. Wiping her eyes with the back of her sleeve, she finally went into the cabin to rest.

Sutter visited her again that day. He noticed that she seemed plumper. He attributed it to ample food and regained health. Physical health, at least, he thought. But then he noticed that in profile most of the weight was in her stomach. She could not have gained that much in so short a time. Her belly was obviously swollen.

He did not mention his observation to her, shifting instead to an expansion of what he had already told her about the American take-over of California. He noticed a hardening of her expression as he spoke of Frémont and his party of "explorers." But it passed, and he forgot it quickly.

Frémont had come to California peacefully, Sutter explained, but then, as the war with Mexico began, he encouraged American settlers to revolt. The first sorties, skirmishes, and ambuscades were farcically one-sided American victories. The tenor of sporadic battle remained essentially the same after the U.S. Navy and Army entered the conflict. The Americans drove southward by land and sea from Monterey in a series of virtually bloodless takeovers from the ill-equipped and dissension-ridden Californios. On January 13, 1847, the day before Sutter spirited Esther off to Miwokan's village, General Andres Pico had surrendered northwest of the Pueblo de Los Angeles and it was all over.

Holding her breath, Esther asked him what had happened to Frémont's men.

Sutter was placing logs in the fireplace for the evening. "Disbanded now. Carson left for his home on the Cimarron but plans to return to California. Many stayed with Frémont through it all. Scattered to the winds now, I think. All but a handful who will settle here. Some tired of the confusing, childish game it was at first and left early. Luther Mosby, a Southerner, was the first to go. I am told he trapped in the Sierras last fall and winter, but I doubt that. There was a rumor that he was seen not long ago at Isaac Claussen's ranch between here and San Jose."

Sutter, intent on his firebuilding, did not see Esther press her eyes shut and fight to regain control of her voice. "Why do you doubt it?"

"Because Mosby spoke to me once, when they were all encamped at the fort. He did not like California or the mountains. He told me he was thinking of going back to Texas. He was once a law officer there, an important one, from what I gathered. He did not like taking orders from Frémont. And he did not think he could quickly obtain a similar position here." Sutter turned to her. "Why do you ask?"

Esther clenched her fists around the arms of her chair and resisted both tears and the sensation that the room was beginning to spin. "I . . . spoke to him briefly at Bent's Fort. . . . Just curiosity."

She could not control the dizziness much longer. When she got up and staggered, Sutter helped her to the bed.

"Are you all right?"

She lay down and closed her eyes. "Yes . . . I will be . . . We have talked for a long time . . . I just need to rest a bit."

"Of course," Sutter said, pulling a fur over her. "I'm sorry."

"It was not your fault. Will you come back after you visit with Miwokan? I'll be fine then, and I will cook something for you before you go back to the fort."

Sutter brushed the back of his hand over her cheek. "We will cook it together—niece."

After dinner, as they drank coffee and nibbled at the English toffee Sutter had brought, Esther asked him of the latest news about the Donner people. Only a few more than half of them had survived. Five separate relief parties had gone to the rescue. One group, led by James Frazier Reed, almost perished in a storm on the return trip from the lake. A sixth, led by a man named Fallon, was now on its way to bring back the last few who remained alive. When Esther asked him for more details, he told her that some of it was unspeakable, horrible. He did not, would not talk of it further with her until she was stronger in mind and spirit.

"One good thing has come out of it," he said. "My story—about the injured 'Californio' woman who was retrieved and taken south by her husband—has been accepted and quickly forgotten. Suffice to say," Sutter mentioned in the doorway before he left, "that you are a very fortunate, very lucky woman, just to be alive."

Lucky, she thought, as she closed and bolted the leather-hinged door and prepared for bed. *Lucky to be alive, when I would rather be dead and do not have the courage to take my own life and risk eternal damnation.* She took the loaded Colt revolver out of the holster hanging on the far wall and contemplated it for a long time before placing it within easy reach under the bed. Lucky to be alive when my wits may never return to normal and physical strength flows back into me as slowly as water dripping from an icicle. She got under the furs and blew out the lamp.

Lucky. And almost continually numb to everything. Lucky. With my beloved son dead, and with—if my swollen stomach contains what I think it does—with the issue of Luther Mosby inside me. Growing. I am not rid of him. . . . He is still with me. . . . And I am too weak, too powerless, too scattered of mind to even construct a plan to avenge myself. The coffee had not slowed her increasing drowsiness. She felt fatigue rapidly overtaking her. *Alex,* she thought, forming the name silently, lovingly on her lips. She was too tired to cry. A last thought crossed her mind before she plummeted into sleep. She was too weak, too mentally exhausted to challenge it, examine it any more than by constructing the thought in the form of a question: *Could it be that God is punishing me for my wanton behavior with Alexander before we were married?*

* * *

She was rolling in Alexander's arms along the riverbank in Ohio. They were both naked, and he was deep inside her. As she began to tell Alex how marvelous it was that he could move in and out of her while they were rolling down the long bank, how wonderful his being in her made her feel, the dream shifted. Suddenly it was freezing cold and Alexander had the face of Mosby. She turned away from him and saw God standing on the flowing waters of the river, frowning. God had Alexander's face. God gestured and the waters under Him turned to motionless waves of solid ice. She was too terrified to move. When she did not attempt to break free of Mosby, God . . . Alexander . . . God raised his right arm and threw a small, jagged stone of solid gold that struck her squarely on the nose.

The almost constant numbness of feeling did not abate. The morning sickness increased in duration and frequency. Within a week Esther was positive she was pregnant. She thought carefully about what she would do. When the plan took its final shape and she acted, the change in her daily pattern almost went unnoticed by the Indians.

That morning, she went toward the river as usual. They didn't see the kitchen knife she was carrying. She stopped halfway and vomited. A short distance from the river she veered off the trail to a small clearing and searched the open ground and the edges of the surrounding woods. They watched until she selected five or six very narrow, straight, and smooth fallen branches. They saw the knife only when she began cutting the branches to a length of a little over a foot. She removed a few small twigs, smoothing the nubs until they were even with the surfaces, then sharpened one end of each short stick to a long, slender point.

When she headed again toward the river, the female watcher followed. The warrior was already running. Covering ground rapidly in a fast, smooth gait, he met Solana halfway to the village. He told her of the sharpened branches, then continued on as Solana, heavy with child, lumbered toward the cabin as quickly as she could.

Esther was still at the river when Solana reached the other watcher. She had done nothing with the sticks. She stood gazing at the water rushing past the riverbank and bubbling over a fallen tree trunk. Absently she rotated the sharpened branches with her thumb and forefinger, then turned and walked quickly back toward the cabin. Solana and the Indian woman followed.

Esther went in and sat on the bed. Solana silently moved closer, to a point where she could see through the unbolted and open wooden window nearest the door. Esther slowly took off her clothes and lay on the bed with the sticks in her hand. Solana glanced at the door. It was closed but not snug against the jamb. Perhaps it was not bolted.

Esther stared at the sticks, then gazed out the window nearest the door. She did not see Solana. Blurred by her tears, the opening was only a brilliant square of sunlight tinged with the green of the coniferous trees beyond the small corral. *Why am I crying,* she thought numbly. *It doesn't make any difference. Even if the idea that God is punishing me is not absurd, I do not want this thing in my womb. And if I should die doing it, it will be a blessing. An accident, God. For that is not my intention and you cannot blame me if that happens.*

She lay all but one of the sticks down beside her. Pulling herself up to a sitting position, she drew her legs inward, knees apart, until the soles of her feet touched. She stared at the point of the stick and gulped in a deep breath. Spreading the folds of her vulva, she found the entrance and began, slowly, carefully, pushing, angling the slender shaft up inside her.

Solana burst through the unbolted door.

Startled, Esther involuntarily jerked the stick out.

"You must not, you cannot do this thing!"

"It's none of your business," Esther said evenly. "Please go away."

"You must not do it!"

"Why?"

"It is the worst thing we can do."

"I *want* to do it."

Solana moved a little closer. "How can you want this? You have already lost one child. I know what that has done to you. You are broken, as I was, when my first was born silent and blue."

"But this one isn't mine!" Esther shouted.

Solana took another short step, puzzled, weighing, sifting. "You knew this could happen if you lay with the man, did you not?"

"I did not lay with the man."

Solana thought for another moment, puzzled again. Then she understood. "You could not stop him?"

"No." Esther began crying, swinging her head back and forth. "No. *No . . . NO!*" Miserable, she let her right hand drop to her side.

Solana moved to Esther and sat down beside her. The stick was still in Esther's hand, on the opposite side of the bed. "Then I understand why you do this."

"Now will you go away?"

"It was not the fault of the child in you, any of this."

"Of course not," Esther said.

"Then you punish it, kill a living thing for some-

thing it has not done. Women of other tribes do
that and they are cursed."

Esther had not thought of that aspect. She fought
the truth of it. "I don't care. *It isn't mine!*" The injustice to the living creature inside her did not go away.

"I will hate you if you do it. You are my friend,
and I will hate you."

"I don't care."

Instinctively Solana used truth to gain time, stall
the act she might not have the strength to prevent,
allow the seed of what was fair to the child to grow
—she had seen it take root in the fleeting change in
Esther's expression. "I will hate you for what you
have done and for making a fool of me."

"How will I do that?"

"My people will laugh at me, speak to me no
more."

"In God's name, why?" Esther's attention was on
Solana now.

"Because I have told them you are Miwokan's sunsister. That the sun made you at the same time; as
with Miwokan, the sun has given you large work to
do. Even Miwokan believes it. And that you also carry
the strong spirit of the great bear in your heart. That
you flew over the mountains and the snow and ice
because the sun will not call you back until you
have done what you have to do for him. That you are
the woman who would not die."

The thought of Mosby, of what she wanted to do
to him, swelled in Esther's mind. She fought it. She
was breathing fast, and the exaggerated sight of her
swollen stomach rising and falling caught her attention. She thought of the unborn innocent. It was *not*
fair to the child.

"Do not do it—for me," Solana said, touching her
shoulder.

"It wasn't the baby's fault," Esther said, crying
once more. "The poor thing didn't do it."

"That is the truth."

Mosby's angry, sneering face and the ugly, rough feel of his hands hung suspended in Esther's thoughts again. "*HE DID IT!*" she screamed, rage enveloping her. She picked up the other sticks and threw them all against the wall of the cabin. "*HE DID IT, AND ONE DAY I WILL KILL HIM FOR IT!*"

"Yes," Solana said, reaching, wrapping her arms around Esther and rocking her back and forth as she sobbed, "I . . . will . . . not . . . kill . . . the . . . baby." She rocked her until the uncontrollable crying and the wracking, deep sobs drained all the energy from Esther and she closed her eyes. She was asleep when Miwokan finally arrived.

Eighteen

South Fork Cabin
September 1, 1847

Solana and Miwokan came today. He is gone now, but Solana will stay with me until the child is born. She says she is sure it will happen within this quarter of the moon. She sits rocking and nursing her three-month-old son, Mwamwaash, as I write this. Miwokan brought a spear for me as a token of his appreciation today. It is fiercely beautiful, carved with bear symbols, its long, hand-sharpened stone spearhead imbedded in an oak shaft. In the wood just below the base of the stone he somehow has set a circle of upturned bear claws. How I would, forgive me, Lord, like to see that awful circle of points in Luther Mosby's heart!

How my hatred of the man persists, grows, the periods

of wrath against him increasing as the blessed days when my mind is clear and my spirit and body do not fail me grow longer in number.

Strange as well how the Indians persist in their somewhat idolatrous beliefs about me. "Bear Woman" indeed! I suppose with this nose and this hand I do look like I have had an altercation with a grizzly and escaped. And no matter what I say, neither Solana nor Miwokan will look upon what I did during Solana's breech birth as anything short of a "miracle."

While it is true that I luckily was able to reach up and ease her unborn child the last bit around, it had already turned in the right direction during Solana's trip here. And it was good fortune accompanying desperation more than anything else. Lucky that I remembered even unclearly the time I watched mother do the same thing midwifing in Vermont, and read more on it in Elisha Canby's medical book at Bent's Fort. In any case, Solana had broken water and not delivered for two days. Surely when they reached here on their way to Mount Diablo, something had to be done immediately or she might have died before reaching Dr. Marsh's place. Still, they ignore simple fact and regard me, subtly, most of them at a distance, thank God, as though I were a saint! I have given up trying to reason with them on the matter.

It would be obvious that summer is ending even without keeping track. The nights grow colder after each sunset, and Sutter tells me his fields of grain are ready for harvest. He, as usual, has been most understanding about my request that he not come so often. I know he believes the issue in me was the true reason I did not wish to rejoin Alex, although he has never spoken directly of it. It is just as well. I wish no one to know of the details on the ribbon-bound pages that I wrote after the events occurred. No matter what course of action fate leads me to. It is better that way.

Forgot again to show Sutter the strange yellow-streaked stones I have been collecting from the river. Must remember to take them out of the small drawer of the armoire next time he comes.

The solitude and the beauty of these parts suits me well. Still do not respond with feelings equal to the profusion of life and color that has surrounded me here each day this spring and summer. Perhaps the feeble emotions I feel from time to time are a sign of further "healing." Perhaps not. Certainly have "felt" things during my time here when provoked and angered. I wonder what feelings I will have when the child is born? It is hard to imagine loving Mosby's child, although I care that it is born healthy and strong for its own sake. Perhaps that tardy portion of my returning senses, once-felt feelings of happiness, delight——dear God, perhaps even joy——will return to me when I no longer carry Mosby's flesh and blood. Foolish musings, all of this. We will just wait and see and try, however difficult it still is, to accept God's will.

Solana is probably right. Even these larger trousers I asked Sutter for seem fit to burst. Saw myself in these male "hermit" clothes in a quiet patch of water yesterday. Must admit they are a sight, but do not care, in fact, prefer the manner in which they hide even from me the otherwise obvious reminders that I am a woman.

Feel forunate to be this far from "civilization," if in Alta California it can be called that. Sutter says the number of settlers who arrived this summer was much greater than last year. One wonders, having crossed all that vast territory, suffering the hardships, why so many do.

I grow weary. Must remember to bolt the windows, having seen the bear tracks about the remains of the trash fire. No doubt a cub, so small and closer-placed were its prints. Nevertheless, would hate to have even a medium-sized cub climb through the window some night in search of food. Will say a prayer for Alex as I lie beside the spear of the "Bear Woman!" So good to hear from Sutter that Alex is equal to his cousin in position, doing so well. I would be proud if I could but feel such things. And grateful as well that I have partially come to accept the self-imposed loss of him. . . . Still unable to think of any possible means to return what is left of Alex's money . . . without revealing I have survived. Someday, dearest husband, I will find a way to replace what I have used of it, and either have the money itself returned to you, or arrange for some gain of at least equal value. Dearest, dearest Alex. . . . Oh, God, how I love and miss you when I allow myself to think of the times gone by. But I must not, cannot waver from a purpose concerning Mosby that is now vague and simply suspended by lack of strength, knowledge, money, and circumstance.

Nineteen

Forty miles southwest of Esther's cabin, at Isaac Claussen's small ranch, Luther Mosby drew on his cigar and blew smoke at one of the Californios sitting opposite him. The heavier, darker man in tooled, silver-studded chaps, embroidered muslin shirt, and waist-length jacket grinned, one large, gold tooth gleaming. He held up his right hand, rubbing his thumb and forefinger together and raising his eyebrows as he nodded his head and smiled again. Mosby scowled. It annoyed him that the Californio was so certain he would win the ten-dollar bet they had just made. The thought that September had never been a good month irritated him further. *And we're just five days into the damn thing*, he calculated. He dismissed the foreboding quickly, certain there was no way he could lose his bet, the way things were stacked.

Isaac Claussen nudged Mosby's ribs. Burly, red-bearded, and gruff, he was about to call Mosby "Alamo," but he thought better of it. "He'll think you stove that smile straight up his ass when he takes another look at the size of the bull, won't he?"

"I can't abide fuckin' greasers," Mosby said.

"I can understand that." Claussen chose his words carefully. "What with you losin' so many friends you left behind to the bastards . . . not bein' able to persuade that dumbass Colonel . . . Colonel . . . ?"

"Fannin."

"Colonel Fannin into gettin' off his ass and helpin' 'em outa the pickle they wuz in at the Alamo."

"That's ancient history," Mosby said, taking stock of the slender, sad-eyed Californio perched next to the one who had made the bet. "Don't really have nothin' to do with it anyway. Just never could stand the oily cocksuckers and never will."

"Don't care much for greasers myself," Claussen chimed in. "But they brought in the grizzly."

"Yeah. He ain't much, though. Seen a lot bigger."

"This bull ought to make short work of him."

"That's the way I see it. And that greaser better have ten dollars or I'll pull that fuckin' gold tooth out of his head with my own hands."

Across from Mosby, Joaquin Alejandro Murietta took it all in. Six rangy *Americanos* sat on the twelve-foot-high, double-thick oak fence that opened on a chute leading to the corral. Thirty feet in diameter, the fence also encircled a stone and adobe outbuilding. Two more rough-looking gringos were leading one of the longhorns in the nearby corral this way. Besides the man next to him with the gold tooth there were two more mestizos—Californios of mixed Spanish, Mexican, and Indian blood. They stood at the latched heavy door to the outbuilding, ready to let the bear loose and climb jutting stones, a small, high window-ledge, and the fence to safety. Twice

as many *Americanos* as them. It could be ugly,
Murietta thought, if the man next to him won his
bet.

Murietta sighed and took a measured swig of the
whiskey from Isaac Claussen's still. It was rotten, but
he did not spit it out. He felt contempt for Claussen,
who had made so much money by selling this barbaric liquid to mestizos, Indians, and whites who
knew no better. He swallowed and sighed. The quality of the whiskey matched what was about to take
place within the confines of the circular fence. Since
the day his father took him to Mexico City as a young
boy and gave him his first exposure to the *corrida de
toros,* this Alta California bull-and-bear fighting had
been to him only meaningless cruelty, the sport of
savages. There was no ultimate test of man's courage
in the face of painful, violent death; simply brutality.

Murietta took another drink, and the alcohol began
to soften the edge of his contempt for Claussen, the
other Americanos, the three other Californios, and
the crude ritual itself. He was here only because he
needed his share of the money Claussen would pay
for the meat and skin of the bear. The thought and
the necessity did not lessen the degree of shame he
felt. Quickly he took another drink.

The two Americans prodded the longhorn bull
through the end of the chute and closed the solid
gate behind it. Enormous, it stood still for a moment,
then saw the two mestizos. One of them had just
thrown a long rope attached to the door handle over
the fence. He was halfway up the side of the building when the other mestizo threw the latch, kicked
the door open, and quickly climbed after him.

The bull charged. For a moment it seemed to
Mosby that there was something wrong with its gait,
that the bull favored one foreleg. But then the bear
appeared on his hind legs in the doorway and roared.
The bull swerved from the fence and the second mestizo. Hurtling through the doorway and into the bear,

he drove it back against the rear wall of the building.

The men felt the impact in their buttocks. The bear roared again, rolled under and away from the bull, and scrambled out into the ring. It stopped in the center, saw the men sitting on the fence, roared in anger again and was about to race at Claussen's dangling boot when the bull cleared the doorway. It came straight on, driving into the bear's back, stunning it and slicing one horn-tip forward along a flank. The bear howled as it flew forward, rolled, and then smashed against the base of the fence. Dazed, the bull paused for a moment, then turned as the shouting and whistling of the Americans distracted him.

Forgetting the bear momentarily, the bull charged the fence under Mosby. When the animal hit it, Mosby nearly toppled over backward. Riding the fence with his thighs as though it were a bucking horse, Mosby recovered, righted himself, and watched as the enraged bull struggled to free one imbedded horn.

The bear, temporarily senseless and riddled with pain, rolled over, tried to stand and collapsed. The Americans jeered at it. The bull, free again, trotted away from the bear, its nostrils flaring, and looked upward at dangling boots as it circled the far half of the enclosure. It reached the man beside Murietta and stopped. Sunlight gleamed on the heavy mestizo's false tooth, confusing the bull. Myopically, the bear watched the circling bull as its senses began to clear. Instinctively, the bear rose up on all four paws, but it was still too stunned to stand.

When the bear fell again, the bull caught the movement, turned, pawed at the ground, and began another charge. Again Mosby saw the odd movement of one foreleg. As the bull reached the center of the enclosed circle, its left forehoof dug into the packed earth and wedged between two large rocks just below the surface. With the sound of a rifle shot, the bone in its left foreleg snapped and it went down, bellowing and sliding to within three yards of the bear.

Both animals lay still for ten seconds. No one made a sound. The bear finally growled and began to rise. The bull was up and ready by the time the bear stood on its hind legs at full height. The bear crouched as the bull charged, its left foreleg buckling under again. Sliding on its chest, the bull slammed into the bear, hooked up and drove one horn deep into its lower belly. Roaring, the bear slashed at the back and shoulders of the bull, its three-inch claws tearing through hide, fat and muscle. Enraged, the bull rose on three legs, swung its head, and the horn pulled free. Escaping the tight area between the bloody horns and the fence, the bear struck the bull along the side of the head and sent it toppling to its side.

The bull bellowed and moaned in pain. Free to maneuver now, the bear took two loping steps and threw itself at the bull's exposed neck. Gripping the other animal in a lethal embrace, the bear snapped its jaws shut on the bull's throat, its hind legs pumping, its hind claws ripping deep into the larger animal's belly. When the bull's neck snapped and it stopped moving, the bear backed off. Tentatively, it moved back to the bull and took a long, slashing swipe at its flank. The bull quivered but did not move.

When the bear rose on its hind legs, Isaac Claussen fired his revolver into the air six times in succession. The other Americans unholstered and fired their guns. The bear, confused by the sharp, ear-splitting sounds, dropped to all fours, searched for an escape through the fence, followed its line to the outbuilding, saw the darker shape of the door, and ran for it. Once the bear was inside, the mestizo holding the long rope yanked the door shut, pulled the line taut, and waited while his companion jumped down, ran over to the door, latched it, and threw the thick outside-bolt home.

For a few minutes, as the Americans reloaded their

revolvers, the bear roared and flailed at the door. Weakened, the bear finally gave up, retreated to one corner, sat down, and licked at the large puncture-wound seven inches above its genitals.

Mosby, Claussen, and the rest waited until the bear was silent. Then they dropped down into the ring. Three of the Californios followed them and stared at the bull. Murietta stayed where he was. The stench of animal sweat, blood, torn intestines, and feces filled the air.

"Get this fuckin' thing outa here!" Claussen snapped. Two of his men quickly trussed and tied the bull, opened the gate to the chute, and began dragging the animal out of the ring.

"Some fuckin' bull you got me," he shouted at one of the men hauling on the ropes. "Well, you got the pleasure of butcherin' him up. And have the job finished before sundown!"

Mosby turned to the mestizos. The heavy one with the gold tooth was smiling.

"There was somethin' wrong with that bull's left foreleg," Mosby said, glancing at Claussen. He took out a ten dollar gold piece and flipped it in the air. As he caught it, he winked at Claussen. "He was all right yesterday, wasn't he?"

"Yeah," Claussen said. "Wasn't nothin' wrong with him."

"When'd these greasers bring in the bear? How long they been here?"

"Couple days," Claussen said, catching the drift.

"Where they been sleepin'?"

"Why, down by the corral. In them sheds."

One of the two men who had hauled the dead bull to Claussen's barn came back. He took his place in a fanned semicircle around the three mestizos as Mosby turned again to the man with the gold tooth.

"So any one of these greasers could have tampered with the bull last night, right?"

"Well, I'll be goddamned," Claussen said. He saw now what Mosby was up to.

"We did not touch the bull, señor," the man with the gold tooth said.

Mosby had his hand on the butt of his holstered revolver. "You're a lyin' greaser son of a bitch."

The man with the gold tooth scanned the Americans around him and his two companions. The flesh under his left eye twitched. There were too many.

"We did not touch the bull, señor," the Californio said again. "But since you have doubt of that, I will forget about our bet."

"He's gonna *forget* about it!" Mosby said, turning briefly to Claussen and laughing. "You need proof, there it is. Anyone ever know a greaser was willing to forget about ten dollars?"

All the Americans laughed.

"I would not take your money now, gringo. I would not let it touch my fingers," the man with the gold tooth said, hard-pressed to control his growing rage. "If Señor Claussen will pay us for the bear, we will be on our way."

"You hear that, Claussen? Thievin' son of a bitch insults me, calls me a gringo, and wants money to boot."

"Señor—"

"Listen, you oily little bastard, you're gonna leave all right. Right now. Without a fuckin' penny from any of us." Mosby's fingers were around the tooled handle of his revolver, ready to pull.

The Californio glared at him. He thought for a moment about pulling on the tall, hawk-nosed man with the moustache, but he knew he and his friends would be dead in less than a minute if he did. He stared at Mosby for a moment longer, then spat down at the dirt. Some of the saliva struck the toe of Mosby's right boot. "*Vámonos*," he said to the two men with him, forgetting for the moment about Murietta. He started to brush past Mosby.

"Wait a minute, greaser," Mosby said, straight-arming him. He pointed to his boot. "You're goin' to clean that off, with your hand, before you leave."

The Californio looked coldly at the hand on his shoulder. His eyes turned to Mosby. "No, señor. Some other day, perhaps." He started to turn, move off again.

"No other fuckin' day!" Mosby snapped, gripping at the man's jacket, spinning him back, and kneeing him hard in the groin. The Californio doubled over. Mosby saw him reach at his boot, saw the knife blade gleam as it came out. He stepped back just out of reach as the knife whipped up toward him. He pulled his revolver. The force of the upward swing tipped the Californio off balance for a second. He watched helplessly as Mosby held the gun on him for several seconds, laughed, and then blew a hole in the center of his chest.

The rest happened quickly. The other two Californios started to make their moves, were grabbed by each arm, held, punched, and kicked in the face, body, groin, and shins. Murietta, who had watched it all without moving, slipped off the fence into the ring while the deafening sound of the gun was still reverberating and they began beating the other two mestizos. Moving quickly, he ran to the door of the outbuilding, slipped the latch, pulled the bolt free, and kicked the door open before moving to one side and flattening himself against the wall.

Inside, the bear was blinded for a few seconds by the sudden light in the doorway. Then his weak eyes picked up the blurred movements of the men in the far end of the ring and, just beyond them, the contrasting light of the open gate. The bear was up in an instant, rushing through the doorway, roaring and racing straight at the cluster of men.

When they heard the sound, they froze. The bear burst into their midst before they had a chance to turn. Slashing and snapping as it hit them, the bear bit off half a hand, bowled another man over, and kept moving for the open gate. Now only Mosby, half-turned, and the dead mestizo lay between the bear and freedom. Mosby swung around. As he did, the bear took a swipe at him in midstride, never stopping. One claw sunk three quarters of an inch into Mosby's left arm just above the elbow. He screamed. In its curving, downward slice, the claw severed the tendons and ligaments in Mosby's left elbow. He screamed again as the blow spun him and sent him sprawling.

By the time the Americans had recovered their wits, regrouped, and chased after the bear, firing ineffectually as it quickly closed the distance to the edge of the woods, the two mestizos were out of the ring, on their horses, and riding fast. Dazed, Mosby rolled over in the dirt, wincing with pain, and saw Murietta at the small window-ledge, climbing. Mosby fired at him and missed. He fired again and grazed Murietta's ribs. The shot knocking him off balance, Murietta fell back onto the dirt floor of the ring.

The shots brought the others back through the gate. Two of them held Murietta up, and two more stood on his boots while Mosby, his left arm hanging limp and bleeding heavily, punched the Californio repeatedly in the face. Mosby broke off one of his teeth. He cracked three of Murietta's ribs. He kneed Murietta in the stomach and groin until he vomited; then, just as he was about to crush the Californio's skull with the butt of his gun, Mosby, staggering from loss of blood, passed out.

"Throw the greaser in there," Claussen said, gesturing toward the outbuilding. "We'll let the son' bitch starve a few days until Mosby's feelin' better. Then we'll have ourselves an old-fashioned hangin'." He tied a neckerchief around Mosby's biceps and pulled it tight. "Take him up to the house," he said. "I'll see if I can't stitch him up." He glanced at the man with only half a hand left. "Nothin' I can do about that, Shorty, 'cept coat it with pitch."

From what seemed to be a long distance, Murietta heard the latch snap shut and the bolt slide into place. They had thrown him onto the tamped dirt floor of the outbuilding. It did not feel like hard-packed earth. It was soft and wet. Then the acrid, musky combination of odors registered through all the pain and loss of feeling. Murietta realized the floor was nearly covered by the urine and feces of the bear he had set loose. The grizzly was probably miles away by now, nursing its wounds, foraging for food. *Imaginese*, he thought. *¡Qué gracia!* What gratitude! His own sardonic sense of humor and the fact that it remained unbroken amid so much pain amused him. He started to smile just as he slipped into unconsciousness.

Twenty

Esther gave birth without difficulty on September 5. When she awoke from long sleep that had engulfed her after Solana had sliced and tied the umbilical cord, the thought of taking the baby to the river and drowning it briefly crossed her mind. But the sight of the helpless infant, its poignantly jerking, spastic movements, wrinkled pink face, and Cupid's mouth erased the notion and unlocked at least a portion of her ability to feel again. Within minutes, as the baby suckled at her breast, she knew that the birth had somehow been cathartic.

She did not know whether it was ridding herself of the last trace of Mosby that had clung to her for so long, or the enormous power of maternal instinct that had torn away a portion of the emotional dam inside her brain. She had never fully understood the almost total loss of normal feelings—all but hatred for Mosby and anger under severe provocation—and she did not understand this sudden, partial restoration of them. But she didn't care. What mattered was that they had returned to her, and she gazed at the baby, Solana, the Indian woman's child, and at each item in the cabin with new eyes. Slowly, with an only slightly muted sense of delight, she examined each thing, each person and felt traces of happiness, contentment, even a whisper of exhilaration. That incipient feeling passed quickly as she turned her attention again to the baby nursing in the crook of her arm.

She lay thinking about the child long after Solana locked the cabin, blew out the light, and went to sleep. Over and over Esther searched her mind, sifted and weighed her true feelings about the infant. For hours she speculated on what would become of the child, what she would do with it, for it; whether she would keep it or give it away. If she kept it, would they stay here? If she gave it away, whom would she give it to? None of the answers crystallized completely. The one that almost did disturbed her.

She thought about this half-drawn conclusion separately, testing it, reexamining it until she became drowsy. There was no way to be certain now. It was too early. But as she drifted toward sleep, she guessed that the feeling, or lack of it, for the child would continue. She knew she cared for it, cared about its well-being, wanted it to be healthy, and would do all she could for it. More than she would for most human beings. But it was Mosby's son. She did not love it. Perhaps that will change, she thought. A part of her hoped it would. In time, she would know. And with that answer would come those to all the other questions.

In the morning, after the runner brought him the news, Miwokan arrived at the cabin. He presented Esther with a second spear, identical to the first, for her son. He looked at the boy and said, "Yes, he will be a fine warrior. Look at the long bones."

Esther hoped he was wrong. She wished for this child a life of peace, as free of turmoil and hardship as God would allow. She watched as Solana picked up the swaddled child in one arm and showed it to her husband. As Miwokan examined it, nodding in approval, Esther noticed there was no difference in the degree of love in Solana's eyes as she shifted her gaze back and forth from her own child, slung in her right arm, and Esther's, in her left. As Solana kissed Esther's boy on the forehead, the beginnings of a plan for the child started to form in Esther's mind. But then it was lost, as Solana took a step backward, laid both infants down for a moment, pulled open the upper portion of the crude cloth garment she was wearing, then placed both infants at her breasts.

"Think if we had two of them!" she said, starting to laugh as the infants made rapid sucking sounds.

Miwokan frowned for a moment, remembering the belief that had persisted down through the generations. "No," he said. "Twins bring only sorrow and suffering."

"I did not say twins, husband. Just two. Two of them close in a line."

The sight of her holding the pair of them, the babies ravenously draining the milk-laden breasts, filling the room with the sound of sucking, smacking, gurgling, and swallowing in frantic haste suddenly made Miwokan laugh. Then Solana began laughing too, and quickly Esther joined them. They did not stop until tears ran down from their eyes. For Esther the tears had an additional source. She, too, saw the humor, the exaggeration in the scene, and that was one origin of the crying. But she was also overcome by happiness. Not only could she see, she could *feel* and respond to what was happening to a degree she had not experienced in almost ten months.

Miwokan stayed the entire afternoon, and they feasted on a wild duck he had caught and roasted. Before he left, he fished a small hide pouch from a carrying bag strapped around his waist. It was a gift for Esther, from the two of them. Esther opened the pouch and pulled out the delicately beaded necklace he had made. Hanging from it was a hollow, heart-shaped amulet of thin, pounded raw gold. Unexpectedly, she found she could open it. Inside lay a tiny, finely woven heart fashioned from silver tips of fur taken from the grizzly skin in his hut. She closed it and looked at the two of them, profoundly touched, unable to speak, remonstrating with herself for dismissing their beliefs, the myth they were building around her. What difference did it make whether or not the concepts were childlike, born of ignorance and superstition, if they sprang from a source that yielded so much caring and love for another human being?

Miwokan, sensing her inability to express her gratitude, put a finger to his lips, then pantomimed a flight of words from his mouth and summarily brushed them away with a sweep of his open hand, signaling that such words were meaningless. He stepped toward Solana. Extending two gently arced forefingers and making a small circle with his thumb and the two smaller digits, he touched Solana's chest and slowly, undulatingly, rolled the arced fingers upward and over toward Esther. Then he repeated the gesture from his own heart. The expression locked Esther's tongue. Finally—awkwardly, she thought—she shaped the fingers of her right hand and confirmed her love for them in the same manner.

Only after Miwokan had gone and she was gazing at the amulet was she aware that she had been looking at its back. She felt impressions on one finger and turned it over. In the center of the heart, Miwokan had painstakingly formed the fine outlines of a sunburst. Something about the pointed, thick-based, curving representations of the sun's rays seemed vaguely familiar. She glanced up and saw that the rays were cut into the hammered gold in precisely the same shape as the bear claws that encircled both shafts of the stone-headed spears.

Murietta awoke in darkness. At first he could not remember where he was. But then the stench around him, and the pain, brought it all back. He rolled over and propped himself up on his elbows. It was too painful, and he lay back down, his head resting blessedly on one of the older, more dried out and solid bear chips. At first he could see nothing, but then the outlines of the bare storage room and its high-beamed ceiling dimly took shape. A distant twinkle of light caught his eye. He started to retch from the cloying, ammoniac stench of the bear waste, forced down the foul tasting matter in his throat, and stared at the star. He could see it through the single, high, foot-and-a-half-square window.

The pain was almost intolerable, and for a moment, as he rose to his feet, the room began to spin. He closed his eyes and willed himself not to pass out. When he was steady again, he opened his eyes slowly and looked up. The window was two feet out of reach and too small for him to get through. There was no sense trying the door. It would only be a painful waste of what little strength he had. He turned slowly, searching the walls. They were absolutely bare.

He looked back up at the window. He could not tell how much time had passed, but guessed he had been unconscious for more than twelve hours, that

it was just after midnight. All he knew was that sometime after the sun was up the next day, the day
that followed, or the day after that, the *Americanos*
would kill him. And probably that was not all. The
gringo with the torn arm would probably have a
few more gifts for him before his neck snapped in a
noose. There was no waiting. The window was all he
had. He stared at it, studied the rock and adobe wall
beneath it until he became dizzy again. His head
finally cleared, and he walked toward the window unsteadily, leaned against the wall, and took off one
boot. He dug two toeholds with a spur and put the
boot back on. Wedging the pointed toe of one boot
into a chink in the adobe, he set his jaw in anticipation of the pain and sprang upward.

His fingertips caught the edge of the window. He
held on, waves of pain washing through him. Chilling
sweat ran down his body as he felt for the second
toehold, found it, and jammed the boot-point in. The
oval rocks lining the window made it a little easier,
but not much. Summoning all his strength, he dropped
one hand, lifted his leg up the wall, and carefully
pulled one boot off. He chipped out a new set of toeholds, lay the boot carefully on the window ledge, and
climbed higher.

His arms were lying on the window ledge now. He
rested for several minutes, regaining his breath. When
the pain subsided, he slipped the boot back on and
began pulling himself through the window. By extending one arm, laying his head on it, tilting his
shoulders toward the floor of the room and flattening
the other arm along his torso, he managed to work
through to his waist. His hips just failed to clear the
opening.

Letting himself back in, finding the higher set of
toeholds, he rested again, then tried to pry the oval
rocks from the adobe. They were too deeply set for
him to gain enough leverage with his fingers. He
thought of the spur again but quickly realized the

rocks were too tightly placed for him to do more than make a lot of noise.

His calves ached now. Pulling himself up, he tried to gain enough purchase on the window ledge to rest them, but the pain in his ribs sent him back down. He missed the toeholds and landed on one foot, toppling over backward. Frustrated, he lay there panting, gripping and squeezing his outstretched hands again and again in frustration. Soft, wet bear feces spurted between his fingers and made a slopping, oozy sound. And then the thought struck him.

When his heart stopped pounding, he rose again, slowly took off his clothes and threw them through the window. Wearing only his boots, he crouched and began smearing the bear waste over himself. When he was coated with it from hip to thigh, he rubbed his palms and fingers clean on one wall until they began to hurt. Buoyed by hope, he returned to the wall below the window, paused to rest, then sprang up again. The wall scraped the skin on his chest but he caught hold of the ledge. Resting at each toehold, he repeated the earlier maneuver until he was hanging half in and half out of the window. The rocks chafed and tore at him, but this time, his flanks as slippery as a basted pig's, he pulled free.

Bracing himself, his hands down on the outside of the building, he balanced on his thighs and then reached back to grasp the upper inside edge of the window. Pulling and turning at the same time, forcing his mind to shut out the pain, he lifted his other hand, grasped the lower inside edge of the window, and jerked himself to a sitting position. Breathing hard, he held on, rested his forehead against the building, and listened. He thought he heard someone laugh up at the ranch house, but then all was still again.

Rested, Murietta pulled his legs through the window one at a time, found a footing on a pair of jutting rocks on the outside of the building, and slowly climbed down to the floor of the ring.

Outside, he wiped down with an undershirt, put on his clothes and inched his way to the corral. He found his horse and led it, one step at a time, toward the tack shed. The other horses suddenly began shying, moving restlessly, spooked by the dark, moving figure. He had purposely circled downwind of them, and they did not pick up the scent of the bear. His own horse balked, whinnied once, and began to rear, but when Murietta whispered to it and gave it several soft strokes on its neck, the horse was gentled by the familiar sound and touch.

His saddle was in the same place he had hung it the previous morning. Somehow he found the strength to throw it up on the horse. He waited for a moment, resting, then pulled and buckled the cinch. When the bit, bridle, and reins were in place, he hauled himself up by the pommel and eased one leg over. He ached, he was dizzy again, and he was sure he would vomit all over the horse's mane. But the wave of nausea passed. Quietly, he backed the horse out from under the shed roof, reined it around, and squeezed gently with his thighs. The horse walked until he was well away from Claussen's place, heading south over the tracks made by the two mestizos who had fled.

He tried loping and found that he could tolerate the pain. He squeezed the horse's flanks harder, and it broke into a gallop. For a minute or two, sitting in the saddle loosely, Murietta was certain he would have to slow down. But then the smooth flow of pain brought on by the animal's rhythmic movements and pounding hooves turned into a numbness that enveloped and held him steady. Following the tracks by moonlight, he rode south—as Claussen and the other gringos would expect him to—until he reached a stream that ran east to west. He crossed it and made a third set of tracks until he reached a loamy, unmarkable stretch of clover a hundred yards farther. Ahead of it was a long slope covered with high grass. It led down into a field of wheat swaying gently in the wind. Satisfied, he backed his horse the hundred yards to the stream he had crossed, turned east in the shallow water, and followed it toward the dim, gray outline of the Sierras.

In the morning, after he slept, he watched from a great distance as Claussen, Mosby, and four other Americans rode south across the stream, stopped, studied the tracks, and continued on through the clover, the high grass, and the wheat. When Murietta was satisfied they would not return, he turned north and headed deeper into the mountains.

Twenty-one

Esther lay in bed with the baby, thinking about what Sutter had told her that morning: Alex stopping at the fort, inquiring about the survivors, then heading off to find William Eddy, whom Sutter had said was one of the last persons to see his wife alive. She glanced at the calendar Sutter had left with her. September 7, 1847. More than half a year had passed since news of her "death" had reached Alex, and he was still searching, seeking, not yet ready to believe. Turning, she glanced at Solana, who was in the rocking chair between the bed and the wall, dozing and toeing the crude cradle in which her son slept.

Esther suddenly thought she was experiencing another spell of dizziness when she saw the door buckle inward and strain both its bolts. Then it buckled and groaned again. This time she heard the sound of wood being sliced. The door creaked a third time after something thudded twice against it in rapid succession. Solana had come sharply awake at the sounds. The two women watched in mounting disbelief, then fear, as the metal base of the smaller bolt lifted nails out of wood and fell to the floor. The wooden cross-bolt continued to buckle inward, then snapped just before the door flew open and they saw the grizzly.

Both women screamed. Startled awake, the two infants shrieked and then began a continuous wailing. The bear stood there, confused and growling as the sounds filled the room. Paralyzed by the sight of the beast, Esther took in the claws, the enormous, fang-like teeth. Then she noticed the portion of the bowel slanting down the lower belly to the animal's groin. Time was suspended, expanded. It seemed as though she had forever to think about it.

A remembrance of Mosby and the torn, raw, chafed feeling between her legs when she awoke alone in the snow and found John Alexander dead flashed across Esther's mind. The bear took a step toward her. The memory, the grizzly's movement, and her resurging maternal instinct galvanized Esther. Forgetting entirely about the loaded pistol within reach, she rolled from the bed, naked, and grabbed the two spears leaning against the near wall. Whirling, she pointed them at the bear and waited. The animal took a second swaying step and stopped, distracted as Solana darted from her chair and picked up her son.

Esther felt the heavy spears tipping downward and apart. She moved her grip on them forward as the bear grunted, looking at her, then at Solana, then at Esther again. Esther's knees shook uncontrollably now, as the grizzly turned its head and looked at the baby screaming on the bed. She tried to shout at the animal. No sound came from her throat. As she stared at the unnaturally dry, leathery snout, pendulous black lips, enormous teeth, broad nose, and piggish eyes she felt the hollowness in her stomach expand. She no longer had knees, legs. She felt herself going, fought it, then froze as a log in the fire snapped and the bear moved forward again.

The points of the spears were separated. As the bear trundled toward Esther, the one held steadiest shallowly sliced the side of his throat. The huge animal backed up a step and roared at the stinging pain. Swiping at the spear, the bear batted it out of Esther's hands.

She hung on to the second spear and swung its point upward as the bear moved again, dropping toward the floor in her direction. As it came down, the animal impaled the skin of its throat on the sharp stone point. Ignoring it, the bear continued dropping, his neck muscles pushing the spear and Esther backward until the butt of the shaft jammed into the wall behind her. The thick stone point stopped as the beast kept moving toward her. It jarred the bear's head upward, and the combination of opposing forces sent it slicing, ripping deep, through skin, fat neck muscle, and arteries before it severed two cervical vertebrae.

The bear let out a choked roar. Its vision blurred completely and began to darken as it lashed out erratically, its whirring claws barely missing Esther. In a surge of spasmodic effort and rage, the bear lifted its body and spun to the right, picking the spear and Esther up off the floor and whirling her almost halfway around the room. She crashed into the armoire as the bear took two last steps toward the draft of cool air from the door and collapsed, twisting over onto its back.

To Solana, her senses blunted by terror and hysteria, her perception reshaped by the amazing sight of Esther pointing two spears at the grizzly, it had all appeared differently. Esther had attacked the bear. Esther, in some awesome manifestation of the powers that had brought her across the deep snow and the great mountains, had literally flown in a circle to slice through the bear's neck. It was all confirmed, set in psychological concrete now, as she watched Esther rise from the floor screaming in rage and release, saw her pick up the first spear and plunge it into the bear's body again and again and again.

She did not see or hear the white woman now, as the panic and hysterical trembling overtook Esther and she collapsed, exhausted, beside the bear, crying and sobbing in both grief and thanksgiving.

When the worst of the crying, the images of Mosby dead and disemboweled, the short bursts of hysterical laughter, the coldness and shuddering were over, Esther crawled into bed and rocked the baby mindlessly. She was still sobbing intermittently in her sleep when Miwokan and the rest of them came and stared in awe at the carcass of what they had always believed was the giant dog of the gods.

Twenty-two

The bear carcass was gone when she awoke, and for a moment she wondered whether it had not been a dream. But then she saw the dried flecks of blood the bear had spewed out in the last moments of his attack. They were all over her body. Solana informed her that the Indians had taken the bear to skin it and dry the hide, butcher and cure the meat. Esther quickly told Solana to pass on a message. The bear meat was her gift to the tribe. The skin to Miwokan, her sunbrother.

They began calling her Sunsister then, and even Solana ignored her brief protestations. They came with gifts—garments of cloth, fur and buckskin, baskets of flour and meal, berries, fruit, dried meat, tallow, and nuts.

When Miwokan appeared, she noticed that he treated her even more lovingly like a younger sister, but now he also showed her the respect of an equal and added to that a shading of what seemed like reverence.

She lay in bed for two days, nursing, watching them come and go, letting Solana tend to her every need. She was certain the experience with the bear would push her back into apathy, another period of numbed emotion. Instead, what the birth had started, the terror and then the rage, the venting of all her bottled up hostility, the violent thrusting of the spear into the quivering, bloody flesh of the dead bear had finished. Somehow the sudden nearness of death had reawakened her to the possibilities of life. She grew impatient with Solana's near-obeisance. After taking only small amounts of food and liquid at first, she became ravenous. To her surprise, the baby's insistent demands annoyed her. She had not felt simple irritation for a long time.

She got out of bed and began planning for the winter. There was soap and butter to make, there were berries and fruit to preserve. She would need jars and sugar, lye. Sutter had them. Perhaps he could also find her a spinning wheel. After a week, she had an unquenchable desire to ride. She felt as though she were sixteen again—instead of going on nineteen! She laughed at that, and weighed the possibility of taking a trip. But no, the baby was too young, she could not impose that much on Solana, and as well as she felt, she didn't wish to be with people yet. She told Solana that she needed to be alone much of the time for a while; that she would like her to come in the mornings for a brief period to help a bit and allow her to leave the baby for an hour or so. Solana quietly acceded to her wishes. Unless it was necessary, none of the Indians but Miwokan, who came only every few days, ventured near the cabin except the two who watched from a distance.

She began riding each morning, slowly at first, then finding each day that she could move her horse a little faster. Most of the time she ambled along the flat portions of the riverbank, drinking in the vistas, the darting fish, and the first tints of fall. She used the rides, the time alone, to think. She had no desire to put on a woman's clothing yet, any more than she wanted to be around other whites. That might take a long time, she thought as she walked her horse along the bank one morning.

Suddenly Mosby crossed her mind, and she was seized with a cold rage that was frightening. *I actually want to kill him!* she said to herself. *A minister's daughter!* She shrugged, guessing that she would never see him again, let alone have the opportunity to take revenge. She guided her horse to a shallow stretch of the riverbed, then crossed to the other side. Turning to her right, she suddenly saw the figure lying on the bank downstream.

At first she thought it was an animal. It was the size of a young male deer, and from a distance of thirty yards she could not see that what looked like mud-caked fur was actually a man's clothing. As she drew closer, a tremor of apprehension rippled through her and she drew the loaded, long-barreled, five-shot Colt out of the sling on the side of her saddle. She noticed his horse, foraging for itself nearby, before she realized the figure was a man and he was unconscious. He was covered with dirt and grime, breathing shallowly, and unarmed.

She dismounted and, still holding the pistol, turned him over, almost recoiling from the stench. There was an odor stronger than that of a man's unwashed body.

She realized, just as she became aware that his face and shirt were crusted with blood almost a week old, that he smelled like the bear.

She brought his horse back. Pulling and dragging, she lifted and laid the man over the saddle and tied him to the pommel with his belt.

Murietta stayed with her for a month. He did not regain consciousness for several days, ate his first moderate meal with Esther on her birthday, October 26, and could not walk until the first week of November. The only words he spoke regularly were *Gracias, señora* and *por favor*. Another long lost sensibility returned to her: deep compassion. She tended him, cared for him, fed him at first. When he was able, he did light chores for her, replaced the poorly repaired door bolt, and made the latch more secure. It surprised her that she was in no hurry for him to leave. She grew almost comfortable with him, became practically unaware that only a few yards separated them at night. When she nursed, she simply turned her back to him.

She asked him questions: about his name, what had happened to him, whether or not he had been attacked by a bear, but he only smiled and shrugged apologetically. She wrote down the initials on his saddle, "J.M.," and he looked at the letters for a minute, thinking, then smiled and nodded.

"What is your name?" she asked.

He smiled, thought carefully for a moment, and said, "*Ah, sí. Mi nombre.*"

"Yes. What is your name? Your *nombre?*"

"Name," he repeated. "Name, Joaquin Alejandro."

She was listening for a surname beginning with an "M," and was certain she had misheard him.

"Yes," she said. "Yes. Your name is Joaquin Malejandro."

"*Sí,*" he said, thinking quickly. "Joaquin Malejandro."

"My name is . . . Esther."

"Esther," he repeated. "Esther *es su nombre.*"

Sutter did not like Esther having the sinewy, slender, good-looking, dark-haired man with her in the cabin, wounded and healing or not. Murietta appeared to be asleep on a blanket and his saddle over in one corner when Sutter stopped by. He was on his way to inspect the progress his hired carpenter, James Wilson Marshall, was making on the sawmill. Marshall and he were going partners in a mill downriver near Coloma.

"Will it pay?" Esther asked.

"*Gott in Himmel,* who knows? It may just be another pipe dream that will cost me more money. You don't know . . . you couldn't imagine the troubles I am going through."

She saw him glance at Murietta and frown. "Tell me about your problems," she said, sensing it would be better to keep him away from the subject of her "visitor."

"*Gott,* you just don't know! I need another tanner, and there's none to be found. Shoes. We need more shoe production. The new flour mill is not finished, and I have to make a payment on it. You would not believe how much the cost of building it has increased."

He turned again and looked at Murietta. "Who *is* this man?" he asked, whispering, before Esther could head him off again.

"A vaquero, I suppose. I found him, wounded, lying beside the river."

"You are a very trusting woman. He may be dangerous."

"He has helped me. He is a gentleman."

"I see." Sutter frowned again, obviously thinking about the sleeping arrangements as he glanced at the bed. "What is his name?"

"Malejandro. Joaquin Malejandro."

"And has he told you how he was hurt? I can see for myself that he has been in some sort of brawl."

"No. He speaks no English."

Sutter put on his hat and walked to the door. "I have to go, but I will be back in a day or two. I speak enough Spanish to find out just who this . . . this Joaquin Malejandro fellow is, and why he is in these parts."

It was time to get him off his protective high horse again. "I have decided to stay on here, John. I want to pay you fifty of the one hundred dollars I owe you for this place."

Sutter pulled her out of the doorway, shushing her with a finger to his lips. "Do not show or speak of money while this . . . this Malejandro is here."

"But why? He—"

"Esther, you do not know what men are capable of doing."

She smiled to herself. *If you only knew.* "We will discuss it when you return, then?"

"As you wish. But not where he can hear us. I will have Miwokan send another man or two to look over things here until I return. In the meantime, be on your guard."

"John, I think you're being silly."

"Do not speak to me that way!" Sutter snapped, exasperated. "You are practically a child. And you are not aware how close danger can come before it is too late."

Murietta was gone when Sutter stopped briefly on his return trip the following afternoon.

"He must have heard what you said."

"If he had nothing to hide, nothing to fear, he would have stayed." Sutter was obviously delighted she was not sharing her cabin with a man any longer.

Smiling, aware now of the jealousy that tinged Sutter's estimate of the situation, however much wisdom it also contained, Esther shook her finger teasingly.

"You are simply a suspicious man, John. Look what he left as payment for food and lodging."

Sutter stared at the solid-silver spur, took on an expression that would have suited a chastised child, then quickly shrugged in deprecation.

It was time to change the subject again. "Will you stay for dinner?"

Still thinking about the stranger, Sutter shook his head distractedly.

"Some coffee then?"

"I do not have time for even that," he said petulantly. "There is so much to do, so much to keep track of."

Esther smiled as she watched him ride off. She sat down to dinner after feeding the baby and retrieving the note she had found that morning after her ride.

It had been weighted with the spur. She read it again with the same sense of astonishment and speculation.

November 20, 1847

My dear Señora Esther:

This is to repay you for your kindness and much needed care. You are an angel of mercy and patience.

I ask your forgiveness. There were things I could not tell you and it would have been unforgiveably rude not to answer someone so generous. The most simple solution was not to speak your language. If I had, I also would have been tempted to ask you a question that you might have mistaken for additional rudeness. And that is, why would someone so beautiful wish to wear a man's clothes?

Again, forgive me, and many thanks.

Adios,

Joaquin Alejandro Murietta

She went to the small mirror in the armoire door and looked at the scar tissue on the tip of her nose. Musing, she reached up and touched her tangled hair, which had grown back to shoulder length. *How could anyone think of me as beautiful?* she thought. She attributed it to excessively worded gratitude and then dismissed it entirely as she realized that, once again, she had forgotten to show Sutter the yellow-streaked stones. To remind herself the next time he came, she opened the drawer, took one stone out, and placed it in the middle of her table.

Twenty-three

The next time Miwokan appeared at the cabin, he brought back the two spears, cleaned and repaired. He set and wrapped them with unknotted rawhide in the form of an X, then hammered a triangle of three wooden pegs upon which to hang the spears over the head of Esther's bed. As he drove the last peg into a chink between two logs, he spoke over his shoulder to Esther.

"Sunsister, you had a man with you, and you sent him away. I know he was broken when he came to you, but he was straight again after you healed him. Was he no good?"

Esther found herself flustered and then a bit too eager to put the matter straight. "I didn't send him away," she said. "And he didn't come to me. And I don't know if he was good or not. It was not that way."

Miwokan hung the spears up and turned to her.

"You need a man, Sunsister. You would be more happy with a man here."

"I'm quite happy, thank you," she said, an edge to her voice. She immediately regretted the tone and tried to make up for it. "You don't understand," she said more softly, wanting him to comprehend. "I found him and I brought him here only because he was injured, sick. It wasn't meant for us to have . . . closeness."

"But he passed many nights in your cabin."

"He slept in the corner, after he was well enough. Before that, I slept in the corner. When he was in the corner, I was in the bed. In any case, I like being alone."

Miwokan shook his head. "I understand what you are saying. But I do not understand him. Perhaps the sickness took away his eyes."

"What do you mean?" Esther said, as Miwokan noticed the stone on the table and walked toward it.

"Anyone can see that you would make a fine wife. I have seen that and thought of it many times, Sunsister." He picked up the stone and studied it.

"Why would you think such a thing?"

"If I did not know how much sorrow it would bring to Solana, I would lay many shells at your feet."

She did not know what to say.

"But I do not share the ways of many of my people," he said, knowing she was uncomfortable. "One wife is enough for me. If you were my wife, I would have to send Solana away, and I could not do that."

Esther finally found the words. "Thank you," she said, not looking at him. "It makes me . . . happy . . . and proud . . . to know that you think so much of me. Happier still to know that you love Solana that much."

He dismissed the subject with a wave of his hand. "There are no more words to speak on it. You are my sister, that is all." He put the stone down on the table again and thought for a moment. "Where did you find this?"

"In the river. Do you know what it is?"

He sighed. "Sit with me for a moment while I think."

She took a chair opposite him and watched as he gazed at the stone, then shut his eyes for a long time. "It is in my mind," he finally said, "to tell you I do not know what it is, but you are my sister and I do not want to be false with you."

"You do know what it is, then?"

He sighed again. "Yes, I think I do."

"Then tell me."

"This is for your ears. No one else is to hear it." She nodded.

"I cannot be sure, but I think it is gold."

Esther gulped. "Gold?" She glanced at the armoire. . . . "My God! I've got a drawerful of it!"

There was an expression of infinite sadness on Miwokan's face.

"Oh, it can't be. It's probably mica."

"It is not fool's gold." Miwokan's voice was firm.

"Then it must be something else."

"There is nothing else the eyes see the same way," he said with double meaning.

"Well, I'm sure it isn't gold. Why, the river near here is practically full of it."

"I know."

She caught herself suddenly becoming excited, hopeful about something that couldn't be true, and she missed his meaning. "It's probably some other cheap metal, made shiny by the water." She had wasted enough time on the subject. She wanted to get back to her preserves. "Well, I'll show it to Captain Sutter. He'll know, and I'm certain he'll laugh at me when I tell him I thought it was gold."

"Sunsister, I ask you not to show it to Sutter."

"For God's sake, why?"

"To stop what will happen, if I am right."

"But you said you weren't certain. And what do you mean—'happen'?"

"The heart you are wearing. Do you think it is gold?"

"Of course. No other metal could be pounded so thin, shaped so, marked so, without breaking."

"Then I am certain."

She fingered the heart hanging just above her breasts. "This came from the river?"

"Yes. My people, my father's people, and back and back have known of it, and picked more than a hundred hundred stones like this from the sides of the river and in the water where it is not so deep."

Esther felt her heart begin to race. "A *thousand* or more stones? Miwokan, do you know what that means? What did they do with it all?"

He could not bring himself to tell her all of it yet. First she must have the knowledge, the legend. "They buried it. It is the law of my tribe."

"They never used it? Never had it tested?"

"No."

"Do you know where it is buried?"

"Yes."

"Good Lord, Miwokan! Do you realize what you have if it is truly gold? You and your tribe are rich beyond your dreams. You can be the most powerful tribe in Alta California without raising a single spear. You can have almost anything you want."

He sighed again. The weight of it made him feel as if he had a mountain on his shoulders. "We do not want to be the most powerful tribe. We do not want to be rich in that way. We are rich now. We have everything we need."

"You don't understand . . ."

"It is you who do not understand!" he snapped. "I am sorry for lifting my voice," he added quickly. "But because my people, many of them, are simple, ignorant, you cannot believe or understand what we believe and understand, what we know, and what those before us knew, forever."

"You are *not* ignorant. You are *not* simple."

"Then listen to me, Sunsister. Listen until it is all told. First, remember that we have all we need because we take from the earth only what we need. There is wisdom in that. Wisdom that has been given to us since before any stories were told, by our fathers."

He saw she concurred with the idea, shifted his weight, and leaned forward in the chair. "This wisdom first came to us in stone pictures. Then in stories —myths, legends. I know of this from the mission fathers' books. You have stories, legends as we do."

"Yes, many of them."

"You also know there is truth in them."

"Yes."

"I must tell you of a story, a legend. Perhaps then you will understand about the gold and why you must not speak of it to Sutter or any other." He paused. "Once, before the time when the people made their journey from the far side of the great waters, across the islands of ice and white bears, and down two sides of the great mountains to where the earth and the sun were more kind, to this place and others like it, the sun became angry. His people were praying to other gods, worshipping things the sun had made himself. The sun is a fair god, and he wished to be sure of their misdeeds before he punished them.

"To do this, the sun made the most beautiful thing. Gathering his fire into strong spears, he threw them to the earth, to seven places in the great mountains that are a shield between the great water and the long flat places. Where the spears bit into the mountains, there was great fire. When the fires died, the mountains and rivers where the seven fire spears fell were filled with gold. The sun knew that if his people did not pray to something so beautiful, he would be wrong and would not punish them.

"His sister, the moon, laughed at him. It was she who first spoke of the betrayal, of the other, tiny gods. To prove she was right, she stopped between the sun and the earth and made the sky cold and black in the day. From the cold sky she made seven spears of ice and hurled them down into the same mountains. Where they cut into the earth and turned the mountains white, there was silver. Some of them fell side by side with the gold. She laughed again and told the sun to wait. His people, she said, would not only make the beautiful gold their god, but the ugly silver also. Then she made the people dream of a great journey to a land not so cold as their own.

"And it was true. They came to the warm land beside the mountains, and they prayed to the gold and silver. The moon laughed, and the sun cried. Then he punished his people. Only the sun and the moon had spears before this. But now the sun gave spears to the people, and great sickness, and war, and greed so the wars would not stop and they would be punished forever.

"When the moon saw this, she cried also. For she saw the people were changed. She wished to have things as they were before she shamed the sun. He would not let her. In the night, when the sun slept, the moon made the people dream of new ways to use the gold and silver, hoping they would trade them for the things of life, and by doing this, make their life kind. She also hoped this would make them worship the sun again. And some of them who learned from the dream did. But not all of them.

"When the sun learned of what the moon had done, he was even more angry. But then he remembered his power and laughed. The sound made the people afraid. He laughed again and made the mountains crack, rise and fall so the silver and gold would be hidden from the people and make them want it more. He left only small bits of it shining in the rivers so that his people would kill each other to have it for their own. Where they prayed to it there would only be sorrow and death. He waited for the moon to appear in the day, and then he punished her also. He took away the fire he had given her for warmth and left her as cold as ice forever. He still laughs when he remembers this. Louder when his weak sister stands between him and the earth and hides the people from his eyes. Loudest of all when he places the earth between himself and his sister, and takes away all the pale light and warmth he lets her keep. His laughter still makes great fear in the people when it moves the earth beneath their feet."

Esther smiled. "Earthquakes have nothing to do with the sun and the moon, Miwokan. But what a marvelous story."

"You must try to understand that in such small stories of small people there are large truths."

"But surely, Miwokan, a man as intelligent as you—"

"Think of the story for a moment. You have read the books of the white man. Has the story not been true again and again? My people have seen and heard proof of it in the time we can remember. We do not pray to gold or silver. We have no war, and we are happy. We have small battles, fights, one man against one man. But not so many. It is true of most of the tribes in what you call Alta California. In the south and across the mountains, where the Mojave, the Yuma, the Ute, the Apache, and the Comanche worship gold, there is war. The whites worship gold, and they have war. The whites from Spain came many winters ago, looking for seven cities made of gold. They were fools. There are no seven cities. Only seven places under the mountains. They all died on spears and swords or by the fire of the desert sun."

He watched her face for a moment. "Now do you understand?"

"Much of what you say is true," Esther admitted. "But are there no people who use gold and do not pray to it?"

"Some would have you believe they do. But in their hearts they pray to it also. That is why we bury it. That is why I ask them to leave it in the river so the light will still dance on the water."

She started to ask where the cache was, but decided against it. "Someone will find it sooner or later."

"When they do, it will change my people and be the end of us. I ask you not to be the one to tell them. I know it will happen one day. All things must end. It is the sun's way. But perhaps it does not have to be now."

Esther was torn by conflicting loyalties and the conviction that what Miwokan feared for his people might not, need not, happen if the metal was gold after all. She wanted to comply, but she also felt she owed it to Sutter to reveal all this to him if it was true. If it was gold, she could pay Alexander Todd back easily. And then it struck her. If it *was* gold, she would also have the wherewithal to have Mosby traced . . . track him down . . . kill him. Or have him killed. Her pulse quickened.

If it was here, it was probably elsewhere on Sutter's land. At least that seemed possible, along the river lands if nowhere else. She suddenly realized that no matter what Miwokan believed about the stones, there still was no absolute proof that it was gold; and that all this talk might be meaningless. The practical side of her New England mind took over.

"I want to think about everything you have told me today. I have many reasons to tell Captain Sutter of the stones, but I will not—until I have thought much about it, and I am certain that it actually is gold. I must know that before I make up my mind. The stone must be tested by someone who really knows."

"An assayer." Miwokan was always surprising her.

"Yes."

"That can be done."

"In Yerba Buena? Monterey?"

"No. There are men there, white men, who could do it. But until you decide, I want no one in these places to know of it."

"But where else can it be done?"

"There is a place, far to the south, near the Mission San Fernando. Gold was found there six winters ago. A small place of gold. They do not dig much there now. But I believe such a man could be found in those parts. Or near the Queen of Angels pueblo."

"Will you take the stone there?"

Miwokan thought for a moment. He wondered again if she had been sent by the sun to begin the end of the Miwok. "No," he said, finally. "My people will need me." He rubbed his angular jaw and strong cheekbones with thumb and forefinger, thinking of all he had told her and the need to bring the teaching home in her mind. He gripped the bridge of his nose and thought about what he was certain would happen to those who carried the stone. It made him more sad than he had been after his first wife died in childbirth.

"I will send my son and my brother."

Esther laughed. "Your son is hardly older than mine."

"I have another son. He has twenty winters. He has lived with his mother's sister since the time, two years after his mother's death, when Solana became my wife."

"I never dreamed you were old enough to have a son of twenty."

"I have forty-one winters."

"And Solana?"

"Thirty-seven."

She was astonished. "The sun and the earth have been good to you. They have kept you young."

"Think of that," he said, "while the two men I

trust more than any others ride south through the long valley of blowing yellow grass with your stone."

Twenty-four

South Fork Cabin
December 25, 1847

Captain Sutter shared Christmas dinner with me today. He came this morning after celebrating his Yuletide in European style at the fort last night. He brought me the comb and brush Alex gave me as a wedding present. It was found by a party of his men who traveled to Truckee Lake to sift through what was left there. He has had it since June, but feared it would upset me unduly in its reminder of Alex. Indeed, I did feel far more than a pang for a time, but that is all in the past. Now it is more than a matter of not wanting Alex to see me as I am, know that I was responsible for his son's death, in a way. I cannot involve him in what I plan to do to Mosby if the means and opportunity present themselves.

Grateful to say the reawakening of my feelings continues. I feel more fully alive each week. I am glad this year is coming to a close. Beginning to study the manner in which the books Sutter continues to bring are written. (Became aware how poorly I write upon reading the fluent sentences of Joaquin Murietta's note. Shameful. And he not even a native! Must improve.)

I think of Murietta from time to time. Handsome man. Lord, what a foolish cow I am. Well, he was too short for me by an inch or two even if I had been so disposed.

And I wasn't. And I am not. And I doubt I ever will be. Toward him or any other male animal. Prattle.

Merry Christmas little . . . I must think of a name for the poor child. Earliest conclusions about my feelings for him seem to be borne out. But will wait still. . . . Solana surely loves him.

The two Indians have been gone more than a month now. Have suspended all thought about the stones and what to do about them until they return. Useless to waste the time. Cross the bridge when you come to it.

Sutter brought a spinning wheel and a volume of the writings of a Roman, Epictetus, to me as Christmas gifts. Read a bit earlier, after he left. Some of it interesting. Particularly one idea—that how we perceive and think of events is the cause of much of our sorrows, rather than the events themselves.

Cannot rid myself of the ridiculous notion that I will someday see Murietta again. Foolishness. In any case, dear Lord, I offer up thanksgiving on this the day of your birth, for staying with me through these last twelve months. My fervent prayers go out to you for Alexander Todd's continued good health and prosperity. I know it has been a difficult year for him as well. Painful, I am sure. Pray that he has come alive again after long sorrow. And hope that the coming New Year will hold for him an end of tribulations and the beginning of a new and happier life.

Forgive me also, dear Lord, for my continued desire for vengeance. As I grow stronger, the urge to have Mosby at my mercy, somehow, someday, fills me and silences the God-fearing young girl I once was. Elizabeth Purdy Todd was not capable of such thoughts. But Esther Cable is. Perhaps it will not be gold and the matter will be put to rest as simply impractical wrath, impossible to act upon. But if it is gold, dear Lord, forgive me for what it may one day make possible. . . .

On the last day of the year Esther sat staring at her morning coffee, pondering the awesome beauty of

the previous day's total eclipse, remembering the brief
terror of the earthquake that followed it, and the
dream she had awakened from before sunrise.

*She was driving a wagon loaded with goods. What
they were was not clear. The team of horses, the
wagon were engulfed in a sea of bearded faces. The
men and women clawed at one another, scarcely able
to breathe any more than she could in their frantic
efforts to exchange gold coins for the objects she
seemed to be selling. One man shot another. A woman
in a shirt and trousers scratched out the eyes of an
old man with white hair who was next to be served.
Then Esther saw that they were standing in moving
water up to their ankles, their calves. They stretched
as far as the eye could see, a virtual multitude. In the
distance, where the ground seemed to rise, Miwokan
stood, watching. The sadness in his eyes made her
weep. . . .*

The sound in the doorway startled her, and she
looked up. Mikowan was standing there with his
brother. He was trembling. He came in and placed
the stone on the table. His brother, silver-haired and
in his fifties, stayed just outside the door. In the sunlight Esther could see the ugly purple streak running
from his temple and through a furrow of burned hair.

"It is gold," Miwokan said.

"What happened?" Esther was suddenly aware
of the ineffable grief in Miwokan's eyes.

He told her.

They had gone to San Fernando, then on to the
Pueblo de Los Angeles. They found an assayer, and
he tested the stone. Either they had been seen with
the gold or someone had told of it. Crossing the valley of San Fernando on the return journey, they were
overtaken by three men. One had a red beard and

was fat. Another had only half of one hand left. He
was short. The third was tall and lean. His left arm
dangled and flopped this way and that, as if there
were no bones in it. The tall, lean man killed Miwokan's son with a pistol. Miwokan's brother had
scattered their horses with a scream, leaped on his
own pony, and outdistanced them after the redbearded
man grazed his scalp with a shot from a rifle. The
three men had asked where the Indians found the
gold.

Esther put her arms around Miwokan, rested her
head against his chest, sobbing. "I'm so sorry. So
terribly sorry. It was my fault."

"It was not," Miwokan said. "I sent them. I knew
the gold would shine in the sun and make the rattle-
snakes dance. I only did not know if two, one, or
no one would return."

"God in heaven, I want to bury it! All of it!" She
ran to the armoire, pulled out the baggy pair of
trousers she had not worn since the birth of her baby,
knotted one leg, opened the drawer, and filled the
pant leg with stones. "Will you take it? *Please*! I understand now! I *want* you to bury it!"

"No," Miwokan said. "It will be more good if my
people see you do it."

As the sun cleared the mountains on the first day
of the New Year, she stood on the ragged lip of ice
again, over the convex waterfall where she had sent
the dust of her firstborn son toward the ocean. The
Indians along the bank watched Miwokan's sunsister
as she gazed down at the white, rushing water arcing
toward the deeper place where they had buried the
golden stones for hundreds of years. For a moment
she wondered how much was down there, buried in
sand. The gold in the water was unreachable, as was
Mosby, no doubt. *Perhaps*, she thought, *this is God's
way of showing me he is against my taking venegance.
We shall see.*

She looked at Miwokan, then Solana, then swept her gaze past the rest of the tribe standing on the riverbank. Sighing, she turned the trousers upside down and watched the small, gleaming pieces of rock drop into the tumbling water and disappear beneath the fall.

Two

GOLD

Twenty-five

Sacramento
May 7, 1869
8 A.M.

Esther retied the black-ribboned pages, rose from her parlor-car chair, and placed the journal, open at the next entry, down on the cushion. She stretched, loosening the muscles of her arms, back, and calves, then bent over to unfasten the clasp of her valise. Searching beneath neatly folded undergarments, she pulled out a broad, black sash, her late second husband's double-barreled, over-and-under derringer, and a slender, corked vial of poison. She stared at the objects for a moment, then walked back through the curtain and slipped them under the quilt covering Charles Crocker's brass bed.

Fishing in the valise again, she pulled out her small black purse and searched through a jumble of personal items for the oval gold locket-watch Murietta had given her almost two decades earlier. She opened the cover, exquisitely engraved with an italic E, and marveled at the time. Only an hour had passed since she had sat down and resumed reading the diary entries. She could scarcely remember turning the pages; the memories they evoked of things both recorded and unrecorded, things she had witnessed or had been told, were so complete, so vivid, she felt as if she were living them again.

She lifted a small writing table hanging by hinges under the window nearest her chair, propped it up, and placed the Swiss watch on its wooden surface, thinking of the entries still to be read. There was enough time. She turned, walked forward, and, on the map spread across Charles Crocker's teak desk, traced the route of the Central Pacific from Sacramento through Dutch Flat and farther past Donner Lake. She calculated the time it would take the Pacific Union Express to reach each point, compared the intervals with the time she estimated it would take to read the remaining portions of the journal, then superimposed both sequences on a mental diagram of where she and Mosby would be and what they would be doing as the train carried them up into the Sierras.

She smiled. The three moving elements dovetailed, meshed like the gears of an engine. The smile faded. *Unless,* she thought, *an unforeseen cog interrupts the movement of the machinery, slows it, stops it, perhaps even destroys it—and me.*

She shuddered and took in a deep, calming breath. Turning, she walked back toward her chair; then, on an impulse, she stepped to a window on the opposite side of the car and curled the edge of the shade open. On the wooden sidewalk in front of the hotel, Sutter stood gazing at the train. Several men came out through the hotel doorway. They exchanged greetings with Sutter, but when he made an attempt to engage them in conversation, they all but snubbed him, hurrying off down the street. Esther watched as Sutter reached out with one hand, pathetically reflecting his desire to stop them, bring them back, and hold their attention. He dropped the arm, turned, and, downcast, walked aimlessly in the opposite direction.

Aside from his ceremonial value as a historical curiosity, the short, portly, overgenerous, and ill-fated man was of almost no significance to anyone in Sacramento now. The irony of it struck her as she wondered whether or not he would play a role in the final moments of her plan. That would depend on chance—and on Luther Mosby's predilection for the added excitement that deception and risk added to his sexual activity. But if Sutter were involved, he—once the most important figure in the Sacramento Valley—would again become the most important man in her life. For a second time he would play a pivotal role in helping her conceal from the world yet another secret within a secret, another act he would not witness, would not know about. Only this time, Sutter might help provide her not only with the opportunity for a brand new life, but also with an alibi that might save her life itself.

Compassion for Sutter gave way to deep maternal pride as young Todd darted out of the hotel doorway and raced across the street in the direction of the train. Solana appeared and stopped him with a firm command. He turned and, looking over his shoulder longingly at the locomotive, retraced his steps, took Solana's hand, and skipped along as she walked him toward the river. Canny old woman. She knew the boats and the activity along the riverfront would hold Todd's attention until it was time to strap him into his seat in the cab of the engine.

The boy brought Alex Todd to mind. She wondered what he was doing at this moment. Whether he had finished breakfast and was on his way to the train, or if he had slept a little longer this morning and was just commencing to shave.

She pushed the idle thoughts out of her mind, picked up the journal, and sat down. Sutter . . . Solana—and Miwokan—Alex Todd. . . . Recollections of that next stretch of time flooded her mind as she began reading again.

Twenty-six

South Fork Cabin
March 1, 1848

Dearest Alex, I know it will seem strange, should you ever read these pages, to see that I have taken to writing them somewhat in the form of letters to you. Letters I will never send, letters that you will only read after I am dead and gone, having previously arranged for this journal to be delivered into your hands. Somehow, the notion of sharing what has happened to me, both bad and good, is a comfort in the midst of my decision to maintain my new identity and let you begin a new life. I must not, CANNOT allow you to become enmeshed in what will eventually unfold in mine. At the same time, I hope it will be possible for you to read these scribblings (you will undoubtedly outlive me!), so that you will not only understand why I have done what I have done, but so that, in a way, you will have been with me during all of it.

I wish you could be here in body as well as spirit, but that is no longer possible. What *is* possible is that you will one day be privy to EVERYTHING. I will attempt, as I continue to write, to be open about even my innermost thoughts. Normally we all conceal our little secrets, even husbands and wives. It will be small consolation to either of us, but I vow to record in these pages even those things I would not tell another soul, not even you, if we were still together. In that way you will know me, in a sense will have lived with me, more fully and in more important ways than if we had slept in the same bed together for however many years are left me.

For the first time since learning of the discovery of gold at Sutter's sawmill near Coloma in late January, my mind is clear and things have finally come into focus. Three elements made for such prolonged confusion. The find itself—by Sutter's partner, James Marshall—would be enough to make anyone giddy. But concern about what the discovery portends for Miwokan and his people adds to my disorientation. Compounding it all, my mind has been pulled one way and another by conflicting interests. I do care deeply about the welfare of the Indians, and do not relish being a part of anything that might harm them, but I have also come to realize what the gold could mean to me in achieving the thing that matters most to me now: Mosby's undoing. I think I have found a way to reconcile the two.

Although I was prepared for it to happen eventually, I was stunned when Sutter visited me in mid-February and told me of the discovery. Marshall and his men were working on the tailrace of the mill and he literally stooped down and picked up "something shining in the bottom of the ditch." At first none of them believed it was gold, but Marshall took the stone, and several others, to Sutter at the fort, and tests confirmed their value.

Ironically, Sutter suggested that I enlist some of Miwokan's tribesmen and pan for gold here. "It is your property," he said. "If there is gold near Coloma, possibly it is in these parts as well." He asked me to keep it a "secret," which I have! Thought better of telling him I had already found the metal here, at least until I speak to Miwokan tomorrow.

Oh, Alex, my strength and my wits have returned to normal, but I tremble thinking of what the meeting with Miwokan means to me. I MUST convince him, persuade him to help me pan for the gold! In my weakness and disorientation last year, in my preoccupation with the birth of the child, and during the aftermath of the bear attack,

I wavered in my resolve about the man who dishonored me and caused the death of our son. I knew I wanted to settle the score with him somehow, someday. But I had neither the strength nor the wits nor even the beginnings of wherewithal to do such a thing. I had no plan, and still I do not. But I know that gold will mean money, and money will mean power——the extraordinary power a woman alone in these times would need to make a man like Mosby pay for what he has done. I must have it, Alex. I MUST have it. To trace him, keep track of him, and then, when the time is right, to formulate a plan, trap him, and have my revenge!

Dearest husband, I know what these words must sound like to you. You would not recognize them as the pennings of your young, God-fearing wife. I am that young girl no longer, no matter what my age may be. Often, when I hear that sweet girl's voice within me, quaking at the prospect of eternal damnation for even thinking of harming another human being, I wish that things were different. Oh, how I wish the sickness had not held me at Bent's Fort. That we had journeyed to California together, and that I was in Monterey in your strong arms at this very moment. That John Alexander were alive and well. But he is not. And I can no longer be with you. For I am no longer Elizabeth Purdy Todd.

Forgive me, Alex, for what it is in Esther Cable's mind to do. Forgive me for denying you what small comfort my presence might mean to you. I long to hold you. I do not ever lay my head to rest without feeling the absence of you in my bed. Forgive me for the decision to forego a life together. But things are as they are. And I must do what I must do. I will not rest. I will not "let the sun take me back," as the Indians would say, until I have accomplished what I hope to set in motion tomorrow, no matter how long it takes.

Dear God, please understand. The Lord smiteth the wicked himself. How I wish I could share this with you now, dear husband, and know that you understand and forgive me as well.

Twenty-seven

Thoughts of Mosby and what the gold might mean to her filled Esther's mind as she rode through melting snow toward the Indian village just after sunrise. She carried the baby boy in a makeshift sling on her back. Solana was waiting for her at the central hut when she arrived, but Miwokan and his horse were gone. The Indian woman wore a slight frown.

"He waits for you by the waterfall. He knows what you wish to speak of." Beyond Solana, a half-dozen women sat repairing nets and weirs. Otherwise the village was unusually quiet, and the older men were nowhere to be seen.

"He has heard, then, of what is happening at Coloma?"

Solana laughed. "We have known since the day Marshall picked up the stones in the tailrace of Sutter's mill."

"And Miwokan? How does he feel about it?"

"You will have to hear his words yourself," Solana said, turning and starting into the hut. She stopped just inside and turned back, her expression softening. "Leave the child here while you speak with your sunbrother."

As Solana took the baby, gazed at it, and broke into a loving smile, Esther realized how uncharacteristically cool the Indian woman had been to her. Steeling herself for resistance, she wheeled her horse around and cantered toward the river.

Miwokan sat watching the water rush out from

under the softening ice at the lip of the fall as Esther
reined the horse up and dismounted. A dozen of the
older braves in the village sat around him in a semicircle, smoking several long pipes and whispering to
one another. Miwokan glanced at her as she approached, then went back to his musings. She brushed
the snow off a low, flat rock and sat down to wait. The
elders grew silent as Miwokan gazed at the tumbling
white water for a full five minutes. The sound of it
filled Esther's ears and calmed her. *No matter what
he says,* she thought, *I must convince him. It is too
important to allow him to stand between me and the
wealth I will need to bring Mosby down. If he re-
fuses . . .*

"Why do you wish to dirty your hands?" Miwokan
suddenly said, interrupting her thoughts. The elders
nodded in approval. "Do you not believe what I have
told you about the gold and all those who worship
it? Was this not proven to you?"

"Miwokan. Sunbrother. I do not worship the gold.
I need it."

"For what?"

"There are many reasons. Some I cannot tell you.
But it is enough for you to know that a woman alone
must have the means to support herself."

"A husband could do that."

"*I do not want a husband!*"

The elders recoiled at the sharpness of her voice.
Miwokan stared at her, his face expressionless.

"I did not mean to speak harshly," she said. "But
I cannot seem to make you understand."

"I understand more than you know." He looked away
as a chunk of ice became dislodged, fell, and sent a
spray of sunlit water across the base of the fall. "I
understand that something has happened that makes
you hate the thought of being with a man. I think
it has to do with the child and its father."

"That may be," she said, uncomfortable with the
tack he was taking.

"And it is foolish. One thieving priest does not mean that the whole church is evil."

"I do not hate all men."

"Only one?" he asked. The elders leaned forward.

She hesitated. She felt outnumbered, her privacy unfairly breached. Their eyes seemed to bore holes in her forehead. *They* know, she thought. *Somehow they know everything.* Then she realized it was the only thing that might persuade Miwokan. "Yes," she finally said.

"Who is this man? If he has wronged you, we will find him and make him pay."

"What is done to him I must do myself."

The elders looked at one another in astonishment. A woman did not speak this way, let alone set out on such a course. Miwokan's brother shook his head disapprovingly.

"And I cannot do it without money," she added quickly. "Do you understand?"

"How do you know the gold you find will be enough?"

"I don't. It is a gamble I have to take."

"I will not help you, then. I know what gold, as well as revenge, do to the human heart."

Esther tossed her head in frustration. "If you do not help me, I will have to hire white men. They will come here and change everything."

"You would do that?" Miwokan was off balance. He had not counted on such determination, defiance. The elders murmured and shifted uncomfortably.

"I'm sorry, but I would have to. I would rather you and your people worked with me. That way the legend would not come true. That way you would share with me, your tribe would be strong in a different way than it is now. Much stronger, in fact. It would not be the end of your people, but a new beginning."

"How can that be?"

"Men are mining near Coloma. Sooner or later, they will come here to search for gold. If no one has staked a claim, they will simply move in, and your people will be driven off."

"We will fight them," Miwokan said. "These are our lands. This has been our place forever." The elders nodded uneasily.

"Don't you understand? They have better weapons! There will be more of them than you! If you have the gold, you can buy weapons to protect yourselves. You can be equal to them in other ways also. In time there will be change. Just as there was change when your people came across the islands of snow and ice. The life of your people must have been different on the far side of the great water. To make it better, you traveled thousands of miles."

"What you say is true. But those changes did not have to do with gold."

"It is time for change again, Sunbrother. This time the gold will help you make a better life, now that the white men are here. As long as you continue to worship the sun, love one another as you do, and stay together, the gold will not be the end of you. Can't you see?"

"I know that you have great wisdom for a woman. But you are too young to know what will happen. Even I do not know that."

"Listen to me. I have read of these things. The new people, the whites, will move in and take your place if they have the gold and you do not."

"You are certain of that?"

"Yes. In other times, it was not gold. Something else, spears, gunpowder, arrows, something, made the new people stronger than those who were there before them. This time it is the gold that will make the difference."

He thought for a moment. "If you hired the white men, *you* would be making them stronger."

"I don't want to do that. That is why I have come to you."

"But you would do it if I refuse?"

"I have no choice. I *must* obtain the money I need."

"Will you tell me more about this man you hate so much?"

"He has dishonored me, and I must make him pay for it." She wanted to reveal more but could not. She saw they still were not satisfied with her response. Reluctantly she resorted to turning their beliefs about her to advantage. "This is why the sun helped me walk across the mountains in the deep snow."

Miwokan turned to the elders and saw they were moved by what she had said. He felt himself swayed by the power of her determination, and the sun *had* protected her, aided her in her mission. "These words are strong. They bend my mind toward your wishes."

"Then you will help me? You and your people will join me in the work?"

"I did not say that. The legend also stands strong in my thoughts. Let me reason this out," Miwokan said, waving his hand as she began to protest. "You have told me what you believe. And the sun is with you or you would not have lived. I must think of a way to do this thing without offending the sun. I will try. Leave me now, and I will talk with you again about it tomorrow."

At noon the next day Miwokan arrived at the cabin with a dozen young braves. Each of them carried a shallow woven basket and a crude, wooden-handled stone hacking tool.

"There is a way to do this thing," Miwokan said after she had asked him in and they were sitting at her table. "We will work *for* you. Not with you. For wages. Just as we have for Sutter."

"But I wish to share what we find. I want you and your people to benefit."

"Can you—how is it said?—stake a claim here and on the river near the village as well?"

"I don't know. I think so. I will have to look into it."

"If you cannot, there is another way. Once or twice in Alta California, the Spanish and the Mexicans paid to use the lands of my people. They . . . leased it. Such a thing has not been often done. But it might work for us."

"I would use the land, pay you for the use, but you would own it?"

"Yes, it would be a way to stop the legend from being fulfilled. For I can see no way harm could come to us from the gold if we were simply working for you. You would gain what you want, we would not be seeking the gold for ourselves, and we would not have other whites here."

"But why not share in the profits with me? That would make you stronger."

"That is the part of it we cannot do without risking the anger of the sun. If we dig not for ourselves but for another, we are simply working at a new thing. It is no different from working in the wheatfields for Sutter."

"Is there no way I can persuade you to take some of the gold for yourselves?"

"No. You will pay my people the same wage Sutter pays us. I will watch over the work and receive a small amount more. I will be . . . the boss."

Esther laughed. "The chief boss . . ." She reached out and touched Miwokan's hand. "Would the sun be angry if I paid you more than Sutter? After all, it is harder work. And the water is cold."

"We have been in the water forever. It does not bother us. But wait until the white men are in it. They will find it not easy to work the riverbeds for long."

"You think they will go away?"

"No. They will want the gold as you do. For reasons not as good, but just as much. They will suffer in the getting of it. From the icy waters and in many other ways."

"I want to pay you twice as much as Sutter."

"That is too much. I do not want to tempt the sun to punish us."

"Your people cannot work all year at it. The snow and ice will stop the work every winter."

"That is true."

"Twice as much, then?"

"One and a half of one," Miwokan said.

"Done. But twice as much for the chief boss."

He smiled then, but only halfheartedly. Normally his sense of humor would have had him grinning broadly, and Esther finally realized how much he had yielded simply to please her. "We will start now," he said. "It is a simple thing when the stones are close to the surface. Later, when those are gone, it will be more difficult."

"I will pay you and your men in gold. Is that all right?"

"It does not matter to me. However and whenever you wish. I ask only one thing of you, Sunsister."

"Anything," she said, already feeling a surge of desire to get started, to begin taking the first steps toward the day of her vengeance.

"Sunsister, I ask only that we do not touch any of the gold under the waterfall. And that you speak of that gold to no one."

"Of course."

"There is enough in other parts of the river to give you more than you will need."

"I will never tell a soul about it."

"Do not be afraid," he said as he slipped the long knife out of its sheath and took hold of her hand. "This is our way of sealing all we have agreed to. It is a swearing." Interlocking his fingers in hers, he pressed their palms together and quickly, lightly, sliced skin deep across the soft flesh at the base of their thumbs.

She felt faint for a moment as she watched the blood emerge from each of their hands, trickle, down and then commingle inside their tightly pressed wrists.

But then, suddenly, in her mind she saw the knife in her own hand and the flesh beneath it was Mosby's and the cut was long and inches deep and the blood was gushing out of it—and she smiled with clear-headed, almost frightening satisfaction.

Twenty-eight

South Fork Cabin
May 27, 1848

Oh, Alex, it seems impossible that almost five months have passed so quickly. I must review what I have written since the turn of the year. Think upon it with a cool head, and be sure that what I am about to propose to Sutter and the Mormon, Sam Brannan, as well as those in charge of things at the Blue Star Shipping Company in Yerba Buena—or rather San Francisco, as it is now called—is sound. I wonder now what you would think of this imminent journey; whether it and my plans are sensible or simply the harebrained ideas of a foolish young woman.

So much has happened since the discovery of gold that I must list things as they happened, in order:

Marshall's discovery was known to the men, several Mormons, and a number of Coloma Maidu among them, working on the sawmill. In the beginning, Sutter wished to keep it all a secret. Yet he told me and, if I recall the conversation immediately wrote of it to his Californio friend, Mariano Vallejo, in Sonoma. Vallejo kept the confidence, but others did not. Little wonder that the word has spread. And now Sutter tells me there are literally hundreds of men searching, panning, then quickly moving on to other sites all around the area of his mill. At first I was alarmed, but thus far I am told the men are orderly, well-behaved, and although they do not pay the Indians equal wages, they have not lifted a hand to harm them.

Miwokan seems a bit reassured by all this—resigned might be a better word. He does not complain and has never tried to dissuade me from my goal. But he is far from happy. I have honored his request that we not touch what is beneath the waterfall and that I do not reveal prior knowledge of the gold to Sutter. I am certain he is satisfied that as long as we do not remove the original cache from its sacred place, his god will be appeased, but I am not sure how he feels about the future and the part I play in it. He does not reveal his deepest feelings to me on the matter. I must confess that instinctively I sense that sooner or later that gold will cause fearful things to happen—some of it to the Indians. It would have come to pass sooner or later anyway, all of this. I cannot do much elsewhere, but I give you my word, Alex, that one way or another I will use some of the power the gold brings to me to see that Miwokan and his people are protected.

Alex, if you could see the astonishing amount of gold nuggets, flakes, and dust that now almost covers the floor of the new storage shed Miwokan's men have built! Already I possess more wealth than I ever dreamed of! And there is no end in sight! At first we panned with close-woven, shallow grass bowls, my skillets, and two wash-basins, swirling the bottom sand out of them, as Sutter instructed, until only the gold remained. Some of the men still do that, as do I, for as long as I can stand the icy-cold mountain water, which is to say for about an hour at a time. Lately we have been using also something Miwokan devised by altering Mwamwaash's and Moses'—rocker cradles. Oh, God, Alex, he IS my son, even if Luther Mosby is his father. And he is named after my grandfather, Moses Purdy. Thank God he is daily showered with love since I gave him over to Solana's care, for such feelings are simply not in me.

I wander from my original purpose. In any case, Miwokan removed a slat from the foot of each cradle and fitted wooden ridges across their bottoms. We shovel in the river dirt, pour in water, and then, tilting and rocking the cradle, wash the dirt out through the opening more quickly and in much greater amounts. The result is much more gold, caught on the wooden ridges, than before. Sutter saw the device on his last trip through here and told us it resembles a larger invention called the Long-Tom, which has been used elsewhere, according to one of his books. He suggested we build a number of them, as he plans to, and dispense with the ordinary panning entirely. No doubt we will.

Now what does it all portend? First, there is no one here but us—for now. But there is gold here as well as at Coloma, and sooner or later prospectors are bound to arrive. Second, Miwokan has heard of nuggets being found in many places by Indians both north and south of here, so it is more than possible that it will soon be "discovered" by whites in a great number of locations in these mountains. How many and how far a distance in both directions from here? Impossible to say. But probably considerable.

Which brings me to my idea. Would you not agree that if the prospectors come, they will need supplies? And that if they do not come in great numbers, surely settlers will, at least at the rate they did last year. Thus, if the supplies are such as might be used by settlers as well as prospectors, they would be equally, if not as quickly, salable. Now, I do not wish to become involved in such a business directly, nor do I desire yet for traffic with so many people as it would entail. But if I were to do what my father did to supplement his meager income from the ministry—that is to say, become a partner to one or more businessmen by providing money for them to increase the number of their transactions—then I could reap the possible rewards of such a venture without direct involvement.

I have read and reread the last paragraph and it seems sound. Why then do I have such a queasy feeling in my stomach? Perhaps, Alex, it is that I am a girl not yet twenty who no longer has you to lean on. And these things seem exceedingly intricate to me because I am ignorant of the workings of business. But then my father was not a businessman by any measure. He cared nothing to learn of every action, every ledger entry. He relied only on common sense and his estimate of a man's intelligence and honesty . . . and so shall I!

There. It is decided. Fears or not. Tomorrow night I will begin mending the slits in the dress I wore when I . . . crossed the mountains. Oh, God, Alex, I cannot think of that time without filling up with hatred and vengefulness. I must suspend that train of thought until it can be implemented . . . think of the immediate task. . . . The long matching gloves are here somewhere. And surely Sutter will have a hat bearing a veil to cover this ugly nose. He has just about everything at the fort! As soon as it is possible, I will go to Coloma to speak with him, journey on to New Helvetia and see Brannan, and thence to San Francisco! Pray for me.

Twenty-nine

When Esther reached Sutter's idle sawmill just before noon on the last day of May, she was shocked by his appearance. There were dark circles under his eyes. His lustrous gray hair was dull, unkempt, and speckled with mud. Normally erect in bearing, he stooped as though the weight of two worlds were on his shoulders. She found him idly setting out a lunch of bacon, frijoles, flour tortillas, and coffee for his Californio friend Mariano Vallejo. Esther had not expected Sutter to have a visitor, and at first she was reluctant even to dismount. She still had no veil. The heavyset alcalde of Sonoma would see her scar. Beyond the embarrassment, he would undoubtedly ask questions. But Sutter would not hear of her leaving without refreshment. Even before she dismounted, he began putting her at ease.

"Mariano, this . . . is . . . the widow of the settler, Cable, I was telling you about. Is she not a lovely lady?"

Esther was relieved by Sutter's introduction but disturbed by the weak, quavering tone of his voice.

Vallejo bowed, took her hand and touched it with his lips. "*Muy hermosa*," he said, looking straight into her eyes and smiling. There was not a trace of sexual interest in his voice or expression. It comforted her when he looked away without so much as a glance at her scarred nose.

"My friend Vallejo," Sutter said too heartily, "is a gentleman, a former general, and a fast and loyal comrade. He virtually rules Sonoma."

Vallejo took Esther's arm and led her to the camp table Sutter had set out. "He exaggerates, señora. I merely see that the law is carried out."

"Were there only an alcalde in these parts," Sutter grumbled, as he sat down and toyed with his food.

Vallejo turned to Esther. "He is beset by troubles. You have come to see him at the worst of times."

Puzzled, Esther caught a glimpse of Sutter's expression. He had been signaling Vallejo to silence. "But the gold . . . ?"

"The gold is the least of his problems," Vallejo responded. "It *could* solve everything else—if he could find enough of it. With gold, he could—"

"Curse the gold!" Sutter shouted, spraying bits of food onto the table. He looked sheepishly at Vallejo. "Forgive me Mariano. But you know I am distressed."

"Of course," Vallejo said.

For the first time she could remember, Esther heard

a note of pleading in Sutter's voice and saw a trace of tears in his eyes. "*Please* speak no more of it, Mariano. I do not want to burden her with any of it."

Vallejo nodded. "As you wish, John."

Sutter could not look straight at Esther. His hands were trembling.

"Is the panning not going well for you?" she asked.

"Yes. . . . We can speak of that . . ." Sutter answered vaguely, his mind obviously on something else. "We are not taking nearly the amount of ore out of the river I expected. Not one quarter as much." He gazed off, distracted for a moment, then turned back to Esther. "Oh, yes, the Indians," he said, as if she had asked about them. "Those who work for me dawdle while their brothers, working for themselves —on the land *I* leased from them up- and downriver —pull nuggets and flakes out of the gravel and the riverbank by the handful."

Vallejo tried to soothe his friend. "It is only a matter of luck."

But Sutter suddenly waved his arms wildly. "Industry!" he shouted, off on another tack entirely. "If only I had a dozen hardworking, industrious men!"

"Can't you hire them?" Esther asked.

"They will *really* work for no one but themselves, these Indians." Sutter's voice trailed off again. He gazed at the rushing water of the Middle Fork, nodding first, then shaking his head, holding a conversation with himself. "On *my* land . . . my land."

"You have leased more than you can control," Vallejo said gently.

Sutter brought his hand down on the table so hard his coffee cup jumped. The liquid spilled and dripped onto his pants, but he didn't seem aware of it. "I have *paid* for the use of this land!" he shouted. "And they ignore my protests, white and red alike! *They* seem to find gold without even trying! Wherever I have my men stop to pan, the stones bearing ore are in pitifully short supply."

Esther was increasingly unsettled by Sutter's behavior. She watched now as his hands moved constantly, touching his lap, the table, his metal camp plate, his hair. "Is there no way to stop them?" she asked quietly, hoping to focus his attention, wondering at the same time what it might be like if the prospectors overran her own claim—and, more frighteningly, the land she was leasing from Miwokan's people.

"What am I to do, *kill* them all?" Sutter snapped. As he continued, his voice shifted eerily from loud to soft and back again in midsentence. "There are too many. Too many men, too many places along the river and its tributaries." He sighed and ran both his hands back along the sides of his head. "Too many . . . other things . . . to think . . . about . . . as well." Silent once again, he drifted into his own thoughts.

Vallejo looked at Esther and shook his head sadly. "I'm sure the two of you have things to discuss privately. I will go down to the riverbank to find myself a souvenir." He stood up. "If you will excuse me for a short while, señora."

Esther waited until Vallejo was out of earshot and then turned to Sutter. He was totally preoccupied now, more dejected than a man of his means had a right to be simply over poor prospecting luck.

"You have so much on your mind," Esther said, bringing him out of his musing. "Perhaps it is the wrong time. . . ."

"No, no," Sutter protested, a little unconvincingly. He managed a smile and took her hand. For a few moments he seemed almost himself again. "What a beauty you are. And so considerate. No, I have always the time for you. What is it?"

"I wish to go into business."

"Good. Good." His eyes were off her again, drifting, starting to go slightly blank. He caught himself and brought his attention back to her. "But you are

. . . already in business. The mining business. And doing well, I hope?"

She was uncomfortable about how much better her yield had been than his. "Quite well," she finally said, adding quickly, "I'm sure your luck will change for the better here."

He shrugged. "It . . . doesn't matter anymore . . . It is too late, anyway."

"What do you mean?"

He waved a hand. "Nothing, nothing," he whispered, realizing he had hinted at more than he intended. "Go on. What sort of business besides mining have you in mind?"

"A wholesale business in general supplies for the miners—or settlers, should the mining not last. Hard goods. Pans, hammers, nails, picks, shovels. Other tools. Cooking utensils. That sort of thing."

"I do not see how you can fail at such a venture in these parts."

"I was hoping you would become my partner, invest with me, sell the goods I will be arranging to purchase in San Francisco—"

"Out of the question!" Sutter barked. He had never spoken to her in such a tone. "I have no time! I have too much to deal with now! My hands are too full to take on even a dollar's worth of additional responsibility! Look at this mill. Idle. The flour mill, unfinished. . . . I do not wish to speak of it, do you hear?"

She was crestfallen, and he saw it. Contrite, he put an arm over her shoulder. "Forgive me, my beautiful friend. If I could only tell you." He sighed. "I have come to the end of my . . ." He stopped and stared off into the distance. "When I first came here . . . the dreams I had. . . . But this is not your concern. Go to the fort, make your arrangements with someone else, and I will provide you with all the storage space I can find. I will have to charge you rent, but it will be reasonable."

"I have heard of a man named Brannan. . . ."

"Yes, he might be willing to join forces with you."

"Do you know him?"

"He is a Mormon. A hard bargainer, but Mormons keep to their word once they have given it. Usually."

"Will Brannan keep to his word? Can he be trusted?"

Sutter frowned. "He is a Mormon. That is all I can say for him."

"In Yerba—San Francisco, I wish to arrange with the man you have spoken of—Mr. Kelsey—at Blue Star. To have the goods shipped from the East."

"Say no more," Sutter said. "It is done. Before you leave, I will give you a letter of introduction. He is an old friend. A good man, and I would trust him with my life."

"Will you tell me what it is that troubles you so much? Beyond the difficulties here?"

"You will understand everything soon enough. Forgive me, but I do not wish to speak of it to anyone. Not even you."

On the ride to the fort, Esther passed dozens of prospectors walking and riding toward Coloma, her thoughts alternating between the purpose of her journey and the possible sources of Sutter's appalling state of mind. But her thoughts were abruptly swept away by what she saw as she approached New Helvetia late the following afternoon.

There were at least two dozen crude houses between the fort and the riverfront now. Stacks of unthreshed wheat sat amid new growth that already showed signs of withering in the sun for lack of water. The Indians were gone. All but two of the white men employed by Sutter had left. Manaiki did the bidding of a domineering man named Kyburz, who had leased Sutter's two-story house for five hundred dollars a month and converted it into a hotel. Merchants, strangers, had opened stores in rented rooms along the walls of the fort. Cattle and horses, sheep, pigs, and dogs wandered and dropped waste everywhere, unattended. A completely new crowd of men Esther had never seen before hauled wagonloads of goods into the fort. Others reined their teams to a halt in front of the general store Sam Brannan had opened in an outbuilding leased from Sutter. Now she understood the look of fear she had seen in Sutter's eyes: the hint of a man drowning economically. Now she knew why he had passed the point of even considering a partnership with anyone. The acrid stench of two thousand abandoned, rotting hides stacked outside Sutter's unmanned tannery confirmed the impending disaster.

She took a room, asked Manaiki to find her a hat with a veil, ate an early supper alone, rested briefly, then, her face sufficiently concealed, went to see Brannan. Burly, chin-whiskered but moustacheless, he was wearing a Sunday-meeting black hat, a colorless, dirty shirt, and black trousers tucked into knee-high boots. His store was crammed with merchandise and dry goods of every kind and description.

"Don't need no partners," Brannan said when she broached the subject. "Doin' right fine by myself."

"I had hoped . . ."

"Say you're goin' to San Francisco? What for? Nothin' to be had there now. Everything's bought up. Goods that isn't, you can't find a man jack to get it here for you. Into the mountains neither. I had the foresight . . ."

"I have made arrangements," Esther said, stretching a half-truth. "The goods will be delivered. But if you do not wish to become partners . . ."

"Now just wait a minute, little missy. You got brass, you do. Don't want a partner, I said. But I might be willin' to strike some sort of arrangement with you—if you can get supplies delivered here."

"I can," she said, trembling.

He regarded her coolly, and she saw a mercenary glint in his eyes as he manufactured a smile. "Tell you what I'll do. I'll receive any goods you get shipped here, store 'em and, ah, attempt to sell 'em. You pay for 'em, pay for storage—reasonable, reasonable, rates the market bears these days—if I don't turn them over. What sells, why, we'll split the profits. What don't . . . well . . . you'll just have to cart it off, say after six months. At your own cost, of course."

Esther thought for a moment. She could not believe he would have any trouble selling anything, anywhere. The storage and carting expense likely would never materialize.

"Sixty-forty on the profits," she heard herself say.

"Good-bye, young lady."

"All right. Fifty-fifty."

"Ought to charge you an extra 5 percent just for your cheek." Brannan fabricated another good-natured smile. "But I like you. Admire your gumption. Fifty-fifty. Do we have a deal?"

"We do, Mr. Brannan."

"No, we don't."

"What do you mean?"

"Got to show me some earnest money. S'pose I get stuck with a whole room full of goods and can't sell 'em? Got to have a little payment against possible storage costs."

Esther frowned. She did not like Brannan, but he was all she had for the moment, and she had to make a start somewhere. She opened her carryall bag and handed him a pouchful of nuggets and dust. "Will this do for now?"

"Plenty, plenty," he said, untying the purse strings and staring greedily as the lantern light gleamed on the gold. "I'm not a hard man, missy. Just had to know you had the means. . . ."

"There is more where that came from."

"I don't doubt it, listenin' to you. Be interestin' to see how successful you are with your arrangement in San Francisco."

"What you're saying is that if my arrangement does not work out, you will keep the gold I just gave you."

"Missy, my time is worth money. But you said you could do it. So what's there to worry about?"

Esther quashed a sudden tremor of fear. "It will take a little time, Mr. Brannan. But you shall have the goods."

"Shall we shake on it then?" he said, coming out from behind a long table upon which glasses and bottles of liquor sat waiting for the tradesmen and transient prospectors who were just now finishing dinner inside the fort. He took her hand, held on to it, and squinted to see through the veil. Esther tried to pull away. "You're a pretty one, all right."

"Thank you."

"Why don't you stay for a while 'fore you go on to San Francisco?"

She pulled her hand free. "My time is just as valuable as yours, Mr. Brannan."

He laughed. "So it is, so it is." He took a step backward. "No offense."

"None taken." She turned. "If you will excuse me now, I will be going back to my room."

"Leavin' on the early boat?"

"Yes."

"I'll tell you a little secret," he said. "Now that we've made our deal."

"And what is that, Mr. Brannan? That you knew all along you could sell just about anything I could lay my hands on in San Francisco?"

He doubled over as a deep laugh rumbled up out of his throat. "That's right. I can tell you there'll be no end to what we can sell in these parts. I was there. Showed 'em the gold I had and they wouldn't believe me. Less'n a month ago, right on the main street of San Francisco. Now look at 'em. Practically crawlin' over one another to get at it, like ants after spilled sugar."

* * *

Esther thought about Brannan as she stood on the
forward deck of Sutter's launch with the cloth bag
containing five pouches of gold pressed firmly between
her ankles. Leaning one gloved hand on the port gun-
wale, she took off her hat and veil and let the breeze
unfurl her long, dark hair as she gazed down the
last stretch of the wide river. There was no cargo
aboard the San Francisco–bound launch, no one else
except the pilot, and he was back in the raised cabin,
not near enough to see the pale scar on her face
even if she turned.

She was glad to be alone; she needed time to collect her thoughts. Despite what Sutter had told her
earlier in the year, she had not been prepared for
the sight of so many tents, crude wooden lean-tos,
shanties, and scores of men working in the streams
and along the riverbanks, riding horses and pack
mules, sawing, hammering, panning, picking, and
shoveling in and around Coloma.

She looked up. Two other boats were moving upstream, loaded to the gunwales with cargo and male
passengers. Self-consciously, Esther put on her hat
and hesitantly returned friendly waves. Even at a distance of thirty yards, she could see the picks and
shovels and metal pans. There was no doubt about
where they were headed. Thinking of them, of Brannan's willingness to sell for her on a consignment
basis, and of what she had witnessed during the last
three days, the last of her uncertainty vanished.

The launch left the mouth of the river and turned
southwest into a stunningly wide bay. For the remainder of the afternoon, Esther sat on a wooden
locker pondering Sutter's predicament and marveling
at the serene, multifaceted beauty of the inland waters and the low hills that encircled them like an
enormous necklace of unmatched, gray-green jewels.
It was still light when the strait John Frémont had
named the Golden Gate materialized out of the sun-

set haze in the distance. Esther gasped as the launch drew closer and the channel's size and splendor became apparent. But even that did not match her astonishment when the pilot turned the vessel around the near headland of a deep cove and San Francisco came into view.

Thirty

The last time Sutter had described Yerba Buena to Esther, more than a year before, he had left her with an impression: a small village of perhaps fifty humble and haphazardly scattered wood and adobe houses and a population of about two hundred. What Esther saw now was a town at least four times as large with more than a dozen stores, two hotels, a number of warehouses along the shore, several wharves, perpendicular unpaved streets—and, strangely, a good deal fewer than half as many people as Sutter had indicated. It did not make sense. Except for the crowd of men waiting among the crates of cargo on the wharf, the town seemed almost as empty as the windblown sand dunes that surrounded it. Esther turned and scanned the dozen or more ships that lay anchored offshore and just outside the cove. Nothing moved on any of them.

When the launch docked, several of the men waiting to board tipped their caps and good-naturedly invited her to join them on their journey to the gold fields. Esther ignored them and walked on, up one street and then right at a corner in the general direction of a "hotel" sign she remembered seeing from

the launch. It was not in sight, so when she came
to another rude intersection, she glanced back down
toward the waterfront. The hotel was not down that
street either, but she noted the building upon which
"Blue Star Shipping Company" was painted in white
letters. A single lamp burned in one window.

Gusts of cold, early evening wind blew up from the
cove and chilled her as she continued on, disoriented
by these new, tightly packed surroundings. She passed
an empty butcher shop, a vacant tailor's establishment, a shoemaker's with the door open and no one
inside. Signs in French, German, Russian, and Chinese increased her unsettled feeling. At the next corner she saw the hotel sign over the rooftops a few
streets farther on. A woman and her child crossed
the street ahead as Esther turned toward it.

Another woman watched her from the window of
a dressmaker's shop as she hurried past. She saw a
few more people and felt comforted. The sun dropped
behind the hills to the west. Although it was still
light, the first coils of a night fog were rolling in.
The entire town suddenly took on an unearthly trans-
lucent amber hue.

She turned the last corner and started toward the
hotel. At first, she paid the relatively tall, well-pro-
portioned man walking toward her from the next cross
street no mind. But then she realized that something
about the way he walked, the way his shoulders were
set, the way his arms moved seemed familiar. Her
pulse quickened as he approached. At a distance of
twenty feet she knew it was Alex Todd.

She saw him smile courteously and tip his hat just
before she tilted her head downward and passed him.
She held her breath as she heard him continue on.
Then his footsteps stopped. She *knew* he had turned
around and was watching her, *felt* it. Three years. A
small part of her screamed silently to turn around,
drop the cloth bag, run and throw her arms around
him, tell him all that had happened, sob it out against

his chest and . . . Three years. . . . She thought of the scar . . . the missing fingers . . . the dead baby . . . Mosby . . . His son . . . Three years. *I cannot stop*, she said to herself, *I cannot go back. I must not give in.*

She was certain he was still watching, observing the way she walked as she had observed him. He could not possibly have seen her face, *but God,* she thought, *will he remember this dress?* She continued on past the entrance to the hotel. The thought that he had *not* come out of this establishment registered in her mind. She began rocking her shoulders, taking wider, swinging steps and bouncing a little on the balls of her feet. Anything; anything to walk like someone else, prevent him from recognizing movements that no doubt were still indelibly traced in his mind.

"Elizabeth?" he called out as she turned the corner.

Without looking back, she began walking faster, uphill, away from the hotel. At the next intersection she crossed the street diagonally and glanced back. He was following her. She began to run. She turned left into a dirt alley behind a row of houses and then right into another. She came to a broad street and briefly slowed to a walk, her breath coming in short gasps. She looked back again. *Oh, God, he is pursuing me now.* He had just come out of the last alley and was walking fast.

Turning at the next corner, she ran downhill toward the waterfront and a street that veered left past warehouses and wharves. A block to the west a lamp turned on in what appeared in the glowing darkness to be a large, barnlike structure. As Esther approached it, she saw that the place had once been a large stable. Now a series of canvass-walled enclosures hung from an attached shed roof along one side. Another lamp, then a third, flamed on behind two separate tent-units.

She peered back through patches of blowing fog

and saw a man's figure at the last corner she had
turned. He was standing still, looking in her direction.
She went into the building. Beyond the bare pine
planks of the entrance hallway, another door led to
the central area of the stable. It had been converted
into an enormous room. An unvarnished subfloor had
been laid in; one wall was painted a garish red, but
the others were only whitewashed. A girl wearing a
camisole dotted with eyelets, long white bloomers,
black stockings, and buttoned, high-heeled walking
boots sat sprawled in a chair reading a newspaper.
Near her a glowing, potbellied stove stood by the
far wall. The girl did not look up.

Another young woman in cheap cloth slippers and
a dirty nightdress came out through a door to Esther's right. Scowling, she glanced at Esther and continued on without a word through a stall and an
opening into one of the tents. Esther turned to the
doorway the girl had come from and found it filled
by a fat, slatternly woman with dyed red hair.

The fat woman puffed on a thin cheroot and gave
Esther a quick, appraising look. "I'm sorry, honey.
But you've come to the wrong place at the wrong
time. All the regulars are up to the gold mines. There
ain't no business. I had to send three girls away this
mornin', and like as not, we'll *all* be packin' up and
movin' to Coloma before the month is out."

"I'm not looking for . . . work," Esther said, moving closer to her. The woman reeked of cheap per-
fume and sweat.

"Well, what is it you want, honey?"

Esther took five silver dollars out of her purse.
"A man is following me . . ."

The woman laughed. "We should all be so lucky."

"No, please, listen to me! A man is following me,
and I must avoid him. Is there someplace I can hide?
And will you send him away if he comes in?"

The fat woman cocked an eyebrow. "I don't want
no trouble."

"There'll be no trouble, I promise you. *Please!* I'll give you five more dollars if you'll do it."

The woman hesitated a moment, then shrugged her shoulders. "That's more than I've taken in since Sunday. Come on in here."

Grabbing Esther by the arm, the woman led her through a makeshift office and into a small storage area screened off by a slit curtain. "You wait in here." She hesitated for a moment, then arched one eyebrow again. "You sure you got five more dollars?"

Esther opened her bag, found a ten-dollar gold piece in a separate coin purse, and gave it to her. "*Please* . . . it's so important to me."

The fat woman put her finger to her lips as they both heard the front door open and close.

"It's *him*," Esther whispered. "I just know it!"

The madam bustled out and greeted Alex. "*Girls!*" she shouted hoarsely. Turning back to him she asked, "What's your pleasure this evening, sir? I don't have but three young ladies with me at the moment, but . . ."

"I'm looking for a young woman who came in here just a few minutes ago."

"Got her all picked out already, do you?"

"You don't understand," Alex said. "I . . ."

"Rebecca just came in awhile ago. Here she is now."

The three prostitutes walked up and stood in a ragged line, facing Alex. He shook his head and tried to explain. "Not one of your girls, I'm not . . ."

"Rebecca," the fat woman said. "Let him see your titties. He's taken a fancy to you."

"For God's sake, the girl I'm looking for . . ."

"Maybe you'd prefer Dora," the fat woman said. "Show him your bum, Dora." She turned to Alex, leering and nudging him in the ribs. "She *loves* it that way."

"I'm not interested in any of your girls!" Alex said, raising his voice. "Can't you understand?"

"Well, there's no need to get sharp about it," the fat woman said. "What do you want?"

"I'm sorry . . . I . . . another girl came in. I don't believe she works here."

"Hasn't no one come in but Rebecca."

For a moment Alex came into Esther's view. Through the curtain slit she saw him tilt his hat back and nervously rub his forehead. The look on his face was so frustrated and forlorn it almost brought tears to her eyes. For a moment she felt an almost overwhelming urge to walk out and spare Alex what he was going through.

"The girl I'm talking about is taller than anyone here," Alex said. "She . . . I know her personally."

"Where'd you see her?" the fat woman asked.

"From up the street. I'm sure she came in here."

"Mister, in that fog out there, Rebecca could'a looked like anyone."

Esther bit her lip. *I cannot help him,* she thought, tears streaming down her face. *I must do what I have to do.*

"Damn it," Alex said tenaciously. "I saw her. I followed her for at least six blocks."

"From where?"

"From in front of the Alta Hotel. She came in here. I know it!"

"Rebecca just come from there," she said, turning to the girl and covertly winking. "Didn't you, Rebecca?"

"Yes, ma'am," Rebecca said.

"She just come back from givin' someone what she could give you just as nice. What do you say, mister?"

Esther winced at the look of revulsion on Alex's face. She watched as the expression faded and he stared at the woman, unconvinced. He started to say something, then gave up. *Oh, dear God, forgive me,* she thought. *Forgive me, please . . .* Forgive me, Alex. . . . I simply cannot . . . I must not . . . now or ever, no matter how much I would like to. She stood trembling, holding her breath until Alex finally shook his head in disgust and she heard him walk back out through the front door.

After a few moments the madam came back into the office. "He's gone, honey. I had one of the girls get dressed and follow him a ways. He won't be back."

"Thank you," Esther said.

The fat woman saw the tears and sighed. "It's gonna be all right." She put one corpulent arm around Esther and glanced down at her bag. "Now don't you worry."

"I'm sorry," Esther whimpered, wiping her eyes. "He . . . he . . . just upset me."

"Happens all the time, honey." She looked at the bag again and thought for a moment. "Why don't you just sit down here and relax awhile. I'll have one of the girls fix us some tea."

When the woman came back, she unexpectedly reached into the pocket of her housedress and handed Esther five silver dollars back. "Ten's plenty. That was the original bargain."

"Thank you," Esther said, surprised at the apparent fairness. But then she saw the fat woman eyeing the bag again.

"If you want, you can spend the night here in one of the tents. Three's empty, so there's plenty of room. Why don't you stay?"

"That is most kind of you," Esther said, her mind racing.

"It ain't nothin'. Now you just calm yourself. My name is Arabella. What's yours? Here, have some of your tea."

"Martha," Esther replied. "I'm most grateful to you." She took a sip of the tea before realizing it had a strange taste and a foreign aroma. She tried to hold the liquid in her mouth, but it was too hot and she had to swallow. It caused an unfamiliar tingling in her throat. Blowing on the tea, stalling, she tried to appraise the fat woman's motivations. Suddenly she knew, and an electric sensation ran up. the base of her neck.

"Finish it up, finish it up," Arabella said, a little too insistently.

A murmur of voices in the large room beyond the office rose to the sound of a heated argument. "Damn those two!" Arabella said, scowling. "They're at each other like cats all the time. You wait right here." She got up and rushed out of the room.

While she was gone, Esther carefully poured the rest of the tea into a waste can and covered it with crumpled papers. She held the empty cup to her mouth and pretended she was finishing the tea when the fat woman came back.

"Feelin' better now, dearie?"

Esther nodded.

"Good cuppa tea'll wash away most of the world's tears. Come on. I'll show you where you can sleep."

When all the lamps but the one glowing in the fat woman's office were out, Esther got up from the foul-smelling cot and searched for the nail file Sutter had given her. Quietly she slit open a line of light stitching that held the back flaps of the tent together.

Ten minutes later, Arabella Ryan came into the tent with a tall, soft-spoken man who had been a steady customer since arriving in San Francisco a week before. When she saw Esther was gone, sweat broke out on her chin and forehead. Each time this man came in, he left her with an inexplicable aftertaste of fear. That part of his nature was what had prompted Arabella to send for him, but now it chilled her.

"She was here, Luther. I swear it. And I put enough in that tea to knock out a horse!"

Mosby stared at her for a moment, examined the

loose tent flaps, then smiled. "Forget it, Arabella. I was losin' in that faro game anyway. Wake up Rebecca, and I'll take her back to the hotel with me."

There was no one behind the front desk when Esther reached the Alta Hotel. Taking a key off a hook, she went upstairs and let herself into a room at the back of the second floor. As soon as she closed and latched the door, she began shaking uncontrollably. Taking off her hat and gloves, she lay down on the bed and started to cry. Pulling the comforter over her legs and chest, she waited until the tears and the shivering subsided, then closed her eyes as the small amount of the drug she had swallowed with the tea took effect.

Thirty-one

In the morning, when the hotel clerk knocked, Esther told him her name was Josephine Caldwell and that she was sick with the grippe, and passed him payment in advance for five days through the still-latched door. She arranged for meals to be brought to her room, after giving him five extra silver dollars and promising five more if he saw to it that under no circumstances would she be disturbed.

She lay in bed the first day, reliving the months she had spent so happily with Alex Todd; she walked with him again, held his hand, kissed him tenderly, made love with him passionately; in the barn, in her bed, by the river, in the Conestoga wagon. The very

happiness of her memories only served to make her
more depressed with the reality of the present.

The second night, she sat by the window, out of
view, staring at the moonlit fog over the waters of
the bay and reexamining her decision to leave her
life with Alex behind. It could never be the same with
him now. Any attempt to be together again would
be haunted, subverted by all that had happened, and,
finally, doomed. She was certain he would never permit her to pursue Mosby; as certain as she was un-
swerving in her determination to track Mosby down
at all costs. Still, the thought of Alex tormented her
until she fell asleep, tears drying on her face as she
began a night of fitful tossing and turning.

The following morning she lay staring at the ceiling, dwelling on the same subject, remembering the
urgency, hope, frustration, and, finally, dejection in
Alex's voice just two nights before. The short span
of hours seemed like a lifetime. She fought the urge
to search for him, find him, soothe him, and drain
away his pain and grief. Her fantasies were interrupted by a thunderous crash in the next room. A
tremor of fear ran through her as she heard a woman
plead: "*Please.* Oh, God, *please* don't hit me!"

Luther Mosby stood glaring at Rebecca Coyle, the
prostitute he had brought back to his room from
Arabella Ryan's two nights in a row. The flat morning
light made him squint. His long johns were open to
the waist. She was fully dressed and ready to leave.
Behind her, the shards of a water pitcher he had
thrown at her lay at the base of a wall. Still drunk
from the better part of a quart of whiskey they had
consumed the previous night, Mosby lurched toward
her. He grabbed the lapels of her jacket with one
fist and jerked so hard her head snapped forward.

"You connivin' little bitch!" He slapped her hard
across the face with an open hand. "You thought I
was asleep, didn't you? Too drunk to know you was

liftin' my wallet?" He slapped her again with the back of his hand, and she screamed.

"I *wasn't* stealing it!" she cried. "You took more'n you paid for. I was just going to . . ."

"You're fulla shit, you little slut." Mosby punched at her.

She ducked, and the blow glanced off her ear. "*Oh, God,*" she shrieked. "Please! *Please don't hurt me!*"

Enraged, Mosby punched her on the point of the jaw, knocking her temporarily senseless. "Rotten little bitch! You're all the same. Every last one of you." Staggering, he threw her on the bed, face down. "*I'll* show you what you'll do for free." Groping under the bed for his socks, he tied both her wrists to the bedposts with them, ripped off her clothes, then pushed at her until she was sitting on her knees. Opening the bottom of his long johns, he positioned himself behind her, shoved her further forward and spread her thighs until her anus was exposed.

At the hotel desk downstairs, Alex Todd let out a disappointed sigh. "Damn. I've inquired at just about every place in San Francisco."

"I'm awful sorry I can't help you," the clerk intoned. "But as I said, there's only one unattached lady in the hotel, and she's a working girl. Come back with Mr. Mosby late last night. So you might say she's attached, too." He broke into a peal of laughter, pleased with the joke and proud of himself for resisting the urge to mention the other young woman, the one who was suffering from the grippe. *Five dollars more to come,* he thought.

"Is she one of the girls from that stable down near the waterfront?" Alex asked.

"Believe she is. 'Course, it's just a guess," the owner added quickly. "I don't pay much attention to that sort, you understand."

"Yes," Alex said, thinking, *I'm sure you don't.*

The barber from the shop next to the hotel walked

up to the desk. "Littlejohn? A Mr. Littlejohn wants a shave in his room," he said to the clerk. He looked at Alex. "You wouldn't be he?"

Alex shook his head.

The barber turned back to the clerk. "What room is he in? I'll just go right on up."

The clerk was about to answer, when all three of them heard the woman scream upstairs.

Esther held her hand to her mouth. The girl had stopped screaming, but she could hear the man shouting in rage. For a moment Esther thought it sounded like Mosby. She dismissed the idea as absurd. She listened at the wall as several minutes passed. Suddenly she heard the girl moan: "Oh, Lord, don't do that. *Please.* I'm too small there. Please get some . . ." Esther heard her scream in pain.

"I'll get *nothin'* to make it feel any better!" Esther heard the man shout. "You thievin' little whore! I hope it kills you!"

"Oh, God. You'll tear me . . . apart . . ." The girl screamed again. "Stop. *No!* Oh, Jesus, *please stop!*"

Esther got up from her bed and pulled on her dress. She heard a loud crack through the wall. It sounded like a slap. Biting at her knuckles, she wondered if the man was going to kill the girl. She moved toward the door, then hesitated. He might kill her too, if she interfered. She considered the prospect of being dead, never having the opportunity to take revenge. *Mosby be damned!* she said to herself. *I cannot just stand here. I must do something to help the poor woman."*

When the girl started screaming again, Alex glared at the clerk. "Well, what are you *waiting* for? Someone may be getting killed!"

"I'm not a . . . a . . . peace officer," the clerk said, unable to look Alex in the eye.

"Goddamnit!" Alex shouted. "Get out from behind that desk!"

The woman screamed again, and for a moment Alex had the urge to grab the clerk by the scruff of the neck and drag him upstairs. But the continued pleading from the woman demanded immediate action. "Give me a passkey!" he ordered. "And, damn you, follow me up there or I'll break your neck when this is through." He glanced at the barber, who seemed rooted where he stood. "You *too!*" The barber didn't move. Alex bared his teeth in anger. "Come *on,* I said!"

Esther quickly pulled on her shoes and ran to the door.

She heard the woman sob, "Oh, Jesus. *Oh,* oh . . . *Oh!* Jesus Christ. Please . . . I'm bleeding."

Turning the doorknob, Esther took a half-step into the hallway and saw Alex rushing up out of the stairwell. Involuntarily, she pulled back and closed the door again. Pressing her face against it, she heard Alex run by and pound on the door to the next room. *He was not looking at me,* she thought. *He did not see me. . . .*

Alex punched the passkey into the door, threw it open, and rushed into the room. The sight of Mosby, still thrusting savagely into the now unconscious girl, stopped him in his tracks.

Mosby turned and glared at Alex. "What the fuck you think you're doin'?" He pulled out of the girl and got off the bed on the far side, eyeing the chair where his holster, belt, and pistol hung. It was too near Alex to make a move for it. "You don't want your skull cracked, mister, you'll butt your goddamn ass out of here."

Alex looked at the gun hanging on the chair. "Not until you get dressed and leave." He heard a footstep

behind him, turned for a second, and saw the terrified
barber peeking into the room from the far side of
the hallway.

"*Get the hell out of here!*" Mosby shouted. "You
hear what I said?"

"And I said I would after you're gone and this
woman is safe." He walked over and picked up the
holstered pistol. "You can get this down at the desk—
later."

Mosby moved quickly, picking up a second chair
and rushing Alex in one motion. Hefting the chair
with his good arm, he swung it in a looping, over-
the-shoulder arc. Alex moved to one side as the chair
caught on an elaborate gas lamp hanging from the
center of the ceiling. Mosby jerked at it and the
fixture crashed to the floor at his feet. Acting instinctively, Alex ran at Mosby. Taller and heavier, he
rammed into him with both forearms and drove him
backward into the wall beyond the bed. Mosby's head
snapped back and cracked against a thick oak beam
just beneath the thin layer of plaster. His eyes glaz-
ing over, he slumped against Alex's chest.

Torn between relief and anger, Alex eased Mosby
down onto the floor. He glanced around and saw that
the girl was coming to. The barber was staring at
him from out in the hall, mouth open and bug-eyed
with terror. It suddenly came home to Alex that he
might have been drawn into killing an absolute stranger because of his own overblown imagination. The
girl he had seen, inquired about downstairs, resem-
bled his wife, to be sure. But his wife was dead. And
so was his son. He was shocked that after three years
he had spent an entire day and two nights convincing himself she was still alive.

He stared at the trickle of blood running down behind Mosby's ear, staining his long johns. For a moment Alex wondered if he indeed *had* killed the
stranger. He crouched and laid his hand over Mosby's
heart. Still alive. Relieved, he beckoned the barber

in and examined the scalp wound. It was superficial.

He turned to the timid, fearful man in the barber's apron. "I don't know this gentleman. Do you?"

The barber nodded, his eyes darting back and forth between Mosby, who had been in his shop earlier in the week, and Alex.

Alex stood up, towering over the barber. "He doesn't appear to be hurt bad. I want you to stay with him. No, get a hot towel and clean his head wound. Then wait with him until he revives. Here." Alex fished a silver dollar out of his pocket and handed it to the barber, who seemed ready to faint. "Can you steady yourself?"

The barber nodded again, went to his shop, and returned a few minutes later with a steaming towel.

"I want no more trouble with this man," Alex said. "So I'm going to leave—with the girl. He'll probably come to in ten minutes or so. Will you stay with him?"

The barber nodded once more and applied the towel to Mosby's scalp. Alex walked over to the bed. The girl was fully conscious now, but still groggy and so frightened she could hardly speak. Alex handed her a towel and her clothing When she had cleaned the blood off her legs and dressed, Alex took one last look at Mosby, who was beginning to stir, and ushered the girl out through the door.

At a restaurant several blocks away, Alex ordered tea for the girl and waited until she had regained a semblance of calm. Her left cheek was swollen and turning purple.

"Are you all right now? Would you like me to take you to a doctor?"

The girl sobbed. "No . . . I'm sore as hell, but I think I'll be all right." She squirmed, extremely uncomfortable. "Listen. I want to thank you. You took a hell of a chance, helping me like that." Her head clearing, she suddenly recognized Alex. "Say, ain't you the fella come into Arabella's the other night?"

"Yes." The urge to make one last effort to find his

wife suddenly overpowered him. "Yes, I was there. And I'd like to ask you a question or two."

The girl frowned and let out a deep breath. "I got no time for questions, mister. I'm grateful to you, but time with me costs money. And that son of a bitch at the hotel's already set me back a bundle, not to mention what he done to my face." She touched gingerly under her eye. "Jesus Christ, no one's gonna want to . . ."

"What's your name?"

"Rebecca." She pouted. "Wasn't good enough for you the other night, huh?"

"It wasn't that. You're very . . . attractive. Listen, Rebecca, you're going to be out of . . . work for a few days anyway, aren't you?"

"Yeah, I suppose so."

"Well, if you have the right answers to my questions, it could be worth twenty dollars."

She thought about it for a moment. "All right. But make it quick. I got to go get cleaned up. Maybe with a little rouge, I *will* be able to work."

"Did a girl—someone who doesn't work for . . . for Arabella, come in and hide from me the other night?"

She weighed the pros and cons of telling him. Stalling, she said, "Arabella told you wasn't no one come in, didn't she?"

"Yes. But I thought perhaps she was lying for some reason."

"Why would she do that?"

"I don't know, but it would be worth even more to me if you told me she was, and knew the young lady's name."

"How would I know her . . ." She swallowed the rest of the sentence. She was suddenly afraid of what Arabella might do if she spoke out of turn.

"Then a young lady *did* come in."

"I didn't say that, mister. I just mean how would I know her name even if she was there?"

"You're lying! I can tell by your voice."

"Listen, mister!" She stood up. "I don't have to listen to that kind of talk! I had enough grief today." She spun on her heel and stalked toward the door of the restaurant grimacing with pain. "Take your twenty dollars and shove it. . . ."

When he finally left the restaurant, Alex thought briefly of going back to the bordello, but his common sense took over, and he decided the best thing was to depart for Monterey as quickly as possible. He had one more appointment—at Blue Star Shipping. After that there was no reason for him to stay in San Francisco. He swore to himself that he would make every effort within his power to put his dead wife out of his mind hereafter. The last thirty-six hours had been insane. It was time, he told himself, to begin a new life without the ghost of her haunting him every time he saw a woman of her approximate age and appearance.

Still trembling, but certain that Alex and the girl had left the hotel safely, Esther undressed and lay down on her bed, exhausted. She wondered how much effort Alex would put into searching for the girl he had seen. She heard the man next door swearing, heard another, more timid-sounding man placating him, but there was no more evidence of violence. She heard someone leave the room next door and walk down the hall, then picked up the sounds of a second person leaving. She lay back in the welcome silence, tension draining out of her, and drifted into sleep. She awoke midway through the afternoon, went to a mirror, and was startled by how disheveled she looked. She walked to the closet where she had left her bag and took out her comb and brush. When she was finished, she returned to get her dress so she could go down the hall to take a bath. On the high shelf in the closet she noticed a yellowing newspaper. Out of curiosity she reached for it and shook off the dust. It was the May 22, 1847, edition of the *California Star*. Realizing it was more than a year old, she started to put it back but then noticed the name "Patrick Breen" in subheadline type on the front page. The issue carried Breen's diary of his experiences at Truckee, or what they were now calling Donner Lake.

She sat down on the bed and read the accompanying story quickly, wincing at every other sentence, remembering vividly each of those who had died or survived, then turned to Breen's journal. The memory of the bitter cold, the camp, the cabins almost submerged in snow, was as clear in her mind as though she were there again. She skimmed over what she had lived through, then read slowly or scanned quickly, in proportion to their gravity, the entries relating to events after she had left Donner Lake with the snowshoe party:

Jan. 15, Clear day again, wind NW—Mrs. Murphy blind, Lanthron not able to get wood, but one axe between him and Keseburg—it looks like another storm, expecting some account from Sutters' soon.

Jan. 21, Fine morning, John Battise came this morning with Eliza Williams, she will not eat hides; Mrs.——— sent her back to live or die on them.

Esther sighed deeply. The accompanying story reported that Eliza Williams, James Reed's cook, had died of starvation.

Feb. 5, Snowed hard until 12 o'clock last night, many uneasy for fear we shall all perish with hunger. . . . Eddy's child died last night. . . .

Feb. 25, Today Mrs. Murphy says the wolves are about to dig up the dead bodies around her shanty and the nights are too cold to watch them, but we hear them howl. . . .

Feb. 26, Hungry times in camp . . . Mrs. Murphy said here yesterday that she thought she would commence on Milton Eddy and eat him, I do not think she has done so yet, it is so distressing, the Donners told . . . that they would commence on the dead people if they did not succeed that day or next in finding their cattle, then ten or twelve feet under the snow. . . .

Esther let the paper fall to the floor. She slumped over, put her face in her hands and wept. When there were no more tears left, she grieved silently for all of them, prayed for their souls. The desk clerk knocked on the door with her supper. Esther had him leave it on the floor in the hall. She couldn't bring herself to touch it. She got up, paced back and forth, stared out the window, then finally slumped down in an easy chair, thinking.

She mourned for the dead and pitied their survivors, but refused to let it weigh upon her any more. She had suffered as they did, and if she had not died, she had lost a son and been crazed for months. She pushed all tormenting thoughts of what had happened to the others out of her mind.

She thought calmly now about Alex. She reconfirmed her judgment, then weighed it against the experiences of the other Donner survivors. Husbands and wives had been reunited after committing the unspeakable. But she was quite certain no other woman in the party had borne a bastard child; that her own and Mosby's part in John Alexander's death were what made the difference, supported her renewed conviction, justified any pain the loss of her was still causing Alex. *Sooner or later his sorrow will pass,* she thought, *and he will meet someone else and find happiness. I am sure of it. He will have his life and his fulfillment.* And I will have mine.

She focused on the purpose of her journey. She was here to continue building the financial power to live independently and accomplish the only goal that mattered to her now. Pursuing her aims might well mean running into Alex. She would try to avoid that, but she would not allow it to keep her a prisoner in this room, send her scurrying back to the South Fork, her mission unattempted, like a frightened squirrel.

And if she did run into Alex? The thought of it made her tremble. She pictured it. Remembering his gentleness, the fear left her. *We will sit down together,* she thought. *Perhaps over dinner. No, we will just talk. And I will tell him everything, except what I plan to do, no matter how difficult it is. I will explain the choice I have made. He will not like it, and will try to dissuade me, I am sure. But I will not alter my decision. It will be painful, impossible to carry out if I allow it to be. I will not. Any more than I will allow unrealistic thoughts of us together again to transform me into a wavering adolescent. When he comes to understand that I will not change my mind, he will accept it. Sooner or later, he will have to, and it will be better for him, and that is that!*

Esther walked to the window and pulled the curtain partly open. She gazed at the orange, setting sun and sighed. *First things first,* she thought. *I need a bath before I can even begin to organize my thoughts for the meeting with Kelsey.* She turned and did not see Alex step out of the shadows down the street diagonally opposite from the hotel.

Thirty-two

Stepping off the wooden sidewalk, Alex walked across the street and through the doorway of the barbershop. When the barber saw him, he dropped his shaving brush and turned away from the customer he had just lathered up. He walked quickly to Alex, glancing back once to see if the man in the chair was still asleep. "Mister, I don't want any trouble," he whispered. "Please."

"No trouble," Alex said. "I just wanted to make sure the gentleman wasn't seriously hurt."

"He'll survive," the barber said nervously, respectfully guiding Alex outside onto the sidewalk. When he was sure his customer couldn't hear him, he glanced up and down the street and said, "The man you cold-cocked ain't no gentleman, mister. No matter how he dresses. And he's looking to kill you. I was you, I'd make myself scarce."

"Gambler?"

"So far as I can see, mister. That's all I can say. I don't want . . ."

"What's his name?"

"Mosby. Look, mister, I got to get back to my customer."

"Well, don't worry about me," Alex said. "I'm just in town for a few days anyway. And I can take care of myself. Just felt conscience-bound to find out if he was badly hurt."

"Worry about yourself, mister," the barber said

from the door of his shop. "You see Luther Mosby again, walk in the opposite direction, fast!"

On the way back to the boardinghouse where he was staying, Alex caught himself glancing back over his shoulder, looking for the tall, wiry man with the moustache. *Mosby*, he thought. *Well, I'm not going to look for trouble, but I'll be damned if I'm going to skulk around or hide from anybody.* In his room he thought briefly about remaining another day. *Just pride*, he thought. There wasn't any reason for him to stay. The intelligent thing to do would be to get back to Monterey. He packed his bags and headed for the livery stable where he had left his horse several days before.

Mosby was awakened by the sound of a woman singing softly in the room next door. He cursed, tried to go back to sleep, but couldn't. His head still ached. He got up and dressed. He heard the woman, humming now, close the door to her room. When he left his own, he glimpsed her entering the bathroom down the hall. She was barefoot, and the sight of her ankles stirred him briefly before she closed the door. He wondered why she was wearing a dress rather than a bathrobe. A torn one, at that. He tried the bathroom door after waiting until he heard water splashing. It was locked. Shrugging, he went down the stairs to the first floor.

At the front desk he asked the clerk if he knew who had burst into his room the day before.

"Man's name was Alexander, I think," the clerk said, unnerved by Mosby's stare and misremembering Alex's name. "Todd Alexander. He forced me to give him the passkey. Held a gun on me. I swear it."

"You told me that yesterday. He staying here?"

"No sir. Never seen him before. Come in inquiring about a lady he thought he knew."

"Rebecca?"

"No sir. He was looking for an unattached lady."

"Let me see the register."

"That's against reg—"

"Let me see the damn thing or I'll stuff you into one of those mailboxes."

"Yessir." Shaking, the owner handed him the guest book.

"Well, you wasn't lyin'. Don't see no unattached ladies, neither."

"No sir."

Mosby reached across the desk, grabbed the clerk by the shirt, and jerked him forward. "Then who's the shapely lady I just saw goin' to take a bath?"

The clerk summoned up all his courage. "I don't know who you mean, Mr. Mosby."

"Never mind," Mosby said, letting him go. "Probably someone's wife."

"Yessir."

"You see that Alexander again, you let me know. You hear?"

"Yessir."

Mosby ran his hand across the stubble on his jaw, walked to the door, and headed for the barbershop.

After her bath Esther ate breakfast ravenously, then headed for a milliner's she had seen on the way from the wharf. Hurrying past the barbershop, she glanced in and fleetingly saw the man laid out and lathered, the barber shaving him. She walked on without a thought about him.

Lying there with the chair tilted way back, relaxed by the hot towels the barber had pressed to his face minutes before, Mosby almost dozed. Through half-closed eyelids, he saw Esther pass the shop but did not get a good look at her. He closed his eyes and let his mind wander over the ten months he had spent in and around Los Angeles after he and Claussen had tried to track the man who had set the bear loose. He wondered where the man had disappeared to. *Greaser never showed his face down south,* he thought. *That's for sure.*

Mosby felt the thinned-out role of bills in his pocket. This town was dead. No money to be made gambling here. Go up to the gold fields? In truth, he was tired of gambling anyway. He thought of Texas and began visualizing alternatives for the future.

Esther stopped at a dress shop and bought two new outfits. At the millinery store she purchased two hats with dark, embroidered veils and several remnants of gauzy material for additional veils if she needed them. Then she stopped at another store, where she bought two pairs of high-buttoned shoes, undergarments, and some stockings before heading back to the hotel.

Mosby smiled to himself as he turned out of the stairwell and glimpsed the woman letting herself into the room next to his down on the far end of the hallway. He stopped and looked at his watch. Turning, he went back down to the lobby, took a seat, and finished reading his newspaper. *Maybe she'll come down again,* he thought. *If she looks like anything, I might just strike up a conversation and see what happens.*

Esther hung up the dresses she had bought, stripped, and put one of them on over a new set of undergarments. Fitting one of the new hats on her head in front of the mirror, she primped a bit and then left the room. At the head of the stairs she decided to go back and take her carryall bag. She didn't like the idea of leaving all but one of the pouches filled with gold unattended. In the room she saw the mended old dress and well-worn underwear lying across the bed where she had thrown them. On an impulse she stuffed the old clothing and the sorry hat Manaiki had given her into one of the milliner's boxes. Going down the back stairs, she dropped the box into a trash barrel and headed for the Blue Star Shipping Company.

She found William Kelsey writing in a ledger at one of six clerkless desks stacked with papers. Middle-aged, a little shorter than Esther, he had a pleasant, slightly florid face with fine, almost handsome features. He glanced at Sutter's letter of introduction —not knowing the "Captain" had taken some liberties with Esther's history—stood up, and escorted her into his cluttered office.

"I see yah from Bahston." Kelsey offered her a chair. "From Maine, m'self, but most of the family stayed around the Cape."

Esther took out the list of goods she planned to buy or have shipped from the East Coast as Kelsey finished Sutter's letter.

"Widah, hah? And so young. Too bad yah didn't stop by yestiday or the day befowah. Could've introduced yah to a fine young man your age. Wonderful, nice young fella. Alex Todd."

Esther's heart began to pound.

"Loyal and hardworkin' as they come. Runs most of Consul Larkin's business down to Monterey, now that his cousin's gone off to the fields. Up here tracin' a shipment of goods. Too bad. Left yestiday."

Esther breathed slowly and deeply, calming herself.

"One of the few workin' for Larkin didn't run off," Kelsey finished.

"Monterey has been drained of men as well?"

"Same as here. All but one of my clerks ah up there. And he's down with the grippe. Not that it mattahs," he sighed. "Now what can I do for yah?"

"Captain Sutter told me you were one of the most decent, honest men he's ever known."

"Don't know about that. But I've known Sutter since he come here in '39. Fine man. Fine man."

"He told me you have helped many people get started here."

"A few. A few," Kelsey protested. "In small ways. What do yah have in mind, young lady?"

Esther laid the list on his desk. "I would like to obtain as many of these items in quantity as are available here, and order what is not, to be shipped to San Franicsco by your company."

Kelsey read down the list, frowning and shaking his head.

"Can you suggest a wholesaler or two I can trust?" she went on.

"That's not the problem."

"I have arranged for storage space at Sutter's, and Mister Sam Brannan will be selling for me on consignment."

Kelsey frowned again. "Nevah liked that man."

"You confirm my own impression. But for now he is the man to whom you will ship the goods."

"Now hold on a minute! I didn't say I'd be shippin' yah anything! I don't even know if I'li be in business through the end of the year."

"But you own, you are a partner in one of San Francisco's most flourishing shipping concerns."

"Need men to do this sort of thing. And they're all gone. Ships rotting in the harbor. Crews, captains and all, jump ship soon as they drop anchor, leave the cargo aboard to spoil or collect dust. Meanwhile, overhead and accounts payable don't go anywhere but up. Keeps on, we'll be bankrupt by Novembah."

Esther began thinking. "It can't go on forever, can it?"

"No. Six months. A year, mebby. But Novembah is a lot sooner than that."

"The problem is simply manpower?"

"No. Money. Cahn't pay them enough to make them stay. Cahn't afford it."

Esther's mind was racing. She saw an opportunity that exceeded anything she had hoped for, and it

made her heart race. She squeezed the carryall bag
between her ankles, taking strength and nerve from
what the solid feel of the pouches represented. "And
the wholesalers?" she asked, controlling her voice,
hoping it would not flutter.

"Same pickle," Kelsey said, throwing up one hand
in frustration. "They're packin' up and headin' for
Coloma just like everybody else."

"If you . . . someone, had the money to equal or
slightly better what the average man can earn in the
fields, could he not last this out until the situation is
back to normal?"

"He . . . or they . . . if there were just a few of
them, would have a monopoly for the short run. And
more than a toehold on being way ahead of the pack
after this passes. But all this is just idle . . ."

"And all it would take is money?" Esther interrupted.

Kelsey sighed again. "More than anyone in San
Francisco has at the moment. It's the old story.
Money makes money."

"You have a partner?"

"Yes, ma'am. Warren Barnett. But what . . . ?"

"Tell me about him."

Kelsey checked his impatience. *Humor her,* he
thought. *After all, she's just a young girl. And she's
a friend of Sutter's.* "Warren's a big, open fella. Always smilin'. Talks a lot. But he's got a heart of
gold, if you'll pardon the expression. Honest as they
come."

"He does not have the money you need?" She held
her breath.

"Same boat as I am. Equity poor."

"Would you consider a third partner?"

"Might. But I don't see . . ."

"Someone to put up the capital you need? As much
as it takes?"

"Yah talkin' about the answer to a prayer, young
lady. And I haven't prayed in twenty yeahs."

"Perhaps you should take the habit up again."

"Now see here . . . !"

"I meant no insult," Esther said, caught off balance by her own capacity for sarcasm. "In fact, you don't need to pray at all, for you are looking at just such a potential partner."

"Young lady, I don't know where yah get your nerve, but . . ."

"Why do you reject the idea of having me as a partner out of hand?"

"Well, first off, you're a woman."

"And that automatically disqualifies me?"

"Wouldn't want a woman meddlin' in the runnin' of any business. For God's sake! You're young enough to be my daughter. What could yah possibly know about the shipping business?"

"Nothing."

"That's what I mean."

"But I have no interest in being involved in the day-to-day affairs of the firm."

"Oh, yah don't, do yah? Young lady, I have work to do." He stood up.

Esther stayed in her chair. "But I am interested in providing you with money you need and making a profit from such an investment."

"I don't know who yah think yah are, young lady, but . . . !"

"Just wait one moment," Esther said, fishing the pouches out of her bag. She placed them on the edge of Kelsey's desk. "*Now* will you listen?" She took one of the pouches, opened its drawstrings, and spilled the gold dust out onto the desk under Kelsey's lamp.

"So yah have four or five bags of gold. So what? Do yah know how much . . . ?"

"This is simply a token of good faith. There is more, much more, where this came from."

"I don't know," Kelsey said, shaking his head.

"What don't you know?"

"A woman. I . . ."

"Because I'm a woman, are you going to turn down this offer and watch helplessly while your company goes bankrupt?"

"That wouldn't make any sense, would it?" Kelsey said, scratching behind his ear. "It's just . . ."

"It's just that women don't do this sort of thing. Is that it?"

"I didn't say that."

Esther stood up and began placing the pouches back in her bag.

"Now wait a minute," Kelsey said, trying to set his thoughts in order. "It's just unusual. Highly unusual and unexpected. Give me a chance to think about this for a minute."

Esther sat back down. "No one has to know about any of it except you and your partner. In fact, I would prefer it that way."

"And yah don't want anything to do with running the business?"

"I would be a fool to get in your way. I said I want to make a profit."

Kelsey stared at the spilled gold and whistled. "This could run into some money, yah understand. Are yah certain—?"

"Are *you* certain I would make a profit from the investment?"

Kelsey sat down and thought for a moment. "All I can tell yah is that if I had the money, I'd do the same thing myself."

"Then I am certain. Do you deal with a bank?"

Kelsey nodded, trying to keep up with her.

"I will be shipping pouches and larger bags directly to you. At the moment there is perhaps ten or eleven times this amount accumulated. As it is delivered to you, keep a third and use it. The rest, put in the bank under my name. E. Cable."

Kelsey simply stared at her, his mouth agape.

"I will expect a strict accounting of every ounce you receive."

"Of course."

"Now, will you help me to come to some fair arrangement about what I shall receive in return for the investment?"

Kelsey reached for a pad and pencil and started to devise something. He looked up at her again for a moment, shook his head, then crossed out his initial set of figures. "Fairest is simplest," he said. "You own one-third of the firm. We'll have papers drawn up. You receive . . . we'll bank in your name one-third of the profits. Once we're under way, writing in blue ink, whatever amount you've invested that exceeds one-third of Blue Star's capitalization and assets— why, we'll pay back to yah fifty cents on the dollah out of our two-thirds of the profits."

"It all sounds perfectly fair to me. As little as I know of such things."

"Yah have the instincts. That's all yah need. If you're dealin' with honest men."

"Your partner will not object?"

"Warren? He'll probably jump into the cove with his clothes on out of sheer joy."

"There is just one condition."

"Yes?" Kelsey felt his stomach begin to tighten.

"That you invite me to your home for dinner tonight. It has been so long since I have eaten at a proper dining table." She smiled. "And I would like to meet the wife of . . . such an open-minded man."

Thirty-three

The following morning Esther rode the raft ferry across the strait and bought a horse on the north shore. Riding northeast toward Sonoma, she found Sausalito practically deserted. Passing empty farmhouses, she saw fields untended, horses and cattle wandering and trampling crops. If all these people had left for the gold fields, she thought, her decision the night before to hew to her original plan of selling supplies through Brannan or someone else seemed wise. However uncomplicated and rewarding her primary arrangement with William Kelsey and Warren Barnett turned out to be, it would not hurt to have something else to fall back on.

As she rode on, she smiled, recalling the pleasant evening she had spent with Billy Kelsey and his wife. Simple and down-to-earth while revealing hints of refined taste and intelligence, Connie Kelsey was a slender, handsome woman, and far too modest about her considerable talent as an artist. She hoped to have Connie as a friend if she ever lived in San Francisco.

She was grateful to the Kelseys for never asking why she did not remove her hat and scoop veil during dinner. They had made her feel completely at home. Neither took obvious note of the odd way she held a fork, left palm tilted upward, clenching her fist, concealing her missing fingers from them as she sliced through a piece of roast lamb. Later, in the lobby of the hotel, she had covered another potential embarrassment. As she was saying good-bye to Kelsey, she realized it was not unlikely that he would mention her to Alex Todd—unless she headed him off. Obliquely, but allowing no room for misinterpretation, she made it plain that it would be several years before she would even begin to entertain thoughts of remarriage.

Three days later, just before noon, Esther crossed a shallow stretch of the South Fork. Riding her own horse and leading by the reins the one she had bought, she worked her way along the bank of a small stream near her cabin. She was astonished, then strangely thrilled to see Murietta lazing against the rail fence surrounding her garden, waiting for her. But then she sensed something was wrong. Miwokan, her pistol slung from his shoulder, stood guard at the shed. His brother, crouched and watching Murietta carefully from a strategic distance, had the Californio's gunbelt lying across his thighs. As Esther reined up and dismounted, she became aware of a party of prospectors in red flannel shirts heading south through the woods beyond the cabin.

She saw Miwokan frown as Murietta stepped forward and greeted her with an exaggerated, hat-sweeping bow. They were both laughing nervously when Miwokan strode over to them.

"He came yesterday and helped us. And again this morning, just before you returned."

"*De nada*," Murietta said. "It was nothing, señora."

"But why have you . . . ?"

"Many redshirts have come," Miwokan said, interrupting her. "Just before sunset one party of six would not leave this place."

"They were not unreasonable," Murietta said. "They simply needed a firm word about your ownership of this property. They only wanted to know why they had no right to prospect here."

"He sent another five of them away before you came," Miwokan added.

Esther glanced at Miwokan's brother, who walked toward them carrying Murietta's weapon. "Is that why you are guarding the shed?" she asked Miwokan. "Is that why your brother has my friend's gun?"

"I could not be sure of him, any more than of the others," Miwokan replied.

"But he helped you! And you seem to be treating him like a prisoner."

Murietta smiled. His tooth had been repaired, crudely, but it looked much better than when she had last seen him. "They only watch over your gold. They meant no insult to me, I am sure."

"This man is my friend," Esther said. "You knew that."

"I know that yesterday's friend is sometimes today's enemy when there is gold."

"I want none of your gold!" Murietta said, anger rising in him involuntarily. He lowered his voice. "Or any other's." He turned to Esther. "I came only to see you again. And to thank you personally."

Esther fought off an urge to jerk her gunbelt out of Miwokan's hand. She saw that he was plainly embarrassed now. "Please give him back his gun."

Miwokan beckoned to his brother to hand it to her instead. "Perhaps there were other things in my mind." Miwokan looked at Esther and then away, and she sensed that a touch of jealousy had colored his behavior.

"It was just a mistake," Esther said, touching Miwokan's arm compassionately.

He turned to Murietta. "I am sorry," he said, offering his hand. "Will you forgive me?"

Murietta grinned and clasped Miwokan's forearm. "I would have done the same thing. You were only showing how much you are the señora's friend. Consider it forgotten."

"Then the matter is settled?" Esther asked. "There will be no hard feelings?"

"If he is your friend, he is mine," Miwokan said evenly.

She spent the afternoon with the two of them, quickly dropping her curiosity about where Murietta had been all these months after it became obvious that he was concealing something. Nor did she pursue whatever it was he had not wanted to tell her when he had resorted to speaking only Spanish while recuperating at her cabin. Instead she addressed herself to planning and arranging the first shipment to San Francisco. Murietta, she saw, could help her. He was full of ideas and knew the territory well. She guessed also that he could handle the gun he was wearing again. Beyond that, she found herself attracted to him, no matter how hard she tried to dismiss the feeling. She watched Miwokan carefully and became convinced that Murietta's arrival had stirred his old feelings for her. *In time,* she thought, Miwokan *will see that there is nothing to be jealous about.* And, of course, he was right. Although instinct told her Murietta would not steal from anyone, let alone her, she had no reason to be certain.

As they talked, party after party of prospectors crossed the river, took note of the armed men with Esther, then veered up and downstream or continued on south beyond the clearing. She detected a brief hardening in Miwokan's expression when she persuaded Murietta to stay and work the claim with them. It passed when Murietta refused to be paid any more than Miwokan was receiving. They worked out a plan for the shipment. Miwokan's brother would take a band of men and, avoiding all mining camps, travel by way of Sutter's Fort and the north shore of the bay to Blue Star.

Later, when Miwokan's men had quit work and started back for their village, she took the chief aside, then walked slowly with him to the river.

"You did the right thing," she said. "I am grateful

to you. It was an awkward situation for me, that is why . . ."

"I understand that it was difficult," he said. "It was like being a peacemaker between two tribes you do not want to make war."

"Exactly."

"And also you feel deep things for this man."

"That is not true. He is simply my friend."

"You do not have love for him?" Miwokan asked, measuring his voice.

"I feel for him as I feel for you. As a sister." She saw Miwokan look at her quickly, then away. "Of course," she added hastily, "I do not know him as well as you. He has not done the things for me that you have. He is not my sunbrother."

Miwokan nodded, reassured. "Do you trust him?"

"You have left one of your men to guard the shed."

"But do you trust him?"

"I think so. But I will test him. I will give him two thousand dollars in gold to take to Kelsey tomorrow. And a small amount more—to purchase weapons. At the fort. If he can buy them there, I will have him leave them at Brannan's store, in a package, for your brother to pick up. If he cannot, I will have him secure them in San Francisco, double back along the trail your brother and the men will follow, then accompany them in case they need him."

"That is what you will tell him. But more of it will be to see if he runs with the gold?"

"Yes. It is not much compared to what is in the shed."

"That is wise, Sunsister. You are very wise for one with so few winters." Miwokan looked off, thinking. "You will watch him until he is asleep in the cabin tonight?" he asked almost casually.

Esther smiled. She had been right. He *was* jealous. "He will not sleep in the cabin again. Tonight or any other night."

For a moment, as he studied her face, the beginnings of a smile turned the corners of his mouth upward. It passed, and she heard him control the sound of a sigh. "Do all white women understand as much as you do? Are they all so wise?"

She touched his cheek with the back of her hand, then drew it back. "Wiser," she said. "Much wiser."

Late that summer, gold was discovered in several creeks to the south of the cabin. Within a week hordes of men moved into the area. Not a day passed without news of a strike. Enthused as well as slightly alarmed by the number of miners passing her place in September, Esther journeyed to Sutter's Fort to check on the possible arrival of goods from Blue Star.

A small quantity had been delivered, and Brannan beamed as he paid Esther off. "Got twice the price you paid for them," he said, handing her an accounting he had drawn up. "Don't see any need to keep the pouch you gave me," he added, fishing it out of a drawer and putting it on the counter beside Esther's half of the profits. "When do you think your people at Blue Star will be sending more goods?"

"I don't know," Esther said, studying the figures and suddenly aware that they didn't wash. "Soon, I would guess. The more normal things get in San Francisco, the more they'll send."

"Good. Good. Well, if you'll excuse me, I've business to conclude with this young fellow." He gestured to a table beside which a slender man scarcely in his twenties stood waiting. He was dressed in a suit tailored in an unmistakably European style. "Perhaps you'd like to meet him," Brannan said as an afterthought. "He's Captain Sutter's son, just arrived from Europe."

After she'd been introduced to August Sutter, she took note of the legal-looking papers and the newly drawn maps that depicted a sizable town between the fort and the embarcadero. Troubled, Esther left

Brannan's store and made her way inside the walls of the fort. As she waited while a dealer in picks and pans served a half-dozen customers, she weighed what Brannan had said when he saw her looking at the maps.

"You're looking at a new city, young lady. A city of the future. One that this young man and his father are going to make possible."

Considering what she already suspected about Brannan, she did not like the sound of it.

When the dealer finally got around to her, she pretended she wanted to buy a half-dozen items he was selling, and asked the prices. They were five times the amount she had paid wholesale for similar goods, two and a half times what Brannan said he had sold them for. *Brazen, unprincipled devil*, Esther thought. *He is keeping me happy by splitting a 100 percent profit with me, while keeping an additional 300 percent return—on my investment—for himself.*

"How long have they been selling at such outrageous prices?" she asked, controlling her fury.

The dealer shrugged. "A month, maybe two. Leastwise since Brannan got his last shipment in. Better buy now. They'll be costin' more next week."

"Everyone is charging the same prices?"

"Well, there's only Brannan, and me, and the Jew, Kellerman, who has that shack down by the embarcadero. Me and Brannan, we talk, see. When one of us ups his price, the other follows suit before the sun rises. And the Jew goes along, *or else*. You know what I mean?"

"Indeed I do. Thank you very much."

"Well, you gonna buy or ain'tcha?"

Esther turned without answering the question. She went straight to the embarcadero, where she found Kellerman, a frail, kindly man in his late fifties, fighting an impossible battle with a broom and a dustpan. Each time he swept up a corner of the open-sided shack, the wind coming off the river undid his labor.

"You need a proper store, with four walls instead of two," Esther said.

"Would be nice. But I can't afford it." Kellerman laid the broom aside. "What can I do for such a nice lady?"

"How would you like to have the money to build a *real* store?"

"It'll never happen. There's a nice profit in these goods, but I can't lay my hands on enough of them to make that kind of money."

"Brannan and the men in the fort seem to be well stacked."

"They got the suppliers all tied up. They fix it so I get enough to stay open, but no more."

"You will be receiving as much as you can handle from now on."

Kellerman scratched his head and smiled. "I wish you were right."

"I am right. I have been selling goods through Brannan, but I will no longer be associated with him. From now on you will be selling my goods, if you are interested."

"I'm interested, young lady, I'm interested!"

"These are the terms. I will pay the wholesale price and arrange delivery. You will sell them at the going rate and share in the profits with me. Forty percent to you, the remainder to me. There will be no storage costs, and you will provide me with an accounting each month."

"What kind of goods can you ship to me?"

"Just about everything you carry." She looked around, taking note of several items she would have to add to her next order. She wrote out her address on a slip of paper and handed it to him.

"Young lady, you got yourself a deal," Kellerman said happily.

She started to turn, then thought for a moment. "You will need more space, a more secure building, right away."

"That'll be a problem until—"

"Here." Esther handed him a pouch filled with gold. "Use this to build a store. Make it big enough for about five times as much inventory. Pay me back with 10 percent of your share of the profits until the debt is liquidated."

She left Kellerman talking to himself in amazement and headed back to Brannan's. As she walked in, he was sitting behind the ramshackle counter, sipping whiskey and beaming.

"Well, it's all signed, sealed, and delivered," he said. "Your friend Sutter's son has just arranged with me to sell the lots that will soon be known as Sacramento City."

She wondered if there was any way she could warn Sutter about Brannan, but it was too complicated to think about now. To control her rage, to do what she was about to do, she needed to concentrate. She would have to wait until she saw Sutter the next day at his sawmill on the South Fork.

"Congratulations," she said. "I forgot something. I wanted to pick up a kerosene lamp. Do you have one?"

"All out."

Esther glanced over at the barrels of kerosene that lined one wall.

"Plenty of fuel, as you can see. But I sold my last lamp yesterday." He saw her frown. "But for a business associate," he added, "I suppose I could let go one of mine. Wait here. I'll get one from the back room."

"Could you sell me a gallon cask of kerosene as well?" she asked when he placed the lamp on the table.

Brannan went to one of the barrels and drew out what she had requested. He placed it on the counter next to the lamp.

"Is the lamp full?"

"To the brim. Here, let me adjust the wick and

show you." He ignited a rolled piece of paper and lit the lamp.

"I am not familiar with that new damping device." Brannan turned the flame down, then up full. "Easy," he said. "Better'n the old one."

"Let me try." She conjured up her best smile, reached for the lamp and as she pulled it back toward her, knocked the cask of kerosene off the counter with her elbow. When it hit the floor, the wooden bung flew out of its hole, the oil poured out and began spreading under the work clothes hanging to her left and toward the kerosene barrels beyond them. "Oh, mercy," she said. "Now look what I've done."

Brannan came out from behind the counter again and surveyed the spill. "No harm done." He let out a breath of unconcealed exasperation, then forced a smile. "Won't even charge you for it. Hell, once it dries . . ."

"Once it dries, there won't be any danger of fire," Esther said, lifting the lamp off the counter and holding it out over the spreading pool of kerosene.

Brannan's mouth dropped open.

"Mr. Brannan, you will now pay me the money you owe me."

"What are you talking about?" Brannan stammered.

"You know very well what I'm talking about. You have been selling my goods at five—rather than two—times what I paid for them. You owe me an additional 150 percent on my investment."

"This is an outrage!"

"Not nearly as much of an outrage as what you have tried to do to me. Now, if you will kindly pay me my due, I will not drop this lamp on the floor, where it will shatter, light the spilled kerosene, and burn its way to the barrels against the wall."

"You wouldn't dare."

"I will count to ten, Mr. Brannan. After which, I believe you will probably lose your entire store." For emphasis, she jerked her wrist. The lamp swung under her hand.

"All right, all right! You've made your point!"

He counted out the exact amount in bills, stacked them, and pushed the money to her side of the counter. "You're crazy, you know that? You haven't heard the last of this." He eyed a rifle standing in a corner to his right.

"And now, Mr. Brannan, as a last consideration for my not dropping this lamp, I would like you to walk at least thirty yards from this store. In the direction I can see through that window. When you are that distance away, I will leave the lantern outside the doorway and make my way inside the fort—where there will be witnesses to any retaliation a huge man like you might take on a smaller creature like me."

A pair of miners came into the store. They were both as large as Brannan.

"Never mind my last request," Esther whispered. "I see there are two strong witnesses at my disposal right here." She scooped up the money, set the lantern down before Brannan had a chance to react, and moved quickly toward the door. Both miners took off their hats, held them to their chests, and moved out of the way courteously as she passed. Brannan watched dumbfounded as she smiled sweetly at the miners and called back, "Good day, Sam. Thank you for treating me so fairly."

Thirty-four

Esther found August Sutter at the door to a room in Kyburz's Hotel. Ironically, it was the same room, unchanged for the most part since the German had leased the building from John Sutter, where she had first awakened after the Indians brought her to the fort. Sutter's son had converted it into an office. Two well-dressed men were talking sharply with him as she reached the second-floor landing and turned into the hallway. They lowered their voices as she approached. Nervously, the pale, well-mannered young man glanced at Esther and unsuccessfully tried to conclude the conversation he was having without her hearing anything.

"It is just a question of a little more time," he said quietly.

"There's been too much time already," one of the men said.

"I assure you, the matter will be attended to as soon as I have returned from Monterey."

"It had better be, Mr. Sutter," the second man said. "Thirty days and no more."

Esther stopped and waited a few feet away from them. "Am I interrupting anything?" she asked.

"No, ma'am," the first man said, tipping his hat. "We were just leaving."

Inside young Sutter's room, Esther sat down and waited while he composed himself. His desk was strewn with papers. More spilled out onto the floor from his father's old trunk. An image of Sutter reaching into the trunk for her diary crossed Esther's mind. Memories of those first days after the ordeal in the mountains followed in quick succession. She thought of Mosby and felt herself grinding her teeth so hard her jaw ached.

"It is almost too much for any one man to deal with," August finally said, bringing her out of her thoughts.

"You know I am one of your father's closest friends. You can speak freely to me. Who were those men?"

"Creditors." He took out a handkerchief and wiped his forehead.

"But surely with all your father's holdings, there is no need to become rattled by one outstanding bill. Or even a half dozen."

August Sutter reached for a ledger book, his hand shaking visibly, stood up, and walked to the bed he had pushed over against one wall. He placed the ledger in one of several packed bags that lay open on top of the quilt. "It is not a matter of one bill or even a dozen." He gestured to the desk and the trunk. "There are scores." He walked back to the desk and sat down, slowly massaging his temples.

"Scores?" Esther was incredulous.

"Perhaps two hundred or more. My father owes tens of thousands of dollars to businessmen and bankers in Monterey and San Francisco."

"But I don't understand."

"He has built an empire on credit. He started modestly, but it has been going on for almost a decade."

"But the fort, the mills, the shops . . . ?"

"As soon as one enterprise was completed, he would begin another. Then two more. Three. Four more. All begun before the funds he borrowed to begin the first were paid off. Material, seed, equipment, blankets, everything. First a snowball, then a rolling boulder of ice, and now an avalanche of debt. The inter-

est alone is staggering. My God, he still owes someone money for the cannons at the entrance to this
place."

"But he bought them years ago from the Russians,
when they abandoned Fort Ross."

"Almost *ten* years ago. On credit."

"And it is all like this, the tannery, the sawmill,
the flour mill . . . ?"

"The flour mill is not even completed, and already
it has cost—I am not sure of the figure—upwards of
fifty thousand dollars!"

"And he does not have it?"

"No. If that was the only thing he was being pressed
to pay, it would be a simple matter. But everyone
he owes money assumes he has become rich overnight because of the gold. They have descended on
him like a flock of vultures. And he has not mined
enough to pay off even a fraction of his debt."

Esther sighed. "Why is he not here? There must
be some way he can arrange to . . . ? At the very
least, he should be here attending to these matters."

"He wants no part of it. They have all come at
once, demanding immediate payment. It is too much
for him. Shortly after I arrived from Switzerland, he
asked me to take over his affairs here in New Helvetia."

"But you, forgive me, you are a stranger to these
parts. You cannot possibly be equipped to—"

"I can only do my best. I have a personal debt to
my father. Indirectly, just by being born, I caused
him much pain and grief, and this is a way to make
up for that."

"That's foolish nonsense! Your father and mother
were the only ones responsible. And you had no
part in what your grandmother did to him. But we
can talk about that some other time. Put it out of
your mind. What's important now is that you understand that Brannan is a dishonest, despicable man."

"Mr. Brannan? I cannot believe that. Why, he has been . . ."

"He tried to cheat me, a woman. Why should he treat you any differently?"

"But is it all not legal? We have signed contracts."

"He has copies of them?"

"Of course. I go to Monterey this very afternoon to record them."

Esther shook her head. "And you are selling off your father's land to pay off the debts?"

"Yes. It is the only way I can see out of this."

"Well, I suppose what is done is done. But do not mention anything I have said to Brannan. Be armed with the knowledge, and watch him carefully. But do not say anything. Do you understand?"

"Yes, of course. But—"

"I will be seeing your father this afternoon, tomorrow at the latest. I will try to persuade him to come back to the fort to work with you on these matters. I mean you no insult, but you are simply not up to dealing with a man like Brannan."

August reached for a glass of water on the desk and spilled a quarter of it on his shirtfront before bringing it to his lips. "Do you think, should I . . . should I go to Monterey?"

"Yes, I suppose so. But do not enter into any transactions until your father is here. Two heads are better than one."

"I hope you can persuade him to come."

Esther sighed, stood up, and shook the young man's trembling hand. "I will do my best. Your father has been like an . . . uncle, no, like a father to me, as well."

On a signal from Manaiki that Brannan was occupied with customers in his store, Esther rode out of a side entrance to the fort the following morning and headed for Coloma. It was late afternoon when she arrived at the abandoned mill. The sight of it shocked

Esther. Canvas tenting had been set up by Sutter's
Kanakas. While they were out panning, passing miners had dismantled most of the sawmill for lumber
and carried it off. The Indians Sutter had hired were
gone. The Kanakas were demoralized, at a loss over
what to do next. Sutter no longer led them out on
panning expeditions. He spent his days in his tent
drowning himself in liquor, the procurement of which
was the only task left for the remaining half-dozen
loyal Kanakas to perform.

Esther found him lying on his cot, caressing a
nearly empty whiskey bottle and talking to himself.
He sat up when she entered and tried to assume a
posture and expression of sobriety.

"I have been too selfish," he blubbered. "You are
my beloved niece, and if you wish for me to become
a partner with you in a business venture . . ."

Esther sat down beside Sutter and kept him from
topping over. "Do not trouble with that now. There
are other things you must deal with."

"Auwgoost is attending to everything," he said, his
accent more pronounced than she could remember.

She took the bottle out of his hands and laid it
on the floor. "Brannan will tie him in knots. You
must pull yourself together . . ."

"He is a fine boy, a fine boy," Sutter said, not
really listening. "You know when he first come here
this summer, I say to myself, oh, *Gott*, a bad sign,
a *bad* sign. But it is not that way at all. I sign all
my property over to him and he takes care of the
whole business. He is a smart boy. Smarter than his
father."

"He cannot—"

"You know," Sutter went on, "it is, how do you
say?—poetic chustice. He was, you know, illegitimate. The mother-in-law, very rich, makes us get
married. I would have, anyway. I would have. But
she makes us gets married, und then she never for-
gives me for spoiling her daughter. She lends me

money to start a business, not so good, and then when I am threaten with debtor's prison, she throws us out of her house. How do you like that? That is why I left Europe, my beloved Switzerland."

"You have told me this story . . ."

"So, when Auwgoost comes here, I say to myself, John, the past is catching up with you. But it is not that way. It is fate balancing the scales. He tells me, Auwgoost, that he knows the whole story. And sees the piggle I am in and says he will get me out of it. He wants to make it up to me the things his *grossmutter* did to me. And it is going to work. He is going to straighten this mess out, you wait and see. Fate is on my side this time."

"He can't possibly handle it all. He's too young and too inexperienced."

"You wait and see. He's a smart boy, Auwgoost. And strong-minded, like you." He reached out and stroked Esther's long hair. "My beautiful niece."

"If you will pull yourself together and go back to the fort, I will lend you what I have to help you through this."

"No. No. I couldn't do that. You don't have enough to even start. I appreciate it, what you are saying. But don't worry. Auwgoost will get it all straightened out. He sells some property, pays the debts, then we build a city. Sutterville. You know the one I show you with the maps?"

Frustrated, she reached out and grasped his shoulders, shaking him. "John! *Listen to me!* Your site is too far upriver! Can't you see? Brannan's parcels are closer. Nothing at Sutterville will match them. No one will set up business there when he can be closer to the docks."

Sutter waved his hand. "We build a new embarcadero. We build a *better* city . . ."

"*It won't work!* Why would anyone . . . ?"

"We beat Brannan at his own game. You think I don't know him? You think I am a child?"

"John, *please!*"

Sutter picked up the bottle and drained it. "Go now. Take care of your business. You are doing well?"

Thwarted, she began to cry. "Yes. But I'm worried about you!"

He put his arms around her. "There, there, little beautiful niece. What are those tears for? Your Uncle John can take care of himself."

"Will you *please* promise me you will go back to the fort?"

"Yes. Yes. Yes. I promise. Now go, and don't worry so much about me. Everything . . . will . . . be . . . "

She felt his head loll over on her shoulder, turned, and saw that he had passed out.

That fall and winter Esther's worst fears for Sutter were realized. She rode to Coloma several times, but Sutter was always too drunk to reason with. The last time she went, the mill was deserted. She sent word to the fort, but no one had seen him for weeks. Esther sent Murietta with a letter to Sutter's son, but she received no reply. She was soon to learn the reason. The poor young man had collapsed from physical and mental exhaustion.

Finally she heard that Sutter was back at the fort. He had taken over what August was handling before he fell ill. But it was too late. While small towns sprang up everywhere in the mountains, as far north as the Yuba River and south to the Tuolumne, Sutter's empire was torn from him. To satisfy all the claims, some of them fraudulent, August had sold off almost all of his father's property. What was left, Brannan wheedled and swindled away, enriching himself as Sacramento City, engorging and enlarging itself on the gold spent in its tent-hotels, restaurants, gambling dens, and shops, sprang to full size overnight.

When it was all over, even the fort had been sold —for approximately $39,000. In a month even that was gone. All Sutter had left now was the Hock

Farm, a piece of property up the Sacramento River he had bought after his arrival in the valley almost a decade earlier. He came to see Esther at the cabin before he packed up the last of his personal belongings and headed north to his homestead.

It was a brief, sentimental visit. Finally Sutter rose to go; when he took her hands in his, there were tears in his eyes.

"I thought they would come sooner, the settlers," he said. "Two years ago, these people coming in now would have saved me. I would have sold them land reasonably and watched over them. Now . . . Now . . . they pay through, how do you say it? Through the nose."

"And you?" Esther said sadly. "What of you?"

"I have the farm, a place to live and raise enough to live on, perhaps even make a little profit. Almost all the debts, the big ones, are paid off. There are a few left, and I suppose someone could try to force me to sell the Hock Farm. . . ."

"If that ever happens, John, I would feel ashamed if you did not come to me for help. I could never live with myself if you were hounded out of your own home."

"I do not think it will happen," he said, uncomfortable, impatient to leave. "It will take time, but I believe the crops I raise will earn enough for me to slowly pay off the remaining debts. But I appreciate your offer."

"You have done much for me, kept my secret."

"I would under any circumstances. . . ."

"I know that." She put her arms around him and kissed his cheek. "And I know you would never take advantage of our friendship. So will you promise that you will come to me if you are ever in danger of losing the farm?"

He coughed and looked away, embarrassed again. "I promise."

"You have promised before and—"

"And I wish I had kept to my word. I do not think I could have changed the course of things, but I often wish that I had tried when you urged me to."

"This time you will keep your promise, then?"

"I will have no choice." He smiled and gazed off through her window at the mountains. "I will miss this place. And the fort. But I will have more than enough company."

"What do you mean?"

"August. For a time he will be with me, helping at the farm." He sighed. "And," he added, smiling again at the irony of it, "I have had another little surprise, another letter from Switzerland. From my wife. She, my daughter, Elise, and another son are on their way here from Europe."

"Oh, my God."

"Is it not interesting, the way things work out?" Sutter attempted a smile. "Perhaps it will all be for the best. The woman has always had some love for me. We *had* to marry, and I *was* 'beneath her station,' but perhaps, without her mother breathing down our necks, we may be able to make a life together after all these years."

"I hope so. I want you to be happy, more than . . . just about . . . anything else."

When he was gone, she sat for a long while on a boulder by the waterfall, gazing at the tumbling, white water, her thoughts turning for some reason to little John Alexander. *I wonder what fate holds in store for me,* she thought. *And if, when it is all over, when I have accomplished what I have set out to do about Mosby, if Alexander and I might come to-gether after long years.* She pictured him working at Larkin's store in Monterey. She saw herself setting supper out for him in a modest little house, then turn-ing and running to him as he walked in the door. The thought held her for a moment, wistful, but then she pushed it out of her mind. She got up, walked slowly for a few seconds, then forced herself into a purposeful stride.

"There is work to be done," she said out loud to herself. "And it is late afternoon. The men will be finished soon. I had better stop this foolishness and see what the yield has been today. Sooner or later, Mr. Mosby, it will add up to enough to bring you to a reckoning."

Thirty-five

There were ten thousand men in the fields by December 1848. Their numbers disquieted Esther. At night she often thought she could actually hear them all breathing. The comfort of being far from civilization —and the things people did to one another—diminished with each passing day.

Blue Star recovered rapidly as prospectors flooded back into San Francisco that fall to spend their fortunes, or to find jobs after meeting with failure in the placers. The additional manpower brought the volume of the firm's shipping back to normal and then some, the profits almost doubling Esther's revenue from her claim. Murietta oversaw the gold shipments, and there were no incidents or losses. The hard goods, shipped now to Hyman Kellerman's new wholesale-retail store opposite the embarcadero in Sacramento City, flowed steadily eastward from San Francisco. Esther's share of Kellerman's sales increased her bank account by another 20 percent. The riverbed was yielding less and less gold, but it was of little concern

to Esther; she had always known that sooner or later
the gold would run out. But now her income from
Blue Star, Kellerman, and the half-dozen other min-
ing-town stores that bought her goods was much
more than enough to satisfy her needs. And the gold
had already provided her with all she required to
deal with Mosby.

A town had risen two miles below the South Fork.
As yet it had no name, but Esther heard a young
prospecting Kentuckian named Coleman and his wife
were opening a general store. She decided to add a
seventh establishment to her list of wholesale customers, and Murietta accompanied her the morning
she took the short ride to speak to Coleman. The
woods were unusually quiet as they loped southward.
They were almost to the outskirts of the tent-and-
shanty village when the sound of angry voices answered their unspoken questions about the absence
of men in the creeks and canyons south of the river.

Standing on one of the hills overlooking the small,
makeshift town, they watched the movements of a
crowd of three dozen men and a few women in a
clearing beyond the tents. The latest in a series of
unseasonably moderate snow flurries had left the
ground moist before dawn that morning. As they stood
there trying to figure out what was going on, their
horses picked up their hooves impatiently, making
sucking sounds in the mud. Snow began to fall again,
the flakes gradually increasing in number as Esther
and Murietta finally saw the isolated man sitting on
a horse beyond the semicircle of people. The crowd
grew quiet. The man on the horse, they suddenly
realized, had a noose around his neck.

"¡Por Dios!" Murietta said.

They moved closer. A tall, baby-faced, strapping
man in overalls and farmer's boots spoke to the prisoner. "Do you have anything to say?"

The accused man smirked at him.

"There are no alcaldes here, no officials, no judges

of the ordinary sort," the tall man said, ignoring the
prisoner's contempt. "You are the first to be caught
thieving in this place. You have been found by your
equals to be guilty, and although you have a physical
affliction, we find that no excuse for your crime."

The snow began falling more heavily as the tall
man continued.

"We do not have time or the luxury of a regular
court to lavish on the likes of you. And therefore we
will now carry out the judgment and sentence of this
miner's court."

Restless, the crowd murmured its approval. "Let's
get on with it, Coleman," one man shouted.

"*You can't do this!*" Esther screamed, spurring her
horse down the slope toward an opening through the
tents that led to the clearing.

From where they stood, forty yards away, the
miners had no idea she was a woman. In addition
to the broad hat, workshirt, pants and boots, the
gauzy veil stitched to her hatbrim and tied around
her neck gave her the appearance of a bandit. Halfway down the slope the sling from her small carrying
bag slipped from her shoulder. As she grabbed for it,
one of the miners mistook the movement for the un-
holstering of a weapon and raised his muzzle-loader.
He pointed and fired just as Murietta caught up with
Esther, bowled her out of her saddle, and spun her
over him as they fell. The bullet nicked Esther's horse
and thudded into a tree trunk just short of the rise.

"*Let me go!*" Esther screamed as Murietta rolled
over on top of her. She wrenched one arm free and
struck him a glancing blow on the head, then began
pounding his shoulder and chest with her fist.

Murietta kept her pinned, watching, as twenty
yards to his right several of the miners moved out
in front of the tents. Their weapons were pointed
straight at him. "*We do not know the man!*" he shouted. "My friend hates violence. She cannot tolerate the
sight of such an act. She can't help herself."

"*Let . . . go . . . of . . . me, you beast!*" Esther screamed, as Murietta grabbed for her free wrist and held it down. "Let . . . me . . . *go!*" Squirming, she bit at him, spat in his face, flushed with rage. "You have no right to do this!"

The tall, baby-faced man emerged from the small cluster of miners watching Esther and Murietta from a distance. "That a woman?" he shouted.

"Yes!" Murietta called back.

"Well, keep her under control—and stay out of this!"

Murietta nodded, then watched as the tall man, inaudible from where he stood, gave instructions. One miner stayed behind when the others went back beyond the tents to the main body of the crowd. Pointing his gun at Murietta, he called out: "Don't you come no closer. You try to interfere, Mr. Coleman says I'll have to shoot you."

Murietta moved Esther's wrists together and held them with one hand. "They would have killed you," he whispered.

"I don't care."

Murietta moved his weight to ease the burden on her without losing control of her movement. In doing so, his pelvis and legs fell between hers. She kicked at his calves as he reached out and gently stroked her cheek, trying to quiet and soothe her. Esther squirmed again and felt the warm, hard pressure of Murietta's body on her. The sensation, amid her fury, was not unlike that caused by a slightly loose tooth; positive and negative, welcome and discomfiting at the same time. "Get . . . *off* . . . me," she shouted, biting at his ear.

Both their heads turned as the tall, baby-faced man named Coleman walked to the prisoner's horse, slapped the animal hard on the rump, and shouted, "*Heeeeeeeyaaaah!*" Murietta gently gripped Esther's chin and tried to prevent her from seeing it. She struggled, forcing her head back around, staring as the man in the noose dropped and the sharp snapping of his neck could be heard in the silence of the falling snow. As the swinging, jerking man's eyes bulged, his bladder and bowels opened involuntarily, and a deep stain spread across his light-colored trousers.

Murietta carefully turned Esther's head away. He lay his temple next to her cheek and, one arm extended over his own head, kept her from seeing any more.

She struggled a moment longer, then heard one of the dispersing miners say, "Teach trash to think twice before robbing an honest working man. This be called Hangtown from now on. And let the name be a lesson."

It was over. There was nothing she could do now. Nothing either of them could do. The finality of it dissolved what was left of Esther's anger. Her shoulders slumped, the rigidity went out of her, and she stared up at the snowflakes spiraling down onto her face. She turned her head and buried it in the crook of Murietta's neck, and began to cry silently.

"I am sorry," Murietta said.

"The man had a right to a trial," she sobbed. "What they did is savagery."

"I know. But there was nothing you could do against so many."

Esther's anger flared again. "You *coward!*"

Murietta winced at the momentary hatred and contempt in Esther's eyes. "I have seen this thief before. He was not a good man."

"So they have the right to kill him?" she snapped.

"I did not say that. If there were more of us, I would have tried to stop them. It was simply a matter of not being foolish, not attempting the impossible at the sure cost of your own life."

He let go of her wrists. Slowly, she brought her arms down and held him until the crying stopped. The faint, not unpleasant smell of his hair and body began pulling her thoughts in another direction.

"I am sorry if I hurt you."

She pushed him away gently and wiped at her nose. "It's all right, Joaquin. I understand. What you did was sensible. It probably saved my life. I'm grateful to you."

They stood up, and he noticed she was still holding one of his hands. She looked down at their entwined fingers, then at him, and finally pulled her hand free.

"Can we go now?" she sobbed. "I never . . . want to set foot in this place again."

Murietta glanced back once, just before the woods between the town and the river closed behind them. He stopped and took one last look at the hanging man's face and the hand that was only a stump just above the place where the knuckles would have been. He remembered the day the bear had bitten part of the dead man's hand off in Claussen's high-walled corral. He shivered and wondered for a moment where the dead man's tall, hawk-nosed friend, Mosby, was at this moment. Shrugging, he rode on toward the cabin after Esther.

He caught up with her at the edge of the clearing, just in time to see Miwokan take note of the stains and mud on Esther's clothing, the tangled mass of her moistened hair. He didn't understand the grimace on Miwokan's face, or the abruptness of Miwokan's movement when he took one jealous look at Murietta's soiled clothing, turned on his heel without a word, and stomped off toward the river.

Thirty-six

The snow fell off and on for three weeks, blanketing the land around the cabin and bringing the placer mining to a halt there and everywhere else in the Sierras. Working during the intermittent stretches of dry weather, Murietta built an extension on the shed for himself. Miwokan had kept silent about his suspicions concerning Esther and Murietta since the day of the hanging. Esther sensed only that he was reluctant to leave when his men retired to their camp, more than ready for two or three months of lassitude, frequent sex, and the supportive, purifying rituals of the sweathouse. Taking some reassurance from Murietta's new bunkhouse, Miwokan held his tongue when she asked him what the trouble was, and glumly followed his braves toward the village.

Late in the day on Christmas Eve, after he had hammered in the last nail on the enlarged shed, Murietta snared a quail. Turning his back to Esther, he snapped its neck quickly and began dressing it for the fire. They had kept a discreet, unspecified distance from one another since the incident at Hangtown. Unexpectedly, the physical closeness had aroused and alarmed Esther. She was not ready for it, and Murietta sensed her need for time to sort the matter out.

Time had softened the terms of their wary sexual armistice, and by now, as Esther watched Murietta finish plucking and trimming the bird, his tactfulness had pushed the concern from her mind.

"I was going to offer you some cured deer meat this evening," she called from the door of the cabin. "After all, tomorrow is Christmas. But now that you have something fresh, I will make a deal with you."

"And what is that?" Murietta said, smiling. "It will have to be equitable for me to give up so much as a morsel of this soft, tender, plump, and obviously delicious creature."

"Well," she said, twisting the end of an apron string with a coyness she did not realize was only half contrived, "if you will contribute your soft, tender, plump, and obviously delicious bird, you may sit at my grand table this evening. And I will provide the remainder of a complete dinner you would not have otherwise enjoyed."

"I will have to think about that. . . ."

"Oh, well, if you would rather—"

"For about twenty seconds," Murietta interrupted, grinning.

Esther pursed her lips. Her veil was flipped back over her hat, but Murietta was oblivious of the pale scar. "*Well*," she said, mock-seriously. "You have had five seconds longer than this exchange usually allows its traders."

"Done!" he said, laughing and moving toward her. He remembered himself and stopped just close enough to hand over the bird.

She took it with her thumb and forefinger by one leathery talon. Making a face and shaking her head, she cocked an eyebrow and sighed. "I don't know, Señor Murietta, it seems to me you have struck the better part of this bargain."

"That remains to be seen," he said, relaxing again. "I must wait until I have sampled your cooking."

The fire crackled as they finished the meal, sipped at their coffee, and stared, smiling, at one another. Murietta's stare became a gaze, and he felt a longing for her he knew was out of place. Quickly, he wiped his lips with a napkin Sutter had given her and stood up. "Well, now I must go out to the shed."

Inexplicably, she was annoyed with him. "You don't have to leave so early, do you? It would be nice to sit and talk for a while. You have never told me much about yourself. Do you realize that?"

"Señora, it is absolutely necessary that I return to the shed. . . ."

"Oh, all *right*," she said, surprised at her pique. "We'll talk some other—"

"For a moment or two," he said, smiling.

She was puzzled, but she waited. He returned with a small velvet pouch and placed it on the table before her.

"Whatever is this?" she asked, surprised again.

"It was obvious to me that I did indeed strike the better bargain." He pointed to the small pouch. "This is a small gesture of appreciation."

She took the velvet material in her hand, immediately aware from its weight that it contained something of substance. She undid the strings. Inside she found a small, oval, gold locket-watch on a delicately wrought gold chain. It was an antique, engraved exquisitely with an italic capital E.

"My God, Joaquin, it's beautiful. I . . . I cannot accept something so valuable from you."

"I wish to trade it for the silver spur," he said, laughing and immediately easing her mild discomfort. "I have kept this to myself, but without the spur, I find it extremely difficult to turn my horse to the left."

She burst out laughing. "Haven't you ever thought of moving your one spur to the other boot before you need to turn?"

"There is not enough time for that. I tried turning around in the saddle and riding backward—but the branch of a tree nearly gave me a haircut."

She was completely disarmed. "Thank you, Joaquin. I will treasure it. Where did you find such a lovely watch?"

"It was my grandmother's. Her name was Esperanza." Seeing her renewed reluctance to accept it, he added quickly, "Many, many times I have almost damaged it. Accepting the watch would be a great kindness. You would be taking care of it for me."

He ached with longing again as Esther opened and closed the locket, stared at the delicate black roman numerals and scalloped hands that stood in sharp contrast to the bone-white watchface.

Unaware of the depth of feeling beneath Murietta's misleadingly easy banter, Esther suddenly thought of Alex, and of what it would do to him if he knew. For a moment she was filled with guilt. *Well,* she thought, *there will be no reason for guilt. It was my choice not to return to Alex. But I am his wife. And I love him still. As long as I am his wife, or at least as long as he is not married, I will try to honor my vows of fidelity.*

Sighing, she stood up. Moving close to Murietta but keeping her arms at her sides, she leaned over at the waist and kissed him on the cheek. "You are a wonderful man," she said, the thought of Alex still strong in her mind. "I only wish . . ."

"Wish for nothing," Murietta said, placing his palms on her cheeks and lifting her gaze to his. "Accept what is in you, and what is not in you. And do not trouble yourself for things that come only in their proper season."

The fleeting hint of disappointment, pain in his eyes cut into her. "Oh, Joaquin," she said, leaning her head on his shoulder. "I . . . a part of me . . . wants . . . to . . ."

"Simply wait. I know the place your heart and mind still ride across. I have been there. I understand. And until you feel such things, if you ever feel them for me, it is enough that we are friends."

They sat facing one another across the table and talked for hours. She stuck to the truth about her life up to the meeting of Alex Todd, substituted a nameless "husband" in his place, and then, paraphrasing, tried to leave Murietta with the impression that she had lost her husband, two fingers, and the normal pigment at the tip of her nose during an accident coming west on the Santa Fe Trail.

He did not fully believe her. The scar was plainly the result of frostbite. He had seen it before. And she had mentioned nothing about winter or the mountains. In time, he thought, perhaps she would tell him all of it. He decided not to probe for additional details.

His own story was just as complicated. His grandfather, Don Miguel Murietta y Guitterez, had been the *padron* of the Rancho de los Encinos, south of the Mission San Fernando. Don Miguel and his wife had adopted a beautiful Gabrieleno Indian girl, Esperanza, when both her father and mother died in a fire at the rancho. Don Miguel doted on the child, treating her as he did his natural son and daughter. Nineteen years later, after his wife died of cholera on a visit to Mexico, he became hopelessly infatuated with his ward.

"At first," Murietta explained, "he flouted his passion and ignored the outrage and the pleas of his family and wellborn friends among the *gente de razon*. He even set a date for marriage. But during the engagement the entreaties of his bishop swayed him. By that time, however, Esperanza was pregnant."

Don Miguel ensconced her on one end of the hacienda just as though they were formally married. She gave birth to a son who eventually married and became Joaquin Alejandro Murietta's father. There were other grandchildren. One of them, Ramonda, lived on the rancho with her parents, Don Miguel's legitimate son and daughter-in-law. During their childhood, Murietta and Ramonda were inseparable.

Neither Don Miguel nor Esperanza gave the affection the children held for one another a second thought.

"She went to school in Spain for several years during adolescence," Murietta went on. "When she returned a young woman, we edged slowly toward what we knew was forbidden. We were in the grape arbor hours past sunset one summer night, locked in each other's arms, half-naked and almost paralyzed with love and fear when my father surprised us. Tears were streaming down his face. He beat me senseless and banished me from the rancho on the threat of death."

Murietta had spent a year in the desert and the mountains, alone, healing both physically and spiritually. During this solitary period, he said, before he passed a second year herding sheep in the hills along the southern end of the San Joaquin Valley, he had come to understand his precise place in the universe. He had reached a state of mind where he could slip off his boots and clothes, dig his feet into the earth, tilt his head upward, and lose consciousness of himself. It was as though, he continued, he blended completely into the earth and sky. He had tried peyote and mescal, and while they were interesting, they did not take him to the amorphously serene place he could reach himself by ridding his mind of all thought.

He returned at least once every few years, he told Esther, to the desolate and nearly unreachable places to renew himself, feel the earth spin, and hear the soothing rhythms of water and wind. Death had long since held no fear for him.

"If all that happens," he said, "is that I return to being part of the earth, the waters, the universe, it is enough. If there is more, all the better, but more is not necessary."

Listening to Murietta, Esther found herself thinking about an eventual confrontation with Mosby. She might fail. Mosby might kill her. Suddenly she saw the possibility of her own violent death in a new light. She had thought of it before. In the past, the prospect had chilled her. Now it didn't seem to bother her as much. She liked Murietta's concept of death. It made sense. It soothed her. After all, she thought, once you are dead, what does it matter *how* you died?"

"You are certainly a different sort of man," she said.

"I do not feel so different. Just fortunate to understand what is important and what is not . . . I think."

"So many do not. So many behave like animals."

"Not all. And I enjoy the company of gentle, amusing people." He sighed. "Those that are not gentle, well, occasionally they force me to do things I would rather not."

She thought of Mosby again and spoke without caution. "Have you ever taken revenge? Killed a man?" Alarmed, she hoped Murietta would not be curious about why she had asked such a question.

He stared at her evenly for a moment. "No. Not for revenge. In self-defense. . . . But there is one man I have thought of killing for what he did to me."

"Just before I found you by the river?"

"Yes. But I wish to talk no more about it."

Esther sighed. "Will you kill him?"

Murietta was silent for a moment. "In time, I believe the desire for vengeance will pass. I hope it does. I do not like the idea of killing another man. But until my blood cools on the matter, I do not know what I would do if I saw him. I hope I do not, for that very reason."

Briefly, Esther wondered if she would ever get over her desire to bring Mosby down. She doubted it. She saw from his expression that Murietta was wondering why she had asked him the question. She led him in another direction.

"One would never know how much there is to you, Joaquin," she said. "Sometimes I want to scream at the lack of such understanding among men—and women."

"That is when you need to be alone, in a wild place where men do not pass." He smiled. "Sometimes I have seen you slip away, when you thought I was dreaming on my bedroll."

"Yes. I go to the waterfall. It washes away the things I cannot stop from troubling me with my own will."

"I have a special place I go to also. It is far south of here, in the land of the Morangos, many miles east of the Mission San Gabriel. There is a place in the high desert, a mile into the sky above millions of strange, tall, cactus-like trees that some say look like monks. From this place you can see at least one hundred miles across the desert and mountains in three directions. To the southwest, across the desert where the earth has come apart and together again many times, there is a mountain called San Jacinto. There is a taller one to the west, San Gorgonio, but Jacinto rises so rapidly off the desert floor that when I gaze at it, I feel as though it draws me, lifts me like an eagle on its air currents, straight up to the sun or the moon. Of all the distant, silent places, it is the one where I can rid myself of my mind and my body most easily, most quickly."

"You must take me there one day. I would love to see it."

"One day," he said wistfully, standing up and taking her left hand. He kissed the knuckle stubs tenderly, then reached out with his other hand and stroked her hair. "I think it will be good for me to be gone for a time now. I think you should have this place and the waterfall to yourself, and I have felt the need to gaze at Jacinto for many weeks."

"Will you come back?"

"Of course. Just as the snow melts, in time for the work." He laughed. "After all, what would you and Miwokan do without me?"

He left before dawn, while she was still sleeping. It was not until noon on Christmas Day, as he watered his horse in a stream deep into the San Joaquin Valley, that he found the two large pouches of gold and the note in his saddlebag.

"*I want you to have these. If you do not come back, I will understand. Feliz Navidad. Esther.*"

Thirty-seven

South Fork Cabin
July 11, 1849

Dearest Husband, I learned, while in Sacramento City on business last week, that you, like almost every other able-bodied male from here to Santa Clara, have succumbed to the lure of gold and that you are working the streams at Mormon Bar. Found out from Sutter who chanced also to be in Sacramento, attending to some business, as I was. Reduced as he is, Sutter certainly has maintained his network of friends. The man knows everything that goes on within 100 miles of the city, and he seems to have taken pains to discreetly stay informed of your whereabouts.

I wish you well, hope that your decision to quit your job at Larkin's store four months ago was a wise one, and pray that you do not become ill from the icy waters, as so many miners have. I understand you passed through the city on your way to Mormon Bar. Can you believe the changes that have taken place? It astonishes me that between the fort, which already shows the first signs of decay, and the embarcadero, has sprung up a sizable town almost overnight.

Went there to talk with Kellerman, the retailer, and was totally taken aback by the city itself, and by the prices Kellerman is getting for the hammers, picks, pans, and other items he is selling for me. (Hammers $8 to $10!) It seems my notion to "go into the hard goods business" was an uncommonly lucky one. Stayed at the still unfinished City Hotel, where I ran into Sutter, and I also happened upon Warren Barnett, who told me that a theater is planned just down the street from the City! Reportedly it will be called the Eagle, the first such in the entire territory. I have never been to a play. But I remember daydreaming once, of dressing gaily and attending a drama with you.

Interesting talk with Barnett. As it happened, he planned to stop at the South Fork during his "tour," as he calls it, to apprise me of developments at Blue Star. Things there progressing marvelously, as predicted, since San Francisco returned to "normal" last fall. Barnett brought me a statement and documents from the Mercantile Bank as an accounting. It seems I have more than $80,000 at this juncture! With that I ought to be able to do something about Mosby, should I ever find him. And I certainly will not have to worry about survival for many years to come. That is, if I do not eat in Sacramento's (and I would imagine San Francisco's) outrageously overpriced restaurants too often.

Cannot quite put my finger on what Barnett's purpose in these parts is. He seems to be interested in something more than gaining additional shipping orders for Blue Star. He relays talk, very preliminary at this point, of a drive for statehood, so perhaps he has a political career in mind. Transparent but fascinating man. Essentially uneducated, but shrewd and knowledgeable, along with being extraordinarily likeable. Big and clumsy as a bull in a china shop, but so sincere, so honest, one wants to overlook the rough edges and occasionally bruised senses. I like him.

In a way, his gentleness and compassion remind me of Murietta. (Thank goodness, *he* has finally returned. Until these last few weeks, I had a growing fear that Miwokan and his men would not be able to hold the line against some of these ruffians that call themselves "forty-niners." Not all, but many, are a far cry from the civilized prospectors from local parts—all but those few in Hangtown—who were here last year. It is to be expected, I suppose, what with the numbers—Barnett says the latest estimates indicate 40,000 men in the fields and another 40,000 settlers between here and the coast. It is hard to believe that many are from places as far away as Chile, the Sandwich Islands, and Europe. With such a mix and multitude, one cannot expect but to find more than a few examples of primitive behavior.)

While talking with Barnett, an interesting subject came up: the absolutely unpardonable length of time it takes a letter of any sort to reach Sacramento, let alone the mining towns, from San Francisco. Suggested, admittedly thinking of you, that someone ought to set up a private or government-supported mail service. One could surely make more out of it, and hauling prospector's gold to San Francisco and back, than from the ore itself. Fortuitously, from the standpoint of finding a way to remunerate you for the $300 left with me at Bent's Fort, Barnett said he would speak to "young Todd" about the mail and express idea. Perhaps, dear Alex, it will be your next step to greater prosperity. I hope so.

Saw little Moses at the Indian village on the way back from Sacramento City. A darling, placid child, serene in the care Solana virtually smothers him with. It may seem heartless of me, but I have accepted the fact that I can never have him with me. I detect an element of the subdued in his nature, young as he is. On those rare occasions when he frowns, the sudden resemblance to Mosby is frightening, and prompts in me so much anger I must look away from the poor child.

As I must look away from Murietta from time to time for other reasons. I wrote earlier in these pages that I would share things with you that women rarely, if ever, speak of to men. It is time for me to fulfill the promise. Oh, Alex, the absence of you and what I am beginning to realize is a strong streak of base physical nature in me, lead me to torment. I have not broken my vow to sustain my fidelity to you, but the lack in my life of those pleasures we shared so joyously together leads me to gaze upon Joaquin, unbeknownst to him, with unpardonable lust. Particularly when he has his shirt off and I can see the sinewy muscles of his torso and arms. I imagine myself doing unspeakable things with him. In order to take hold of my senses, I think of you with me, naked, instead, but it does little to satisfy my craving. Such desires, I would guess, led to the strange experience I had in bed the other morning before sunrise.

I had been dreaming of you, us, together, in the barn in Ohio. When I awoke, I found myself rocking, my hand on my privates, which were as moist as if you had spilled your seed in me, and astonishingly, I was in the midst of one of those quivering, tingling flights during which my whole body seemed aflame. It was exactly as I felt on more than one occasion toward the end of our love-makings.

I was really not fully awake, for as if in some sort of trance, I continued to move my fingers over myself, and the same remarkable sensations repeated even more intensely. I must confess that the feeling of peace and contentment that followed, the absence of my lustful cravings for some days, has tempted me to the same again—intentionally. I have deliberated on it, and although I recall vividly all the words spoken of such things from the pulpit, I cannot for the life of me see anything wrong with it. It would harm no one. And if it diminishes my desire for Murietta, perhaps it may even be a positive thing.

I want you to know that there is little likelihood of Murietta ever pressing his own unspoken desires on me. He came here this evening concerning the use of small amounts of blasting powder to clear boulders upriver where he and the men are camped. Our friendship is somehow diminished. He is caring and gentle, as usual, but there seems a gulf between us. Much the same as the unspoken barrier of near-formality that Miwokan has erected and slowly fortifies. Can he as well still be harboring thoughts of me in this vein? It is sad, but perhaps men cannot in any other way deal with a woman they desire.

Useless and irrelevant misgivings, these, my dear husband. I have too much to attend to. Too difficult to remain at peace with what surrounds me. So many people! And, more to the point, I have a much stronger desire to keep my quiet, unheard promise to you, dear man. Rest assured that I will continue to do the mental exercises I must employ to rid myself of such thoughts concerning Murietta. In much the same way as I banished the sadness and remorse that washed over me after seeing little Moses recently.

I feel the way I feel. Do not feel what I cannot. For Moses, or Murietta, or anyone. And that is that. I will not torment myself over what simply is.

Enough. I must remember to talk with Murietta about going for a look at the new sluices and flumes being built north of here. The power of the water reduces almost unworkable banks to flowing silt and mud out of which the gold can be practically plucked! Perhaps you and your fellow miners are using such at Mormon Bar. I will pass close to where you are, I would imagine, but of course I cannot go near that place, no matter how much I would like to.

Just thinking about such a thing prompts me to pine for you. I will not. For I cannot and still go on in my purpose. Good night, dear Husband. And may God keep you well.

Thirty-eight

Unexpected labor troubles delayed Esther's tour of the northern camps until mid-August. "Coyote-hole" digging under the bed of the river was required now that the surface deposits were thinning out. A dam had to be built; then a trench, through which to divert water so the bed would be exposed for working. The additional labor and the exhausting work set some of Miwokan's men to grumbling, then to open rebellion. Despite entreaties by Miwokan and his brother, a half-dozen men decided to pack up and move north for less arduous and far more remunerative independent panning. Esther renewed her offer to share her profits with them if all the others became equal partners as well. But Miwokan and those loyal to him refused the increase, and the discontented men left.

The evening before she and Murietta were to leave on the tour, Miwokan inexplicably flew into a tirade about the trip.

"There is no need for you to go!" he shouted when the conversation had reached a stalemate.

"And there is no need for you to raise your voice, Miwokan!" Esther remonstrated. "What is the matter with you? You are acting as though you were my father, and an unreasonable father at that!"

Miwokan glanced coldly at Murietta, then turned back to Esther. "I will send two of my men. They will draw pictures of these, these . . ."

"Flumes," Murietta said.

"You do not have to tell me what they are called!" Miwokan said, shouting again, his underlying feelings slowly being exposed. "I know the words 'flume' and 'sluice.'"

"I did not mean to—"

"Why should you go with her?" he said, cutting Murietta off. "You are needed here. We are six men short now."

Esther, preoccupied with other things, had let Miwokan's jealousy of Murietta slip her mind. Now she understood why he was so agitated. "Do you wish me to go alone?" she said gently.

"I wish you not to go at all."

She placed her hand on Miwokan's shoulder. "Can we walk, just the two of us? I would like to speak with you alone."

Grudgingly, barely concealing his annoyance with Murietta, he followed. When they were out of sight and earshot, Esther put her arm through his and looked up at him. She smiled and cocked her head and saw that he knew she knew.

"You are not yourself today. I understand. But there is no reason for it. There never has been."

"He goes with you, and I do not."

"You are more important to me here. Don't you know there is nothing between Joaquin and me?"

Miwokan sighed. "I am sorry I behaved that way. Perhaps I needed to hear it from your lips again after so many sunsets."

"Well, you have heard it."

"I have no bad feelings for him. He is my friend. This comes to me from a place in my heart I do not understand."

"You have a wife. You love her."

"I know," he said. "And I am sometimes like a spoiled child. It makes me betray her in my thoughts. She has done nothing to make me feel less for her." He stopped and turned to her. "I am sorry. I will not let my heart do this to me again. I promise you

that. I will go to the village now. Tell Murietta that
it was the leaving of my people that made me speak
sharply."

For five days Esther and Murietta worked their way
northward to Georgetown and west to Auburn. While
staying there overnight, Esther read in *The Placer
Times* that an enterprising young miner named Alexander Todd and his cousin had recently given up the
quest to establish a much-needed and already profitable mail and limited express service to and from
the gold fields. The following morning, Esther and
Murietta angled up toward the Yuba by way of Dutch
Flat, Yankee Jim's, then on through You Bet, Nevada City, Blue Tent, and Goodyear's Bar. The beginnings of a new system of mining were springing
up everywhere. Where the riverbeds were starting
to play out, in the claim-jammed creeks and canyon
areas where the water was insufficient to the task of
washing at this time of year, miners threw in their
lot together. Jointly they built lengthy wooden sluices
and enormously long flumes to carry the water from
higher points in the mountain. The resultant flow was
more than enough to wash pans and rockers full of
deeper gold-bearing dirt. In a few locations it was
funneled and hosed in primitive ways for carving into
the banks and canyon walls to unearth new and even
richer placer deposits.

But more than just the methods of mining had
changed. They arrived at Downieville late in the afternoon. As they turned their horses into the town's
rutted dirt street, both of them suddenly reined up in
stunned disbelief. Halfway to the end of the double
line of tents and shanties, a woman hung from a
rope, turning slowly, her legs extending down through
the crude trap door of a hastily built scaffold. Beneath
her, on the ground under the wooden platform from
which she had dropped, lay a lump of moist matter
the shape and color of a jellyfish. Esther, shocked but

also puzzled, glanced at Murietta. The blood had drained from his face. Pulled almost against her will by the unsettlingly strange form beneath the hanged woman, she walked her horse nearer. Murietta shook his head sadly and followed.

To the right, a few doors down from a shanty bearing a crudely lettered sign reading: *Justiss of the Peese,* a tall, stately woman with fine features was loading suitcases and personal belongings onto a wagon. A well-dressed man wearing a wedding ring carried an armload of clothing out from their tent-shanty and laid it carefully in the well behind the seat. Esther reined her horse toward the woman and dismounted.

"In God's name, what has happened here?"

The woman turned and took a moment before deciding to answer. "These barbarians have done the unspeakable."

"But what did the woman do?" Murietta asked.

"It was not what *she* did," the tall woman said, suddenly angry. "But that made no difference to these . . . these . . . animals." She glanced at the dangling corpse and, for a moment, tears welled in her eyes. Collecting herself, she went on. "A drunken miner broke down the door of a house last night. Inside was the Mexican lady who has been hanged, and her paramour. Ugly words were exchanged. This morning the miner returned to the Mexican woman's cabin. His friends claim he meant only to apologize. He apparently used insulting Spanish words, the Mexican woman was angered, and he in turn threatened her and her . . . male friend. At which point the Mexican woman pulled a knife from beneath her apron. The minor was *inside* the cabin, well inside it, when they found him after she stabbed him to death. I have no doubt he was up to no good."

"And they hanged her? For defending herself?" Esther asked, appalled.

"Yes. Despite the finding of my husband, Dr. Carson, that she was at least three months pregnant."

Esther and Murietta turned and looked again at the semitransparent form lying on the ground under the scaffold.

"God . . . Oh, good God," Esther exclaimed. "Then that is . . . ?"

"It is indeed the fetus," the woman said, giving a scathing look to a trio of miners walking by. "Two other men who *claim* to be doctors examined the woman at great length, I might add—and gave the opinion that she was not with child. A half-minute or so after they hanged the poor creature, the unborn baby dropped from her womb."

Esther gasped. She turned to look again and saw a miner scooping up the formless mass beneath the dead woman with a shovel. Expressionlessly, he walked off toward the edge of the woods. "I cannot believe this," Esther said. "I *cannot* believe it!" Lightheaded, she started to sway.

Murietta, still ashen, got down from his horse and steadied her.

The doctor's wife started toward her tent-shanty, then hesitated. "I would leave this place if I were you. These mountains, in fact. There is an evil growing here that passes understanding."

"It is the gold," Esther murmured, trembling as she thought of Miwokan's words.

The woman nodded her head. "Yes, you might be right. I am beginning to believe that it contains the seed of the devil himself."

Or the wrath of the sun, Esther thought.

After that, Esther had no stomach for additional surveying of the new water-machinery. Turning about abruptly, she and Murietta rode half the night to Allegheny Camp, put up in a vacant tent, and continued south in the morning. They hardly spoke during the entire trip. When they finally reached the South Fork, Murietta stayed drunk on the claim and then in Placerville, the new name the miners had given Hangtown, for three days. The business at Downieville had shaken him as much as it had Esther. When he sobered up, she called him to the cabin.

"I no longer wish to live here," she said after pouring him a cup of fresh coffee. "I do not want to be near all these people—and what some of them are doing."

He shook his head, not sure he had heard her right, certain that his hangover was playing tricks with his ears.

"I want you to become a full partner with me, run the claim after I leave."

It took a minute for him to let it sink in. "Where will you go?" he finally asked, sadness fast coming over him.

"I don't know. San Francisco first, to make arrangements. Then someplace where I will be away from all the madness. Will you accept?"

"Miwokan will not like this."

"He is not my guardian! I own the property! I shall do as I please!" Esther shouted.

"I meant only that he will not like my being the boss."

"I'm sorry, Joaquin. I haven't been myself since Downieville. Will you run the claim for me?"

"Not as a partner. But as a foreman, for wages, yes."

"You do not want to become rich? Do you think there is something wrong with that?"

He thought carefully about his answer. He did not want to betray his thoughts about the subtle hardening in Esther's personality over the last year. Or his belief that the gold had caused it. "For others, not necessarily . . . For me, it would not be a good thing."

"As you like. I will pay you as much or more than any foreman in the fields."

"Whatever you decide, Esther. But what of Miwokan?"

"He will simply have to get used to it. He does

not have to know everything. You handle the shipping of the gold, anyway. Simple deduct your salary from the shipment privately, and keep an accounting of it only for me."

"It is all in the way I handle it, in other words?"

"Yes. The way things are done doesn't have to change. You will simply know that I consider you the foreman. And Miwokan will not be unhappy about us being apart."

Murietta sighed. "I suspected he had such feelings."

"It will pass. Especially if I am no longer here."

"In time," Murietta said, wondering how long it would take him to get used to her absence himself. "Everything will be carried out in the same way, then?"

"Yes. You will continue shipping the gold to Blue Star. Since you will need to be here, I will arrange in San Francisco for Adams and Company to carry it. I will let you know where I settle as soon as I can. I want you to inform me if the new mail and express operation established by—a man named Alexander Todd, begins servicing Placerville. If it does, I would like to shift the business to his firm."

"As you wish," Murietta said, betraying curiosity about Esther's wish.

"Todd is—a friend of Warren Barnett," she quickly added. "He——he comes highly recommended."

That night at the village, she informed Miwokan of her decision. He accepted the change more stoically than she expected. After visiting with Solana and Moses, she said good-bye to them all, "For the time being, anyway," and returned to the cabin. She pored over its contents, deciding what to take and what to leave. When she said farewell to a glum Murietta the following morning and rode for Sacramento, she had with her only her clothing, her diary, toiletries, the comb-and-brush set Alex had given her, Murietta's gold locket-watch and the heart-shaped amulet fash-

ioned by Miwokan. The night before, for the first
time in all these months, she had realized she no
longer had the antique watch "Uncle" Billy Graves
had given her the day she became separated from
the snowshoe party. Now, as she continued toward
Sacramento, she wondered if Mosby had it; or if one
of Sutter's Kanakas had taken it—surely Sutter himself wouldn't; or if it had simply been lost as she
made her way down out of the mountains.

Two days later, as she waited to board the paddle-
wheeler *Sacramento*, she was too preoccupied with
the city's unusual post office, which had been established aboard the docked bark *Whiton*, to notice or
hear the big-bellied, red-bearded passenger from San
Francisco who brushed past her as he came down
off the gangplank.

Isaac Claussen did not fail to notice Esther. Turning to the man carrying his mining equipment, Claussen laughed. He nodded back toward the attractive
woman in the veiled hat. "Like 'em plumper, myself.
But that's just the sort of machinery drives old Mosby
wild. Skinny with big tits." Claussen looked back one
last time as he headed away from the embarcadero
dock. "Maybe old Alamo knows somethin' I don't,"
he said, laughing again. "I'll have to ask him." His
face went curious. "Wonder where the son'bitch is
keepin' hisself these days?"

Thirty-nine

Esther stood staring out through the window in William Kelsey's office, wondering where fate or luck

would place her next. Before her lay what seemed like a forest of tall trees denuded by a raging fire. Between eight hundred and a thousand sailing ships sat crowded together in and beyond the cove, abandoned, stripped of their sailcloth and rocking gently in the still, midmorning interval between the fog and the formidable afternoon wind. Here and there a stately vessel cut slowly through an open channel dissecting the marine graveyard.

A block down Montgomery Street on the waterfront, one huge ship had been shoved up against a wharf, demasted, leveled to the deck, and rebuilt to serve as a giant warehouse. Another, its decks ripped off and turned over on its side, had been partitioned and fronted with canvas compartments. In and out of the tent flaps, men, women, and children moved back and forth, carrying furniture, personal items, and provisions.

Esther walked back out through the office and gave William Kelsey a comforting look. Harried, he had spent a few minutes with her earlier, then, after sending someone for Warren Barnett, had excused himself. He was virtually surrounded by clerks, each of them holding a ledger, a sheaf of lading bills, consignment orders, or correspondence that needed his attention. The din of a hundred hammers pulsed through the doorway as Esther stepped back out onto the wooden sidewalk to reconfirm what she had seen from her room at the Parker House on Portsmouth Square early that morning.

Everywhere men were busy building, teams of them nailing down roofs, others raising preconstructed house frames into place; draymen hauling lumber, barrowmen wheeling shingles to waiting carpenters. Here and there bricklayers moved incessantly, scooping, slapping, placing, and setting in a continuous rhythm. The walls they were erecting seemed almost to grow, back and forth, line by line, by themselves behind the blurred movements of the craftsmen.

The city was three times the size it had been when she last saw it. Wooden houses, many of them enlarged by canvas extensions, and a veritable sea of tents spread across the flatlands and crept up the hills like an enormous living growth of multihued ground-cover. Clusters of shy, narrow-eyed Chinese hurried across intersections. Several Frenchmen argued volubly with an express agent across the street. Twenty Chileans, their heads poking through ponchos, labored under the weight of mining equipment on their way to a steamboat and Sacramento. Malays, Sonorans, Yankees, Kanakas—Esther was certain she had counted a dozen nationalities, not including the fairer faced men whose clothing did not immediately identify their origin. Finally she saw Warren Barnett step out of the door of his newly established assay office down the street.

"Well, what do you think?" Barnett said as he guided her back toward Blue Star's private offices. "Do we not have a city abuilding here?"

"Indeed you do."

"It will one day be one of the world's great trade centers."

"Gold or no gold," Esther said, thinking beyond the present.

"Exactly." Barnett ushered her to a chair and then sat down himself. The desk seemed like a toy from a child's playhouse with his bulk behind it.

"You are comfortable at the Parker House?"

"Quite comfortable, and fascinated by the gaming establishments on the plaza."

"Yes," he said, noting her expression of tolerant amusement. "Well, we have a city, and with cities come problems. We are looking for ways to unseat some unscrupulous men in office who are busy lining their pockets by allowing such things to get out of hand. It will all end well, though. I think the outcome of the convention—one outcome, at least—will be the legislative and judicial tools to deal with these rascals."

"Convention?"

"It will be a glorious thing. Just between you and me—and William, of course—I think a great deal more will be framed at Monterey. The Frémonts will be there—drumming up support for a U.S. Senate nomination."

The incongruity of a senatorial campaign before California achieved statehood was lost on Esther as she wondered if the Frémonts might know of Mosby's whereabouts. *My God,* she thought. *Why haven't I thought of them before?* Suddenly she was filled with excitement. Aware that Barnett was watching her, she quickly said, "I hope something will be resolved about the lack of law in the gold fields. And steps taken to ensure the rights and safety of those who lived here long before we arrived."

"The Indians? Yes, something has to be done. Why, just the other day, near the Mokelumne River, a band of drunken miners amused themselves by taking target practice on a Maidu encampment!"

"Miwok," Esther said absently, still thinking of Frémont and Mosby.

Barnett looked puzzled.

"South of the American and in beyond the foothills, the Indians are of the Miwok subtribes," Esther explained.

"Yes, of course. You would know that, living near Placerville."

"I mean for it no longer to be my home."

Barnett was surprised. "You're moving here, to San Francisco?"

"No. That's one reason I wished to talk with you. As William may have told you, I am . . . ah . . . of a somewhat reclusive nature. I find it no longer tolerable to live in an area so overcrowded."

"Are you planning to sell your property?"

"No, it's in capable hands. Mr. Murietta, whom I

believe you have met, will be running things for me at the South Fork."

"I'm happy to hear that. He's a good man, and I'm convinced you haven't even touched the potential of the country."

"You may be right," she replied, remembering what Sutter had once told her: Mosby had left Frémont soon after arriving in California. Still . . .

"In any case," Barnett went on, "where do you wish to live? There is much land here, although I wouldn't advise building in town. There's a lack of privacy, and I foresee a danger in the central areas. We have already experienced several disastrous fires."

"Really? One would never know from the look of things."

"Rebuilt within a matter of days." Barnett shook his head in wonderment. "It is as though nothing, not even God, can stop the growth of this city."

"Yes. Well, for the moment, I don't wish to live here. I would like to remain in the foothill area." *Frémont must know,* she willed silently.

"It will be difficult to find a place not teeming with prospectors. They range as far north as the Yuba, and there are literally hordes of Sonorans as well as native miners down around the Stanislaus and the . . ." Barnett paused. "There *is* one area," he said, musing. "The Frémonts are building a ranch near a place called Mariposa."

Esther's heart leaped. *If they do not know now, perhaps in the future, if I am situated near them . . .*

"It's wild and beautiful country," Barnett continued, "relatively unsettled at the moment. It's more than possible another tract of land could be obtained for you with the help of Consul Larkin."

The name triggered a burst of nostalgia and longing for Alex. She fought it off. "I would like that very much." Her mind churned again about Frémont and Mosby. "Would it be possible for me to meet with Mr. Larkin?"

"I am sure I can arrange it."

The strong possibility that John Charles Frémont could provide her with information concerning Mosby's whereabouts made her hands tremble. "Would it be too much trouble to make another request?"

"Name it, dear lady. If it is within my power . . ."

She pretended she could not look Barnett in the eye. "You will think me foolish. . . ."

"Never you mind about that. What is it?"

"I have . . . I have heard so much about . . . John Charles Frémont," she whispered, feigning a shyness she did not feel. "And his extraordinary wife. He is . . . has become a . . ."

"Sort of a hero to you?"

Esther put her glove to her lips and lowered her gaze. "Yes." She wondered if acting on a stage was this easy.

"And you would like to meet him?"

"How did you . . . ? Yes. And his wife, of course."

"Consider it done," Barnett said as Kelsey walked into the office. "And don't be so shy about your admiration for the man. It's shared by many. John Charles Frémont may be too conservative for *some* political tastes, but he's nonetheless a hero of the first order. Am I not right, William?"

Kelsey glanced at her, then at Barnett, glared briefly before deciding to avoid a political debate centering on Frémont. "Of course." But then, unable to control himself, he added, "Everyone knows he conquered California all by himself."

"Oh, William!" Esther said, maintaining her pose, "you're just jealous."

"Of that vain little squirt? That windbag?"

"Well, Warren and I think he is a patriot, don't we, Warren? And I would like to meet him."

"No harm in that," Kelsey said, backing off. "Just take along some cotton."

"Cotton?" Esther said.

"For your ears. The man never stops talking."
I hope not, she thought.

Forty

Barnett and Kelsey took her to lunch at Tong Ling's
in Jackson Street. As they argued about Frémont, she
toyed with her food and wondered how she would
get The "Pathfinder" to talk about Mosby without
being obvious. The dishes were too hot for her taste,
but Esther's first experience with the delectably milder
chow-chow took her mind off Monterey for the moment. Over steaming tea she made arrangements for
a shift in procedure at Blue Star. She had long since
paid for her third of the company's privately held
stock, and she wanted any funds due her henceforth
to be deposited at the newly established banking arm
of Adams and Company.

"What's wrong with the Mercantile Bank?" Barnett
asked. "Blue Star has been doing business with them
since—"

"I engaged Adams and Company to haul my gold
yesterday. This will simplify matters."

"The Mercantile people are powerful," Barnett said.
"We don't want them as enemies."

"I'm not suggesting Blue Star shift its account. I
simply find that the Mercantile seems to be far less
efficient and much more rude these days," Esther said.

"She's right about that." Kelsey was enjoying having her on his side now that the Frémont discussion
was over. "That bank not only is putting people off

by smugly assuming there are few other places so secure, it's resting on its laurels. Eventually, Adams might be a better place to have your money."

They got up, and Barnett paid for the meal with gold dust. The Chinese proprietor slowly weighed it on a small set of scales.

"Why aren't you paying in bills or coin?" Esther asked.

"Dust is handy to me at the assay office."

"And there is a shortage of coins and bills," Esther said as they left the restaurant. "I learned of it yesterday."

"That's true," Barnett said as they passed a market displaying squash from Hawaii. "A lot of people are finding it inconvenient to pay with dust."

"I asked if something could be done about the problem yesterday at the Mercantile," Esther said. "All I got was exasperated looks—and rudeness."

"Too cocksure of themselves," Kelsey said. "Keep it up, theyah gonna lose all theyah customers."

They picked their way across a street reduced to a quagmire by heavy rain two days earlier. The lids of a score of submerged cast-iron stoves served as stepping stones.

"Mind you, don't snap one of them open," Kelsey said, taking Esther's hand. "It was a fine idea to set them in the mud. They were going to waste. But yesterday one of the lids flew up and cracked a man's shinbone."

They reached the wooden sidewalk in front of a hardware store.

"Can't anything be done about this coin and currency business?" Esther asked.

"Until the government establishes a mint here," Barnett said, "I doubt things will get any better."

"Mebbe they will if we become a state," Kelsey said, nudging Esther and winking. They passed a man throwing brush and branches under the rear wheels of a buckboard stalled in the mud. "Myself, I'd just as soon see us get some cobblestones first."

"*If* we become a state?" Barnett said defensively. "There's no question about it. You can bet the matter will be settled in Monterey."

"Monterey is one thing," Kelsey said, "but Washington is another."

"Oh, come on, William," Barnett went on. "Polk is for it. The Congress can't ignore us. We're too rich, there's too much gold flowing eastward for statehood to be delayed very long."

So much gold and not enough coins, Esther thought, as an idea struck her.

"And in the meantime," Barnett continued, "if I judge the temper of those headed for Monterey correctly, we will function as a state with or without the government's blessing."

"With or without coin of the realm," Esther mused out loud.

Barnett turned to her, puzzled. For a moment Esther stared at several men unearthing a carriage that had sunk up to its windows into the mire on Kearny Street. In front of it, the head of a dead mule protruded from the surface of the street.

Esther shuddered and turned back to Barnett. "Is there any law against coining gold privately?"

"Why, I don't know," Barnett said, a bit flustered. He prided himself on his self-taught knowledge of the law.

"I'm sure you can find out," Esther said. "You run an assay office, through which a formidable amount of gold passes. For the price of some machinery, which could be made at the foundry I saw from my hotel-room window, you could turn out coins from that gold. Would there be any profit in it?"

"Why, I'd never thought of it," Barnett said.

"What did I tell you about this little lady?" Kelsey nudged Barnett in the ribs, enjoying every minute of the big man's being caught off balance.

"Yes. Yes," Barnett said, thinking. "She has a fine mind for business."

"It was just a thought," Esther said, smiling knowingly at Kelsey. "I don't know if it could be turned to advantage."

"Easy," Kelsey said. "Just start turning out coins."

"That wouldn't sit well with the Mercantile," Barnett said.

"The Mercantile be damned!" Embarrassed, Esther sucked in a breath and put her hand to her mouth.

Barnett's jaw dropped open. Kelsey roared.

"If they don't like it," Kelsey said, "tell them we'll just have to pull our account out of the bank."

Barnett suddenly enjoyed the prospect of it all. "Why, it would be simple. You must add another metal to a gold coin to keep it from bending, breaking up with use. If a five-dollar gold piece, for which a minter received five dollars in nuggets or dust, contained only four dollars' worth of gold, there would be a dollar's profit in each coin."

"Less the cost of the additional metal," Kelsey said.

"Minimal. Minimal," Barnett responded, his mind racing as they started downhill toward Montgomery Street and the Blue Star offices.

"If you stayed within a reasonable proximity of what the government puts into its coins, that would be fair, would it not?" Esther asked.

"Honest. Honest. Couldn't be fairer than that," Barnett answered.

"Why don't the three of us go into the mint business?" Esther wondered out loud. "At least until the government takes it upon itself to remedy the situation."

"It *would* be a natural outgrowth of the assay office," Kelsey said.

"A third each for the equipment," Esther suggested.

"And a three-way split of the profits," Kelsey added.

"Less a shared expenditure for additional space and the men you will have to hire," Esther said.

Barnett was beaming like a child with a new toy. "Why, we might get rich on this."

"Richer," Esther said.

"Richer is right." Kelsey laughed, putting his arm around Esther and giving her a fatherly squeeze. "Now, will you pack up your things and come stay with Connie and me? You're too valuable an asset to be left alone at night in a hotel on Portsmouth Square, fancy Parker House or not."

Forty-one

Esther put off accepting the Kelseys' invitation to stay in their guest room for several days. She wanted to be alone, have time to think. But then she gave in. She had grown tired of the noise and bustle around the Parker House. Barnett had left for Monterey. She could not join him until the end of the week, and she realized that no amount of planning would guarantee the Frémonts would not be curious about questions concerning Mosby. She would simply have to wait and improvise her approach.

Bill Kelsey offered to pick her up at the hotel, but Esther declined. Not wanting to impose, she hired a buckboard and driver for a late afternoon departure. It was well past supper when the apologetic driver arrived, explaining that he had broken an axle shortly after noon. Disgruntled because she was keeping the Kelseys waiting, Esther had the driver load her bags on the buckboard while she crossed Portsmouth Square to a small shop. She hoped to find an appropriate gift for Connie Kelsey as a token of her gratitude.

The wrapped porcelain figure of a child under her
arm, she started back toward the buckboard. Guitar,
banjo, and violin sounds wafted out onto the plaza
from the Aguila de Oro and other gambling houses
amid a loud murmur of voices and occasional peals
of laughter. As she glanced into the Verandah gaming
tent, the sound and sight of a dextrous musician drew
her attention. She stopped and watched as the man
alternately sang hoarsely and blew through a set of
penny whistles on a makeshift brace around his neck.
Simultaneously, he clapped a pair of miniature cym-
bals together and beat out a tattoo with sticks attached at his elbows on a drum hanging down his
back.

She smiled and started to turn, but then she saw
the mustachioed player sitting at a monte table directly in front of the one-man band. Esther had only
a three-quarter view of the gambler's face because
of the angle of his chair. From where she stood, he
looked like Mosby. *It cannot be,* she thought. *My
mind is playing tricks.* She moved to the left for a
better view of the man. The profile matched Mosby's
perfectly, right down to the aquiline nose. The man
laughed as he drew in a winning pot, and the sound
electrified her. She was certain it was Mosby.

She felt the certainty take on the color and tem-
perature of cold rage. Her heart pounded, her hands
grew clammy, her breath came in short, deep gasps.
Suddenly past examining danger, weighing consequences, she was overwhelmed by the urge for vengeance. Recrossing the square, Esther took a small
pouch of gold out of one of her bags and directed the
driver to wait for her behind the hotel.

She walked back across the corner of the plaza and
turned into the Bella Union. Three steps into the
smoky, crowded gaming room, she saw a man wearing
a holstered pistol. Ignoring the cool glances of several prostitutes, Esther beckoned the man outside.

"Is that pistol serviceable?"

The man, half-drunk, laughed, spraying her with liquor-sweetened saliva and sickening her with his breath. "Shoot the eye out'a Digger fifty yards away."

"Is it loaded?"

"Shore is, ma'am."

"How much will you take for it?"

"Won't take nothin' fer it. Need it. Can't get to sleep without it. This here's a crazy town."

Esther held out the gold pouch. "Will you take one hundred dollars in dust for it?"

"A hunnert dollars? You crazy? You kin buy one in'a mornin' fer less'n half that over't Folsom Hardware on Sagra . . . Sagramendo Street."

"I have to travel a ways tonight—without my husband. I need a weapon for protection."

"Can't do it, ma'am."

"One hundred twenty-five?"

"You say a hunnert twenty-*five*?"

"It's all I have."

"Can't pass that up," he said, unbuckling his gunbelt.

"I just want the pistol." She handed him the pouch and extracted the weapon from its leather holster.

"Here. You might as well take these." He fumbled with the bullets, trying to thumb them out of the snug pockets stitched into the black belt. When he looked up, she was already walking away.

She circled the Verandah once, holding the pistol in her open purse and noting the exits from the building. At the doorway, she glanced at the men hanging onto the bar and the half-dozen women in frilled corsets and high, colored stockings. The entire room blurred for a moment. She stopped and closed her eyes for several seconds until the faintness passed. Coldly, without thought, she eased her way through a cluster of bearded miners intently watching a game, then sidled past three Mexicans pleading for seats at one of the crowded tables. Above the din, the one-man band fought to be heard, but this time Esther scarcely noticed him.

She stopped a yard or so behind the rangy man with the moustache and looked around. No one was paying any attention to her. She scanned the table: a polyglot mix of bearded miners and more neatly dressed businessmen, all of them absorbed by the cards they had been dealt. Crouching as if to pick up something she had dropped, she slipped the pistol out of her purse. She could hear the man with the moustache say, "You're gonna lose this one, too," and then laugh again. It sounded exactly like the laugh she'd heard from Mosby as she lay semiconscious, face down in the snow. She struggled to keep from tearing at the back of his head with her hands.

Rising, she reached out and rapped the comb-back of the man's chair with the gun barrel. "Excuse me," she said, steeling herself for the noise the gun would make, the sight of him with his face torn apart, flying backward over the table.

The players looked up and paled. An old miner dropped his cards. Another gambler involuntarily put his hands up, palms out. A third with a plump Latin face pushed back from the table, his eyes bulging with fear.

The man with the moustache turned and froze in his seat when he saw the muzzle of the pistol pointing straight at his forehead.

Something is wrong, Esther thought. "Now hold on a minute . . . *please*," she heard the man say as her vision blurred again. The room was suddenly silent.

One of the professional dealers, wearing a stove-pipe hat, evening clothes, and a red sash around his waist, moved at the far end of the table. Retrieving the derringer he had strapped to his ankle, he pointed it at Esther and pulled the hammer back.

Esther's vision cleared. The man with the moustache, the man she was about to kill, had one cast-eye and a cleft chin. In full view, he looked nothing at all like Mosby. Paralyzed, Esther stared at the derringer pointing at her, the hand holding it flexing slightly. Realization that she was a woman had slowed the dealer's reaction; now her innocent, curious expression stopped his trigger finger in midsqueeze.

Esther lowered the barrel of her pistol. Her voice breaking with fast-draining emotion and embarrassment, she asked the gambler with the moustache: "Is this yours, sir? I . . . I stumbled on it as I was passing your table."

Ashen, the gambler wiped a hand across his mouth. "No, ma'am. I think . . ." He looked down at his own holstered weapon. "I think this here's mine . . . right here." He glanced up and saw the pistol Esther held was now pointed at his groin. He winced. "Would you *please* aim that thing someplace else? You're makin' me awful nervous."

Esther looked down at the pistol in her hand as though this were the first time she'd realized what it was. "Oh," she said, summoning as much innocence as she could muster. "Please forgive me. I know nothing about firearms."

There was a collective exhaling of breath around the table as the man with the moustache reached out very slowly and eased the barrel aside with the back of his hand. "Whooooooeeee," he said, as the dealer behind him put the derringer down. "Will someone buy this nice lady a drink? And count me out of the next few hands. I need a little air."

Lying in bed later that night at the Kelseys', Esther waited for the emotions she thought she had held in check to envelope her. Delayed fear, shame, guilt, embarrassment, anger—something. None came. After thinking about it vaguely, generally, disjointedly for more than a year, she had *wanted* to kill Mosby. That truth did not bother her. She wondered briefly if she were no better than Mosby in her hatred, her wanting revenge. She decided that was foolish. They had reasons for their behavior as different as fire and lightning. What did bother her was that such intense emotion and desire could rob her of common sense and reason. *Any one of those men could have killed me on the spot,* she thought. *It is a wonder I am still alive. Again.*

She got out of bed and stared through the window at the sea of lamp-lit canvas rectangles washing over the hills and hummocks below the Kelsey house. *I mustn't ever let my feelings overcome my wits again,* she thought. *In that direction lies nothing but failure.* And even if she had killed him, she wouldn't have survived the event herself. No, a way would present itself wherein she could have her revenge and live, kill him and still survive. Undetected. It would take time, and luck, and it would all begin with the knowledge she obtained from the Frémonts. And then, no matter how long it took her, she would do it properly, in a way that was foolproof. Letting her mind rule, rather than her passions.

Long after midnight she lay imagining the possible ways it might happen, savoring with each new setting the remembered feel and heft of the gun in her hand, the silken smoothness of the trigger under the soft flesh of her finger.

Forty-two

In Monterey, Esther could not at first believe her good fortune. Within an hour of her arrival, Barnett had given her Larkin's assurance that there would be no problem in acquiring land in the Mariposa region.

Then, not only did Barnett arrange for an introduction to the Frémonts, he somehow managed to have Esther invited to stay at the spacious hacienda they had rented that summer after Jessie Benton Frémont's arrival in California. She was ecstatic.

But Esther's hopes for an unforced, early conversation with Frémont about Mosby were quickly dampened. She found herself almost isolated, not easily in the presence of the "Pathfinder" or his wife, situated as she was in a guest room on the far end of a newly constructed wing. Not that it would have been a simple matter to gain their attention had she been given a room closer to the main portion of the house. Frémont was consumed by the convention, which had begun in early September. He was absent most of the time Esther was there. His wife was just as preoccupied. She had opened her home to forty-eight delegates from every district in California.

Cordial and hospitable, Jessie Benton Frémont nonetheless hurried on about her business each time Esther encountered her. Frémont himself scarcely noticed her after their first introduction. It was obvious that one thing was uppermost in both their minds: securing John Charles Frémont's senatorial nomination. Esther found herself with nothing to do. She began taking long walks through the quaint town, enjoying the look of the Spanish-tile roofs on the low, sprawling haciendas and the port's picturesque setting near the southern lip of an enormous halfmoon bay.

Four days slipped by, and the most Esther got out of Jessie Frémont was a passing: "Isn't it wonderful? They have signed into law a bill allowing women to control all property in their possession before marriage." Esther tried to engage Jessie in further conversation then, but the eyes of her attractive, indefatigable hostess drifted immediately to a group of delegates' wives who had just arrived for tea.

"We will talk another time," Esther said.

"Yes, forgive me," Jessie answered, her mind already on how she could win the new guests—and indirectly, their husbands—over to Frémont's cause. "You do understand? I will make it a point to spend time with you later this week."

Esther waited, read, for the most part avoided the endless gatherings in the patio and the hacienda's huge dining room, and walked—for hours. One afternoon, as she passed the general store Alex had run for Larkin, nostalgia and a painful sense of loss rocked her. Shutting it from her mind, she hurried on. Approaching the sandstone schoolhouse where the delegates were meeting, she saw John Sutter step out through the doorway of the building. He sat down on a bench, as though exhausted. He had aged drastically, his clothes were shabby and mended. And now, as he rested his head against the wall of the building, his eyes suddenly brimmed with tears.

Esther walked toward him. Unaware of her presence, he drew out a handkerchief, wiped at his eyes, blew his nose, and took a deep breath. She stopped several yards away, saw him try to shake off whatever was bothering him and pull himself together before going back in to the convention. As he stood up, he finally saw her.

"My child, my child," he said, beaming. "What a wonderful surprise."

She moved toward him, and they put their arms around one another. "You look well," she said.

"You flatter me. I look like something the dogs dragged in."

"I was watching you. What's the matter? Are you not feeling well?"

"Tired, my child," he said unconvincingly. "Just very tired."

"You are not telling me everything."

"Such a woman. You see through me so easily." He sighed. "It is just that . . ." He could not go on. The tears were brimming again.

"Please tell me. Perhaps I can help."

"I will not go into all of it, but I will say that it saddens me to be here."

"But you've aways wanted statehood for California."

"It is not that."

"Then why . . . Are things going well with your family—your wife?"

"She is an angel of patience and understanding. She has never once spoken harshly of my leaving Europe. We could not be getting along better."

"Then . . . ?"

"It simply pains me deeply to be here, partaking in this great endeavor when I . . ." He paused.

"Tell me, *please*."

"When I am . . . in such reduced circumstances. That is all I can say, *will* say, to you."

"Do you mean you wish you were still . . . ?" She didn't want to elaborate. "Before Brannan and the rest of them . . . ?"

"Yes," he said, gazing off. "That is it, essentially. I am no longer the man I was." He took a deep breath and gave Esther another squeeze. "You look so beautiful, my child. I must go back in now. They will be taking a vote on whether California will be a slave or free state. And everyone against slavery must be heard. We will spend some time together again?"

"Of course. I'll be here a short while longer before returning to San Francisco."

"We will have dinner together. I will send you a note at the Frémonts', yes?"

"Please," she said. "I do so want to talk with you more."

When Sutter went through the doorway after embracing her again, Esther turned and saw Jessie Benton Frémont riding toward the Calle Principal in an open carriage with the wife of Andres Pico, the Californio delegate from San Jose. Jessie smiled coolly

and noddded at Esther before the carriage continued
on.

Barnett came bounding out of the building. "We've
done it!" he shouted, as elated as a schoolboy. "California will be a state of free men!" Before Esther had
a chance to respond, Barnett added, "Forgive me. I
must hurry to post the news to San Francisco. I spoke
to Larkin this morning, and it is all arranged. Your
land purchase. As soon as I have a moment, I'll have
the builders begin work. You did say Spanish rancho
style?"

"Yes . . ."

"Then that's that," he said, turning. He glanced
back as he hurried off down the street. "I'm sorry
I've so little time. I'll make amends in San Francisco
when all this is over."

She watched him disappear around a corner and
then resumed her long walk toward the high bluff
that overlooked the Pacific. There, away from the
noise and bustle of the town, the convention crowds,
the drummers and tradesmen hawking everything
from pencils to hosiery, she turned her attention back
to Sutter. *He knew I was staying at the Frémonts'*,
she thought, *yet he made no effort to contact me.*
Something was wrong. There was more to what was
troubling him than he revealed.

No word, no invitation came from Sutter. But three
days later her suspicions were confirmed when she
walked out onto the Frémont patio. Jessie was putting
last-minute touches on a dozen table settings.

"You're not angry with me for my unforgivable
rudeness?" Jessie said, not stopping. "I have meant to
spend some time with you, but . . ."

"You've been overwhelmed. I know how busy you
are. And I understand. Of course I'm not angry.
You've been more than kind to have me as your
guest."

"This business will be the death of me," Jessie said,
waving a hand histrionically over all the elaborate

tables, as though she didn't actually relish it. She
sighed and collapsed into a chair.

Esther sat down beside her. "There is someone I
would like to ask you about. An acquaintance of
mine. . . ."

"Mr. Sutter?" Jessie asked, raising her eyebrows.
"My dear, he seemed, if you will forgive me, far more
than an acquaintance."

Esther fought off the urge to impale her verbally.
"Captain Sutter? Oh, no. I wasn't speaking of him.
He is a dear friend. Like a . . . like an uncle to me.
He has been very helpful."

"Well, that's a relief to hear. This is a land of,
shall we say, peculiar relationships. One never knows
what to expect of anyone. Of course, I try to keep
a broad mind about such things."

For a moment, Esther felt a surge of jealousy as
well as annoyance. *Her heart-shaped face is so perfect,* she thought. And her figure . . . so exquisite.
The daughter of a U.S. Senator. The wife of . . . for
a fleeting moment, Esther wondered what it would
be like to have a normal life. A home. A husband.

"Poor man," Jessie went on. "It's a pity he will not
allow his friends to extricate him from his troubles."

"I haven't spoken to him for some time, except for
the other day, briefly. What troubles?"

"As you probably know, he's already had his share,"
Jessie went on. "And now this Peter Corbett thing.
Totally unjust. Just the same, one would think Sutter
might have learned his lesson. No one denies he was
cheated, or that stripping him—and others—of title
to lands granted by the Mexicans is unjust, or that
the squatters already overrunning what remains of
his property are in the wrong; but it still makes no
sense for a man who has lost so much through prof-
ligacy to continue being a spendthrift."

"How do you know that is true?" Esther asked,
finding it increasingly difficult to contain her pique.

"How does anyone know? My Lord, the man enter-tains friends and hordes of strangers alike in a manner that would tax a millionaire. Nonetheless, this Corbett business is shameful."

"Corbett?"

"A Sacramento land-trader who will have nothing less than the governorship. It would be a disgrace to the new state, I tell you. Imagine such a man in the executive office!"

"What has he against Sutter?"

"Sutter is a strident voice against him at the convention. Corbett knew he would be, and tried to prevent him from coming here as a delegate. First he disgraced Sutter publicly during the delegates' election. By having a man Sutter still owes several thousand dollars press for repayment. Sutter didn't have the means, as Corbett knew from the outset, and the next step was to initiate a legal action to dispossess Sutter from his farm. It's a valuable piece of property, I'm told. Corbett and Brannan have coveted it for some time."

Shocked, Esther couldn't believe the extent of John Sutter's pride. "He's lost the Hock Farm?"

"Not yet. The convention has delayed the case. But Corbett hasn't missed an opportunity to make the matter public here. He's succeeded in humiliating Sutter completely. And you can be sure he'll have the property when all this convention business is over."

"How much did you say Sutter owes?" Esther asked, exasperated. Why had he let things go so far without asking her for help!

"Four thousand dollars is the figure I've heard."

"Perhaps one of his friends will pay the debt for him."

"Perhaps," Jessie said, getting up. "And now I must . . ."

"I was going to ask you a question before we were sidetracked by this sad business about Sutter," Esther said quickly. "It will only take a minute."

"Just a moment, then. I *must* get back to the kitchen."

"I . . . had the pleasure of meeting a gentleman once . . . while I was journeying west. A man who was a member of one of your husband's remarkable expeditions."

Jessie smiled proudly. "Yes, which man, dear? I must hurry."

"A man named Luther Mosby. Whatever became of him?"

"I don't have the faintest idea. But perhaps John does. He's kept track of most of those ruffians." She paused for a moment, staring at Esther. "Perhaps I speak out of turn, but I would be wary of Mosby. Beneath his silky, Southern manner there lurks a male beast. Oh, my goodness, I've spoken out of turn. Is he a friend?"

"No, I met him only briefly."

"Then why do you ask of him?"

"It seems he was at the Alamo, or near it . . ."

"Far enough away to avoid the fate of braver men," Jessie cut in acidly. "From what I hear, he has tried to mask that act of cowardice with brutality and violence ever since."

"I believe a relative of mine was either at the Alamo itself or with Colonel Fannin's troops, where Mr. Mosby repaired just before the siege. I thought perhaps Mosby might have some word of him. My . . . cousin didn't return home at the close of the Mexican War."

"Why didn't you ask Mosby when you met? Where did you say it was?"

Apprehensive, Esther hesitated a moment. "It must have been at Bent's Fort, in '46," she finally said. "I meant to ask him, but he and Colonel Frémont were gone the following morning when I sought him out."

"Well, as I said, *I* don't know." Jessie was obviously restive. "But John might. Why don't you ask him

this evening? You *are* going to be with us for dinner
and the dance that will follow? We've hardly seen
you at table."

"For dinner. . . . I'm not too taken with dancing,
with large crowds." She paused for a second. "Your
husband . . . is so *busy*. I'm sure he'll not have
time—"

"I'll speak to him. Surely he can spare a moment to
help someone seeking information about a patriotic
relative."

"Thank you. You've been most kind, and I must let
you get on with your preparations for this evening."

"Think nothing of it." Jessie started to turn away,
then hesitated. "Would you mind if I asked you a
personal question?"

"Why, no."

"It is none of my business. But I simply cannot
control my curiosity at times."

"Please," Esther said, steeling herself, sure Jessie
was going to ask something that might possibly lead
her to reveal her intentions about Mosby.

"It's just that . . . I . . . I simply cannot understand
why you wear a hat and a veil so often. Almost
. . . without fail. I can see that you have a lovely
face from its outlines, and I cannot for the life of
me . . ."

"I have a scar," Esther said, relieved, drawing in
a deep breath, controlling her feelings. "Suffered in
an accident coming west." She lifted her gloved left
hand. "And two fingers missing on this hand. That
is why I wear gloves around strangers, as well."

Jessie winced, sucked in an embarrassed breath,
and brought the back of her hand to her mouth. "Oh,
dear. I'm *so* sorry. I should never have asked."

"It's quite all right. I suppose avoiding crowds of
people and preferring to dine alone does seem odd."

Jessie gently put her hand on Esther's forearm.
"You poor dear. And so young. Well, don't you worry,

I'll see to it John and you have a moment alone in the study before dinner. You can be sure of it."

The early arrivals were mingling and talking in the patio when Jessie ushered Esther into a book-lined room off a long hallway toward the front of the house. Frémont, preoccupied with a map of California, turned when they came in, and his wife explained Esther's quest for information.

"You are in luck, young lady," Frémont said, gazing at Esther with the most soulful eyes she had ever seen. "I have had no call to keep in touch with Mosby myself, since he chose, characteristically, to desert my forces when we were in the . . . pitch of battle . . . here in early '47. But I did receive a letter from Kit Carson just a week ago. Kit mentioned he heard Mosby is now a U.S. Marshal . . . in south-central Texas, I believe. Some vague business about studying the law in his spare time. I would not have been informed, I would guess, but that Carson thought it amusing. The idea of Mosby a lawyer, I mean—or, God forbid, a judge."

"I don't know the man well." Esther's heart began to beat faster. "The humor of it escapes me."

"Let us say," Frémont said, weighing his words, "that Luther Mosby has yet to show the integrity, the loyalty, one would expect of a man of the bar."

"I would like to write him, regarding my . . . my cousin." Esther held her breath.

"His exact whereabouts I cannot give you. Kit did not mention precisely where he was. But I would imagine you could obtain it easily enough by writing the proper agency in Washington."

And that, Esther thought, crestfallen, numb with disappointment as Frémont droned on about how to go about writing the letter, *might reveal to him that I am alive.*

Frémont came around from behind his desk and

put his arm around her. "Have patience, dear woman," he said consolingly. "And faith. God usually helps someone with as much familial love as you obviously have in your heart."

Forty-three

Mariposa Ranch
December 28, 1849

Moved into this half-finished ranch house in November. (Barnett, bless his soul, has seen to everything, including the building.) I wish you could see it, Alex. When it is finished, it will be a home you would be proud of. I know you would love the silence of this wild and beautiful country. As I look out my window, it glistens even in this damnable rain that has hardly let up since the beginning of the month. It snows higher in the mountains, but here the roads have turned into rivers of mud.

No chance to write in this journal until now. . . . Busy arranging for furniture to be shipped here, and a thousand other little items that one is swamped with when establishing a new residence. The builders are proceeding apace, but what a racket they make! Some of the furniture has arrived. Thank goodness Murietta saw fit to bring the hide bed after I informed him of my whereabouts. A marvelously subtle hint, if those were his thoughts. But you have nothing to be concerned about, Alex. My intentions will not change in the matter, and although Murietta was more at ease with me during his visit, he knows where I stand and takes great pains not to crowd me.

Have thought many times about that night in San

Francisco when I believed I saw Mosby. A small voice within me would like to banish such vengeful tendencies, but I tell you, a larger voice shouts it down. I know I will not be at peace until I have dealt with him. It took me several weeks to get over the deep disappointment, no, despondence I felt when Frémont informed me of Mosby's return to Texas. For a time, I despaired also that there was no way on earth that anyone, let alone a woman, could bring a U.S. Marshal down on his home ground. But while that is true, I began thinking about the extraordinary turns my life has taken since we last held one another. One simply never knows. And for the time being I am simply going to wait to see what happens. It is possible that Mosby may one day return to California. If he does not, I will simply continue to build my financial strength against the day when I can seek him out, wherever he is.

So much for him. Happy as a purring cat with the old Mexican woman, Marianita, and her husband, Emilio, whom I have hired to help me. The Frémonts' place is some ten miles southeast of here. They have invited me to dinner, but thus far, I have declined. Much as I find the woman small and abrasive, I am happy for Jessie about John Charles's election, along with the Southerner William Gwin, as U.S. Senator. Considering that California is yet to be recognized, it would seem more practical being elected State Senator, as was Warren Barnett's good fortune following the convention in Monterey.

Received a note from Barnett concerning the Sutter business. All has worked out well for the poor man. After returning to the Kelseys', I arranged to have a draft of four thousand dollars transferred to the Bank of Monterey and delivered, anonymously, to Sutter. I would like to have seen the look on his dear face when he opened the envelope. And on Peter Corbett's, when he learned that Sutter had paid the debt. I suppose Sutter could find out who sent the money if he had a mind to and was persistent. I hope he will not.

I do not know just what Frémont will do as a senator in

Washington until California is admitted to the Union. But whatever that spellbindingly ascetic-looking gentleman accomplishes, it will not be without wifely support. I must confess to you, Alex, that I found myself exceedingly jealous of the woman. Of the way she looks. Of that enviable mind. It is always ticking, strategizing, arranging, and manipulating the strings for future puppeteering. How well I could use such mental capability in an effort to ensnare Mr. Mosby. Jealous, too, of the life she has, the home, the husband, all the things I do not. But most of all, now, her beauty. I would admit such a thing only to you. Is it not silly of me?

The prattle of a jealous girl of twenty with a horrible nose! I will try the face-colors and rouge I bought in San Francisco from the little peddler lady outside the Bella Union. Perhaps a delicate application will conceal the whiteness, with equally subtle blending of cheek color, without making me look like a strumpet. Little need of it here, however. But it will be interesting to try in the event I travel abroad of these parts.

Which, of course, I will be doing early in the coming year. I do not like the continuing reports of depredation and viciousness directed against the Indians. I must speak of such matters to Miwokan. The thought of placing little Moses in a mission school grows more practical, and now, a matter of safety, one would guess, with each passing month. I will think on it and perhaps make a decision before journeying to Sacramento City in January. I pray for your health, dear husband, and do miss you so.

Forty-four

In early January, Esther rode up to the South Fork by buckboard, old Emilio at the reins and one of her saddle horses trailing the rig. It rained off and on during most of the trip, and more than once the old man had to lay logs and branches where the road had turned into a quagmire. Noting how exhausted he was, she sent Emilio back to Mariposa after a night's rest at the cabin, then spent most of the following morning going over accounts with Murietta. Shortly after lunch they unharnessed the buckboard team, saddled up, and headed for Miwokan's village.

All the way up from the ranch she had been excited over the prospect of attending her first play at the new Eagle Theater. Barnett's last letter mentioned he would be in Sacramento City during the first week of 1850. In a postscript he had added that, should she happen to be there for any reason as well, he would take her to see Mrs. Henry Ray, of The Royal Theater of New Zealand, in *The Bandit Chief*. The timing was perfect, but her eagerness was diluted by a mixture of concerns as she made the long, wet journey northward. Violence against the Indians had increased everywhere in northern California, and her fears for Moses—and everyone else at Miwokan's camp—had been the source of several nightmares.

Now, as she and Murietta worked their way eastward along the muddy bank of the South Fork and it began to drizzle again, he put her at ease: There had been no signs of trouble. The village was far enough out of the way to be overlooked. He saw no reason why things would not continue as peacefully in the future, at least in this area. Still, more of Miwokan's tribesmen had left after the work had been halted in December.

"He has held half of them together," Murietta said, "in the face of constant temptation to disband and go their separate ways."

"Into a white world he is certain will destroy them."

"That is what he believes, and I believe it will happen, also, to those who try to live as we do."

Esther sighed. "Their leaving saddens me for many reasons."

"It has been a great strain on Miwokan," Murietta continued. "He wishes to keep them together, and he is also deeply troubled that soon there will not be enough left to keep his promises to you."

Esther was shocked to see how much Miwokan had aged when he greeted them at the village. There was something else, something beyond what she knew was eating away at him, but she could not put her finger on it. When she embraced him, he quickly pulled away and called out to Solana. The Indian woman burst out of their hut, trailing the two boys behind her, delighted to see Esther after so long. Solana kissed Esther on both cheeks and hugged her, but then she glanced past Esther and saw it: Miwokan couldn't keep his eyes off her. Quickly, she turned her attention to the two children. Esther couldn't understand why Solana, too, had retreated emotionally, but she let it go for the moment as each of the tribesmen and their wives came out into the heavy drizzle to welcome her.

Later, Esther asked Murietta to accompany her to Sacramento the following morning. Over her shoulder the Californio saw a fleeting but unmistakable look of pain and longing cross Miwokan's face. Esther missed it, and she was somewhat surprised when Murietta wisely decided to return and wait for her at the cabin.

Then she couldn't understand why Miwokan suddenly found things to do in the rain and did not reappear all afternoon.

For a moment she wondered if it had to do with the feelings he once had for her. *But I have been gone for months,* she thought. And Murietta has been here. Remembering what Miwokan had said about never letting his jealousy dominate him again, she dismissed the idea. Still troubled, she sat with Solana in the central hut watching two-and-a-half-year-old Moses, dressed in deerskins, resolutely playing simple games with Mwamwaash and several other children their age. For a while she was preoccupied with the boy and what she should do about him. Aside from the ripple of unexplained uneasiness in Miwokan and his wife, a feeling of peace reigned at the village. Her apprehensions about Moses' safety suddenly seemed exaggerated, and she decided to leave him with Solana for a while longer. Finally, her thoughts back on Miwokan, she turned to the Indian woman.

"Your husband acts strangely toward me. Is he not well? Is there something I don't know?"

Solana remained silent.

Esther reached out and took her hand. "Tell me. Please. Is he ill?"

"Only here and here," Solana said, touching her temple and then her heart. "He is saddened by the loss of so many brothers. Saddened more by how many he knows will leave here."

"It's the gold," Esther said, thinking of the legend. Suddenly, she was so forlorn she had to bite her lip to keep from crying. "And he thinks it is my fault."

"You are a part of it," Solana said guardedly. "But not in the way you think. In many ways you have helped him keep them together. They work for you, their chief's sunsister, and Miwokan. They love both of you, and that binds them. They have some of the gold without leaving, because you are generous to them."

"I wanted them to share . . ."

"I know. They could have had much more. I think it is wise that Miwokan did what he did. And no one here would speak against it. But they hear how much more they can have elsewhere. They believe what Miwokan says about the sun's anger is true only here. Their brothers come and show them the bright things they have bought, and pour Claussen's whiskey into them. It does not take much after that."

"Claussen?"

"If not from that man's still, there are many others who make it."

"But whites are forbidden to sell liquor to them."

"Some here are secretly going to the store Claussen has made in Placerville. I have seen them go in."

"But the new laws—"

"Mean nothing," Solana interrupted, "when an Indian has gold and men like Claussen want it."

"The gold again. And I am a part of it all."

"Do not trouble yourself with that. He knows that if you had never been born, this would have come."

As they ate by firelight in the central hut, one side of which had been torn away and enlarged with canvas, Miwokan drifted off in his own thoughts. He scarcely looked at Esther. When she spoke to him, he answered as briefly as possible. With his fur cape off and the dancing light of the fire etching the deep creases in his wan face, his loss of weight was startlingly obvious. When he finally rose and left the hut, most of his meal uneaten, Esther experienced a sudden stab of anguish.

She weighed the effect on Miwokan if she stayed at the cabin with Murietta, and she decided to remain overnight at the camp. Settled in an abandoned hut, wrapped in furs and wearing only her chemise, she lay staring for hours at the fire. Unable to sleep, she pulled one of the furs around her, slipped on some moccasins, moved the bark door covering to one side, and stepped through the entrance flap into the clearing.

The rain clouds had passed. Moonless, the night sky was awash with brilliant stars. She looked straight up and saw the pale white streak of the Milky Way overhead. She wondered for a moment how far away it was, but then a sound and a movement to her right caught her attention.

Two human shadows played against a thin, canvas-covered enlargement of Miwokan's shelter. At first Esther was puzzled, but then it became obvious that inside, Solana was attempting to arouse her husband's sexual interest. Esther felt a tremor in her loins. Embarrassed, she began to turn away, but the shadows moved again, riveting her attention and overriding her normal sense of propriety. The breasted shadow of Solana hovered, now, over her husband. She massaged and then mounted him and moved slowly up and down. Almost overcome by long-suppressed desire, Esther forced herself to turn away. She had just entered her own hut when she heard Miwokan growl, *"No!"*

Esther turned just inside the entrance to her hut and saw Miwokan push Solana off, rise, and come stalking out of the hut. He stopped and looked around but did not see Esther watching him. For a moment he gazed straight ahead, then glanced quickly at her hut. She saw him take in a deep breath, let it out, then walk, head bent, across the central clearing. Esther waited a moment, then stepped outside. Across the camp she saw Miwokan disappear into the sunken sweathouse. *It is I*, she thought. Sadness enveloped her. Sighing, not knowing what she could do, she was about to return to her sleeping throw when she saw Solana watching her from in front of the main hut. Gathering the fur around her again, Esther walked slowly to where the Indian woman stood. There were tears in her eyes. Esther reached out and embraced her.

"It fills me with pain to see him this way. I couldn't sleep. I came out of the hut for a moment, and I couldn't help but see . . . "

"Go to him," Solana said, quickly regaining control of her emotions.

"Go to him? I don't understand."

"Go to him and heal him—any way you can."

"But *you* are his wife. He loves you."

Solana looked at her and smiled sadly. "Know that I have no bad feelings for you as I speak this. I know you have done no wrongs. But you are more of his pain than anyone or anything else. He feels a hollow place in him since you are gone. He would have it another way, I know that. He would be done with it. But he cannot kill what is in him for you."

"But he loves *you*. And you love him."

"Each is true," Solana said, her eyes drifting downward. "That is why he has not sent me away. And that is why I ask you to do this thing."

"But I do not feel . . . I have never . . ."

"You make too much of it, as all whites do. It will be no different than lying with someone sick and cold."

"You don't understand! It *is* more than that to me. I can't . . ."

Solana's eyes flashed with anger. "You will not do this for him, your sunbrother? Or for me, when I care for your child as my own?"

"Oh, *God*. I can't!"

"You can. And you will. You have the strength to do it. He lay upon you when you were like ice. He carried you to Sutter when that was not enough to heal you. For two of your years, his people have worked in the icy river so you would have the gold. He found a way to do this only because *you* wanted to. *Go to him!*"

At the entrance to the sweathouse, Esther trembled as she watched Miwokan inside. Stark naked, he stood a yard or so from the central firepit, fanning embers and new logs he had placed beneath an ingeniously suspended platform of smooth, round stones. There was no one else in the large, open-peaked enclosure. Torn by conflicting emotions, she stared, mesmerized by the sight of his extraordinary body. Confused as well as fascinated, she watched as he poured a finely ground powder into a large bowl of water and threw it on the heated stones. A cloud of steam rose above the fire as she stepped into the hut. Lost in his own thoughts, he did not see or hear her. She could not take her eyes off him. In the soft firelight, the loss of weight served only to accentuate the remarkable musculature of his torso, arms, and legs, the perfect shape and proportion of his dark genitals.

She inhaled silently, and her lungs were filled with the pungent steam that was rising and spreading out from the stones. He put more of the powder in the bowl, refilled it with water from a barrel, and placed it on the warm rock-wall of the firepit. Her heart raced as she inhaled deeply again, trying not to be heard. Suddenly, then, in the midst of her indecisiveness, her soul searching, the tension left her and she began to feel as if she were floating.

She looked at his face as he tamped some of the finely ground powder into the deep bowl of a long pipe. She found herself wanting to reach out and smother the sadness in his eyes with a mother's kisses, take his head in her arms and soothe him like a child. Her gaze dropped to his loins again, and a wave of raw animal desire washed over her. For a second, as she continued to breathe in the moist, aromatic steam that now filled the hut, fear and reluctance licked at her mind. Then, in rapid succession, she thought obliquely of Alex, Murietta, and John Alexander. Desire, compassion, tenderness, and sexual arousal blended together, flooding through her and wiping away all thought. She dropped the fur on the earth floor of the hut and took a step toward him.

He heard the sound, turned, and frowned. "This place is forbidden to women."

Slightly giddy now, she stopped two yards from him and smiled. "You are the chief. You can change the rule."

He sighed. "I have changed one rule too many for you already."

"What is it you put in the water? In your pipe? It makes me feel wonderful."

"You cannot be here," he said evenly. But she had seen his eyes fastened on her breasts, rising and falling beneath her chemise.

"Tell me what you put in the water."

"The crushed seeds of a desert flower."

"What is it called?"

"In your language it would be called 'the dust of living dreams.' Why have you come here?"

She took another step toward him, breathing deeply. She no longer felt her body. She could scarcely remember who she was. "I have come to offer myself to you."

"You would do this?" Within the aroma of the steam he could smell her hair, the scent of lilac water, and faint traces of her body. He forced his eyes away from her.

"I have caused you much pain," she said, swaying. "I will wash it away."

"I have a wife." He looked at her again, saw the exquisitely tapered silhouette of her legs through the thin fabric.

"She sent me. She asked me to heal your pain."

He was astonished. "She did this thing?"

"Yes. She loves you. You are her husband. And I love you. You are my sunbrother."

He felt himself begin to engorge, rise, then saw her smile as she watched it happen. He took a step forward and pulled the chemise up over her head. For a moment he stared at the long-imagined lines of her full breasts and pale, slender body, the dark hair at the base of her flat stomach. Almost overcome, he swung his right arm back, throwing the chemise behind him. Wadded, it hit the bowl of steaming water on the wall of the firepit and knocked it over onto the red-hot stones. The water hissed, and a spray of boiling droplets struck both of them. Tears formed in Esther's eyes from the sharp, brief, stinging pain. As the droplets burned against his leg, Miwokan suddenly understood.

It is a sign, he thought. *The sun is testing me.* In the clarity of that fleeting moment of pain, he realized the full extent of his wife's love, how much Esther loved him to be here, doing what she had no wish for. Then, as he reached out and gently brushed away the tears brimming on Esther's eyelids, it became clear to him that lying with her would only make things worse. She would hate him for it. She would be gone again, and the remembered joy would haunt him. Solana would be with him, but no matter how much she loved him, thought this would heal him, it would change things forever between them. *They are women,* he thought. *They mean well, but they cannot see what this would do to all of us. I will not be a woman, and I will not fail in this.*

Esther moved forward and touched his cheek. *My God,* she thought, *his face is beautiful.*

"We will smoke this together first," he said, relighting the pipe with a glowing twig and handing it to her.

"Why?" she asked.

"It will make it easier for you. Better."

"I have never smoked. How shall I do it?"

He placed the tip of the pipe shaft on her lips. "As you would breathe the air in with your mouth."

She sucked at the pipe and coughed. "Wait," she said, recovering. "I will try again."

He watched as she drew in the smoke and inhaled it this time. "Again." She took in a long draw. "Close your mouth and hold it in your body until you cannot any longer." He saw her eyes tear and glaze over and caught her as she staggered. She let the smoke out. "And again."

When she passed out, he gently dropped the chemise back over her body, wrapped the fur around her, and picked her up in his arms. Still naked, he carried her across the snow-covered clearing. Twenty feet from the entrance to her hut, he veered and went into his own. Smiling at Solana, he laid Esther down next to the sleeping boys in one corner, covered her, then turned and walked to his waiting wife.

Once, when the effect of the narcotic had almost worn off, Esther opened her eyes in the middle of what she thought was a dream. She heard gentle laughter from beyond a fire that glowed inexplicably in the center of Miwokan's hut, rather than her own. She drifted off, then awakened again. She saw and heard them together, Miwokan above his wife, the two of them moving rhythmically beyond the embers, shadows playing on their bronze, moist bodies, until, finally, she heard them both moan with joy.

Forty-five

An overcast sky obscured the early evening stars as Esther emerged from the doorway of Sacramento's City Hotel just after dinner. The rains of December and the first week of 1850 had turned Front Street, along the Embarcadero, into a bog. Turning left, Esther began walking the short distance beyond the C. M. and T. Company building to the Eagle Theater. She was early, and though the clouds were threatening again, she decided to stroll a block or two before coming back to meet Warren Barnett for the evening performance.

She passed G. B. Stevens's store on the corner of Front and J Streets, glanced left, and shook her head. A half-block away a crater at least two-dozen feet in diameter marred the middle of the street where an oak tree had been callously ripped from the earth. On both sides wooden houses and stores had been built almost as far as the eye could see. Crossing J, Esther passed a long, clapboard warehouse, the Eldorado Exchange, and then a grocery. She stepped around a Maidu Indian dressed in a red-flannel shirt and rumpled trousers two sizes too big. He was too drunk to feel the nip of a raw, slowly rising wind on his bruised, bare feet. Up the street, a group of winter-idled miners brushed past another intoxicated Maidu, jostling and almost knocking him off his feet as they entered the Elephant House Hotel, bulging pouches hanging from their belts.

They have "come to see the elephant," Esther thought gloomily, employing the forty-niners' slang term for California and the gold fields. They are seeing it—and the Indians are feeling its sharp-pointed tusks.

Esther turned back as a light drizzle began to fall, and took a seat in the back row of the empty theater where Barnett could easily spot her when he arrived. *How long will it be before more of Miwokan's men succumb completely to the whiskey, the gold and the gambling?* Esther wondered. She sighed as her thoughts turned to Solana and her husband. As clearly as though it were happening again, she pictured saying good-bye to Solana three mornings earlier.

She had awakened in their hut, groggy and beset by the worst headache she had ever experienced. The village was so silent she could hear the rush of the rain-swollen river more than fifty yards away. Mortified, she stared mutely out through the hut entrance at the sweathouse. Solana prepared breakfast and helped her dress without mention of the previous night, her husband, or how Esther had ended up sleeping near the children. Miwokan was gone, off on a hunting sortie with several young braves. Despondent, scarcely aware that the sun had finally broken through the storm clouds, Esther slowly prepared to leave. She was about to climb into her saddle, ride to the cabin and then on to Sacramento in the buckboard with Murietta, when Solana reached out and touched the amulet hanging from her neck.

"Perhaps the gold heart made it work out well," the Indian woman said, smiling.

"Work out *well?*" Esther gasped. "I can never come here again!"

Solana stroked Esther's hair. "But nothing happened."

"Everything happened!" Esther said, trying not to cry.

"You passed out from what was in the pipe, and the sweating air."

"But that doesn't mean he . . ."

"What I thought . . . what I hoped would happen, happened. He saw what it would do to us, to his friendship with you. He knew how much I loved him to do this thing. And he carried you back here after giving you enough of the smoke to make you sleep. Then he came to me in our bed as he did when he was a young brave. And again, before anyone was awake this morning."

Esther's mouth dropped open. "And we did not? Nothing happened?"

"Nothing," Solana said, smiling happily.

"You actually thought it would not happen?"

"I knew two things could happen. That he would see things clearly, as he did. Or that you would lie with him, and afterward you would never come back. In time, knowing you hated him for it, knowing you would not be with him again, the pain in him would pass and he would force you from his mind. Which way did not matter. I knew that one or the other would give him back to me."

"But he might have hated you."

"No, Sunsister. . . . In time, he would see how wise it was for me to do this thing. He might not love me as before, but he would not send me away. But that does not matter. The dream dust and the amulet have been kind to me. He loves me now as he has not for many winters. And that is good. It will help him live with the changes as the end for us draws near."

"The end? It doesn't have to be that way!"

"It will come, Sunsister. And we will change. Not as you said it might be when you spoke to him at the waterfall. We will eat mice, but we will live, and we will be together. And that will be enough until the sun takes us back."

Remembering their final, half-happy, half-sad embrace, Esther wiped at her eyes as she waited in the partially filled theater. When Barnett arrived and sat down next to her, it was practically jammed.

"Forgive me for being late. Minor, unexpected difficulties. There has been a change in my plans, and I have the time to accompany you back to Mariposa, if you like."

For a moment Esther had a fleeting suspicion that Barnett might also be succumbing to an infatuation. "I had tentatively planned to go back with Murietta."

"Oh, well," he said, glancing at the program, obviously only slightly disappointed. "I thought I'd see for myself just how well my orders have been carried out by the builders."

Relieved and embarrassed by her quick assumption, she thought for a moment about how much less awkward it might be for her if Barnett did accompany her, rather than the Californio. "The plans are

not definite. . . . Why don't you? You could go on
from the ranch by stagecoach."

"Yes, I thought I'd stay briefly, a few hours, and
then, if you were kind enough to have me driven
to Coulterville, go on to San Jose from there."

"We could stop at the South Fork to let Murietta
know. I'm sure he'll be delighted not to have to make
the long round-trip."

"I can attend to some business in Placerville. Would
you mind stopping there briefly?"

"I'm not too taken with that place. But I can visit
with Joaquin at the cabin until you've finished."

"Fine," he said, craning his neck, fascinated by the
people around them. Chuckling, he leaned over and
whispered: "We certainly have a mixed lot of characters here tonight, do we not?"

Well-dressed women and their merchant husbands
sniffed and murmured disdainfully as the last of the
bench-row seats were filled by miners coming in
through a side entrance from the Round Tent, a saloon and gambling hall adjacent to the wood-frame,
canvas-covered building. An usher removed someone
from the seat next to Esther, and a well-dressed young
man with muttonchop whiskers took his place. He
nodded at Esther and took out a notepad bearing a
stamped *New York Tribune* on its cover. The air in
the auditorium was stifling, and the sound of rain on
canvas rose appreciably in volume.

Toward the end of the melodrama, the New Zealand–born leading lady threw herself prostrate in the
middle of the stage. Turning to a knight in purple,
attempting to outdo the now pelting raindrops and
flapping canvas along the walls, the actress moaned,
then shouted, "You're me only 'ope. *Me only 'ope!*"

The *Tribune* correspondent turned, smiled, and
whispered to Esther, "*Me* only 'ope is to get out of
'ere before I suffocate from the lack of air and talent."

Suddenly with a roar and tearing of canvas, a wall
of water burst through the side of the building and

flooded the stage, taking the entire cast with it. In seconds, the orchestra was inundated, each man swimming for himself in the pit, instruments floating like jetsam from a sunken vessel. Next the audience received the brunt of the cascade; the playgoers, dressed in heavy overcoats, knee-high boots, and long, full-skirted dresses, were floundering, falling, screaming, and attempting to climb up on submerged benches. The correspondent next to Esther grabbed one arm just as Warren Barnett took the other, and together they lifted her onto a bench.

"Bayard Taylor," the *Tribune* correspondent shouted, reaching out to shake hands, still clutching his notepad.

"Barnett. William Barnett," Warren said, more than unnerved. "I mean *Warren* Barnett."

Esther broke into a peal of laughter. It rose to a hysterical pitch as she watched another wave of water smash in under the flapping canvas siding and bowl the three of them off the bench. Before she went under, she saw Barnett and Taylor picked up and tossed yards away like life-sized dolls. She came up and a heavy-set miner washed into her from two rows forward. Scrambling, he pushed her under and clutched desperately at the bench. It toppled slowly in the water, turning until it wedged beneath a nailed-down seat and trapped Esther.

She could not move. The coldness made the bridge of her nose ache. Opening her eyes, she saw the hazy light of the gas lamps not four feet above her, beyond the surface of the frigid water. The man who had pushed her under was gone. She started to gasp for air involuntarily, felt the water trickle down her throat, and fought the urge to breathe. The water gagged her, and she coughed. Closing her mouth quickly, she put one hand over it and tried not to panic. Reaching down with her other hand, she pushed at the bench pinning her to the floor of the auditorium. It moved, but then it wedged even more firmly as one end slipped beneath another bench to her left. Someone scrambled by, stepping on her and sending sharp stabs of pain through shin and shoulder. Only seconds had passed, but it seemed infinitely longer.

Oh, God, she thought. *Just one breath of air.* An image of Alex floated through her mind. Then her father . . . sister . . . old Miss Cable . . . John Alexander. *I'm going to die.* She was surprised that she felt no fear—it was simply a fact: *I'm going to die.* Her stomach tightening in spasms, she was numbly, clinically aware of the strange, swollen sensation of crying under water.

Now it was Mosby's face hanging in front of her, laughing. *I will never have the chance to kill you now . . . Bastard!* The anger galvanized her. *I will not die. I . . . will . . . not . . . die. . . .* Her lungs knotted. She took her hand from her mouth and pushed at the bench with both arms as hard as she could. It wouldn't budge. She knew it was useless and gave in. Staring up through the water, she wondered when she would be forced to open her mouth and let it in. She thought of Alex again.

Oddly, it was not Alex she saw hovering over her just above the surface now, but Barnett. She watched as a frantic miner pulled at Barnett's coat, saw him push the man away and take hold of the bench lying across her chest. He pulled at it, and the cords in his neck grew taut. He moved to the right, grabbed the bench again and, bracing his forearm under it, heaved up with every muscle in his enormous body just as she passed out.

Barnett relaxed once, then yanked upward again, tearing the bench free. Throwing it aside, he reached down and picked Esther up in his arms. Semiconscious, she coughed up a half-pint of water and began sucking in deep breaths of air. Surprised that she was still alive, Barnett waded, hip-deep, toward the door of the theater. Still spitting up small amounts of water, Esther hung dazed in his arms as he pushed toward the City Hotel, two buildings away.

Once, before they reached it, she saw the body of an Indian drift past. Even through half-closed eyes she knew it was the drunken Maidu she had seen sprawled on the sidewalk earlier. Near the flooded hotel entrance, an old man floated by on a cot, pleading hoarsely for help. She tried to lift her arm and reach out to him, but all her energy was spent. The strain of the effort made her close her eyes for a moment. When she opened them again, the old man had disappeared in the darkness.

Soaked through, she began to regain full consciousness as Barnett carried her up the stairs and sat her down on the second-floor landing. Cognizance of how close she had come to death caught up with her, and she began trembling uncontrollably. Barnett found a blanket, wrapped it around her, and began wringing the water out of her dress. She tried to thank him, but her teeth were chattering wildly. Below, amid the screaming and hysteria of those who lived, bodies floated face-down in the foyer and the first-floor hallway. Near the foot of the stairs a small boy sat on a step, water up to his waist, holding onto the hand of his dead two-year-old sister.

Pointing to the child, Esther nodded to Barnett. When she stopped shivering and regained her wits, he went down and carried the little girl's body back up to the second floor, then went back for the boy. Numb with fatigue, speechless with horror and shock, Esther simply gazed at Barnett in stunned gratitude as she put her arms around the boy and tried to comfort him.

In her room Barnett averted his eyes as he undressed Esther and put her to bed. He broke up a chair and laid pieces of it on the dying coals of a Franklin stove that sat over in one corner.

Esther beckoned to him. "Just hold me, Warren. Please."

Self-consciously, he put his arms around her.

"I can never tell you how grateful I am."

"I'm just thankful you're alive."

She leaned back and looked at him. "There will always be a special bond between us now." Her breasts were almost bare, and his eyes darted nervously. "Like a brother and sister," she added quickly. "That's all I mean."

"Thank you for saying that." He paused. "There is something I must tell you, Esther. I . . . I have always cared deeply for you . . . in a spiritual way." He gazed past her. "Often I have wondered why I've never felt more . . . wanted you. . . ."

She stroked his head. "It may sound strange, but it means more to me this way."

"Sometimes I've wished I *did* feel more," he went on, not really hearing her, needing to tell all of it. "It's just that my whole life . . . is . . ."

"Politics," she said, smiling.

"Yes." He laughed nervously. "Physical needs, when they arise, I attend to in a casual way . . . with . . ."

"Those women who know how to do everything."

"Yes."

She leaned forward and kissed him on the cheek. "I understand. I think no less of you for it."

He sat silently with her for a moment, then stood up. "You're all right now?"

"Yes."

"Then . . . perhaps . . . perhaps I should go and see if I can help elsewhere."

When he was gone, she lay back on the bed and began drifting off to sleep. *Dear, good Warren,* she thought. *He is with his first love now. His people. And I am one of them.*

In the morning Esther stared out through the window at the whaleboats and skiffs still carrying people to high ground. The Sacramento and American rivers had crested, and the entire city had been submerged in three to four feet of water. Across Front Street, large boats drifted at odd angles, splintered where they had smashed into one another. Several more were overturned or partially sunk. Bales and crates, equipment, supplies, foodstuffs, and clothing, washed from temporary storage points, littered the street and the banks of the river. *God knows how much more has been washed downstream,* she thought, for the first time remembering that Kellerman had built his new store on a knoll some distance from the now submerged Embarcadero. In all likelihood his losses would be minimal.

She was suddenly struck with the stupidity—and irony—of the disaster. If the scene within her view was any indication, the city had been devastated in several minutes. She guessed rightly that scores of lives had been lost. At least a half-dozen people in the hotel had been drowned sleeping in their beds. No doubt, she thought, more than a hundred thousand dollars in goods had been destroyed, and God knew how much it would cost to repair the damage when the waters subsided.

All of it preventable. All of it forewarned. For as long as she had been in the region, she had known that the Indians never built camps nearer than fifty to one hundred yards from a stream or tributary of any size. They were well aware that the waterways swelled and washed over their banks predictably each year when the snow melted. Down here in the valley there was no snow of any consequence. But by the end of each December, with a formidable snow-mass accumulated to the east, there was always a chance that rain would melt the western edges of the white blanket and sweep it downriver toward the settlements. No doubt the Indians had told others, as Miwokan had told her, of the danger. Undoubtedly the Indians had been ignored, as they largely were on almost any matter worth discussion. Common sense alone should have dictated that the city be protected, at least by

raising levees such as those she had read about along
the Mississippi. The only thing that could have prevented such prudence was a preoccupation that robbed
men of normal good sense.

Had there been any question about what the pre-
occupying, insidious element clouding otherwise sharp
minds might be, it would have been answered while
she stood there. Diagonally across Front Street a
bearded miner lay drowned in his stove-in rowboat.
Clutched in one of his hands was a packed belly bank
holding all his gold.

Before it is through, she thought, *how many will
be pierced, impaled on the elephant's tusks? And
will I be one of them?* Indeed, in subtle ways, was
she already one of the changed, destroyed slowly by
the ugly truth contained in Miwokan's legend? She
went back to bed and fell asleep wondering if she
had enough to use against Mosby, if it was time to
divest herself of all direct involvement with gold, or
if it was already too late.

Nine days later, as Sacramento City finally dried
out and the inhabitants began repairing and rebuild-
ing, a note reached Esther just as she and Barnett
were about to leave for the South Fork:

> Sent Kit Carson, who has returned from the
> Cimarron, to inform you at your home, but you
> had already departed for Sacramento City so
> forwarded this. Gold discovered on our property.
> Not placer gold, but a rich underground vein
> several feet wide, more than a yard in some
> places. Due to its direction, it is likely that the
> same vein or a similar formation extends through
> the mountains on your property. May have left
> for Washington before you return, so wished to
> inform you and let you know we plan to begin
> mining operations here as soon as possible. Have
> discussed methods and procedures with those

knowledgeable in such matters, and it seems
likely we will build a quartz-stamping mill in the
vicinity sometime later this year. Should the presence of "mother lode" vein or veins bear out on
your property, we would be happy to have you
join us in the building and, of course, use of
such a mill.

Please extend my regards to Mr. Barnett the
next time you see him. Jessie sends her best.

Faithfully yours,

JOHN CHARLES FRÉMONT

Forty-six

Murietta was not at the cabin when Esther and Barnett arrived. There were warm ashes in the fireplace,
and although Murietta's horse and saddle were gone,
the rest of his gear lay on the floor. Since it was Sunday, Esther assumed he had gone into town for provisions or to amuse himself. At first she was reluctant
to go with Barnett. But then she decided her vow
never to set foot in Placerville again was foolish. She
would certainly not go out of her way to visit the
mining community, but having Barnett double back
seemed unnecessary. She decided to pass the time
with Murietta while Barnett attended to his political
affairs.

Constant traffic had packed down the widened
wagon-road into Placerville. Only a little of the surface was slick with snow, and they quickly covered

the distance from the river to the ridge overlooking the town. The silence of the pine forest didn't seem unusual or in any way alarming this time. It was winter, and snow covering the ground and the heavily laden evergreens muffled all sound. But now, as Barnett slowed the horses on the crest between two sloping hills, Esther thought she was dreaming, reliving an expanded version of the nightmare that had unfolded the last time she was here.

The town had grown so much it was almost unrecognizable. There were ten times as many people. Most of them were gathered now, a lake of bearded faces and flannel shirts, undulating, hissing and growling like lava, around the hitching rails in front of a saloon on the main street. Off beyond the far edge of town, incongruously, a small group of people was holding a religious service, singing a hymn. As Esther and Barnett drew closer to the larger mass of miners, they saw the rifles and clubs.

A sick feeling spread through Esther's stomach. "Warren, I want to turn around. I don't want to be here."

Barnett reined up fifty yards from the crowd. "Esther, I've got to find out what's going on."

"Your business can wait, can't it? . . . *Please.*" Then she saw the two men tied to the hitching rail. One of them was Murietta. "Oh, God. . . . It's Joaquin. They have Joaquin. *Do something,* Warren."

Barnett eased the team of horses into the rear of the mob. "*Make way!*" he shouted. "*Make way!*"

"Who the hell do you think you are?" one miner barked, raising a length of oak and seizing the reins.

"My name is Warren Barnett, sir. I am a state senator, and I demand to know what is going on here!"

"Get down off that fuggin' wagon," another man bellowed. "Or they'll be takin' you back to San Jose in a pine box."

A tall, strapping man in a suit, vest, and string tie pushed through the crowd. Esther recognized him immediately. He had slapped the horse out from under the man they had hanged here thirteen months earlier.

"Hold on," he said. "Let's not go off half-cocked." He turned to Barnett. "Would you kindly get down, sir?"

Barnett hesitated for a moment, then climbed down off the buckboard. Esther's eyes darted from Barnett to the tall man with the pleasant face and enormous, square jaw, then beyond the crowd to Murietta, who stood glaring at a fat, red-bearded man. Beside him, the second man lashed to the hitching rail winced with pain as he struggled to free his wrists from their bonds.

"My name is William Coleman," the tall, strapping man said, his extremely pale-blue eyes as cold as snow. "Are you indeed a member of the state senate?"

Barnett glanced around him and took in a deep, chest-swelling breath. "I am, sir. And I wish to know what the charge is against these two prisoners."

Coleman regarded him coolly. "Do you have any credentials? Can you prove you are who you say you are?"

"I have identification."

"I'd like to see something official," Coleman said.

"I have letters addressed to me. And I came seeking *you* out at the suggestion of Senator Gwin."

"Gwin spoke about a matter he wished me to discuss with Barnett, but since I have never met the man, I cannot vouch that you are he."

"Good God, aren't letters addressed to me enough?"

"Unless you have something official . . ."

"I do not. And this is outrageous. I will see to it . . ."

"See, my *ass*," the red-bearded man shouted. "You got nothin' official, you got nothin' to say in this affair."

The crowd roared in approval. Esther slipped down from the buckboard and, emotion overriding reason, began making her way toward the edge of the buildings.

"You will answer for this indignity," Barnett said.

"Go to hell, you goddamned windbag!" someone shouted.

"What is your name?" Barnett said angrily, as the red-bearded man pushed through the milling prospectors to where he stood.

"Claussen. Isaac Claussen, if it makes any goddamned difference."

Esther heard the name, remembered Solana's comments about the man, and stared at him for a moment from the edge of the crowd.

"You will answer—"

"I will, shit," Claussen cut Barnett off. "One of these two greasers shot a man last night and another an hour ago. And we're about to try 'em."

"You can't do that!" Barnett said, taking a step forward. Immediately Claussen and three other miners seized him by the arms and neck.

Esther moved cautiously along the edge of the building toward the hitching post.

"Let the man loose," Coleman said. "He has done nothing—as yet. Sir, this is the way here. They have been accused of a crime, and they shall be tried for it."

The man tied up beside Murietta shouted at the top of his voice. "*We have done nothing . . . nothing!*"

"Shut up," Claussen bellowed.

Esther was within ten feet of the hitching rail when the miners turned their attention to Murietta.

He spoke calmly. "If you would examine the bullet in the wounded man, you would find that it is from a rifle. We carry only . . ."

"*Examine the bullet?*" a small, wizened old miner shouted. "You crazy goddamned greaser. The man may be dead in an hour, and you want someone to tamper with him?"

Barnett jerked free of Claussen's grasp and faced

Coleman. "You seem to be a reasonable, intelligent man. Surely only one of these men could have fired the shot, if indeed one of them fired at all."

They had all turned back to Barnett and Coleman again. Esther moved immediately behind Murietta and began working on the leather thongs around his wrists. He showed no sign of her presence, remained perfectly still.

"That's true," she heard Coleman say. "But which one?"

"The point," Barnett said. "The very point. How can you try two men for a crime only one man could commit?"

"You think one'a them's gonna own up?" Claussen shouted. The crowd roared again, eager to get on with it.

"Can't you *wait*?" Barnett pleaded. "Hold these men until you are able to examine the bullet?"

"Who says we ever gonna be able to do that?" Claussen sneered.

Suddenly a burly arm curled around Esther's throat, pulling her away from Murietta. "*She's tryin' to cut 'em loose!*"

Squirming, Esther broke free and fell in the mud at Murietta's feet. Two miners grabbed her and held her arms. Claussen broke through the crowd and confronted Esther. "What the hell you think you're doin'?"

"*Setting these men free!*" Esther screamed, struggling. "You have no proof that they did anything!"

"You cannot reason with this animal," Murietta said, gazing levelly at Claussen. "He is out for blood. He has a personal grudge against me."

Claussen punched Murietta hard in the face.

"*You beast*," Esther screamed as she wrenched loose and lunged at Claussen. Clawing at him, she grabbed at his beard and yanked violently.

Claussen howled and threw her off. "Take hold of her," he ordered. "This here's gone far enough."

"Hang 'em," someone shouted. *"Hang all of them!"*
Several miners seized Barnett again.

"You will answer for this," he shouted. *"Take your
hands off her!"*

Coleman, carefully weighing the mood of the
crowd, took a step forward. "Isaac . . . it can wait
for a moment while we talk."

"Talk, shit."

"If this is really Barnett," Coleman said, lowering
his voice, "it could spell trouble for you—us—if anything happens to him or the woman."

"We're all in this together," a prospector shouted.

The crowd responded, *"Yeah!"*

"There *is* some question about who is guilty," Coleman said quickly. "It would be better not to hang
them."

"What are we supposed to do?" Claussen countered. "Let 'em off clear and free?"

Coleman scanned the crowd. "No. Punish them."
He leaned over and whispered something to Claussen.

The man next to Murietta on the hitching post
worked at the leather loops encircling his right wrist.

"Better'n hanging," Claussen said, nodding his head.
"Yeah. We'll horsewhip 'em and send 'em packin'."

"Just the two prisoners," Coleman said. "When it
is finished, we will let the others go."

"What do you say t' that, boys?" Claussen shouted.

The crowd roared its approval. Someone produced
a mule whip. Two men jerked and twisted Murietta
over by his ankles until his arms crossed; two more
men quickly snugged lariats around his ankles, holding him, legs splayed, as Claussen spit on his hands,
rubbed them together, and took the whip.

"You will be tried for this!" Barnett shouted.

Claussen eyed him, thought for a moment, smiled,
then handed the whip to one of the miners. "Twenty
men, twenty lashes. One lash each man. You'll have
to try us all."

Coleman whispered to Barnett, "They are almost

out of control. This is better than a double hanging, isn't it?"

Barnett groaned, and Esther gasped as Murietta's shirt was ripped off and the first man laid the whip into him. A long cut opened across Murietta's shoulder blades.

"Don't say anything," Coleman whispered to Barnett. He turned to Claussen. "Twelve will be enough," he said, raising his voice. "And take that woman away. Take her into the saloon where she cannot see or hear this." He motioned to one of the miners. "You. Stand guard over her."

"Sit over there on one of them benches, ma'am," the enormous miner standing guard said, after two others had deposited her inside the saloon. His piggish eyes were too small for his face.

Esther stared at him for a moment, her mind whirring. "Would you tell me your name?"

"Carter. Bull Carter," he said, taking his hand off the holstered pistol he was wearing.

"Please help me," Esther pleaded. "I must stop them!"

"Can't do that, ma'am."

Esther's mind raced. "I'll give you five hundred dollars if you'll help me."

Carter thought for a moment. "Like to," he finally said. "But there ain't nothin' I could do with a crowd like that."

Esther heard the whip snap outside. Almost hysterical, she rushed toward the door.

Carter caught her by one arm, took out the pistol, and held it on her. He glanced around. "I'm not goin' to have no trouble from you, lady." He pushed her toward a curtained door off the main room of the saloon. "Git in there and stay quiet. I don't want to hurt you."

The room was a large parlor that led into the living quarters of the saloon-owner and his wife. She was rocking in a chair, staring at the red calico material that covered the wall behind her husband. He was lying on a pine plank, his face covered by a muslin dish towel, his hands folded neatly across the vest of his Sunday-best suit. Esther saw that the dead man was wearing his gunbelt, glimpsed the handle of the pistol protruding from the holster. A little girl of five rolled a hoop around the room with a stick.

When the child finally noticed Esther, she smiled and ran up to her father's bier and lifted the dish towel. She frowned and came back to Esther.

"Daddy got shot by a greaser. Momma said so."

"In that icy water all day long, runnin' this house of the devil at night," the woman in the rocker said. "All for nothin'." She got up and stalked out through the curtain past Carter.

Esther crouched and took the child in her arms. "You poor baby," she said comfortingly. Noticing that Carter was watching the whipping outside through a window, she whispered in the little girl's ear. "If you will get me your father's pistol, I'll give you a dollar. But it has to be a secret."

The child put a finger to her lips, eyed Carter, then ambled over to the pine plank. Hiding the pistol behind her, she came back and handed it to Esther. Rising and swinging in one motion, Esther brought the butt down hard on the side of Carter's head.

Murietta's punishment completed, Claussen approached the other Californio.

Suddenly, the prisoner pulled his hand free, whipped a short knife out of a pocket, and held it to his own throat. "Hang me," he said to Claussen. "Hang me, but do not whip me like a dog! If you do, I will kill myself!"

Claussen eyed him. "He's bluffin'. Greaser's bluffin' to get outta it." He snapped the whip he was holding suddenly, coming up from the ground with it and curling the tip around the prisoner's free forearm. The man screamed. Claussen jerked at the whip. It pulled free, but the knife was still in the Californio's hand.

"God knows it is *you* who do this," he said to Claussen. "Only you."

Murietta pulled himself upright and stood swaying on buckling knees. He had never seen the man before this morning and had not particularly liked him, but that did not lessen his sense of horror as the Californio dug the blade of his knife deep under his own Adam's apple and slashed quickly to the right. Blood flooded down over his dirty frilled shirt and short, embroidered vaquero jacket. He dropped the knife and stared vacantly at Claussen just before his head lolled to one side and he crumpled to his knees.

Claussen turned to the crowd uncertainly. "Son 'bitch was crazy!"

Uneasy, some of the silent miners started to move off.

"Anybody do that rather'n be whipped *got* to be crazy," Claussen bellowed as more miners moved away. He turned to a few who stood gaping at the raw slash and the pulsing blood. "*He deserved it,*" Claussen shouted. "He knew he shot . . ."

"Enough, Isaac," Coleman said.

Claussen's eyes were wild now. He was not prepared for this. "The other one here, I seen him before. He's no-count. Tried to rig a bull-and-bear fight."

They had all turned and were heading back to their tents.

"I would advise you to leave," Coleman said.

"I didn't lift a finger," Claussen whined, his eyes shifting back and forth from Coleman to Barnett. He turned to Murietta. "*He did it to himself, didn't he?*"

Half-turned, Murietta spat in his face. "One day I will kill you for this, Claussen."

Claussen raised a fist and spun Murietta around.

"*Don't do that!*" Esther shouted, standing in the doorway of the saloon. She pointed the dead saloon-owner's pistol at Claussen's face. "Step a little closer to me. . . . I don't want to miss."

Barnett stepped in front of Claussen.

"Esther," he said, softly. "Don't lower yourself to the likes of this man."

Claussen opened his mouth and started to say something, then checked himself.

"He'll be punished, Esther. Please . . . for me . . . for yourself. . . . God will punish him sooner or later." Barnett walked toward her slowly. "You must not throw away your own life for such scum. Listen to me. . . ." He kept talking until he had the pistol and Esther slumped dead away in his arms.

Forty-seven

Murietta lay on his stomach. She reached out and traced a finger, barely touching him, along one of twelve purple, healing scars running diagonally across his back. She stopped, leaning over as she sat on the edge of the hide bed to see if he had awakened. He did not stir. She bent over and let her hair fall onto his shoulders, swaying her head gently, letting the mass of it brush down to his waist.

He turned over, eyes still closed, and whispered something in his sleep. He reminded her of a baby. She pulled the patchwork quilt down slowly and looked at him. He was not a baby. He was not as large as Mosby, nor was he small. Nor was he as perfectly shaped as Miwokan, or as compelling to look at as her husband. She thought about Alex for a moment and a wave of remembered love washed over

her. It passed and she wanted to touch Murietta. Then
she did not want to touch him. She touched him. She
watched, fascinated, as her hand and his penis somehow remained attached to each of them, but were unattached at the same time, moving independently,
taking on lives of their own.

She heard a faint murmuring of voices. She turned
from Murietta and noticed that the bed was made
of slowly melting metal. She looked back and saw
Murietta's eyes were open. He wore an expression of
hatred and—what was it in his eyes?—fear, behind
the hatred, barely discernible. The murmuring grew
louder until it hurt her eyes, and she saw the miners
surrounding them. . . .

It was no longer a bed but a heavy platform suspended beneath enormous, solid-metal cylinders. They
were flat on one end, and there were more than she
could count. Somehow they were melting and solid
at the same time. Several of them began descending
toward Murietta's legs and waist. His hands and feet
were tied to the metal platform with mule whips.
When she reached out to free him, rough hands pulled
her back, and someone shouted, "What the hell you
think you're doin', lady?" Then she saw him dragged
along the ground and tied motionless on the platform
simultaneously. He was surrounded by chunks of
gleaming stone waiting to be crushed by the descending stamps of the mill. Horrified, she watched her own
arm and hand reach out and pull the starting lever
of the machine. She screamed but no sound came
from her throat.

The crowd of miners watched, then applauded, as
the stamps reached Murietta's legs and genitals first
and began grinding them into pulp. He groaned
through gritted teeth, screamed, and jerked one arm
free. She shrieked continuously and the sound shut
out all others. In his agony, Murietta flipped over and
she saw the blood being squeezed out of him through
a dozen open cuts across his back. Beyond him, Mosby

*laughed, Barnett strained to free himself from the grip
of Coleman and Claussen, Miwokan wept helplessly,
and Alexander Todd glared at her just before he
turned and walked away. Suddenly, a wall of water
as high as a house washed everything from view. . . .*

Esther awoke from the dream full of fear, her
breath coming in short gasps, her heart pounding.
She sat up, and for a full minute she stared at the
oak beams above her, not fully believing she was in
her own bedroom. The details of the dream were still
so palpable, the beginning of it so like that first night
after she and Barnett had brought Murietta to the
ranch two months earlier, that she expected at any
moment to find that what she saw now was a dream
and the dream reality. She was certain that in the
blink of an eye she would be standing beside the
maw of Frémont's stamp mill again. *God, I own part
of it!* Strangely, it did not look exactly the same as
it had the first time Jessie Frémont took her to see
it. She felt the wooden frame of the bed, the fur
quilt, the fabric of her nightdress. She pinched the
flesh under her biceps, touched at her cheeks and
breasts.

When she was certain she was not dreaming, that
she was in her own bed in her own house, where
Murietta slept in the unfinished room next door, she
lay back again and waited for the sick, hollow feeling
to pass. She tried to sort out the unreal elements of
the dream. And something else. She touched absently
between her legs and recalled how conflicting emotions had pulled at her as she spread butter across
Murietta's wounds that first night back at the ranch.
Barnett had retired and she had stayed with Murietta
for hours, sitting on the edge of her bed after the
whiskey and fatigue had pulled him down into a deep
sleep. She remembered easing the cover and the
quilt back, at first curious and then aroused as she

had not been since the night in the sweathouse with Miwokan. She had reached out to touch him, it, then pulled her hand back, overruled by the part of her that still loved Alex. She loved Murietta as well, more than she had ever realized, but not enough to make sexual contact permissible.

During the two months he was healing, growing strong again, she had examined her feelings with greater scrutiny. She rationalized, concluded that her love for him was essentially that of a sister, and that her arousal was simply a physical phenomenon she would have to guard against. When she found herself stirred again one morning in late February as she watched him feebly chopping wood behind the long kitchen and dining room wing of the rancho, she redoubled her efforts to will away such thoughts. And then his silent, preoccupied unawareness of even her presence much of the time had begun to annoy her. Each time she thought it through, ridding herself of anger and irritability, she found that arousal and desire invariably took their place.

He had grown restless, more silent and moody with each predominantly idle day, and she was certain that he, too, felt the strain of living under the same roof in separate beds. At dinner the night before the dream, she had finally drawn him into the first semblance of a full conversation since the whipping.

"I am curious about something," she said. "When . . . it happened . . . you said that Claussen had a grudge against you. And then, as I was coming through the door of the saloon, I heard him say something about seeing you before. Something about a bull and a bear fight. Had you known Claussen?"

As Murietta explained what had taken place at Claussen's ranch, Esther realized with growing astonishment that the bear he was talking about had to be the same one that had burst through the door of her cabin. She was still recovering from the shock of that extraordinary coincidence, when Murietta used a brief descriptive phrase recalling what Claussen's friend had done to him following the bear's escape.

"Would you please repeat what you said when you described the man who made the bet with the other Californio?"

"Tall, with the nose of a hawk. I will never forget that face."

"Did he have a moustache?" Esther asked, an electric sensation spreading across the skin of her arms and the back of her neck.

"Yes," Murietta said, almost lost in memory and revived hatred. "And now he has also a scar where the bear clawed him open, from here to here." Murietta smiled sardonically as he drew a curving line down the back of one arm with his fingertip.

Trying to control her emotions, Esther spread her hands on the table on either side of her plate. She felt a numbness in her fingers as she pressed down, a pulsing in the stubs where two were missing. "What was his name? The tall man with the moustache?"

"Mosby. Luther Mosby. That name I will never forget either."

Involuntarily, Esther's hands jerked outward, one of them knocking over her coffee. She stared at the spilled liquid on the table, and for a moment it seemed as dark as blood.

"Why do you ask?" Murietta said, getting up and sponging up the spilled coffee with his napkin.

"Just curious." She wanted to change the subject. "I'll never get the stain out of that napkin."

"Let me soak it in cold water," Murietta said, cupping the cloth in his hands and walking out to the kitchen.

While he was gone, Esther gripped the edge of the table until her knuckles whitened. Thoughts came spinning through her head. *Oh, God, the same man. Murietta would recognize him. He bears Mosby almost as much hatred as I do.*

Murietta came back in and sat down, silent and

totally absorbed by his own thoughts again. Esther released her grip on the table and tried to relax herself. She realized it was impossible to work with this new information, form something with it, in the state she was in. When her mind was cool, after she had slept on it, she thought, she would go over the possibilities. A tremor of guilt rippled through her. *It is unfair of me even to think of drawing Joaquin into this. I might be risking his life. Perhaps there is a way he could simply locate Mosby for me . . . and then . . .*

"I have been thinking of riding south to spend some time in the high place above the desert," Murietta said, recalling Esther from her thoughts.

"*I don't want you to go!*" she shouted, not realizing how loud her voice was until she had finished the sentence. Quickly regaining control, forcing herself to speak softly, sweetly, she added: "You are not completely healed."

"The cuts are closed."

"But you're still weak. It would be better if you stayed. I know it would be . . . and I need you," she added, ashamed but determined.

Murietta smiled. "You can do without me . . . for a while." His eyes drifted away from her and the line of his mouth hardened, almost imperceptibly.

"You'd come back soon?"

"In time," he said unconvincingly.

"*I don't want you to go!*" She lowered her voice again. "I . . . I'm concerned for your safety, your . . ."

"All right," he said, sighing. "I will think about it for a while longer." He got up. "I wish to sleep now. Will you excuse me?"

After he left the dining room, Esther tried to devise a way to bring him into her plans without endangering him. Distracted by the possibility that he might leave and not come back, she found it impossible to think straight. Suddenly, she was exhausted. The weight of Murietta's revelation and her own emotions had drained her. *Sleep on it,* she advised herself. Get-

ting up, she walked down the long hallway and undressed for bed. I must keep him here, she thought.
And find a way . . . She couldn't even finish the sentence in her mind. "In the morning," she said out loud
as she got into bed. "In the morning, it will all become
clear."

The terror, disorientation, and lingering disquiet
that followed the dream were almost gone now as
she closed her eyes again. When she thought she
heard the faint metallic sound of a spur clinking outside, she went to a window and opened the wooden
shutters a crack. The sky to the west was still dark,
but beneath the stars the pines were emerging slowly
as visible black forms. She was about to close the
shutters when she caught a movement out of the corner of her eye. Down at the corral Murietta had
thrown his saddle up on his horse and was fastening
the cinch. The sight of it stunned her.

When he had finished, he led the horse quietly
back toward the house and stopped. He stared straight
at the window, not seeing her. There was a look of
infinite sadness in his eyes. He pulled the pistol out
of the holster hanging from his bullet-laden belt and
checked it. Then, after a last look at the ranch, he
took hold of the pommel, swung up on the horse,
and turned it north instead of south. She suddenly
realized he was *leaving*, that this was not a dream.
And that his preoccupation, his distance, his growing
restlessness had had nothing to do with her.

He was already walking the horse slowly away from
the house when she threw open the shutters and whispered, "*Wait!*" He didn't hear her.

He was trotting when she reached the front door
and cried, "*Joaquin!*" He didn't stop or turn. Frantic,
she pulled up the skirts of her nightdress and began
running barefoot through the shallow layer of snow
between the house and the corral. She climbed through
the split-rail fence and pulled herself, up, bareback,

onto her horse. Gripping the mare's mane, she leaned down and opened the gate. Then, riding as hard as she could without falling, she pointed the horse with her knees until it was headed for the opening in the line of trees through which Murietta had disappeared.

She caught up with him a quarter mile into the pine forest.

"You're going after Claussen," she said, out of breath, not feeling the cold, grateful that he had slowed his horse to a walk. The mounts snorted simultaneously and stopped.

"It would have been better if you . . ."

"You're going to kill Claussen, aren't you?"

He leaned on his pommel and sighed. "Yes. I have thought about it, and that is what I must do. Please go back."

Her body felt twice its weight. *"They will kill you,"* she said, biting at a knuckle. "Claussen is drawing you into the filthy, childish game men play with guns."

"I will wait until it is just the two of us, alone."

Desperate, she ignored the fact that he was doing nothing more than she hoped to do to Mosby; perhaps even with Murietta's help. "This is not you. You said you would not . . ."

"There are some things no man can avoid, no matter how much he would like to."

"And killing Claussen is one of them?"

"Yes."

"You are as stupid and prideful as the rest of them," she screamed, conscious now of how much she might need him. "I hate you. You deceived me. You led me to believe you are different from them."

The irony of what she was saying struck her full force. Desperation overwhelmed the shame she felt. Her frustration turned to anger. She saw Mosby for an instant in her mind and suddenly edged her horse nearer, swinging an open hand at his face. She was not near enough to hit Murietta, and as the force of her swing sent her toppling off the horse, he reached out, grabbed her wrist, and broke her fall. Swinging a leg over, he slid out of his own saddle and dropped down on his knees next to her. She swung her other hand, and he blocked it with his palm. He took hold of her wrists and she struggled for a moment, then gave up. He let go of her and they stood up, staring at each other in the humming silence beneath the sheltering branches of the giant evergreens. He started to remount.

"Is there *nothing* that will stop you?" she pleaded. Murietta's Appaloosa nuzzled her mare. Esther was suddenly aware of the musky aroma of lathered horse-flesh. *No matter what it costs,* she thought, *I will keep him here.* "Could something, anything, be important enough to make you choose it rather than what you are about to do?"

He turned to her, one foot in a stirrup. "I do not think so. My feelings are too strong."

She reached out and touched his cheek. "There are other feelings, just as strong. I don't want to lose you. I couldn't bear the thought of you dead."

"I do not want to die," he said. "But I would rather be dead than . . ."

"Don't you understand what I am saying?" She could feel the pine needles under her feet as she reached up and undid the tie-strings of the night-dress. "I want you *alive.*"

"Esther . . ."

"*I* want you alive." She pulled at the buttons and let the nightdress fall to the ground. "More than you want Claussen dead."

He tried to turn away. "Esther . . ." He couldn't keep his eyes off her.

She moved closer to him, saw his expression soften and his nostrils flare. "I know you have wanted me for a long time," she said, inwardly astonished at what she was capable of doing. "Do you want me more than you want Claussen?"

He stared at her for a long time, then smiled and shook his head in wonder. And then his arms were around her, his lips were on hers, and they were sinking slowly to the carpet of pine needles and snow. He stopped after a moment, got up and unrolled his poncho and his bedroll. He spread the poncho and her nightdress and pulled the blanket over them after stripping naked and lying by her side.

When he was in her, she felt relief and release along with a moderately, then increasingly pleasant feeling. There was no rapture, none of the convulsive, intense response she had experienced with Alex Todd. Murietta's stiff, moving presence was simply a positive physical sensation. The part of him that was in her felt like the smooth fabric of the nightdress beneath her; no more, but no less pleasant. *If this will keep him with me,* she thought, *then I will do it; as often as he wishes. The rest will be scarcely more difficult than being affectionate to a brother or sister.* She thought of Alex, and guilt rose in her. *Forgive me,* she thought. *I have to do this.* She banished the guilt from her mind.

She watched Murietta's face tighten, his eyes grow slightly blank, and then she felt the cool film of perspiration break out all over his body just before he pulled away and his thick, warm liquid pulsed onto her abdomen. She smiled at the pleasure and contentment in his face as he lowered himself and they rolled over, facing one another. A tender, warm feeling for him lifted her out of her detached frame of mind. She kissed him softly on the eyes and cheeks. When he rested his face in the hollow of her neck, she stroked his head the way she would that of a child.

Esther wondered if this was all any woman could feel if she loved someone else. She stared up at the rapidly brightening sky. When she finally turned and saw he was watching her, she knew there was a trace of sadness behind his otherwise contented expression. She wondered if a man might know if a woman was not in love with him by subtle variations in the sexual act. She felt a moment of apprehension as he began to speak, fearful that he would ride on after Claussen because he knew the limitations of her feelings, and they would not be enough to outweigh his need for revenge.

But he simply said, "*Querida*, you have probably saved my life." He laughed at the way it sounded, at the way he had been saved.

She understood and laughed with him. Feeling a surge of relief, she smiled happily and put her arms around him. It occurred to her that he might take her mood and the way she was expressing it as evidence of deep love. She knew that allowing such misinterpretation was deceit, manipulation, but decided she would have to live with that. There was no one else to help her. No matter how much gold she had, she did not think she could do it alone. And she would never find a more natural ally than Murietta. Somehow she would make it up to him. She hoped the limit of her feelings was obscured to him, for his sake. For a moment, as they lay silently in each other's arms, she thought he did not know.

"I have been very lucky today," he said, gazing past her. "Perhaps I will be even luckier in the future." He nodded to a snow-covered clearing beyond where they lay. "For if *that* can grow at this time of year, perhaps your love for me will grow also."

She followed the line of his gaze to an oval patch of white gleaming in a slanting shaft of sunlight. In the center of the exposed clearing, a tiny flower had thrust its yellow petals up through the surface of the snow.

"But I love you now," she said, praying that somehow, someday, it might not be a lie.

Forty-eight

Mariposa Ranch
July 20, 1852

Sunday. Oh, Alex, how can I begin to tell you? It has been more than two years since I have written in these pages. I wish I could say that it is simply because I have been busy, here at the ranch, with the mining operations and so forth. But while that is true, the main reason has been my reluctance to convey in these pages what my life has been like with Murietta. The last time I wrote, I begged your forgiveness and asked you to try to understand my reasons for becoming involved with him. Now that so much time has passed and I have not even spoken once to Murietta of Mosby, the uneasiness I feel about breaking my vow to you weighs on me heavily.

Things change, Alex, and I sense a shift in me concerning Murietta. Perhaps this will cause you additional pain, should you ever read these pages. Banish such feeling, for the changes I detect in myself do not have anything to do with my continued love for you. That will never change. It is just that so much time has passed, and without Murietta I would be alone. That was acceptable to me for a long time, but it is no longer. I have tried to make it up to you, by pulling a string from time to time to assist in increasing your good fortune and prosperity. And surely you have become involved, had your affairs, by this time. I hope so, indeed cannot imagine that you have not.

Or that anything would change the feelings you had for me when we were together.

Nonetheless, I shall make you two promises. First, I will speak to Murietta about Mosby as soon as possible. I have been thinking much lately about how I have let my preoccupation with running things here and the comforting hours with Joaquin lull me in my resolve concerning Mosby. To be fair to myself, I have to say that no way occurred to me in which I could enlist Murietta's aid without sending him into a situation that might easily cost him his life. Perhaps it has been dense of me, but I did not think to tell him all of the story, thereby making him understand that *I* must be the one to finally confront Mosby and do what must be done. And that he must simply help me find the man and arrange his final hour. I will do that—along with keeping a second promise to resume sharing everything with you—as soon as Murietta returns.

He has been gone since Monday. To San Francisco and Sacramento again to spare me the burdens of business. I ask you to please remember how much has transpired since we were together: that each of Joaquin's brief absences has seemed longer than the year and a half (almost) that has passed since that morning at dawn with him under the pines. I suppose missing him so much means that I love him in a way. It may be a comfort to know that I have not experienced those additional ranges of feeling that were part of my love for you. Still, Joaquin is more than a comfort, and I must confess the sweet languor of our occasional nights together gentles me considerably. (I pray that you have found similar affection and relief.) There is some disquiet in me about it. I still see your face occasionally when Joaquin and I lie together. And although the ingenious wrapping of . . . himself . . . with sheep-gut seems indeed to work and I have not become pregnant, I still so much fear such a calamity that it robs me of some of the modest pleasure I feel.

I hope Joaquin keeps his promise to avoid Sonora and Coulterville on his way back. Thank God the bestiality and injustice being heaped upon miners of Latin origin and ancestry in those places has not reached into the larger operations such as this one. Why the Sonorans, Mexicans, and South Americans stay is beyond me, reduced as they are to underpaid laborers for the combines and larger companies that now predominate. They are insulted and attacked at every turn, as you probably know. No wonder so many of them have succumbed to drunkenness and retaliated with murder and banditry. I cannot say with certainty that I would not respond in the same way if I were harshly taxed simply because I was a foreigner, and accused of every crime committed anyway.

Moses will be five in less than two months. I wish my attempt last month to have him here had not resulted in such a turmoil of bad memories and renewed hatred for Mosby. One good thing came of it: I suspect my renewed attention and—I have told Murietta only that Moses is illegitimate—resolve concerning Mosby were triggered by Moses' presence. I wish my feelings were such that I could raise the boy myself. It will be difficult for him—and for Solana, I am sure—when I place him in school. But sooner or later it must be done. He regards Solana as his mother, obviously, and loves and trusts her as he does no one else. But he is white, and it is my duty to see that he is educated, prepared for survival in the world outside her village. And try as I will to remember there has been no trouble there, the knowledge of violence against Indians elsewhere keeps me fearful for his continued safety. It is time. It must be done this year. . . .

I hope Murietta is able to see the "Lieutenant Governor" while he is in Sacramento. Happily, Warren affects little of the trappings and certainly none of the self-importance of most politicos of even modest rank. I have often wondered what you think of him. The more I know Barnett, the more I love and admire the truly decent man that resides within that huge body. Upon reflection, he seems the only man under fifty I have ever known, other than yourself, whose interest in me was untainted. Perhaps men who can accommodate a purely spiritual bond with a woman are even rarer than true friends seem to be in general. . . .

I am eager to hear what has developed in Blue Star's six-month-old business relationship with the new Sacramento firm, Huntington and Hopkins, which I recommended on reports received from Mr. Kellerman. Perhaps it might be prudent for me to extend my private whole-sale-retail arrangements to include Huntington and Hopkins as well. From all indications, the intense competition may well "do in" Kellerman, and that would leave me without an outlet for my goods in Sacramento. That prospect displeases me, not least because I take a particular pleasure from every penny anyone keeps out of Sam Brannan's pockets. I must hand it to him—and to Coleman. They have wasted no time in establishing themselves, everywhere, it seems, from the gold-field towns to San Francisco itself.

I wish things were not so drastically changed on the South Fork. It is true that since Barnett and Kelsey persuaded you—at my oblique suggestion—to take over the new hydraulic mining operations for the absentee-owner, "E. Cable," efficiency and profits have risen steadily. (The irony of the arrangement! What a shock it will be to you when you finally read this!) But it pains me that Miwokan is no longer involved, retreating to his hut as he has since his brother and so many more of his men went off on their own last year. Of course, I could not feel as secure as I do about the management of the South Fork Mining Company without you there. How I wish I could personally praise and congratulate you for what you have done for yourself. Somehow it does not surprise me that you are able to manage both the mining company and the stage and express line you and your cousin, Talbott, developed out of the original mail service. I am glad you resisted selling the line to Adams and Company.

Good Lord, they are so high-handed in their business and banking dealings! Were it not for the intricate financial relationship between Adams and Company and Blue

Star, I would take my account to another bank just to show them what I think of their haughty attitude!

When I think of it, it is strange how little the figure $450,000 registers with me. That, as they say, is "what I am worth" according to the last account. Does that astonish you? It does me. I am unable to grasp what that much money means, beyond the knowledge that I have at my disposal wherewithal unimaginably beyond that available to the average person. And that when fate ordains, I will have more than enough financial strength to deal with Mosby.

It seems ironic to me that I could hire, through third parties, Murietta—whomever, a half-dozen assassins—to find and kill Mosby tomorrow, for far less than I now have. But I could not even begin to entertain such thoughts. It seems clear to me that it would be morally different from taking revenge with my own hands. Perhaps such a distinction would seem like splitting hairs to some, but it is not to me. Moreover, it would seem to be injudicious to reveal to anyone my part in whatever happens to Mosby. How could I avoid that, and subsequent entrapment—perhaps even the gallows—if I hired someone to kill him? And now that I have focused sharply on the subject again, after weakly allowing my determination to wane, the urge to do him in by my own hand is so strong it alone would preclude paying someone else to do it.

God, I cannot believe it! Just thinking about Mosby again for more than a few seconds after so long has my hands trembling. I swear I will not let the matter drift again. I cannot wait until Murietta returns!

Forty-nine

Esther was picking tomatoes in the new, expanded garden between the ranch house and a stream that ran across the quiet, northwest corner of her property. She had just worked out a way to introduce the subject of Mosby to Murietta, when she heard the sound of hoofbeats. They were rapid, and they echoed ominously from beyond the edge of the pines. She had been concerned about Murietta. He was several days overdue. And now, as she saw him clear the line of trees without slowing, her pulse rose.

He veered when he saw her and reined up his snorting, lathered horse so abruptly he almost pitched out of the saddle.

"There is little time," he said.

"What's happened?"

"They are sure I am a man called Joaquin Ocomorenia, or another bandit who calls himself Murietta."

"Who does?"

"A man, a peace officer named Love. Colonel Harry Love. He and a band of—how do you call them?—rangers, have been scouring the area around Chinese Camp, watching the roads between Sacramento and Placerville, Coulterville, looking for the outlaws. I took the southern route, as I promised. But someone at the place where I stayed in Merced believed me to be Ocomorenia, went to the alcalde, and they locked me up and sent for Love. I gave the man who

sweeps out the jail, a mestizo, a pouch of gold for
the keys hanging on the wall. The alcalde came back,
and I had to shoot him to keep him from killing me
and the mestizo."

"Oh, God!"

He put his arms around Esther and kissed her.
"There is no time, *querida*. I am certain I have no
more than half an hour on them."

"Where will you go?"

"I do not know. South first, through the mountains.
Perhaps across them and then north. I will make up
my mind as I go."

"They will listen if Senator Frémont—"

"Frémont is not even at his ranch. And I may have
killed a man. They are out for blood."

She was torn between an instant, blinding awareness of how much she needed him and the certainty
that he had to run, leave her for God knows how
long.

"Wait," she said, running to the house and motioning him to follow. He got up in his saddle and waited
at the front door, watching the line of trees and then
hearing the low, distant rumble of more than a dozen
horses. She came back out quickly, handing him a
fistfull of bills and stuffing a chunk of dressed beef
into his saddlebag. He gave her the papers he had
brought, then leaned over and kissed her fiercely before wheeling around and galloping toward the mountains. She dropped the papers and sobbed. Collecting
herself, she was ready when the thirteen men carrying rifles burst out of the woods and stopped.

Esther watched for a moment as they examined
the open ground looking for tracks. Casually, she bent
over to pick up the two dozen or so letters, ledger-
entry copies, and bills of lading that had scattered
in a wide circle after Murietta rode off. She picked
up three of them, then stood holding one hand to
her back as the men rode up slowly, their attention

shifting from her to the house, then to the cottage where old Marianita and her husband, Emilio, stood watching.

Esther had started to bend over again to pick up another piece of paper when the rangy man with the light-brown handlebar moustache, battered top hat, and mud-splattered yellow slicker got down off his horse. She stopped halfway through the movement, put her hand to her back again, and winced.

"Would one of you gentlemen help me, please? I'm afraid I have wrenched my back and . . ."

The rangy man wore a small, official metal shield. He turned and motioned rapidly to three men, who dropped from their saddles and began chasing the papers, now blowing in another gust of warm wind.

"Name's Love, ma'am. Colonel Harry Love. Looking for a man rode this way. Little taller than you. Mexican. Seen him?"

"Why no, Mr. Love." She turned and pointed to the paper that was farthest away. "Please don't forget that one." She turned back to Love. "You and your men look parched. Can I get you something to drink?"

Love stared at her for a moment. He turned and pointed two fingers at another man. "Take a look down there around the corral and them sheds." He tilted his head at still another deputy. "Take Willens, there, with you."

"Yessir." The two men wheeled and, drawing their guns, loped back toward the outbuildings.

"*Marianita*," Esther called. The old woman came running. "Fetch these men some water, please."

"Thank you, ma'am," Love said. "Tracks lead straight here. You sure you haven't seen anyone?"

"Seems I would have. I've been out here working in the garden . . ."

"With correspondence?"

"I beg your pardon?"

"Workin' in the garden with them letters?" He smiled coldly.

"Why, no. They were in my apron pocket. What do you mean?"

"Nothing, ma'am. Nothing. Fell out of your pocket, did they? Blew all the way here to the front of the house? You don't mind if we search the servants' quarters over there, do you?"

"They fell when I came back to . . ." Her voice trailed off as she watched the two men Love had waved over to Marianita's cottage stop and take a long look at old Emilio. "Do you always behave so rudely?" she asked, conscious now that her heart was beating rapidly.

Love was looking at the ground near her feet. "Sorry, ma'am, but the man we're looking for has killed a number of people. Highwayman. You understand."

"I see. Would you like to search the house?"

"Judgin' from these hoofprints, yes."

She looked down at the tracks Murietta's Appaloosa had left. "They're fresh, aren't they?"

Love stared at her again. "Yes, ma'am, they are."

"You think I'm concealing someone?" She wondered how many minutes had passed, how much time she had gained for Murietta.

"Didn't say that, ma'am. Now, if you don't mind, I'll just take a look around. . . ."

"You just walk into my house, into my home," she said, stalling as much as she could, any way she could, "and I have to stand still for it?"

"Ma'am," Love said, exasperation beginning to show in the set of his face. "You might not have noticed him. Could have snuck into the house while you were out here. Might be hiding somewheres."

"I doubt that." She calculated how long it would take them to look through the ranch house. "But do go in and see for yourself."

"Thank you, ma'am."

"Just one moment. . . . I believe I left some . . . unmentionables . . . on my bed. I would like to put them away before you enter."

"Certainly, ma'am. But be careful."

"I'll just be a moment."

Marianita waddled out with a wooden bucket of water and a ladle.

"Much obliged, ma'am," Love said, sipping as Esther backed slowly in through the doorway.

She was in her bedroom, peering out from beside the window, when one of Love's men ran around from behind the house.

"Fresh tracks, same as these. Headin' east."

"Let's go," Love barked, dropping the bucket at Marianita's feet.

Back outside, Esther put one arm around Marianita and wiped at the old woman's tears. "It's all right. They'll never find him. I just know it." She hated herself for not believing what she was saying.

They both turned when they heard the low whistle from the direction of the pines. Murietta sat there on his Appaloosa, barely visible behind a low-hanging branch. He waved, and she could see the white of his teeth as he grinned in the sunlight. He wheeled then and was gone, back in the direction from which the posse had come.

Esther smiled. Until Mosby finally crossed her mind once more, and the numbing certainty suddenly came over her that she would never see Murietta again.

Fifty

The poster hung on the varnished, wood-paneled wall
of the new Wells Fargo Express depot in Sacramento:

> **$5000**
> **REWARD!**
> For the Capture
> of the Bandit
> **JOAQUIN**
> Alive or Dead

Sitting in the waiting room, Esther put her arm
around little Moses. She stared at the "wanted" poster
and thought of the dozen crimes reportedly committed by Murietta during the two months since she
had last seen him. She laughed to herself at the absurdity of at least some of the charges. On several days,
bank and stage robberies that had taken place hundreds of miles apart and within an hour or two of
one another had been attributed to him. A pamphlet
written by a San Francisco journalist claimed that
Murietta was a Mexican miner of good breeding who
had turned to crime in revenge. A band of prospectors had raped his young wife. The Americans had

DANIEL KNAPP

in turn hanged his brother. They had left Murietta
for dead after lashing him to a tree and whipping him
for an hour.

Barnett had shown her the pamphlet at dinner in
a restaurant on K Street the night before.

"It is patently ridiculous," Esther said, wondering
if there was any way to enlist Barnett's aid in con-
tacting Murietta. The idea seemed totally improbable.

"Obviously a fiction. But the business about the
whipping is an extraordinary coincidence. The man
who wrote it is talented, but taken to gambling. He's
so heavily in debt he would probably write anything
to turn a dollar."

"Is there *anything* we can do to help Joaquin?"

"I'm afraid it's hopeless," Barnett sighed. "Now
that the Merced alcalde is dead . . ."

"But Joaquin was not the man they were looking
for in the first place!"

"That no longer matters to those who are hunting
him. I understand how it all started, but I'm only
one voice." He saw the tears brimming in Esther's
eyes. "Esther, I promise you I will do everything
within my power to see that Murietta is taken alive."

Esther absently fingered the gold watch hanging
from her neck. It was all she had left of Murietta. She
doubted either she or Barnett would ever see him
again. Murietta was wily enough to know that even
the best lawyer in California could not save him from
the gallows now. She was certain he would never
allow himself to be taken alive.

For a moment the thought of him dead and the
task ahead of her with little Moses became too much
to bear. Barnett didn't know anything about Moses,
was not aware that Esther even *had* a son. She had
purposely kept it from him and almost everyone else.
Now she had the sudden urge to share the secret,
to relieve herself of some, *any* part of the mental
burden she was carrying. She was about to tell him

about the boy, reveal that an elderly woman was watching over him at the hotel, and that she was taking Moses north to enroll him in school. But then the waiter came to clear the dishes and bring them coffee. It is too complicated, she thought. She was too tired to parry the questions Warren would ask about Moses' father.

"You are going to Marysville to look at property?" Barnett said, interrupting her thoughts.

"Yes," she answered, suddenly thinking she might do just that after she had taken Moses north to the school. Perhaps it was time for her to be away from the mountains, away from direct involvement with the gold. It occurred to her that if she moved, she might persuade Miwokan and Solana to come with her. If she could, it would prove that she had no intention of dropping them from her life now that Moses was no longer with them. And it might spare them any more heartbreak. She was suddenly aware that Barnett had asked her a question. "I'm sorry, Warren. I wasn't listening. What did you say?"

"I asked if you are taking the new Wells Fargo stage to Marysville?"

"Yes, I thought I would have a look at Adams's competition."

"I'll be interested to hear what you have to say. I've heard glowing reports, but Adams is too powerful to be threatened by them, I would think."

Unconsciously, Esther seized on the welcome distraction the subject of Wells Fargo provided. Concentrating, she suddenly hit on an idea. "Too powerful *now*."

"What are you getting at?"

"When will the Blue Star merger with Pacific Mail Steamship be official?" she asked.

"In a matter of days, I would think. A week at most."

"And if Wells Fargo becomes a serious rival to

Adams, it will be a dog-eat-dog affair. Wells Fargo will need cash to survive, to gain an enduring place here in California."

"True . . . but what is your point?"

"I was just thinking," Esther said, weighing, sifting, calculating. "If they do become serious rivals, and we joined forces with them—became partners by providing the cash they will need—the combination of Blue Star, Pacific, and Wells Fargo would be the foundation for a mail, express, and banking company of even greater power than Adams."

Barnett raised his eyebrows and whistled. "My God, Esther. Is there no end to the things that marvelous brain of yours can imagine? It's a marvelous idea. It will bear watching, careful watching. But I'll speak of it to William when I return to San Francisco."

Absorbed, Esther's mind was still ticking. "We might want to assist them in the early stages, help them reach the status of serious competition more quickly."

"I don't see how. . . . The risk. . . . We rely heavily on Adams."

"It could be done secretly."

"But how . . . ?"

"There are numerous independent mail and express companies operating in the shadow of Adams . . ."

"Such as Todd's."

Esther smiled to herself. "Wells Fargo would need immediate cash to do it, but if the new company absorbed some or all of the smaller operations . . ."

"Ingenious!" Barnett exclaimed. He calculated for a moment. "Why, they'd become a threat to Adams almost overnight."

And Alex could take a step to even greater success, Esther thought. "We would need someone we can trust, someone who had proven himself to us, on the inside, to look out for our interests."

Barnett thought for a second. "Todd. He has done an excellent job for us, don't you think? He would be perfect. Part of the arrangement might be that he be given a substantial managerial job in the enlarged firm. If he's willing to be bought out."

"I have no mind for such decisions," Esther said casually, positive that Alex would leap at the chance to tangle on even terms with his brutally competitive rivals. "I have nothing but praise for Mr. Todd, but I would leave that choice up to you and Bill."

Esther smiled now, thinking about the maneuver, as the Wells Fargo stage pulled in. Five minutes early. It was almost certain that Barnett and Kelsey would choose Alex, if such a merger ever took place. And Alex's impression that it had been the idea of his good friends, Kelsey and Barnett, would be sustained. For the time being, however, she would see for herself if Wells Fargo was all it was cracked up to be.

She watched as four Chinese and two heavily rouged women emerged from the stage and came into the waiting room. There were no complaints. Esther listened as the courteous clerk explained a schedule to one of the Orientals. She glanced at the "wanted" poster, felt a pang of longing; then fought it off by turning her attention to the two men coming down off the driver's seat of the stage.

Waiting for a moment to observe the care and efficiency of the firm's freight-handling, she gathered up little Moses as the driver took their bags, and they walked out to the open stagecoach door. In minutes they were at the magnificent new Embarcadero levee, waiting for the ferry to take them across the river. On the ride north through what had once been Sutter's enormous land-grant from the Mexicans, Esther's bitterness over Murietta was replaced by resignation and a small measure of thanksgiving. At least he was still alive. Then melancholy superseded her faint hope that Murietta would continue to elude the persistent hunting of Harry Love and God knows how many others.

She turned to little Moses. The suit, shirt, and shoes she had bought him the day before fit perfectly, seemed almost made to order. Still, they did not look right. They fit him physically but in no other way. With his longish black hair and permanently wary dark eyes, the predominant impression he gave was of a subdued but still wild creature trapped in a tight cage.

He looked at her now and then, expressionlessly. Most of the time he gazed out through the window, intently studying the countryside slipping past. She wondered if he was storing the route in his mind, preparing himself to retrace it if he could escape from the school. He had not uttered a word to her since the painful parting at the village.

. Strangely, it was she who had nearly wavered, not Solana. The Indian woman had grown as attached to Moses as she was to her own son, and at first she wept uncontrollably. Moses, too young to know or have anything to say about what was happening to him, nonetheless seemed as totally accepting of the change as an ancient shaman. He stared calmly over Solana's shoulder, first at Miwokan, then at Esther, and then, comfortingly, almost patiently, he stroked Solana's hair as though he was the parent and she the child.

"You see? He knows this is best," Solana said, standing up, wiping her eyes, and taking Esther's hand as she walked out of earshot.

"But now I don't," Esther whispered, holding back tears.

"You know that I love him as my own."

"Yes."

"But I must be strong in this, as you must be. I must live with the pain of his going away, accept the empty place in me that will be there all the years he is no longer here. As you must, in your own way. I cannot know why you will not have him with you, but I know you. And I know you would not do this unless the reasons in your heart are strong."

"Someday I will tell you what those reasons are."

"It does not matter to me. I believe you do what you must. And I know that Moses, as much as he is loved here, is different. He will always be different here, not an Indian. . . . Not a stranger—he could never be that. But never completely one of us."

"That wouldn't be good for him."

"No it would not. I hope it is not too late for him to be one of his own. But what you are doing will be a chance for that."

Esther gazed off for a moment, wondering if the four years here had already shaped him enough to make him a permanent outsider in the world he was about to enter. She turned back to Solana and smiled sadly. "You and Miwokan always remind me, when I least expect it, of how much wisdom and strength I lack."

"Come," Solana said gently, putting her arm through Esther's. "We will go back to him now. And there will be no tears. We must do what is for him and not ourselves."

When she rode out of the village with him, his expression was as blank as it was now. She brushed at his hair with her fingers as the stagecoach finally rocked him to sleep. *He probably knows there is nothing he can do about what is happening to him,* she thought. *No more than I can alter the emptiness and increasing uncertainty I have felt in Joaquin's absence.*

He is accepting it as I must accept. But God, the lack of Murietta is so dreadful.

It was not the same palpable, hollowed out longing she had experienced during her year without Alex at Bent's Fort. That had been like the absence of a limb and a lessening of the warmth of the sun. Aside from what the loss of Joaquin meant concerning Mosby, this was more like an increase in weight around her heart; and an unexpected unsteadiness, a feeling that the earth was about to shift beneath her feet, to open and swallow her up. Until now, she had not been aware of how much she had come to rely on Murietta. She sorely missed his honest, objective advice about her business dealings, his confirmations and gentle corrections of her judgment, the way his calm reason cut through her often emotional reaction to things and helped her see them more objectively. She could almost *feel* the absence of him, *see* the gap where a living, physical barrier once screened her from loneliness. She also recognized now how important he had been in providing a focus of attention outside herself.

Magnifying her disquiet was the strange disbelief that began when she glanced at the accountings Murietta had hurriedly left with her that final day. Inventory, Blue Star holdings, and mining properties aside, $501,475 was deposited in her name at Adams and Company. When she translated the figure into the words "more than a half-million dollars," she had begun laughing hysterically. She had watched the figure increase on each bank statement over the past four years, but now she wondered whether there had been some simple but enormous mathematical mistake somewhere along the line. She was only twenty-three years old. She could not comprehend how she had come to be a rich woman. During the hours when she believed the figure, she was not sure she could continue playing such a game without faltering, committing some disastrous error, and losing everything.

As the day she planned to take little Moses to the school approached, an unsettling hollowness grew within her. Vague fears and sieges of inexplicable remorse drifted through her mind like patches of ground fog, all the more unsettling, puzzling, because they did not last.

Thinking of it now, as the stagecoach jounced over a rough stretch of road, she wondered whether the source of that additional disquiet was Moses himself. She had long since accepted the impossibility of having him with her, she told herself. She was sad about separating him from Solana, but she was sure that she was doing the best thing for Moses. The thought buoyed her spirits until the boy spoke to her for the first time.

She was saying good-bye to him outside the entrance to the school. The old priest who met them when they arrived stood watching. She was certain the Jesuits would provide him with a good home, moral guidance, proper food and care. He would have an education. Barnett had spoken highly of this new school once, when she had drawn him into a general conversation about California's educational needs. Esther realized that in all likelihood, the end result for Moses here would probably be a seminary and the priesthood. Although the prospect went against her Protestant grain, no other denomination had established a similar institution in northern California. And the thought of Moses once-removed from what she knew of the world made up for her reservations. But then he said his first words to her.

"Are you my real mother?" he asked, eyeing the gold, heart-shaped amulet hanging next to her locket watch.

She was suddenly sure he remembered it from their time together. Guilt stabbed at her as she saw that he could not look her in the eye.

For a moment she was about to answer, "Yes. Oh, God, yes, I *am* your mother," and sweep him up in her arms and kiss his little face and take him back with her.

The priest who had come out to greet them took

Moses' hand, turned him, and pointed to a hand-carved Virgin near the vaulted door of the Spanish-style school.

"That, my son, is your real mother."

Esther fought down mounting doubt, self-recrimination, and anguish as Moses' face brightened. The boy walked over and hesitantly touched the wooden woman whose outstretched arms and loving smile were directed toward three small children carved at her feet. Esther felt a brief but shocking twinge of jealousy. She had not seen Moses smile at her like that since his infancy. But now, as he stood there mesmerized, he was beaming.

"When will I see her?" he asked the priest.

Two voices argued in Esther's mind: "He is Mosby's son and you cannot bear the constant reminder when you are with the boy for more than an hour." Then softer, but almost as powerfully: "Moses is *your* son as well. And *you* are his mother."

Moses turned again to the statue.

She took a step toward him, but the brown-robed, aging friar gently laid a hand on her arm and held her back.

"She comes here every night," the priest said to Moses. "When we are all asleep."

Esther's expression had become a plea as well as a question now. But the gray-haired Jesuit wisely shook his head. A small voice within her whispered that he was right. Surely it was better for Moses to be here rather than with her, seeing, every day, the loathing that he could only think was directed at him. Surely, not telling him that she was his mother, rather than telling him and leaving him here, wondering how his mother could do such a thing, was best. For a moment the logic was almost overwhelmed by emotions that seemed to pull her apart.

"Will she ever come in the day?" Moses asked.

The priest sighed. "Yes . . . one day . . . one day you—all of us—will see your real mother."

"I would like to go inside the great hut now," Moses said.

"Go," the priest said, smoothing the boy's wild black hair. "Father Bernardo is waiting for you inside the door."

The boy stared at Esther for a moment. Her moist eyes and the resignation in her face confused him for a moment. He saw her try to smile and innocently interpreted her tears as happiness for him. His huge brown eyes were no longer wary. She thought she saw the beginning of a grateful smile at the corners of his mouth. But then it and he were gone through the solid oak door.

She wiped her eyes and bit her lower lip until she thought she would draw blood. The priest strolled with her briefly, recounting the contents of her letter, reaffirming the wisdom of what she was doing, then bade her farewell.

In the hired buggy on the way back to Marysville, she refused to break down and have the driver see or hear it. She knew, now, that no matter how much she missed Murietta, *this* had tied her mind in knots, torn at her even more. She held herself in check until she was alone in the stagecoach, headed south again. Once the tears started, she thought they would never stop.

Fifty-one

It was late in the day when Esther debarked from the stagecoach in Sacramento. She was immediately reminded of Murietta and, tangentially, of Mosby.

The city was buzzing with stories of how the bandit and four companions had stopped a stage near the mining town of Angel's Camp, then inexplicably let it pass untouched. It had been one of Alex Todd's expresses, carrying gold from the southern mines. On board was a shipment from Frémont and another from E. Cable's Southern Sierra Mining Company. Some wags had it that Murietta was in the employ of the two mines. Others thought it possible that the bandit and the Todd cousins were in league with one another.

Esther had her bag taken to her rooms at the Hotel Orleans and headed for a real estate office owned by a sharp-faced man named William Sharon. She looked at two houses with him and found them unsuitable. Sharon showed her another, and she began to suspect that he was trying to unload at ridiculously inflated prices properties he probably owned himself. There could be no other reason why the houses were empty when they were in such short supply.

On the way back to the Orleans, Esther passed an eating establishment and could not believe the sign outside:

"The Donner Lake Restaurant. Proprietor: Lewis Keseburg."

She shuddered and shook her head in disgust. The sound of harsh male laughter drew her attention to an open-front saloon and beer garden just ahead. She started to cross the street, but then she had an even darker reminder of Joaquin. At one of the tables underneath a broad, striped awning, Isaac Claussen sat with his arm around a silver-haired Indian. Anger rose within her. As much as she hated Claussen for what he had done to Murietta, his association with Mosby made her wish even more that the red-bearded man were dead.

She had the urge to walk up to Claussen and smash his face with one of the whiskey bottles on the table. She took a deep breath to quiet and control her-

self, adjusted her veil, and slowed her stride. The
Indian was so drunk Claussen had grabbed his chin
and propped his head up. Claussen was talking non-
stop. Four other rough-looking white men nodded in
agreement with him. Two of them braced another
Indian much younger than the first. There was an
empty chair next to Claussen. It was pushed back as
though someone sitting there had left the table, but
Esther paid it no mind. The pale-brown men wore
miners' clothing. Their faces were partially obscured.
For a moment Esther got a good look at the Indians.
She could not tell if they were Miwoks or Maidu,
but something about the older one, whose silver hair
hung forward and partially obscured his face, seemed
familiar.

She was almost abreast of the saloon now, and
Claussen glanced out at her. Fear suddenly took its
place beside her anger. *I am only a woman,* she
thought. *And there are five of them. What chance
would I have?* Quickening her pace, she looked away
and hurried on. Turning a corner, she skirted a row
of charred, empty houses that had gone up in a
four-block blaze only two months before, and continued toward her hotel.

Luther Mosby looked at his watch as he stepped
out of the privy behind the saloon. Absently, he
brushed the back of a sleeve over the silver marshal's
star pinned over the breast pocket of his coat. Working his way back through the pantry past a Chinese
dishwasher, he went through the kitchen and the
main room of the saloon toward the front door. Outside, under the canvas awning of the open, beer garden area that fronted on the street, Mosby started
to sit down again next to Claussen. But the red-
bearded man stood up and motioned with his head
for Mosby to follow him out onto the wooden sidewalk.

Claussen waited until a man and woman passed

out of earshot, then whispered, "It's *him*, Luther, it's got to be. Ain't no two Indians in California with a scar like that."

"It's hard to believe," Mosby said, looking back at the older Indian.

"It all fits together. I *know* it's there. I can feel it!"

"Well, you must of slept in horseshit last night, if it *is* him. . . . I wish you luck," Mosby added with a touch of envy.

"You gotta come with us, Luther."

"I got a prisoner to think of."

Claussen glanced at Mosby's star. "Shit. You been gone how long comin' out here to find him?"

"Six weeks, maybe seven."

"Couple more days ain't gonna make no never mind."

Mosby pushed his hat back on his head and took in the bank across the street. He glanced up at the legal offices on the second floor and clucked his tongue against the inside of his teeth. "You think it could amount to more than just a piece of change?"

"You're damn right it could. I'm bettin' on it."

"I could use a stake like that," Mosby said, thinking. He glanced at the sign on the law offices again. "I got some plans go beyond bein' a marshal."

"Well, how 'bout it? You comin'?"

"I suppose I could let my man rest up in the jail for a few days more. It's gonna be a long trip back to Galveston."

"Now you're talkin'," Claussen said, putting his arm over Mosby's shoulder as the two of them headed back into the saloon.

Esther turned into Second Street and made her way to the entrance of the Hotel Orleans. Walking past the reading and billiard rooms, the saloon and parlor, she climbed the stairs to the second floor. In her suite she tried to distract herself with how quickly and precisely the proprietors had duplicated the original Creole decor of the hotel. It, too, had burned to the ground in the conflagration that summer, but the owners had replaced the old wood-frame structure with a larger one of brick.

Esther's distraction could not compete with the hatred she felt for Claussen—and something more; an uneasiness that surfaced now, refused to be ignored. Something about his friendly expression, the brotherly arm over the Indian's shoulder, the grinning camaraderie of the other four men with a second "Digger" went beyond simply being incongruous, inconsistent. She thought about it as she took off her hat and poured water from a pitcher to wash her hands and face. As she was drying her hands, she realized she was so upset, so preoccupied she had forgotten she wanted to take a bath rather than just freshen up. As the hot water in the tub calmed her and soaked away the stiffness brought on by the long ride back from Marysville, Esther searched her mind for a clue about the old Indian. She found nothing and gave up.

The discomfiting feeling that Claussen was up to no good persisted as she ate a light, early supper in her room. Finished, she opened a book the priest at the school had given her after she'd paid a year's board, room, and tuition in advance. She gazed through the open connecting door at Moses' empty bed in the next room. She began to think about him and had to bite her tongue to keep from crying again. She got up and closed the door to shut away the reminder. The sadness and guilt did not abate. She turned to the book again to escape. The volume was a whitewashed history of the California missions. She started to read, but her thoughts wandered back to Claussen. *No doubt,* she thought, *whatever it is Claussen and his cronies want, they will have before sunrise.* She wished there were something she could do. But she knew there was no way even Barnett would come to the aid of the two intoxicated Indians unless she could somehow substantiate her fears. Realizing that was impossible, she forced herself to read.

On the road to Coloma, Isaac Claussen reined up in the darkness and waited with Mosby and two of the men with them. Two others, leading horses carrying the drunken Indians, drew abreast ten minutes later.

"Goddamnit," Claussen said, "I want to be there by this time tomorrow night."

"We got 'em tied to the saddles, Isaac," one of the stragglers whined. "But if we ride any faster, they liable to pitch out, and we won't have no guides."

Claussen belched and thought for a moment. "Shit, I know the village they's talkin' about."

"You sure, Isaac?" Mosby asked. "Too much at stake if you ain't."

"Sure I'm sure. Ain't no other place like the one the Digger spoke of. Sheer cliffs on both sides of the river."

"You think they got it hid in the village?" one of the men asked.

"Where else? Probably got it buried somewheres." Claussen laughed. "We'll know soon enough."

Another man hesitantly spoke up. "Why's it have to be tomorra night? Can't we take an extra day travelin'?"

"You blockheaded bastard," Mosby snapped. "This's got to be fast and clean. Anyone gets wind of it . . ."

"It's be your ass, you mean," the chastened man said. "You bein' a marshal and all."

Mosby lashed out and struck the man with the back of his fist. "*You never heard that, never knew it*," Mosby growled, his eyes glaring. "You understand, you stupid son of a bitch? You better. 'Cause if you don't . . ."

"Take it easy, Luther," Claussen said, looking up at the pale quarter-moon. "You ain't wearin' your star. And none of these boys ever laid eyes on you. Ain't that right, boys? Anyways, it'd be *all* our asses. We'll travel by night, both nights. Goin' and comin'. No one ever sees us anywheres near the place."

"All right," Mosby said. He glanced around at the four men. "But just remember. *All* of you." He turned to Claussen again. "Now, what do we do with these two Diggers?"

Claussen eased his horse around and edged in next to the younger Indian. He started to pull his pistol, then decided against using it. Unbuttoning his jacket, Claussen pulled his bowie knife from its sheath. He pushed the unconscious Indian upright and sliced smoothly and deeply across his throat. A gurgling sound rose from the pale-brown man as his jaw dropped open. He stared at Claussen in hazy disbelief until his eyes rolled up under their lids and he slumped forward. Untying the leather thongs holding the Miwok to his saddle, Claussen let him fall to the ground.

Mosby watched as Claussen moved to the older man and removed a knife from under his belt. He grabbed a shock of the Indian's silver-gray hair and jerked him to a sitting position. The unconscious man's eyes opened briefly, then closed once more. As Claussen lifted the blade, he saw the old furrow over the Digger's left ear again. He hesitated for a moment, staring at the scar and remembering how the Indian had gotten it. Smiling with certainty, he drove the knife in hard under the old man's breastbone and left it there.

He cut the thongs around the older Indian's wrists and let him drop near the first one. Claussen motioned to the man Mosby had hit in the face. "Jenkins, git down and lay the young one on top of him. Sideways, kinda. Wrap his hand around that knife butt. Make it look like they's in a drunken brawl." Claussen pondered the two dead Indians for a moment. "Git me the knife in the young one's sheath," he said. "And that necklace the old geezer's wearing." Claussen smiled in self-satisfaction. "I got a notion how we might be able to use 'em."

Esther sat bolt upright, perspiring and wide awake. The book about the missions had fallen to the floor beside her bed. She looked at her watch. It was well past midnight. She could not remember falling asleep. She looked up and saw the pale quarter-moon hanging in the center of the open window beyond the footboard. A light breeze stirred the gauzy curtains for a moment, and from somewhere she heard the wail of a baby. Filling out in her mind, the moon suddenly was transformed into the rounded, heart-wrenchingly sad-eyed face of little Moses. The painful image faded as her thoughts progressed to Mwamwaash, then Solana—then Miwokan. Suddenly she knew why the Indian Claussen had been talking to had looked vaguely familiar.

She had not seen him in at least two years. His silver hair had grown inordinately long, and the old scar over his left ear had been concealed. Had she seen it, gotten a better look at him, she would have known sooner that the Indian was Miwokan's brother.

Fifty-two

Barnett was unreachable until almost noon the following day. Red-eyed and exhausted after a sleepless night, Esther caught him on his way to a carriage he was taking to the new state capital at Vallejo. She still had nothing to support her suspicions, and she could not bring herself to tell Barnett about the cache of gold buried at the base of the waterfall. Tightened like a guitar string from fatigue and frustration, her emotions snapped, and she could not hold back the tears. To put her mind at ease, Barnett instructed an aide to enlist a handful of deputies to accompany Esther to Miwokan's village.

It took until late afternoon to round up even two lawmen. They were uninterested at best, plainly annoyed that they had to ride more than a hundred miles going and coming for what they assumed was nothing. They were already talking about finding a place to stop for the night when they saw Miwokan's brother and the younger Indian. Two crows that had been plucking at the dead men flew off as they approached.

Esther gasped and turned her head away. The more heavyset of the two deputies took off his hat and stared down at the bodies for a moment. "Well, that's that, ma'am." He started to wheel his horse around for the ride back to Sacramento.

"*Just one minute!* Certainly you are not going to leave them here?"

The second deputy, a tall, gaunt man with enormous ears, stared at her. "Nothin' we can do for 'em now, ma'am."

"For God's sake, you can at least bury them."

"No shovels, ma'am. Besides, we don't do that."

She looked at the bodies and a faint awareness that something was incongruous about them flashed through her mind. The off-key note was lost for a moment in rising anger. "You don't *do* that? *You don't bury people lying dead along the side of a road?* What kind of law officers are you?"

The heavy-set deputy rolled his eyes up in exasperation. "That's undertaker's work. We'll send someone out . . ."

"You'll do no such thing!" she shouted. "By the time anyone gets to them, they'll be mutilated."

"You got no right to get sharp with us, ma'am,"

the gaunt deputy said. "You got no authority to tell us what we have to do. Anyways, you're actin's though these here was white folks. Plain to see they's just two drunken Indians killed each other in a fight."

"They shoulda thought about gettin' a decent burial before pickin' this place to kill each other," the other deputy said.

Esther was looking at the two dead men again, and what she began to realize overrode her urge to lash out with her reins at the face of the nearest peace officer. She got down from her horse and, fighting back nausea, reached out and pulled the younger Indian off the body of Miwokan's brother. She started to wretch at the sight of the wounds and blood, but the gagging stopped as she looked away and thought about the element that seemed to be missing. Then it struck her.

"There is only one knife."

"So what?" the heavy-set deputy said. He got down from his horse, not yet aware of what she was driving at. "Could've been throwed or knocked away in these bushes."

"Look for it," Esther said.

"Now lissen . . ."

"You *idiot*," Esther hissed. "Can't you see it would be practically impossible for them to stab each other in this way—in the heart and in the throat, at almost the same instant—even if they *had* two knives?"

The gaunt man got down now and looked more closely at the bodies. "She's right, Lemuel. Either one of these cuts would've stopped the other in his tracks. Couldn't have struck the second blow, stabbed the first one back."

The searched the underbrush carefully, then covered a circle of ground as far as a knife could possibly be thrown. They found nothing.

"Looks like they's murdered, all right," the gaunt man said.

"And more will be killed unless we get to the village in time," Esther said, getting back on her horse.

The two deputies looked at one another uneasily, then at Esther, both of them aware that she was a friend of Warren Barnett. "How many men you say was with these two?" the heavier man asked.

"At least five."

The gaunt man whistled. "We better stop by Negro Bar on the way, see if we can round up a few more men." He looked at Esther and sheepishly dropped his gaze. "Afraid we won't have time to bury 'em, ma'am. But maybe we can get someone to come down from the Bar and do it."

"Perfect," Claussen said. Lying next to him at the edge of the woods, Mosby nodded. Twenty yards away the watchman circled the storage shed on the eastern end of the sprawling South Fork Mining Company complex. Claussen waited until the watchman was beyond the building, then moved to the shadows underneath an enormous ore chute. The watchman circled back, and Claussen waited until he passed, a yard away, before stepping out from behind the braced chute support. He took one step, cupped his hand over the watchman's mouth, shoved the dead young Miwok's knife into his back, and held him until he stopped squirming, his knees buckled, and he fell.

Mosby watched as Claussen dropped the Indian necklace next to the dead watchman and waved the other four men over. When they were at his side, he gestured to the storage shed. Three minutes later, the four men returned with axes, picks, and kerosene. Mosby bent down and took a half-finished pint of whiskey out of the dead man's pocket. He found a small pouch of gold dust in the watchman's money belt and took that as well. He held the pouch up and saw the initials that had been burned into the leather: *SFM Co.* Smiling, he handed the bottle and the pouch to Claussen. The red-bearded man looked puzzled for a moment. But then he understood and nodded in approval.

"I'm sorry for the delay, but we got to rest the horses for an hour or so, ma'am," the gaunt deputy said.

Exhausted herself, Esther nodded and looked at her watch as the other deputy and the five miners riding with them dismounted. It was four in the morning. One of the men, a muscular black cook well over six feet tall and with a completely bald head, walked over to her. "Kin I lay out your bedroll, ma'am?" he asked in a gentle voice. "You might ought to git some rest."

"Thank you. I'm very grateful to you for coming."

"I seen this kind thing before," the black man said. "Done to mah own kind. Wa'n't nobody willin' to do nothin' 'bout it. Wasn't gonna be like them folks."

Esther nodded. She calculated the time it would take, riding hard, to reach the village. "Do you think we'll be ready to leave in an hour?"

The black man turned a corner of her blanket back and stood up. "First light, ma'am. Deputy say we be leavin' at first light."

Solana stirred, turned over under the fur blanket, and then awoke, listening for the sound that had aroused her. She heard it again—a faint *wooosh,* like the flight of a bird, followed by a soft, thicker noise that was accompanied by an almost inaudible crack. She thought one of the small boys in the village had risen early and was trying his skill with a bow and arrow on a tree stump. She clucked disapprovingly. There were only three dozen people in camp now. Most of the fathers were gone. A score of those who remained were children, and the boys were difficult to manage with only five men left.

She got up and went to the rear entrance of the

hut. She heard the sound again just as she stepped outside. This time she noticed that the hushing of the arrow in flight seemed unusually short. What seemed like the quick splintering of light bark and the noise of the arrowhead as it lodged in the soft core of a young tree followed the *wooosh* almost immediately. She had only the light of the false dawn to see by. She had taken three or four steps when she stumbled over the body of the sentinel. She crouched down and saw it was the young male who had just gone through his initiation ritual. There was a dark, gaping split in his head from crown to eyebrow.

She heard the sound again and waited as her eyes adjusted to the darkness. A white man in miner's clothing emerged from a hut twenty feet to her left. He was carrying an ax. The blade did not shine. Another man and then another moved from one hut to the next. Across the clearing, a heavy, bearded white man and a taller one with a moustache walked toward the dying campfire. She recognized Isaac Claussen from Placerville. In the faint glow of the logs the tall man's long, broad knife glistened and dark liquid dropped from its tip. The bearded man motioned to a sixth white carrying a pick, and they started toward Miwokan's hut.

Solana's mind was still not keeping pace with her quickening pulse. She heard a child wail and simultaneously remembered Mwamwaash just as she started back toward the rear entrance. She screamed, veered, picked up a spear lying against the hut and ran at Claussen.

She was halfway to him when someone knocked her down from behind. She rolled over and saw the tall white man with the moustache lift the long rifle by its muzzle, crouch, and adjust his swing as she rolled over on her stomach again. The flat of the stock came down hard on the back of her head, but the grip and part of the barrel hit the flesh across her back and shoulders, cushioning the blow so it

did not kill her. She heard Claussen say, "She's finished. Let's get on with it, Luther," before she blacked
out.

She felt herself rotating slowly, pulling at the earth
with her fingers because her legs did not work, as
she regained partial consciousness a few minutes later.
Blood ran down around her ears and over her cheeks.
She opened her eyes and saw that they had Miwokan,
three of them, and the bearded man was talking to
him. She saw the man with the moustache then, holding Mwamwaash upside down by his ankles. The boy
was sobbing. She tried to call out, but she could not
open her mouth. She attempted to crawl but could
not move. The blackness enveloped her again, briefly,
then she heard Claussen's voice.

"Where's the fuckin' gold?" he said, swinging up
with the thick, solid butt of his knife into Miwokan's
stomach. "Where you heathen bastards got it hid?"

Miwokan smiled at him. Claussen smashed him in
the nose.

"No one's gonna help you," Claussen said. "They
all gone. You better tell me."

Blood seeped down over Miwokan's split upper lip.
"There is no gold for you. Only the death it brings."

Claussen punched him with the knife butt again,
this time under the diaphragm. Miwokan choked, then
retched. He forced the bile down and pulled himself
erect. He locked his knees so his leg muscles would
stop quivering.

"You think you're smart, don't you, you Digger
bastard?" Claussen nodded at Mosby. "Dip that boy
into the fire for a minute, Luther. We'll just see if
his daddy don't want to talk."

Solana watched, helplessly immobile, as Mosby lowered the screaming boy until his hands were almost
touching the logs. Mwamwaash shrieked in agony as
the heat seared his fingertips and palms. The higher
pitch of his voice and his pleading eyes unleashed

something in Miwokan, a surging power he had not felt in years. He lifted himself from the men holding him and spun left, then right, throwing them off. Diving at Mosby, he bowled him over with his shoulders and pulled his son away from the fire in the crook of his outstretched arm.

The boy was under Miwokan now as he rolled and got up on all fours. He heard the other white men coming behind him. He gazed briefly at Mwamwaash's terrified, pain-filled beseeching face. "Forgive me," Miwokan said, turning the boy over on his side. He lifted his arm and brought the side of his hand down sharply on the flank of his son's neck, snapping it and killing him instantly. He started to get up, but the men were already on him.

Mosby waited until he got his wind back, then stood up and brushed at his clothes as two of the men held Miwokan again.

"Sand," Claussen said, whistling and raising his eyebrows. He turned to Mosby. "Got to hand it to him, Luther. He's got sand."

"You can no longer harm him," Miwokan said.

"No, but I can hurt you, Digger. An' I'm goin' to, 'less you tell me where the damn gold is!"

Miwokan was silent. Claussen turned to one of the men. "Get me an arrow. Caleb, Jared, get him on his feet."

When his man brought the stone-tipped shaft back, Claussen removed the arrowhead and sharpened the wooden tip with his knife. After he finished, he held the sharp point up and showed it to Miwokan. He flicked at it with his fingertip, then traced a red welt across Miwokan's chest.

"You ought to know about this little trick, Digger. I seen one o' your Apache cousins use it." Claussen turned to Mosby and smiled coldly. "This don't make him talk, nothin' will. Hold him steady. He ain't gonna like this at all. Hold them goddamned legs tight."

Claussen stepped up to Miwokan and inserted the point of the arrow shaft into one ear. "How's 'at feel? Huh? Feel good?"

Miwokan moaned, gritted his teeth, and tried to think of something else. Claussen slowly pushed the point farther in. Cold beads of sweat broke out all over Miwokan's body as the excruciating pain spread from his ear to the side of his head, then his jaw, his neck, and one shoulder. A low, animal sound came up from his throat and through his clenched teeth.

"*Goddamnit it,*" Claussen screamed. "*Why'n't you tell me where it is?*" He pulled the point out a bit. "You tell me now, won't you?"

"No," Miwokan muttered.

"*Why, goddamnit? Why?*" He held the point poised.

"Because you will kill me anyway."

"You heathen son'bitch," Claussen bellowed. Enraged, losing control completely, he jammed the point through drum cartilage and brittle bone into Miwokan's brain.

"Goddamnit, Isaac, now look what you done!" Mosby said. "There's none left to tell us where it is."

"We'll find it," Claussen snapped, angry with himself. "Look around. See if any of 'em's still alive."

While they were searching, Claussen spilled the contents of the whiskey bottle on Miwokan's upturned face and chest. He took out the pouch of gold dust and scattered it by one of Miwokan's hands. Prying open the fingers, Claussen inserted the empty pouch in his palm. With one foot he pushed the Indian's head over on its side. Picking up a long rifle by its barrel, he lifted it high and stamped the butt down hard on Miwokan's skull.

Solana felt Mosby turn her over. She stayed limp and held her breath. She was certain he would detect the pulsing beneath her eyelids, the thundering sound her heart was making in her ears. Mosby stood up and turned, and she got a good look at him before he shouted, "They're all dead. We'll never find it without help. Let's get the hell out of here."

Full consciousness slowly returned to her. She lay there watching surreptitiously as they spread the kerosene and set the village afire. When they were gone, she dragged herself to Miwokan, listened for a heartbeat and, finding none, slowly rolled him into the campfire. She pushed along the ground to Mwamwaash. He was not breathing, but except for his hands, there were no marks on him, no blood. Hoping against hope, dragging him by one arm, she crawled until they were beyond the searing heat of the blazing huts.

Isaac, she thought, trying to take her mind off the terrible pain and pulsations at the back of her head, down her neck, and across her back. "Isaac Claussen and Luther—something," she said out loud. "I am only an Indian, only a woman. But one day, if it is in my power to do it, I will kill you both for this."

The sun was up when Esther and the men found Solana, propped up against a tree, staring blankly and rocking Mwamwaash back and forth in her arms. Feeling as though the blood had been drained out of her body, Esther walked dazedly to the river and soaked a piece of her undergarments to wash Solana's head wound. The rest of them moved through the smoking village. She didn't need to go and look herself or hear the details. She knew them from the stunned silence of the men as they picked their way through the hacked and charred bodies—five men, ten women, and twenty children.

The tall, gaunt deputy came back after what seemed hours. "Found this." He showed Esther the pouch bearing the *SFM Co.* brand. "And this." He held up the whiskey bottle. "There's a bunch of axes and

picks scattered around, and a couple of kerosene cans.
. . . They all got the South Fork Mining Company
mark on 'em."

Appalled, Esther wondered for a moment if he
knew she owned the company. The thought that
Claussen had used SFM Co. equipment suddenly
made her nauseated.

The heavy-set deputy looked at Esther, shook his
head, and pulled the gaunt man aside. "Looks to me
like them miners down the ways come up here to
get even for somethin'. What do you think?"

"We better go have a look in at South Fork," the
gaunt deputy said. "Might could be touchy."

Esther stared at them as she wiped at her mouth
with her sleeve. She started to tongue-lash them, but
she was too numb, too tired to even cry, let alone
speak. She knew it was no use anyway. They would
believe what was easiest to believe. Later, when the
inconsistencies were more apparent, they would know
it had been rigged. But by then it would be too late.
For a moment the only positive thought she could
muster consoled her. Had she waited another few
days, Moses also would have been lost. She grasped
at that fact as though it were a buoyant piece of
wood in the wake of a shipwreck. But even it did not
keep her from sinking further into the numbing horror and grief that enveloped her.

The black miner stayed and helped her build a
small, makeshift pyre over the dead campfire and the
remains of Miwokan. She tried not to look at the
body but found that impossible. It was as though her
brain were forcing her eyes to the focus of her guilt-
ridden thoughts. *If only I had begun thinking of them
sooner—acted more quickly, taken them away from
this place, they would not be dead.*

Solana was too weak to participate, too shocked to
speak, so she simply watched through dulled eyes as
Esther placed Mwamwaash's body on top of the
stacked branches and set them ablaze. At first, Esther

had in mind to wait until the fire died, cooled, and then take a handful of the ashes to the waterfall. But the sight and the stench of the charred, smoking village, the sorrow and grief rocking her, and the vivid memories of the larger, even more emotionally devastating pyre upon which she had placed little John Alexander, were simply too much to bear.

The snow will soon do the same thing, she thought. *It will fall in a month or two. . . . It will be essentially the same purification. . . . It will all be gone by spring. . . . Oh, God. . . . Forgive me, Sunbrother. I cannot . . . I cannot . . . I simply do not have the strength to stay—even until the fire reaches its peak.*

She waited limply as the black man brought back one of the scattered Indian ponies for her, then lifted Solana up onto Esther's horse. At Negro Bar he helped her purchase a wagon for the remainder of the trip back to Sacramento. When they parted, she gave him every ounce of gold, every coin she had.

Fifty-three

Sacramento
May 7, 1869
8:45 A.M.

Esther looked up from the account of the massacre in her diary and realized she was coated with a light film of sweat. The air in the parlor car was close. She could hardly breathe. She got up, still thinking about how, years earlier, Solana had finally recounted

that terrible morning at the village, mentioning only
Claussen's name. She walked back to the rear of the
car. Pulling the bolt free, she opened the door and
stepped outside onto the open observation platform.
Shutting from her mind all thought of what might
take place on this small metal rectangle later in the
day, she took deep breaths to regain her composure.

Settled, cool again in mind and body, she glanced
across several sets of railroad tracks toward Front
Street. Down near the station, members of a band
were gathering at a wooden stand decked with patriotic bunting, arranging sheet music and taking
seats. Already passengers were headed toward the
train from Front Street. Some, Esther guessed, had
already boarded the forward cars. She looked the
other way and saw Solana and young Todd in the
distance, near the riverbank. She wondered if Solana
had ever seen Mosby during the massacre. She knew
he had been there; a chance remark had told her
that. But the Indian woman had never described anyone but Claussen, who had sold his ranch and vanished. But what if she *had* seen Mosby and simply
never said so? It suddenly registered with Esther that
Solana had seen Mosby last night, when she delivered the rendezvous message at the hotel. Esther
chided herself for not thinking of the possibility that
Solana might remember him, of what seeing him again
might have provoked. But Solana had said nothing.
Undoubtedly, Esther thought, *she was unconscious
during the massacre and never really got a good look
at him. Thank God, considering the complications
that might have developed and crippled* my *plans.*

Memories of the two years following the massacre
unfolded in Esther's mind as she gazed out over the
river to her right. Numb with guilt and grief, she
had sold the mining properties and the Mariposa ranch
in early 1853, had bought and moved to a farm on
the outskirts of Sacramento. She had nursed Solana
back to health and then virtually collapsed from men-

tal and physical exhaustion. In all, nine months passed before she was even remotely herself again.

Esther stepped to the back railing and sighed as she remembered how the abating grief and lethargy had returned in full force when she learned that Harry Love and his rangers had finally caught up with Murietta and killed him. After two months of keeping to her bed she had decided that activity and absorption were the only things that might heal her almost incapacitating sorrow. She established a school for orphaned and abandoned children, plunging into the work with an almost maniacal fervor. She insisted that the school be open to Indian as well as white students, and for a time the project and its problems had preoccupied her. But then, after six months, Esther found herself becoming short with her young wards, slipping back into apathy and, finally, indifference to almost everything.

Turning from the railing Esther caught sight of Alex Todd coming out of the hotel on Front Street. As he tipped his hat to a passing woman in a full-bustled dress, Esther thought about Judith Britten, the lovely young teacher she had found to run the school in her place. Even now, the similarity of their facial and bodily appearance seemed remarkable to Esther. She had taken Judith to San Francisco during the summer of '54 and introduced her to the Kelseys. It had occurred to her that Alex might well be attracted to Judith. He was still unmarried after seven years; and her resemblance to his "dead" wife, Elizabeth, might prove an overpowering lure.

They were having dinner with the Kelseys and Warren Barnett. Esther had simply asked Bill Kelsey how well Alex was looking after Blue Star's interests in his new post as vice-president of Wells, Fargo and Company. Judith was sitting directly across the dinner table from Kelsey, and as he responded to Esther's question, he glanced at the young woman. Esther had virtually seen the wheels in the inveterate matchmaker's mind begin to turn as he put together the thought of his friend Alex Todd and the sight of Judith Britten's lovely face.

Esther turned and went back into the parlor car now, absently leaving the bolt on the rear door open. She sat down and stared at the journal, thinking about how much had developed at that otherwise unremarkable dinner gathering. Beyond what had been set in motion for Alex and Judith, it had been the first time Esther had had any idea that Mosby was involved in the massacre. Barnett, commenting on the terrible incident over coffee, had thought for a moment, then cryptically shaken his head.

"No," he had said absently. "I don't suppose it would have made any difference."

"What wouldn't have?" Esther asked.

"Another man. A marshal. There was another peace officer in Sacramento the day you told me of Claussen's suspicious behavior. A man from Galveston who had pursued an escaped prisoner, caught him here in California, and was preparing to take him back to Texas."

"What of him?" Esther said.

"I was just wondering if it would have made any difference, if the marshal had gone with you, considering how few men my aide was able to round up."

"Perhaps. But Claussen had too much of a head start, I think."

Galveston, Esther thought. *South-central Texas.* She upbraided herself silently for such a ridiculous notion. Still, the question would not go unasked, unanswered. "I don't suppose you remember the name of the peace officer from Texas, do you, Warren?"

"I don't think so. So much time has . . . Mosby. His name was Mosby. I remember it because someone mentioned he had escaped death at the Alamo by taking a message to an officer encamped some distance from the old mission."

Esther clenched her fists and bit her lip to keep from crying out in astonishment.

"Remarkable luck, don't you think?" Barnett said.

"Yes, remarkable," Esther replied, almost faint.

"Is there something the matter? You don't look well."

"I've been feeling poorly all day," Esther said, excusing herself. Upstairs in the Kelseys' guest room she had lain awake all night, filled with rage and frustration.

Footsteps on the gravel separating the railroad tracks just beyond the window of the parlor car jarred Esther from her recollections. For a moment, she thought she had imagined the sound. But then she heard it again—someone moving down the side of the parlor car. One of the trainmen, she thought. She stood up, cracked the shade beside her, peered out, and saw Luther Mosby walking slowly toward the rear of the car.

Paralyzed with surprise and sudden fear, Esther watched as he walked to a point just below the rear-platform railing and glanced back toward Front Street. In the midst of wondering why he was here now, rather than later in the day at Dutch Flat, Esther saw Mosby turn again, glance up at the windows of the car, and start around the rear platform to the obscured side of the car.

Esther let go of the shade and fell back into her chair. She heard him walk past the window opposite and continue on toward the front of the car. There was silence for a minute, but then she heard him climb the metal stairs onto the forward platform. After another moment of stillness she saw the handle turning slowly as he tried the front door.

When he found it locked, he went back down the stairs on the side of the car screened from Front Street and began walking toward the rear again. He was almost abreast of the window opposite Esther when she remembered she had not rebolted the rear door. *Oh, my God,* she thought, jumping up and moving quickly and silently across the compartment. *It will all be ruined if I confront him now. I'm not prepared. I'm not ready.*

She reached the rear door just as she heard him step up onto the stairwell. Gripping the tiny bolt-handle firmly, she slowly began easing the metal cylinder into its socket, praying that it would not click and alert him to what she was doing. She had just slipped it home when she felt the door handle in her other hand begin to turn. Holding her breath and pressing her face to the broad shade covering the small window, she relaxed her grip as the force of his turning lifted her hand. When she realized suddenly that his face was no more than six or eight inches from hers on the other side of the door, she almost fainted. She let go of the handle, eased her head back carefully, then waited to be sure he had not seen the depression her cheek had made on the shade.

"Mizz Carter?" she heard him say, her legs shaking uncontrollably. "Mizz Carter?"

The door handle rattled as he tried it again, and she was so frightened she thought she would urinate. Slowly, she backed away from the door into the hallway, through the pantry and kitchen, and sat down on the bed. She heard him go down the steps and then cross the gravel as he started back around and up toward the passenger cars. Gathering her nerve, she peeled back another shade in the sleeping area and watched as he picked up two bags and boarded.

Behind Esther, out of view, Solana approached with young Todd. When she saw Mosby her eyes narrowed, and she involuntarily squeezed the boy's hand so hard he let out a yelp. Esther neither saw nor heard. When her heart was beating normally again, she relieved herself in the bathroom, then retraced her steps to the chair she had been sitting in and picked up the journal. She wondered if her nerve would crumple the same way later that morning when she would need to be as firm as the steel tracks upon which the parlor car sat. *I cannot know,* she thought, *until it happens. But I will do my best, and I will be prepared. The reading will steady and strengthen me. I know it will. It must.*

She looked at the entries tied with the black ribbon and clenched her teeth. *He is on this train,* she thought. *And I will do what I have set out to do!* Opening the journal, flipping past the ribboned entries and the pages she had already covered, Esther began reading again, letting go of the present as her handwritten sentences, some of them no more than skeletally descriptive, brought all of it back fully, clearly in her mind.

Fifty-four

San Francisco
October 27, 1854

Dearest Husband, it is difficult to believe that I was twenty-five years old yesterday! Almost as difficult to believe as the fact that Yerba Buena Cove no longer exists, what with the continuous process of land-filling and creation of new streets toward the east for this extraordinarily growing city! Have not written in this journal for so long a time. It seems fitting to begin again now that I have fully recovered from the after-effects of the massacre and

Murietta's death. Moved here from Sacramento last summer, after being jarred back to a sense of purpose once again upon learning of Mosby's part in what happened to Miwokan and Mwamwaash. The thought of it fills me with renewed hatred for the man, along with the frustration that comes of knowing how impossible it would be for me to take revenge on him now. I have thought long and hard upon the matter. There is simply no way I could bring it off under present circumstances without giving up my own life in the bargain almost automatically. I not only must do the deed myself, I wish to savor such a retaliation. What good would it be, what satisfaction, if I were dead along with him? I would not know it, or feel it. It would be the same as if I had never done it at all. No, I will continue to wait. Time may bring the opportunity, unforced, to me.

Moved here not a moment too soon, considering the fire that recently wiped out seven-eighths of Sacramento. My farm was not touched, but all the hastily built houses they so unexpectedly surrounded my land with went down. I must think about the substantial offer I received in the mail two weeks ago for the property. Perhaps I could sell off the acreage but keep the house. I would not like to dispossess the handsome and grave mercantile man, Leland Stanford, to whom I am renting the place, and his lovely young wife.

I babble on about such things to delay telling you how I really feel about your announced engagement to Judith Britten. Oh, God, Alex, I should not be jealous! I should be happy for you, grateful that my machinations have brought you a measure of comfort and joy after so many years. What a rare example of good nature your prospective bride is. But what is in me now, churning, tearing, keeping me awake each night, is a longing to be in your arms more powerful than I have felt in half a score years. Oh, Alex, I still love you as I did as a girl. . . . Dear God, let this burning in my mind and my loins cease!

There. I have wiped away the torrent of tears from my face, and I take some comfort in your happiness. After all, it was I who brought the two of you together, indirectly or not. And there is some small consolation in the fact that Judith looks enough like me to be a sister. I must be stronger, less selfish, Alex. This is the price I must pay for the course I decided upon when I came down out of the mountains. Even now, I still dream of the two of us together someday. But, of course, that is impossible. And I will stop thinking about it.

It interests me, Alex, that amid all your activities at Wells Fargo, you are studying law at night. . . . God, I cannot believe the meanness that just ran through my mind. As a measure of how strong my feelings for you are still, I took momentary pleasure in the notion that your studies will reduce the time you and Judith can spend together in bed! Forgive me. I will try to strengthen my resolve not to have such thoughts. . . .

In any case, Kelsey thinks you are secretly planning a political move, rather than simply arming yourself with legal knowledge to perform effectively in your post as vice-president of W, F & Co. I wonder. Are you simply acquiring an additional skill to use should you find yourself unseated someday? I suppose such could happen in the light of the fierce competition between Wells Fargo and Adams and Company.

I want you to know I have left my money at Adams simply out of laziness and disinterest, drawing from my account only for my monthly needs and the purchase of this house. I truly love this place, situated as it is on the crown of this hill, which for some reason is called Lone Mountain. It is far enough to the west of the city to be tranquil and unpestered by drummers, advertisers, and the like. The view is magnificent. One can scarcely hear the hum of the city, let alone the often boisterous noise of the crowds.

But I wander. I must make a note to myself to transfer my account to Wells Fargo. The ridiculous figure—$991,087—is simply there, as far as I am concerned. But leaving it at Adams seems disloyal to you, since it might be of some use to Wells Fargo. I suppose if your fight with Adams comes down to the wire, it might even be a significant deposit, however much, W. F. already has in its vaults. I promise to begin transferring it next month, a portion at a time so as not to cause a ruckus and entreaties from the Adams management.

I wish I could persuade Solana to ride with me into town. I do not cotton to going in alone. She is worse than I am, even more reclusive, sitting there in her rocker on the porch, day after day. Of course, she has much weighing upon her. At least when Emilio and Marianita were still with us, the old woman could occasionally bring Solana to life in the kitchen. I miss them. And I fear Emilio simply wanted to return to his home village in Mexico to wait for death.

Still find it difficult to believe that Murietta is gone. Strange, but upon reading the news that Harry Love and his rangers had killed him, something in me said it was not Joaquin. Of course, that is more hope than realism, considering they exhibited his head—barbarians—and the hand of his supposed accomplice, Three-Fingered Jack, in every town of any size in California. In jars of alcohol! Good God, there is no end to man's capacity for the vulgar and sensational.

It is almost as difficult to believe that Billy Ralston, your old friend from Ohio, has been working these past five years in Panama as a manager for the Pacific Mail Steamship Company. And that he is being transferred to the main offices here in San Francisco. (In a sense, he will work for me!) Barnett says he is an extraordinarily convivial and outgoing young man. Can you imagine! I have been invited to the dinner celebrating your engagement, at which Billy will also be present! I wonder if he would recognize me? Pointless question, since you certainly would. I have had to maneuver so many times in order not to be in the same room with you it begins to vex me. But I must find a plausible excuse for declining once again.

It would otherwise be enjoyable, since I see so little of Warren Barnett these days. It pleases me that he is virtually the leader of the Democratic Party in California, even though he has decided not to run for reelection as lieutenant governor. The slavery issue that divides the party spurs him, I know, in his incessant hegiras about the state. Sometimes I think he would travel a hundred miles to speak to a meeting of two laborers under an oak tree in a thunderstorm! I worry about him. If he is not more careful of himself, he is bound to be taken ill.

All of a sudden I have a growing desire to be out in the world again. I suppose two years of keeping essentially to myself, reading for endless hours, and mothering my flower garden have been enough. In any event, I feel as though a pall has been lifted since moving here. Perhaps I might go to the theater, if I can persuade Solana to accompany me. The praise heaped on the Booth family's Shakespearean performance tempts me. I do not know if I care to see Lola Montez, aside from my feminine craving to discover what all the fuss is about. (Half-naked on a horse, indeed!) No doubt I will find excuses to put off a visit to town. But I shall not let a month slip by before I go in, with or without Solana.

Indeed, I have the very thing to justify the shedding of my hermit's cloak. I loathe the curtains left by the previous owner. There is an upholstery-and-materials shop that carries a variety of draperies. Next to that abominable sideshow tent on Sacramento Street, if I recall correctly. Moreover, I must begin transferring my deposits. I will set my mind to it and go.

Fifty-five

Esther turned her carriage into Sacramento Street and slowed the horse to a walk. The drapery shop was just a block ahead. For a moment the throngs of people made her think of turning around and going home. There were fifty-thousand souls in San Francisco now, a thousand new buildings—more than half of them of brick and stone. It was no longer an infant port. Now it was what Barnett had expected it to be, the United States gateway to the Orient. It boasted more than a hundred and fifty boardinghouses and hotels. New telegraph lines connected the city with Sacramento, San Jose, Stockton—and Marysville.

For a moment Esther thought of little Moses. The latest report from the school near Marysville was that he could not be more content or doing better in his studies. Then, contemplating one of the numberless gambling tents and saloons she had driven past, Esther wondered whether coming into town had been a wise idea after all. She was unsettled, ill at ease in the presence of so much unwashed humanity. She saw a man carrying a gun and recalled newspaper articles she had read about the proliferation of dueling. She shuddered at the thought of such violence, then smiled to herself at the irony of such normally delicate sensibilities juxtaposed with what she planned eventually to do to Mosby.

As she reined the horses to a halt in front of the store, she glanced up one of the hills in the distance and gasped at the size of a mansion being erected on its crown. She had read of such homes, had driven by several that afternoon on the way in from her house, but the size of this one was staggering. She guessed that three houses the size of her own could easily be fitted into it, and she speculated for a moment about how much material it would take to curtain the windows in such a dwelling. Getting down from the carriage, she snugged the reins into the ring of a hitching post and started toward the store.

Halfway across the sidewalk she noticed the sign hanging on the front of the old carnival tent standing in the lot next door. She stopped, suddenly feeling as though the blood had drained out of her and she was encased in an enormous, soundproof bubble of glass. The sign, surrounded by others touting the carnival's exotic attractions, read:

SEE
THE HEAD
OF THE RENOWNED BANDIT
JOAQUIN!
and the Hand of
Three-Fingered Jack!
on Exhibit here Daily!

Esther swayed and reached out for something with which to support herself. She felt soft material beneath her hand. Turning, she saw that she was gripping a frilled gold epaulet. For a few seconds she was certain she was dreaming, but then the portly, bearded man wearing one epaulet on his tattered military jacket—along with a top hat fitted with an ostrich feather and a sword in a scabbard—spoke to her.

"Have no fear, madam. I am Joshua Abraham Norton, Emperor of the United States and Protector of Mexico. And seeing you sorely distressed, I am at your service."

"Forgive me . . . but I felt faint for a moment."

"That sign would make anyone feel faint," the oddly dressed man said. "It is a monument to man's base nature."

Esther finally realized who Norton was. He had lost a fortune in gold during one night at the gambling tables and gone mad. He was harmless, at most a nuisance, supported and in an odd way revered by the citizens of San Francisco. *Perhaps they see in him what any one of them might have become,* Esther thought. But for the grace of God, John Sutter might be standing beside her instead. She dug in her purse and handed Norton a dollar.

"Thank you, kindly, ma'am. Is there anything I can do for you before going on about the business of government?"

"No." Esther glanced at the sign on the carnival tent again. "Wait," she called as Norton started to move on. She had to go in and see for herself. She could not allow the shred of doubt that Murietta was dead linger in her mind a moment longer. The urge took hold of her and carried her through the repulsion she felt for all carnivals and sideshows. She could not possibly go in alone. "Will you accompany me into the tent?" she asked Norton. "I will pay for your ticket and give you another dollar."

"There will be no need for you to pay additional taxes," Norton said, taking her arm and guiding her forcefully down the sidewalk.

Esther's apprehensions about seeing Joaquin's severed head were overridden by Norton's propellant grip on her arm. Inside they passed a man covered from shoulders to ankles with tattoos, a cageful of reptiles, a fat woman with a beard. When Norton saw Esther hesitantly edging toward the two glass jars on a table set up at the rear of the tent, he stopped.

"I have no stomach for such things, madam. I will wait for you here. Perhaps the man who eats fire will put on a display in my honor."

Esther nodded and eased her way past a dozen people watching an act in one of the alcoves. When she reached the table, she could not at first look directly at the two jars filled with alcohol. Forcing herself, she glanced at them out of the corner of her eye.

On the left, a ghastly white hand, severed at the wrist and missing two digits, hung fingers-down in the colorless liquid. Next to it, the head rested at a slight angle on the glass bottom of a larger jar. There was no odor, other than the stale smell of sawdust underfoot and the faint aroma of an elephant chained to a post ten yards away, but Esther felt nauseated. Fighting down the queasiness, she took darting looks at the head, turning her eyes away every few seconds until she was sure she would not be sick.

She quickly read the small, lettered rectangle between the two jars. It described the two bandits, their infamous careers, and the details of their capture. She forced herself to look steadily at the severed head. The eyelids were closed. The hair was long and straight, straighter than Joaquin's wavy, dark locks. The nose was flattened, too big. The cheekbones, almost Indian in their breadth, were too wide. It did not look like Joaquin at all. Oddly, the head seemed to be smiling. And then Esther noticed the gleaming gold tooth.

Outside, after Norton had gone, she tried to recover, distract herself from the horror of the exhibit, by wrestling with the conviction that it was not Joaquin. She had no idea if alcohol could render such changes in a face after death. He might have replaced the false tooth with one of gold, she thought. She was standing by her carriage, trying to remember which tooth it was that Joaquin had lost. But then all thought of him vanished as she saw Luther Mosby step out of the doorway directly across the street. Scarcely able to breathe, she scanned the front of the building. Across two windows on the second floor the black-bordered, gold letters seemed to scream out at her deafeningly: "LUTHER MOSBY—ATTORNEY AT LAW."

Still stunned, Esther watched him walk to the right and cross an intersection. Unconsciously, she felt in her purse as though she were carrying a gun, as though it were that night on Portsmouth Square when she thought the gambler with his back turned was *he*. Snapping out of it, she climbed into the carriage, pulled away from the curb, and followed Mosby at a discreet distance. The information Kit Carson relayed to Frémont had been right, she thought. He had studied for the bar. And Sutter had been right. Mosby would only come back to California if he could command a position of status or authority. *I will not panic,* she thought. *He is here. In San Francisco. There is time. There is no need to blunder into it. I must watch, and wait, and find the best way to do it. I will control my emotions. I will not let them rob me of the day I have waited for these past eight years.*

Mosby turned a corner several blocks away. When Esther eased the carriage into the street he had entered, she saw no trace of him. For a moment panic rose in her. But then she remembered the sign on the window of his office. *He isn't going anywhere,* she thought. *He is here to stay. There is plenty of time.*

She sat in the carriage, as though she were waiting for someone, for an hour. She took note of a hotel on the near side of the street, then finally saw

Mosby come out of a cheap-shingled house onto the opposite sidewalk. He headed back toward his office. She waited until he was out of view, then walked across the street. In front of the two-story, shingled dwelling, Esther hesitated. She looked both ways and, sure no one was watching, lifted the door-knocker and let it fall twice.

The door opened, and Arabella Ryan peered out. "What can I do for you, dearie?"

Esther put her hand to her veiled face in shocked surprise.

"Well? Cat got your tongue?"

"I'm terribly sorry," Esther said, gathering her wits. "I seem to have the wrong address."

"Think nothin' of it," Arabella said, closing the door.

Esther smiled as she climbed back into her carriage and drove back to the drapery shop. She hardly saw the material the proprietor showed her. The only evidence of preference she gave him was for those bolts laid out by the front window. She let him chatter on about the advantages and beauty of each sample as she gazed past him, through the window, at Luther Mosby's office across the street.

"I can't make up my mind," she finally said. "I'll come back again tomorrow."

Esther returned to the drapery shop each afternoon for five days, playing the role of a silly, indecisive, rich young woman with nothing but time on her hands. When she was certain Mosby went to the bordello each afternoon at two, she placed an order for material, then bought a spyglass and took a room on a monthly basis in the hotel directly opposite Arabella Ryan's "boardinghouse."

Aside from Mosby, only one other man returned to the house across the street regularly. Late one night, after telling Solana she was taking a two-day trip to Sacramento, Esther saw the second man arguing with Arabella Ryan through a window of one of the

second-floor rooms. She watched as the man turned
on his heel, then stalked out through the front door
of the bordello a minute later. Pleading, Arabella
ran out after him. When the madam contritely handed
him a roll of bills, the man smiled, kissed her, and
strode off down the street.

Esther put on a coat, raced downstairs, and followed him to a gambling hall several blocks away.
Sitting at a table off in one corner, she sipped tea
laced with brandy and watched as the man lost every
penny Arabella had given him. One of the men at
the faro table with him frowned and said, "Should've
paid what you owe 'stead'a playin' again, Cora. When
are we gonna see the money due us?"

"Soon," the man named Cora said, obviously uncomfortable. "Soon."

"You keep up like this, Charlie, you're gonna be
in deep trouble," another gambler said. "People been
known to find themselves dead owes less than you
do."

"You'll have your money!" Cora said, turning on
all the bravado he could muster. "And don't threaten
me, understand?"

Waiting several minutes, Esther followed Charles
Cora back to the bordello. In her hotel room she
turned her spyglass on the second floor across the
street. Cora was sitting on the edge of a bed, his
head in his hands. Arabella Ryan seemed beside herself, gesturing in a way that made it obvious to Esther that she was saying there was nothing she could
do to help.

Esther smiled. Undressing, she got into bed and lay
sifting it all in the darkness. She did not yet know
how, but she was certain that Charles Cora and Arabella Ryan would play a part in the undoing of
Luther Mosby.

Fifty-six

After the plan took form in Esther's mind, she continued observing Charles Cora and following Mosby, carefully, on foot and in her carriage. For two more weeks she weighed the possibility of an alternative, but none presented itself. Mosby's hotel room was inaccessible except by its door. The lobby and hallways were never empty, even late at night. In his hotel any move she made would be detected immediately. There was a staircase up the side of the wooden building in which Mosby had his office, but he never stayed past sunset. During the day, there was simply too much activity, too many potential witnesses in Sacramento Street. And the saloons and gambling dens he frequented were out of the question.

In mid-December, when she was certain there was no other place where he was as vulnerable, she waited until dark in her hotel room, put on one of her heaviest veils, and went across the street to Arabella Ryan's front door.

Cora's bad luck at the gambling tables had remained unchanged during the month Esther had watched both him and Mosby. As she raised the bordello's doorknocker a second time, there was no question in her mind that the madam would jump at almost any chance to obtain money to help Cora. She had no doubt, after watching him come and go, after seeing them locked in each other's arms through the second-floor window, that Charles Cora was Arabella Ryan's lover. It was plain to see that she was almost frantic

about his predicament. And it was virtually indis-
putable that Luther Mosby had a sexual appetite of
mammoth proportions. More than once Esther had
seen him go into this house on his daily visit, then
return later in the evening, stay for another hour, and
then leave with a Chinese prostitute on his arm. On
occasion he took a tall girl with long, dark hair and
Latin features back to his hotel. Mosby's taste for
the unusual was not lost on Esther. The hat, veil, and
gloves she planned to wear when she finally confronted
him might just prove to be pivotally disarming dis-
tractions.

Esther held her breath for a moment as Arabella
Ryan opened the door a few inches and stared at her.
The only nagging doubt she had about her plan lay
in the possibility that Arabella would somehow recognize her. More than six years had passed since that
night when the madam thought she could rifle Esther's
bag after drugging her tea in the converted stable
on Montgomery Street. Despite that, and the heavy
veil Esther was wearing, she trembled as she watched
for the slightest sign of recognition. There was none.

"Thought you said you had the wrong address."

"No, I merely lost my nerve last month. May I
speak with you privately?"

Arabella sized her up and decided from the conservative cut of Esther's clothing that there was no
money to be made from her. "I'm awful busy, dearie."

"It's about Charles Cora."

The madam's eyebrows rose. "What about him?"

"I think I can help you—him. He owes a considerable amount of money, does he not?"

"How did you . . . ?" Arabella glanced over her
shoulder, then turned back, still skeptical but too desperate about Cora to ignore even the remotest possibility of extricating him from the hole he had dug
for himself. "Come in, dearie. Please come in."

The madam ushered Esther through a dimly lit
foyer and then a parlor done up in red flocking, sec-

ond-hand couches, and frayed soft chairs. A half-dozen women lazed about in undergarments and flowing, diaphanous nightgowns. One of them yawned as Arabella opened a curtained French door at the rear of the room and let Esther into a small office. An oil lamp fitted with a green eyeshade sat flickering on the madam's desk.

"Can I get you some tea, miss?"

"Missus," Esther said as her eyes adjusted to the darkness. "No, thank you kindly." The irony of it struck her, and she almost laughed. She noticed the rumpled cot pushed up against one wall.

"I was just takin' a nap," Arabella said defensively. She gestured to a chair. "Sit down, sit down."

"A nap? Your friend Mr. Cora was here just a while ago, wasn't he?"

"Now look here! That's my . . . How did . . . ?"

"I didn't mean to pry. I know you are lovers. And I know how much you want to help him. How much money does he owe?"

"Why should I tell you that? I don't even know you. What's this all about?"

"Let me explain. I'm a newly married woman. I . . . I'm inexperienced in the ways of . . . sex. My husband has . . . demanding tastes, and I do not wish to lose him. I want to learn a few things by observation, and I'm willing to pay for the knowledge. Enough to help your Mr. Cora with his difficulties. Now, how much does he owe?"

"Who are you?"

"Don't be ridiculous! I'm certainly not going to reveal my identity. If my husband ever found out . . ."

"Yeah, I can see what you mean. How much does Charlie owe? I'd say in the neighborhood of seven thousand dollars."

"And he could lose his life if he doesn't repay it?"

Arabella winced. Her fingers moved nervously. "Yeah. It's possible." She sobbed and put one hand over her eyes. "Oh, Jesus, what am I gonna do with him?"

"I can help you."

"Seven thousand's a lot of money to pay for . . ."

"I didn't say I'd pay all of it."

"I see. How much are you willing to spend?"

"Two thousand dollars. Initially. . . . There may be an opportunity for you to earn the balance by performing another—favor—for me."

"What kind of favor?"

"First things first. I promise you I'll give you the opportunity, and that it will not be a burden. It will be easy, in fact. But first there are things I must learn. Is the Oriental woman who works for you the most skilled of your . . . employees?"

The madam's eyebrows rose again. "You know an awful lot about—"

"Does that matter? Beyond the fact that you must know by now you are not dealing with a fool?"

"No, I suppose not. But you sure been studyin' up, all right." Arabella hesitated, thinking a moment. "Yeah, I'd say Ling Wu is right up there with the best of them. Maybe one other girl here's as good."

"The Latin girl?"

"No. French. She's dosed up, though." A look of apprehension followed by one of relief passed across her face. "She sure as hell won't be workin' *here* no more."

"You looked troubled for a moment. Is something the matter?"

The madam sighed. "No. But there could'a been. One of my steady customers sees the French girl from time to time. It's just lucky he hasn't had a taste for her the last few weeks. He's a mean one."

Esther had no doubt who the customer was. "Well, in any event, I'd like to observe the Chinese girl . . . at work. Would that be possible?"

"For two thousand? You bet your life it is!"

"I wouldn't want the girl, or whoever is with her, to know."

"'Course. 'Course. That's no problem. You're not the first—well, person—wanted to watch. We got men come in here do nothin' else. You're the first woman, though."

"How is it arranged?"

"We got a peephole—behind one of the pitchures —upstairs in one of the bedrooms. Looks right into the next room." The madam laughed. "Through the eye in another pitchure—of an angel—on the other side."

"There is no chance of detection?"

"The girl might know. But like as not, the boy'll be too interested in her and what he's doin'. We've never had no problems."

Esther reached into her purse and pulled out a thousand dollars in large bills. "Half now, half after I've seen all I want to see."

"Suit yourself," Arabella said, counting the money. "You set your mind to something, you sure—"

"When will I be able to watch?"

"Tonight? Tomorrow? Ling's got customers regular, every night."

"Tomorrow night, then. I'll be here at ten o'clock. And I'd like to be let in through the back door." She thought again of Arabella Ryan's attempt to rob her six years before and the madam's present desperation. "Remember, if all goes well, I'll find a way for you to earn the balance of Mr. Cora's debt—at a later date."

"Everything'll happen just like you want. Trust me."

Esther stared through the peephole and watched the Chinese prostitute working on a fat man she recognized as an officer of the Adams and Company bank. She was disappointed that it was not Mosby but realized there was less risk the way things were.

Beside her in a second chair, Arabella Ryan peered through another opening she had drilled into the wall that morning.

"You notice the way she wet her fingers with spit?" Arabella whispered. "Before handling him? That drives 'em crazy. She's smart, that one. She knows enough of that—and what she's doin' now—with her mouth, see? —'ll get 'em to shoot their spunk all the quicker." She laughed. "Less work for mother."

Esther felt herself stirred as the Chinese girl ran the tip of her tongue along the lip and cleft of the man's glans. The customer reached out and fondled her breasts. Esther experienced a vicarious tremor along the inside of her thighs. She reminded herself that this was simply a weapon she would be using, a lure. There would be no pleasure in it. She forced herself to contemplate the customer's enormous, flabby stomach until disgust at the sight of him wiped away her awakening desire.

" 'Course, the business with the wet fingertips, and what she's doin' now—My Christ! He's gonna gaha-muche her. I don't believe it!"

"You were saying?" Esther whispered.

"The finger and tongue work, the mouth business, it can be drawn out. It don't *have* to bring 'em off so quick when they get in you. Careful like, it just gives 'em more pleasure—before and during."

The Chinese girl eased the customer's head from between her thighs, rolled him over gently and mounted him.

"See how she rotates her . . . ?"

"Yes."

"That, and tightenin' the muscles of your, you know, snapping it, gives 'em a great deal'a pleasure, too."

Esther marveled at the Chinese girl's virtuosity, astonished by the number of things that could drive a man to look and sound like a helpless child. Finally the customer lay back, spent. Esther could not determine how much of the excitement she felt was from what she had just witnessed and how much sprang from envisioning how she would use the new knowledge. She smiled. *Woman's ultimate weapon,* she thought. *And it is all so obvious, so simple, if one is merely armed with full knowledge of a man's sexual anatomy and uses her imagination!* Between what she had seen and what Arabella had explained, she doubted there was much more she needed to learn.

She turned and handed the madam an envelope. "The second thousand dollars. Easily earned, since I feel no need to watch any more."

Arabella got up and handed Esther her coat. "Any questions?"

"No. You've been more than helpful." Esther wondered whether now was the time to broach the subject of the additional five thousand dollars Cora needed. She hesitated for a moment, then decided to let the bait hang in the air unmentioned, at least until they were down at the door to the back stairs. The more eager Arabella was, the better it would be. "Well, I must be on my way. Will you see me out?"

"You won't be comin' back for another look-see?"

Esther walked toward the door. "That won't be necessary. You've taught me more than I need to know."

"Wait a minute," Arabella Ryan cleared her throat. "You . . . I . . . There was a mention of my . . . You said I might be able to do you another favor."

"Oh, yes. I hadn't really forgotten. It's just . . . difficult for me to speak of it."

"Come on. We're friends now, ain't we?"

"Why, yes, Arabella. We are. And surely, if anyone could understand, you would."

"What is it, dearie? Tell me."

"I don't know how to begin. There is . . . a man. A man I have an unquenchable lust for, I'm ashamed to say."

"Nothin' to be ashamed of."

"But I'm a married woman. And I wish to . . ."

"Get into bed with someone who ain't your husband."

Esther feigned embarrassment. "Yes. . . . With someone who is a regular customer of yours."

"Well, ain't that a bitch! Who is he?"

"I don't know his name. He's tall, of a slender, muscular build, darkly handsome, sharp-nosed, and wears a moustache."

"Luther. You must mean Luther Mosby."

Esther steadied herself. "The name means nothing to me. I've seen him in Sacramento Street and been seized by an uncontrollable urge to . . ."

"I understand. But what do you want me to do? I can introduce you to him."

"No. No. That would never do. I'm married. I can only indulge myself once without fear of being detected by my husband. Mr. . . . Mosby, did you say his name was . . . ? Must never know."

"I don't see . . ."

"I have a plan. If I were here, in your establishment, for one hour, one night, you could arrange for him to be with me, could you not?"

"I suppose I could," Arabella mused, weighing the proposal. "Don't see why not."

"That is the favor I spoke of. I wish to be with him. Once. To satisfy this thing that leaves me sleepless nights on end."

"I know what you mean, dearie. I've had cravings for someone like that myself."

"Mr. Cora?"

"Yeah. I can't get enough of him. He's no good. But I love the rotter. I'm crazy about him, and the thought of him gettin' himself killed makes me even crazier."

"Then you do know the torment I'm going through."

"Yeah. I don't know if once is gonna cure it . . ."

"It will have to. It must. If you will arrange it, I'll pay you five thousand dollars. Enough to cover the rest of your Mr. Cora's gambling debts."

"When do you?—wait a minute. There's a problem. Luther's gone."

"Gone?" Esther felt her heart sink into a suddenly hollowed-out stomach.

"Yeah. He's up to Sacramento. Lawyer by trade. Used to be a marshal. But he's got political notions. Went up to Sacramento to put his head together with Senator Gwin, the Southerner."

Esther let out a sigh of relief. "He won't be gone long, then?"

"No. Just a couple weeks, I'd guess. Maybe less. Said he'd be back in time to celebrate New Year's with us. Wanted me to think up somethin' special."

"You'll arrange it, then?"

"Soon's he gets back. How'll I reach you?"

"You won't have to. I'll know when he is back. And I'll contact you."

"Shouldn't be any problem. He comes in everyday when he's in town."

"I know," Esther said. "You will receive half of the money the night it takes place. Ahead of time. Half afterward, delivered the following day in an envelope."

"You sure play it careful."

"I must. I have to be sure he never knows who I am, cannot possibly cause me problems with my husband after it's done."

"But he'll see you in the room here. He'll be able to recognize you after."

"No. I plan to wear my hat and veil. And my gloves. Do you think he'll object?"

Arabella thought for a moment, then smiled. "He'll love it! He goes for the unusual, a little mystery. Fact, I'll use it when I tell him it's the somethin' really special I dreamed up for him."

Esther's mind raced. "Tell him I will not wear the hat and veil the second time we are together."

Arabella Ryan laughed knowingly. "You're a devil,

you are. Planned all along to see him again, didn't
you?"

"Yes. But only here. So he will think I'm a . . .
prostitute. And I will make sure you are taken care
of generously for continuing to keep my secret."

Fifty-seven

She was lying on the brass bed—naked except for
the new deep-lavender hat, veil, and long silk gloves
she had purchased before—when Mosby entered the
room. He was smoking a cigar. She trembled when
he sat down next to her on the bed, touched at the
pale birthmark between her breasts, and smirked. She
thought she could actually hear the rapid beating of
her heart. She pictured the pistol hidden under the
two pillows beneath her head and suppressed an urge
to claw at Mosby's face.

"Old Arabella wasn't lyin' when she said she got
up somethin' special for me. You new here?"

"Yes." Trying to look relaxed, she folded her hands
behind her neck and calculated how long it would
take to pull the pistol, shoot him, put on her clothes,
and get down the back stairs.

"And you like bein' a little mysterious, do you?"

"Yes," she said, forcing herself to reach out and
put one hand on his thigh.

"And you don't like to talk much."

"No."

She started to slip her other hand under the pillow
when he glanced away for a moment, but then he
turned back.

"Well, the less talk from you, the better, and I like the mystery. What I can't see's made up for by what I can."

"Thank you." *Oh, God, how I hate you.*

"You any good?"

"You will soon see."

"That I will."

He stood up and unbuttoned his jacket. She could see the derringer he wore under one arm. She decided to wait.

"You mind if I finish this cigar before I get undressed?" he said, walking over to a partially open window. "Just lookin' at you is gettin' me ready."

"I can see that." *You animal.*

"Goddamn, I never seen such a body!" He took a drag on the cigar and smiled. "Well, if this is as good as the rest of the day has been, I might as well've slept in horseshit last night."

"You've had good fortune today?"

"The best. Can't go into all the details, but what it amounts to is a shoo-in for a really fine legal position in about six months."

If you are still alive, she thought. *Which you won't be.* "What sort of legal position?"

He flicked a glowing cylinder of ash out through the window. For a moment he turned away from her and watched the wind scatter it across an attached shed-roof. His gaze was on her again before there was time for her to make a move. "Funny. I wouldn't tell this to anyone I know. And you got to promise you'll keep it . . ." He laughed. "Under your hat."

"It's always easier to reveal things to a stranger. . . . I won't tell a soul. Not even Arabella."

"She knows, so she's all right." He waved a finger. "But no one else, you hear?" He drew on the cigar again between clenched teeth as he took off his jacket and laid it on a chair.

When he has the gun off, Esther thought, her heart beginning to race, *then I will do it.*

"You're right, you know. I've told more secrets to whores than you can shake a stick at. Anyways, I'm a lawyer. And some friends of mine in Sacramento are fixin' it so's I become a judge later this year."

"That's wonderful," she said, attempting to look happy for him, trying to will her heart from pounding so rapidly.

"Yeah, ain't it? Bought me a bar examination in Galveston, and now I'm gonna buy me a seat on the California Circuit Court. Ain't that a bitch?" Absently, he tossed the cigar butt, still lit, out through the window, walked back, and sat down next to her on the bed. "Give me a kiss."

"But you will see me and the mystery will be gone."

He grabbed her painfully by one wrist, jerked her up to a sitting position, and locked an arm around her waist. "No, it won't. I'll close my eyes. Lift that fuckin' veil up now, and kiss me like you mean it."

Full of revulsion, she kissed him, remembering how the Chinese girl had plunged her tongue into the banker's mouth. She reached back with her free hand toward the pillows. They were out of reach.

"That's good. Now let the veil back down and I'll open my eyes again."

He got up and slipped off his low-cut boots.

"Take all your clothes off," she said. "Please. I want to see you without anything on." *You beast . . . you filthy, rotten . . .*

"At your service, ma'am." He slipped off the shoulder holster and hung it over the chair, still staring at her breasts. "Git down by the end of the bed, by the brass railing. Bend over and spread your legs so I can see your bumhole."

Esther saw the long, snaking scar on his left arm before she reluctantly moved and exposed herself. The thought of what he had done to Murietta, to Mwamwaash, to Miwokan, to her son and herself steeled her as she heard him remove the rest of his clothing and pad over to the bed.

"All right, turn around now."

She gasped when she saw the size of him again. For a moment, vague recollections of that night with him in the mountains almost made her cry out and smash at him with her fists. Breathing hard, she fought to control her rage. She was aware of the derringer hanging over the arm of the chair, and of the distance to the pillows. *Not yet,* she thought. *Not until he is on the bed.*

"You like that, do you? Like the old boy's pego? Ever seen the likes of it?"

"No."

"Well, what are you waiting for?"

"Aren't you going to get into bed with me?"

"I like to have it sucked standin' up for a while. Makes it bigger. And I can feel what you're doin' on the bottoms of my feet." He laughed.

She eased over to the edge of the bed and sat, feet on the floor, in front of him. She looked at the scar and the notched leather brace encircling his left elbow, became aware of how limply his left arm hung, then closed her eyes for a moment, knowing he could not see her face. *Let me have the strength,* she thought. *Let me have the skill.* She opened her eyes and reached out, gripping his penis firmly and squeezing it in successive, tightening, and releasing holds.

"Goddamn, that feels good."

She watched it rise a fraction more as she worked her dry mouth and finally produced some saliva. She spilled it carefully onto her gloved right fingers and began working him.

"Jesus, you know what it's all about, don't you?"

She lifted her veil slightly and took him, almost gagging, unable to do nearly as much as the Chinese girl had done to the banker. Improvising, she caressed him with the sides and roof of her mouth. She pointed her tongue and probed, then worked alternately with her mouth and the moistened gloved hand.

"Lie on the bed," she said. "Please."

He lay down with his head on the pillows.

"Not that way. Across the bed."

"Fuck that. I want to be comfortable. . . . Now do what you were doing some more."

She worked and fondled him, finally pulling herself up and slowly easing down onto it. She began moving up and down slowly, hurting, fighting rage and disgust, and digging her gloved fingers into his arms as she tried to shut the thought and feeling of what she was doing from her mind. She glanced at his face as she flexed her genital muscles, rose, relaxed, eased down, rotated, leaned slightly backward, then flexed again, increasing the tension and friction he was feeling. His eyes were closed. She leaned forward and lay on his chest, still moving. Slowly, she slid one hand up toward the pillow.

He opened his eyes. "I love those fuckin' gloves and that hat," he said as the veil brushed against his chin. "Turn over."

She was shocked for a moment, dreading the thought of him in her anus. But then he lifted her bodily and rolled over on top of her stomach.

"Wrap your legs around me, you wild little bitch!" He shoved into her hard, and she almost screamed from the pain. Lying there, she tried to focus on the sounds of a piano and loud singing in the parlor downstairs.

In the alley next to the shed beneath the windows, Luther Mosby's cigar butt ignited a dry, wind-scattered half-bale of straw that had fallen from a wagon earlier that day. Spreading quickly, the flames hit the fences on either side of the narrow passage. Blown by gusting wind, sparks landed on the curtains hanging in Arabella Ryan's vacant first-floor office. They burned rapidly, almost matching the speed of the flames beginning to devour the empty carriage stable next door.

A portion of one of the curtains fell, still burning,

and wafted onto Arabella's desk. It set a newspaper and several letters ablaze. In minutes the desk itself was burning. Then the kerosene lamp exploded onto the carpet, and the room was suddenly an inferno. Outside, shingles caught fire rapidly, and the flames lapped up and along the side of the building.

Next door, the roof was ablaze now, sending wind-blown sparks onto the bordello's overhanging eaves.

Just outside Arabella's office, flame broke through the base of a thin wall and raced up and forward through the decorative flocking along the hallway. Before anyone in the parlor or the rooms upstairs knew what was happening, the fire had taken hold over half of the first floor. Fed by a draft from raised windows, it leaped a half foot, then a foot at a time, up the carpeting and railings of the front and rear staircases.

Holding Esther's arms down, Mosby drove into her again and again. She couldn't move. Each time he rammed home she thought something would tear open. *I never meant for it to be this way,* she thought, appalled and ashamed that around the rim of her disgust, the pain, her hatred, she was experiencing the beginnings of a delicious sensation. She fought it off, waiting for the moment he released her arms and she could reach under the pillow for the gun.

She remembered how her emotions had overruled her, almost brought her down in the gambling tent on Portsmouth Square. She tried not to think of Mosby inside her, about to release his seed in her again. I must let it happen. *I must give him his complete pleasure. When he is done and lying beside me with his eyes closed, perhaps even dozing, then I will do it . . . and I will succeed . . . and be gone before anyone realizes what has happened.*

She felt Mosby suddenly grow limp in her and saw him gaping in disbelief at the window.

"*Jesus Christ!*" he shouted. "Will you look at that!"

She turned and saw the flames leaping up past the window, covering it in a matter of seconds. Tendrils of smoke filtered around the sash and began extending into the room. She thought it strange that she felt no fear.

"The whole fuckin' place is on fire!" Mosby shouted, leaping up and pulling on his pants.

Almost in a state of shock from the sight of the flames and what had taken place on the bed, Esther reached under the pillow and searched for the gun. Distracted, she inadvertently pushed the weapon out under the backs of the pillows and heard a faint thud as it fell to the carpeted floor. She froze.

Mosby pulled on his boots. "Get the fuck up and get dressed, 'less you want to roast right here!" He left his shirt and jacket on the chair. The belt and holster hanging from his bare shoulder, he rushed to the door and opened it.

Esther saw a naked man run past and topple down into the stairwell as a blazing hallway railing gave way. A giant hand seemed to hold her rigid in its grip. She willed herself to move, turned over, reached down, and groped for the gun. She could not find it.

Mosby turned and saw her lying face down on the bed. "Are you fuckin' *crazy?*" He came back and jerked her up off the bed. "Where are your clothes? In that closet?" Without waiting for an answer, he charged to the closet door, opened it and recoiled as smoke billowed out and around him. An instant later, flames surged up through the floor of the closet as he grabbed Esther's dress and threw it at her.

She was on her hands and knees now, trying to reach the gun on the floor under the bed. He pulled her to her feet and slapped her face. Pointing to her high-buttoned shoes beneath the skirt of the mattress cover, he snapped: "You're on your own now. I got my own hide to think of."

Numbly, Esther sat down, pulled on the shoes, and put on the dress after he raced out through the door of the room. She was standing, immobilized again by shock, terror, and frustration when he came back. The curtains in the room were ablaze, and the wallpaper had begun to peel and roll up around the window. There was a wild look in Mosby's eyes.

"There's no fuckin' way out!" He glanced out the window and shook his head. The shed-roof along the side of the house was afire. "Those bastards! They could have shouted, let us know . . . !"

He came over and shook Esther by the arm. "What's the matter with you?" he snapped. "Come on!" He jerked her forward and out into the hallway. The floor was ablaze at either end. The stairway was gone. Fingers of blazing heat clawed up under Esther's veil and tore at her face. She backed into the room again.

"Wait here!" Mosby bellowed.

She peered out through the door and saw him leap a low wall of flame and try the door to another room. Moving quickly to the bed, she pulled at its brass foot-post and moved it away from the wall. Picking up the gun, she cocked it and ran back to the doorway. Mosby was at the door to another room. She saw him open it as she raised the pistol, but halfway through her upward swing, the floor beneath Mosby gave way in a shower of flame and sparks, and he dropped from sight. She heard him scream in pain, but then there was nothing but the deafening, unearthly sound of the fire. Staring down through a gap in the hallway floor, she tried to see where he had fallen but couldn't make him out. Enraged, she flung the gun after him. Smoke blew into her eyes and mouth, and she backed away involuntarily and closed the door.

She looked around and saw all four walls going up in flames. She coughed as the smoke level dropped rapidly from the ceiling and a shaft of fire suddenly roared up through the floor beside her. Jumping back, she felt the flames licking at her right calf before she saw the hem of her dress was afire. Quickly, she bent down and slapped the flames out. When she stood erect again, she felt herself almost go. The heat was almost unbearable. Another column of flame shot up in front of her. Dizzy, she turned and saw the curtains were completely consumed now, a pile of sparkling, paper-like ashes below the window. She realized the lower half of the sash was partially raised. Rushing to it, she gripped the smoldering lower slat and tried to open it further. It wouldn't budge. She choked on a billow of smoke. Forcing herself not to give up, she threw Mosby's shirt and jacket off the ladder-back wooden chair where they lay, lifted it, and smashed the glass out of the window.

She looked out. The overhanging shed-roof on the side of the house was gone. A thick oak beam ran out and away from the building just left of the window to an upright stanchion. It was smoldering but still not ablaze. She got out onto it and slowly, carefully, walking foot in front of foot, eased her way to the stanchion, crouched down, and leaped into the alley. She felt a sharp pain as one of her ankles twisted when she landed, but the heat of the burning house next door was so intense she ran out into the street without stopping.

Only then, when she glanced left and right, did she realize that one side of the street was afire for a block in either direction. The entire bordello was ablaze now, flames reaching thirty feet into the sky from its glowing roof. Scores of people were standing dazed or running about, almost haphazardly, not knowing what to do. She thought she saw Arabella, but then the face was swallowed up in a throng of people running straight at her. Esther stepped back so she would not be trampled.

She heard bells ringing and turned. A team of horses pulling a tank wagon full of water churned into the street. Half-dressed volunteer firemen dropped from it and began uncoiling hose. She looked up and saw sparks and small bits of burning debris floating across the street onto the roof of her hotel and the adjacent buildings. Suddenly, as though her hearing had just been restored, she realized people were screaming.

Limping, she made her way to the first intersection and, pushing through gaping onlookers, turned away from the area of the fire. When she was about a block away, she stopped and leaned against the side of a building. She glanced up and saw that the sky was almost as bright as day. Small sparks sailed over, even at this distance. Crowds of people ran toward the fire. She moved on and rested against a street lamp. In the flickering gaslight, she watched as another fire wagon rushed by. A man in a buggy carrying a woman who was either unconscious or dead raced past in the opposite direction. Only then did the recent imminence of her own horrible death reach her consciousness. For a moment she imagined herself back in the doorway of the room and gasped. She began to weep, at first silently, then uncontrollably, shaking and sobbing in the aftermath of terror. She sat down at the curb and held her head in her hands, trembling.

She didn't realize almost an hour had passed before she got control of herself. All she knew was that she was lucky to be alive and that Mosby was dead. She stood up and suddenly heard the voice of Elizabeth Purdy Todd in her brain. "I am glad it was not I who killed him," she heard the voice say. But then Esther Cable took over, and she felt cheated.

Still partially dazed, shaking, exhausted, she walked aimlessly for hours. Her dress was charred along the hem and on one shoulder, her shoes covered with soot. Dark charcoal fingermarks ran diagonally across one of her cheeks. She could shake off neither the chagrin of having failed to have her revenge nor the small measure of relief she also felt about not killing another human being.

The shivering and the constriction in her throat passed. She walked on, numbly, stooping to pick up

a newspaper when she saw the word "Adams" in the
headline. It was an afternoon edition, dated the day
before, the first Friday of 1855. She had been so involved in preparing herself for her confrontation with
Mosby that she had not even bothered to eat, let
alone leave her hotel room until after dark. She
opened the paper:

"BLACK FRIDAY. ADAMS AND COMPANY
FAILS."

Below, in a subheadline, she scanned the words:
"Run on Page Bacon & Company Causes Bank To
Close Doors."

For a moment it did not register. But then the
meaning emerged in her mind. She had not transferred
much of her account to Wells Fargo. Most of it, perhaps over $900,000, was still at Adams. If they were
bankrupt, so was she. At least to the extent of her
deposits. Strangely, it did not seem to matter.

Walking slowly along the side of a gambling establishment, she dropped the paper and looked at her
locket watch. It was two thirty in the morning. She
suddenly felt faint. Stopping for a moment, swaying,
she fought the feeling off and continued on around
the corner. Her head tilted downward, not looking
where she was going, she ran straight into a man
walking in the opposite direction. The force of the
collision knocked her down.

"Forgive me, señora," she heard the man say.

She was still dizzy from the collision when he
reached down and began helping her to her feet.

Partially bent over, she brushed at her skirt. "I'm
terribly sorry. It was my fault. I wasn't paying attention." Only then did she look up into his face.

It was Murietta.

Three

SILVER AND STEEL

Fifty-eight

Sacramento
May 7, 1869
9 A.M.

Absorbed by the almost total recall the diary pages evoked, Esther didn't hear the ceremonial band begin playing fifteen minutes before the scheduled departure of the Union Pacific Express. Thoughts of the massacre, the night with Mosby, the fire, the reunion with Murietta, and the complex eighteen months that had followed shut off all sense of the present. She turned another page and remembered her short-lived relief and thankfulness for not having killed Mosby in the bordello. The irony of that righteousness and her subsequent discovery of Mosby's survival made her laugh out loud. Only then, as the sound of her bitter laughter reverberated in the parlor car, did she become aware of the military air the band was playing, the festive noise of the crowd.

She glanced at the locket watch, and more thoughts tumbled across her mind. *If I had told Murietta everything during that first six months of 1855, before Mosby rode to—God, the absurdity of it—to a judgeship on Gwin's coattails. If I had told Joaquin everything then, he would have helped me, it would have been over and done with, come what may . . . and so much more could have been prevented. But then again, considering how much Joaquin had changed, he might not have lifted a finger for me, as amazing as that seems now. . . .*

Esther sighed, stood up, and peered out of the car. She couldn't see the bandstand. Curious, she walked back and opened the door to the rear platform. Making sure no one was back this far, she stepped out and went to the railing. A twin-stacked paddle-wheeler nearly startled her out of her wits as its steam whistle sent a loud, congratulatory note across the river toward the train. Glancing forward, she saw Solana. Above her, Mister Sam nodded in the locomotive window. Young Todd's excited face was visible just beyond him. The music and the sound of the crowd milling around the main station building rose to a deafening level as the last of the passengers boarded. She thought of her late husband Bull Carter's partners, then saw Billy Ralston hand some coins to a young man who had carried his bags from the hotel. Finally, Alex Todd came through the throng and boarded the train.

She wondered if he and Mosby would be sitting near each other. *No matter,* Esther thought. *There are too many of Alex's friends, too many witnesses for Mosby to attempt anything on board.* And, God willing, he would never see the other side of the Sierras.

Esther glanced up the side of the train again. Two cars forward she saw John Sutter leaning out of a window, watching her. Sutter nodded, his bald head gleaming in the morning sunlight, and she smiled back. *He has the note in his pocket.* She pictured what she had written before handing it to him just after dinner in the hotel lobby the previous night.

To the Conductor or Trainman:
My instructions to you notwithstanding, Captain John Sutter has my express permission to

visit with me, should he wish to, at any time following the train's departure from Dutch Flat.

ESTHER CABLE CARTER

Esther recalled Sutter's surprise when she had said, "I'd like to spend some time with you tomorrow. This note will allow you to come back to the parlor car. Can you join me one half-hour after the train leaves Dutch Flat? I'll be resting until then."

He had been delighted. And after expressing his opinion that Mosby's intention to do Alex Todd harm was probably just talk, that time had undoubtedly cooled the firebrand's anger, Sutter had said good night.

But it was not just talk. And Mosby's anger would never cool. Esther knew better than to entertain even a hope of that. Once he set his mind to something. . . . He had spent a year badgering Arabella Ryan in his attempt to find the woman he had been with the night of the fire. Fruitlessly. But he had.

Esther dismissed thoughts of the past for the moment as she scanned the crowd for Solana. Giving up, she reentered the parlor car and locked the rear door. Inside, she cracked one window to reduce the rising heat. Once the train was rolling, the overhead vents would cool it down. It will be hell until then. But it would be a small price to pay if she could send *Mosby* to hell when the sun reached the western heavens. Holding the journal closed on her lap, she began rehearsing the elements and timing of her plan as it would unfold after the train pulled into Dutch Flat.

Forward, on the side of the locomotive obscured from the station, Solana stood on her tiptoes in the gravel between two sets of tracks. She smiled, motioning to young Todd Carter, and the boy leaned out of the cab window, straining against the belt strapping him to a built-in metal seat. She hoped the boy would not suspect her motives for wanting to be aboard the train.

"You will be good?"

"I wouldn't do *anything* to make Mister Sam put me back in one of the passenger cars."

"You are lucky to ride in such a—machine." She wondered if he would understand and act on what she was saying, make it easier to stay aboard the train by reducing the amount of time she would have to remain concealed in the equipment bin. "I am just an old Indian woman," she went on. "I could never be so lucky, to have such a ride, even for a short distance."

"You are *not* just an old Indian woman! You're special, and I love you very much—almost as much as mother!" He thought for a moment. "Do you want to ride in the locomotive?"

"They would not let me." She saw the sudden determination in the boy's expression.

"Maybe Mister Sam will. I'm going to ask him."

"No! I cannot ask you to do such a thing for me."

"Why not? You do all kinds of nice things for me. I'm going to ask him."

She watched as he pulled himself back into the cab and waited until the engineer stopped talking to his coal-heaver.

"Mister Sam?"

Sam Collett turned away from his gauges and levers, looked at the boy, and winked. "Busy now, son. Talk to you after we git goin'."

"I just have one question to ask. Please."

The engineer's handlebar moustache curled down in a slight frown. "All right, then. What is it?"

The boy took a deep breath. "Can . . . can Solana ride with us?" He thought quickly. "Just . . . just to Dutch Flat? She's . . . she's an Indian. She's never been on a train."

Collett moved over, his massive body towering

above the boy, and glanced down at the Indian woman.

Solana held her breath.

Collett ran a hand over his moustache and scowled. "Well . . . I don't know. Against regulation for you to be here, even." He turned to the boy. "Skeered of goin' alone? I'll take good care'a yah."

"I'm not scared, Mister Sam. Honest I'm not. I just know Solana would love it. She's . . . she's been so good to me. *Please?*"

"Well, all right. But just to Dutch Flat. She kin kitch a ride back here on the first empty supply. Have to stay out of the way, though. You tell her that."

When Solana climbed up into the cab, the engineer took one look at her broad-boned, pale-brown face, exchanged deprecatory glances with his Russian assistant, turned away, and stifled a laugh. The white woman's purse and the black dress with the white, Quaker-style collar were one thing. But the tiny hat sitting askew on her head and the contrasting Maidu moccasins on her feet were an absolute sketch.

Esther fingered one corner of her journal, thinking: *We stop at Dutch Flat for ten minutes or so. Mosby gets off and comes to the window, as instructed last night. I then tell him to return, via the ladders and the roofs, exactly one hour after we have left Dutch Flat. The danger will appeal to him. He will go forward first, out the front door of his car, before he returns this way. No one will see him come, no one will ever know he was here in this car.*

Before that, a half hour after we have left Dutch Flat and Mosby is forward, in his seat in the passenger car, Sutter shows the note to the conductor. Sutter stays with me until I ask him to leave—so I can "freshen up a bit." He leaves five minutes or so before Mosby arrives—unbeknownst to anyone—by the roofs. I will have already asked Sutter to return after

*we have passed Donner Lake. He will understand
why I would want to be alone passing that place.
And that will give me time enough to . . . it will be
done by then. And afterward, the conductors will
know the doors have been locked and only Sutter has
been here. As time passes, it will amount to having
someone with me during the entire time it happened
. . . if it ever comes to that. . . . In the unlikely event
I would even be suspected. . . . If his body is ever
found. . . .*

*There. I am satisfied. The rest is in the hands of
. . .*

She was wondering whether "God," "the Devil,"
"Fate," or "Luck" was the appropriate word when the
train lurched once, then again, and finally started
rolling forward. The sound of the bandsmen, outdoing
themselves now, grew louder. She got up, pulled a
shade aside, and watched the passing faces of the
noisy well-wishers and celebrants gathered at the station. She sat down again and raised the shade by her
side; as the train continued to move forward, Esther
raised the shade farther. To her left, smoke rose from
thousands of chimneys in the sprawling state capital.
The river, close by to her right, was lined with
streamers, launches, barges, small boats, and at least
a half-dozen paddle-wheelers. It was a far cry, she
thought, from the days when there were only a fort
and a few ranches. And even farther, mentally and
spiritually, from the night Miwokan and Solana had
brought her to that fort. Miwokan . . . John Alexander . . . Moses . . . Murietta . . .

She bit her lip. *I would not die,* she thought. *I did
not die, you scum. You will learn that today, and it
will be the last entry in your vicious brain.*

She glanced at the time as the train picked up speed
beyond the station and began circling eastward around
the city. Opening the journal, she began scanning
quickly; turning, scanning, then turning again. Oh,

God. What the years in hiding had done to Joaquin.
. . . She knew there would not be enough time to
read every word now. The significant entries would
be enough. Her mind would recapture all the rest.
By the time the train left Dutch Flat, all that would
be left would be the rereading of the ribboned entries. She would relive every word of those during
the half hour before Sutter knocked on the forward
door of the parlor car. Every single word. And then
she would be ready. Ready . . . and waiting.

Fifty-nine

San Francisco
May 18, 1856

Solana and I buried "Jack Marin" today. On a quiet
knoll beneath a sycamore on his property just to the west
of Twin Peaks. He would have liked being interred away
from the city, in one of his beloved quiet places, no matter how changed he was during the year and a half we
were intermittently together after we chanced to meet
again. How shocked you must be, Alex, to read of Murietta's survival. How surprised this city would be if it knew
"Jack Marin's" real identity! I dare say the double hanging that took place today would have been postponed
indefinitely while William T. Coleman's resurrected mob of
vigilantes and Luther Mosby's opposing "Law and Order"
hoodlums recovered from the stunning knowledge that
Joaquin Murietta lived among them, sold goods to them
from his profitable saddlery, for more than two years!

I have not written of "Jack Marin" or Joaquin in these pages in a year and a half for fear that, had this journal fallen into the wrong hands, it would have spelled his doom. Nor have I addressed myself to you, Alex, since shortly after your marriage to Judith Britten. It was a comfort once, and I tried to continue. But I found that doing so, late of an evening, as is my habit, knowing you might at the same moment be in Judith's arms, stirred longings and jealousies within me that were intolerable. (Is that not remarkable after all this time?) And so I have written since only as one does normally. That will explain the inclusion of so many things you should know about. Your dear friend Billy Ralston's rapid rise to a position equal in importance at Blue Star with those of William Kelsey and Warren Barnett, for example. You might be surprised to know that I was introduced to him at one of the few Blue Star board meetings I have ever attended. Did not expect him to be there. Heavily veiled. Even had I not been, I seriously doubt he would have recognized me after so many years.

So, too, would you have known about Warren's reelection to the state assembly at the same time you, not six months admitted to the bar, also joined that august body. (I was so proud for you.)

I have written little of Luther Mosby, who this very moment languishes in the Committee of Vigilance jail. Believe me, I have not forgotten him, nor my intentions, as you will soon discover in these pages. But beyond my comments that he has been virtually untouchable since Gwin engineered his rise to a seat on the California Supreme Court, there has been precious little to say, until today.

You know, undoubtedly, that Mosby had a hand in "Jack Marin's" death, even if he did not strike the killing blow himself. But what you, and everyone else in San Francisco, cannot know, is that "Jack Marin" was actually Joaquin. Let me go back over the events of the past week, nay, past year and a half. Let me recount it all, so that you will understand . . . and so that I can share the bur-

den of a grief so deep it cannot be described . . . other
than to say it could only be deeper had you been the one
killed this past Friday.

Sixty

The morning sun warmed Esther as she waited for
Murietta in the swing seat on the porch of her two-
story house. Mayflies swarmed above the oval of green
lawn and the circular driveway bordered with lavender Johnny-jump-ups. She could smell the fragrance
of the flowering shrubs skirting the porch and the
thick blanket of white alyssum blossoming between
the house and her carriage stable. The warmth lulled
her. She nudged a toe impatiently at the *Evening
Bulletin* lying near her feet. Murietta was due at nine
sharp; she would read the paper when they returned
later in the day.

Gazing instead toward the new houses being built
on Rincon Hill, south of the city, she smiled ruefully.
Fitting, she thought. Sides were being taken in Congress on the increasingly explosive issue of slavery,
and they were being taken there as well. The houses
barely visible in the distance on Rincon Hill were
being built for a dozen or so of San Francisco's wealthy
Southerners, the Gwins among them. Set apart from
the rest of the city, the area was to be called South
Park.

The Southerners were not the only hostile faction
in the city. Editors railed at one another, at corrupt
politicians and businessmen, even personal enemies.
The newly named Republicans vilified every Demo-

crat, including Barnett. Esther knew Warren was above the rapaciousness, election rigging, and strong-arm tactics of his fellow party members, but her conviction didn't matter. A rising malice was transforming San Francisco into a savage arena. Daily there were insults, brawls, challenges, and duels. There was talk of reviving the Committee of Vigilance, which in 1852 had taken the law into its own hands and rid the city of numerous criminals—as well as innocent people—in a series of beatings and lynchings. This time, if the rumor was true, the target would be political exploiters.

But here, on her blossom-covered hill far to the west of the city, Esther felt protected from it all. Her gaze swept northward past a hill too steep to be settled, then on to the clapboard and brick dwellings that sprawled south and west toward her ten acres. Some of the new Romanesque, stone business buildings were four stories high. She knew the land she owned would hold the city at bay if the growth reached out and surrounded her, but the prospect rankled.

She traveled into the city with Solana regularly now, enjoying the visits, the myriad diversions San Francisco had to offer. The reassuring knowledge that she had more than enough breathing room here had been a major factor in once again abandoning her semireclusive ways. But she knew that sooner or later this hilltop retreat would be lost to "progress." And that was the main reason she was faintly excited and expectant about accompanying Murietta to see the acreage he had purchased to the west of Twin Peaks today. She was eager to look over the surrounding land. If it was as beautiful as he said it was, perhaps she would purchase some herself as a hedge against the day the city engulfed her.

There had been a hint of something else in Murietta's tone when he asked her to inspect his purchase. She wondered if he were planning to propose marriage. She doubted that, but it was not beyond possibility. She had no idea how she might respond, although she guessed her answer would be no. True, they were more married than many legally bound couples she knew of; Alex was married, and she still cared about Joaquin. But changes in him had prompted a gradual lessening of her feelings.

"Not the physical changes," she said out loud to the cat curled in a chair on her porch, as if it would nod in agreement. He did look different, had shaved off his moustache and grown a bit plump in the face. There were deep lines around his eyes, he limped slightly from a bullet wound in his left leg, and he stooped a bit to one side, like a much older man. No, not those outward and visible signs. Nor the store-bought suits and top hat he wore. Esther thought they looked ridiculous, but she understood their value. Combined with the facial differences, they made him virtually unrecognizable to almost anyone who had known him in the past. Even Solana looked at him disbelievingly over the first six months he had come visiting her in the new house.

The inward changes were the ones that had dampened her regard for him. They were not total, and for that reason her feelings were still ambivalent, rather than entirely gone. She remembered a day a year earlier, when one part of the old Murietta emerged clearly, sharply defining all else that was gone in him.

They were picnicking on the boulder-braced cliffs to the west of the Presidio, on the Pacific. Below them more than a hundred seals blanketed a jagged outcropping just offshore. Waves crashed against the rocks and sent sunlit spray thirty feet up the cliffs.

"Why won't you tell me about the years you were —away?" She toyed absently with the edge of a cucumber sandwich, knowing full well how uncomfortable the same question had made him in the past.

"Why won't you share that with me? Do you think I would tell someone about it?"

He stared off at the horizon. "No. I have told you many times. It is simply a time of my life I wish to forget."

She knew she was being unreasonable, but still it piqued her that he would not share that information, help her to understand more fully why he behaved more than carefully now. In spite of herself, she prodded him. "It seems obvious that you were not herding sheep," she said almost waspishly. She tried to stop herself, but the slender thread of bitchiness and sarcasm she hated in herself would not be silenced. "The saddlery you own, the building itself, let alone the inventory, would require a considerable outlay of money."

"And where did I get it? Is that what you want to know?" He turned to her and the sight of her face triggered in him a surge of love that checked his anger. He had pictured that face countless times in the mountains, in caves, at night, alone on a bedroll in the wilds, and longed to hold it, kiss it. He did not want to lose it again. He laughed, and for a moment displayed his once casual ability to sidestep almost any issue through sardonic amusement. "There are such things as banks, Esther. They lend money to men who wish to establish a business."

"But not without—"

He put his hand to her lips, smiling again, patiently. "No more," he said. "All right?" Finally, he took his hand away.

"All right," she said guiltily, subduing unreasonableness and wanting to make it up to him. "But if you've borrowed money, why don't you let me pay you your fair share from the sale of the Southern Sierra Mining Company? You could—"

"I have told you before. I asked you to hold that money for me in your account at Adams—"

"I don't remember you ever asking me that."

"Well, I did. And therefore it was the same as if I had been a depositor, too."

"But—"

"No 'buts.' When the bank failed, I lost my money just as you did. And I will hear no more about it." He smiled again. "Now, can we finish our picnic and enjoy this lovely afternoon."

She sighed, ashamed that she had pried at him again but still slightly irritated with not having the information she wanted. "Yes," she said. "Let's enjoy it." For a moment she contrasted his independence and fairness with the solicitous mercantile life he was leading now. She understood the need for some of it, but . . .

"Look at them," Murietta said, pointing to a bull seal and his mate, basking near the top of the offshore rocks. "Growing old together, sharing a life of peace. Perhaps that is in store for us as well."

"Perhaps," she said, not convincingly, still half-lost in her own thoughts and betraying how much she was beginning to doubt such a thing would happen. When she became aware of the subtle change in his voice and turned, the look in his eyes made her feel as though an arctic wind had knifed through the hot summer sun and sliced a path between them.

Getting up from the porch swing, Esther glanced again at her locket watch, and felt a twinge of irritation. It was well past nine. Murietta had not been like this when she first knew him. He had always been prompt. But in the last year and a half, he was late more often than not. Invariably, his excuse was the press of business. But she knew it was more often caused by extra time he spent ingratiating himself with customers. Their friendship, he thought, would make him more "respectable" and therefore less vulnerable to discovery.

Even more annoyed now, she plumped back into the porch swing. *That's all he seems interested in*:

mercantile stature, security, and creature comforts,
she thought. His friends were so old, so stuffy; and
he had adopted their ways, their atitudes, even their
causes. It seemed as if he were attempting to become
another person entirely! As though those few years
spent in the mountains and on stagecoach trails, wearing a bandanna over his face and holding a gun in
his hand, had aged him twenty years, robbed him
of the better part of his sardonic humor and, worse,
stripped him of his courage. It had all been brought
home to her just a week earlier when she had decided to combine the need to replace a damaged
buggy harness with the prospect of an unexpected
lunch together at the little restaurant near Joaquin's
shop.

She paused at the entrance to the saddlery when
she saw Murietta was just completing a sale to James
King, the vitriolically righteous publisher of the
Bulletin. Murietta had just convinced King that a
snaffle bit would do less damage to a horse and be
just as effective as a curb bit for the sort of riding
he did. Behind him an array of hand-tooled saddles
and brass-studded tack hung from pegs on the rear
wall of the store. King—short, bearded, and wiry—
did not notice Esther's entrance.

"I thought you gave that fellow Casey exactly what
he deserved in the paper this morning," Murietta
said, deferentially nodding his head as he wrapped
up the snaffle bit.

"Ah, you mean the account of his ballot-box stuffing to gain his seat on the City Council." King turned.
When he saw a woman was listening as well, he
took on an even more theatrical air of indignation.

"Yes," Murietta continued, coming around from be-
hind the counter even though there was no need to.
"The business about Casey having been in prison in
New York State . . . that is true?"

"True? Of course it's true! I would not have printed

it if it were not. The man is a scoundrel of the first order."

And the publisher of a rival paper, The Times, Esther thought.

"Were it not for your editorials, God knows what men like Casey would get away with," Murietta went on, glancing somewhat guiltily at Esther.

She sensed he was weighing whether or not to introduce her to his "friend." She had no interest whatsoever in meeting King, who so fancied himself above the average citizen he had legally adopted for himself the appellation "James King of William," to distinguish himself from a number of other men in the city with the same name. But she still felt slighted when he turned back to King.

"You do the God-fearing citizens of this great city an unending service exposing those in high office who abuse power."

Late for something, King looked at his watch, then succumbed to holding center stage for just a minute longer. "Marin," he said, putting an arm over Joaquin's shoulder and walking him to the door, "good men like you have no conception of the extent of it. Ninety-five percent of the men holding public office in this city are tainted."

At the doorway he paused and glanced over to be sure Esther was taking it all in. "And it goes beyond that. San Francisco is overrun with gamblers, prostitutes, pimps as well." He bowed toward Esther. "Forgive me, madam. Mark my words, Marin, a day will soon come when we citizens will take it into our own hands again, as the vigilantes did in '52. We will rid this city of the vermin our elected officials and police are either unable or unwilling to exterminate."

"You know I will be on the side of right that day, Mr. King," Murietta whispered as the publisher started out through the doorway.

"I'm sure you will, Marin. I consider you a friend, and I appreciate your support."

Murietta watched him walk off, then turned to Esther. "A good man, a good man," he said, nodding again. "Now, what brings you into town?"

She stood up. "A harness," she said, feeling slightly nauseated. "I need a harness to replace one—damaged beyond repair."

"Then why are you frowning? Surely a broken harness isn't enough to darken that sweet face. Is something troubling you?" He reached out to put a hand on her shoulder, but she pulled away.

"No. It's nothing, Joaq—Jack. I'm just not in a very good mood."

He looked at his watch. "Almost time for lunch. Would that cheer you up?"

"No . . . I'd like to, but there is too much to do. Would you just pick out a rig for me and put it in the buggy?"

She was thinking of James King now, and of the threat he had reported in the *Bulletin* two days before, when she heard Murietta's carriage turn up the road to her house. James Casey had boasted that he would shoot King on sight. She dismissed the idea. Surely, as biased and vindictive as King's editorials sometimes were, there was much truth in them. And Casey would not dare to . . .

Murietta came into view. Gathering her parasol and trying unsuccessfully to hold her annoyance in check, she went down the front steps as he reined up his lathered team.

"Joaquin, I've been waiting an hour! Did you forget?" She noticed he seemed breathless, agitated.

"For God's sake, will you *ever* remember to call me Jack? Someday you will forget in public!"

"Jack, then. I'm sorry. But you're almost never late . . ." Then she noticed the bayonet-fitted muzzleloader propped up beside him.

"What in God's name are you doing with that weapon?"

He ignored the question. "I simply came to say we must postpone our ride. I'm sorry, but I have to get back to town. Too much is happening."

"Wait a minute! *What* is happening? What are you talking about?"

"You haven't read the papers?"

"No. Not for a day or so."

"Casey shot King. He's dying. I witnessed it from the doorway of the Pacific Express Company."

"When?"

"Yesterday. It's the last straw. We're forming our own city government. We're going to put a stop to what's happening in San Francisco."

"Who is forming a government?"

He cracked the buggy whip and started to rein his horses around.

"Wait!"

"I have to go!" he called over his shoulder. "A group of businessmen. I'll be a witness against Casey. I'll tell you more about it tonight—if I'm still invited for supper."

She nodded, and he cracked the whip again. He was out of earshot by the time Esther collected her wits. Her first impulse was to hitch up her own team and race after Murietta, but she realized he was already a quarter of the way back to the city. She needed to think. Spotting the paper lying on the porch, she walked over and picked it up. It was all there: The account of the shooting. . . . Eyewitness quotes from several men, including "Jack Marin." . . . Casey's subsequent surrender to the authorities. . . . The prediction at the end of the story that James King would likely die.

And then she caught sight of the notice printed on the lower left corner of the front page:

The members of the Vigilance Committee in good standing will please meet at No. 105-½ Sacramento

Street, this day, Thursday, 15 inst. at nine o'clock A.M.
By order of the Committee of Thirteen.

A feeling of predestined dread rose in her as she
turned to the third page and saw Charles Cora's
name. It was in a reprint of a James King editorial
entitled "The Heavens Be Hung With Black."

"Thieves and harlots will rejoice," the column rant-
ed, "with the acquittal of Charles Cora in the murder
of Marshal William Richardson."

She had heard Murietta mention an upcoming trial
in which a gambler was accused of the unprovoked
killing of a U.S. Marshal. But she had no idea the
gambler was Charles Cora. When it had happened, she
and Solana had been visiting little Moses in Marysville, and she had been busy trying to find a second
teacher for her expanding school in Sacramento.
Esther also remembered Murietta saying the man
owed him a gambling debt. She had not pursued the
matter, never asked his name.

Astonished by the coincidence, she read how Cora
had surrendered himself to his own employer; how
Arabella Ryan had spent $10,000 tampering with jus-
tice and hiring as counsel Edward D. Baker. A masterful lawyer, Baker had secured a hung jury. Half
the panel had been bought off: Cora, in fact, had almost been acquitted. He sat in jail now, King's editorial went on, but it was almost a foregone conclusion that Baker, Arabella Ryan, and corrupt city officials would set Cora free. Something, King had
raged, had to be done.

Esther pondered what might happen and tried to
understand why Murietta would be a party to any
of it. All she could guess was that the vigilantes' ac-
tions would be a repetition of the kangaroo courts,
trials without due process, whippings and hangings
they had sponsored, carried out in the early fifties.

She guessed that he saw joining them as a final
maneuver that would forever screen his past from

view. She could understand that, but she couldn't believe he would ever participate in mob violence. Perhaps he thought this time it would be different, lawful. She doubted that. Worse, Murietta's life might be in danger. The thought chilled her. Somehow, at dinner that night, she would find a way to guide him to an objective appraisal of things.

The glowing fire at the far end of her long, oak-paneled dining room did little to warm Esther as she listened to Murietta go on and on about the developments of the day. Eight thousand men were under arms, among them policemen who had turned in their badges, at least temporarily, for the white-linen buttonhole markers of the vigilantes. William T. Coleman, active in vigilante affairs in 1852 and now a prosperous San Francisco businessman, had been elected Chairman of the Vigilante Committee. Coleman had requested the delivery of Cora as well as Casey. The new marshal had refused. In forty-eight hours the committee would take the prisoners by force if they were not turned over voluntarily. Tomorrow, Friday, others would be arrested. Opposing forces were organizing, calling themselves the "Law and Order Party." Among its leaders: Luther Mosby.

How ironic! Esther thought, hardly touching her food. She let Murietta go on until Solana retired to her room and her nightly ritual of prayers for Miwokan and Mwamwaash before going to bed. Sitting there, gazing past him, Esther feared for Murietta. The enthusiasm in his candlelit eyes sickened her; his earnest expression appalled her. Beyond the walnut harvest table where they sat, a fog as thick as lamb-fat blocked from view everything beyond the sixteen-paned windows. She felt as if they were sailing blindly in some unearthly ship on a collision course with doom. She recalled a similar sensation crossing the Missouri on a river ferry with Alex, years before. They had hit no shoal, just the opposite bank, slightly off the waiting slip. It had been startling for a moment, but no more. This time, on this imaginary vessel, Esther was increasingly certain the landing for Murietta would be a graveyard.

"You're not listening to me!"

"I *am* listening! It's simply that I can't believe it's you speaking." She had been stunned, speechless, but now disappointment and rising anger unlocked her tongue. "Do you honestly believe it will be any different this time? That Coleman and the rest of those animals will wait for legal juries to convict, authorized judges to sentence?"

Murietta glowered. "They're *not* animals! Some of them are my friends."

"Friends?" Esther laughed scornfully. "They're the same men who hunted you like a beast! Who laughed and made jokes about the 'greaser' whose head they displayed all over California! The man who leads them helped put the scars on your back! *Friends?*"

He shifted uneasily. "That's all in the past. This is different. This has to do with the life I now lead. I have to forget Joaquin Murietta. Don't you understand?" He lowered his voice. "They are simply replacing corrupt men who bend the law any way they choose." His voice grew more emphatic again. "It is *their* law, *their* courts, isn't it? Everything will be as it should be." He fished into a jacket pocket, pulled out a handbill Coleman had hastily printed up, unfolded and handed it to her. "Here. Read this."

At the top of the page the all-seeing eye in the center of the vigilantes' seal stared at her indifferently. Around it were circled the words:

"*Fiat Justitia Ruat Coelum* ° *No Party. No Creed. No Sectional Issues.* ° *Committee of Vigilance* -°- *San Francisco.*"

Below the seal, the self-justifying first paragraph read:

"*Who made the laws and set agents over them? The people. Who saw these laws neglected, dis-*

*regarded, abused, trampled on? The people. Who has
the right to protect these laws, and administer them
when their servants had failed? The people.*"

Enraged, not a little because Coleman had seized
on some truths that galled her, she balled the handbill up and threw it at Murietta. "And you're swallowing this self-righteous trash?" she shouted. "It's
nothing less than well-dressed anarchy. The rule of
the mob—again. You must have lost part of your
brain while you were robbing innocent people in
stagecoaches."

Murietta pushed away from the table, stung by her
sudden attack. "You don't know I did that."

"I'm sorry," she said, appalled that she had cut at
him in such a humiliating and unjust way.

"And even if I—even if Joaquin Murietta—did such
things, the Murietta who was driven from a lawful
life, driven to rob simply to survive, would he not
be forgiven? Understood?"

Revived feeling for him washed through her. "Yes.
Yes, he would be." She reached out and touched his
hand. "I didn't mean to speak the way I did. I'm
afraid for you. I can't just sit here and let you take
part in something so evil."

"It's the others who are evil, Esther. And you're
in no position to allow or not allow me to do anything. This is the life I live now. These are my
friends, business associates. I'm with them because
their cause is just."

Born of unspoken terror for his own life or not,
the piety of his words made her furious again.

"*Hogwash!* You're with them because you think
they will never suspect anything about you if you
take part in this despicable business! Admit it! You
live in fear despite the fact that no one in the world
believes Joaquin Murietta is still alive! They'll provide you with a little more insurance. A little less
uncertainty. At the expense of God knows how many
lives!"

"You have no right—"

"Listen to me! Continue with them and you will
cease to exist as far as I'm concerned. *Do you understand?* You *will* be dead."

"Esther—"

"Don't 'Esther' me! I mean it! I want an answer
now. This instant!"

He couldn't look her in the eye. "Esther . . . *please
. . .*" he whispered. "Please try to understand why—"

"*Get out!*" she shrieked, slapping him in the face.
"You coward. *Get out of my house!* I never want to
see you again!"

Sixty-one

She awoke drained from a near-sleepless night, her
first thoughts a vivid recollection of a dream that had
played over and over in her mind as she tossed fitfully the last few hours before dawn:

*Murietta swallowed up by the fog enshrouding the
house the night before. Then nothing but the fog and
a distant wailing of women, her own voice recog-
nizable above the rest. Then pelting, choking, blinding snow driven by a freezing wind. Rain and head-
high waves that turned from muddy gray to red.
None of it touching her. Then the fog again. And
Murietta finally emerging from it, his face shattered
and bloodied, his jacket covered with spreading stains.
Dark liquid dripping from his string bow tie . . .*

She tried to dismiss the dream. Her anger had

cooled. In its place, as she bathed, dressed, and ate breakfast, were compassion and hard-won awareness that losing control of one's emotions was always self-defeating. Getting into the buggy and starting for town, she chided herself for having lost any influence she had over him, any chance of persuading him to reconsider. Then she turned from self-recrimination to more hopeful thoughts: *There is still time. I will find him. Talk with him. Point out that, if these men, Coleman in particular, have not recognized him now, in these circumstances no one ever will . . . I mean* something *to him still.* Somehow, if reason failed, that depth of feeling would provide her with the means to divert him from this madness.

Within a four-block-square area around Sacramento and Front streets, the thoroughfares were impassable. Hundreds of men carrying muskets and rifles drilled on hard-packed earth and planks set between stone or wooden sidewalks. Other groups stood in squads at intersections or idled, their weapons at rest, in orderly fashion at various storefronts.

In Sacramento Street, she found number 105-½ deserted. Pushing back through the crowds, she turned left and started eastward toward a concentrated din coming from the direction of four vacant lots not far from the waterfront. She could make out long lines of vigilante troops standing in formation. Brushing past onlookers, she stepped away from the buildings and first heard, then saw a team of carpenters starting the foundation for a huge gallows in the center of the vacant area. Beyond the heads and shoulders of the armed men in the columns, she could see another team of craftsmen constructing hinged platforms just below two third-floor windows of the building at number 41 Sacramento. Above them, on the roof over a sign reading "Mills & Vantine," cannons pointed out over the open area. Armed men lined every visible rooftop.

She worked her way around the perimeter of the vacant lots and moved toward an eight-foot-high wall of gunnysacks filled with sand in front of number 41. The three-sided temporary breastwork was pocked with slits for rifles. A police lieutenant wearing an incongruous military cap from the Mexican War blocked a narrow, baffled entrance through the wall of sandbags.

"I haven't the faintest idea, madam," the lieutenant intoned, when she asked him how she could locate Jack Marin. "He could be in that formation out there, or anywhere in the city."

"Would anyone inside know where he is?"

"Not likely." The lieutenant grimaced and raised his eyebrows importantly. "Wait a minute . . . Marin? Isn't he the fellow witnessed the King shooting?"

"Yes, he is. One of them."

"Well, the committee'd likely know where he is."

"Could I pass through to speak with someone who might know."

"Not allowed, madam."

"Could you send someone in to inquire? Please? It's extremely important. A—a family emergency." She fished in her purse and took out a gold coin.

The lieutenant glanced around, saw that several men were watching him. "There won't be any need for that, madam. Let me see what I can do."

He beckoned to a police sergeant standing nearby, whispered in his ear, and sent him in through the sandbags. Esther stepped back a few paces. While she was waiting, a tall, fully-bearded man walked toward the entrance and stopped to shake hands with the police lieutenant. Esther didn't recognize him at first. The last time she'd seen him up close he had been much thinner and he'd worn only chin whiskers. But as soon as she heard his harsh, booming voice, she knew it was Sam Brannan.

"Got you out of the hoosegow soon enough, didn't we?" The lieutenant laughed ingratiatingly.

"*Soon* enough? Shouldn't've been jailed one minute for demanding the hanging of that son of a bitch Cora."

"Unjust. Unjust," the lieutenant nodded. "How were you to know that crowd would go wild?"

Brannan grunted in agreement.

The police officer glanced at Esther to see if she was aware that he was on privileged speaking terms with Brannan. He turned back.

"What's the latest from our friend the governor?"

Brannan sneered. "That horse's ass? Neeley's appointed William T. Sherman, the banker, commander of the state forces. I just tried to talk some sense into Sherman. Damn fool. He's taking the assignment seriously. Couldn't budge him. Well, we'll shove that West Point diploma of his up—" Brannan noticed Esther for the first time. She was sure he did not recognize her. "Well, you know what I mean," Brannan went on. "Wait 'til he finds out there *aren't* any state forces to command."

Both of them broke into loud, deprecatory laughter before Brannan slapped the lieutenant on the back and went in through the sandbags. A minute later, the police sergeant returned and passed a message to the lieutenant. He walked over to Esther.

"Your Mr. Marin is out with a group making arrests this morning," the lieutenant said. "It'll be difficult to find him. I shouldn't be telling you this, but you might have some luck if you keep an eye out in Sansome Street or thereabouts. I'd be careful, if I were you."

Esther thanked him and hurried off. She had no idea how she would manage to pry Murietta loose. She would have to improvise, possibly follow him back here and await an opportunity. Passage through the street was difficult and slow. When she finally reached Sansome, she searched the length of it, then doubled back. There was no sign of Murietta. She veered off into adjoining streets with no more success. She was beginning to despair when she passed a bank and caught sight of the list of its officers in gold letters on a glass panel in the massive front door.

"William T. Sherman," she read. Remembering, she felt once again an overwhelming sense of interconnected destinies. William Tecumseh Sherman. As a young army lieutenant he had been one of the first men to see a sample of Sutter's gold in Monterey. He had surveyed Sacramento's Embarcadero, been a part of the city's rise—and, unwittingly, Sutter's fall. He had obviously done well for himself in San Francisco during the years she had also lived here. Acting on a sudden impulse, she pushed in through the doorway, asked where he could be found, then nearly bowled over a clerk blocking her way and burst in on Sherman in the middle of a meeting.

"Can *nothing* be done about the insanity that is gripping this city?" she pleaded.

Embarrassed for a moment, Sherman looked from Esther to each of the concerned-looking, well-dressed men who turned to her from his conference table. One of them, an aging man with rectangular Ben Franklin eyeglasses, laughed half-heartedly. "Madam, we have been discussing just that for the past hour."

Sherman scowled, then took in a deep breath as he tried to control his frustration. "I do not know who you are, or how you got in here, madam, but I assure you—"

"Can anything be *done*?" Esther snapped.

Sherman sighed, exasperated, toying with the tip of his carefully trimmed beard. "Our hands are tied for the moment, madam. Without men, without arms, I can accomplish nothing."

"And what are you doing to get them?"

"Everything I can," Sherman said, his annoyance mounting.

"Which is precious little, from the looks of things."

"You will be apprised of my resignation as com-

mander by the press if the present situation continues—*madam.* I bid you good day!"

Incensed, frustrated, increasingly forlorn, Esther
searched several streets again without success. She
was about to make her way back to vigilante headquarters when she saw him. Two blocks ahead, Murietta moved resolutely across the street in a diagonal path toward a restaurant with a cluster of armed
men. She started running, shoving aside those who
did not make way. There were eight men with Murietta. They were heading toward six others standing
on the opposite side of the street. In the midst of the
second group she saw a tall man in a top hat and
formal clothes directing those with him to fan out.
He was affecting chin whiskers now, his moustache
was gone, but the moment she was within twenty
yards of the two groups, she recognized the scowl
and the glaring eyes. It was Mosby.

As a member of the Supreme Court, he has *to op-
pose the vigilantes,* Esther thought, her breath coming harder with each step. One of the men with
Murietta pointed toward the Law and Order man in
a top hat and frock coat standing near Mosby. Three
of the vigilantes moved to seize him, and Mosby
barked a series of commands, shoving the man on his
left toward Murietta. She was within ten yards of
them and still running when she heard the first shot
fired.

Murietta saw her, and she stopped.

He was holding the bayonet-fitted muzzle-loader in
front of him. Surprised, he paused for an instant, and
the man rushing at him took the opportunity to pull
the rifle out of his hands. For a few seconds Mosby
obscured Murietta from view, his left hand grasping
the barrel of a rifle held by another vigilante. She
saw Mosby's right hand flash under his broad bow
tie and inside his vest. When it came into view again,
jerking straight forward at the elbow, Mosby was

holding a bowie knife. The blade gleamed as it crossed the distance between the two men, and Esther gasped as Mosby drove it deep into the vigilante's neck.

Two other men grabbed Mosby from behind and, as they fell struggling in the middle of the street, she saw the rifle-stock swinging hard toward Murietta. It struck him squarely in the face. She heard the bones crack as his nose shattered and his forehead split open.

The rest of it she could hardly recall later. She dimly remembered the vigilantes overpowering Mosby and most of the men with him as she sat cradling Murietta's pitifully smashed face in her arms. She heard someone give an order to take Mosby and the rest of them to headquarters. After they had gone, it seemed as if an hour passed while she sat there quietly weeping. She was aware of the crowd gaping at the woman sitting in the middle of the street with the corpse lying across her lap. She knew Murietta was dead, but she did not fully believe it until the undertaker and his assistant talked to her gently and finally pried her hands loose from his head.

Sobbing and quivering in the darkness of her bedroom that night, her eyes swollen and her limbs made leaden by grief, she realized that she had to pull herself together. There was no one else to attend to the details of Murietta's funeral, no one she wanted to share his secret. The grief would have to wait until he was in the ground. She owed him a proper burial, at least that much courage and efficiency. Then, in the early morning hours, as the mental armor she was building for herself began solidifying, she realized there was something else that would strengthen the protective shell. Someone else she could focus on so she could hold up for the next seventy-two hours. She seized on the idea like a blacksmith shaping iron, hammering, plunging it into the fire of her

anger, tempering it, cooling it, until by morning she
had set the terrible hollowness aside.

On the Sunday morning she buried Murietta, Esther
arranged to ride back into town with the undertaker.
Before stepping up into the black, horse-drawn hearse,
she instructed Solana to drive her own buggy home
and wait. At three that afternoon, Solana was to take
the buggy to the entrance of Delmonico's restaurant.
She was to bring Esther's green shawl and a carriage
blanket. She was to sit there until dark, if necessary.
If Esther did not meet her, if anything unusual happened, she explained vaguely, Solana was to deliver
the journal in the bottom left-hand drawer of her
desk to Alexander Todd at the state capitol in Sacramento. Along with the sealed envelope beneath it.
She did not tell Solana that the envelope contained
her will, or that the document provided generously
for the Indian woman.

She went over it once again in her mind as the
undertaker drove back toward the city. King had
died of his chest wound. From the tenor of the previous day's newspaper accounts, they had probably
seized Casey and Cora by now. The man Mosby had
stabbed would recover. Equivocating, Coleman had
merely asked Mosby to resign. By the time she got
to Sacramento Street, she guessed they would have
tried Cora and Casey and that preparations for a
hanging would already be in progress.

There would be throngs in the open air in front
of number 41 Sacramento Street. The vigilantes would
be there, out in force to control the crowds. She
hoped only a handful of men would be inside the
headquarters building. Perhaps only one or two,
armed and watching the prisoners. However many
guards there were, if she got through, one would
be enough to provide witness to her act. *The consequences be damned,* she thought. *I will do it this*

*time. Let them do with me what they will after I
have told them the whole story. Perhaps they will
leave me alone with him for a moment, and there will
be no witness.* She doubted that. She wondered, as
the carriage skirted the more crowded downtown
streets and pulled to a halt in front of the undertaker's establishment, whether, ironically, the vigilantes' sentiments would support her after it was
done. . . . Whether Alex would come to her aid if
she sent word to him. . . . What he would think
of her. . . .

Once the undertaker had helped her out of the
carriage, all such thoughts gave way to total preoccupation with the plan she had developed in the last
forty-eight hours. The crowds forced her to move off
the sidewalk as she walked eastward. A block from
vigilante headquarters she turned right on Davis
and found the thriving restaurant she had reconnoi-
tered the previous afternoon. It was nearly deserted.
She ordered the Sunday roast-beef special, extra thick
cut, with all the trimmings, and a thermos of coffee;
paid extra for a tray and clean dish towel the grateful proprietor used to cover it. She pulled out of her
purse a Bible she had bought and tucked it under
her arm before picking up the tray and going back
out onto Davis Street.

As she turned left into California Street, which ran
parallel to and south of Sacramento, she glanced back
toward the Unitarian Church. In front of it, James
King's funeral cortege waited for the memorial service
inside to end. A clock in a store window read 1:20.
Esther could have been no less aware of the time
or the brilliantly sunny skies if she were in the bowels
of a mine. There were fewer vigilantes posted along
the way than there had been on Saturday. She was
grateful for that.

She passed a shop window: "G. R. Fardon. Da-
guerreotypist." *I must have a picture taken of me—
one day* . . . She crossed Front Street and approached

the alleyway between two buildings that led into the enormous backyard area behind number 41 Sacramento. Yesterday afternoon a squad of men had covered its entrance. Now a single county sheriff stood watch.

"I'm glad you chose the right side to be on, sheriff," she said, not stopping.

The peace officer eyed the woman in black Sunday-go-to-meeting clothes, the Bible, and the covered tray. He couldn't see through her heavy veil, but she was moving so resolutely, so authoritatively, for a moment he almost let her pass unquestioned. "Hold on a second, ma'am," he finally called out. "Uh, could you please tell me your business here?"

"The Lord's work," Esther answered, still walking. The sheriff trailed her. "The ladies of the First Baptist Church have delegated me to take a decent Sunday meal to Judge Mosby. We must not be sparing in our charity—even unto a man who has had a hand in another's death."

They were halfway through the alley. Esther's heart was beginning to pound.

"Ma'am? You say the First Baptist—?"

"With Mr. Coleman's approval, of course." Esther stopped. "There is a signed authorization from him in my purse. My hands are full and the poor man's meal is cooling. I will show it to the officer in charge at the rear of the building. Will that be all right?"

The sheriff shrugged. *Damn women.* "I reckon so, ma'am. You go on in."

There was a man posted at the end of the alley, but he had seen the sheriff let her through. Esther nodded courteously at him and went on without missing a step. In the rear yard, a makeshift corral held a half-dozen horses. There was room enough for dozens more. Out on Sacramento Street, she thought, controlling the crowds watching the carnival. Artillery pieces and gun carriages sat at odd angles in

454   DANIEL KNAPP

the enclosure. She walked on. At the rear of number
41, another peace officer, a marshal wearing a new
tin star, stood in the doorway looking at his watch.
Behind him, on a wall, there was a clock: 1:25.

"Ma'am?"

"Sunday dinner for Judge Mosby. As a gesture of
mercy from the First Baptist Church. I gave the letter of authorization signed by Mr. Coleman to the
sheriff at the entrance to the alley back there." She
cocked her head over her right shoulder and held
her breath.

"Yes, ma'am," the marshal said, ushering her inside. "Will you please set that tray down on the table
there? I'll have to look it over. Procedure, you understand. Judge Mosby may be charged with murder.
Of Jack Marin, that is. Ah . . . I'm afraid I'll have to
see the contents of your purse, too, ma'am. Orders."

"Perfectly understandable," she said. "I don't think
you can be careful enough." She sighed audibly.
"Dear, dear. I must be more forgiving. But there are
so many questionable characters lurking about."

"Right, ma'am," the marshal said, placing the dish
towel back over the tray. He peered into Esther's
purse as she pulled the contents out one by one and
dropped them back inside. She wondered if he could
see how her hands were trembling. She could feel
the cold metal of the gun where it lay snugged against
her skin, under the bustle, beneath the corset. He
turned and knocked on a door leading inside. A
young man opened it partway.

"Corbett, escort this lady to Mosby's cell."

"I have been asked to read a psalm while I am
in his company," Esther said. "That, you see, is why
I have the Bible under my arm."

"Perfectly all right, ma'am," the marshal said. He
nodded to the younger man, who quickly opened the
door and gestured for Esther to follow.

They went through another small room, a hallway,
and then into a large warehousing and stable area.

Along two sides, the stalls had been turned into make-shift cells. The bars were flagpole-thick wooden rods that ran up into overhead beams in the ceiling. A number of cells on the far end contained men, but several between the first group and the corner cell where Mosby stood watching them approach were empty. She glanced to her right at a second, perpendicular row of cells and took note of another exit directly onto the rear yard. She did not see the man lying on the cot in the cell directly next to Mosby's. It was the first one on the rear wall, Mosby's the last in the other line. As they stopped, the young deputy blocked most of the adjacent cell from view.

"Lady here's brought you a fine Sunday dinner, judge."

"That so?" Mosby glanced sharply at Esther, trying to make out her face under the veil.

"Gonna say a psalm over you, too, judge. Ain't that nice?"

"Wonderful," Mosby said. "Just what I need. To whom do I owe this act of Christian charity?"

"The ladies of the First Baptist Church," Esther said.

"That's right nice," Mosby purred, calculating. He looked at his watch. "Makes you feel the Good Lord hasn't forsaken a body, after all."

The young deputy took the tray from Esther and carefully set it on the base of a rectangular, slat-framed opening built into the wooden bars. Mosby picked it up and put it on a table just as the huge bell the vigilantes had borrowed from the California Engine Company tolled on the roof above. In seconds they could hear church bells all over the city echoing back the knell.

"They're hangin' Cora and Casey!" The young deputy's eyes widened. "Ma'am. I don't want to miss this. It'll be somethin' to tell my grandchildren. You say your psalm over the judge and I'll be right back." He tipped his hat, turned, and ran toward the front of the building. "I just want to take one fast look," he called over his shoulder.

She could not have asked for more. She took in a deep breath as Mosby turned to her.

"*Over* the judge. Sounds like I've already been laid to rest." He laughed. "Which psalm you going to read?"

"Why, the twenty-third." Esther stepped a bit closer, holding up the Bible.

"My land," Mosby said, "looks like one my mother used to read me from. I mean, the brown leather cover. But you said Baptist. That couldn't be a Methodist-Episcopal Bible, now could it?"

"I suspect not," she said, trying not to remember her father's sermons on violence.

"You mind if I just take a look at it for a minute? Before you read? It'd satisfy my curiosity. Just want to look through the first few pages to see who printed it up."

She could hear the bells tolling, the one on the roof ringing loudest. Briefly, there was a sudden, muffled roar of thousands of voices from out beyond the front walls of the building. She thought quickly. *It will be easier if I have both hands free, if I give him the Bible. One hand to hold and fire, one to steady my aim.* She moved up to the wooden bars and held the Good Book out to him.

Mosby reached past the Bible, grabbed her wrist, and spun her around. The Bible fell to the floor as he hissed, "Who sent you, little angel? Who made the supper? I'll bet it's laced with arsenic. Here! *You* eat some of it!"

He had surreptitiously palmed a piece of the beef. Now he swung his left hand up, the arm moving a bit freely, until he had the meat pressed against her lips.

She opened her mouth and took the beef on her tongue. *If he sees me eat it, he will let go of me,* she thought. And then I will remove the pistol and kill him. She chewed obediently as he slid his hand down from her mouth and chin to her throat, let go of her wrist, and quickly threw his other arm around her neck. He waited until he felt her swallow the beef. *He will let me go now,* she thought. *He must.*

Instead, he pulled her head and neck against the bars until she began to feel faint. He raised his weak arm and fumbled at her veil. "Let's just get a look at you, see who the hell you are."

"Jesus Christ!" the young deputy said as he came walking back through the door at the far end of the room. He started running. "*Jesus . . . H . . . Christ!* Earl! *Mr. Coombs!* For God's sake, come in here and help me! *Marshal COOOMBS!*"

He was at the cell now, trying to pry Mosby's arm loose from Esther's throat.

"I'll kill her 'less you hand me your gun, you son of a bitch!" Mosby whispered hoarsely. "I'll choke her to death. The gun and the keys! *Now!*"

The young deputy stopped for a moment, moved to the right, thought about drawing, firing at him. There would be hell to pay if he killed a Supreme Court judge, committee or no committee. He threw himself at Mosby's arm again.

Esther started to black out. She could hear the bells tolling. The man on the cot in the cell beside Mosby's got up and quietly moved behind the young deputy. Reaching through the bars, he pulled the deputy's pistol out of its holster, raised and fired it into the young man's back just as Marshal Coombs came bursting through the rear door.

"Get the damn keys, judge. *The keys!* Forget the woman. Get the keys!"

Esther felt Mosby let go of her, and she fell. Opening her eyes, she saw Coombs drop to one knee and flinch as the man in the cell next to Mosby's sent a shell burrowing into the hard-packed earth floor be-

side him. Then she saw the sheriff point and fire into
the cell, heard the man she could not see scream and
fall just before she passed out.

When she came to on a cot in one of the rooms
along the side of the stable area, a short, fat man
with weasel eyes was hovering over her.

"I'm Dr. Leander Sims. How do you feel? You've
had one heck of an experience."

"Give me a minute," she said. She waited, regaining her senses, taking hope as she felt the bulk of
the pistol beneath her, still snugged to her back by
the lower portion of her corset.

The doctor saw her glance down. There was a
towel covering her upper body. "I took the liberty of
loosening—I didn't remove anything, mind you—loosening some of your undergarments. It was immediately apparent that you suffered no serious harm, but
you had the wind knocked out of you. The shock of
it—you needed to breathe more freely than those
contraptions allow. . . ."

"I understand," she said.

"Are you all right? Do you think you can stand
up?"

"Yes. Give me a moment." She glanced at the door.
"Would you—?"

"Of course, of course. You just take your time."

When he was out of the room, she made sure the
pistol was secure, fastened the corset, and buttoned
the top of her dress. She reached for her heavily
veiled hat and put it on, then stood up. For a moment she swayed, but then her equilibrium returned.
She wondered if anyone had checked her story about
the authorization from Coleman in the aftermath of
the shooting. She looked at her watch—half-past two
—went to the door, and opened it.

"How are you feeling?" the doctor asked again.

"I'm fine. A bit shaken, but fine."

"You'll have a bruise on your neck, young lady, but you can be thankful it's no more than that."

"Yes. Thank you. I feel fine now. I just want to go home."

"I can understand that. Come with me. I'll escort you out to the plaza."

There were a dozen men in the corner near Mosby's cell, talking and gesturing. She saw Coleman glance at her, then turn back, absorbed. No one called to the doctor or Esther as they went out the front door.

Outside, the crowds had dwindled. Only a small number of vigilante troops stood at ease nearby. The police lieutenant outside the sandbags looked at her, and her heart stopped, but he simply tipped his cap, smiled at the doctor, and turned away. She looked back once, just before thanking the doctor again. The bodies of Cora and Casey were still dangling on ropes hung from rafters above the top-story windows. The hinged platforms they had stood on lay flat against the side of the building.

"My Lord, I almost forgot," the doctor said. "I was asked to take your name."

"Cordelia Plaggett."

"And your address? I should have it for my records, and they'll undoubtedly want to ask you a question or two."

"Perhaps I should go back and write it all out for them."

"No need, no need. I recommended they wait until you have a chance to recover. You should get some rest. I can pass it along."

"Four hundred aught seven, Orchard Street. Cordelia Plaggett. With two *t*'s."

The doctor fished out a notepad and pencil and wrote it down. "Orchard Street. Coincidence. I have a patient at three hundred aught six. Are you sure you'll be all right? I have a carriage nearby. It would be no trouble to take you."

"No. I'll be fine. Someone is waiting for me at a restaurant. She'll be half out of her wits with worry by now."

"If you have any difficulty, please send for me." He gave her his card and tipped his hat.

Quickly, she put distance and people between them. Her throat hurt. The pistol was bruising the lower portion of her spine. *Small price to pay for the chance I had . . .* She felt chagrined and disappointed, grateful, thankful, all at the same time. *I am still alive. . . . If I can get to Solana and get home before they learn of my ruse . . .* No one but the doctor had seen her unveiled face, and she had never seen him before. With luck she would never see him again. No one had seen anything but the clothes she wore—and hundreds of women wore similar outfits every Sunday of the year.

She kept walking, not looking back. *I will stay at home . . . perhaps even travel, leave San Francisco until enough time has passed so no one, not even the doctor, could identify me with certainty. . . . If I can just reach Solana . . .*

Anger over her failure began blossoming again. She squelched it. *First things first . . . Get away . . . Get to Solana and get away . . . So there can be another time, another opportunity . . . if I am patient enough . . . lucky enough. . . .*

Solana was waiting in the buggy in front of Delmonico's. She seemed to look knowingly at Esther, had almost the beginning of a smile on her mouth. But the Indian woman said nothing, simply turned, clucked, and snapped the reins. As they began the ride out of town, Esther took off her hat, reached back, and threw the forest-green shawl over her head, shoulders, and chest, then covered her black skirts with the beige carriage blanket. Sitting back and letting out a deep breath, she watched the people they passed. No one took particular notice of her. It was already cool enough for a woman in a carriage to want cover, warmth. She sighed with relief. Wrapped in the shawl and blanket, she no doubt looked like a different person. There was nothing to connect her with the black-clad "Baptist lady" at number 41 Sacramento Street.

Later, in her bedroom with the door closed, the pistol put away, after her pulse had slowed and her hands had stopped shaking, she felt only the hollow, bone-deep loss of Murietta. She still could not believe that he was gone, that she would never see him again. She wanted to talk to someone about him. Not Solana, who had long since retreated into a shell of virtual silence. Not Barnett, who knew nothing of Murietta's return. But who? She thought of Alex. Dear, sweet Alex. She had not addressed herself to him in the pages of her journal for some time. It had been necessary to stop. But now she needed him. He was the one. He was the only one she could "tell," the only one who could really understand how she felt, know why she needed so to write to him again.

She went to her desk, yearning for the blessed relief she knew she would feel when she picked up the pen, began forming the letters, the words. She sat down and opened the journal. She noted the date and place. Then her mind went blank. She did not know where to begin. A minute passed. Then, as she sat there detached, watching her hand, it began to move. Almost independent of her, it wrote the first line:

"Solana and I buried 'Jack Marin' today."

And then the rest of the words flowed as freely as her tears.

Sixty-two

Esther and Solana were sailing through the Golden Gate aboard the clipper *Flying Cloud* by the time a messenger surprised William Kelsey with her letter. In it, she explained that she wished to be away from San Francisco for the duration of the vigilante madness, that she felt a need for a temporary change of scenery, and she apologized for not saying good-bye. She also requested that he have Billy Ralston look after her affairs. Half of the profits accruing to her from Blue Star and her wholesale business were to be placed in her security vault at the Miner's Exchange Bank. A separate letter of authorization and a key were enclosed. The remaining half, Ralston was to invest for her as he saw fit. She added that he was to receive 20 percent of any income he made for her, nothing if he did not.

At first she planned only to spend a few months in New York and New England, then return to California. But after a surreptitious carriage-drive one painfully nostalgic fall afternoon past her Vermont home and the old school where her younger sister now taught, she decided a trip to Europe would do wonders for Solana as well as herself.

They spent an enthralled month in London, then moved on. Establishing an apartment in Paris as a base, they traveled the Continent for almost a year. She wrote to and heard from Sutter, Kelsey, and Barnett several times, learned in one letter that Warren had been a target of the vigilantes. He had come

out of it unscathed politically and, more important,
unharmed. Kelsey's life was still as placid as Sutter's
was troubled. The petitions for title Sutter had sent
to the U.S. Government were getting no further than
they had with the State of California.

The extended tour broadened and restored her. But
by the end of eighteen months she began to feel
homesick. She was sure even Dr. Sims could no longer
be certain she was the woman who had visited Mosby's
cell. Twenty-two months after the vigilantes disbanded, she returned to San Francisco by way of
London, New York, and a second, eighty-day clipper
voyage around the Horn.

The first thing she did after reopening her house
and unpacking was to check on Mosby's whereabouts.
U.S. government, state, and military officials had put
pressure on Coleman. Mosby had been charged only
with assault, let off with a fine. He was back on the
bench in Sacramento. She would go there, observe
his movements, and find out where he lived. Perhaps
then she could begin planning again. But that could
wait for the moment. He wasn't going anywhere,
and there were other things she wanted to do first.

Initially she had enough on her hands simply adjusting to all that had happened while she was gone.
Discomfitingly, the city had crept to within two
miles of her hilltop. There were thousands more people, among them a growing number of Chinese who
had worked off their contracts with the large hy-
draulic- and shaft-mining combines and set up small
businesses.

Going over her accounts, she discovered that Ralston had done far better with her money than she'd
ever dreamed he would. She had spent almost all of
the profits she'd made during the year and a half
following the panic. But more had accumulated while
she was away. Ralston had quadrupled that base with
investments in commodity firms, real estate, a foundry, and a railroad that someone named Theodore

Judah had built from Sacramento up into the gold
fields. She recalled the extensive railroads of the
Eastern seaboard, two of which she'd traveled on to
Boston, and briefly considered the importance such
transportation might play in California if Judah's
system could be expanded. She would have to look
into that. Setting the matter aside, she went back to
the accounts. Ralston had provided funds for three
separate coffee merchants: the Hills brothers, James
Folger, and Max Joseph Brandenstein, whose coffee
sacks, Ralston informed her, bore his initials. All were
thriving. The last item on the list was a relatively
small investment in a silver mine in Nevada called
the Ophir.

Impressed, she read the letter Ralston enclosed. He
had continued to represent her interests after leaving
Blue Star to become a bank manager. She thought
of the advantage money had meant in setting Mosby
up in the bordello. It seemed prudent to have Ralston expand his activities for her. She had just decided to find a way to meet him without danger of
being recognized when she glanced at the front page
of the *San Francisco Journal* sitting on her desk. Alex
Todd was campaigning for a judgeship. He was better qualified than his opponent, the article said, but
the man he was running against was favored because
he had unlimited financial support from the city's
Southern faction. And, as if that were not enough,
the piece added, Todd's own efforts were curtailed
because his wife was gravely ill.

Esther gazed out through her bedroom window at
the city. She suddenly had an unquenchable urge to
see Alex again; to just look at him. She thought of
how she could meet with Ralston, then of Alex's political predicament. Slowly, a means of fulfilling both
wishes began to materialize. A dangerous means, to
be sure, but, surprisingly, the danger—along with
the possibility of succeeding—excited her more than
any of Europe's endless wonders.

The following day she scoured the financial district and found a vacant office with western exposure in a four-story brick building. It was September, and by midafternoon the sun streamed through the windows of the small room, casting everything before them in silhouette.

Satisfied, she bought handsome office furniture: a couch, a leather desk-set, and a calendar. She had louvered shutters installed on the windows, nailing all of them shut except those directly behind the desk. Of the three lamps she acquired, one was a floor model. She placed it behind her leather desk-chair. The smaller fixtures on the desk itself and the end table next to the couch, she left empty. If she had to turn on a lamp, the only one operable would be behind her. Even in the unlikely event that someone could see through the heavy veil she planned to wear, it would be impossible to make out her face.

"You won't understand why I'm asking this," she said to Solana, "but if for any reason I faint while they're here, you're to make them leave immediately. Just tell them I'll see them another time."

The sun had just dropped below the upper frame of the office windows. The louvered shutters slanted down, and the brilliant light spilling through them blacked out every vertical, eastward-facing surface in the room.

"You do not feel well?" Solana asked as Esther sat the Indian woman in the desk chair for the third time. Solana's features were barely discernible even without covering.

"It's nothing," Esther said, satisfied.

"I will not have to speak?"

"Not unless I'm taken ill."

Solana grumbled, then sat back down on the couch. She wondered why Esther was going to so much trouble to remain unseen. They would hear her, recognize her voice. . . . She decided the matter did not

concern her. She was beyond wondering about the inexplicable things Esther occasionally did. If it was part
of the large work the sun had given her, then so be it.
Esther would tell her if she cared to, or if she needed
help. Still, Solana was aware of how nervous Esther
seemed, then puzzled when she flinched visibly at the
knock on the door. She listened and watched, fascinated, as Esther began speaking in a loud whisper,
dragging the words across the back of her tongue so
she gargled slightly and sounded like someone else.

"Forgive me for not getting up and shaking hands,"
she said, after they had been introduced to Solana and
seated. "I have a touch of the ague."

"Pleasure to meet you again, ma'am," Ralston said.
"I'm excited about the business ventures you outlined in your letter, and Assemblyman Todd here is
sure grateful for the support you've offered."

She had not looked at Alex when they came in. She
still did not trust herself. She had to become accustomed to the pounding of her heart and the tremor in
her limbs. When he spoke, she gripped the arms of her
chair until her knuckles turned white under her gloves.

"I certainly *am* grateful," he said diffidently. "And
I want to say it's a privilege finally to meet you after
all those years associated in business. I hope you were
satisfied with my handling of things at the South
Fork."

"More than pleased," she whispered, shifting her
eyes toward him slowly. When she finally looked
straight at him, she was certain her voice would crack.
He looked marvelous, even if his suit was a bad fit and
slightly rumpled. Alex would do justice to burlap. She
glanced at Ralston's meticulously selected, carefully
pressed clothing. By comparison, he looked like a
dandy.

Thirteen years since the day Alex had left her at
Bent's Fort; eleven since their near encounter here in
San Francisco. And yet he still looked young, had not
lost that endearing touch of awkward shyness. She

felt as though a tiny bird was trapped beneath her chest, beating its fragile wings against her rib cage in an effort to free itself. His face was even more handsome than she remembered. His pale, slightly sad blue eyes made her want to fold him in her arms.

She looked at Ralston out of desperation, anything to take her eyes off Alex. He was still fit. Ralston was also trim, but she guessed he had to work long and hard with barbells to stay that way. Alex would probably retain his athletic build through his fifties with half the effort. *They age better than we do,* she thought, the strangely detached observation floating in a sea of emotion.

She looked back at Alex. "Much more than pleased," she heard herself say. She had to shift her gaze back to Ralston again to keep from breaking, giving in to the impulse to rip her hat and veil off, plead with Alex to leave his wife and take her back. She had not turned her head, and she knew Alex thought she was still looking at him. "You had a great deal to do with our success, right from the start." She did not dare take her eyes off Ralston's solid-gold stickpin. "That's why I want to help you now. I feel I owe you that."

"No need to feel obliged, Mrs. Cable."

His voice made her ache inside. "But I do, and nothing you say will change that."

Ralston shifted impatiently, trying to avoid the sunlight shining in his eyes.

"Please forgive the glare. I have to have it behind me. My eyes are very sensitive to light."

"No trouble, Mrs. Cable," Ralston said. "I just can't see you."

Esther took in a breath, trying to work up moisture in her mouth so her speech would remain glottal. "I'm sorry about the veil, Mr. Ralston. As you may know, I am of a retiring nature. It is most unusual for me to meet with anyone this way—" Out of the corner of her eye she caught sight of Alex moving his chair slightly closer, and nearly panicked. "And as you can plainly hear . . . the ague . . . is sufficient to affect my voice. I wouldn't want to pass it on to either of you gentlemen."

She glanced at Alex and felt a little calmer. Satisfied that she could carry it off, she asked Alex's forbearance and went over the expanded activities she wanted Ralston to undertake. He was delighted. Finally she knew she could put off speaking to Alex for only a question or two more. She gathered her courage as she asked Ralston, "You don't mind working for—" She corrected herself, sensitive to the notion most men had of a woman's place "—*representing* a woman?"

"Not at all," Ralston smiled. "I don't really care who or what a person is when they're giving me what might be the opportunity of a lifetime. I think a man who does has got to be a jackass, if you'll pardon me."

"I'm glad you feel that way."

"You might be surprised at the number of ladies who—ah—quietly, secretly have their hand in things."

Esther smiled at the double irony. "Would it be any help to you personally if I transferred my savings to your bank? To an account rather than a safe deposit?"

Ralston beamed. "*Very* helpful, Mrs. Cable. It would also be more convenient all around."

She steeled herself. "Mr. Todd . . . Thank you for your patience. What I had in mind was something like this. I'd like to contribute nine hundred dollars to your campaign." *Three times what he left with me at Bent's Fort. Nearly ten times the interest a bank would have paid. I hope he will one day consider that fair.* "Use it as you see fit," she went on. "I'll also ask William Kelsey to lend a hand. Perhaps he can enlist some business acquaintances. If you need more than that, I'll be happy to advance it." She wanted to give him all of it, anything he needed. But that would raise questions in his mind. She was certain of it. "Anything above the nine hundred I will expect you to pay back. Whenever you are able, of course, without interest."

She wondered if he could sense that her eyes were

sweeping back and forth beneath the veil, resting on his face for only seconds at a time.

Alex shook his head in disbelief. "I don't know what to say, Mrs. Cable. I can't thank you enough." He looked down at the floor. "You know, I was never cut out to be either a borrower or a politician."

"Thank God for that," Ralston said, echoing Esther's thoughts.

Alex laughed self-deprecatingly. The sound sent a current of memories down Esther's spine. "I suppose I could go back into business. But I . . . I have a hunch I'd be suited—I think I could do a good job as a judge."

"I'm sure you will," Esther said, trying to hold on. "I wouldn't be doing it unless I knew what a decent, conscientious man you are." She wondered if she sounded too familiar, if she had gone too far. It frightened her. She looked at her watch. "Now . . . both of you will have to excuse me. I'm expecting my doctor any minute." She smiled to herself. She might need a doctor. She turned to Ralston. "You'll be sure . . ." Her voice was beginning to fail her. She cleared her throat. "The railroad business. You'll be sure to look into it?"

"Yes, ma'am. As quickly as I can," Ralston said as he and Alex got up and turned toward the door. "As well as that rumor I mentioned about the Ophir mine. I think we ought to buy more of it."

"Thank you again, Mrs. Cable," Alex said softly, looking back.

The sound of his voice and the imminence of his departure sent a pang through her. As relieved as she was that they were going, she wanted to prolong his presence, if only for a few seconds.

"Your wife, Mr. Todd. Is she any better?"

"Thank you for asking. I'm afraid not."

She searched for something else to say, going headlong over the limit she usually placed on personal questions. "Is it . . . the nature of your wife's illness . . . is it serious?"

"It could be. She's having early complications."

"Early . . . complications?"

"She's with child, Mrs. Cable."

Esther bit her lip. "Well . . . I do hope she's feeling better."

When they were gone, she sat silently for a moment, stunned, unable to do anything but stare at the door. She felt herself beginning to come apart. She asked Solana to wait for her in the lobby, and after the Indian woman had left, she rested her head on her arms and wept. The hollowness in her chest and the knots in her stomach were ample evidence of the truth. Now she had to find a way to deal with it. If there had ever been any doubt, any rationalized belief that her feelings had diminished, it was gone now. She still loved him, wanted him as much as she ever had. Enough to disregard willfully the pain this meeting might have held for him as well as her. And there was nothing she could do about it, other than find something to occupy her mind totally, shut him out as she had in the past.

She sat there for almost half an hour, going over what she could do, what would most absorb her. A few minutes before she collected herself, dried her eyes, and got up, Solana quietly came back and peered through the door at her, unseen.

The Indian woman went back down the hallway and the stairs and waited. She weighed the extreme measures Esther had taken not to reveal herself to Ralston and Todd. She thought of the day they had found her on the river ice . . . pictured the baby, ice blue, cradled in her arms . . . remembered the heretofore unexplained slightly wistful look in Esther's eyes whenever Todd's name had come up in conversation with Miwokan and Murietta. And then she nodded to herself as it finally began to come together.

There was little doubt in her mind that Alex Todd

was the dead child's father, that he thought Esther had died with the baby in the mountains, and that Esther wanted it that way.

Shaking her head sadly, Solana turned her thoughts to the newspaper picture she had seen of the man who had killed so many in her village. She had carried his first name, along with that of the red-bearded man who had killed her husband, in her mind for years. She knew the moustachioed man's last name: *Mos-by.* She turned the name over in her thoughts as she recalled vaguely the questions she had once overheard Esther asking Murietta about him. *Mos-by. Clauss-en.* She remembered something about Mosby beating Murietta. She pictured Esther clipping a line drawing of Mosby out of the paper, placing it in a pigeonhole of her desk, and wondered if what he had done to Murietta was all there was to it. Instinctively, she sensed there was more, and guessed that it went back as far as the time before they had found her, halfdead, walking on the ice.

And then her eyes narrowed and she nodded to herself, smiling as it began to fall into place.

Sixty-three

"The man in the top hat, the judge with the whiskers. You watch him always. Why?"

Esther felt a burst of annoyance with Solana. "I'm not watching anyone!" She softened her voice. "We're simply out for a ride. I needed some air."

"He is always there when we go in the carriage together."

"He is? I hadn't noticed. Just coincidence."

"Many coincidences." Solana clucked and snapped the reins.

"*What are you doing?*"

"We are out for a ride, you said."

"Stop the carriage. I . . . I want to rest from the . . . jouncing."

"As you wish, Sunsister." Solana gave no hint she knew Esther was trying to conceal her continued observation of Mosby. The tall man and his friends walked up the steps of the state courthouse and disappeared beyond its ten massive pillars.

"I'm sorry I spoke so sharply," Esther said. "We can drive on now."

Solana smiled.

For a moment Esther wondered what Solana knew, if somehow she recognized Mosby. *Ridiculous,* she thought. *She was unconscious while it happened.* She toyed with the idea of telling the Indian woman everything. Mosby *had* been a part of the death of her husband, her son. For an instant she was seized by the conviction that she owed it to Solana, and briefly, guilt over her concealment almost prompted her to speak. But then she wondered what the Indian woman would do, how she would react. Overcome by emotion, would she attempt to kill Mosby and be killed herself? Short of that, she might rob Esther of the chance to take revenge. Sighing with a measure of guilt, Esther decided to remain silent.

It is true, Solana thought. *I feel it.* Mosby was the one who had given Esther Moses when she did not want a child. The boy looks too much like him for it not to be true. . . . If it was only what he did to Murietta, she would not be doing this, watching him, thinking of him and almost nothing else when she was not with the children at the school. That is why there was not only one picture of him in Esther's desk now, but many. And if he was a part of the death of Esther's firstborn, then all this could only mean she would one day try to kill him. She had the power of the sun, who was with her, and the power of the white man's money turned from gold. She would try to do it! If she destroyed or changed the place of the pictures in her desk, then it would be clear that the time had come.

He was the man who had held Mwamwaash in the fire. Solana was certain now. He did not kill Miwokan, but he had been a part of it, and he had killed many others. And she would kill him someday. She was only an Indian. Only a woman. But she would wait until her sunsister found the way and the place, and then she would be there and be the one to kill him. For herself and for Esther.

Riding back to the school, Esther mused about the year that had passed since they moved to Sacramento. Scarcely two months after returning from Europe she'd closed the San Francisco house again, in the wake of her painful meeting with Ralston and Alex. She recognized now that her move here initially was just to be nearer to the man she had always loved. But after Alex had won his election, resigned from the assembly, and moved back to sit on the bench in San Francisco, Esther had stayed on.

She worked hard at her original intention—to shut all thought of him out of her mind. She plunged into expanding the Sacramento school; converted its attic into an apartment containing two small bedrooms. Nights, she pored over Ralston's reports. Most of her investments had dipped to only average returns, but the money was literally pouring into her account from the Comstock. She had given Ralston leeway to use his own judgment, and he was shoveling at least a quarter of everything he made for her into the Ophir and other mines he virtually controlled now, after pulling together a dozen investors besides Esther. She had been the first, so when the others came in with them, the value of her stock jumped even higher.

Last but not least, she had avidly followed the activities of Theodore Judah, the builder of the Sacramento Valley Railroad. Ralston kept her abreast of Judah's unsuccessful efforts to form a stock company to underwrite a railroad across the Sierras. After reading Ralston's latest report, she had taken it upon herself to speak to Leland Stanford, her tenant, and two men she was indirectly associated with through Blue Star: the Sacramento hardware merchants, Collis P. Huntington and Mark Hopkins. They had reluctantly agreed to attend one of Judah's almost evangelistic presentations of maps, charts, and figures at the St. Charles Hotel this coming week.

Other things kept her mind off Alex, as well. The Butterfield Overland Mail was making the trip from St. Louis to San Francisco in twenty-three days. With the inception of the transatlantic cable, news from Europe was reaching America in twelve hours. Dispatches from New York and Washington as well as London and Paris were on the presses in San Francisco and Sacramento more rapidly than ever before. The news from the East was ominous. From the tenor of the reports, secession and war seemed inevitable.

Barnett had been in Washington since his election to the U.S. Senate the year before. He had outmaneuvered Gwin in California, won most of the political patronage Gwin controlled as a condition for supporting the Southerner's reelection. Outspokenly antislavery, Barnett had been received icily by President Buchanan, who saw to it that the patronage remained in Gwin's hands. Barnett was back in California now, for the state Democratic convention currently being held in Sacramento. She hoped he could regain some of the political power that was slipping from his grasp. They planned to have dinner together. Perhaps she could be of some help to him.

By the time the convention had started, thousands of Californians had crossed the Sierras, drawn by the extraordinary yields of the Comstock. Ralston was increasing what were now their joint holdings in the mines. Her profits were beginning to rival the initial sums she had made in the gold fields. At first that had bothered her, but she quickly suppressed her distaste for precious metal. She knew now that she would probably need all the money, all the power she could accumulate if she were ever to have what she wanted most.

For despite all the other interests that absorbed her, her greatest preoccupation was with Mosby. During that year in Sacramento she took every opportunity to observe his movements. She knew where he lived, where he ate, the women he spent time with. She sat in the gallery and watched him, contemptuous and coldly efficient, in his courtroom. By now she knew he was virtually unreachable. Hated by political opponents, former vigilantes, and those he had dealt with harshly on the bench, he was accompanied by a bodyguard everywhere. During the day, cronies surrounded him. At night, two Sacramento policemen watched his house until midnight, when a pair of state militiamen took over. He was inaccessible at the courthouse. In the streets she rarely saw him unaccompanied by other men. On the rare occasions when he went to a restaurant, the bodyguard kept the curious away from his table, and friends usually occupied several tables around him.

Esther had again contemplated having him assassinated, but the chances for success were slim and the risk of exposure too great. In any case she still considered that method morally unacceptable. And she still wanted to strike the avenging blow—in a manner that would provide at least a chance of bringing it off undetected, of surviving and savoring her accomplishment.

So she had continued to observe him, follow him and his cluster of bullies at a distance whenever she could. She knew just about everything she needed to know about him now. Sooner or later he would reveal an

Achilles heel, uncover for her the ways and means she was watching for. Now, as she and Solana returned to the school from the latest of her rides, she knew she would have to devise methods of surveillance that were less obvious. If Solana were suspicious, others might react the same way.

The next time Esther rode out in her carriage on a reconnaissance mission, she did not take Solana with her. She saw no sign of Mosby that day. And in the late afternoon he did not return as usual to the Supreme Court offices in the Hastings Building at Second and J Streets. On the ride home she did not recognize the red-bearded man carrying the case into the gunsmith's on M Street as she drove past. Five years of trapping in the Rockies and a prison term for manslaughter in Texas had slimmed him down considerably.

"French dueling pistols," the gunsmith said, fingers splayed on the counter of his immaculate shop. "Beauties. I don't see nothing wrong with them."

"There *ain't* nothin' wrong with 'em." Isaac Claussen pointed one of the long-barreled, understocked weapons at the gunsmith's face and pulled the trigger. He laughed as the hammer snapped home and the gunsmith flinched. "Nothin' wrong at all. Want you to file down the trigger mechanism for me, that's all. On both of 'em."

"Hair triggers, huh? Now why would you want me to do that?"

"You'd be smart to mind your own fuckin' business," Claussen said, glaring. "Now and in the future, if you know what's good for you."

Esther passed the swarm of children playing in the schoolyard. At the mailbox the happy noise of their shrieking and laughter faded as she opened the evening edition of the *Sacramento Union* and began reading the first of two adjoining stories on the front page. Her mouth dropped open. Luther Mosby had been one of Gwin's most vitriolic allies against Barnett in the past, but this time he had gone even further:

Barnett is an arch traitor to the Democratic Party. The men who follow him are personal chattels of a single individual who has not even kept his pork-barrel promises of make-work jobs. A man they are ashamed of but beholden to for pathetic political crumbs he has fed them through the years. They belong heart, body, and breeches to the hoodlum son of an illiterate Irish, New York City Tammany shoulder-striker and ballot-box stuffer. Their souls are owned by the devil incarnate, Warren Barnett.

Esther grew more apprehensive as she read Barnett's caustic response:

I once called Luther Mosby the only honest man on the California Supreme Court. That was when he was one of the few who stood up against the vigilantes. I was mistaken. I donated two hundred dollars to a San Francisco newspaper to defend Judge Mosby when he was incarcerated by the Committee of Thirteen in the matter of the stabbing of a vigilante. I realize now that that was a mistake as well. As much as I detest all the vigilantes stood for, California might have been better served if they had had their way with the man. If I were to be asked now, I have no doubt whatsoever that I would not offer the opinion that Judge Mosby is an honest man.

Esther was temporarily stunned, almost as much by the discovery that Barnett had once helped Mosby as by the severity of the exchange. She was so engrossed

by what she had read, so gripped by an inexplicable
certainty that things would get worse, she didn't realize the children around her were shouting playfully
that the dinner bell was ringing. One of them finally
brought her to her senses when he tugged innocently
on her glove and almost pulled it off her disfigured
left hand.

"Hold your forefinger out straight, judge, against
the front of the housing when you lift it. And don't
move sudden with it. Otherwise, the hair trigger'll—"
Mosby turned to Claussen icily. "You really think
I need telling how to handle a weapon, any kind of
weapon?"
"Just—"
"Just shut up, Isaac." Turning, Mosby slowly lifted
the dueling pistol and aimed at the target tacked to
the privy behind his house. Holding the ball-and-cap
model steadily, he fired off the single round. Dead
center. He smiled at Claussen. "Here. Load it up. I
want to see you do it just in case the son of a bitch
surprises us and shows some courage sooner than I
expect."
Claussen carried the loaded pistol to the same spot,
aimed, and fired. The ball went through the rim of the
outer circle.
"Stay here and practice until you can put two or
three shots in a row right in the center circle," Mosby
said. "Unless you want to lose the chance of gettin' fat
as a bloated pig again."
"Ain't no need to talk to me that way, Luther."
Mosby stopped without turning back. "I'll talk to
you any goddamned way I please, and don't you forget it! And the name is Judge Mosby, you hear? You
might also try to remember, if your pea brain is up to
it, that a letter from me got you out of prison five
years early. Wouldn't take much to have you thrown
back in."

* * *

Fear for Barnett preoccupied Esther as she drove to the St. Charles Hotel the following evening to attend the Judah presentation. For the sake of convenience she had arranged to meet Barnett in the dining room after the meeting. In a second-floor suite, she listened absently while Judah made his fiery pitch to Huntington, Hopkins, Stanford, and a small group of men Stanford windily introduced before they all sat down. One of them was an enormous, ill-tempered man named Charles Crocker, a dry-goods wholesaler she had been competing with through the past ten years. With him was one of his two half-brothers, William "Bull" Carter.

Esther had seen no reason to wear a veil.

"Haven't I met you somewhere before?" Carter asked.

Esther pictured him toppling over after she'd struck him with the pistol the day they whipped Murietta in Placerville. "I don't believe so, Mr. Carter." She smiled and quickly turned away, hoping his eyes were weak as well as piggishly small.

Carter smiled at her several times as Judah slowly won the cautious support of the men, but she knew from the transparent expression on his face that he was interested in far more than determining where he had seen her. To avoid him, she went downstairs to join Barnett before Huntington, Hopkins, Stanford, and Crocker had themselves voted officers of the company and formally concluded the meeting. Barnett was waiting for her at a table in the far corner of the buzzing, smoke-filled dining room. The waiter had scarcely taken their order when Esther voiced her apprehensions about Mosby.

"Just political barbs." Barnett laughed, waving the matter off.

"But you don't know what a vicious, evil man he is. He's capable of murder."

"Now what brings you to say something like that? Fiery, aggressive, yes. But vicious? Evil?"

She was searching for a way to answer him when Barnett's eyes moved up over her head, and she heard the hoarse voice of a man standing directly behind her.

"Senator Barnett, I take personal offense at your remarks about my friend, Judge Mosby, in yesterday's paper."

Her skin prickling, Esther turned and gasped in surprise. He was thinner, but there was no mistaking the man. It was Isaac Claussen.

"I'm sorry you feel that way," Barnett said calmly, not moving.

"Sorry's not enough, senator. Or should I call you *almost ex-senator?*"

"You have the right to any words you choose, so long as they are spoken with the knowledge that you are in the presence of a lady."

Frightened, Esther nonetheless felt the urge to leap up and slap Claussen across the face. He glanced down and, not recognizing her, shrugged.

"I said sorry wasn't enough," Claussen repeated.

"What did you have in mind, sir?" Barnett countered. "Perhaps I could arrange for a free meal in the kitchen—if you are as hungry and impoverished as you look."

The waiter punctuated Barnett's remark by delivering the salad. Several men at nearby tables cackled. Claussen stared them down. He turned back to Barnett. "Now you gone and insulted me, too!" he bellowed. "How does you gentlefolks say it? If you will do me the honor, senator, I'd like to settle this up the river aways. Tomorra mornin' at dawn."

The room was suddenly silent.

"You must have practiced that little speech for some time to recite it so well," Barnett drawled sarcastically. Delighted, the men at the surrounding tables laughed again. "But to no good purpose, I'm afraid. I do not accept challenges from gentlemen who are—if you will forgive me—beneath my station in life." Barnett turned from Claussen and commenced on his salad.

The onlookers howled.

"You . . . you can't get away with that kinda crap with me!" Claussen barked, his blotchy face turning red.

"Your only alternative is to pull that pistol you are hiding beneath your jacket and murder me—right here, in front of all these witnesses. I suggest you think seriously before doing anything so patently guaranteed to send you to the gallows. Beyond that, this discussion is closed."

Esther suppressed a snicker as Claussen stammered, and the men nearby laughed so hard they had to hold their sides. The big, red-bearded man swung his head left and right like a confused bull, turned on his heel finally, and left.

"A year in Washington has done wonders for your delivery, not to mention your sense of humor, Warren. But that man is almost as dangerous as Mosby, believe me."

Barnett reached out with his free hand and rested it on Esther's arm. "You fret too much, dear girl. All of it is just talk. No one's going to do a damn thing but that. Talk. As soon as the convention and the election are over, we'll all be smiling at one another again. Now, I don't want to discuss it any further. Just stop worrying your lovely head about it."

"But . . ."

"No 'buts.' Let's not spoil our dinner. I haven't seen you in over a year. Tell me what you've been up to. Why are you living in Sacramento?"

She tried several times during dinner to bring the matter up again, but Barnett refused to talk of anything but their activities over the past eighteen months. He had just asked her for more details about the meeting with Judah, when Mosby entered the dining room. A combination of rage and fear froze Esther as Mosby walked slowly over to the table, looked at her, searched his mind, and then not thinking back as far as ten or more years, shrugged and turned to Barnett. There were more pressing matters on his mind. Again the room was as silent as an empty church.

"Good evening, judge," Barnett said.

"Understand you'll only accept a challenge from an equal."

"You are correct."

"And I suppose you'll find a way of thinking I'm not either."

"Not what?" Barnett smiled, annoyed and slightly apprehensive but enjoying it as well.

"Your equal, you horse's ass!"

"Obviously we could not be equal if I am a horse's ass, as you put it, since you are wearing a different kind of tail at the moment. I might add that it does little to conceal your true nature."

Esther shuddered as the patrons nearby broke into appreciative if hesitant laughter.

"What's it going to take then? *This?*" Mosby moved quickly, slapping Barnett hard across the face with his gloves.

"I will be the only one who obtains satisfaction from that stupid action," Barnett said, dabbing his napkin at a small nick where a button had sliced across his cheek. "In court, where these things are rightly dealt with." Barnett got up. "If you will excuse me, *judge,* I am having dinner. After which I plan to report your barbaric conduct to the police. You prove how unequal you are by thinking for a moment that I would be drawn into your crude little game."

Mosby shoved Barnett back into the chair. "You spineless son of a—"

Screaming, Esther threw herself at Mosby. "Leave him *alone,* you *filthy beast!*"

Half turning, hardly taking notice of the blow she landed on his shoulder, Mosby grabbed Esther by one arm and threw her sprawling into a cluster of people and plates at the next table. The onlookers gasped, but no one moved. Mosby turned back to Barnett. "Your lady friend is actin' like a whore, Barnett."

"You were born of one, you worthless scum!" Barnett shot out of his chair and seized Mosby by the throat. Livid, beyond his senses, he lifted Mosby off the ground and was shaking him like a dog worrying a cat when Claussen and two other men rushed in, grabbed him from behind, and pried his hands loose.

Mosby staggered for a moment, choking, as Claussen hit Barnett in the stomach, doubling him over. Recovering quickly, Mosby barked, "Turn him loose!"

"You've gone too far this time," Barnett coughed out, trying to regain his wind.

"You can have your satisfaction anytime you want it," Mosby hissed. "We *gentlemen* shouldn't brawl in public this way."

Still stunned, Esther swayed and screamed, "Warren! . . . Don't listen to him!"

"Tomorrow morning will be fine, you whoreson!"

"Tomorrow morning it is then. A mile north of the city, on this side of the river. Pistols?"

"It will be a pleasure."

Regaining her wits, Esther started to get up. *"For God's sake,* Warren!"

"If you're agreeable, I'll provide the weapons. You can have first choice between the pair."

"That will be fine. When I'm through with you, Mosby, your foul-smelling friend here can have *his* turn."

Mosby smiled, then swept out of the room with Claussen and his cohorts. Esther got up and walked unsteadily toward Barnett. Crying, she put her arms around him. "It's *insane,* Warren. For God's sake, can't you see that? The man is a crack shot."

Barnett smiled coldly. "He may be. But at twenty paces, that won't come into play."

"Warren—!"

"And I'll have the hand of God steadying me." There was a frightening look of certainty in his eyes as he fished a bill out of his pocket, paid the waiter, and took Esther by the arm. "Come, I'll take you home," he said, guiding her toward the door.

She attempted a dozen times to persuade him to reconsider. Nothing she said got through to him. When he finally stood in her doorway and noted he had much paperwork to attend to—just in case God saw fit to call him—the look of righteous invincibility on his face was gone. In its place was the blank stare of a man considering the possibility that he was living his last hours on earth.

He was not dead when she was called at his hotel room the following afternoon. He had asked to see her. She winced at the blood-soaked bandages the doctors had wrapped around his chest after removing the bullet.

"Now, don't you spend a minute thinking you had anything to do with this," Barnett rasped. "It would have come to a showdown sooner or later. I just couldn't let him do what he did without answering it like a man." He waved a nurse and several political cronies out of the room. When they were gone, he motioned Esther closer and kissed her on the cheek. "I have always loved you as my own sister."

"I know," she sobbed. "And I you, as a brother."

"I want to share a secret with you. Nothing, no election I have ever won, no amount of money I have ever made, has given me the satisfaction of finding the courage not to run this morning. All the glib talk, the windy bravado, the sarcastic bluster has concealed a coward until today. I want you to know how happy that makes me. Particularly since I have paid for it with only a superficial wound."

"But the nurse said it is gravely serious."

"Doctors and nurses. What do they know? I am more alive at this moment than I have ever been in my life. And I will recover. Count on it, little sister. Now let me rest awhile. As soon as I'm better, up and about, we will have that dinner Mosby so rudely interrupted."

She hoped fervently that he was right, but word of his death was sent to her that evening just after she read the newspaper accounts of the duel. She didn't want to believe it. Almost obsessed, she kept reading the articles over and over, hoping she would find that it was not Warren Barnett's name she saw there. Finally she read the report in the *Democratic Standard* one last time, accepting the reality and noticing for the first time the peculiar way Barnett had been left defenseless almost immediately.

. . . as the seconds stepped back and Mr. Ryder gave the word, the principals raised their pistols, which they had held pointed to the ground. On the rise, Mr. Barnett's weapon went off, the ball striking the ground a few feet short of his opponent . . .

She scanned the rest, her mind already at work on how to find out how such a thing could happen to a man who had fired guns skillfully at recreational targets. *A gun expert will know,* she thought, still reading.

. . . lowered himself . . . reclining position . . . then fell full length . . . Surgeons present . . . passed through . . . cavity of the chest . . . mattress litter . . . conveyed to the city . . . sat up . . . concealed the great pain . . . the weight of a thousand pounds upon him . . . internal hemorrhage . . ."

She glanced back up the page. *"On the rise . . . ball striking the ground . . ."* Before she could even think of where to find a gunsmith, she knew instinctively what the man would tell her.

Sixty-four

Aboard the *Pacific Union Express*
May 7, 1869
9:30 A.M.

Esther glanced through the window beside her as
the train slowed in its ascent through the Sierra foothills. It had long since left behind the spot on the
river where Mosby had fatally wounded Warren Barnett. More than enough to justify revenge at that
point, she reminded herself, let alone now. She moved
her gloved fingertips over the pebbled leather of the
journal cover, recalling the furor that arose when it
was discovered that Mosby's pistols had been tampered with . . . that he had practiced with them on
two successive nights before the duel . . . his resignation . . . her fruitless search for him after his sudden disappearance. He had resurfaced almost a year
later in Nevada, carrying with him an appointment
as governor from Jefferson Davis if he succeeded in
aligning the territory with the Confederacy. Then
there had been the election of Lincoln . . . the in-
terminable winter of 1860–61, waiting to cross the
Sierras, to find and face Mosby once and for all, no
matter what the consequences were . . . the ridiculous attentions Bull Carter paid to her . . . Alex . . .
    Shaking her head at the irony of the unexpected
events that delayed her departure for Virginia City
that subsequent spring, she opened the journal again.

San Francisco
April 18, 1861

No matter what I have revealed about my continued feelings for you, Alex, you must believe me when I tell you that my heart is shattered with the news that your lovely wife, Judith, is gone. I rejoiced, despite my longings for you, when she recovered from her miscarriage nearly two years ago. And I prayed for her well-being during the untroubled period of her latest pregnancy. And now this. Oh, how I wish I could comfort you personally, soothe you in your grief. You have done nothing to deserve this. Whatever the telegraph message I send to you as Mrs. "E. Cable," when I return to Sacramento, know, if you ever read this, that my true feelings could never be expressed . . .

Esther lingered in San Francisco for a month after the death of Judith Todd. Repeatedly she found excuses not to make the journey back to Sacramento. She arranged a series of meetings with Ralston, to ask him redundant questions about the Comstock, the railroad, her other investments, until he almost lost his temper. Reopening her house, she surprised the Kelseys with a dinner invitation, then surprised them again by immediately accepting a reciprocal meal three days later. News of the firing on Fort Sumter and the start of the Civil War reached San Francisco. Several days later she attended a pro-Union rally with Ralston, and through him offered financial support in the effort to thwart secession maneuvers by Southerners throughout the state. When she spotted Alex standing at the far side of the noisy crowd just across from the Road Depot Saloon, she finally admitted to herself why she had remained in San Francisco.

And then Bull Carter showed up at her door.

He was holding a nosegay of flowers. It was almost hidden in a hand the size of a small rib-roast. Respectfully, he held his hat in the other.

"Why, Mr. Carter, what a surprise."

"I hope not too much of a one," Carter stammered. "I mean callin' on you . . . uh . . . this unexpected . . . way." His hair was slicked back with what appeared to be half a pound of chicken fat. He rushed on. "I was in San Francisco on business for my brother . . . half-brother . . ."

"Mr. Crocker."

"Yes . . . and . . . I . . . ah . . . thought I'd bring you these flowers." He handed them to her, his tiny eyes blinking repeatedly.

"That's quite all right, Mr. Carter. And thank you."

"I know I bothered you . . . in Sacramento. That is—"

"You weren't a bother, Mr. Carter. I was simply too busy with things at the school."

"Well, it was stupid of me, what with you bein' in mourning for your friend Senator Barnett. I didn't show no tack." He glanced in through the door for a second, stared at her oddly. She guessed he was trying to remember again where he had seen her before.

Esther reached for her hat on the mirror rack just beside the entrance. "I wish I could invite you in, but I'm expected in town in just a few minutes."

"Quite all right, quite all right," Carter said, following and trying to keep up with her as she headed for the carriage stable. "I just wanted to . . . pay my respects."

She lost Carter easily once she reached the outskirts of the city, then doubled back to her house fifteen minutes later. The following day she wrote a note to Ralston, requesting a meeting.

"What do you know about William Carter?" she asked Ralston, after setting out chairs on the porch when he arrived after dinner. On the pretext that the mayflies had been noisome in the unseasonal warmth that evening, she was wearing a gardening hat with light mosquito netting draped down over the front brim. For a moment she thought he recognized her features, but then she realized it was simply male appreciation. Casually she moved the lamp on the table beside them so that it shed less light on her face.

"Carter? He's a climber. Wants into the Big Four so bad he can taste it. But he doesn't have any money. Best he'll manage is a handout from Crocker. A good job, probably. But, knowing Crocker, it will be about as secure as an ice cube in Panama. Why do you ask?"

"Oh, just a woman's curiosity. I spoke briefly with Mr. Carter yesterday. I ran into him unexpectedly—in town."

"He's here in San Francisco?" Ralston frowned. "I'd watch out for him, Esther. He didn't pay a call on you, did he?"

"Why . . . no. Whatever would he do that for?"

"I *said* he wanted in bad. To be more specific, he's sidled up to more than one wealthy widow, looking for a bankbook. Wants to pry his way into a silent partnership with Crocker and the rest of them."

Esther's mind began ticking. "Oh, Billy, are you sure of that? Or is it just rumor?" She thought of the marvelous act Carter had put on the day before. At least in part. No doubt some of it was authentic awkwardness with a woman as well as embarrassment about what he was doing. "He seems such a nice man."

"He's about as nice as his half-brother. And that's like calling a grizzly bear a Quaker!"

Esther laughed. "Well, I'll certainly be on the lookout. Not that he would ever be interested in me." She thought of Carter's enormous size and physical strength, and the power-potential attached to being even tangentially involved with the railroad suddenly struck her.

"Why not?" Ralston smiled. "You're not only wealthy, you're a beautiful woman. I can see that, even through your veils."

"Oh, Billy, you don't need to flatter me. There are many women in San Francisco far more attractive than I am."

"But most of them don't have money."

"No, they don't," Esther mused. The thought of beating Carter at his own game, turning it to her own advantage, intrigued her.

"And the ones who do often don't realize that under California law, anything a wife owns becomes her husband's property once they're married, unless she declares it beforehand."

"Well, that's only right," Esther said, concealing a righteous indignation. "Isn't it? Aren't we the weaker sex? Don't we need the guidance of a big, smart, strong man?" She suddenly *knew* she would use Carter's physical strength someday against Mosby. She quickly parsed the premonition with reason and probability. More likely, it would be the strength of the railroad she would employ. Or at least the privileges that being the wife of a silent partner might afford her.

"You don't seem to need a *big, strong man,*" Ralston said, smiling. "You really don't believe that at all."

"Oh, but I do—at least occasionally. It would be a comfort."

She thought she saw a fleeting expression of pleasure cross Ralston's face; but then it was gone, and she couldn't be sure. The notion was quickly lost in considerations of Alex, what she had really asked Ralston to meet her about, and the discomfiting thought of being Bull Carter's wife.

"I never figured you had any interest in marriage," Ralston said, interrupting her thoughts.

"I never said I did."

"Well, if you ever do, be wary of Carter."

"What a pity. He's such a fine figure of a man."

"I think he'd look good on a serving platter—with an apple in his mouth." Ralston looked at his watch, suddenly a little nervous again.

"I'm not keeping you, am I? I did want to ask you if there's been any news from Judah."

"No, I have plenty of time. And yes, there has been some word. It will take some time, perhaps another year, to get an act passed, but Judah's convinced Congress that the road is a military necessity to the Union."

"That's marvelous news," Esther said, thinking about Carter as well as Alex again.

"Yes. It means the financial support that's needed. I have to go up to Sacramento before they draw up the papers."

"Papers?"

"Incorporation papers. The Central Pacific Railroad Company will be formed sometime before summer." He looked at his watch again, then glanced left to where the carriage road came over the crest of the hill. For a moment he seemed preoccupied, but then his face lit up with enthusiasm. "Esther, you won't believe what they're going to ask for—Huntington and the rest of them. Thousands of dollars per mile. An even higher rate for the mountains. They plan to set up their own construction company, so even if the damn thing never gets over the Sierras, they stand to make an enormous profit. Right now we're in a position to buy a small piece of it, since you helped put Judah and the rest of them together. But I want to get us more. It won't be a huge share, Huntington's too smart and too greedy for that. But I think we can increase our position."

"Whatever you think, Billy. You're the financial wizard." She was about to begin a series of circuitous questions she hoped might lead to an "accidental" meeting with Alex, when Ralston looked at his watch again.

"I am keeping you." She would wait for a more propitious time.

"No, it's just—I told someone I was going to be . . . I . . . ah . . . said he could meet me here. I hope you'll forgive me."

"Nothing to forgive. Who is coming?"

The clinking sound of a buckboard harness drew her attention as Ralston said, "Alex Todd. Poor devil. He's thinking about taking a leave of absence, doing some legal work for . . . for the railroad people. He's . . . he thinks he needs a change. It's probably just temporary confusion. I want to talk him out of it."

Although she had been thinking for weeks about a way to be briefly with Alex again, the sight of him pulling up in front of her house, just ten yards away, made her knees weak. She could not just sit here. She couldn't just leave them, either. She had to get into the house somehow, put on a hat with a heavy veil. It was an impossible situation.

As Alex stepped down from the buckboard, she quickly turned to Ralston. "I feel a chill. Will you excuse me for a moment? I must get a wrap. Tell Mr. Todd I'll be right back. I'm sure . . . you two men will have things to discuss for a few minutes."

Upstairs she gripped the edge of her dresser, staring into the mirror without seeing, trying to get hold of herself, searching for a way to avoid going back down to the porch. Her mind wasn't working. The muffled sound of their voices increased the feeling of helplessness. Then she heard what sounded like the tones of a mild disagreement. Seconds later, reins snapped, and she heard one of the buckboards roll out of her driveway and down the hill. Certain Alex had interpreted her hasty retreat as an objection to his coming, sure he was gone, she went back downstairs still wearing the garden hat. But it was Alex who was standing at the screened front door. She froze, waited for the expression of shock to transform his face.

"I stayed to apologize, Mrs. Cable. I'm mortified, but that won't stop me from being honest. I'm afraid Billy was making an awkward stab at matchmaking."

Esther was certain she would faint. Disoriented, she forgot to disguise her voice. "What a lovely compliment," she heard herself say, immediately conscious that only circumstance had caused her to whisper.

"I think it was stupid," Alex said, not looking at her. "He knows I have no interest in anything like that. Knows I've told all my friends to stop doing this sort of thing. Some of the women they've thrown at me . . . I'm sorry. I don't mean you. I just never would have come if I knew what he was up to. If you'll excuse me, I'll be going."

She watched him turn and start down the steps. She knew her voice had deepened slightly over the last dozen years. That might make it possible. How much could he possibly see through the screen and the mosquito netting? She realized the porch lamp would not reach this far, became aware that the one behind her in the hallway would lessen rather than improve his view of her. Pulled forcefully by her desire to see him again, she regained her courage. If she had succeeded once, she could do it again.

"Wait!" she called out. He turned, and she shivered, certain that this time her voice would register. But he simply stood there, poised, pulling at her in a way that could not have been more powerful if he had thrown a rope over her and tugged it with all his might. She began half-whispering again. "There isn't any need to feel bad about what Billy did. He was . . . obviously . . . well-intentioned."

"I suppose so. But—"

"Why don't you stay for a few minutes? Would you like a cup of tea? I'm afraid I don't have any spirits in the house."

"You're very kind, Mrs. Cable. But I think—"

"I have some port, now that I recall."

"I've had a little too much to drink already."

"Just one, Mr. Todd. It would be a graceful way to extricate ourselves from this awkward situation."

He thought for a moment. "I'd be pleased, and I thank you. You've made it less uncomfortable already."

"Why don't you sit there on the porch swing? I'll go in and get the bottle and some glasses."

"But just one—"

"Of course. You might blow out that lamp. It's drawing all kinds of insects."

Her hands were shaking as she placed the port and glasses on a tray and carried it back out. Near the front door she blew out the lamp in the hallway. Her eyes adjusted to the darkness. She could barely see his features. She put the tray down, poured, and handed him a glass.

"What's that you're wearing? I can hardly see, it's so dark."

Her heart almost stopped. "Just a garden hat, with mosquito netting."

"You really are shy, aren't you? I can understand that. I've seen you a few times in town—at a distance. And in your buggy at the rally last week. You always cover your face, don't you?"

She gripped the rattan arms of her chair, making them squeak. "Not always. And it's . . . it's not just shyness," she said, still whispering, "although . . . that's part of it. I have a scar. And I wear these gloves because I have two fingers missing. Gruesome, isn't it?"

He looked away and sighed. "It could be worse. And your face certainly has a lovely outline, from what little I've seen. Listen to me! I sound like somebody courting."

"You're still grieving over your wife. I was so sorry. She was such a lovely woman."

"Yes, she was. She liked you. Told me she loved

working with you during her brief time at the school."

"Yes, it's a small world, isn't it? I liked her very much, too."

He drained his glass. "That was a lovely note you sent. I appreciate it. God, I have this urge to tell someone how I really feel."

"Why don't you? It will ease the pain." She fought down the desire to get up out of her chair and sit with him in the swing.

"That's just it. There is no pain. Oh, I feel sad about her passing. Very sad. But it doesn't compare with what I felt when I lost my first wife. Can you understand that?"

I must remember to keep whispering. I must. "I think I can. I . . . I didn't know you'd been married once before. . . . You must have . . . loved her very much."

"More than life itself. There was so much sorrow, so much numbness after she . . . she and my son . . ." his voice began to break. "She and my son were with the Donner Party. . . . It felt like *I* was the one who died. . . . I didn't have any feelings left. Not for years. I don't think I ever got all of them back. I cared deeply for Judith, loved her, I suppose. But it was never the same. Elizabeth was . . ." His voice trailed off.

Tears brimmed in Esther's eyes. To control herself, she took a deep breath, then reached out, took his glass, and refilled it. She prayed he wouldn't notice the way her hands were trembling. "I . . . can understand that, too. I know . . . that . . . I will never feel again . . . what I felt for my husband."

"When did it happen?"

"A long time ago."

"It creates the damnedest feelings in a man. But I don't ever remember going through what plagues me now. This time I feel a total indifference to women —except in a way I try never to act on."

"Physical need?"

"Yes. God, it's so good to talk to someone. A woman, particularly." He sighed and started to get up. "Forgive me. I probably sound like a complainer."

"You needn't apologize. A man needs to talk to a woman about some things. Things men never have the courage to tell one another."

Relaxing, he sat back again.

"I know that . . . Mr. Todd," she went on, "the physical business. It can be so intense . . . I . . . I know."

"Yes. It can. Almost uncontrollable at times. That's why I've been drinking so much these last few weeks. To dull it. That's not like me, either. I talked to my doctor about it. Righteous as it sounds, it bothers me. Oh, I joke about such things with friends. Men friends. It's a cover-up. Down deep, I've always . . . it sounds conceited, I suppose . . . but I've always wanted to be better than most men in that way. Never wanted to let animal craving control me. We deserve, owe ourselves more than that. Men as well as women. I . . . I haven't always been successful . . ."

She wanted to wrap her arms around him, rock him like a baby, tell him how rare he was. Moved to the limits of caution and suddenly, giddily beyond the first stages of arousal, Esther got up, poured Alex another glassful, and sat opposite him on the swing. "What matters is that you try. What did the doctor tell you?"

"Says it's a common experience. Has some foolish notion that death and grief stir a man's . . . Well, you know what I mean."

It was so dark now she could scarcely see him, three feet away. He started to get up again. She moved over to him involuntarily, put a hand on his forearm. "Don't go just yet."

"I'm making a fool of myself. I sound like an idiot."

She could smell the liquor behind the port on his breath, and she could smell *him*. "No you don't. It all seems quite natural."

"You probably think—"

"No, I don't, Mr.—Alex. You don't mind if I call you Alex, do you?"

"Not at all."

"Did it ever occur to you that women experience the same feelings? I know we are not supposed to. But I have . . ." She forced herself to say, "I am . . . feeling them this very minute."

She had lost her senses. She thought she would fall off the edge of the earth when he reached out, gently lifted the mosquito veil on her garden hat, and touched her face with his fingertips.

"You're a beautiful woman. I suspected that, even with the veils you wear. Now I know it, just from the way your face feels."

The pulse in her neck actually ached. She reached out and took his hand, bravely, short of breath, terrified, not knowing what would happen, knowing full well that she might be revealed at any moment. And that if she were, he would probably hate her. She could not stop herself. Kissing his fingers, she pulled him gently toward her, lifted her face, and brushed her lips against his. He looked up and away for a moment, not sure, then kissed her; tenderly at first, then passionately. He stood up and pulled her to him. She let him wrap his arms around her and pressed her cheek against his. She wondered if the moon would rise and betray her, if the stars would fall and burn her alive for what she was doing. She no longer cared.

"You feel so good against me," he said, swaying, revealing how close to drunkenness he was.

"You're lonely. Just as I am."

He kissed her again, hesitantly pushing his tongue just inside her lips. She felt moisture, then a sudden pulsation between her legs. Waiting until she was sure she could stand on her own feet, she pulled away gently. "I don't want to talk anymore. Will you come inside with me?"

He stumbled once as they went up the stairs hand in hand. "I'm a little drunk."

"That's perfectly all right."

They reached the upstairs hallway. Soft light spilled out through her bedroom door. She turned her face away from him. "Will you wait here until I call you?"

In her bedroom, she blew out the lamp and looked in the mirror. Even after she grew accustomed to the darkness, she could not see herself. She experienced a wave of terror, pushed it away. *He cannot possibly see me,* she told herself. *He does not recognize my voice. . . .* I have borne two children. . . . I will not feel the same. Larger there . . . She remembered the skills she had learned from Arabella Ryan. He would never expect that from me. . . . I will use everything . . . it will throw him off if he even begins to suspect.

She placed the snuffed lamp on an armoire shelf, closed its door, undressed, and got into bed.

Somehow her fear made it even more remarkable. Once, while they were making love, he whispered, "I don't have to see your body to know how beautiful it is. . . ."

"Shhhhh."

Afterward, while she drifted back down through a sequence of her own aftertremors and he lay nestled on her breast with his eyes closed, she asked him what he was thinking about.

"Nothing," he said, his hand cupped tenderly over her hip.

"Tell me."

"You'd be angry."

"Why? Please tell me. I won't be angry."

"All right," he sighed. "But you won't like it. I know you won't."

"Tell me."

"It hasn't felt like that since—"

"Your first wife."

"Yes. You're . . . much more . . . knowledgeable. She was just a young girl. But I don't mean in that way. I mean the rest of it. The tenderness. What I felt like . . . in my mind. It reminded me so much of being with her. You even wear the same lavender scent."

She held her breath. Then, relieved but still on guard, she stroked his hair. "That doesn't make me angry. It's . . ." She was almost crying. "It's a compliment."

He got up and dressed, walked back to her unsteadily, and kissed her on the cheek. She heard him stagger slightly as he went toward the door, then hesitated.

"Will I see you again?" he asked. "I'd like to . . . after a decent interval. Perhaps we could have dinner."

"We shall see." She wondered how on earth she could have allowed herself to do it, knew she could never get away with it again. "In the meantime, I think it best we forget this."

"If you really feel that way—" The touch of sadness in his voice cut into her.

"I want us to remain friends, first of all. Seeing each other again . . . this way . . . might . . . spoil that."

"You're a very generous woman," Alex said, bumping himself with the door as he closed it behind him. "I hope I . . ."

The door shut, and she didn't hear the rest. Only then, as she began to tremble at the thought of what might have happened, did she realize how much the alcohol had dulled his senses, made it possible. She heard him stumble in the driveway, ask himself where in hell he had left the buckboard. After he was gone, she put on a bathrobe and went downstairs. For the first time in her life she drank herself senseless. Short of laudanum, she knew there was no other way she could blot out the shame she felt about deceiving him.

Erase the aching wish that things could be different. Wipe out the icy determination concerning Mosby and Carter that was crowding her thoughts again. Make her forget that she could never risk being with Alex this way again.

Sixty-five

She was aware of the hesitant, tapping sound before she opened her eyes. Sunlight streaming through the windows nearly blinded her, and she felt as though her head would split open from the pain. Everything seemed on its side. Then she realized she had passed out, had slumped over and slept with one cheek pressed to the kitchen table. She sat up, wiped her mouth, and heard the sound behind her again. Turning, she saw Bull Carter standing on the steps just beyond the rear screen-door.

"In God's name, what are you doing here at this hour of the morning?" She glanced at the clock. It was almost noon.

Sheepishly, he glanced down at his shoes. "I . . . I come to the front door first. When you didn't answer and I seen the carriage out there, I thought . . . I thought somethin' might be wrong."

She got up and unlatched the door, trying to control the wretched mood she was in. "Well, come in. I'll make some coffee."

He didn't move.

"Well, *are you coming in or aren't you?*" She suddenly realized her bathrobe was partially open. She jerked at the lapels and snugged the cloth belt tight.

Ignoring him, she padded to the cupboard barefoot and reached for a mason jar full of coffee. She heard him come in and almost laughed when she realized he was tiptoeing. When she turned, he stared at her, bug-eyed.

"For God's sake, haven't you ever seen a woman in a bathrobe before?"

"I'm . . . I'm just not used to it, that's all."

She knew before he had finished speaking that he was looking at her nose rather than at the fullness of her bosom. Turning, she jerked her coffeepot off its hook on the wall, walked to the stove, and set it down on an adjacent counter. "Frostbite," she said. "Lovely, isn't it? Do you still want to bring me flowers?"

"It don't matter, the scar. I wasn't lookin' at that."

She bent over a bin and removed some kindling and a few sheets of old newspaper. "Well, what were you looking at, then?"

"Your face. I never seen such a beautiful face before. I never dreamed—here, let me help you with that."

She let him take the wood and the paper, absently measured coffee into the pot as he placed a small shovelful of coal over the kindling. "I'm sorry. . . . I don't feel well this morning."

He glanced at the empty port bottle on the table, then reached under his arm. "I . . . I brung you a paper. Fresh from Virginia City with all kindsa news from east of there. Come by Pony Express just this mornin'."

"How *nice* of you, Mr. Carter." Her back turned to him, she rolled her eyes toward the ceiling. "Are you hungry?" She opened the paper and glanced at the front page. A pen-and-ink sketch of Luther Mosby stared up at her.

"I could eat somethin'." Carter said, lighting the kindling.

"Yes . . . well . . . I'll fix some eggs . . ." Mosby

was gone, so far out of reach it made her dizzy for
a moment. She steadied herself and scanned the story:

*. . . failed in his attempt to win alignment with . . .
left for the South this morning . . . Confederate Army
commission . . . likely, he said, before departing . . .
serve on the staff of . . . his distant relative . . . John
Singleton Mosby . . .*

Bull Carter's voice seemed to be coming from deep
in a mine shaft. "Won't be much longer for the Pony
Express. Telegraph across the Sierras ought to be
finished this year. That'll kill it."

Three thousand miles, she thought. Across mountains, desert, the plains . . . at war . . . months. Perhaps years. "Is that right?" she finally responded,
aware of Carter again. She put the coffee on and went
to the cellar door. "I'll get the eggs. Sit down and
make yourself comfortable."

In the coolness of the basement she weighed it all
—Mosby, Carter, the need to construct an artificial
barrier that might prevent her from giving way to
her yearning to be in Alex's arms again. The ends
were clear, the means—as far as Mosby was concerned
—still vague. But it *would* work, somehow. That she
knew. By the time she went back upstairs, she had
decided.

He was putting her glass in the sink, and the bottle
was gone. "Tidied up a bit for you. Hope you don't
mind."

"That was very nice of you." She scrambled the
eggs and poured the coffee. When she set the plates
down, she reached out hesitantly and put her hand
on his. He stared at it incredulously. "I hope you
don't think I'm a heavy drinker."

It took him ten seconds to find his voice.

"One bottle don't make a drunk."

She sat, sipped her coffee, put it down, and massaged her aching temples. "I . . . I was seized with a fit of loneliness last night. Oh, dear. I'm getting too personal."

"It's all right. It's all right. I get that way sometimes." She shoveled in some eggs and washed them down.

"You do? I would think you'd have all the company, a handsome man like you."

He couldn't look at her for a moment. "Don't know about that. And there's difference between company and . . . and . . ."

"A woman you admire."

"That's it."

"Do you know, I have admired *you*—from a distance?"

His mouth dropped open, and he stared at her. "You have? I can't believe it." He looked away.

"Tell me, Mr. Carter—this will seem terribly forward of me—but are your intentions honorable?"

His eyes darted back to her. "As pure as the driven snow. And now that I've really seen you . . ."

"You like what you see?"

"God, yes."

"You would like to marry me?"

He nearly choked. "Why . . . why . . . yes. After a decent period of . . . of . . . courtship."

"I should hope it wouldn't be too long a period. I never want to feel the way I did last night . . . never want to drink out of loneliness that way . . . again."

"Are you sayin' . . . you'll marry me?"

"I will have to think about it, Mr. Carter. I'm not an experienced woman. . . . I don't care too much for the physical aspects of marriage, you understand. But it's been too long without someone I can lean on. I need a man like you. Strong . . . decent . . . honest."

He stared at her wide-eyed. "I don't believe it. Are you sayin'—?"

"Yes, Mr. Carter. I am. I fully expect my answer to be Yes."

"Gaaaaaaah-damn! Uh, excuse me."

"It's all right, Mr. Carter. I understand *exactly* how you feel."

Billy Ralston sat behind his massive desk at the bank, wiping his forehead with a handkerchief. "There's nothing I can say that will dissuade you?"

Esther leaned back in her chair. "No. We will be married this weekend."

"It wasn't what I did the other night? Having Alex Todd—?"

"Don't be silly. I have known Mr. Carter for quite some time."

"But not as long and as well as some do. Forgive me, Esther. I just have your interests in mind."

"And your own."

"That's true . . . but a little unfair."

"I'm sorry. I didn't mean to sound cutting. You've been extraordinarily skillful with my investments. Totally honest. And a friend. Always. That's the primary reason I'm here. I want you to help me arrange things so only enough for Mr. Carter to buy a silent partnership will be available to him."

Ralston's eyebrows shot up. Then he thought for a moment and smiled. "Esther, you amaze me. It could easily be done. All we need is to sign most of it over to someone you trust. With an accompanying document, signed at the same time, that returns all of the stock, cash, whatever, to you the moment you exercise it. Or transfer it to an heir automatically, in case of your death. We'll need an alternate holder in case the first one dies. . . . I need the names of two people you not only trust that much, but who would do it."

"Why not yourself? And . . . Alex Todd?"

"Esther, I don't want to be in a position where you might even suspect I was acting purely out of self-interest. And you hardly know Alex."

"He's . . . a friend. And I know he's an honest man. If I'm wrong about that, well . . ."

"All right. Alex as an alternate. Who first?"

"William Kelsey?"

"Fine. If you want me to, I'll sign as a second alternate—in case, God forbid, both of them should—"

"Let's not even think about that." She smoothed her skirts, adjusted her veil, and got up. "I'll be going back to Sacramento after a short"—she almost gagged on the word—"honeymoon."

"I'll have the papers drawn up this afternoon. You can sign the initiating document late today or tomorrow, whichever's more convenient. By the way, who'll be the heir?"

"I'd like to keep that private." *Who else but Alex?* she thought.

"All right. I can have a separate document drawn up for that. I'll send it along. You can fill in the name. Just be sure to put it in a safe place."

"I'll be seeing Bill Kelsey this evening. I'm sure he'll agree to do it. Would you see Mr. Todd? I . . . I'll be somewhat busy the next few days. It would be helpful if you could get his signature."

"Consider it done, Esther. I'm having dinner with him tonight."

"Are you still playing matchmaker?"

Ralston laughed nervously. "As a matter of fact, I am introducing him to a young lady this evening. Katherine McDonnell . . . ah, an acquaintance of an acquaintance. Do you know her?"

"I can't say that I do," Esther said, fighting down a wave of regret. She paused at the door. "You're wasting your time, Billy. He's really not interested right now."

Ralston hurried to join her at the door. "He will be. She's an extraordinarily beautiful woman. And he needs company, if nothing else."

"You may be right. Well, thank you for taking care of this for me."

"Glad to. You're certainly nobody's fool, Esther." He opened the door for her. "I can't tell you how much better I feel about this now."

"I'm a bit more comfortable myself. I hope you don't think any less of me."

"Why should I? You're just protecting yourself. Wisely, I might add."

"Yes, you might. But it is calculating. Someday I hope I can explain why I did this. . . . All of it."

Bull Carter brought the lamp over to the bed where she lay with the covers pulled up to her neck. "You're not mad at me for asking you to postpone the honeymoon, are you sweetheart?"

The sound of his voice almost made her sick. "No. I'm just cold." She tried to appear cheerful. "And driving back to Sacramento *is* like a short honeymoon, isn't it?"

"Kinda." He slipped out of his shirt and trousers.

She could see the outline of his genitals beneath the stained front of his long johns. She was surprised and then relieved that he was so small.

"This is a nice little inn, isn't it?" He got into bed with her. "Benicia used to be the capital."

She stared up at the beamed ceiling. "It's lovely."

When it was over, a mercifully few minutes later, she waited until the revulsion subsided, then turned to him.

"What is it, sweetheart?"

"You're not going to like this, Mr. Carter."

"For Christ's sake, call me Bull. And what won't—?"

"No. I will call you Mr. Carter now and in the future."

He frowned. "What the hell does *that* mean?"

"It means that I have never for a moment fallen for your stupid little scheme. And that you have had all you are going to have of the marriage bed with me."

"*What . . . ?*"

For a moment she wondered if he were going to hit her. But then she saw that he was too shocked even to speak. "Listen to me, Mr. Carter. I have known all along what you wanted. And now you have it. I want to leave it that way."

"But . . ."

"But nothing. There will be a transfer of my savings and the money from all the stocks I have liquidated to a bank account in both our names as soon as we reach Sacramento. It will not be quite what you expected, but it will be enough. You can take it to Mr. Crocker and buy your way in. Do you understand? I won't get in your way. It suits my purposes, as well. You can have it. But that is all you can have."

"Sweetheart, you're all wrong about me. I—"

"Oh, I've seen the change in you since the other morning in the kitchen. The moony eyes. The fear of displeasing. No doubt it's authentic. But it comes too late. You have a choice, Mr. Carter. You can leave me alone and get additional money as the few stocks I have kept in my name turn their investments. Or you can be made a laughingstock when I leave you and inform your half-brother that *I* am his silent partner as well."

"But, Esther . . ."

"I will live in your home, undertake all the other duties of a wife. I will say nothing. No one has to know. But I will not spend another night in bed with you."

"For God's sake, Esther. *This ain't fair!*"

"If you raise your voice to me, lift a hand, I will do the same thing. And you will look like an utter fool, to Crocker and everyone else."

He stared past her, his face frozen in a scowl for a moment, then collapsing in resignation. "I can't believe you'd do this. I never—"

"You did, and you know it. Why don't you act like a man and accept this for what it is? A business arrangement. That's what you had in mind to begin with."

"But now it's different."

"That's too bad."

"You're a bitch, ain't you? A twenty-carat bitch. I can't believe this."

"Believe it. In time, you'll accept it, if you've got half a brain. You have what you want. No one need be the wiser. And I certainly won't expect *you* to live up to your vows."

"You mean . . . ?"

"Yes, I mean. Whoever, wherever you want. As long as you don't cause either of us embarrassment or bring attention to what the truth really is."

"I'll have to think about this."

"No, you won't. Just sleep on it, Mr. Carter. I'm sure you already understand it's to your advantage. Just remember what I said."

"Do you . . . do you want me to get out of bed right now?"

"That won't be necessary," she said, turning her back to him. "It will be the first of many penances I must undertake for doing this just the way you would have."

Sixty-six

She knew she was pregnant even before the doctor confirmed it. Now, sitting in the parlor of Bull Carter's surprisingly comfortable and well-kept house on the far end of I Street, she had a passing thought about finding a way to safely rid herself of the baby. But she knew the unborn child might have been fathered by Alex. There was at least a 50 percent chance of that. She had received both their seeds within the space of a week—and Carter had pulled out of her hurriedly, for the most part spending all over her thigh. The irony of it made her smile.

She got up and walked through the house. Carter would not be back from Crocker's dry-goods store before supper. He had railed off and on about her sexual embargo for a few weeks, then pleaded for a few more. Now a cool, polite truce existed between them. She climbed the stairs to the second floor. His brother had moved out of the third bedroom and into a hotel the day she arrived. She glanced in through the door. It could be fitted out nicely as a nursery. The house would not be a bad place to raise a child, she thought. The fenced rear yard was ample. There was a loft over the carriage stable that could be made livable, if she decided to have Solana move here from the school to help her.

Turning, she started back down the hall and went into the room where Bull Carter grudgingly slept by himself. She began to make the rumpled bed. *In time*, she thought, *it will not even matter to him*. She finished, went into her own bedroom, and glanced at the tintype of herself taken in San Francisco the day of their wedding. The other daguerreotype, of the two of them smiling, was downstairs on display in the foyer.

She went to her desk and looked at the calendar. Eight weeks had passed since the wedding, and it seemed to be working well enough. Carter had his "nights out" once or twice a week. The rest of the time he read his paper and went to bed early. She fulfilled her promises, kept the house neat and clean, cooked, saw to it that the Chinese man who came in to do their laundry attended to his shirts, socks, and underwear properly. She had even darned a bit, repaired the seam in one of his jackets. Twin pangs of regret and remorse stabbed at her for a moment. She no longer believed Carter was an evil man. Just morally small, dense, and overly ambitious. He hated the arrangement. She was certain that he had indeed experienced a sudden infatuation for her that morning in the kitchen. Nonetheless, he spoke to her courteously and avoided arguments. When she carefully suggested several ways to negotiate cleverly and protect himself from Crocker, he not only listened but implemented the advice. As a result, he had been able to buy for himself the superintendency of the construction company Crocker, Huntington, Hopkins, and Stanford were putting together. He had not fared as well in acquiring stock in the Central Pacific Railroad; he and Esther owned only one-quarter as much as each of the four principal officers. But he was satisfied, and so was she.

Esther sat down at her desk, thinking about what she had heard the icy-eyed Huntington say in the sitting room downstairs the night before. They were going to ask the government for alternate sections of land on either side of the entire line as one consideration. It was outrageous, but after her first careful look at Huntington and two sentences from Crocker, she had no doubt they would get what they wanted. And a joint, one-twentieth ownership of just the acreage alone would probably make her richer than she had ever been prior to the crash of '55. Richer and more powerful, in an indirect way. The thought warmed her as much as the summer sun coming through the window.

She thought of the other men involved: Hopkins, the accounting genius, was painfully shy, timid. He probably wouldn't even plant a radish in the backyard from which he still sold vegetables to neighbors without his wife's permission. She laughed to herself. Bull Carter weighed twice as much as Hopkins, and he was behaving just as meekly for her. She surmised that if Huntington would steal the gold out of his mother's teeth, Crocker would *beat* his for it at the drop of a hat. It was also obvious, from what she had overheard during the previous night's meeting, that they all thought Stanford useless—save for his ability to impress people with his overly dignified verbosity—and that Bull Carter both hated and worshipped his half-brother.

It would be interesting to see them jostling one another for dominance, she thought, wondering how Judah would fare with them in the long run. She shuddered as she weighed it, suddenly conscious that if the railroad did make it over the Sierras, and was joined by lines from the East, Judah, Crocker, Huntington, Hopkins, Stanford—and, in a lesser way, her husband—could rise to a place among the most powerful men in the nation. If there was a nation left after the war. She guessed there would be, despite the dark news of a Confederate victory at Bull Run.

She opened the latest letter from Ralston. It described in glowing terms the frenzied expansion of the Comstock, outlined the astronomical rise in value of her mining stocks, then went on to summarize quickly the gains the rest of her investments were making on the swell of the silver boom. A trace of

concern danced through her mind. Although Ralston
had tried to hide it, it seemed apparent that some of
what was now going on at the Comstock was paper
speculation, not a solid reflection of ore ripped from
the mines. How widespread and potentially dangerous the inflation might be, she could not tell. Then
the ripple of concern was lost in waves of apprehension and anger as Ralston turned gravely to a personal
matter in a postscript on the second page. Alex was
in trouble.

"And she claims Alex is the father?" Esther asked.
Ralston put his hand over his eyes. "I feel like a
fool. Worse. A Judas goat. It's a setup. She's after
social position and the money Alex's put away all
these years. And I introduced them!"
They were sitting in his carriage at the wharf. She
had disembarked from the paddle-wheeler Senator
just minutes before. Beyond a thick latticework of
square-rigger masts and spars, the heat of a warm
August sun rose from the waters of San Francisco Bay
and made the Golden Gate shimmer in the distance.
It was Sunday, and there was little activity on the
waterfront. The last of the passengers from Sacramento hurried past and funneled into the streets of
the city as Esther sat there, thinking.
"When does this Miss McDonnell say they were
. . . together?"
"Two nights after we had our discussion about the
stock transfer."
"What does Alex say?"
"That he was alone, all evening. And I believe him.
The irony of it is that he seems to have driven up
to your place. But you weren't there. I don't know
what he wanted to talk to you about, but he says
when he didn't find you, he went directly home."
Esther was rocked by guilt for a moment. "God
. . . the Wednesday night before my wedding. I was
with Connie Kelsey until late in the evening. She

was helping me with alterations on my wedding dress. Has Alex seen the woman since?"

Ralston snapped the reins, and they started off toward Esther's home. "A number of times. He says they haven't been intimate. It seemed strange at first. He didn't particularly take to her the night we all had dinner together, and I didn't think he'd see her again. But then about two weeks later he had a sudden change of heart. It wasn't like him. Usually, when he makes up his mind, that's it. I was glad at first, but now I could kick myself."

"It's simply her word against his, then?"

"Not quite. That would be difficult enough, considering what even an unsubstantiated claim like this would do to his reputation. But she's got a doctor who'll testify she became pregnant when she says she did. And an aunt who says she was with Alex that night—and has spent time with no one else."

"Who is the doctor?"

"A man named Leander Sims."

Esther remembered his name immediately. If she proceeded with what she had in mind, it was conceivable that Sims might recognize her from that Sunday at the vigilante headquarters. She had no idea what might come of such a revelation at this late date, but it seemed likely that it would cause her more than just embarrassment. She thought of Carter, then of Alex and the prospect of having almost all of it uncovered, having to face him and try to tell him why she had deceived him all these years. She sighed. His honor was at stake, not to mention his money. *If it comes down to revealing myself*, she thought, *I will simply have to. I must help him.* It might be that the time had finally come to be honest with Alex. Reluctant about that, she made one more stab at finding a variation on the strategy taking form in her mind. "What if you, or another of Alex's friends, testified that he was with him that night?"

"We've discussed that. In a case like this the woman's word would probably carry more weight. She and her lawyer know that they'd have better than a fifty-fifty chance in court. And by then, even if they failed, Alex's name would be tarred."

"And if another woman gave such testimony?"

"That might do it. It would be worth a try. Might even head her off before it ever got to court. But she'd have to be pretty convincing."

When Esther arrived at Ralston's office the following day, she was ready with her story. Alex, so mortified he could hardly raise his eyes, stared at the floor. Katherine McDonnell, her doctor, and the lawyers for both sides were already there. Esther nodded at Ralston and Alex's lawyer, whom she'd met in a hastily called meeting held the day before. Then she turned again to the McDonnell woman. There was something vaguely familiar about her, but try as she might, Esther could not place her.

"I think we should get right down to business," the opposing lawyer suggested confidently. "I see here in your deposition, Mrs. Carter, that you claim you have had . . ." He smiled at Alex. "Ah—congress with Judge Todd."

"That is correct," Esther said, her eyes on Dr. Sims. His attention on her was disquieting. "I was with Judge Todd the entire evening in question. And the night before. And the two nights before that. And each night following until the day of my wedding." She remembered that Carter had made a preliminary survey trip into the Sierras with Crocker as soon as they had returned to Sacramento. At the time, she had been sure he had arranged it simply to be away from her, weigh their arrangement, and adjust to it. Now she used his absence in a way that would cause her endless difficulty if the truth ever came out. "My husband was out of town immediately after we returned to the capital. He was gone for . . . over a week. . . . During that time I returned to San

Francisco and spent several more nights with Judge Todd. The entire week, in fact."

The lawyer's expression went from smug to uncertain. "You are saying that just before and immediately after your marriage, you . . . had relations with Judge Todd?"

"I am."

"You realize what this could do to you in a court trial?"

"I do."

"I take it that is why you have not, ah, spelled it all out in your deposition."

"That is correct."

"Well, it's an interesting story." The lawyer frowned, thinking quickly. "That leaves only Sunday, the night of Mrs. Carter's wedding." He turned to Katherine McDonnell. "Is it possible you have your dates wrong?"

"No, she hasn't," Ralston interjected. "She couldn't have been with Judge Todd that Sunday evening, either. He was with me—until well past midnight."

Esther wondered if Ralston were telling the truth. Alex put a hand over his eyes as the lawyer turned to her, a narrow-eyed look of utter scorn on his face.

"I'm sure my client hasn't mistaken the dates. As sure as I am that Mrs. Carter's story is a fabrication."

Alex's lawyer stood up. "It is no fabrication. Mrs. Carter is carrying Judge Todd's child."

"What?" Katherine McDonnell's lawyer looked as though he had been hit in the stomach with a shovel. He quickly collected himself. "You mean to tell me that—? This is absurd. She's been . . . cohabiting . . . with her husband for two months."

"My husband and I sleep in separate bedrooms. We do not . . . have not . . ."

Alex shifted uncomfortably as Dr. Sim's eyebrows shot up. "Are you telling us that you and your husband have"—the doctor cleared his throat—"never had relations?"

"That is exactly what I'm telling you!" Esther thought of the agony she would go through with Carter if she had to implement what she was about to say. She steeled herself and went on. "I am also telling you that I will testify so in court, and that I will also force my husband to verify it."

"My God," the opposing lawyer said, shaking his head. He turned back to her, bearing down. "You would reveal this, despite what it would do to you, to your marriage, to your reputation and your husband's—not to mention Judge Todd, here? Why?"

She gazed at Alex for a moment, wished he could have been spared all this, hoped he would not put two and two together and realize who she was. Then she turned back to Katherine McDonnell. "Because I love Mr. Todd. He is a dear friend and an impeccably honest man. I will not allow a conniving . . ."

Alex's lawyer put his hand on her arm and gently shook his head, stopping her. He turned to Katherine McDonnell and her counsel. "Mrs. Carter and Judge Todd are not the only ones who risk defamation in court. Should an examination—by a doctor of our choosing——show that Miss McDonnell is not with child, she will face not only civil action for damages, but criminal charges as well."

Alex, pained by the thought of fighting a lie with a possible untruth, stared straight ahead at a wall, fighting off the urge to end the proceedings and pay the woman off. There was a look of despair on the opposing lawyer's face. Dr. Sims shifted uneasily in his chair, and Katherine McDonnell, who was as beautiful as Ralston had described her, touched nervously at her carefully arranged hair. Her lawyer fought to regain his edge. "We . . . won't be threatened! Miss McDonnell has a bona fide paternity claim here . . ."

Alex's lawyer spoke softly. "Then the next step is to have both women examined. We will be happy to have Dr. Sims see Mrs. Carter first, at his office.

Should you subsequently decide to notify us by legal means that Miss McDonnell has decided not to press her charge, a second examination—by a doctor we select—will not be necessary, and we will let the matter drop. Right where it belongs, I might add."

"Please open your eyes," Leander Sims said, after lingering all too long over his pelvic examination. "I want to give the rest of you a thorough look-see." He stared at her nose for a moment, not bothering to cover her with the sheet he had pulled aside.

She reached down and tried unsuccessfully to tug one corner of it across her thighs. "You're finished . . . there, aren't you?"

"Yes. No doubt about your being pregnant. For just about the length of time in question." He lifted her eyelids, then stared at the pale birthmark between her breasts and, finally, at her nipples. He half-smiled. "I've seen you before, haven't I?"

Lying there on the examination table, she was suddenly aware that the front of his pants were beginning to bulge slightly. "No. You haven't."

"I think I have."

"You're mistaken."

"I . . . can't recall where, but I'm certain of it." He let his hand trail over her breast.

Esther pushed up off the table and slapped him hard in the face. "You filthy lecher! You've finished your examination! Keep your damnable hands off me!"

He backed away, holding his cheek, startled at first, then sneering. "I thought you might be one of those rare women who enjoy it—with anybody."

She quickly began dressing. "Well, you were wrong! Just as wrong as you were about thinking you could profit by your stinking little scheme."

"My, you are a spitfire. Just like it with Judge Todd, do you? I don't believe that for a minute!"

Esther picked up a glass jar filled with cotton

swabs. "*Get out!*" she screamed. "Get out or I'll smash your face with this."

Sims backed toward the door of the examining room. "I *know* I've seen you. It's been five years, but I couldn't forget that nose. I tended to you after—"

"If I ever hear a word from you again," she hissed, "if you *ever* cause me an ounce of trouble—for any reason—I will bring charges against you."

"For what?"

"You rotten, scheming fraud! You of all people know Miss McDonnell would be showing slightly by this time. Even in a dress. There are witnesses to the fact that she isn't. Even her own lawyer. Now get out, or the next time we see one another it will be at a trial that brings so much down on your head you'll be lucky to ever practice in California again."

He paused for a moment. "You people with money. You won't stop at anything, will you?" He glared at her and went out through the door, slamming it behind him.

She stayed in San Francisco for a week, expecting Alex to arrive at her front door to thank her after the charges were dropped. She was prepared to tell him almost everything, but it was Ralston who came instead.

"You were really something. *I* even believed you. For a moment there, when you said you loved Alex, I thought I was listening to someone else."

"I was . . . only stretching the truth. I care . . . deeply . . . for Alex Todd . . . as a friend."

"Well, you certainly proved your friendship. I hope someone goes to bat for me that way, if I ever need it."

"You won't, Billy. You're too aware of what people are capable of. Alex will . . . I am only guessing . . . always be vulnerable to someone like the McDonnell woman. He . . . acts in the belief that most people are as honest as he is."

"You may be right. I doubt he could do what you did for him. It would be against his principles."

"It's against your principles, as well. But you could do it, couldn't you?"

"In a small way, I did. He wasn't with me the night of your wedding at all. I saw him earlier in the day, briefly. Had to take him home he was so drunk. Can you imagine? Alex? At noon on a Sunday? He'd been up all night. Kept repeating over and over, something like 'Wish her luck for me.' God, I think Judith's death had him a little out of his mind for a while."

Esther felt as though her insides were going to come apart. "Is he . . . has he continued the drinking?"

"No, I was able to talk some sense into him. He's been moody as hell, and he's done something I think is foolish, but other than that—by the way, before he left yesterday, he asked me to thank you again for what you did."

"Left?"

"Yes, he didn't think it would be wise to say goodbye personally. Didn't want to risk embarrassing you."

"Left *San Francisco* yesterday?"

"Yes. Didn't he tell you? He said he'd written to thank you."

"He sent a beautiful letter of appreciation."

"Well, I tried to talk him out of it but he wouldn't listen. The whole thing mortified him. He took his extended leave of absence, after all. Got himself a commission as a major from General Sumner over at the Presidio."

"In the Union Army?"

"Yep." Ralston looked at his watch. "Could have served here in the West, but he wouldn't hear of it. On his way to Washington for assignment. I'd guess the clipper he's on is a third of the way to Panama by now."

Sixty-seven

Esther knew the baby was Todd's the moment she saw the shape of its body. Bull Carter didn't seem to notice, nor did he object when Esther requested that the child be named Todd—after "her grandfather." He doted over the infant, softening toward Esther even though she continued to say no to his less and less frequent entreaties. He had enough on his hands to keep his mind off her. Since passage of the Pacific Railroad Act that spring, he had been working sixteen-hour days at Charles Crocker's dry-goods warehouse and the Central Pacific's modest offices over Huntington and Hopkins's hardware store on K Street.

That was the only thing that could be called modest about the Central Pacific. They were already pushing Stanford's nomination for governor. Through Judah, Huntington had obtained a thirty-year government loan granting $16,000 per mile for work on the flatlands, $32,000 for the foothills, and $48,000 per mile in mountain terrain, far more than the construction cost.

"That Huntington is a fox," Bull Carter said one evening over dinner. "He's got a geologist who will testify that mountain soil can be found four miles east of Sacramento. Can you beat that? Son of a bitch —excuse me—is gonna move the Sierras forty miles west on the survey maps so we'll get the higher rate almost from ground-breaking time next January."

Esther toyed with the food on her plate. She had

been thinking of Moses lately, wanting to give him a taste of the outside world so he could make his own decision about going into the priesthood. It was the least she could do for him. He would be fifteen in the fall, old enough to work this summer if Carter would find a job for him. Now was not the time to comment acidly on the rapaciousness of the Big Four.

"What does Judah think of all this?"

"He don't like it at all. But he's keeping his mouth shut. He better keep on keeping his mouth shut, too. If he tries anything, they'll force him out quick as look at him."

"I hope that doesn't happen."

"Hope so too. He's not a bad little fella. I don't hardly understand what he's talkin' about half the time, but I like him."

He was in a good mood. She decided to seize the opportunity. "Bull . . . I . . . I want to ask you a favor."

"What kinda favor?"

"I want you to find a job this summer—at the construction company—for . . . the son of a friend of mine."

"There won't be no jobs 'til winter. Just preliminary stocking, preparations. I don't see how I can do it."

"Please? I would appreciate it."

"Who's the kid? How old is he?" Carter looked at her, thinking.

"Fifteen. He's . . . Solana's son. He's away at school."

"An injun kid? Forget it."

She thought for a moment. "I said I would appreciate it. I think you know what I mean."

His eyebrows rose, and he shook his head slowly, not believing what he was thinking. "Esther, I ain't as smart as you. You'll have to spell it out for me."

She measured out the difficult words. "While he is here, working at the construction company—and no longer—I would be . . . willing to . . . accommodate . . . you. Occasionally."

Carter laughed nervously, still slightly incredulous. "You mean? The two of us . . . like . . . uh . . ." His voice dropped to almost a whisper. "Once a . . . once a week?"

Esther looked away for a moment, then turned back. She nodded.

"Gaaaaahdamn! Esther, sweetheart, you got a deal." He laughed again, completely forgetting his usual "Excuse me."

"Just while he is here."

"I know, I know." He was more delighted than she had ever seen him. "Maybe . . . maybe I can talk him into staying on 'til the whole damn railroad's finished." He saw her frown. "I was just joking, Esther," he added quickly. "Just joking, for God's sake."

She knew he wasn't being facetious at all, but for now she had enough to think about. She had received the third of a series of letters from Alex. He never said as much, but she sensed from the tone of his letters that he had seen combat. She also knew instinctively that there was more to his writing than the desire to remain in touch with a "friend," as he put it, during the lonely hours between battles. He never came right out with it, but she wondered if, upon reflection, he had begun to suspect who she really was. She thought several times of writing him more than just an encouraging letter, telling him everything, but then decided against it. She would go to him after he returned home. It was not the sort of thing to write about. Not while he was at war. And there was no way to convey all she wanted to. No, he must see her face, know from the look in her eyes that she loved him still, despite everything that had happened. She was convinced it was her only hope of ever winning his forgiveness, if that were still possible. She began to long for that meeting, that confession, and the more she yearned for it, the greater her fear became that he would be killed.

When Moses arrived that summer, reawakened sadness and a measure of guilt were added to the whisper of fear for Alex she carried with her every day. The loose-limbed, natural coordination he inherited from his father counterbalanced the awkwardness of adolescence. As he stepped down off the stage from Marysville, Esther was struck by another similarity to Mosby: the boy's rawboned features and even gaze. He had a handsomer face than his father and less of Mosby's flat, almost reptilian stare, but the similarity was still enough to make Esther shudder.

She wondered if the ripple of remembered hatred engendered by the sight of the boy showed as he looked at her for a moment, hesitantly studying her face, then walked toward Solana, finally relaxed, and embraced the Indian woman.

Solana immediately sensed the question in the boy's mind as he turned again and stared at Esther in confusion. "You see?" she said, laughing, coming completely out of the shell of withdrawal she had retreated to since the massacre. "He has grown to be a fine man." *He is Mos-by's son,* she thought. *There is no question with that face.*

Esther held out her hand.

"This is the woman who . . . found you in the snow, in the mountains, when you were a child," Solana quickly said.

"Then you are not my mother?" Moses asked Solana, still staring at Esther.

"It is time you knew that we could not know who your mother was, and that I . . . adopted you." Solana said wisely.

Esther noticed Solana was studying the boy's face, then saw her nod to herself almost imperceptibly, as though she had finally confirmed something. But then Moses pulled her thoughts in another direction as they picked up his bags and headed for the waiting carriage.

"Then who are *you?*" he asked, glancing again at Esther.

"I . . ." The words stuck in her throat.

"Mrs. Carter is your friend," Solana quickly intervened. "She was my friend first, then after she . . . found you . . . and gave you to me to care for, she helped you go to the school."

"I never knew who paid for the school," he said, obviously deep in thought. "It costs a lot of money. I wondered about it."

"Mrs. Carter pays for all of it because she wanted to help you."

They got into the carriage and started off for Esther's place.

"I've never had the chance to thank you," Moses said. "I didn't even know it was you."

"That's perfectly all right, Moses. It was really nothing. I simply had the money, and we wanted to help you. It was Solana who did the important thing —raising you when you were a baby."

"I remember much of that time," Moses said as he began playing absently with young Todd in his wicker carrying crib. "Sometimes I think I can remember all the way back to the time I was born. Isn't that strange?"

"No one can go back that far," Solana said, uneasy.

"I know," Moses responded, "but sometimes it seems that way. Sometimes I have a feeling that I know about some things I couldn't possibly know."

Esther turned, and for a moment, as she caught Moses stealing a darting glance at her, she was sure he knew she was his mother. She was aware that he was watching her again when Solana suddenly reined the carriage team toward the Indian school rather than continuing toward Esther's home.

"It will be better if he stays with me," Solana explained. "There is room for him in the . . . apartment, and there are two boys from the village at the school. Perhaps he will remember them."

"Yes," Esther said. "Perhaps that will be better."

She was sure there was no way he could possibly know she was his mother, but the eerie feeling that he sensed it lasted until he came home from work the following day. Bull Carter's arm was over the boy's shoulder when he brought him back unexpectedly for dinner that night. He had clearly won Moses over, and whatever questions about Esther had arisen in the boy's mind, they were obviously buried now in his fascination with the railroad and his unalloyed worship of her husband.

Throughout that summer Carter treated Moses like his own son, teaching him mechanical skills, telling him of the outside world. In September the boy pleaded to stay on for several more months, telling Solana he was still undecided about what he wanted to pursue. Esther consented. Moses seemed so happy she could not bring herself to send him back to Marysville.

He had stayed with Solana in the apartment over the school the entire time, coming to dinner with Esther and her husband each Sunday afternoon and occasionally during the week. In early December Esther asked that they spend a weekend at her home. It was time to help him come to a decision. Solana had gone to bed after dinner on the Sunday Esther finally mustered the courage to bring up the subject.

"Moses don't want to be no priest, do you?" Bull Carter responded, slapping the boy on the shoulder.

"I would rather work for you, Mr. Carter—"

"Come on, boy, I told you you could call me Bull. We're friends."

"—or fight with the soldiers in the war."

"Now who put that idea into his head?" Esther frowned at her husband.

"He ain't gonna be no fool as to volunteer," Carter said, laughing. "Are yuh, boy? Wants to learn all about the railroad business. Be a railroad man. Don't yuh?"

"I want to stay with you, Bull. You're . . . better than a father."

"See? What I tell you, Esther? I told him about the California Battalion they're formin' up in Frisco. But he knows how much fun this railroad buildin's gonna be once we get started next month, don'tcha boy?"

"Well, Mr. Carter and I will discuss this further. I think it's time for you to turn in, Moses. Don't you?"

Moses kissed Esther on the cheek and obediently left the dining room. At the foot of the stairs, he decided to go back into the kitchen for a glass of water. Returning, he stopped for a moment near the dining room door, not believing what he was hearing.

Carter was certain the boy was upstairs in his room. "Why don't you stop fightin' it? He may be a goddamn half-breed Injun, but he's not as stupid as his mother. He don't want to be no namby-pamby priest. Damn Catholics. Can't stand them hardly no more than Injuns."

"Bull . . . !"

Carter rolled right over Esther's words. "Goddamn it! The only reason you're talkin' this stand is . . . Esther, I've done what you asked, put my arm around that goddamned, stinkin' little Injun bastard and made him feel welcome. Against everything I feel about them heathen . . ."

Moses eased backward in the hallway, stunned, tears spilling down his cheeks.

"You have no right to speak about another human being that way," he heard Esther say. "The boy thinks you're really fond of him. . . ."

Moses needed to hear no more. Going up the back stairs, he quietly packed his bag, looked at Solana for a moment as she lay sleeping, then started down the hall. At the door to Esther's bedroom, he stopped and stared at the daguerreotype sitting on the night table next to her bed. Moving quietly, he walked to the table, removed Esther's picture from its frame, then stole down the back stairs again and out through the kitchen door.

They didn't discover Moses was gone until the next morning. It took Esther the better part of three days to journey up to the school at Marysville and then return after learning he was not there. An hour after coming home she finally put two and two together, turned around without unpacking her bags, and, taking Solana with her, boarded the paddle-wheeler *Sacramento* for the trip downriver to San Francisco.

When she arrived at the recruiting center at Platt's Hall, the officer in charge told her the California Battalion had sailed for Boston two days before, December 10, 1862. No one recalled a young, dark-haired boy with somewhat sharp features. In any case, she was told, there was no possibility that a fifteen-year-old would be accepted for service.

She hoped Moses would be there, at her house, or at least at the school for Indian children, when she and Solana got back. He wasn't. Only when she sat on the edge of her bed, damning Bull Carter and crying for Moses, did she notice that the daguerreotype was missing from its oval frame.

Sixty-eight

Sacramento
December 20, 1863

No sign of Moses in over a year. I pray the boy is safe. Not a word from Alex since his letter of June 28, at which time he was preparing his battalion for Gettysburg. I fear, no, by now I am almost convinced, that he rests in that bloodied earth where Pickett's long gray line was finally turned back. Save for the fact that young Todd, who will be a year old in February, is robust and healthy and brings me a measure of joy each day, there is little to kindle the Christmas spirit. Thank God Mr. Carter has informed me he will remain at the railhead through the New Year . . .

She continued to busy herself at the school, where she had begun teaching again as soon as she had weaned the infant. Blessedly, Bull Carter was rarely home, and Esther spent most nights in the apartment over the school with the baby and Solana, who cared for him during the day. When Carter was in Sacramento, she moved over to his house and went through the motions of their marriage. She would keep their bargain, but she hated him now, rarely spoke with him unless it was absolutely necessary.

It went beyond Carter's part in Moses' disappearance. She loathed all of them now—Huntington, who

had duped his own country in time of war; Hopkins;
Stanford, whom they had successfully stuffed into the
governor's mansion; and Crocker, whose brutality toward his laborers sickened her. She knew Carter vied
with his half-brother in these horrible acts out at
the railhead each day. What they had done to Judah
she could never forgive them for. The fiery little genius
had finally taken a stand against the false survey.
They had in turn offered to buy him out for $100,000
or let him buy them out, if he could raise the millions
they asked for. Optimistic until the very end, Judah
had started on a trip east with expectations of rounding up the necessary investors. But his long battle
with the Big Four had taken its toll. Crossing the
Isthmus, he contracted cholera. Esther read of his
death in New York in the *Sacramento Bee* just as 1863
came to an end.

In the same edition she learned that General John
C. Frémont had been relieved by Lincoln of his supply command in the wake of a kickback scandal. It
was only one of many articles about the war she read
avidly. She followed the progress of the Union Army
southward and prayed that Alex would be mentioned.

By late summer of 1864, she gave up even the rem-
nant of hope for him she had somehow maintained.
For distraction she turned her attention once again
to the Comstock. Almost miraculously, Ralston had
stayed on his feet and kept the value of their investments rising through several crises. When the mines
were flooded in late 1862, dropping the bottom out
of what had been partially an inflated market built
on worthless desert land, Ralston bought up depressed
shares on credit after prices were driven down, then
helped finance a pump system, and came out ahead
of almost everyone. Somehow he walked the wire
over the most rapacious mining market the world had
ever seen. Dozens of men around him had fallen,
ruined by swindling, natural disasters, lawsuits, and
the luck of the draw. But Ralston not only kept on

making money for himself, Esther, and two dozen other investors, he made enough to establish the Bank of California.

By the time she stopped in at Ralston's new offices during a visit to San Francisco in the summer of 1864, his bank had millions invested in foundries, suppliers, factories, and forges as well as the mines themselves. Stocks in the Ophir, Yellow Jacket, Gould and Curry, Chollar, Belcher, Kentuck, and Empire mines were selling for as much as $22,000 a share; dividends were exceeding an unheard-of $100. Twenty thousand men working for huge companies had already ripped $20 million-worth of ore out of the Nevada earth.

Esther frowned when she recognized the real estate man, William Sharon, as he hurried out through Ralston's crowded, buzzing waiting room. Ralston leaned out of his office and glanced around. There was an uncharacteristically troubled look on his face when he spotted Esther and quickly motioned her inside.

"Do you know the man who was just in here very well?"

Ralston frowned. "Sharon? Well enough. Former real estate man who just lost his shirt—one hundred fifty thousand dollars worth of shirt. Just like I may lose mine in that damn Comstock. I should say my shirt, and, ah, possibly your dress, if you'll pardon me."

"He's a dishonest man."

"Sharon? Never heard that before. Sharp poker player. Hardnosed. The meanest expression I've ever seen. But dishonest?"

"He tried to cheat me once when I was looking for a house in Sacramento."

"Well, there's a little dishonesty in most of us, isn't there, Esther?"

"I suppose there is." *More than a little in my case,* she thought.

"I'll be wary of him. But in a way, I hope he's dishonest enough to deal with that pack of sharks in Virginia City. I'm banking on Sharon."

"Banking on him?"

"I just gave him a job as our branch manager there. I have a hunch he'll come through with his promise to find ways to get the mines working, and the profits rolling in again. Just out of pure hatred. He was sold back his own shares in one mine just before it closed down."

"I don't understand. It's summer? What's happened?"

"The mines are flooded again. They reached about five hundred feet and ran into an underground river. No one's figured a way to get past it."

"What does that mean to us financially?"

"It means a nightmare for me, considering all the bank has invested. You? I've restricted your Comstock investments to one-quarter of what's coming in. But I have reinvested all the mining profits, as you agreed. Some of the other things I've sold and shifted to mine-oriented items. Of the two million you're worth on this end, Esther—"

"*Two million dollars?*"

"Two million dollars. But I'd say about three quarters of it is in mining paper and allied stock-holdings."

"Billy, this frightens me."

"Don't worry, Esther. We'll find a way out of it."

"I hope so, for your sake. You've done well enough for me, despite this setback. And I'm well taken care of now, no matter what happens in Nevada. But I don't like it, Billy. And I think you'll be sorry you ever got involved with Sharon."

"You'll be worth *three* million after we pull out of this!"

Esther smiled. She had grown attached to Ralston, wishing only the best for him. "Billy, listen to me. I don't really care about that. It's you I'm concerned about. I see you looking at the calendar, getting ready for your next meeting before this one is even through. Harried. Worried. Tired."

"Esther—"

"Listen to me! *Please!* I don't care half as much about what happens at the Comstock as I do about what's happening to you. It's changing you, all this. And it worries me."

She was right about Sharon, and right about Ralston as well. Just as right as he was about pumping the value of her stock even higher than it was before Virginia City's second Mount Davidson flood. She didn't like what he was doing any more than she cared for the increasing changes in Ralston as the months quickly passed.

Esther had moved back into her own house after the tenant who replaced Stanford pushed on with the hordes moving to Virginia City. She had reached a tacit understanding with Carter—she would not bring down the scandal of divorce or the embarrassment of a formally announced separation if she saw him only when he picked up young Todd for an occasional outing. Once settled into her old home, she resumed teaching and kept track of Ralston's increasingly indefensible tactics.

She learned that Sharon had discovered tons of hastily dumped waste at the mills as well as the mines. The leavings were loaded with ore. It was also evident, he reported, that the veins ran well below the water level. Rather than solve the underground water problem immediately, he suggested the Bank of California take advantage of it in a way that would result in control of practically every mine in the Comstock.

Ralston went along with Sharon's scheme. When other San Francisco banks refused to lend small-mill owners additional funds, the Bank of California offered it to them at 2 percent a month interest. With pumping stalled, the owners quickly failed to meet their notes. Sharon then foreclosed, and Ralston took the small mills over. They worked the same financial squeeze on as many of the still partially operating mines as they could, then forced their new partners to send their ore to the bank-controlled mills. The larger processing plants soon went into bankruptcy. In turn, they were bought out at depressed prices as well.

Esther pondered the vicious cycle of starving and buying out competitors as she sat on her porch watching young Todd, now three and a half years old, playing in her fenced front yard with a new puppy. It was Indian summer, the foliage was still green, and the atmosphere of warm peace that had followed the end of the Civil War and the death of Lincoln was in sharp contrast to events just across the Sierras in Virginia City. The tactics Ralston and Sharon were using were just as inexcusable as the bullwhip, bone-crushing approach Crocker and her husband were employing as they pushed the railroad farther up into the Sierra foothills toward Dutch Flat. She could see little difference between men dying from exhaustion at the railhead every other day and others who starved financially in Virginia City and took their lives in the wake of ruin.

She knew she was a part of it, at least indirectly, and her conscience demanded she remove herself once again from involvement of any kind. But, clinging to the undefined notion that her wealth, her connection with the railroad would be of use when Mosby inevitably returned to California, she rationalized, found arguments for her position, and finally repressed all though of disengaging herself. . . .

Until that Sunday morning, early in 1866, when Bull Carter arrived at her house to pick up Todd and take him to see his first locomotive.

"Letter came for yuh up to the house," Carter said, picking the child up in his arms. "Somethin' in it besides words. Here . . . I'll, ah, have the boy back to you by midafternoon."

She waited until Carter had driven off with her son in the buckboard before opening the unsettlingly heavy envelope. Enclosed she found the daguerreotype of herself that had been missing since Moses' disappearance. Quickly, she unfolded the letter itself.

Dear Mrs. Carter:

Please forgive the long delay in getting this to you. I have been preoccupied with reestablishing myself here since the close of hostilities, and at first did not even know your name. The enclosed tintype was among the personal effects of Private Moses Cable, who gave up his life in battle at Aldie, Virginia, while serving under my command. Upon returning to San Francisco, I took the liberty of inquiring at the shop of Mr. G. R. Fardon, whose imprint I found on the back of the daguerreotype, as to your identity and address. I do not know your relationship with young Private Cable, but assume you are family.

I deeply regret bearing such sad news, but be assured that Private Cable was conspicuous in his valor and died bravely for his country. I have several of Private Cable's personal effects, including an exquisitely wrought stone spearhead, a set of rosary beads, and a heart-shaped amulet, woven, apparently, from the fur of a wild animal. Since I am sure you would want these articles, I have enclosed my new address at Bear Point, just across the bay from San Francisco. Should you find difficulty in locating my home, it is just up the shore to the west of General James Atterbury's former residence.

Please feel free to call on me at your convenience, as I expect to be here preparing a report of the battalion's experiences in the late war for

the State Adjutant General during the coming
weeks.

Once again, I am so deeply sorry, and share
with you the grief I know you must be experiencing with this unhappy news.

Your most obedient servant,

D. W. C. THOMPSON, MAJOR (RET.)
CALIFORNIA BATTALION
2D MASSACHUSETTS CAVALRY

Esther fingered the stone spearhead set in a base
of bear claws, as Thompson tried to explain why he
could tell her very little about the circumstances surrounding the boy's death. There could be no other
reason for Moses adopting her last name unless he
instinctively *knew*.

"I had no idea he was so young. He seemed to
have attached himself to a fellow, eventually given
a field commission as a lieutenant, in San Francisco.
Lied about his age, I suppose, and got away with it
in the confusion of early '63."

"Didn't anyone bother to check his age?"

"Madam, please forgive me, but I must point out
it was an extremely hectic time. Had he been more
closely connected to me, personally, I might have
noticed."

"You didn't know him well, then?"

"Well enough. I knew all my men. But he was not
among the cavalrymen and officers I spent most of
my time with. There were four hundred men under
me, you understand."

"You say he wasn't with your cavalry?"

"No, he was assigned to a detachment of unmounted.
They served primarily as picket guards. In battle he
was a flag-bearer."

"And you didn't actually see him killed?"

"No, madam. I was told of the peculiar nature of his death by his friend, Lieutenant, then Sergeant, Harlan Cooper."

"What do you mean, peculiar?"

"We were unexpectedly overrun by a superior force of Mosby's guerrilla cavalry at Aldie. Most of our engagements were with the raiders, as they were called. Very difficult business for almost a year. Back and forth across the Potomac and just about every hill in northern Virginia."

Esther's mouth was suddenly dry.

"Mosby?"

"Yes. Colonel John Singleton Mosby. In any case, they caught us by surprise. Overran us and took quite a number of prisoners. Killed and wounded many of our men, Lieutenant Cooper among them, and then they were repulsed. The battle was over, and we were peppering their retreat from across a meadow when Private Cable inexplicably dashed after them across the field. He was ordered back several times. At least once by Lieutenant Cooper. To no avail. For some reason he seemed to have lost his senses. Kept rushing across the field in an apparent attempt to kill one of the Confederate officers with the point of his flagstaff. He was carrying the regimental colors, you see. They were already in the woods, continuing their retreat, when Private Cable reached them and was—killed."

"He was buried there?"

"I'm sure he was. I did not witness the burial myself. We were quickly in pursuit of Mosby and his men. Never quite caught up with them." Thompson paused, staring sadly out through the windows of his study at the waters of San Francisco Bay. "That is all I can tell you, madam. You might gain additional details from Lieutenant Cooper. I can give you his address."

Thompson walked with Esther to her carriage. "I grieve with you, madam, believe me. Your nephew was a popular young lad. The pity of it is that his death was unnecessary. Aldie was our last serious encounter with the guerrillas."

She found Harlan Cooper at the wayside inn he ran just north of Sausalito the following morning. When she told the slender, bearded man with deep hollows under his eyes who she was and why she had come, he limped out from behind the beer traps and sat down with her at a table half-lit with shafts of sunlight. A thousand dust motes danced between them in the dark, sour-smelling tavern as he covered what Thompson had already told her, then described Moses' last moments of life.

"I was lyin' there, couldn't move with this leg shattered, you see, and he was tendin' to me and several other men who was wounded. Keepin' his eye on the Rebs across the way. It'd grown so quiet, 'cept for an occasional peppershot, you could hear yourself breathin'. Of a sudden, a look come over Moses' face the likes of which I never seen. Like he saw somethin' or someone that crazed him. I don't know what it was, anger over what happened to me—we was close, you know—or what. But as I said, of a sudden he gets this look in his eyes, like . . . like a wild creature, and ups and sets out across that field after 'em, colors in hand. I don't know what he was thinkin', or whether he had one of 'em picked out, but when he gets near the woods on the other side, he runs straight at this officer on horseback, pointin' that flagstaff right at the bloody Reb's chest. Captain he was—"

"An officer. A staff officer?"

"Yep. Seen that bird many a time before. We was at 'em off and on maybe thirteen, fourteen months, you know. Mean-lookin' man as I've ever seen. Rumor had it he was a relative of that devil Mosby himself."

Esther closed her eyes and began to shake her head, but Cooper, eyes blank and caught up in the memory, stared past her all the way back to Aldie, Virginia, in July 1864.

"Anyways, Moses run at him and he backed his horse so's the little fella missed him. Wheeled and come down on the boy full force with a saber."

Esther put her hands to her face and began to sob.

"I'm sorry, ma'am. Really sorry. At the time it struck me down worse than this ball I'm carryin' in my hip. If it's any comfort, I hear tell this officer, this relative of the guerrilla king himself, was killed— in an accident—about a month later. More than a rumor, actually, though I didn't see it myself. We'd pulled back to the Potomac by then. Blown to bits by one of his own artillery pieces. I'd seen him cut down so many men, I couldn't a' been more glad if I'd done it myself. Johnny Reb bastard."

"Thank you," Esther said, getting up. She was too numb even to cry now. Cooper limped with her to the doorway.

"I'm sorry, ma'am. Like I said, I took it hard when he was killed. He was a good boy. No better. You might say he was like a son to me. Hope you'll pass my regrets along to his mother."

Esther turned to him. "He was buried properly?"

Cooper had seen the sorrow etched around Esther's eyes many times on many faces during the past year. "Had the boys carry me on a litter to where they put him in the ground. Placed a cross of thick branches on it myself."

He did not have the heart to tell her that they had all moved on, either in pursuit of the raiders or to the medical area at Fairfax County Courthouse, within minutes of the incident. Or that Moses, along with two dozen others in darkly stained blues, had been left there in the meadow grass under the scorching summer sun and the dark swarms of eagerly keening flies.

Sixty-nine

Aboard the *Pacific Union Express*
May 7, 1869
11:55 A.M.

John Sutter gazed out through the window beside his
seat as the train slowed, then emerged from the pine
forest and rolled across a trestle high above a deep
canyon. He could feel the express begin to climb
again as it left the trestle behind and moved on into
wild mountain country. Sutter got up and walked
to the forward door of his car. He turned for a moment, tipped his hat to Alex Todd, then went out
the door and stood on the platform, thinking. He
stepped to one side so he could see through the port
in the opposite entrance. Luther Mosby was laughing
as he drew in a winning hand in the card game he
was playing with three other passengers. Sutter recognized the men. Southerners. The war was not over
yet. It had simply taken on a more subtle complexion.
Sutter saw Mosby look at his watch and wondered
how the pieces he had begun to put next to one another in his mind would all fit together. All the elements added up to more than the simple fact that
Mosby would undoubtedly attempt revenge on Alex
Todd, no matter what he had said to the contrary.
Sutter hoped neither Alex nor Esther would be
harmed. But there was more to it than that, and
Sutter sensed vaguely that it had something to do

with the pages in Esther's diary that he had read
almost twenty-two years before. He could not remember them in detail, but the gist of it was enough.
Esther had been in those mountains, and so had
Mosby—at roughly the same time. That much Sutter
was sure of. Less certain was that somehow Esther's
part in whatever was about to happen went back far
beyond the incident involving Todd and Mosby the
previous year.

It would all be foolish conjecture, he thought, if
he had not seen Mosby move down Front Street,
then double back and head for the parlor car late
the night before. Ralston had gone to bed, and he
had remained in the second rocking chair on the
third-floor porch, smoking his cigar. Puzzled, curious,
he had waited almost an hour until Mosby reappeared
and then saw Esther hurry back from the direction
of the parlor car five minutes later.

Considering Esther's feelings and Mosby's obvious
hatred for Alex, none of it made sense. Particularly
the fact that she seemed to have asked him to meet
her in the parlor car. Sutter shook his head. The look
of unmitigated hatred on Solana's face, a look she
had concealed until she turned away from Mosby—
after she had delivered what was no doubt a note
from Esther in the lobby of the hotel before dinner
—was even more puzzling. It was the first time he
had ever seen Solana display more than a minimal
degree of emotion. Where, he wondered, could she
have seen Mosby before? And what could he have
done to her to elicit such intense wrath? Sutter stared
out at the green blur of the conifers sweeping past,
oblivious of their beauty, hardly hearing the roar and
racket the locomotive and the cars were making as
the train rushed onward. Many times he'd wondered
about exactly what had happened to Esther in the
Sierras. Now he was sure that somewhere between
here and Promontory he would find out.

*　*　*

Luther Mosby dealt, looked at his hand, and decided to fold.

"What's the matter, judge?" one of the players joshed. "Cards turned bad on you?"

"No, it's my stomach. Don't agree with me, all this rattlin' and shakin'." He thought about the questions that might be asked if he stayed in the parlor car with the woman all the way to Promontory. "Keeps troublin' me, might just get off and stay off at Dutch Flat. Excuse me, gentlemen. I think a little air might do me some good."

On the platform up forward, Mosby checked the ladder leading to the roof, then looked up at the space between the cars. They were rocking slightly, but he anticipated no difficulty in jumping from one to another when he went up later. Back in the car he got his bag down from the luggage rack. "Think I'll try to trade for a seat in the one up ahead. Ain't rockin' as much."

"Hope you feel better, judge. We'd hate to see you miss the festivities at Promontory."

Mosby smiled, thinking of Alex Todd. "Wouldn't want to miss it for the world. You boys stay honest, you hear?"

Solana huddled beside young Todd in the engine cab, fighting the fear engendered by this strange metal monster and the incredible noise it was making. She glanced back over the low, attached fuel-unit at the two infantrymen, rifles across their laps, sitting on the crates lashed to the bed of the flatcar. Looking past them, she studied the platform of the first passenger unit. The ladder was within easy reach. She knew there were similar ladders on each end of the car she could not see. She pictured the other platforms farther back that she had observed the day before. They were all the same, except that the forward platform of Charles Crocker's parlor car contained a large, wooden equipment-bin.

* * *

The roar of the train doubled in volume, and the parlor car grew suddenly dark as the train rattled through a long, wooden snowshed at the base of a steep ravine. When the car grew light again, Esther uncorked the vial of powder and poured a small amount into a glass. It was ground from four red and black jequirity-bean beads removed from the rosary Colonel Thompson had given her along with the rest of Moses' personal effects. Harmless when lacquered, even if a child sucked on them. When stripped and ground to a fine dust, two of the beads contained enough indigenous poison to kill a man. She shook the glass, one of a set carefully selected for their color-match with the jequirity powder, until the poison lay in a fine coating across the narrow bottom. Then she set the glass down with five others on a tray containing a decanter filled with sherry. Placing the tray on the hinged table between her seat and the one facing it, she arranged the glasses so they appeared to be placed at random.

Leaning back, she thought of the numbing grief that had enveloped her after she learned of Moses' death. For a month or so it had been as immobilizing as the bone-deep mixture of lethargy and hatred that gripped her for almost a year after she came down out of the Sierras. Added to that were the frustration, anger, and then disappointment born of being certain she would never have the opportunity to get back at Mosby.

Her chair swayed slightly as the train rolled over another trestle, and she remembered how her rage at being cheated of her revenge had actually outweighed sorrow over Moses' death. All her accumulated wealth and power meant nothing. There was little to live for—except young Todd. That was just enough to sustain her at first, and then more than enough as she invested all her love and attention on the boy.

In the soothing, distracting light of her young

son's love, the sorrow, anger, and frustration faded. Then, as the spring of 1866 burst forth magnificently all around her, she began a parallel process of rebirth. She started closing the door on the long spiritual winter she had lived through. Adjusting, rationalizing, she attributed her preoccupation with Mosby to an understandable kind of madness. Now that it had all ended fruitlessly, she remonstrated with herself, no matter what Mosby had done, revenge did not seem worth lowering herself almost to his level, giving up Alex, and living the life she had led for the better part of two decades.

Briefly she punished herself with questions about what it might have been like if she had rejoined Alex in 1847. But then she put even that aside as her duties at the school and the demands young Todd was making on her time and attention pulled her bodily back into the present and started her thinking of the future.

Esther listened to the clanking sound of the train wheels for a moment, pictured the miles they were crossing, then translated them into the months of her life. She opened the journal again, smiling as she recalled Todd's first day of school, and then frowning as she skipped several entries and began to read.

Sacramento
September 30, 1866

Astonished to read today, after months of not being interested in newspapers, that Luther Mosby is alive! Good God! He is not only a survivor of the War, but a beneficiary! He has won election as U.S. Senator from Nevada after having been back in Virginia City for a mere six months. His picture and the mention of his name evoked an intense sequence of feelings. The old urge to get back at him, then an awareness of futility, what with his imminent departure for the East. Followed by a slow return to the state of mind I have been in since spring. Let fate have him. Sooner or later it will all come home to roost, and someone will make him pay for everything he has done. Perhaps God, in the end. Do not know how I would feel were I placed before him again. But that seems unlikely for some time to come, in any event, and I have spent enough time, wasted enough of my life in that obsession. Perhaps I am getting older, more tired, less able to pursue such a thing. After all, I will be thirty-seven years old in less than a month. Or perhaps I am simply growing wiser. But it does seem as though such preoccupation would simply be still more self-inflicted punishment I no longer deserve. If, indeed, I ever did. Who is to say what might happen if he returns to northern California? Perhaps I would maintain my present attitude in the matter. Or possibly the hatred would be fanned to uncontrollable flames again. I do not know, even though at this very moment I am feeling the beginnings of my old lust for his destruction. But I certainly feel no urge to travel to Washington City after him. And I will not waste time even thinking of him while revenge is almost an impossibility. After all, what chance would a lone woman have of gaining satisfaction while he is ensconced in the Senate? To hell with him! For now, at least.

Ironic is the coincidence that Sutter will also be in Washington. Since the fire that leveled all but the "shack" he and his taciturn wife now live in, he has become almost a mad Don Quixote, jousting with the Federal Government over his land claims. He actually plans to move there, take rooms until he either dies or gets his due! I fear there is little hope for that, but seriously doubt he will not return, at least from time to time, for his unending "public appearance."

There are other matters to consider. Todd seems well-adjusted here, so I see no reason to move him to a normal school. Much as I detest Carter, perhaps I should think about selling this place (and the house in San Francisco as well?) and moving back into his. Todd has begun to ask questions about why we live here rather than at his "father's" house. Considering how much Bull is away, it might be tolerable. Then there are the investments. I have thought long enough about them. I can find no justification for remaining even indirectly involved in the vile madness of Virginia City. And the other stocks have lost their meaning to me. Ralston's latest report: an unbelievable three-and-a-half-million dollars in assets! There is nothing I can do about the railroad stock, since it is in Carter's name. But there is no reason now not to liquidate everything else. Blue Star holdings included. Let the money sit in the bank and draw interest, for all the use I will ever put it to! Let Todd have it all when he reaches maturity and Carter is no longer in a position to do anything about it. I suppose there may be some legal complications in keeping it out of Carter's reach, even after Todd comes of age. I will have to speak to Ralston about that next week. I am still unaccustomed to thinking of Billy as a married man. Such a sudden shift of heart for what appeared to be a confirmed bachelor. Well, she is young and quite lovely, and I wish him well. But it pains me to hear of the lengths he goes to for her. He will probably still be engrossed in that ridiculous marble barn he has built for his new bride at Belmont. He mentioned that he had a surprise for me. Wait until he hears that I have decided to liquidate all my holdings! No matter what he has to tell me, I doubt it will be as surprising as that. I must resolve not to alter my decision no matter how hard he tries to dissuade me.

Seventy

During the twenty-mile ride south from San Francisco in Ralston's coach, Esther decided to move back to Carter's house, at least until the railroad was completed. By then Todd would be old enough to understand a permanent separation. She had just decided to sell her Sacramento property but keep the house in San Francisco, when the coach pulled around a bend and Belmont absorbed all her attention.

The coach rolled across a miniature bridge, and its weight triggered a mechanical system that opened massive gates to the courtyard outside the mansion. Built along the lines of an Italian country villa, the house itself seemed large enough to hold several sailing ships. Ralston greeted her at the enormous front door.

"Well, how do you like it?" Eagerly, he ushered her into a vaulted entranceway brightened by skylights.

"It—leaves me speechless."

"One hundred twenty-five rooms, last time I counted. That ought to be enough guest space for a rollicking weekend, wouldn't you say?"

Esther glanced at the long stairway and balcony railings, then all the doorknobs within sight. They were made of silver. Ralston pushed open a pair of etched glass-doors and led her by the hand into his ballroom. It was large enough to house one of San Francisco's three-story granite buildings.

Esther could no longer hold her tongue. "Don't you think this is all a bit extravagant, Billy?"

They were standing in the middle of the ballroom, and Ralston looked up, his eyes sweeping across an expanse of ceiling. "It's only money, Esther. What good is it if you don't spend it? You could build a house like this now. Do you know what you're worth?"

"I read your last report."

"Add another quarter-million dollars to that, Esther. Sharon continues to work his miracles."

"I wouldn't exactly describe what he does in religious terms, Billy." She decided not to comment any further. She knew how much Ralston gave away, the considerable sums he had donated to the city for public works, the orphanage. "But that's your business," she went on. "And his." She girded herself. "Billy, what I'm about to say has nothing to do with Sharon, or you personally. I hope you understand that. But I think it's time for me to liquidate."

"Everything?"

"Everything."

Ralston thought for a moment, then beamed. "All right. I see no problems with that. It's about time you enjoyed some of that money, anyway."

"I'd like to place it all in trust for my son."

"That can easily be arranged."

"Can it be held in the bank's name? After all, Bill Kelsey is sixty-eight now, and with Alex gone . . ."

For a moment, Esther thought she saw a slightly amused, somewhat devilish look in Ralston's eyes. But he quickly turned away, and, as he went on, she forgot it.

"I'll set it up so you can draw from the account, as well. Anytime you wish."

She took one of Ralston's hands. "Thank you, Billy. I was so certain you'd take a dim view of all this."

"But why?" He laughed. "It will give me the opportunity to buy your stocks and get even richer. Now, on to more important things. You *will* stay the weekend?"

"I haven't brought anything. I—"

"That's no problem either. My wife will find some suitable things. I won't hear of you not staying. You'll spoil my surprise."

"Can't we just have lunch? Can't you just surprise me now?"

Ralston walked over to a window and reached for a bellpull. "Impossible. It has to be tonight. At the dinner dance."

"Dance? Billy, I *can't*—"

"Come on now, Esther. Please. Don't spoil it for for me. Haven't I always done everything *you've* asked? You'll love it. You'll have more fun than you've ever had in your life. You've got to start living, Esther."

"All right," she said, relenting, tempted by the idea of 'living.' "But remember, I'm a married woman."

"No one said anything about romance. Just dancing, good company, and good fun. And none of your veiled-hat business. It just won't do." He looked at his watch, took her arm, and they walked back to the swinging doors. "My wife should be making one of her grand descents down the stairs by now. She'll take you to the room we picked. And for God's sake, don't fill the tub up. It's five feet deep. I don't want you drowning before you have had the most pleasant shock of your life."

Esther stood watching the hundred-odd guests who had arrived during the afternoon. Half of them were dancing to the light strains of a violin ensemble Ralston had installed in a bandbox over in one corner of the ballroom. At first she was self-conscious without a veil in so much company. But after Ralston and Kelsey introduced her to a dozen people, and they took no notice of her nose, she began feeling at ease. Now, as Bill and Connie Kelsey waltzed by, she experienced a wave of delight, just watching. She had begun living again, just as she'd planned.

A tall man she'd been introduced to asked her to dance. She declined at first, but when he came back a second time, she mustered her courage, began awkwardly, then quickly put into smooth practice the simple steps she'd learned as a girl. By the time the number soared to a close, she was swept up in the rhythm, the sound, the sentimental meaning of the lyrics, and a sense of pleasure so foreign to her it made her slightly light-headed. When the music ended, the gentleman bowed, then turned as they both heard Ralston clap for attention halfway across the floor.

He was standing precariously on the low, flower-bedecked trellis fence surrounding the musicians.

"And now, ladies and gentlemen, your attention, please!" Ralston glanced down to his left at someone. He broke into a broad grin as a number of people near him turned and began buzzing in astonishment.

Esther stood up on her toes, but her view of who or what had caused the commotion was blocked.

"Back, ladies and gentlemen," Ralston shouted, "from the horrors of the Rebellion, back from two years in the abomination of Andersonville—and the even more torturous clutches of buxom nurses at St. Simon's Hospital in Washington D.C.—back, ladies and gentlemen, from the dead! I give you . . . *Judge Alexander Todd!*"

Ralston jumped down from his perch and embraced Alex as the crowd around them parted, and, turning, they both walked toward the center of the ballroom. Struck dumb, Esther watched as Alex shook hands repeatedly, smiled, nodded, and then finally glanced her way. The smile on his face froze grotesquely when he saw her. He stopped for a moment; then, certain, he began pushing slowly through the clutch of well-wishers.

His second step galvanized Esther. Panicked, she

spun around and rushed toward the doors of the
ballroom. Almost knocking over an elderly man, she
raced through the entranceway and the foyer. Startling the butler, she pushed violently through the
front door. Cabs and carriages lined the courtyard
driveway. Running to the buggy nearest the open
gates, she climbed up into the seat and frantically
snapped the reins. As the team of chestnuts clattered
across the decorative bridge, she glanced back. Alex
stood alone in the doorway.

In the dim light just before dawn, the sheets covering the furniture in her San Francisco house seemed
like ghosts from the past. She sat there on the couch,
watching the open front door, certain Alex would come
sooner or later. She was calm now, as prepared as she
would ever be for the confrontation. Still, her hands
trembled and she held her knees together tightly as
the buggy rolled around the circular driveway and
stopped. The pounding of her heart almost drowned
out the sound of his footsteps on the gravel.

He stood in the doorway for a moment, ironically
outlined in silhouette by the first rays of the sun.
Then he slowly walked in through the foyer, crossed
the room, and sat down beside her. For a minute he
simply stared at her, the same look of utter disbelief
locking his features in place.

"It *is* you, isn't it?" he whispered. "I'm not imagining this."

She dropped her eyes, hesitantly reached out and
laid a hand on his. "Alex . . . I . . . this is . . . the
most difficult moment I have ever known."

"Good God, it's almost too much to bear! I am so
confused. How? Why?" He put his hand to his forehead and massaged his temples, as though that would
help his brain function normally again. "For a time,"
he finally said, "while I was in the field, I . . . made
believe that it was you." Tears welled in his eyes.

"That somehow you'd come back to me that night."

"I sensed that, in your letters."

"But I . . ." He took out a handkerchief and brushed at his eyes. "I finally knew, I *knew* I was just dreaming, putting together coincidence, similarities. Out of disappointment you'd married, loneliness, need . . . fear of dying out there . . . God, I don't know."

"As you can see, your instincts were right," she whispered.

"Then, in the prison camp, even though I knew by then it was a fantasy, I built all my hope of surviving around you—getting out, healing, getting better, coming home, finding you. I . . . lived for a dream, another night like we spent together here. A dream I didn't know was real the whole time."

"I've never stopped loving you, Alex."

He took a deep breath. "That's hard to believe, Elizabeth."

"I know it is. But it's true."

"That night? How could you have—?"

"Because I loved you so much, I was willing to risk discovery as well as giving you pain. With you sitting there, next to me, I was simply overcome."

"Esther Cable. Esther Cable Carter. Good sweet Jesus, I just don't understand."

"As much as I wanted that night again, every night until eternity, I couldn't risk what it might do to you. Risk what now has happened."

"But why didn't you come to me after . . ." He suddenly thought of John Alexander. "The boy. Our son . . . ?"

She began to cry softly. "Our first son. He died, Alex. In the mountains when . . ."

Conflicting emotions disorienting him, he didn't realize what she had said. "*But why, damn it? Why didn't you come back to me, tell me?*"

The look of confused, hurt, sudden anger tore at

her. For a moment she was so completely off guard
she almost blurted all of it out. But there was enough
for him to accept as it was. She took both his hands,
bent over and laid her moistened cheek against them.
"I was more confused than you are right now. I was
so . . . *ashamed* . . . I couldn't face you. Can you
understand that?"

"Ashamed? Many people, other children, died."

"But my willfulness . . . was . . . a . . . factor in
. . . I made a tragic mistake. *I . . . helped cause John
Alexander's death.*"

He stared at her, his features softening, beginning
to comprehend.

"And I couldn't face you," she sobbed. "I felt I
didn't deserve you anymore. Can you understand?
And then, as time passed, it became impossible to
turn back."

"All these years, all the things you've done for me.
The South Fork Mine, all of it. You arranged everything."

"I wanted to make things up to you in a pitiably
small way, wanted to be part of your life, even if
you didn't know it. It was all I had."

"God, it boggles the mind. I still can't believe it's
you, Elizabeth." He leaned over and tilted her face
upward.

"It isn't me anymore. It isn't Elizabeth Purdy Todd.
Look at me. Can you understand why I couldn't face
you looking the way I do?"

He brushed his fingertips tenderly across her nose.
"It's hardly noticeable."

"It was then."

"You're more beautiful now than you were when
we were married." He thought for a moment. "You're
married. Are you happy?"

"It's simply a marriage of convenience. Nothing
more. I plan to separate from him in time."

"But you have a son."

She started to tell him, but decided to wait. "Alex, I married William Carter so I wouldn't be tempted to—"

"See me again?"

"Yes. Stripping it to the truth, yes. There were . . . other considerations, a business arrangement. But, yes, that is the main reason why I married him."

The anger was leaving him. In its place he felt compassion for her. "I was married, too, Esther. You know that."

She couldn't help herself. Tears streaming down her face, she still had to laugh. "I was so *jealous!* Did you know that I . . . well, I put the idea in Kelsey's head. To introduce the two of you. Can you imagine?"

Alex shook his head, then smiled. "It will take some time to accommodate all of it."

"You don't hate me?"

"Esther . . ." He laughed. "Look, *I'm* even calling you that. . . . I've learned not to hate anyone or anything. We're all human. All capable of God knows what, if circumstances push us far enough. I learned that and a good deal more about tolerance in the war. No, I don't hate you."

She threw her arms around him, sobbing again. "I was so certain you . . . would."

"I don't. I'm angry. Happy. Sad. Grateful you're alive. God, it will take months for me to understand it, accept what you did. Perhaps even more time to absorb the fact that so much stands between us, that we can't be together, under the circumstances. But no, I could never hate you."

"I love you, Alex."

He eased her back, smiling, trying to calm her. "Here, now. A married woman isn't supposed to talk that way."

"I am married to you!"

He thought about that for a moment. "I . . . suppose you are."

"I . . . I've never . . . I don't sleep in the same bed with Carter."

"But the boy?"

"When you see him, I won't have to tell you whose son he is."

Alex looked at her incredulously.

"His name is Todd."

He put his arms around her, rocking back and forth, trying to assimilate all of it. "That night?"

"Yes. That one night. In the dark. Upstairs. I wish . . ."

"If I told anyone all this, they'd think I was as crazy as Emperor Norton. Twenty years. Good God! Twenty-two years!"

"Twenty-one this past summer."

"If I told Billy, even he wouldn't believe me. He's looked you square in the face and not recognized you."

"I've gotten fat."

"Fat, hell. You're—"

"Don't tell anyone."

"Don't—?"

"About me. It doesn't matter. We know. That's all that matters. And if you still want me . . ."

"Oh, God, Esther, a part of me wants to horsewhip you for all the years we've lost . . . but another part of me . . ."

"If you still want me, I will see to it that we are together as often as possible."

He kissed her cheek. "Twenty-one years. And yes, I do still love you, want you . . ."

"Then it's been long enough, hasn't it?" She laughed nervously, stroking his hair. "All but once. That night. God in heaven, married or not, I want you to carry me upstairs and . . ."

"Begin an affair—with my own wife." He smiled, still staggered by it all, but happy for the moment.

"Yes," she whispered, leaning over and kissing him softly. "Can you? Will you . . . ?"

"Oh, yes." He picked her up in his arms and started toward the stairs.

"Yes," she whispered, covering his mouth, his cheeks, his eyes with kisses. "Yes . . . yes . . . yes . . . yes . . . Oh, God, in heaven, *yes!*"

Seventy-one

It was far from easy at first. From time to time, what she had done reached out from the past and tore at him. Sometimes, during the weekends they spent together once or twice a month, he hardly spoke. Moods came upon him suddenly, locking away his desire as well as his voice. For a time he urged her to leave Carter. But then, after seeing his son, he recognized the need to protect the child, allow him time to reach an age when he could adjust to such a drastic change more easily.

He was uncomfortable about becoming Todd's godfather, but Carter was in eastern Nevada at the railhead, and Alex realized during the solemnity of the church service that the connection would permit him to visit the child—and Esther—occasionally in Sacramento. In mid-1867, he won an appointment to the superior court. The work absorbed him and accelerated his acceptance of things as they were. The months passed, Esther traveled to San Francisco more frequently, sometimes with Todd in tow, and Alex eagerly took the steamer upriver once a month. The days they spent together were carefree, happy. The nights, the sweetest either of them had ever known. He did not ask her how she had come to be so skillful with a man's body until almost a year had passed. They were in the bedroom of her San Francisco house.

"From a book I found in Dr. Canby's library. A French book. Do you remember him? At Bent's Fort? I have been saving the knowledge all these years."

"Well, you certainly have a good memory!" He laughed, not quite believing her, but content as she lay nestled in his arms. He decided to change the subject. "They say the railroad will be joined late next spring."

"I know. I've been thinking about it."

"Todd will be seven. That may not be quite old enough to—"

"He will simply have to adjust to it. I couldn't bear being under the same roof every day with Carter. Not now, if I ever could. The few times he's been here during the last two years have been almost unbearable, even sleeping in separate rooms. Do you have any idea how many deaths that man and Crocker are responsible for? Hundreds. Perhaps thousands. Men crushed, blown to bits by dynamite and that new liquid they're using."

"Nitroglycerin."

"Hanging by ropes down sheer cliffs, falling to their deaths. All for an extra mile of track, a day's lead on the railroad coming west from Chicago. I despise him! All of this!"

It was time to change the subject again. "I have a surprise for you."

"Tell me!"

"I'll be moving over to the Sacramento court for a spell come the first of the year."

"How wonderful!"

"We'll have to be discreet."

"I'll sneak over at midnight, just the way I did when you were waiting for me in the barn in Ohio."

"Sneak over where? I'll be in some hotel. It won't be that simple with people about."

Esther propped herself up on one arm, staring past Alex out through a window at the ships in the harbor. She estimated a third of them had brought iron, rails, coal, lumber, locomotives, and cars built in the east for the Central Pacific's lethal battle with the mountains. "I'll sell you my house," she mumbled absently. "At a reasonable price, of course."

"Why should you sell me this house?"

She came back to the present. "Not this one. The one in Sacramento. I've been thinking of getting rid of it anyway. It's been empty for more than two years."

"Marvelous. I'll probably make a profit on it when I move back to San Francisco."

"When *we* move back," she said, touching him, bringing the physical part of him she loved most back to life quickly. "And we begin a new life together."

She had scarcely even thought of Mosby for two years. When she read that he had been defeated for reelection in Nevada, she wondered briefly whether he would return to the South or stay in Virginia City. For an hour she daydreamed about seeking him out, having him killed, but then she dismissed dwelling on it. She was too happy, too hopeful to go back to that state of mind permanently. Sooner or later, she reminded herself, God would make him pay for all he had done.

For a time she felt almost as if she had returned to her girlhood. On her trips to San Francisco she had to be careful about being seen with Alex. She experienced almost an adolescent excitement when she spent an extra day in the city before returning to Sacramento, covertly sitting in the gallery of Alex's courtroom and watching him at work. Perched there, high above the bench and the jury box, hidden, she thought, by other spectators, she was thrilled by the contrast between her casual outward appearance and the tingling, illicit pleasure of being so close to Alex in public.

"You think I don't know you've been sitting up there in the gallery, don't you?" he said, carrying in a block of ice for the new cooling box she had bought for her San Francisco house.

"Why, I—"

"Six months in the workhouse for long-distance lust over a judge." He laughed. "Now, what's for dinner?"

"Bread and water for me, roast beef for you, your honor."

"Sentence suspended. By the way, do you have to leave tomorrow?"

"I should. It's stretching things enough getting back to the school on Tuesday."

"Too bad. I'll be trying an interesting case."

"Oh?"

"Some woman, one of those ladies who flit around the stock exchange looking for tips and then capital-izing—"

"A female curb-broker."

"Right. One of them is trying to capitalize on a night or two in bed with Billy's partner, William Sharon."

"I don't like that man."

"Well, that doesn't justify some woman taking him to the races, does it?"

"Who is she?"

"I know what you're thinking. But it isn't Katherine McDonnell. Wouldn't that have been a twist? I haven't seen her, but the woman's name is Lovell. Marcy Lovell."

Esther decided to stay one extra day, just to see Sharon in an uncomfortable situation and satisfy her curiosity about what his Jezebel looked like. Neither Sharon nor the woman had appeared when the clerk suddenly came out through the door to Alex's chambers and announced that session had been postponed until the following day.

"I had to disqualify myself," Alex said that evening as they sat at her dinner table. "You might as well go on back."

"But why?"

He hesitated for a moment. "I wasn't planning to tell you. But it *is* Katherine McDonnell. I held a conference with the attorneys for both sides just before the session was about to start. She was with her lawyers in the waiting room. You should have seen the look on her face. Both her attorneys resigned the case when I told them I'd disqualify myself and I'd testify against her. I'm not crazy about Sharon, but I'd be derelict if I didn't."

"Do you have to get involved in it? There's sure to be embarrassment for you."

"Not enough to amount to anything. And I'm conscience-bound to do whatever I can now that she knows there's even a possibility that I'll be testifying."

"What do you mean?"

"It's my guess she'll try to find the most persuasive counsel she can lay her hands on."

"Does that matter? Sharon has a good attorney, doesn't he?"

"Damn fool is representing himself. I'm told he practiced law briefly somewhere in the midwest, but he hasn't set foot in a courtroom in fifteen years. If McDonnell gets herself anyone of consequence, he'll wrap Sharon right around his finger."

In his new offices on the fourth floor of the Miner's Exchange Bank on Montgomery Street, Luther Mosby stared down at the picture of "Marcy Lovell" on the front page of the morning newspaper. There was something familiar about the woman, but he could not place her. He had been following her case in the papers; with a deft suggestion or two, he had arranged for her to be referred to him by a former political ally after her lawyers had resigned. He had not been back in San Francisco a month. Representing the woman, no matter what the results of the trial were, could do nothing but help in reestablishing a clientele here.

He sat down and gazed at the full-length picture of Marcy Lovell. Early thirties, he guessed. Wonderful tits; what appeared—under all that goddamned fabric—to be a thoroughbred pair of legs. And God, what a face! *I know her from somewhere, goddamnit!* Looking up, he glanced at the picture of himself in Confederate officer's uniform hanging on the wall opposite his desk. *Won't be too long'n I'll be sixty fuckin' years old. Well, five or six more years, anyway.* He turned his attention back to the picture, feeling stirred as he had not been for years as he studied Marcy Lovell's features. She would be here within a matter of minutes. *Wouldn't be too bad havin' a woman like that around. Save a lot of trouble and effort. I could get rid of that goddamned Chinaman cleans the place. Might cost me less in the long run. Sixty. Goddamnit!*

After she'd arrived and they'd introduced themselves, he caught himself staring at her face for such lengths of time that there were long pauses between his questions.

"Is anything wrong, Judge Mosby?"

He cleared his throat, put totally off-balance by the beginnings of infatuation. "No, you just . . . seem very familiar to me."

"I think I have seen you before, as well, Judge Mosby." She looked down, feigning shyness. "No one could forget such a striking man."

He sensed she might be open to "pursuing things," if the approach was acceptable enough, and he regained some of his confidence. "You've lived in San Francisco all your life?"

"No, I grew up in the midwest, studied there, then came here to seek—a teaching position."

"How long ago was that?"

She glanced past him at the window. "Oh, the mid-'50s, or thereabouts."

"And you think you've seen me before too? When do you suppose it was?" In the midst of his commingling calculations and authentic, incipient feelings for her, he caught a hint that she was being very careful with her answer.

"Many years ago, I would think. Probably when I—first came to San Francisco. You were here then, were you not?"

Mid-'50s. Had to be before the vigilante business. His mind ticked off all the possibilities. He knew somehow that it would be an advantage to know where he had seen her. "Before the War of Secession? Yes. I was here. I was a lawyer then, too—"

"Before your term on the State Supreme Court."

He beamed, his ego temporarily stifling his efforts to recollect. He plunged into it then, as another rush of desire, and—he had never felt, could not precisely identify the additional feelings—something more urged him. "I want you to know that I'll be honored to take your case, Miss Lovell. Honored. It's time a man stood by you."

"Why, judge, how—"

"I want you to know something else. I want to be completely honest with you from the start."

"Yes, judge?"

"Please call me Luther. I want you to know—it's hard for me to say this—that there's more than my wanting to see justice done in this case." He rushed on. "That . . . this has never happened to me with a client . . . that I'm . . . taken with you, Miss Lovell. Honorably taken. And when all this is over . . ."

"Judge—Luther, you don't have to say another word. I want you to know that I, too, have been experiencing . . . feelings . . . since I walked in this door." She was certain now that he did not recognize her, could not possibly remember her from the

few days she had been at Arabella Ryan's, before
the fire, just after arriving in San Francisco. He had
looked at her once or twice in the parlor, on the way
upstairs with the Oriental girl. But he had never
been with her, never been closer than ten or twelve
feet away.

Mosby stood up, walked around his desk, leaned
over gallantly, and took her gloved hand. "I think this
is the start of something much bigger than your case
against Mr. Sharon."

When she was gone, he remembered. She could
not have been more than sixteen or seventeen, fresh
off the train when Arabella picked her up. He would
never tell her he knew, never use it obviously. God,
she was beautiful. And unless she was playing him,
she was ripe for the long-term alliance he had in
mind. Well, he might not use the knowledge so she
would know it, but he might damn well press her
a bit, carefully, so that he could begin enjoying her
long before "all this is over."

Worked her way up, just the way I did, he thought.
*Well, what the hell. From what I've heard, some of
them make damn good wives.* He smiled as he thought
about how skillful she would be.

The case was postponed again until mid-September. During the three weeks Esther was back in Sacramento, she decided to be in court if Alex took the
stand. Sharon was confident that would not be necessary, and at Ralston's urging he agreed not to call
upon Alex unless he was certain he would otherwise
lose the case. The week before Esther returned to
San Francisco, Alex wrote to tell her Katherine McDonnell had indeed found herself the powerful lawyer she needed. He did not mention the new lawyer's name, but he was certain Sharon would need
his testimony in the face of the man's prominence and

expertise. He suggested that Esther remain in Sacramento, considering the "circumstances."

She quickly made arrangements for a substitute teacher at the school and gave Solana enough money to cover expenses while she was gone. She did not understand what Alex meant by "circumstances" until she took her place in the court gallery the morning the trial began.

She was early; in another twenty minutes the spectators would jam the rest of the balcony, eager for the circus they expected the case to be. As she sat there, she pondered the effect Alex's testimony would have on both of them should he have to take the stand. All hope that he would not sank in eddies of hatred and fear fifteen minutes later, when Luther Mosby, wearing only a moustache again, rather than Lincolnesque chin whiskers, walked to the defense-counsel conference table with Katherine McDonnell on his arm.

Outwardly it seemed obvious even at a glance that Mosby was smitten with her. And that, authentically or not, she was displaying far more than the feelings of a client. As the courtroom and gallery filled, Katherine McDonnell repeatedly made physical contact with Mosby. In turn, he leaned close, whispered, laid his hand on hers, reached out and gently removed a speck of soot from her cheek, and generally kept every man who approached to a distance of at least a yard.

The judge who had replaced Alex quickly brought the court into session. Sharon railed for half an hour, repeating himself, and displaying a singular lack of humility and a glaring insensitivity toward the members of the jury during his opening statement.

The jurists were all middle-class merchants; most of them, Esther guessed, were likely to have taken part in and been burned by the artificially induced fluctuations of the Comstock market. She shuddered, then felt a sense of hopelessness as she watched Mosby walk calmly over to the jury and shake hands with each man.

"Gentlemen," Mosby said, turning on the mellifluous, grammatically precise voice he had developed for the courtroom and pausing theatrically. "No matter what our political persuasions, I want you to know I have great respect for men like you. You are the people who make this country what it is."

Esther caught a movement at the back of the courtroom and saw Alex slip in and sit down in a chair held for him by one of his marshals.

Mosby paused again. He smiled warmly, with just enough restraint to be convincing, at each member of the jury. Then he walked forward to the end of the jury box nearest the witness chair and leaned almost casually on the railing.

"Gentlemen, I don't have to spend a half hour and ten thousand words stating the realities of this case. It is a simple matter of breach of promise, in writing, by a man we all know has broken hundreds of promises—not to mention lives—in the past. I do not have to recount the deceits, the savage acts of greed the defendant has engaged in while manipulating the Comstock market for his own profit. You may not know that he is now a silent partner in the Bank of California, that he enriches himself personally every time he sends another man home to his family penniless or on the verge of suicide. But I trust a majority of those sitting in this jury box, perhaps half of the people in this courtroom have been, directly or indirectly, victims of the plaintiff's heartless disregard of fairness and honesty."

Mosby walked over to where Katherine McDonnell was sitting. "Gentlemen, here is another of his victims. A woman, chaste when she met him, a woman honest and courageous enough to earn her own daily bread alongside men in the rough-and-tumble of the stock exchange. A woman with mettle enough to stand up to a man with a thousand times her means. A woman seduced and despoiled after being promised the sanctity and safety of marriage—in writing."

In a calculated action, Mosby walked half the distance back to the jury and stopped. He looked at the floor and shook his head. "Gentlemen, under threats from a place so respected in our judicial system I cannot believe them, this poor woman's original lawyers abandoned her. They were cowards and fools. You do not have to be a former State Supreme Court Justice to know an open-and-shut case when you see it. You do not need much courage to stand pat with three aces when a knave is bluffing."

Mosby turned and stared confidently at William Sharon. "Oh, the defendant will attempt to establish that his hollow promise is a forgery. But we know, do we not, what falsehoods he has put his signature to in the past."

Mosby turned and looked back over the heads of the spectators and witnesses to where Alex sat. Remembering Alex from the morning "Todd Alexander" punched him out at the hotel, Mosby glared for a moment. *Better no one knows I have any animosity toward him in the unlikely event he testifies*, Mosby thought, and quickly turned away. "The defendant may also call upon a witness of outwardly impeccable reputation to besmirch further this good woman's name. But—should he do that—we will show, through cross-examination, the testimony of a medical doctor, and—if necessary—a married woman patient . . ." Mosby quickly glanced to his left, and Esther caught sight of Dr. Sims sitting two rows diagonally in front of Alex ". . . just how *peccable*, if you'll excuse the expression, that respected witness's reputation actually is."

Esther stifled a moan as the court broke into restrained laughter.

"In short, gentlemen, the defense will prove, point by point, something that you already know. That there is a liar and a thief in this courtroom. A man capable of stopping at nothing, not even the humiliation of a defenseless woman, to get what he wants without paying for it. His base character is so well known to you, I do not even have to speak his name. The merits of the defendant's case are so patently clear, I do not even feel the need to ask you to come to a verdict in favor of this lovely, innocent, physically bankrupted woman. For I know you will be just. Gentlemen, that is all I have to say."

"You were masterful in court today, Luther. Simply masterful."

They were in the rooms registered to Marcy Lovell, after returning from dinner at an out of the way restaurant. He had run out of talk, large or small. "Lawyering isn't what I do best, either."

She looked puzzled but knew exactly what he meant.

"Come here," he said, pulling her toward him and kissing her. He saw the effect on her, gauged that her desire was as strong as his. "I don't want to leave you here alone tonight."

"Luther, it's too soon. What would it look like if anyone found out."

"No one will know," he whispered, kissing her again and brushing a hand across her breasts. He heard her stifle a small, involuntary sound of arousal. "I'll leave before dawn."

He kissed her again.

"Luther—"

"Come here, I said." He pulled her slowly down on a couch, rolled over on top of her, grew more certain of what he was doing when the feel of his genitals on hers made her close her eyes.

"Luther—"

"You want it just as much as I do."

"Yes, but—"

"But nothing. It's not too soon, the way we feel

about each other. We don't have to act like two kids."
And then he heard himself say, "I want to marry you,
don't I?" It shocked him for a moment, but he did
not retract a single word.

"You *can't* testify!" Esther pleaded as they sat in
front of her fireplace late that night. "It will ruin you!"

Alex sighed. "It's not me I'm worried about, Esther. It's you. And I don't see how I can avoid hurting you."

"I don't care a damn what's said about me! There
are other places to live besides San Francisco or the
state capital. But think of what it will do to your
career; think of what you'll be put through!"

"I'll just have to resign."

"But why? Sharon doesn't deserve such sacrifice."

"I no longer have a choice, Esther. I was informed
today that Sharon applied for a subpoena. During
the recess following Mosby's opening statement."

"Oh, God."

"Mosby's in love with her, you know."

"Either that or he wants her badly, for whatever
reasons."

"What an irony. Once, a long time ago, here in
San Francisco, I had an altercation with him. That
time I told you about, when I thought I had seen
you in the street? I beat him pretty badly. Caught
him—abusing—a young woman. I'm sure he must remember."

She pondered telling him that it was a double irony,
then decided not to. She put one arm around him
and gazed into the fire. "You didn't want me to come
at first because of circumstances. You thought it would
stir up grief over Warren."

"Yes. And now there's all the more reason you ought
to go back to Sacramento."

"Why? Mosby will simply issue a subpoena, and
I'll have to come back." All the hatred, all the desire
for revenge was flowing back into her. She wished she

had hired an assassin, had had Mosby killed when it was possible. She wondered for a moment about having it done now, but she knew Alex might easily be implicated. "I will simply have to speed up my plans for leaving Carter. We will take Todd and—"

"You were in the restaurant when Mosby challenged Warren. Do you think he'll recognize you? Not as Esther Carter, but as a friend of Barnett's with an ax to grind."

"I—I don't think so." She hadn't thought of that, hadn't even considered what would happen if Mosby not only remembered her from that night in Sacramento but realized who she actually was. She wondered for a moment whether telling everything to the jury would make any difference if he did. Alex's name would still be tarred, their relationship would still be revealed. Beyond that, it would probably rob her of the opportunity, later, of doing what she now knew she would never abandon again for as long as she lived.

"Perhaps it won't be necessary for me to testify," she whispered, leaning over and pressing her head against Alex's shoulder.

"I hope not. Perhaps I can cover things in such a way—"

"Let's not think about it. If it's necessary, then we'll do it with all the stops pulled out. We'll make a life together somewhere else. Start all over again, just as though you'd never left Bent's Fort and we came west this year."

He put his face in his hands. "I love this place. I wanted to make my life here."

"So did I." She felt the sadness in him as much as her own. *To hell with it,* she thought. *To hell with having my private revenge. If I tell all in the courtroom, Mosby will be as good as dead, anyway. At least in California. God knows if he's still punishable by law for what he did to me. But surely it will ruin him, and Alex will come out of it with sympathy enough to continue on the bench.* She gently massaged his neck. "We'll find a way to stay here. I know we will."

And then she began thinking about what Mosby might do after she had told it all.

Seventy-two

The trial dragged out over an eight-day period. Sharon kept to his word about not calling Alex until it was absolute necessary. From the gallery, Esther watched Mosby outmaneuver Sharon and his witnesses; it was like observing a cat toy with a field mouse. He displayed an artist's representations of Sharon's signature traced and enlarged from a dozen documents. Then, after Sharon objected so stridently the judge threatened to have him removed from the courtroom, Mosby showed each member of the jury the promissory love letter the banker had written to "Marcy Lovell," individually, handing over the letter, waiting patiently until it was read, taking it back, holding it, staring for ten seconds at the jurist who had just read it, and then moving on to another without saying a word.

During the first five days Esther lost all appetite and ability to sleep. Tossing fitfully despite the detective Alex had hired to act as a watchman when she was at the house, she was plagued by expectations that Mosby would kill Alex or have him killed, come climbing through her window to murder her in her bed. As each day passed, her hatred for Mosby rose to the levels it had reached in the years before Alex returned from the war. Yet each day she grew more certain that Mosby would not strike at them during the trial. He knew there was no need to as he demolished every claim Sharon made, thwarted every one of his strategies in the certainty that the banker would never bring a scandal down on Ralston's best friend by calling Alex to the stand.

By the time the second week of the trial opened, Sharon had turned his case over to another attorney. Alex had not been asked to testify, and Sims had remained in his seat at the rear of the courtroom. Ralston was nowhere to be seen. Mosby had never even glanced up toward where Esther sat. There had been no mention of her, no suggestion that anyone but Alex knew she was sitting in the gallery, and there had been no word of a subpoena being delivered to her home in Sacramento. As the clerk called the court to order, she wondered if Sharon would take a new tack. But then his lawyer stood up and intoned, "The prosecution calls Judge Alexander Todd."

Esther glanced at Mosby. He had his hand on Katherine McDonnell's arm—Esther could never think of her as Marcy—as Alex was sworn in. There was a look of shock on his face, then wrath as he pulled his hand back and let it drop beneath the conference table strewn with notepads. It was clear from the sequence of expressions that Mosby never dreamed his own efficacy in the courtroom would push Sharon to approve this costly, desperate move; and that he fully understood Alex's testimony would seal the case against the woman he loved and make the two of them the laughingstock of San Francisco.

"You are acquainted with the plaintiff, Marcy Lovell?" Sharon's lawyer began.

"Yes."

"Would you please state to the court under what circumstances you met her, and what that acquaintance led to during the year prior to your departure for service in the Union Army?" Sharon's lawyer turned, placed his fragile-looking fingertips together, and started slowly toward Mosby and Katherine Mc-Donnell. Even before Alex began his answer, there was a look of knowing superiority written all over the lawyer's face.

Alex cleared his throat. "I was introduced to Miss Lovell—she called herself Katherine McDonnell then —by a friend who was slightly acquainted with her. Within the space of a month, Miss—McDonnell instituted a fraudulent—"

"You mealy-mouthed, lying son of a bitch!" Mosby shouted at the top of his lungs, lifting the conference table in front of him and flipping it over on its side with an earsplitting crash. "You'll never have the chance to foul this woman's name." The crazed sound of Mosby's voice paralyzed Esther. He rushed forward, hurdling a leg of the table and bowling Sharon's diminutive attorney over as he ran straight at Alex. She caught sight of the bowie knife, and gasped as two marshals finally stopped him a yard short of the witness chair.

Alex recoiled involuntarily.

"*You sniveling, cowardly bastard!*" Mosby screamed as the marshals wrestled with him and locked tightly on the hand holding the knife. "*I'll kill you for this!*" Freeing his left arm, Mosby leaned forward and reached out, grabbing Alex's shirtfront and pulling him forward. "*You're not worthy even to look at a woman like Katherine McDonnell!*"

The crowd, silent after a shocked, audibly collective intake of breath, broke into an uproar that drowned out the judge's startled gaveling. The marshals dragged Mosby away from the witness box and struggled to pull the knife from his hand. For a moment Esther was immobilized by fear and rage. Then she jumped up and ran down several steps to the gallery railing, looking for a way to climb down into the courtroom. It was impossible. She looked at Mosby, saw him spit at Alex and then almost break loose again as one marshal tried to pull his arms behind his back. She turned and raced up to the gallery exit, rushed down the hall and the stairs, and pushed through the door to the courtroom.

A sheriff was assisting the marshals now as they hauled Mosby toward the door to an anteroom. She saw Katherine McDonnell moving slowly toward Alex with her hand hovering over her partially open purse. Esther shoved through a half-dozen people, eluded the clutches of another peace officer, scrambled, then fell over the railing separating the crowd from the bench and the witness chair. Katherine McDonnell had almost reached Alex as Esther regained her footing, rushed forward, and caught up with her.

"*You no-good bastard!*" Katherine McDonnell shrieked. She shoved her right hand into her purse and grasped something just before Esther threw herself into the woman and drove her back against the judge's bench. Moving fast, Alex climbed over the rail in front of the witness chair and pulled Esther up off Mosby's dazed lover. A marshal raced over to them as the judge continued to pound his gavel and call for order.

"Marshal, this woman is a friend," Alex said quickly. "She acted only out of concern for my safety. Please take her, carry her if you have to, back into chambers, and stay with her until I join you."

After they had locked up Katherine McDonnell as well as Mosby and the trial had been recessed, Alex collected Esther and insisted on driving her home.

"That was a foolish thing to do," he said when they had ridden in silence for ten minutes. "You could have been hurt."

"I wanted to kill her."

"My God, what a temper." He laughed. "You would have done that just to save me a lump on my head?"

"She had something in her purse. A gun. Something."

"Perhaps you're right. She did request that a woman friend take her purse just before she was removed."

"I *hate* them. Hate both of those vile—"

He reined the carriage to a halt. "Wait a minute, wait a minute! Take it easy, Esther."

"I'd like to kill both of them."

"Easy . . . easy." He put his arms around her, and she pushed her face into his shirt as she finally began sobbing.

"He . . . he . . . he . . . might have killed you."

"They'll take that into account at his trial."

"They . . . they'll put him away? Lock him up?"

"No doubt about it."

She wiped her nose with the handkerchief in his breast pocket. "And her?"

"Contempt, at least. Assault for Mosby."

"They should both be put in prison for the rest of their lives."

Alex brushed Esther's hair out of her eyes. "Well, I doubt they'll do that. But I'm sure he'll be convicted and given a stiff sentence."

He leaned over and kissed at her moist cheeks, then her mouth. "You really must love me to do something like that."

"Have you ever doubted it?"

He looked at her and smiled. "Doubted?" He thought carefully for a moment, then laughed again. "No, I've had a few questions. But I guess I've never really doubted it. In any case, if I had, the doubts would be over now."

She pulled close to him again, grateful that she could feel his warmth, the strong beat of his heart. "I know what some of those questions might be, Alex. Someday—not now, not anytime soon—I will answer all of them for you. And when I do, you will understand many things and love me just as though we were never apart."

He kissed her softly. "But I do now."

"Then perhaps you'll even love me more."

"That's not possible," he whispered, cradling her head in his hands. "Not in this life, anyway."

Seventy-three

Mosby represented himself when he was brought up on charges of aggravated assault and contempt. Held at the courthouse jail without bail during the hours court was not in session, he proposed, then arranged to be married to Katherine McDonnell in his cell. Newspapers seized on the romance and argued profitably over the merits of leniency for Mosby. The trial took only two days. Mosby pleaded loss of his senses under the provocation of defending the woman he loved. There were four Southerners on the jury. To them he pleaded additionally, "on the basis of his record in the late war." The rest of the panel he wooed with reminders of his years of creditable service as a Supreme Court Justice and U.S. Senator. In terms of gaining sympathy, the marriage had been a masterstroke. Additionally, there was rumor that two of the jurors had been bought off. Out of greed, compassion, allegiance, or a combination of all three, he was found guilty of only simple assault and contempt. Under existing statutes, the maximum sentence was six months in the Alameda County jail.

Katherine McDonnell fared even better. She had dropped her charges against Sharon, and the silver baron decided it would serve his interests better if he let it all blow over quietly. A suit for fraud would only keep his name in the wrong columns of the papers. As a result, Katherine McDonnell could be tried only for contempt. A second jury, softened by a continuing series of sentimental newspaper articles, found her guilty but also recommended leniency. She was sentenced to ninety days in a cell at Alameda overlooking the exercise yard where Mosby strolled every day.

Now, with McDonnell free and Mosby's sentence about to expire, Esther read an article quoting his reiteration of one thing he had professed in court:

"The threat I made to Judge Todd was born of passion and the heat of the moment. I bear no malice toward Judge Todd, plan no retaliation against him. What I said should be taken in light of circumstances. My only wish is to return peacefully to society. I am a chastened man. I wish only to work to reverse my disbarment, and I once again offer Judge Todd my most sincere apology."

Esther did not believe a word of it. She knew Mosby too well. Sooner or later he would attempt to gain satisfaction. He might wait for years, but as long as he lived, she knew Alex would not be safe. It didn't matter that Alex had arranged to have his tour of duty on the bench in Sacramento extended. There was scarcely a place on earth a man like Mosby could not reach to get at Alex if he wanted to. She was as certain of that as she was about the necessity to cut Mosby off first. She no longer cared how it was done—by her, by someone else—just as long as it was accomplished without implicating her. It was late March 1869. In a little more than six months she would be forty years old. She wanted to spend whatever years she had left with Alex. The railroad was due to be completed in early May. She glanced again at the front page of the *Sacramento Bee* and ran her finger down the list of those invited to ride the Pacific Union Express to the golden-spike ceremony commemorating the joining of the Union and Central Pacific railroads somewhere in Utah. She stopped tracing when she came to Alex's name.

The irony of it made her smile. When Alex came back from the trip, he would be coming home to her. When Bull Carter returned, he would find only the legal papers requesting a formal separation, along with her note suggesting that she would sign over all their jointly held stock in the railroad if he did not contest a divorce. As embarrassing as that might be, she didn't think Carter would object, considering the extent of the benefits. All that remained to be dealt with was the threat Mosby posed. She did not know yet how she would go about it, but she guessed she had time enough to come up with a plan. Possibly, she thought, someone she might meet in circumstances that would not reveal her identity. Such a person might be persuaded by enough money to come up with a plan of his own. A quarter of the money in advance, the remainder would be too much to forego.

She doubted Mosby would attempt anything for at least six months after he was released. He was too shrewd to risk that, too cunning not to take the time to establish an elaborate, watertight alibi for himself.

She relaxed a bit, fairly certain she would find the proper person to do it. Methodically, she began making a list of the names of those who might be willing, even eager. She thought of going to the Sacramento courthouse to record all the defendants to whom Mosby's decisions had caused great damage. Then she remembered the man he had stabbed the day Murietta died. An auctioneer, he had been left mute by the wound, and she had heard he'd fallen on extremely hard times. She was pondering ways to reach and meet with the man covertly when events suddenly began pulling her in another direction entirely.

She jumped involuntarily as the sharp sound of someone knocking on the front door reached the kitchen. Mosby had been free for almost a week, and as sure as she was that he would not attempt anything so soon, she had been quaking and trembling each time someone arrived at her house, each time Alex was even a few minutes late.

"You stay here and finish your lunch, Todd," she said to her son, waving a finger. "No cookies until you've eaten that sandwich and finished that milk, do you understand?"

The boy nodded obediently, then went straight to the cookie jar when he heard her talking to someone in the foyer.

"My, what a surprise," she exclaimed, concealing her distaste. "I thought you . . . were out at the railhead. I never imagined you'd be back in Sacramento before the ceremony next month."

Charles Crocker seemed speechless for the first time in his life. He glanced at the mirrored seat-chest in the hallway. "You'd better sit down," he said, nervously revolving his hat by its brim. "I have some bad news."

She could not imagine why Crocker would be telling her of anything that might have happened to Alex. Her entire body suddenly felt empty. "All right, perhaps I'd better," she heard herself say. "What is it?" She clenched her hands, expecting the worst as Crocker started once, stumbled, then began again.

"I'm not much good with words at a time like—I better just—your husband. There's been a terrible accident. We were laying track parallel to the Union Pacific bunch. Competing. I know that sounds crazy, but there's been no order about where and when we stop and join up. The pranks started about three weeks ago. They were trying to outdo one another, the crews. There's no love lost between them, and things got out of hand. Badly out of hand." Crocker paused. "Someone from our gang set fire to their paymaster's car. They got angry as hell and buried bottles of nitro where we were scheduled to lay track three days ago. The whole damn thing went up when we set down the first two sections, killed a dozen men. I'm afraid Bull was one of them."

She sat silently for a moment, letting it sink in. Then suddenly one part of her wanted to laugh, another to cry, and a third not to respond at all.

"Will he go to heaven?" Todd asked from the doorway leading into the dining room. He was still munching on a chocolate cookie.

She burst out crying then, not for Carter, although she did not wish him dead, but for the boy.

"He's in heaven right now, son," Crocker said. He walked over to the child and rubbed his tousled hair. "He's up there right now building a railroad for Jesus."

"Then he'll be happy," the seven-year-old said matter-of-factly. He turned on his heel and went back into the kitchen for another cookie.

"You want me to stay while you talk to the boy?" Esther shook her head.

"I'm sorry, Mrs. Carter. Really sorry. Is there anything I can do for you?"

She shook her head again, crying silently.

"I'll have Mrs. Crocker look in on you. Will that be all right?"

"Yes," Esther whispered.

"Well, if you'll forgive me, I'd better be going. Got to get back out there. Trip'll take a few days, you know."

"It's all right. I understand."

Todd came back and put his arms around his mother. "Don't cry, mommy. You know what daddy always said. We all got to die sometime." He turned to Crocker. "It don't hurt when you die, does it?"

"Doesn't, son. No, it doesn't hurt." He turned, walked to the door, then paused and turned around. "We'll be driving the golden spike next month, son. If you'd like to come, I'll arrange it for your mother and you to be there. I think your father would have liked that." He thought for a moment. "If you want, you can ride all the way to Utah in the locomotive with Mister Sam."

The boy's mouth dropped open, and his eyes grew wide. "You mean that? In the *locomotive?*"

"I certainly do, son. You know Mister Sam, don't you?"

"Sure I do."

Crocker walked back to Esther and placed his hand on her shoulder. "Of course, it'll be up to your mother. . . . If you feel up to it by then, Mrs. Carter, I will see that my private car is at your disposal." He went back to the door and again said, "I'm sorry about all this."

"Thank you," she said, wiping her eyes and getting up.

"You're a brave woman, Mrs. Carter. I have to leave now. I hope I see you at the ceremony. It's true, you know. I think your husband *would* have wanted you to come."

The reverberating, double irony of Crocker's words did not become fully apparent until a week later, when John Sutter called on her unexpectedly and asked her to accompany him to dinner. She was puzzled as well as delighted that he was back from Washington for an appearance at the golden-spike ceremony. She had seen him occasionally in Sacramento through the years, but rarely for dinner. When he had come to her house, it was usually to let her know he needed money, to refuse help when she offered it, and then to write back gratefully from the Hock Farm when she sent the funds by mail. He had paid back some of the money during the last two decades, but the last time he came to see her after the close of the Civil War, vandals had set the main house of the Hock Farm ablaze, and he was desperate. This time he didn't have the same woebegone look in his eyes. He said nothing to indicate he was hard-pressed. Still, there was a hint of urgency in his voice.

"As usual, you're concealing something from me until the right moment," she said after they picked up Solana at the school and left young Todd with her. "What is it?"

"I told you. I want to take you to dinner. After all you have done for me, my child, is that so strange?"

"But there is more to it than that, isn't there?"

He laughed, but his face quickly resumed an expression of poorly concealed apprehension. "You are one of the most intuitive people I have ever known," he said, suddenly reining his buckboard toward Sacramento's Chinese quarter. "Yes, there is something more. I want you to listen to something someone told me yesterday."

"Who, for goodness sake? Why all the mystery?"

"Lewis Keseberg."

"Keseberg? For God's sake, John! He's one of the last people on earth I'd want to talk to."

"You won't have to talk to him. Just listen. I think you will want to hear what he has to say."

"That he didn't murder anyone at Donner Lake? At this point, I don't care if he did or not. He's done enough since—that restaurant, for one thing—to turn my stomach."

"Be charitable, Esther. I have stayed in touch with the poor man since they tried him at the fort. No matter what he did, he has more than paid for it. I have befriended him through the years, out of pity. Now I am glad I did, and you will be, too, when you hear what he has to say."

They pulled up in front of an unpainted pine building at the end of a row of shanties. Chinese in pigtails, baggy pantaloons, and broad, straw sunhats stared at Esther as though she were the first white woman they had ever seen. She noticed a man weave out of the weatherbeaten pine house with a glazed look in his eyes. Another two went inside in quick succession.

"Wait here," Sutter told her. "I will bring him out. He is usually here at this time of day."

"It's an opium den, isn't it?"

"Yes."

"I want to come with you."

He started to object, but he saw that look in her eyes and decided he was too old to argue with anyone so strong-willed. "Come," he said. "They will not like it, but I doubt they will throw you out."

Inside, only the light from a few candles illuminated the hallway as a diminutive Chinese led them past a succession of tiny rooms lined with double-tier bunk beds. Men and women, some of them white, reclined on bare, ticking-covered straw mattresses, smoking pipes. A cloying aroma filled the hallways, making it difficult for Esther to breathe.

Sutter peered into several rooms, finally found Keseberg, and pulled him up off his mattress as though he was also made of straw. He seemed to glide, float next to Sutter as the old man guided him out, nodded down the hallway to Esther, and then steered Keseberg toward a thin rectangle of pale light coming through the outline of a rear door.

Sutter propped him up against a shed covering stairs to the building's cellar.

"Tell me again what you told me at the Hock Farm about Judge Todd."

"Judge Todd, he is a good man." Keseberg's head lolled.

When Sutter tilted his face up, Esther tried to remember what Keseberg had looked like when he was young. All she could recall was a bulkiness of body, and that he had been fair and somewhat handsome. The man standing before her on rubbery knees bore no resemblance to the Keseberg she had known. Thin, hollow under the eyes, spittle forming on the corners of his mouth, it was all he could do to keep from falling over.

"Tell me, Lewis. I would not disturb you unless it was important. You know that. I am your friend."

"He is a good man. I voted for him."

"And what else did you hear? About Judge Todd?"

"Kill him. They going to kill him."

"*Who*, Lewis? *Who* said that?"

"Tall man with moustache. I don't now . . . The man with moustache hit me . . . give me this." He turned his head and pointed to a purple bruise in front of his ear. "I joost make mistake. I forget . . . girls are upstairs. I joost make mistake. I don't know they in room . . . no close on . . . with three woman."

Sutter let him go back inside. "He was in a place like this about two blocks from here. There was another man in the room, apparently also a Southerner. Occasionally, Lewis shows up at the Hock Farm. He did yesterday, and when I asked him about the mark on his face, he told me what he overheard before stumbling against the door and crashing in on them."

"My *God!*" Esther said.

"Do you have any idea who this tall man might be?"

She stared past Sutter for a moment, then said, "No. Not the faintest idea. I've got to tell Judge Todd."

Sutter looked at her, recalling the newspaper accounts of the Sharon trial, remembering Mosby and Barnett, hoping she would say more. When she didn't, he took her arm and started around the side of the house toward the waiting buckboard. At the end of the alley, just before they stepped into the street, he stopped and turned to her. "My God," he said, shaking his head. "How could I forget? Lewis said the man mentioned Utah. That they would kill him in Utah."

Seventy-four

Aboard the *Pacific Union Express*
May 7, 1869
2:20 P.M.

Esther closed the diary as the five-car train sneaked
around the final portion of a narrow wedge cut into
the sheer face of an immense mountain. She glanced
at the invitation, no doubt sent and signed by Charles
Crocker for all four men responsible for this gleaming ribbon of steel so brazenly thrust through terrain
that had once barely offered purchase even to an
eagle. *Their work,* she thought. The ribbon and the
agony of so many who worked on it. Death was no
stranger to these tracks. An army of Chinese, "Crocker's Pets," had virtually clawed and picked with their
bare hands into the ice-cloaked mountain just past,
hundreds of them never to see the lush green paddies
of their homeland again.

She wondered how many of these laborers had
fallen or been blown off that ledge, when it was just
a series of chalk marks on a giant granite blackboard,
dotted with scores of men dangling a thousand feet
in the air on all too fragile ropes; how many Bull
Carter, the other supervisors, foremen, or more favor-
ably treated Caucasian workers had put a bullet
through over the slightest provocation. Disquieting as
the thought was, it gave her a measure of comfort.

What she hoped to do to Mosby was in a different category entirely.

Cursing the years she had slowed and then abandoned her pursuit, then remembering her revived determination, she turned back to her journal.

Sacramento
April 10, 1869

Oh, God, despite hours of pleading, nothing I say to Alex is any use. I know his promise to carry a weapon to Promontory is merely a sop to appease me. He does not believe Mosby would be so foolish as to take revenge upon him surrounded by so many. He does not realize the merits of my theory that Mosby will not strike the killing blow, that an accomplice or two or more will do it at the very moment Alex and everyone else would least expect such a thing. At the height of the ceremony, for example, when the crowd is roaring, the band and the train whistles drowning out all other sound. Or in a saloon, on a pretext, Mosby far enough away and with enough prestigious companions to preclude complicity.

Alex points to the fact that Mosby smiled at him! In the Tehama Theater the other night, and then came over and shook hands with him. Well, I know differently. I know that he and his political cronies have won over Governor Stanford to the degree that Mosby will be reinstated to the bar. I cannot believe what money can do! No doubt that among the public so sharply divided on Mosby there are those who not only sympathize with him but contributed to Stanford's campaign, or lent the railroad money in the lean early years, as even Ralston did. They have obviously won Stanford over, called in their favors. Mosby's name on the revised list of those invited to ride the Pacific Union Express is evidence enough of that.

Well, I too have accepted Crocker's invitation, and at least Sutter will be on board the train. I have slightly less than three weeks to decide if Sutter will play a role, and also to devise the means to put bullet, blade, or poison into Mosby's despicable frame, develop the manner in which I dispose of the body, and come out of it not only alive but unsuspected. Three weeks. I must think carefully.

No doubt Claussen is already in Utah, awaiting the final moments. Fearing and beholden to Mosby. More likely enslaved in a subtle way. He must hate that. What would he do if Mosby does not arrive? Go on with it, one would guess. I need to find a way to prevent Alex from reaching there as well. What will he do if neither Mosby nor Alex arrives in Promontory? Return to California? Await further instructions? Yes. And when he realizes Mosby has disappeared, may be dead, he will probably not only withdraw but rejoice.

The parlor car. The train. Across the Sierras. Over the pass and by Donner Lake. It will come to me. It has to. And it must be before we reach Utah. Mosby is untouchable here, too many at the Sacramento Hotel where he stays. The train. The train. Somehow it must be on the train. Must go again to Carter's office, study once more the maps, the notes, the timetables. Three weeks. Oh, God, I must find a way.

Dutch Flat
May 7, 1869
2:30 P.M.

Esther put on her veiled hat, raised the shade beside her, and eased the window up a bit more. Across the tracks several children played in the midafternoon shadows of an idle railroad sawmill, indifferent to the fanfare along the other side of the train and the passengers who had detrained during the half-hour station stop. She crossed the aisle of the car, looked

out and searched for Alex. She couldn't see him for
the swirl of miners and railroad men who crowded
around the forward cars. Beyond the station and central buildings of the mining town, houses perched on
the mountains that rose almost vertically from the
hollow where Dutch Flat lay.

Mosby was standing there, just below the window,
alone, when she went back to her seat. Casually, to
anyone else just out for a leisurely smoke, he stood
loose-limbed, with his back to the parlor car.

She leaned closer to the partially open window.
"One hour and five minutes after the train leaves
Dutch Flat, Mr. Mosby."

He nodded.

"And no earlier. The doors will be locked until precisely that time. And remember, no one must see you
come. Go forward, then back by the roofs. I will open
only the rear door." She caught her breath. "You will
love the danger, *won't* you?"

He shrugged and turned slowly, never looking at
her, then walked back around the rear of the parlor
car.

Certainly Katherine McDonnell had told Mosby
about her connection with Alex. So Mosby undoubtedly knew who she was. But he could not possibly
know she was Elizabeth Purdy Todd. That was what
mattered. She guessed he would wait until he'd taken
her physically before gloatingly revealing he knew
her identity. And that would give her time enough.

Solana waved to young Todd, then slowly worked
her way back through the noisy crowd in front of
the rude station. No one paid any attention to her.
At the rear of the first passenger unit, she paused for
a second, looked about, saw the trainmen had their
backs to her, then climbed the stairs. Crossing the
metal platform, she quickly went down the steps on
the other side and onto the gravel between the two
sets of tracks. Turning left, she walked back along

the side of the second passenger car, slowly, close to it, directly under the windows. She did not look up.

At the rear of the second passenger car she glanced up at the platform but kept walking. She knew exactly where she was going. Reaching the gap between the third passenger car and the parlor unit, she looked up and stopped. The large equipment bin was on the outer side of the forward platform on the private car. Just as she had noted the day before, its lid was upright, latched to the forward wall of the parlor car itself.

She turned, saw the boys playing in the sawmill near the saw-toothed blade of a buzz saw. They disappeared behind a shed wall for a moment, larking, chasing one another. Glancing down, she gauged the size of the train's enormous wheels. Taking two steps backward, she crouched, spun around, and waddled underneath the last passenger car and pressed herself out of sight behind one wheel.

She peered out. The boys were in sight again, whirling around a wooden column under the gable of the sawmill. No one had seen her. She glanced up and looked for a handhold. She knew she would have to move quickly, or she would either die or be left behind. As far as she was concerned, one would be as bad as the other.

As the last passengers reboarded, Luther Mosby waited on the track side of the second car, out of sight. When he heard the forward door close, he pulled himself up onto the steps of the leading platform and crouched, hidden to anyone in the car or along the sides of the train. He guessed the trainmen were aboard by now, leaning out and checking along the station side. As soon as the train rolled, he would rise, cross to the first car, back in casually, and wait in the lavatory until he heard the increased roar as the head trainman opened the door and went forward to his seat. There were two of them. Mosby saw no reason, short of an emergency, why either would be out on the nearby platform again.

Solana started moving a second after she heard the trainmen call out "Awwwwwwlllbooooooord." Her joints creaking, every muscle in pain, she swung left on a chassis beam, cleared the housing, then scuttled as best she could across wood and steel until she was beyond the outside rail. She glanced across at the sawmill. The boys were lined up, gazing forward toward the locomotive. They had not seen her. She heard the train lurch forward, thought briefly of what would have happened if she had been pinned underneath one of the shrieking wheels. Suddenly the boys shouted and began racing to catch up with the engine.

Fear limbered her. She rose quickly, turned and ran, trundling awkwardly, to the ladder beside the rear platform of the last passenger car. Swinging up, she held on until the sudden, exertive pain in her right arm subsided, then edged back and climbed over the platform railing. She stood there motionless, out of breath, her head bent down, until she heard the shouts of the young boys grow louder, then fade as the train picked up speed and left them behind. She moved quickly then, crossed the collapsible metal lips above the coupling and looked into the equipment bin. Five flares and a lantern lay on a piece of burlap a quarter of the way down from the rim. She pulled the burlap up and saw well-worn picks, shovels, a megaphone, two cases of blasting powder.

She turned, noted the long, curving low trestle the train was approaching. Beneath it, a latticework of wooden beams and piles rose from a partially graded bank of fill on either side. The train bulged outward along the clockwise curve. Even if only at a modest angle, she calculated, the windows to her left and right were temporarily pointed away from her. Quickly she picked up all but one of the pieces of equipment

individually and dropped them down through the
bowels of the trestle onto the sloping mound of fill.

The muffling sound of the train filling her ears,
she climbed into the bin, pulled the burlap up to her
chest, arranged the flares and lantern almost as they
had been, took a knife out of her purse, and quickly
punched a hole in the burlap. Then she curled down
and pulled the material up over her face. When her
heart quieted, she peered up through the small punc-
ture in the fabric. She could see only the gap between
the roofs of the two cars. Afraid to open the rent any
further for fear of being discovered, she wondered
how she would hear anyone proceed rearward across
the two platforms to the parlor-car door.

Swaying slightly as the car oscillated on its wheel-
springs, Esther took one last look at the section of
Charles Crocker's survey map where the tracks ran
in a serpentine line across the twin-breasted carapace
of Calafia Mountain. East of it, the terrain subsided
into a series of ridges, gorges and canyons, eventually
leading to the Donner Pass. Across one of the gorges,
Crocker and his army had erected Long Trestle, a
monumental span three hundred feet high at one
point and almost a half-mile long. She had seen a
picture of it. Either the trestle or the thousand-foot
drop from the single-track bed chiseled along the
north side of Calafia Mountain would do.

Turning, she walked back to the table by her seat,
poured a glass of sherry for herself, and took a sip.
Replacing the glass on the tray, she went back through
the curtains, pulled back one corner of the eiderdown
quilt, picked up the wooden-handled kitchen knife,
and slipped it under the head of the mattress. She
took her late husband's derringer and the partially
empty vial of jequirity powder and went back to the
rear door. Outside on the platform, she opened the
vial, spilled its contents over the railing, then threw
the glass vessel down a steep embankment. Taking

hold of a handgrip, she climbed carefully up onto a railing rung and wedged the derringer into a ribbon of space that ran around the metal skirts of the overhanging roof.

Rocking, she held onto the grip with both hands for a moment, then reached up, banged at the pistol with the heel of her palm, and took hold of it with two fingers. Satisfied that it was secure enough, she slipped her fingers around the handle of the gun. It was a tight fit, but with the trigger housing facing this way and a small portion of the grip protruding from the narrow aperture, she was certain she could pull it free when the time came.

She got down and once again took in the structure of the platform, going over in her mind what she would do here if the poison and the knife could not be employed. A rectangle four by eight feet in size, the platform was enclosed by a railing slightly more than waist-high. Two sets of rungs, the lower one a foot off the platform and the second a foot higher, encircled and reinforced the railing's upright iron rods. The fence was broken only by the latched gate directly over the receding tracks. She would not employ the gate, so she quickly dismissed it from her mind. Where the railings formed a perpendicular angle at the rearmost corners, heavier iron supports ran up through them to the end of the overhanging roof. On the outer side of the rear railing, a cast-iron ladder ran up and curled over to a point where it was bolted to the rear end of the roof.

She walked over, swaying with the train, and took hold of the outer stanchion and then the ladder. Neither budged even a fraction of an inch in her grasp. *Secure enough to hold onto with one hand,* she thought. *He will see that, however risky sitting on the outer railing will seem. He will know, as long as his feet are curled under the bottom rung and he is gripping either the ladder or the corner support as well as the railing with both hands, that the danger of falling off will be minimal.*

Back in her seat, she went over it again. The poison first. And if it does not work or cannot be used for any reason, then the knife. And the knife only if he has taken the poison but it has merely slowed, dulled his senses and ability to react. The platform only if it is necessary. She weighed once more what she would do on the platform. He would be most vulnerable there. Perhaps it would be better to move directly to it whether he had taken the poison or not. She pondered it for another moment. *No, I will proceed as planned, following the three alternatives as things unfold, adapting as circumstances dictate.*

She smiled coldly. She felt toward Mosby the charity of a wasp. The smile faded from her mouth. Wasps could be crushed. Unless they were moving so quickly, so surely, that they could not be caught. She opened the journal and untied the black-ribboned entries again. Rereading these pages, she was sure, would carry her past hatred and into the icy, efficient, eleventh-hour rage beyond it.

South Fork Cabin
July, 1847

Predating these pages. Recording after the fact, as best as I can recall . . .

. . . December 22, 1846 . . .

Separated from the rest of the snowshoe party this day. Down on the west side of the mountain crest, far from the pass. My own fault. Decent motives, but foolish. Willful, ignoring, forgetting that my first responsibility was to John Alexander, then myself, not the two women, who . . .

* * *

She pictured the campsite. The women gone. The indescribable fatigue. The rising fear when she became lost, then the terror when she stumbled on Stanton, dead, frozen in a shell of ice. His boots. The baby. The stick of jerked beef. The note from Mary Graves. The long unbearably cold slog after the other snowshoers. The numbness in her hands. The wish to lie down and let sleep take her away to a warm, gentle place. The snow. The savage, stinging wind. The baby. The rock ledge. Sleeping. Nursing. The baby. The silence. The incredible distance and the forbidding mass of the mountains all around her. The drifts. The snowsquall passing. John Alexander's half-opened eyes. The thinness of her milk as she licked drops off her own gloves. Standing there, no energy in her, unable to go on, even though she knew if she stopped she and the baby would die. And then, the smoke, the top of the ridge, the two men. The baby . . .

Aboard the *Pacific Union Express*
May 7, 1869
3:20 P.M.

Sutter looked through the port into the first car, scanning the passengers. He could not find Mosby. He went in and tried the locked lavatory door, shrugged, and turned back. In the last car he showed the note from Esther to the trainman and passed through to the locked door of the parlor unit.

Solana smelled the smoke from the cigar. For a moment she considered throwing the burlap off and leaping up, but then she heard Esther's voice. She

had peered around the shade and opened the forward
door.

"John . . . you're ten minutes early. And I . . . I
. . . I'm not feeling well. Could we postpone our
visit until we've passed—"

"The lake?"

"Yes." She put her arms around him. "Yes. How
sensitive you are. I'm sure these queasy feelings, memories, will pass once we're on the other side of the
mountains."

"I understand." Sutter started to turn, then hesitated. "Esther—" He took her shoulders in his hands.
"I know how worried you are for Judge Todd's safety.
But . . . please . . . be careful. Don't do anything
foolish."

She mustered a questioning look. "I don't know
what you mean."

Sutter stared at her, thinking. "At Promontory."

She looked away from him just long enough to increase his suspicions. "Of course I won't. What could
I possibly do, in any case? Please . . . can we talk
about this later?"

"Of course. Shall I come back . . ." He paused again,
thinking as he looked past her and saw the open
diary lying on her seat. ". . . when we are approaching
Truckee Meadows?"

"That will be fine."

Solana caught the aroma of Sutter's cigar again
when he came back out of the car and went forward.
She settled, listening, all her senses sharpened, and
stared up through the hole in the burlap. Only ten
minutes had passed when she saw Mosby stop up on
the roof of the last passenger car, pause, look down,
then darken the light of the sun briefly as he jumped
across the four-foot gap.

Inside, Esther did not hear the footsteps on the
roof, the slow turning of the locked rear-door handle

a minute later, or Mosby's soft, mocking laugh. Trembling, she took a sip of sherry and turned another page.

South Fork Cabin
July, 1847

December 25, 1846 (predated)

Came upon Luther Mosby's lean-to in the mountains north of Squaw Peak this day. Thought at first it was a Christmas miracle, the food and the fire gifts from God . . .

. . . The warmth. How cold his eyes are. An Indian. Two of them. Horses. The long ride north, then west, then south. Blood on the snow on the ledge over the ravine where both the horse and the Indian lay dead now at the bottom in the whiteness and the fear and the need to trust and hope. And the baby. Oh, God, the baby. Hold my tongue. The leer in his eyes. The second horse, lying in the snow, its eye staring skyward, blank, above the metal bit covered with ice and blood . . . *"Get up, goddamnit!"* . . . "I can't." No feeling in my nose, two fingers. Nurse the baby. What is he doing? Oh, God, you must not do that! The baby needs it. I cannot move. Cannot keep my eyes open. John Alexander? Why do the sparks fly up over the fire that way? He is untying . . . This is a dream. . . .
Awake . . .
There is John Alexander, sleeping . . .
I will sing to him so he is not afraid . . .
Must go on . . .
Bodies . . .
Four, or is it five? Bodies . . .
Must eat . . .
Must sleep . . .

Must go on . . .
Snow . . .
John Alexander sleeps so peacefully . . .
Squaw Peak . . . ?
A stream . . .
Is this a river . . . ?
I cannot go on . . .
Waterfall . . .
I must go on . . .
I . . . WILL . . . NOT . . . DIE . . .

Seventy-five

Aboard the *Pacific Union Express*
May 7, 1869
3:50 P.M.

She was as ready as she would ever be when the train emerged from a short snowshed and she heard the noise of the rear-door handle. For a moment she was immobilized by sudden fear, but it passed. She took another sip of sherry, collected herself for ten seconds, then put the journal in her bag and snapped it shut. Putting on her hat, she got up and walked back, lurching slightly, to the rear of the car. Her knees were liquid for a moment as she opened the door and Mosby smiled, then gently pushed her backward with his body."

"You're . . . early."

He took out a gold pocket-watch attached to a buttonhole of his vest and glanced at it. "What's the difference?" He moved past her, eyeing the kitchen and pantry, then walked farther and looked at the bed. "So that's what the wonderful contraption looks like."

"I told you all the mysteries would be revealed today." She took deep breaths, slowly, trying not to let him hear. She was stunned by the certainty that the antique watch Mosby was wearing was the one "Uncle" Billy Graves had loaned to her the day she became separated from the snowshoe party in the Sierras.

"A little nervous, are you?" He smiled and sat down on the edge of the bed. "Come here and we'll take care of that."

She walked past him quickly, sidestepping to elude his outstretched arm. "We don't have to rush, Mr. Mosby. There is plenty of time. We—won't be in Reno for some time." She continued through the curtain and sat down in her chair.

"Sometimes rushin' it's all right, too, but have it your way." Mosby came forward and sat down in the chair opposite Esther.

For a moment, as she saw him smile self-confidently, she took in all of his features in detail—the hawk nose, sharp gash of mouth, saber curves of moustache, even the web of fine, thatched lines under his deep, flat, calm reptilian eyes. Evil incarnate. She found herself savoring what she would do to him, how it would feel to see him dead at her feet. From out of nowhere she heard her father's voice from the pulpit, years ago:

"Vengeance is mine, saith the Lord."

She shut the train of thought off, smiled at Mosby, wondering if he could see it through the veil, then responded to the sworl of conscience that was still eddying in her mind.

It will be no different than killing a wolf. A predator who has taken a newborn lamb, let alone more mature creatures. I will have you. No one, not even God would judge revenge as anything but justified in this case.

"Perhaps it would be nice to have a little sherry first," she said.

He glanced at the decanter and glasses and smiled. "Nothin' better to start the juices flowing." When he added, "Here, let me pour," the hair stood up on the back of her neck.

She tried to ignore the increased beating of her heart as he reached toward the tray. She searched for something, anything to say to stop him from doing the pouring himself. "How . . . how was your trip over the roofs?"

He paused, his right hand suspended over the hinged table between them, and looked at her. "Loved it." He smiled and started to move again.

"You have a great curiosity about what I look like, don't you?" she asked, searching frantically now, wondering if she should take the hat and veil off, ask him if he recognized her. It was too risky. If he remembered her, she would never have the chance to set the next steps in motion. If he knew who she really was, not just that she was intimate with Alex Todd, he would have to kill her.

He stopped again. "Sure do. You gonna take that veil off now?"

"No . . . no, not now. I want that to whet your appetite. Here—" She reached toward the tray, but he had already taken hold of the decanter. "There . . . there is an interesting story about my . . . face."

"That so?" He pushed her glass aside. "Ought to drink a toast out of fresh ones, hadn't we?"

Would he recognize me? Would taking the hat and veil off—? It was academic now. She felt her throat constrict as he poured sherry into the glass nearest him and pushed it toward her across the table. She knew if she knocked it over or spilled it, "accidentally" he would know.

"Know what the Romans did, don't you?" He poured a second glass and held it up.

"What . . . what was that?" Her mouth was unbearably dry.

"Always had anyone offerin' 'em wine drink first. Case of poison. Well, anyway, here's to you."

She stared at the glass.

He paused, frowning. "Well? Ain't you going to pick it up?"

On the convex roof, Solana edged slowly toward the rear of the parlor car, carefully placing her steps wide apart. In one hand she held the mountaineer's ice hammer she had left in the equipment bin. Behind her, the locomotive roared toward a long, low-hanging snowshed. She heard the sudden change in the pitch of the engine just as she reached the curving top of the ladder bolted into the roof at the rear of the unit. Turning, she saw the eaves of the snowshed rocketing toward her, four feet above the second passenger car. Dropping instinctively, she flattened out, splaying arms and legs on the roof and holding onto the ladder frame with her free hand. She stayed there, listening to the wild sound of her heart, until the train cleared the shed and the sun gleamed again on the curved, awl-and-pick blade of the ice hammer.

Sutter walked forward and stopped beside the card players in the second car. "Have any of you gentlemen seen Judge Mosby? I would like to speak with him."

One of the men looked up at him. "Take a look up in the next car. He isn't there, he probably got off at Dutch Flat."

Sutter looked puzzled.

"He was havin' some trouble with his stomach."

"Wait a minute," Mosby said, reaching out and lightly grasping Esther's wrist. "Let's do it the way they do in them novels. Here." He pushed his glass past hers and under her veil until it was an inch from her lips. "Now you put yours over here with your arm touchin' mine."

She could not believe her ears. Trembling, she took in a breath and extended her arm.

"Now, don't you spill it on my pants." He laughed. "Wouldn't look too good. Go ahead, drink up. Wait a minute! We haven't clinked." He curled his wrist around and tapped his glass against hers, then moved the one in his hand back up under her veil. "Take a good belt. It'll loosen you up."

He tilted the glass and watched her drain half of it. "That's the way. Now I'll drink some of mine."

She held her breath again as he took a few drops on his tongue, swallowed, then pulled back, grimacing.

"*Damn!*" He growled. "That ain't for me. Can't stand anything sweeter than Amontillado."

Sutter listened as the head trainman told him the last time he had seen Mosby was when he got off at Dutch Flat, then shrugged as he pointed to Mosby's empty seat. As Sutter turned and walked toward it, he glanced up and saw there were two bags on the overhead rack.

He stopped and looked at the man sitting in the window seat. "Are those both yours?"

"Just one of them. The other belongs to the gentleman who asked to sit here awhile back."

"You haven't seen him?"

"Not for a half hour or so. He might be back playing cards."

"You got anything else to drink?" Mosby asked.

Esther thought of John Alexander, Miwokan, Murietta, Barnett, Moses, Alex, and herself, in quick succession. Her mind grew reasonably cool, and the trembling in her arms and legs subsided to a controllable level. "No . . . I don't know. Look back in the pantry."

She got up when she heard him open one closet, then walked back and stood by the bed as he found a bottle of whiskey, uncorked it, and took a long swig.

"Old Crocker, he sure knows how to live." He looked at her, then at the bed. "Why don't we get comfortable?" He walked over and sat down right over the knife, smiling.

She was certain for an instant that her heart would flutter right up out of her throat. She smiled and paused, waiting for the pounding in her ears to slow, then weighed the possibilities: He may have ingested none of the poison. He may stay between me and the portion of the mattress I would have to reach under to get the knife if I get into the bed with him. It is too much of a risk. Better out back, on the platform; even if I have to go through with the whole detestable business to have him at his most vulnerable.

"You want to go back and get your sherry? Might be a way to ease into things."

She thought again for a moment. "No, I won't need it."

He motioned to her with the bottle of bourbon. "Then why don't you sit down here next to me?"

The fear was gone now, the trembling almost unnoticeable as she stared at him in mock softness, mustered another faint smile, and gathered herself. "I had something more exciting in mind than a bed."

"You did? What could that be?"

"How would you like . . ." She coughed. "I'm sorry. But the prospect excites me. How would you like to . . . ?" She breathed deeply, knowing now the platform had offered the best chance all along.

"Go on."

"We could go out on the rear platform, while the train is moving, and there would be a slight element of danger . . . of being seen."

He smiled and shook his head. "You sure are somethin', ain't you? Never met a woman like you in my life." He stared at her veil. "When am I gonna see what you look like? I know you're not bad lookin'. I could tell that in the light by the window."

"Outside. On the platform. While we are . . . doing it."

"How the hell are we going to manage that?"

"In a way that will make it even more exciting."

He smiled again. "If you'll pardon the expression, lay it out for me."

"You could . . . sit on the outside railing—"

"You're crazy!"

"No . . . wait. Listen. You could hold onto the railing with one hand, the ladder or the support with the other, and tuck your shoes under the lower rungs."

He shook his head. "I don't know. Sounds pretty dangerous."

"How? You'll be gripping the rail, the ladder, firmly, with both hands, your feet will be securing you, and I'll be holding onto your lapels . . ." She saw he didn't completely understand. "After . . . after you are ready . . . and . . . I have straddled you."

He burst out laughing. "Well, I'll be goddamned! You got a mind, all right. . . . Still . . ."

She moved past him toward the rear door. "You're not *afraid*, are you, Mr. Mosby? Frightened of something a woman is willing to do with you?"

She saw him touch at his stomach and wince after he followed her out onto the platform. "Is something the matter?" She wondered if the miniscule amount of poison was working on him, slowing him just enough to reduce his edge.

"No. It's nothin'." He staggered slightly, but she couldn't be sure it wasn't just the train."

"Okay. Where do you want me?"

"Over here," she said, fighting the urge to glance up at the derringer. Leaning out, she looked forward at the nearing ledge along the face of Calafia Mountain. "It will be thrilling."

He stared at the railing and paused. The train lurched once, but then rolled on evenly.

"Can you feel it? The train is slowing down a bit. It will hardly be dangerous at all, so long as we keep a firm hold on the railing, the ladder, and the rungs."

He took a step toward the outside rail and looked over just as the train swayed again. "Jesus!"

"I'm not afraid, and I'll be . . . on top of you. Are *you* afraid?

"Please," she continued, feeling the train rock again gently, "I know you'll love it just as much as I will. It will be something we'll never forget for . . . the rest of our lives."

Mosby shrugged and grunted, "I'm with you." Turning, he leaned back against the railing; then, holding tightly with both hands, he eased one boot up behind and under the lowest rung. Then he lifted the other and snugged it as he hoisted himself into place. The car swayed yet another time. "My life is in your hands," he quipped, laughing. "*Goddamn!* You're right. Neither one of us *will* ever forget this!"

She took a step toward him. "Oh, my. You've forgotten to . . ."

He glanced down at his pants and laughed again. "Open my fly. Unbutton it for me, will you? And my long johns. Say, you're gonna have to take off your bloomers, aren't you?"

She smiled. "I don't have anything on under this dress."

"Think of everything, don't you? Take your hat off, too. So I can kiss you without that damn veil bein' in the way."

"Not yet. Let us sustain the mystery—as well as the slight element of danger."

"Goddamn, you are one hell of a woman! Got to say that."

She finished loosening the second set of buttons, hesitated, looked away, then lifted his erect member through the gaps in his clothing. "I'll take my hat off when—we are, in the midst of it."

"Suit yourself."

She summoned up a devilish laugh, wondering for a moment how firmly he was locked onto the railing. *Too strong to risk pushing him,* she thought. *I must begin it, loathsome as it is.* Be patient and calm.

She put one foot up outside his on the rung, then, both hands gripping the top bar, carefully swung the other foot up into place. She forced herself to laugh. "There. I did it!"

She eased down, the skirts of her dress spilling over his legs, and immediately felt that he had grown limp. "Oh, dear."

"Havin' a bit of a problem, am I?" He smiled sheepishly.

"Wait." The pounding in her chest and neck had reached a crescendo again. She took a deep breath. "Here, let me reach up and grasp the overhang so I can get down easily. Then I will . . . bring it to life."

"Go ahead."

Carefully releasing one hand from the railing, she extended her right arm upward toward the spot where she had wedged the derringer. She felt along the opening in the roof skirt all the way to the wall of the car and gasped as a mountaintop to the west suddenly blocked out the light of the waning sun.

"What's the matter?" he asked evenly, his face hardened by the dark shadow cast by the mountain behind the train.

Wondering whether the gun had been jarred loose and fallen off the platform miles back, she didn't notice the slight change in Mosby's voice. "I . . . I can't seem to get a grip." Terrified now, she looked up to make sure she was not mistaken.

Mosby shoved her backward onto the floor of the platform, then didn't even bother to get down as he reached into his jacket pocket and pulled out her husband's derringer.

"You lookin' for this?" He laughed and tossed the gun over his right shoulder. Stunned, Esther watched it arc in the air, bounce once beside the single set of tracks, and disappear down the sheer face of the mountain.

Seventy-six

She got up on her knees, screaming. "*You filthy bastard! You rotten, filthy scum!*" Pushing herself up, she rushed for the door. His fingers were on the handle when she reached it. "*Murderer! Bastard!*"

"Got beat at your own game, did you?" He jerked her around by one arm and pulled her against his chest and legs.

"Let *go* of me!" She tried to kick him.

"Let's see what the fuck you look like!" He let go and ripped her hat off. For a fleeting moment there was a trace of vague recollection in his eyes.

"*Scum! Filthy . . . murdering . . . scum!*" she screamed, punching at him with her fists.

He grabbed her wrist, pinned it behind her back, then took hold of her other arm. "Least you can say Todd's got good taste in mistresses."

"*I'll kill you, you sickening . . . vile . . . beast!*"

"Now, how you gonna do that?"

Pressed against him, she felt the holster inside his jacket. "Let go of me! Let *go* of me! *Please!*"

"Now it's please, huh? Not on your life, you connivin' little bitch! You think I didn't know who you

were, what you might be up to? You think I don't
know—now that I've seen your pretty face—that you
were Barnett's woman before you started layin' down
with the judge?" He spun her around and bent her
out over the railing.

Panting, she stared in horror at the tops of the
evergreens hundreds of feet below her.

"Take a good look, 'cause that's where you're
headin'." He pulled her back. "But not before I take
a little of what you were offerin', you snaky little
whore."

He let go of one arm again as he spun her around.
As soon as it was free, she shoved her hand inside his
jacket and clawed at his holster.

"Wrong again!" he barked, slapping her across the
face and shoving her backward toward the other side
of the platform. As she fell, she struck her head just
over her right ear on one of the rungs. She felt blood
begin to trickle down through her hair as she looked
up, dazed, and saw him pull his derringer from his
jacket pocket.

"Get up!" he shouted.

Solana had heard her screaming. As Mosby took
a step toward Esther, he did not see the Indian woman
come quickly down the ladder, swing to her right, and
throw herself over the rear railing, looping the
ice hammer in the same motion.

The cylinder of the blade struck him at the muscled
base of his neck just before Solana crashed into his
pelvis and legs, knocking him down and stunning him
as he crashed against the wall of the car. Ignoring
the incredible pain in both her kneecaps, she rose
quickly, lifted the ice hammer, swung, and gaffed the
point deep in over his left collarbone.

Mosby shrieked in pain. Then, as she bent over to
free the pick, he lashed out at her face with the gun
still clutched in his right hand.

She staggered backward, blood pouring out of a
gash over one eye, then threw herself on him. Scream-

ing in rage, he blocked her arms and took hold of the fabric of her dress with his teeth. Maddened by the pain in his shoulder, blood pumping out around the buried pick-blade, he lifted, then carried her bodily, spinning and driving her against the wall of the car.

They were locked together now, as Esther rose groggily, unsteadily to her feet and staggered toward them. His teeth were snapped shut on the bodice of Solana's dress, his left hand wedged against her right arm, the pistol between them, suspended in his right hand, held there by their bodies and the fingers Solana had wrapped around his wrist.

Esther saw no way to get at either the gun or the pick still lodged in Mosby's shoulder. Solana pushed forward and bit hard at Mosby's face. Spinning as Mosby howled, Esther pushed into the car, ran to the bed, and found the kitchen knife. She heard the shot just as she got back to the rear door.

Outside, Mosby and Solana, still clutching one another, had revolved to a position on the outside railing. Solana had slipped down until her shoulders were against the upper bar. Weaving, Mosby raised the butt of the derringer over her head.

Lifting the knife to waist-level and gripping it with both hands, Esther staggered two steps forward and plunged the blade into his back.

Mosby groaned. He let go of the derringer in mid-swing, watched it arc away, then began to turn.

She pulled the knife out and pushed it into him again.

"Bastard . . ."

And again.

"Murderer . . . !"

And again.

"*Rapist* . . . !"

She was crying now, as she tried to spin him around so she could slash at his face. She saw Solana's arms clasped around his upper back. Then, aware again of the Indian woman, she stared over Mosby's shoulder into Solana's glazed eyes.

"Solana! Oh, God. Solana!"

Mosby began to slide downward. As he did, Esther saw the broad expanse of blood darkening the black fabric under the gold, heart-shaped amulet Solana was wearing.

The Indian woman closed her eyes, then opened them again. Her arms relaxed slightly.

Enraged, Esther pulled Mosby partially away from her and pushed his face up. His eyes were still half-open. *"Look at me! Murderer! Do you know who I am?"*

Mosby stared blankly at her, listening numbly as the life ebbed out of him.

"I am Elizabeth Purdy Todd! Do you remember?"

His head slumped forward.

She grabbed his hair and jerked it up again. *"Do you remember? In the snow, in the mountains, after you killed Seeswash?"* She saw his pupils begin to roll upward and yanked violently at his hair. *"The baby and the woman? Do . . . you . . . remember?"*

His eyes widened slightly as he realized who she was.

"I am that woman!" She raised the knife again, this time in one hand, ready to drive it into his chest.

"No."

Esther turned to Solana, the knife high in the air.

"Throw the knife away. Give me the pick."

She hesitated.

"Give me the pick. You owe this to me."

Startled, confused, she lowered the knife and dropped it to the platform. It skittered and fell over the side onto the receding gravel beside the track.

"He is almost gone," Solana said wearily. "Help me to be standing."

Esther let go of Mosby, and he fell against the Indian woman. Together, they managed to bring her

to a standing position with Mosby leaning against
her, his head slumped on one shoulder, his eyes half-
closed.

"The pick."

Esther circled Mosby and saw that the tool had
worked loose and fallen to the platform. She lifted it
up and turned back to Solana.

"Give it to me!" Solana extended her left hand and
took the ice hammer from Esther. She hefted it as
blood began to trickle from one corner of her mouth.

"Lift his head."

Esther took hold of his hair again and pulled back.

"For Miwokan . . . and my son," Solana murmured.
Then, raising the pick and measuring, she snapped her
wrist sharply and drove the point deep into Mosby's
ear.

Esther stared at them, dumbfounded, as Solana
choked and tightened her grip on the ice hammer.

"Tie my other wrist to his with your scarf."

Esther obeyed her. When she finished, she looked
at Solana again. The Indian woman smiled. "You are
my sunsister, and you will do what I say."

Esther nodded, suddenly aware that her legs were
terribly weak.

"Stay strong until it is done."

"Is there no way I can help you?" She moved to
do something about Solana's wound, but the Indian
woman slowly shook her head.

"I will be gone soon. It is what I want."

"Oh, God, please! Don't say that!"

"It is the truth. I am glad the blood is filling me."

"What do you want me to do?"

"Wash the blood off the iron after it is done."

"What is done?"

"After you throw us from the train."

Esther fought for breath. "No! I won't do that!" she
sobbed. "Please don't ask me to do that to you!"

Solana turned her head and looked forward, along

the side of the train. "When it is right, you will do it. For me. You will do what I ask."

Esther was suddenly aware that they had left the face of the mountain behind. Green conifers whipped past in a smear of color. "I *can't!*"

"You can and you will. Not here. But when it is right. If I am not gone, it will stop the pain. If I am, it will still be better. For me, and for you, later."

Esther stared at her, tears streaming down her face. Suddenly she felt faint.

"Hold on to my arm," Solana whispered. "Then, when you are not dizzy, do it. If they find us, they will think nothing about you. Do it. . . . Do it for me. . . . Do it for—" Her head fell forward onto Mosby's shoulder.

"Miwokan . . ." Esther sobbed.

She waited, holding onto them tightly, until the train began crossing the long trestle just west of the pass. Scarcely aware of what she was doing, she ripped "Uncle" Billy Graves's antique watch from Mosby's vest and slipped it into a pocket of her dress. Almost at the center of the span, she got behind Mosby, slipped her arms beneath Solana's legs, lifted and sent them toppling over the railing. Leaning over, staring back, she watched as Solana, still clutching the handle of the ice hammer, and Mosby slowly cartwheeled together through space, hit a piling, and continued downward until they struck the surface of the bubbling stream. Desolate, leaden in body, she covered her face with her hands, unaware that the slender ribbon of water flowed southward through a labyrinth of gullys, canyons, and gorges; not knowing that it would carry Mosby's blood past the site of the lean-to, then farther, through a ravine a mile east of the place where John Alexander had died; before it snaked past Lucifer Peak and spilled into the waters of the South Fork.

* * *

Only the rapping on the front door of the parlor car stopped her from immediately lying down on the bed. Numb, she took a bucket from the lavatory, filled it with water, and washed down the floor of the rear platform. Back inside she hesitated for a moment; then, steadying herself on the chairs, she walked forward and pulled the shade aside. Sutter was pounding on the door now. Disconnectedly, she decided she had better let him in before someone heard the noise. Unlocking the door, she stepped back, watched him turn into a blur when he came in, then toppled unconscious into his arms.

Sutter carried her to the bed. When he searched her bag for a handkerchief to clean the superficial gash above her ear, he noticed the journal. As he turned, he saw the two glasses containing sherry. He left the journal in the valise until he saw that an inordinate amount of blood discolored the unexplained water on the rear platform. He went back and checked Esther's pulse and breathing, lay the cool handkerchief over her forehead after cleaning her wound again, then quickly washed down the outside metal floor. He put the bottle of bourbon he found on the bed back into the open pantry closet. Washing out the two sherry glasses, he placed them back on the tray.

Sutter didn't tell her he had the journal when she came to and asked that Alex take her back to Sacramento. Nor did he mention it to Alex or the conductor when he went forward, searching for a doctor, and told them Esther had accidentally fallen while standing on the observation deck. When she awoke with all of them hovering over her bed, he insisted that she was too weak to talk, and that she had already told him what had happened before passing out.

The journal was in his valise when the yardmen uncoupled the parlor car in Reno and he said goodbye to Alex, Esther, and the disappointed boy. A month later, when Sutter received word that she had recovered, he drove downriver to bring her a gift.

It was the gold wedding band he had slipped off her hand two-dozen years earlier, just before Marsh had removed her fingers at the fort. He did not mention Mosby's name during the dinner they shared, and neither did she. He left the journal, wrapped in brown paper, beside the well-worn, pearl-backed comb and brush set in her bathroom. Then he rode home in the weak but sufficient light of the setting moon.

Epilogue

South Fork, American River
April 18, 1906
5 A.M.

The sound of the waterfall rushing out from beneath the lip of ice filled Alex Todd's ears as he gazed up the riverbed, watching for the first light of the sun to rise over the Sierras. She had asked him to scatter her ashes here—at sunrise. It was the least he could do, he thought, marveling again at the woman he had married, been separated from, "involved with," "re-married" in 1870, and then had lived with for the past thirty-six years.

He was seventy-seven years old, and despite his robust health the trip from San Francisco had tired him. He was cold, even with the overcoat and boots and the blanket wrapped around him. It had been years since he had spent the better part of a night out under the stars. But she had asked him to do it, and, by God, he would. At precisely sunrise. He had not carried out her other request—to wait until after he scattered her ashes before reading the diary. But then again, she had warned him in their last conversation that the contents might be a shock. That he ought to read it sitting down. And then adding, her frail face wrinkling mischievously as she burst into a peal of pitifully weak laughter: "Perhaps at the doctor's office, in case you have a heart attack!"

He chuckled, remembering her wry, often sardonic wit: It had not left her, even at the last when she was a silver-haired shadow of her former self. He turned briefly, his gaze sweeping downriver to the new dam going up just beyond the point where her cabin had once stood. Turning back, he looked up at the sheer cliffs on either side of the fall. *All of this will be gone,* he thought. Buried under the new lake the dam will create. The river, the cliffs, the waterfall—and the gold down there. All traces of her life during those first years after it happened.

He understood now why she had saved the clipping that reported the hanging of Isaac Claussen for an obscure murder in Virginia City. But he still could not believe all the diary contained. That would take time. Knowledge too sudden. Almost more difficult than the night he had learned she was alive. *Almost . . . incredible,* he thought. But he knew Esther; knew she would never tell him it was true unless it was. All of it. *Good God, what they can hide from us.*

He thought of the quiet life they had led for more than three decades at the ranch they built on the property Murietta left her just west of Twin Peaks. Unremarkable, pale by comparison to what was on those pages of hers.

He wondered whether she had actually killed Mosby herself. No one would ever know. He had never been found, and neither had Solana. Sutter, even if he had known anything about it, was long since dead. Whatever the facts were, Alex did not wholly approve of what Esther had done. He wished he had never left her at Bent's Fort, or that somehow he had been a part of a more lawful means of bringing Mosby to justice. But done was done, and he couldn't be certain he would not have been moved to the same vengeance. The irony that he might easily have killed Mosby himself once, in that hotel room, did not escape him.

He didn't care a damn what anyone else might think. It had been Esther's request—in the letter he found inside the cover—that he have the diary sealed, placed in trust under irrevocable arrangements to have it delivered to her oldest surviving direct descendant in the year 1945. He had been so puzzled by that distant date, one hundred years after she began writing the diary, that he sat down and read the journal then and there. It was not until the following day that he recovered his wits enough to remember her comment about the doctor's office, or the typical closing sentence in her letter:

"By 1945, perhaps some use could be made of this material by a writer of fiction, since surely no one will ever believe it."

The diary was sealed, rested now in a vault at the Crocker bank. Appropriate, he thought, trying to remember what Charles Crocker's private car looked like. She could have died in the damned thing. Or in any number of other places. But she hadn't, choosing instead to take her leave two days earlier as the sun set on the Pacific and the wind hushed in the evergreens surrounding the ranch.

Even if it all came to light now, he thought, *few would deny she had tried to atone for what she'd done*. He wondered for a moment if God had forgiven her. Her school in Sacramento now housed, fed, and educated two hundred homeless Indian and Mexican-American children. She had poured half her wealth into the school, the San Francisco Orphan Asylum, and other charities. With everything else she had done, she still found time to be an exemplary mother, a good wife. He was certain God would take all that into account.

He suddenly remembered her as a girl—in the barn in Ohio, dark-haired, laughing, long-legged, and beautiful. Then silver-haired and still lovely, her leg over his in bed, giving as much warmth and security as she received. His eyes filmed over.

She always had the time, never denied him anything within reason, had been a fine companion and friend during those last thirty-six years. Secretly—people simply wouldn't understand—he had felt himself blessed to be married to a woman whose strong sexual appetite had carried through into her early six-

ties. He knew that somehow that had kept him young.
And if she was a bit domineering at times, occasionally reminded him of things even a fool could remember, well, she had more than made up for that, too.

Among other things, she had given him two more
children. He tried to picture all three of them when
they were young, but the memory faded. He saw
them instead in their present surroundings. Todd
(whose name they'd legally changed to Todd Carter
Todd; known to one and all as "T. C.") on the floor
of the San Francisco Stock Exchange, barking out an
order. Alex, Jr., in the cloakroom of the U.S. Senate,
wearing the scar from a Mauser bullet along his jawline like a badge—a memento of the Spanish-Amer-
ican War that had helped get him elected. And Eliza,
as she liked to be called, whirling on the dance floor
of an ostentatiously oversized ballroom in a mansion
on Russian Hill. He wondered about her. She was
as headstrong as Esther and, Alex guessed, just as
sexed. She was married to the deputy mayor of San
Francisco. But rumors that the child she gave birth
to on the day Esther died was not the deputy mayor's
were almost too substantial to be ignored.

Well, it is her life, he thought. *And whatever Eliza
gets herself into, she'll have to travel a far piece to
match the one Esther lived.* He sighed. Glancing eastward, he saw the first hint of light over the mountains. Getting up, he tested the ice to see if it was
firm, then walked out to the middle of the fall carrying the urn containing Esther's ashes. He waited to
make sure it was not a false dawn, then looked at
the antique gold pocket-watch that Esther had unexpectedly left to him . . . 5:13. He wondered about
the antique watch for a moment—where it had come
from; how long it had been in the desk drawer with
Esther's diary. *No way to know or ever find out,* he
thought. Shrugging, he tipped the urn, and the second
line Esther had written in her diary, at Bent's Fort
sixty years earlier, rang in his mind:

"I did not know one could love and miss another human being so."

As the last of the ashes disappeared in the water of the fall and his eyes became moist again, he felt the tremor in the ice beneath his feet, saw the earth along the riverbanks ripple. For a second he thought it was just the tears, or that he had lost his senses for a moment, but then the trees shuddered and waved slightly again as the second tremor rocked the ice and he heard it began to crack behind him. For an instant he had the impulse to scramble for the safety of the bank. But then he decided he would rather stay where he was.

The ice crumbled, falling away in huge shards as he plunged downward. He smiled as the shockingly cold, rushing water enveloped and swept him downstream, knowing that Esther could not be far ahead, that nothing could ever separate them again. He did not hear the sound of the great earthquake as it reached the South Fork from San Francisco two minutes later. Like the dark, satisfied laughter of Miwokan's sun god, it echoed between the sheer cliffs flanking the fall, then raced on toward the crest of the Sierras.

Dell Bestsellers

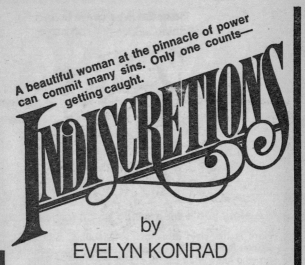

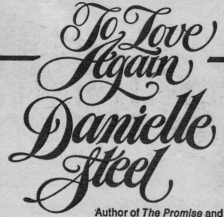